AN AUDIENCE WITH THE Sleeping *Dragon*

The Spear of Longinus

G L ABRAR

authorHOUSE®

AuthorHouse™ UK
1663 Liberty Drive
Bloomington, IN 47403 USA
www.authorhouse.co.uk
Phone: 0800 047 8203 (Domestic TFN)
+44 1908 723714 (International)

Published by AuthorHouse 12/16/2019

ISBN: 978-1-5462-8911-1 (sc)
ISBN: 978-1-5462-8912-8 (hc)
ISBN: 978-1-5462-8910-4 (e)

Print information available on the last page.

CONTENTS

The story of a young girl who wins her heart's desire, and earns the love of a very special friend and companion in the caves beneath the ancient City of Vezelay.

Our heroine can be found in the dark caves beneath Vezelay, made of stone carved partly out of the great granite rock that forms the foundation for this most beautiful of towns. She dwells in an island of mystery within the valley formed by the Camut and Lot rivers and overlooking the misty towers of fair Avalon on the adjoining hillside.

Vezelay is of course the last resting place of Mary Magdalen, brought here by Joseph of Arithamea and honoured by the first Princes of the Clovis family. They built a great church in her honour, long ago, and set in place the Oyster Pilgrimage, the shells of which run from Vezelay in the south to the resting place of the Holy Grael near Camulodenum in the north (in a secret location found amongst the grimoire in the library of our heroine's great great grandfather, one of the last of the lineage of de Clare family and the Angoevin kings).

Beneath her "ancient" home are the cellars: caves of shadowed mystery which as a child became her haunt, a place of quest to find the tomb of Mary ... or the sword of Artor ... or the Spear of Longinus ... or the Round Table of his paladins ... or the hidden treasure of the Knights Templar. Used in recent years to store wine, these caves had once been the burial place for an early community of Christians, fleeing the persecution of Lyons.

But for a seven year old child, born in the steppes of southern Russia, and brought up as a nomad in the deserts of ancient Persia, these caves were the home of Al ad Din or S in Ba'id, the forty thieves, the Djinn ... and her ***dragon.***

Bearing the flickering flame of a lantern carried unsteadily in her quivering young grasp, Ra'el trod the silent maze of the Troll-carved tunnels, shying away from the lime-formed giants and monsters, their reflections in the pools of pure obsidian-black water following her as she ran and hid, then ran again, until she came to her cave of crystal: a line of diamonds the shape of a dragon's tail upon the high domed roof of one final cathedral-like cavern, pillared and majestic at the end of which she could see a deep red glow.

Immediately she could imagine that this would be the home of some great and mighty winged lizard, a draco of awesome magic and wisdom, guarding a treasure accumulated over centuries of bloody massacre. And, as often happened, and happens still to this day, when she began to imagine a dragon …

… then there before her was **the real thing**!

He was sitting in a semi-circle, half asleep, two thin wisps of sulphurous smoke drifting from his nostrils. His coat was a gleaming mass of emeralds, his breast the purest scintillating diamonds, his wings, though folded, still stretched the span of a large aircraft, his head was proud and fierce-some, his mouth and lips sinuous and enticing, his eyes mesmerising, a glowing warmth of humour that showed both love and death … and from his slavering jaws hung the remains of the leg of a young man, the dragon's half-eaten breakfast.

She was paralysed with fear and just stood stock-still, but, fortunately for the young girl, the dragon was replete and also had caught her initial look of admiration. Proud worm that he was, he had decided in that instant that company was the order of the day.

"Come here child and do not be afraid. For you can see I have already eaten. Come and admire me … for am I not magnificent?"

His voice reminded her of the warm desert winds, a foretelling of storms ahead but also the bringer of release and comfort from the heat of the sun. Both welcomed and feared were those winds and she shivered in joy and terror at his gently delivered command.

So she stepped forward and stood before him, to ask timorously:

"Will you eat me?"

"No little one," replied the monster, the gleam in his eyes noting her blonde hair, elfin face and deep blue eyes (a combination that was a favourite delicacy for dragons she would discover later).

"I have eaten and will not eat again until I break my fast on the morrow. It is your company I seek only, conversation to ease the ache of an old lizard's withered soul. I am wise and yet find more wisdom in every chance encounter and so would ask you, of your kindness, to spend some time with me."

"Great and mighty dragon," she replied in courtesy, "I am young and have little wisdom," then seeing a flash of anger in his orange whirling eyes which then turned to yellow and crimson, blood-red, she hastily added: "But I am a teller of story amongst my former people of the desert lands and if you will accept this alternative, I shall tell you a tale that shall be a companion to us both."

At this, the dragon sat up, and shook himself abruptly awake. Then, so fast it was a blur to her young and untrained sight in the dimness of the cavern, his right claw shot out unsheathed and he dug five long sharp hooked nails into the rock around the girl to surround her in a natural but impenetrable cage. She could see him and he could see and hear her, but she was otherwise trapped within his malicious grasp:

"Tell your tale, fair maid, and make it a fine one. For it shall be your last, and on the morrow I shall feast on your fair looks and golden hair, and suck the blood from your veins until your dried bones bleach the floor of my home that you have so foolishly invaded. Tell your tale, little maid ... but know this also: one tear shed by you, or show any fear or lack of respect and I shall kill you now. Your story shall earn you this one day of life prolonged, provided it shall entertain me; make the most of it."

Perhaps another might have been cowed into submission, the horror of their situation depriving them of words, disabling them such that they fell silent before such malevolence, and thus they would have died, incinerated in the wrath of disappointment that followed the shaking silence of fear? But our heroine had faced death and evil intent before and yet lived. So she drew courage from those experiences to stand tall in her prison and glare angrily back at the mighty worm, replying:

"Lord Dragon. I have never shown anything but respect for the creatures of this earth: magical or natural. Nor do I need your caged embrace to force me to tell a story! For this is something I do willingly for friends and strangers alike. Give me leave to choose the subject of my fable but threaten me not ... for I already know my fate is in your grasp and my end is likely to be a cruel one."

This silenced the dragon. Indeed, his heart (deeply buried and rarely seen or felt) was touched by this brave yet poignant speech. Despite many years of converse with the victims of his ancient hate, for the first time in a thousand years, the worm felt the loneliness of his own species and thought to himself: "Some company would not be amiss. I shall see how the day shall pass. For this maid pleases me."

To the girl, he said simply: "Tell your story then, as if to a "friend or a stranger". I make no promise other than that you shall die. But I can make that death swift rather than cruel if you shall satisfy me with thy words."

"Then I shall tell the *Tale of Oweine, the Lady of the Fountain*, as writ upon the crusting, curling, yellowing vellums of an ancient tome within the very caves in which we now converse. It is one of the many tales told of the court of Artor, who lived in this place above our heads, and once named his seat or capital after the rivers that combine here: the city of *Camut et Lot* or Camelot.

It is this same Artor, whose grave is found beneath the fountains of Avallon on the far hill across from here, whose sword I see in the treasure you seek to guard, and whose knights have fallen in holy quests in the long millennium since his death to find the chalice and spear hidden in the land of Arboria to the north. This is the story of one of his knights, the fair lady he found ... and left to die."

THE TALE OF OWEINE

Perched precariously above the Forests of D'Elcemer, stood the Castle of Caer Malice; its fanged towers and turrets were an evil maw standing seer, sorcered sentry over the winding pass from the deserted town of Heneth to the enchanted city of Carillion.

The seneschal of that castle was a knight whose armour was as black as his soul was dark with deeds of dastard and deadly distasteful delight. Those passing within his realm could expect a warm welcome, a repast of splendid munificence, followed by foul ghoulish murder in the shadows of the night.

This black-hearted knight had a lady: her name was Oweine and she was fair-haired, tall, slender as a reed, gentle of heart and demeanour. She had been taken captive when her father had been strung from the roof of the Great Hall after dinner, to be roasted slowly over the fire that dominated the centre of the banqueting hall for the humour of he who was lord of that mesne. She watched in silent tears as her honoured and much-loved patron tossed in agonised screams to turn into a blackened hunk of smouldering meat, become carcass fed to the hounds that padded the corridors of that terrible place.

That night she had been taken in drunken ferocity, her maidenhood torn asunder in ire and contempt, to be left broken in bloodied disarray, made wife against her will to a heartless heathen, whose one sole object in life was the nihilistic destruction of all that was beautiful.

Her new lord sought to quench her soul and diminish her beauty through his constant malcontent: he beat her night and day, removed her food, left her bound or locked away for days on end. If a guest appeared whom she offered even the slightest of smiles, that guest would be the subject of her lord's greatest cruelty and torture - the lady forced to watch the torments and her pleas for mercy prolonging the agony for her master's victims. And so she learnt silence, to look away, to steel herself and appear as stone untouched by the mayhem of her husband. To those who met her she seemed immured and immune to the sin that lay waste around her and in time became as condemned as her lord for the dark deeds in his domain.

Alone at night, she wept and prayed for the repose of the dead, then silently withstood the ritual beatings and rape of her husband. Unknown to her lord, she would then walk the corridors alone and be comforted by the hounds he kept - man eaters tamed by the kind and careful touch of her soft hands, caressed to love by her whose heart remained pure, no matter the despite she suffered.

Then one day she realised she was with child and fearing her lord's reaction did her utmost to hide this fact from him. His attentions continued each morning and night. Her blood ran from the marks of the lash and the blows to her face but she became radiant, and if anything he grew more angry, incensed by the glow that appeared in her cheeks and so renewed his beatings with fresh vigour.

But with life within her, she could no longer be cowed by him, and this finally drove him from her bed, for he hated to see her in such radiant health. For three months she was confined in peace - in that time the black knight attempted to starve the lady, but the hounds she had befriended would bring her morsels and scraps from their own plates and keep both her and the child in her womb fed. For her, this was a time of blessing and bliss and her spirit began to be refreshed. She remembered her voice and would sing in the mornings and laugh at the stories of the stars at night. Her gaiety became infectious, and the birds and creatures of the forest that had studiously avoided the castle, would come in the dark of night to visit her, bringing news of a world beyond her lord's demesne where peace and joy and love reigned.

The day came when she was to give birth.

Her lord had for many months left her to herself so she was forced to go through this ordeal without the aid or comfort of a birthing woman. She made what preparations she could, and ensured that she had to hand clothes and bowls of water, herbs and spices to relieve the pain, and a knife ready to cut the cord. She stepped into the fountain at the centre of the courtyard that formed part of her apartments and relaxed into the pain of birth. In that pain she discovered the joy of creation and from the thrashings of agony that night came the hope of new life in the morning.

On the morrow, tired but overjoyed, she held the fruit of her labours in her quivering arms. A son with deep blue eyes as her own whose first cries had welded her heart to his, and who now slept latched on to her lactating breast in the God-made clasp that is his greatest gift to women.

She sent word to her master by the good offices of the guards that stood sentry at the entrance to her apartments. A short message of great tidings: "To my loved and honoured lord, greetings. This day I have great pleasure in bearing for you the gift of a son" and it was her hope (alas in vain) that through this one act she would be reconciled to her husband and bring him into love with her.

Her husband commanded a feast be held that night in celebration of the news. He summonsed the people of Heneth and Carillion to join him in rejoicing at the news that he was a father with heir. Hundreds of the local nobility were invited to dine with the Black Knight and his lady Oweine in their castle and most accepted the invitation, curious to see whether this would mark the beginning of a new era of tranquillity for the Forest of D'Ecemer.

Into the banqueting hall walked the slender lady of our tale, her child held snug and secure in her arms, whilst she, though wan, still shone with the peace and joy of her fulfilment.

"Bring me my son!" commanded the laughing baron, whose manners and courtesies that night as host had brought all to believe that the demons that tormented him had finally been cured.

Oweine curtsied then proudly presented their son to him. He took the child carefully and then spoke to the assembly:

"Know you this. My wife and I have never lain together and she therefore has been false to me," he lied. "This child is not mine but rather the result of her adultery. I condemn her and it," then he dashed the child to the ground, crushing its skull on the stone floor before throwing it in death into the fire in the centre of the hall in whose conflagration Oweine had seen her own father die.

Oweine stood momentarily stunned, then turned and grasped a scalding poker from that same fire. As her lord stood still laughing at his cruel act, she drove it, red hot and aflame, through his breast to strike him dead in a single blow.

The nobles sentenced her to death: a slow death. She was placed in her apartments and walled within them with no company (save the animals of the forest that would visit her balcony). Their judgment was that she should die of starvation as had been her lord's original intent.

And in time word spread of an evil lord, a Black Knight, whom had been slain by a serpent disguising herself as his evil wife - a woman whom had watched without remorse as the Black Knight's guests had been murdered for her entertainment and had slain her own husband when discovered to have been unfaithful.

The forest and lands around the Caer Malice appeared cursed: no crops would grow to term; the towns and villages nearby were deserted; birds were rarely seen in the sky; a malignant silence descended upon the place. After a few years, the curse was blamed on she who had been shut away in the castle. A few years more and those who still lived in the shadow of the castle spoke openly of the need to strike down the serpent imprisoned in the black towers above them if they were ever to have release. The odd brave soul would make the attempt but be frightened off by the hounds that now held sway over the keep or by the image of a ghostly lady, whose hand rested spectrally upon the still waters of a fountain in the centre of the deserted bastion.

In the kitchens of far away Camelot, a new apprentice had begun the task of heading the pile of turnips long-gathered in the buttery and awaiting preparation for the stew that would be the main course of the feast in the Great Hall that evening. The young man had arrived from the far cold mountains of Erindor, Fyfedom of the Celt, a stark place but made warm by the bearing of its people. He had announced little about his birth or standing save his name was Gareth, which he liked not for the memories it brought of his homeland. So they looked at his hands and saw they were fair and gentle and named him Gentle Hands (Beaumains) and set him to peel the vegetables for the dinner.

In the fullness of time, but mere days after the arrival of Beaumains, came the story of the black serpent of D'Elcemer who was imprisoned in Caer Malice and had cursed the lands around. Aid was sought from the Knights of the Round Table of Artor at the centre of Camelot.

Alas, the young maid sent as messenger from the villages beneath the castle had met no joy in her task to seek a Knight to quest against the serpent. Those knights present, when the request had been made, had been touched by the girl's earnestness and clear need for help. But their liege lord, the King, had decreed that Camelot must at all times be defended by a minimum of one third of the Knights of the Table and was himself with the remaining Knights on quest still for the location of the Holy Grael.

In sadness and grief, the maid had been sent to the kitchen to make provision for her homeward journey, to return empty-handed with news that would drive her people to despair. And it was in this state of clear distress that Beaumains first saw the child; his gentle heart wept for her whilst his kindness and charity bid that he do her what assistance it was within his power to command. He knelt before her and asked softly:

"Of my honour and for the sake of my heart, what ails thee fair maid that I might remove the badge of thy distress and replace it with the joy that should always adorn thy face?"

"I seek a knight to slay a serpent" was the sad reply between the gulps and sniffs of the sobbing girl.

Beaumains paused. Every fibre of his body wanted him to leap forward and accept the challenge of this lady's quest, yet he had a purpose here in Camelot and feared the journey to a far-off land to defeat a serpent would distract him from his own intent. But her sobs unmanned him, so he stood before her and then went down again on one knee to make the oath as he had been taught:

"Fair lady! I am quested now to do thy bid. My life held now within thy grasp. Should I succeed in thy bidding then honour awaits me here before the grande cathedra of our good liege-lord Artor on my return. Should I fail, but die in honour, then there shall be sweet memory of my passing whenst ere I came. Should I fail and lose all honour then my name shall be cursed for all time in both this place and my place of birth. My body, my might, my honour, my skill and my courage are at thy command. Let me have the details only of thy quest and I shall ride to its ruin or fulfilment, the choice be God's not mine."

But she laughed then scorned him:

"Kitchen boy, what use are you to me? I need someone whom can smite a serpent's head in a single stroke and yet here are you amidst the turnips ... and I note not one hath had its head removed clean! Enough of your stupid words and of this cursed place! I am leaving now for my home and I hope my people will receive my news with less mockery and more sense than you have shown, you silly boy."

In great dignity, Beaumains stood before her and pledged: "I will follow you and I shall amaze you by rescuing your village from the thrall of this serpent. I am pledged now to do this"

"You my do as you wish" she replied. "But you are an ignorant kitchen boy and I will ignore you" at which she turned her back on him and walked towards the stable to make ready to leave.

"Drat the girl," thought Beaumains, "and curse these turnips" he added as he sliced the top of his finger in his distraction. But his mind was made up and, abandoning his culinary chore, he headed for the stable, to find his old horse and saddle bag, intent on following the lady.

They rode in procession, the lady ahead, alone, aloof, ignoring the stumbling of the kitchen boy who followed to her rear. Our hero in her train, on his father's aged horse, faltering of gait, frail of foot, doggedly determined to carry the young master through the trials ahead. Our knight supplicant, astride, grasping his saddle bag to his chest, with its precious and yet undisclosed contents, adjusting to the rolling ride of his mount, staring earnestly at the rear of the lady whose quest he must accomplish, hoping for her favour, and receiving nothing but her spiteful scorn in return.

Such was the obvious ordering of this "merry" party that soon the inhabitants of the villages through which they processed came to their windows or stood on their doorsteps to point and laugh. It did not take long for Beaumains to see the humour in his own situation and join in their jollity, but the lady grew more and more angry until finally she spun round and rode up to him on her destrier:

"Must you follow me, boy. You are making me look ridiculous. Go home to your turnips and leave me alone."

Beaumains smiled in good-humoured response:

"My lady, I have accepted your quest and no matter what you say or whatever fears you may now have for me, I shall not go back until the quest is completed or I am dead. If you would avoid the laughter, then stay with me and tell me your name and about yourself. They laugh at your anger and my presumption, so let us show them a better face than this and give them no fuel for their scorn."

The lady huffed but then her own sweet nature rose finally to the surface and with a little smile then gay laugh she admitted generously:

"Well, you are polite and good-natured company at least. I was in danger of getting a cricked neck from looking around at you to see if you were still behind me. Come, join me. Ride at my side. For I am the Lady Jocelyn and my father is the Notaire in our village."

"My sweet lady Jocelyn, I am named Beaumains and am a knight supplicant at your bidding."

"What is a supplicant?" the lady asked her curiosity aroused.

"It means merely that through the performance of this quest I hope to earn the right to go before King Artor and plead my case to become a Knight of the Table" replied the boy with gentle hands, at which the lady laughed and then had a fit of the giggles before finally restraining herself enough to chortle:

"Are the Knights of the Table beset by turnips? Shalt gentle hands replace the need for gauntlered main? Boy, you shall be mocked ... if ever you survive the serpent!"

Thus in silence they rode, until sheepishly looking at him from below her long lashes, Jocelyn laughed once more then nudged him in the ribs and as he nearly fell from his horse cried:

"Catch me my hero" then smiling at him encouragingly took off at a gallop chased slowly and steadily by her protector, now happy to be in her favour (if not yet in her respectful grace).

In the evening he found them board and lodging, which he paid for from his meagre savings: for her the best room, for him a mat to lie on across the lintel of her door as he guarded her with his life. That first night he saw her briefly, without the cape and cloak in which she hid her features, wearing the green girtle, with raven hair and emerald green eyes, on fire as they looked momentarily at him to wish him peace and convey her thanks for his good service.

On the morrow, he broke fast with her: she was groomed and glittering with the best pearls of her father's household arrayed in the curls of her hair. Then he saw to their horses that they also be fed and groomed and that their party be well-provisioned, before offering her his escort as though she were a queen and he the kingdom's champion.

As they rode, still the villagers came and looked. But they no longer laughed as they saw the lady made graceful in the company of such a courteous knight. The days passed towards their destination of the city of Carillion, and Jocelyn and Beaumains grew close, such that they recognised each other's mood and manner, whim and wish, deed and desire. With friendship firmly set, the foundation for further and fuller fealty between these gentle folk settled, they arrived at their destination and the contest that Beaumains must win to retain his honour and thus seek his avowed destiny.

Beaumains stood at the gates of Caer Malice, the parting words of the lady Jocelyn still remembered:

"The serpent is guarded by terrible hounds with many heads that will tear out your throat. The serpent is locked within the centre of the castle and beyond those doors lies a spectre - a white lady whose touch is death. The serpent is also the wife of the Knight who once held this castle. You must defeat the hounds, serpent and the lady for any one of these will overcome you. Slay the serpent and the curse is lifted."

Beaumains marched through the barbican beneath the portcullis and into the main courtyard of the castle keep. It was daylight but the courtyard was in shadow and before him was the entrance to unlit corridors leading to the serpent's prison. He carried on bravely and then the howling began, at first from a distance within the bowels of the castle, but increasingly louder as he heard the rapidly approaching bounding pad-fell of one of the guards of the palazzo he sought to enter.

Then before him stood a monster with shoulder span of at least six feet, bloodied and slavering jaws, sharp ferocious fangs, deep sharpened unsheathed claws, a hound become wolf through hunger and solitude. It ran ... as Beaumains placed a large juicy slab of red meat before him and stepped back. The hound made a startled joyous yapping barking sound and then bent to sniff before picking up the meat. It started to eat, keeping an eye on Beaumains but the boy was no longer the centre of its attention.

Our hero used this chance to walk slowly around the hound, stopping briefly to allow his gentle hands to caress the point between the hound's front haunches that was the gateway to a dog's soul. The hound recognising that kind touch from the daily loving embrace he received from his mistress, straightway stood with the meat hanging from his mouth and followed Beaumains into the keep itself.

Other hounds joined them and each received the gift of food, something they had until that point only been granted by their mistress. To each one the young man became bonded as he offered the touch of brotherhood to the hounds and they accepted him as brethren of the lady of the house, for only she had shown them this kindness before. So they guided him to the lair of the serpent.

Finally they brought him to a circular domed chamber, at the far end of which were two enormous oak doors with intricate iron metal work and stud work, which had been sealed by tearing the great stone shafts for the water causeway that used to run to the fountain within the chamber beyond. Great stones had been piled in a mass of rubble across the entrance way. The chamber in which Beaumains now stood was awash with water from the spring that had obviously once fed the fountain but now pumped out into its antechamber. Through this man-made indoor lake of cold water swam our hero in order to reach the handles of the door on the far side.

On reaching the entranceway, he could see immediately that the doorway had been blocked to prevent anyone from escaping from the chamber beyond, but that on this side the hinges were exposed and could be easily levered out if he could find a cross beam to place beneath one of the heavy oak doors. Such a beam was resting nearby, a roof rafter that had fallen from its original resting place when the causeway had been torn asunder.

Beaumains dragged the beam towards the door then ducked under the water to place it upon a block of stone before easing one end beneath the bottom of the door. The other end of the cross beam was now standing several feet out of the water at an angle.

He swam beyond the beam then dived beneath the water once more: this time to check the depth for where he would be landing as he opened the doorway - he wanted to be sure he did not hit any obstacle beneath the water.

All was now ready. Beaumains climbed a pillar near the door until he was some twenty feet above the cross beam, then leapt and landed feet first on the very far end of the beam. It buckled then sprang back, the force of its energy levering the base of one door off its hinge such that the door crashed down to lie flat beneath the waters that were now rushing into the once sealed chamber beyond.

Meanwhile, Beaumains himself had been sprung forward by the beam to perform a perfect swallow dive into the black waters in the centre of the chamber ... only to be dragged by the head of water as it plunged through the open doorway into Oweine's apartments.

Oweine stood up from her prayers in time to be drenched from head to foot by a wall of water as it found its former path to the fountain and from there to the aquaduct that had once fed the crop fields in the villages beneath the castle - seer soil would become fertile again.

She turned to face Beaumains, who held his father's sword in quaking hand and was ready to run her through for the ghast and serpent she truly was. And then she laughed ruefully at the mess he had made of her once tidy chamber. Oweine herself was bedraggled: her hair hung like rat's tails, her gown clung to her frail thin form, her blue eyes in innocent gaiety captured his gaze and he lowered his blade to return her smile ... as love smote him deeply.

"My room needed a spring clean," she chuckled then held out her hand and asked:

"To which Knight of great valour do I owe the honour of my rescue? For I am the Lady Oweine. I was imprisoned here by the local people for the slaying of my husband, the Black Knight. My husband slew our only child; and only this last foul act would make me harm him or any other man.

I withstood his blows" (and briefly she turned to show Beaumains the thousands of lash marks upon her pale white and emaciated back) "and his insults and his forced attentions. But he took from me my new born son and that broke the peace within my heart. I regret my act of murder but ask if this punishment I must suffer, to die alone here, is not too severe given the provocation I have received?"

At this, Beaumains looked down, temporarily confused, before replying:

"My lady Oweine. I am no lawyer or judge and cannot tell you if you are justly punished or not. I can offer to take you before better men than I to judge of this. But I am come to slay a serpent within this chamber that has cursed the land beyond with drought."

At which Oweine laughed so much the tears streamed down from her eyes and then gently stepping forward to take his arm, guided the young man to the balcony of her room where a great water fall of running water could now be seen cascading below them and onto the ancient aquaduct below.

"You have succeeded in your quest, my knight" she whispered and kissed him gently on the forehead as he turned to her in astonishment at her words "For the serpent was no more than the folly of those who trapped me in this chamber. They used the stones of the water causeway to enclose me in here, little knowing that in so doing they would also seal off the water to their own crop fields. The 'serpent' is slain, and I am your prize, if this is consistent with your honour and your desire?"

He took the fair lady to her bed chamber where his gentleness touched her soul and the manner of his kindness undid all the harm that many years of abuse had rendered upon her. Such was her rapturous response to his careful love-making that he was likewise healed of the lack of confidence that had dogged him in his early maturing years. He found a lover to fulfil his dreams, whilst she found a man to treat her as the child she still was, with care and attentiveness but above all with kindness and loving grace.

But this story is not to have a happy-ending alas. For as time passed and Oweine became increasingly content with her new found love in the peace of her home, Beaumains began to hanker for the Court of Artor, for the destiny that lay in his heart, and above all, an almost lost but still lingering memory for a raven haired girl with emerald eyes. All that is tragic finally came to a head on the day that Oweine told Beaumains with eyes brimming with misty joy that she was once again with child.

"You must finish this tale quickly" demanded the dragon eyeing the approaching dawn through a crack in the roof of his chamber.

"Would you have me ruin the tale in too rapid a telling and thus miss some important part that will leave you afterwards wondering if the tale could not have been improved upon?" Ra'el replied and stood once more before the dragon meeting his fiery red gaze with the innocence of her blue eyes.

"Wait!" responded the dragon and she knew from the paralysis that she now felt that the dragon had used all of his daily magical quotient to cast upon her a spell of wish, that most powerful of ensorcelments but one that can only be used sparingly. To be the subject of such a spell was an honour indeed, although she did not feel particularly flattered at the time.

The dragon flew to the far end of the chamber and then beyond and out of the girl's sight. She waited for a seeming age, but in reality for a few minutes, no more, and then he returned, blood flecks across his nose and jaws demonstrating that he had broken his fast. Not on the girl, I am glad to say, but still she felt great guilt that her actions had condemned some other poor soul to be the victim to sate this monster's hunger. She lived on but was unsure that the price paid was something she could willingly bear again - better to die than to be the source of death for another. Yet the wish to survive is strong especially in the very young.

The dragon looked at the girl then smiled and released her from his spell. He held out his claws once more but this time cupped as if a seat for her to sit in.

"Come" he said. "I like this story well. You have recounted it to me long through the night and into morning. And now we must both sleep ... but later today I will require you tell me the end of your tale of the Lady Oweine and then on the morrow I shall eat you. For now, sleep in the warmth of my hand and have no fear of me. My name is Roaring Flamebringer and I am most pleased to make your acquaintance, my little queen."

"My name is Ra'el, recently brought to live amongst *'the people who are deaf'*. I am likewise pleased and honoured to be in your care ... if only for this one night" and Ra'el settled down to sleep, and to dream, she prayed, of stories new to entice this most severe of critics and thus prolong her young and fledgling life.

Ra'el awoke suddenly to a dousing of cold water as Roaring Flamebringer held her gently beneath the clean waters of a waterfall - she shivered in shock and then pleasure as his warm breath heated the water and she had the first of many unforgettable showers in the crystal cavern beneath the Hill. He watched as her shift clung to her, wistfully noticing the lack of meat or anything much to chew, then smiled and with a last blast of hot air, dried her hair into an aureole of silver and gold. Ra'el could see in the green and blue flecks in his eyes that he was content and she herself looked back bravely in respect and awe at his controlled use of his inner flame.

"My little queen" he spoke respectfully "you have slept so deeply I begin to think you must have dragon's blood in your veins. But my patience is limited and I apologise therefore that I must wake you so abruptly. You have a story to finish and already the sun is past its zenith and night soon approaches. Tell your story to its end and then we shall discuss the manner of your own end."

Ra'el smiled in return at the courtesy of the monster and thanked him for the comfort of the warmth of his breath and his un-shaking claw that had been her bed these hours past. Then, no longer caged by that same claw, but trusted to sit now cross-legged before him as the story-tellers of old, she returned again to the tragedy of Oweine.

Beaumains was overjoyed at the news of the fair Oweine and the child she wouldst bear, yet doubt still ate at his heart. Thus it was, as the lovers sat on the balcony of her apartments to regard the fertile croplands and vineyards that now lay as far as the eye might sweep, he spoke carefully of the sorrow in his heart:

"Knowst thou, my fair lady, that there is a thing that doth grieve me despite the solace and majesty and tranquillity of our time together. I am torn, if truth be told, in two. For my love and gratitude to you for the confidence and maturity that your love has enkindled in me and for the joy of a son or daughter that short time shall gift to us, knows no bounds nor boundaries ... and yet."

Here, the young man paused, then stood from the table where they sat and walked to the chamber in which they slept to return with the saddle bag that he still kept from his departure from Camelot. He brought it from its hiding place beneath their marriage bed to rest upon the trestle before them.

He opened it slowly to allow the fair lady to see its contents for the first time: a ring, a quartered, sur-coated tabard and the hilt of a sword.

"These are my fathers. The dying gift of the King of Orkney to me, his youngest of son's, with a final blessing and a loving behest that I should go to Artor in Camelot, prove my worth and pledge my oath and thus take up arms at the Table where already sit my brothers: Gawain, Yvain and Mordred.

"I sought a quest to prove my worth - to destroy a serpent and free a land from oppression. I found instead a fair and loving maid who has bewitched me and holds me life and soul in her gentle palms," and he smiled reassuringly at his companion who sat head bowed attentively but with a growing sense of concern and loss "and for whom I would do anything to protect from harm."

"My lady, I shalt live with you all my life if you say this must be so and thus break the oath I made to my dying pater. I shall never say more of this and love you unceasingly and without doubt or remorse if this is your desire. I ask merely that you have thought of me and answer this simple question: may I have your leave to fulfil my quest or am I to live as your swain for the rest of my days?"

The lady stood unsteadily but her wise and graceful soul already knew the answer she must give though it break her fragile heart:

"I wouldst know your name, my gentle handed lord and prince."

"I am christened Gareth yet prefer the loving title given in the castle where I once served: call me Beaumains, e'en though I shalt bear another name shouldst I return to Camelot to fulfil my quest."

"Then, my lord prince Gareth, my love, my Gentle Hands, my dearest man; my answer is this: you must in honour complete your quest to the letter and return to the company in which you shall have praise and the fulfilment of your destiny. I ask one favour thus from you: that when you leave, you take our son (for this child seateth forwards in my womb and I feel in the strength of the kicks that he doth give that he is a warrior to be born).

Our son shall grow to be a champion of this world if guided at your side in the company of the greatest Order of Knights this world hast ever known. Let him earn honour as you have in the defeat of evil. I ask therefore that you wait with me three months until our child shalt be born then ride to Artor with my living gift to you and my loving blessing."

At her gentle and considerate words, Beaumains was abashed and yet also joyful in his heart in equal measure; unable to decide how to greet the gift of this loving lady, he stepped gingerly forward to hold her in his arms as she silently wept at the loss she would one day have but still generously proposed.

"I will make these three months for you a time of such wonderful remembrance that they shall see you through the brief time I return to Artor. And when the King shall determine my role in his company then I shall send for you that we shall be together again for all time."

She nodded mistily but knew in her heart this would not be true.

Some days later, the nature of her pregnancy meant that she must retire to rest - her body and womb weakened by many beatings in the past, her physicians advised her remain in bed and abhor all exercise even the gentle love-making that had been her greatest joy and comfort.

Beaumains became frustrated; for he was young and lusty whilst passion for the touch of a woman had been awakened in him by the fair Oweine. So, alas, his mind wandered to thoughts of Jocelyn and her raven hair and saucy smile. His cold bed merely served to bring back memories of the nights lying at her door as her protector. Until finally the heat of his desire took him from the castle of Caer Malice to the town beneath it's still gaping maw and the humble house of its Notaire.

Had he been discreet then no more need be said of this tale save that tragedy would have been averted. But Jocelyn had likewise thought and dreamt of the boy made man whom had rescued her village and was now lord of the manor. She welcomed him and that night began the affair that would finally destroy the lady of our story. Alas, Jocelyn was proud, and could not prevent talk in the taverns in the town of the new "trophy" she had won through the sparkle of her eyes.

The young knight supplicant gave her a ring as a token of her prowess beneath the sheets of their adulterous bed - a ring given to him by Oweine. It was foul mischance that took the fair lady of the fountain, mere days before her confinement, to enter the village beneath the castle for one last walk amongst its market stalls. She sought out some small gift of silver for the child and some finery as a memento of the birth for the father... but saw instead her own already gifted ring upon the finger of the lover, knew its significance, and her heart was torn apart.

The birth went well, a lusty child was born. A son, named Bedevere by the lady (a foretelling of the hiding place of the Grael haft Beaumains but have known) in rude and clamouring health. She handed the child to her lord and gave him also a parchment which she instructed him read when he wouldst reach the Court of the King Artor:

"This is my reference and recommendation to the King; my account of your quest; my last gift to you that will aid you in your quest to be accepted into the company of Knights."

Then she grasped him tight one last time before releasing him as she knew she must to go to the destiny that awaited him.

By her lady in waiting she also did in secret send one further gift for Beaumains: a second letter. Thus it was that Jocelyn did receive a visitor from Caer Malice bearing a message for her from the Lady of the Manor. It was brief but poignant:

"To the fair lady Jocelyn, my greetings from the Lady Oweine.

Alas, that we should never meet, but I knowst thou lovest my prince and it is from that love that I ask this favour of thee. This day he rides for Camelot with our son to become a brave knight in the company there.

It is not my fate to follow him and so I have released him. The church shalt say I was 'in sin' for I married the gentle Beaumains whilst still convicted of the murder of my own husband. The court of Artor shalt say I was 'a demon' bewitching Beaumains until finally he shouldst be able to achieve his own rescue.

Only you shall know the truth: I love him and it is that love that lets me release him into YOUR care.

Do this one favour for me, I beg. Look after my lover and our son as if both were your own. He loves you, not I, so marry him and make him whole; follow him to Camelot and be his lady. Do not be ashamed of your kitchen boy for he is a prince and the son of King Lot of Orkney, now dead. Marriage to him shalt be the making of you both and this is my last and parting gift to the man who rescued me once from prison and a slow and lonely death.

Oweine, the Lady of the Fountain."

The lady Jocelyn caught up with her prince and their reunion was joyful. She immediately took the child to her own care and loved that child as if her own bringing her much solace when in years to come she was brought to realise that the gift of a child was one denied herself. Together, this new family arrived at Court and Beaumains asked for and was granted audience with the King. That night he stood before the whole assembly to make known his deeds and take his place in that select gathering.

"Liege lord, the most noble and honourable King of Briton, I kneel before you, a humble knight supplicant, having completed my quest in order to demonstrate my worth and right to be seated at this most hallowed table. I am a prince and brother to three other Knights already members of this august company but this wouldst not be sufficient were it not also that I come quest-fulfilled to hear your judgement on my actions. The parchment I bear is testimony from the seneschal of the castle and surrounding estate that I have rescued that land from a terrible oppression. I seek your leave to read this statement of support for my supplication."

Beaumains was given leave to read the testimonial and so broke the seal and stood, at first in quiet confidence and then in growing dismay at sight and sound of the words of the Lady of the Fountain as they echoed across the King's chamber, a telling of the death of a gentle soul whose love for her husband and child had become the focus of her life:

"This brave Knight who stands before you this day has wrought great deeds to the aid of my people.

Know this:

The estate he has freed from a curse was once held under the sway of a 'serpent' in the guise of a fair lady known as the lady Oweine. This 'serpent' didst hold the lord Prince Gareth captive and captivated for a year and a day in which time the land around saw drought and plague banished through his acts of rescue and love.

This knight didst finally overcome both the 'evil' lady's ensorcelment and the curse laid upon this place to break her charms and slay the 'serpent' whose death will see life and prosperity continue in these lands once laid waste in despite by their former lord and senescal.

I swear that this Knight hath both lifted a foul curse through his deeds and also has slain she who was known as both the 'serpent' and as the lady Oweine.

Sworn this day by the lawful seneschal and chatelain of Caer Malice.

The Lady Oweine"

As Beaumains read the parchment in distant Camelot, Oweine laid herself gently down into the Fountain in order to fulfil her words to the Court of Artor and thus let her princely lover with the gentle hands achieve her death. She sacrificed her life and her reputation to allow the man she loved to attain his dream. She let the cold crystal waters take her rushing through the waterfall to fall hundreds of feet to the aquaduct below where her crushed and dying body inhaled: and water flooded her lungs. She ignored the dreadful pain as her mind was deprived of oxygen (for she had suffered greater pain before) and turned instead to the white light that approached until it suffused her, blinded her, then finally released her into black nothingness, her sacrifice for her lover accomplished.

She had given birth to two sons by two very different men: the first infant had been slain by the evil of the Black Knight but she had borne the resulting punishment with courage and grace. It was the loss of her second son to a kindly man whom she loved that had slain her: for lost love is far more cruel than hate to a heart that loves.

Beaumains became the favourite of Lancelot and, but for his treatment of Oweine and more particularly the shadow of guilt he felt, Beaumains was the Knight who came closest to the Grael until it was finally found by Lancelot's son, Galahad, and Beaumain's own son Bedevere.

Tragically, Lancelot would kill Beaumains by accident when rescuing Guinevere from the trap of Mordred and Yvain whilst Jocelyn was the lady who held out for the death penalty for Guinevere that sent Artor mad and broke the peaceful kingdom of Briton once and for all. Gawain and Yvain also died at Lancelot's hands leaving Mordred to achieve the final betrayal and allow the pagan Saxons into the land of Albion.

Thus ends the story of Oweine, who gave her broken life to let her son and lover achieve a destiny that would both hold the memory of Camelot alive and also destroy it."

Roaring Flamebringer breathed out a sigh of contentment:

"Well told, my little maid. Bravely spoken and cleverly contrived. It is a long time since I have been thus entertained and I wilt be honest and say it doth please me greatly. But now I am in quandary ... for there are still five hours left until dawn and when I break my fast. Howst propose thou we spend such time?"

Ra'el laughed in response skipping and dancing before him then said over her shoulder:

"I have another story I didst dream of last night. Let me but have something to eat myself of thine kindness and I would be honoured to share this new tale withst thee."

"'Tis a new story?" asked the dragon tremulously.

"None save thee shalt ever hear the telling of it o mightiest serpent" she replied smiling up at him.

"There is time and your company is delightful. I grant you leave to tell me this second account. If the story is good then I shall bring you some fruit to break your fast before I break mine. I wouldst have you tasty after all, my queen" and the dragon lay back, his eyes half open in contented expectation as she drank some of the water in the dark pool beside them, then sat once more before him in the customary story-teller's pose.

"The tale I tell is of the freeing of the great Pallas, civil servant to Emperors and the tutor of the mistress of Vespasian. There is a single line in the account of Suetonius which opens the door to a story of love and adventure. This is the story I shall tell and it begins in the chamber of Tiberius, where a Knight by name of Gallius in his early forties, and with a successful military then legal career to his name, has been granted audience to approach the Emperor and seek admittance to the ranks of the senate."

AELIA

Tiberius Julius Caesar Augustus sat in the presbyterium of his palace, his close friend Aelius Sejanus lounging nonchalantly with his arms folded across the back of the great carved curule chair on which the princeps of the whole of the known world sat in state.

"He is rich," muttered Tiberius rebelliously.

"I can smell the reek of the provinces from here" replied Sejanus.

Tiberius was already in his sixties and time had not been kind. Unhappy marriages, an embarrassing political retirement, military campaigns in plague-infested barbaric provinces, an ambitious mother who appeared to have wiped out half of his adoptive family to get her son on the throne, had all left their mark on both his visage and character. Augustus in the last years of his reign used to cry "Give me back my legions!" of Varus's defeat in the Teutobregen Forest. Tiberius would just as often cry: "Give me back my hair!" when he recalled his tortuous route to become the princeps of Rome.

Sejanus, on the other hand, was heroically handsome. Whilst his military career had not been as successful as his friends, it had seen him in combat in much warmer and gentler climates. It had also brought him command of the Praetorian Guard and he was now become Tiberius' right hand man.

Tiberius' mother was dead and this had lifted the princeps' spirits considerably in recent months. His adopted heir Germanicus had yet to be poisoned by the Pisonis, precipitating Tiberius' disgust at and retirement from politics to Capri, and leaving Sejanus to attempt to become Emperor himself in his friend's absence. Germanicus, rather, had just successfully celebrated his triumph on the defeat of the Germanic tribes and the recapture of the standards lost by Varus.

Tiberius was very proud of his heir but the three year military campaign with no trade benefit or significant booty in sight followed by the lavish triumph (the first in decades) had emptied the Treasury. The Emperor was very broke.

"He is rich ... and we need money," repeated Tiberius.

"Tax him or trump up charges and confiscate it!"

At that the princeps had laughed out loud and then chided his confidant:

"Unlike those good-for-nought senators we keep sending out to my provinces who suck them dry and send me nothing in return, Gallius makes money. If I leave him some money, he will turn it into more to give me. No, my friend ... we do the deal and find out what he wants to do with the money we leave him. Only then do we come for that also."

Sejanus smiled in reply: "I feared you were going soft, domine! I should have known you were one step ahead of the game. I will go fetch the old man and let us see what he wants ... apart from the obvious: a place in the most select company in Rome."

Gallius was grey-haired, in his late forties, with a slight stoop, but with the clear blue honest eyes of a child. He was an immensely successful business man; an equites with the reputation for honesty in his dealings that meant people would return to him for advice and for his investment.

He had been an uninspiring soldier until one day he had found himself and his primus pilum cut off from the rest of his century. No-one knew what possessed him but he had stood bravely over his wounded man, a young lad from his own estates, and held off the attack of four Numidian spearmen. For so doing, he had won the coveted grass crown and the right to become a magistrate.

His magistracy had been a by-word for justice and this had brought him to the attention of several of the patrician families in Rome who were now sponsoring his application to enter the senate; an honour for which he was prepared to pay handsomely whilst he would have no difficulty in demonstrating he had the necessary 1m sesterces of land to his credit.

Gallius bowed to Tiberius and then was invited to join the two other men in the triclinarium. Briefly, they talked of the rumours of the city, mainly of the games Germanicus had proposed for the ensuing week to show off his Germanic captives, but the princeps could not keep his impatience in check and eventually blurted out:

"So you want a place in my senate?"

Gallius answered carefully:

"My lord, I would be honoured. I should explain my purpose however in being so presumptuous as to ask to join such patrician ranks, when I myself am a mere knight. My wish is to place a significant proportion of my wealth at your disposal to help with your proposed military, political and municipal programme, and to use my remaining wealth to further your ambitions from the advantageous position of that of a senator."

"How much?" the ruler of the civilised world demanded in far less than civilised interest.

"I offer you a third of my wealth: just over 100 million sesterces. I also agree to put the same again to use through the senate in support of programmes that you propose ... but I shall want your support in return for a project of mine" Gallius added.

The silence with which this last comment was greeted almost overpowered Gallius but he had a vision and he was not about to give up on his dreams lightly, even though he faced and feared to antagonise the two most powerful men in the world.

"What do you want, old man?" asked Sejanus, barely concealed contempt deepening the timbre of his voice until it was husky with suppressed anger and emotion. "*Another power-greedy knight*" the praetor thought privately and disgustedly to himself.

But when Gallius explained his wishes, both men relaxed. Indeed, as Tiberius allowed the knight to expand on his vision, Tiberius could see massive benefits for his own administration and reputation. When finally, dry-throated and nervous, Gallius had completed his description of his grand design, Tiberius stood immediately, lifted the gentle magistrate from his triclinium and embraced him, saying:

"I shall recommend you personally to the senate and I accept your kind offer of investing in my political programme. I ask merely that your own great plan be done also in my name as well as thine own. Will you agree to this?"

Gallius had nodded amazed and then knelt in gratitude at his new patron's feet. But Tiberius would have none of this and lifted him once more then chuckling mischievously asked him:

"Were you planning to go to the games tomorrow? There is a spectacle I think you will enjoy in the Coliseum. I ask you to join me as my guest. If what I hear is true, I may have found you just what you need to make your dream come to fruition."

Perplexed, Gallius had looked questioningly at his imperator but the man's gaze was impenetrable save for a glint of what he took to be malicious humour in the other's eyes.

Gallius sat nervously on the podium, a mere six feet from the arena sands, in full view of the thousands of spectators who had come to see that day's spectacle. He waited in trepidation for the vestal virgins to take their seats on the opposite side of the Coliseum which would mark the imminent arrival of the Emperor entering via his personal tunnel from the palace.

Tiberius' predecessor, the God Augustus, had decreed the seating plans in every arena and theatre in the world and (until that day) Gallius had always queued to gain entrance through one of the many numbered gates and then taken his place on the second tier.

But today, his membership of the senate unanimously accepted by the censors that morning, he had passed without the need for a ticket through one of four unnumbered entrances and been guided by a praetorian in full crested armour to the elevated pulvinar (a raised dais on four statues of victory above which hung a gold awning and which was affectionately known by the Romans as 'the bedroom').

He had been shown to his sella curulis alongside that of Sejanus (already seated) and immediately to his right was the bisellium on which the Emperor would recline during the games. On the far side of the bisellium was the fair-haired Germanicus in whose honour the games were being celebrated. And now he bit his lip fearfully, unsure why the princeps had wanted him to attend on this day but nonetheless honoured to be so prominent before the people of Rome.

The fanfare sounded, and all stood to greet Tiberius in a deafening roar of appreciation as he walked slowly and humbly into the Imperial Box, held his right hand aloft in acknowledgement of their salute, before sitting as the signal that all should be seated.

Immediately, Tiberius beckoned Gallius to lean over and talk to him:

"My dear friend. This initial contest is one I hope you will enjoy. But first I must give you a bit of background. In a few moments, we will witness a bout between a German princess, captured by Germanicus in her forested retreat, whom he has pitted against four very hungry lions. This is no ordinary combat however for the girl will be unarmed whilst the lions are notorious man-killers.

Germanicus tells me reliably that our German barbarian held off a whole cohort of his best men to protect the children in her village who had been left under her guard and care. His men were only able to capture her when some of them got above her and dropped a net, else, no doubt, she would still be fighting them now!

And so I shall put this remarkable feat to the test and have ordered four of the children captured with her to be staked out on the arena sands. The girl must rescue the children and defeat the lions. If she does this then she must also survive my judgment and that of the crowd.

But, if she lives, then Sejanus and I feel she will be of great help to you with your plans, Gallius. She is a protector of children after all!" and Tiberius had laughed chillingly.

Gallius watched in horror as four young and terrified children were dragged out by their hair into the arena and each tied to a vertical pole at the four corners of the Coliseum. Then, the arena went silent as the girl was brought out.

She was tall, incredibly so, thought Gallius. She was fair and pale-skinned as were all of the people of the north with long straight silver hair and sapphires as eyes. She was beautiful and young, so thin and frail he could scarce believe she could stand before the raucous baying of the crowd.

She wore the simple slip of a gladiator but had no armour or weapons; her feet were bare also. She was a girl, not yet a woman, small-breasted and straight hipped but despite the modesty of her attire her bearing was regal.

"Is she not magnificent? She will make a tasty meal for the lions!" laughed Germanicus.

The girl looked slowly around her and took in the four children stationed on all sides of her. Then she tensed as the first of the lions was released.

The crowd gasped …

. . . for she had run straight at the lion without fear and at incredible speed. The starving animal, intent on the fearful child before it, had been caught by surprise at her pace and direction and been flung backwards as she had launched herself both feet first to strike it in the rib cage.

The lion staggered, winded by the double blow. From the careful way it carried itself, clearly something had been ruptured by the lady's precisely delivered kicks. But the girl did not stop there; rather removing her slip to the delight of the spectators she had wound it rapidly in strips into a thin rope caught the injured lion by the throat and tossed it onto its back, tethering its four feet as it fell thrashing to the ground.

She turned then kissed the child she had rescued reassuringly before looking across the arena for the next hazard.

The arena master knew his trade well and seeing how easily the first lion had been despatched decided to send two lions at once to confuse the girl. She, however, was ready for this also. Again she ran, but this time for the centre of the arena whilst emitting a high-pitched whistle. Both lions had walked carefully out onto the arena sands but at the sound of the sprinting girl their heads turned away from the vulnerable children and towards this larger prize. At this she spun around and ran from them, drawing the carnivores away from the innocents as they gave chase.

She timed her run carefully at first pulling away from them as she flew like the wind but then slowing up when a limp appeared; she had pulled a muscle perhaps? The lions sensed an easy kill. One circled at speed to the left, the other to the right, then both charged before leaping at her exposed back ...

... and she flung herself to the ground beneath them as they flew over her head and smacked into the arena walls. The lions were stunned for only a few seconds but that was long enough for her to grasp their tails and tie them together into a Gordian knot!

The crowd laughed with delight ... even the Emperor smiled to see the lions snapping desperately at each other and their tails in an attempt to break free. But the girl had no time to take this all in for the arena master had released the final lion and it was already stalking the fourth child, tied and defenceless beneath the Imperial Box.

She ran ... how she ran! Even mercury could not have covered the sands with her speed. But, alas she was too late, as the princess was still fifteen feet from the child when the lion leapt for its throat.

At what happened next, the crowd rose as one in awed amazement and even the Emperor stood in wonder.

In the split second when the lion had launched itself, the girl had also leapt, flying many feet through the air to interpose her own bare arm and thrust it down the tearing maw of the lion. Instead of ripping the throat of a young child, the lion had mangled her left arm and flung her to the ground in shock from terrible blood loss.

The lion scented her death now and turned swiftly to remove her as a threat before it could return to feast on the child. She lay still and bleeding as it rocked back on its haunches then it sprang at her …

... only for her to roll to her left and flip herself one-handed onto its back before vaulting across to where the last child was still staked out.

In her left hand she clutched the tooth she had ripped out of the lion's jaw when she had plunged her arm into his mouth and with her prize she quickly cut loose the child.

But now, the lion was at her again: this time striking with its claws. She swung, side-stepped, ducked and dodged clear of each blow with lightning speed before stamping on the lion's tail at which it let out an agonised scream and she used this one chance to grab the child, run up the lion's back and onto the podium, where the Emperor was watching in astonishment. Flashing him a courteous smile and a hasty bow, she turned to deposit the child in Gallius' lap and then jumped back into the arena to finish the fight.

The crowd were now in raptures but the girl was weakening and this last lion might still be her undoing.

The lion circled her warily. It was in no hurry and recognised the nature of the injury it had already inflicted. For it knew that time would give it victory and that each second would see its foe weaken and eventually collapse. From years of fighting its instincts told it that all it need do was keep clear of the lady and her wound would do its job for it.

The girl was no buck or doe, however, going meekly to its death through the loss of its own blood. She also was a veteran of many fights and she knew precisely what now must be done. Slowly they circled ... and then she stumbled.

The lion leapt once more, fooled by her feint, and she flung herself onto her back then pushed upwards with both feet into its stomach to fling the lion head over heels into the air and down, as intended, onto the pointed tip of the stake on which the child had earlier been tethered as bait. The lion crashed down, impaled through its neck, and quivered in surprise then in horror and finally in submission of its own death.

The girl stood: to acclaim, to uproar, to the plaudits of an astonished and gratified crowd and to the gay laughter of a more than satisfied Imperator.

"She is yours if you will take her Gallius" Tiberius twinkled at the old man. "I reckon you might need a partner in your enterprise and she will do nicely. Her name is 'Aelia' named by me after my friend Sejanus here. Look after her for me!"

Gallius sent a message to his house that Gallippa should join him 'quam celerime' at the entrance to the Mamertine, where Aelia was being held prisoner. The Praetorian Guards had warned the old man that it had taken eight of them to hold her down when they had taken the children from the arena.

She was now shackled and they intended her to remain that way. Gallius had no need to ask why as he could see they were sporting several bruises and the odd black eye from their struggle with the wild cat.

Gallius spoke to Germanicus who, hugely amused at the idea of this kind and gentle man being given charge of the ferocious German princess, gladly acceded to his request for aid and went off in search of the arena master.

When all was ready, Gallius prepared to enter the vixen's den. The door to her cell was opened by a guard who was clearly struggling to stand straight.

"Basta bella got me" was all he could mutter holding his battered tackle carefully as he staggered off to the infirmarium. "You can have her with my blessing!"

Gallius gulped but nonetheless persevered and entered into the tiny and lightless room. She was chained to the wall, still naked and bleeding from her injuries yet madly defiant. Her blue eyes were ablaze with angry fire but the innocent admiration in the gentle man's gaze made her hesitate. She straightway recognised him from the podium and started to smile then remembered she had given one of her cares into his safe-keeping and now they were gone. She put back her head and howled like a wolf at which Gallius asked his German slave and secretary, Galippa, to enter.

Galippa spoke softly to calm the princess and at his words she ceased her careening, her head swung down and she looked in sudden hope and then, as the import of what he said sunk in, she became still in tranquil reassurance:

"Genadste beolanc die vest perfunden gast."

"Tell her I have her children safe in my care. Germanicus has had them released into my custody. Tell her that if she will come with me and do me no harm then it is my wish she look after them in the safety of my household. Tell her that I mean her only good things; indeed, I have never hurt any woman or child" had whispered Gallius to Galippa.

"Ai preotan di wunds" the lady had replied gently in return.

"What does this mean?" Gallius had asked urgently and impatiently. "Does she say 'yes'?"

"Hush, domine" replied his slave. "She is tired and hurt, that is all. She needs our aid. But yes, she will come with us and offer us no harm."

Then to the girl he said: "Faúr-bi-gaggan" and pointed to Gallius. "Master, I have said you will go on ahead of us to get things ready. With your permission, I will stay here and tend the lady's wounds, also see if I can find her some clothing and then we will follow. Can you send the litter for us?"

Gallius nodded then gave Galippa a gentle hug of gratitude before, with a smile for Aelia, he left. She raised her eyebrows at Galippa in turn and then asked a simple:

"?Bleips? Sels" at which the slave chortled then chided his own master: "He is too kind if you ask me."

For those not familiar with ancient Gothic:
Genadste beolanc, die vest perfunden gast
Hush princess, all will be well for this is a good man
Ai preotan di wunds
I am weary and I am wounded
Faúr-bi-gaggan
He will go on ahead of us
?Bleips
Is he merciful?
?Sels
Is he kind?

Gallius was at his scriborium deep in thought when his house mistress Elysium came running into the study. "Master, she is here!" cried the out of breath freedwoman.

"*Heavens!*" thought the kindly senator, "*Is the whole household in turmoil already and the girl not even had a chance to settle in?*"

"She must not be frightened!" he admonished. "Tell everyone to receive her with calm respect and see she is taken to the room we have prepared then send the children to her."

"Pah" the lady replied "I know my job. Now you make sure you show the lady respect too. Get your head out of those papers and straighten up your toga. This is a real princess we are to receive and you look like a gutter slave rather than a senator and proud representative of the glory of Rome!" and off she stormed to ensure that all should know the pater familias' orders leaving Gallius to reflect that his entry into the senate had made absolutely no discernible change to his standing in his own household.

Aelia stood in the vestibulum admiring the cold marbled walls with the purple grain for which the villas of Rome were renowned. Before her was the atrium, with its fountain and statue of Zeus Omnipotens, a piece by the famous sculptor Polyprax in the style of Phineas had she known it, but all she could see was its majestic lines and muscular build. She blushed at the sight of its manhood and then looked at the face ... and recognised the image of the kindly child-like face of Gallius, her new master.

Gallius drew back the curtains that covered his tablinum slightly to stand silently, secretly admiring the new lady of his house through the clear waters of the same fountain. Galippa had performed wonders and found a gown of exquisite Parthian silks (soft mauve and rust red) for Aelia to wear as her stola over a simple chiton and peplos). The girl's height and lack of weight meant the outfit hung loosely on her but this did not matter for it was merely the backdrop to her hair and her eyes.

His slave had made no attempt to do anything with Aelia's hair and so it hung in long thin strands of burnished silver and gold that glistened in the Roman sun.

Her hair would have brought any Roman street to a stand-still but only for as long as it took the populus to then notice her eyes. She gazed slowly and carefully around the atrium at the cubicula on either side and then smiled as she noticed the curtain twitching in front of her and bowed towards the tabinum. Gallius hurriedly stepped out of his study in embarrassment, still mesmerised by the clear blue waters of her laughing eyes.

She held out her right arm for him to greet her formally and only then did he notice the bandaging to her left arm and the sign of blood still seeping from the wounds beneath. All sense of embarrassment vanished as his natural concern for her took over and with a clap of his hands he ushered her through to the triclinium where she could be seated whilst he commanded the immediate presence of his physician to look at her arm.

Aelia watched carefully as the physician examined her arm who then told his master that he must both cleanse it to prevent infection and stitch it to allow the wound to heal and strength to return.

"Will she bite me?" the physician asked in genuine anxiety.

"I will ask Galippa to explain and also ask for the children to be brought in. If she sees the children she will be reassured that we mean her no harm." Gallius had replied thoughtfully.

The four children burst into the room and to Aelia's surprise but also secret delight their first action was to bow before Gallius and then surround him in one massive group hug. He pretended to be affronted but she (and they) could see the smile in his eyes and the joy he felt in being with them. Aelia had chosen rightly after all when she had placed the little one she rescued on this kind man's lap. "*Sels*!" she reflected wisely and delightedly to herself.

Then the children mobbed her also and it was Gallius' turn to see her own caring reaction and her face light up in their presence. He also knew that the right choice had been made and this gave him the spur he needed to complete the task he had begun that morning in his study.

He watched carefully as Galippa explained the physician's intent and took her simple nod as affirmation that she would accept the pain without response. He stayed for a few more moments to watch her stoically accept the poultice of herbs on her arm and then see the edges of the wound stitched together to hold the curative herbs in place without any pain relief. She merely bit her own lip, rather than the physician, drawing some blood but showing no other sign of the considerable physical pain she must have felt. Instead she played skittles with the children besides her using her other hand to distract both them and herself from the doctor's ministrations.

In the end, it was Gallius who could bear her pain no longer and took himself off to collect his papers from the study before calling his litter to take him to the nearest magistrate. His final instruction was to Elysium and Galippa:

"The lady's name is Aelia. When she is recovered from her time with the physician see that she has something to eat and then take her into the City to see the sights. The Forum should impress her! But also I want her to know she has complete freedom to come and go as she pleases. I shall not see her caged. For the memory of her in the Mamertine shall haunt me my whole life I fear.

If you need me urgently, I will be with Marcus Ahenobarbus in session at the curiale court."

The curiale magistrate had just overseen the official witnessing of Gallius' documents when Galippa burst into the auditorium seeking his master. Ahenobarbus ignored the interruption as if Galippa did not exist and completed his signature with a flourish then appended the hot wax and sealed the parchments with his signet ring.

"Facit" he said proudly and then rolled up the scrolls, attached the bronze scroll ends to each, before returning them to the former knight. Then the magistrate and the senator shook hands and Gallius turned at last to discover what ailed his slave.

"It is Aelia. Oh master, she is in a fight. She will be taken by the Praetorian Guard and will be whipped in the Forum or worse. Come, please come quickly!"

Aelia had started a riot at the slave market explained Galippa as the two men hurried towards the Forum. She had taken exception to a child-slave being struck by the auctioneer and attacked both the slave-marketer and his bodyguard. A decurion and his Praetorian Guards had stepped into the ensuing mayhem.

On seeing she was an unbranded slave, they had proposed to lash her then execute her on the spot as was their right. Except they seemed to be having difficulty pinning her down - Galippa himself had seen her bite one of them whilst she had raked another with her nails and poked a third in the eye.

The Decurion, rapidly assessing the tactical situation, had sent word back to his camp to get help.

"What shall I say?" had asked one of his legionaries.

"Tell the camp commander we are invaded by Goths - millions of them!" had replied the exasperated decurion taking hasty cover as a brazier full of hot coals had been flung at them both.

By the time Gallius reached the Forum, the girl had finally been caught and was being held down by two of the guards, a third tore her stola and pestos and a fourth brought the lash, with its iron stones, down onto her bare back. Gallius gasped as the girl screamed in pain and then, for the first time in his life, he filled with blind-rage and roared into the silence of the gathered crowd:

"Enough! Halt this nonsense at once."

All eyes turned towards the old man and recognised instantly from his white toga that he was a man of the highest rank. The decurion, however, knew his rights and spoke courteously but unwaveringly to the old man:

"This is an escaped slave who has started a riot in the Forum Augustus and is therefore under my authority. I have commanded that she be whipped and then executed by strangulation as is the law. You may not interfere with this, senator."

"The lady is a virgin" replied Gallius "and so may not be executed except after trial by the Vestal Virgins."

"One of my men can see to that!" replied the decurion and nodded to one of the legionaries who begun to unbuckle his belt all the more readily to raise his tunic and do his duty.

"The lady is a freedwoman and I have her manumission papers with me!" continued Gallius which briefly stopped the decurion in his tracks but after a moment's reflection he was able to rejoinder:

"She is still guilty of riot and her status as a freedwoman will only delay her execution. We shall take her to the Mamertine where she can await sentence by the City Prefect."

"The lady is named Aelia after her patron Aelius Sejanus, your commander in chief, and this day I have made her my adopted daughter!" Gallius gasped to the astonishment of the crowd.

Finally, he had silenced the decurion. The soldier knew the law and, unwittingly, his men had struck a senator's daughter. Not only that but one who bore the name of his commander and no doubt his patronage too. Now his life and that of his men was forfeit. Turning to his men, the soldier ordered them to release the girl and then he stood proudly and fearlessly before the senator, saying:

"My life is in your hands. Had you been in my position, you would have acted as I."

"No" replied Gallius. "All our lives are in the hands of the lady, for it is her that you have harmed. Let us ask her what she would wish done?"

Saying a quick prayer to Athena to give the girl-child wisdom, he asked Galippa to translate for him:

"Aelia. Great wrong has been done to you. These men however can be of great service to you in the future. I ask for your mercy on their behalf. You have the right to demand compensation but I beg you show tolerance and forgiveness, despite your hurt."

Aelia looked at Gallius and next at the soldiers. Then standing regally, she frowned before pointing at one of the child-slaves and speaking to Galippa in her native Goth.

"She wants the child to be released into your care, master" translated Galippa.

"He is worth 100 sesterces!" muttered the auctioneer but was silenced by the decurion with a growl and an angry: "Your men struck the lady too and you face death as we do. Take the loss, shut your mouth and keep your life!"

Seeing the child being unshackled, a gleam came into the girl's eyes and suddenly she laughingly spoke her first Latin word: "Tutto!" Galippa gulped then turned in anguish to his master and said: "I think she wants **ALL** of the children released.»

"I will pay for them!" Gallius hurriedly told the auctioneer thus preventing another outburst from the slaver whilst the decurion grinned at the senator, saying: "I have a daughter just like that one. Give her a pace and she will take a league!"

Then Aelia stepped towards the decurion and bowed. She offered him her hand, speaking again in faltering Latin:

"Forgive me, the fault mine not yours. There is no blame here for you!"

"Domina" replied the decurion taking her hand and bowing over it. "My men and I owe you our lives. If you are ever in need, send word to the Praetorian Camp and ask for Velco."

Aelia stood on the balcony of Gallius' villa on the banks of the Aelias Bridge over the Tiber, near the Campus Tiberinus, and gazed in awe at the world's largest city, the home for over two million people. Never had she seen so much marble whether from the Circus Maximus directly below her or the newly re-furbished Forum Augustum, Ara Pacis and Theatre of Agrippa.

Aelia shuddered briefly at the tall dark brick and timber structure of the ancient Coliseum which had near been her death-place (only fifty years later to burn to the ground and be rebuilt as a magnificent amphitheatre by the Flavians) before gazing on the splendour of Tiberius' own palace on the Palatine just before the camp of the Praetorian Guard.

"I am told there are seven hills" she thought and began to count them: Quirinalis and Palatine, easily picked out besides the Forum; Hortorum and Pincius protecting the approach to the Praetorian camp; Caflius and Viminalis either side of the Coliseum; and the Aventine with its gardens and temples, and containing the 'secret treasure' that Gallius had promised to show her later that day.

In the very centre of her view was the Subara, tall towering tenement blocks: a city within a city; untouched by Octavian's building programme and thus still timber and brick rather than the soft gold of marble but from which she could smell the constant delight of baking bread and cooking meat.

This was not the sacred groves that she missed so dearly since her capture. Instead, there were olive and plane trees to replace her oaks; and aquaducts and fountains of mythical creatures or Gods to remind her of the bubbling brooks of her home - but it was not the same!

No, this was how she imagined **heaven**: a place of so many people living together in safety and comfort and health, surrounded by craftsmanship and architecture of which she could never have dreamed until that day. She sighed contentedly and began to plan her day.

She was still bemused by the events of the last two days. When Galippa had explained that Gallius had adopted her as his own daughter, she had wept then hugged the senator then fallen on her knees. He had blushed and hastily raised her before allowing Elysium to show her to her own private rooms beyond the triclinium. She had a courtyard with its vestibulum, atrium, olive trees and a fountain, and the balcony over-looking Rome on which she now stood in admiration.

As yet she could not understand what was to be her purpose: for what reason had Gallius claimed her and then freed her? But she trusted him: for he loved children. She intended to make him delight in her and to do all she could to learn his language and his customs; to be a daughter of whom the gentle man could be proud and perhaps more? Her studies (Gallius had promised to teach her Latin and the literature of the time) would begin today and she would throw herself into these with gusto. But first to see how her children had settled in after their adventures of the day before and to find some salve for the lash marks on her back which had begun to pull as they healed.

That afternoon, Gallius summonsed her to his scriborium with Galippa in attendance to announce they were to go on a trip to the Aventine and that both of the household's litters had been ordered for them.

"Today I introduce you to my grand design for Rome," pronounced the senator portentously whilst both Galippa and Aelia shrugged their shoulders and decided to humour the kindly man.

Their journey took less than an hour, initially through the bustling streets on the approaches to the Forum, before turning south and then west to climb the gentle slopes into the olive groves that marked the boundaries of the Aventine. Narrow streets with high brick and marble buildings gave way to winding gravel paths, manicured lawns and arboretum. On one of the many outcrops in the Aventine they turned a corner, were carried between two copses, to arrive at a large villa set in sloping gardens with a shallow lake and a riot of statuary of animals and mythical creatures.

Aelia gasped ... but not at the gardens nor at the simple but majestic beauty of the villa, not even at the quiet serenity of her surroundings but rather at the tumultuous noise of hundreds of children playing in the gardens.

"This is my secret, my treasure, and my gift for you," the senator spoke quietly and then pleadingly. "The Emperor himself has given me his blessing for this project. I call it an 'orphanage': a place for the young without family to be brought up in peace, to receive their education and to have a chance to go into the world as freed men and women. But I need help. The children need a mother-figure to guide them and protect them. They need someone special to dedicate her life in their care. It is a lot for me to ask, my daughter, but would you help me make my wish come true? For I cannot do this alone and can think of no-one I would rather have as my partner in this endeavour."

Aelia held his head in her hands and kissed him on the lips. Then turning, she ran towards the children in perfect answer to his request and he smiled joyfully as he watched her join in their games. For she was still a child herself; yet he knew, as Tiberius had secretly hoped, that his orphans would come to no harm with her guardianship and under her devoted protection.

In the months that followed, Aelia would spend her days at the orphanage, playing with the children but also keeping careful eye over them. They adopted her readily and indeed many she discovered to her delight were from her own village, bought out of slavery by Gallius who had made it part of his mission to locate and find all of those originally under her care when she had been captured by Germanicus' men.

In the evenings, she would throw herself into her studies desperate to learn the language, customs and mores of Rome and thus to take her place in its society. She learnt quickly and soon could find her way about the city without the need for Galippa in attendance. Once she was ready to go on her own, she quickly discarded her litter and instead would run ... **everywhere**! She became known as the Golden Atlanta to the folk of the Subara but was well-liked for she would always stop to talk to the shop keepers and stall holders as she passed by.

One evening, instead of joining Gallius for supper, Elysium brought news that Aelia had shut herself in her rooms and would not stop crying. The whole household had gathered in the vestibulum outside her rooms in deep concern. Gallius came himself and had to force his way through his anxious slaves and freedmen to gain the doorway to her chambers where he knocked carefully.

There was no answer except for renewed and anguished sobs.

"Explain!" growled Gallius turning on his household.

"Fetch the tutor," replied Elysium, frightened of her master for the first time as she saw the steely anger in his child-like eyes. The tutor was bustled forwards and looked fearfully at the senator: "It was my lesson," he admitted. "Something I said has made her overwrought."

"What was it you sought to teach my daughter?" was the stern enquiry.

"We studied the Oppian laws on matrimony, domine."

The senator was surprised at his own reaction. For the tutor's words had made his heart wrench and his head to whirl. He realised, suddenly, that he had feared this might happen ever since he had brought Aelia into his household: that one day she would find someone she loved and would seek to marry and thus he would lose her. He had not expected it to happen so soon, that is all, he thought sadly. And, the old fool that he was, he had hoped she might live with him as his daughter until he died and then take over the orphanage after him. But now, he must make other plans. Only with this news did he realise he loved her so very much that he would unselfishly ensure that her dreams of marriage would come true.

"My daughter wishes to marry. We must see to her wishes with all of our hearts and charity. Does any here know of the suitor?"

His words were greeted with silence for none knew of any who had sought the hand or grace of the fair lady of their house.

"Then I must brave her den, enter, and ask in hope that she shall not slay me" said the senator determinedly and knocked loudly this time on the girl's chamber door, demanding entry.

Aelia opened the door to him, her eyes swollen with tears, her nose running from her weeping, had she but known it more adorable to Gallius for her new-found fragility than he had ever seen her before. He sat on the end of the bed as she lay there in silence, sniffing occasionally but otherwise refusing to speak or acknowledge her own tears. Then he asked her gently:

"What ails you, my loving daughter?"

Roaring Flamebringer looked up to see dawn had broken and that he must therefore break his fast. His appetite to hear the end of this story was as great as his hunger, if not more so, yet he knew he must eat each day to stoke the great fires within him.

"My queen! I must leave you and find something to eat. Will you wait for my return?"

"I shall" Ra'el replied, standing before him, "if you will do me one favour?"

"Verily" spoke the dragon. "Is it food that you require?"

"Nay, my lord dragon. I ask that you touch not one of my people if you wouldst eat now. For I wouldst rather die than know I have lived one more day because you have eaten another of my kind."

At this the dragon began to become angry and retorted in growing ire:

"Is this how you show me respect?"

"I shall respectfully not finish my story unless you do as I ask!" the girl ventured looking straight at the dragon fearlessly and in blue-eyed innocence.

"Very well," he smiled good-humouredly. "If you shall promise to remain then I shall promise to refrain."

"I do so promise" Ra'el replied relieved. And then to demonstrate her good faith, she sat down again on the floor of the cavern whilst the dragon took flight in quest of a meal. He soon returned, carrying the remains of a pig he had slaughtered, and sat before her to eat it. Once sated, he then asked the girl courteously to continue:

"Aelia stood up, walked over to the small desk at the end of her cubicula and picked up a scroll, now wet with her tears, before pointing to a single line of text two thirds of the way down the parchment. Gallius took it from her and read the passage she had indicated:

"Marriage between a senator and his adopted daughter shall be forbidden on pain of sacrilege."

At which she flung herself on the bed and began to howl with distress whilst Gallius looked genuinely dumbfounded. Then he began slowly but surely to chuckle. At first a gentle quivering sound but then it rose gradually until it had completely overtaken him in joyous guffaws of laughing delight.

Aelia, however, stared at him as if he had gone quite mad which only made his laughter more uncontrollable until he was doubled up and unable to stop. Finally, he staggered over to her desk and began to rummage through the other scrolls there until he came to the Lex Augustus and then plonked it down in front of her, pointing in his turn to a passage for her to read:

"I, therefore, propose to repeal and to reinforce a number of the Oppian laws. My intent is to both ensure due piety amongst the people of Rome, whilst also removing clauses within the ancient laws that create an unfair barrier to marriage and inheritance. I shall enforce correctness of behaviour and rectitude, but balance this with compassion for those who find themselves in love but unable as laws currently stand to be married. Today, I propose to repeal the following sections of Oppian law:

(i) ......
(ii) ......
(iii) ......
(iv) marriage previously forbidden between a senator and an adopted daughter shall be allowed provided that proof can be given before a magistrate that there is no coercion. To ensure this is the case, possessions of the daughter shall be held in trust by the state until such time as the daughter shall be of an age to determine their use."

Aelia read and understood immediately then turned enquiringly to Gallius, who, still smiling, answered her unspoken question:

"Why am I laughing? Not at you, my dear, I promise. It is notoriously difficult to prove there is not **coercion** in such cases of proposed marriage. But you, dearest Aelia ... no-one is going to believe you have *ever* been coerced nor that a man alive exists that could do so! This is why I could not help laughing: for the idea I could coerce you is so ridiculous. If you will come with me now, I can set all in motion to have you un-adopted and then ... "and at this point he hesitated briefly, before stepping before her and holding both her hands in his own, he continued timidly, yet in hope:

"... and then, if you will, I would be honoured that you become my wife."

Her response was instant, passionate, unrestrained and left him in no doubt of her love for him. His heart leapt and in a state of near delirium, he ordered their litters to be fetched to take them to the magistrate's court. The household cheered and then applauded the couple as Gallius led his daughter but soon to be bride by the hand to the waiting chaise.

Galippa and Elysium rapidly organised for the nuptial procession - they had no need to hire dancing girls and flower bearers from the Forum, for they had a whole orphanage full of children, all of whom had known of Aelia's love for Gallius and had secretly been plotting for this moment for months now.

The whole household lined the street that marked the approach to Gallius' villa; the decurion Vecto was summonsed and had an entire century turn out in their purple crested and black finery; the Subaran shop-keepers heard the news and in a rare gesture of solidarity, closed their stalls to ensure they could be waiting to shower the newly-weds with gifts.

Gallius and Aeilia made their triple vow before Ahenobarbus and thus, in marital bliss, were conveyed back to Gallius' domus. The first thing that greeted them was the noise for a party had already broken out along the approaches to their home. Then when they saw the gathered crowds, they wept at the gift of such friendship before stepping out of their litters to walk amongst their many companions, sharing the great joy of this moment.

The celebrations went on well into the night, until finally the senator and his lady stood on their balcony arm in arm before he lifted her to carry her to their marriage bed to the raucous cheers of the gathering.

The next day, the new wife of Gallius required no encouragement in doing the social rounds of the elite of Rome. She was on a mission as powerful as Gallius': to ensure his dreams were taken up by the Roman matriarchy. Aelia was instantly recognisable as she ran through the streets without time for a litter, with her startling looks, silver-gold hair, fair skin, considerable height and crystal blue eyes - traits seldom seen amongst the shorter patrician families with their bronzed skin and predominantly auburn hair.

Because she was a princess amongst her own people, doors were opened to her out of curiosity. Her humble and quiet courtesy won her respect and further invitations to visit. Her abiding love for children made her much in demand amongst the off-spring of Rome's matrons. She became an adored and favourite aunt to hundreds. But it was her indomitable spirit and remarkable energy that attracted the ladies of Rome like a beacon to visit her orphanage on the Aventine and see first-hand the personal and unselfish love she lavished on Rome's weakest and most vulnerable children.

It took very little time for hearts to thaw, bend and succumb to the charms of the lady and the clear needs of the young whom she tended. Thus, Roman society adopted her orphanage: its continued and growing patronage was assured. Gallius' dream of a place of safety for the children of Rome rapidly saw many orphanages grow up around the city in Aelia's name. She had taken his dream and multiplied it in love and honour of him.

Tiberius himself played his part, reminding the senate and the people of Rome of the special honour they had given children when allowing them all to wear the white toga of a senator in the days of the republic. He exhorted all of Rome to live up to the meaning of this honour by investing in its children through the new schools and orphanages of Gallius and Aelia. Rome, itself, became known throughout the world at that time as the Capital City of Children.

The Emperor also showed considerable restraint in only diverting ten per cent of the vast funds raised by the people of Rome for child welfare to his own personal coffers!

To everyone's surprise, Aelia died suddenly soon after her twenty-eighth birthday. Gallius had planned to leave her everything he possessed in his will and always assumed he would go first, so was left shocked and totally bereft when the news came that Aelia had fallen whilst running between two of her house calls, allowed a simple wound to become infected because she would not take time from her busy life to care for it and died of the fever that followed the infection.

Thus, Gallius approached the Emperor, this time in his retreat in Capri, with a second and final offer: to grant the Emperor all of his remaining fortune if Aelia's forty-two orphanages could be taken under imperial patronage, in return also for the choice of a resting place for his dead wife. Tiberius hugged the grieving senator, in genuine distress himself, then drying both of their eyes with the sleeves of his own toga, said grimly:

"I am building just the place for our Aelia."

So Gallius laid his love to rest in the Theatre of Pompey the Great. Aelia would have been pleased to know she lay alongside one of the most honoured of Rome›s patricians. Above the finely polished marble entrance, he had commissioned with his Emperor's blessing a new tessaraed frieze of the goddess Venus, with fair hair and (unusually) blue eyes, holding the hand of a young child. In years to come, the Theatre of Pompey became the place where parents who had lost their children would pray for aid from Venus Protector of the Young and the frieze was the inspiration for the first paintings of the Madonna and Child when Rome turned in later years to Christianity.

Gallius himself lived another fourteen years and by the time of his death he had established many more orphanages, run by the wives of senators in memory of the quiet young Germanic princess who had run incessantly amidst them, in her quest to save the orphans of Rome. At first, they gave their money and time for the lady but then they also came to realise it was the children for whom they had been ultimately called to give aid.

Meanwhile, Tiberius smiled from his place of retirement in Capri at the memory of Aelia. He was an old man, soured by a lifetime of politicking, war and greed, but glad to have left a peaceful legacy for Rome that was for him more important than the marbled buildings of his predecessors. His legacy was a city where children would be nurtured and where every child would be entitled to wear the toga of a senator with the respect that this endowed.

Little did he know it but two years later, the *emperor of all emperors* would bless those who protected and saved children before he was tortured and crucified to death at the orders of one of Tiberius' own governors. The "old man" never could see eye to eye with his provincial governors (he particularly detested Pilate who had been appointed by Sejanus). Doubtless, the princeps would have got on famously with the quiet young man, Christos, had they ever met, for they both loved children ... but instead Tiberius would be damned for all time for being the Emperor in reign when the Messiah was slain.

Meanwhile, the little boy that Aelia first rescued the day she was scourged by the Praetorian Guard grew up to read and write with such skill he was taken into the household of the noble Antonia, later to become secretary to the Emperors Claudius and Nero. Suetonius once said: "*Perhaps the greatest of all freedmen and the most loyal of civil servants, Pallas came from an obscure background to be brought up in the orphanage of Aelia in the groves of the Aventine, only to meet his end when he sought to restore the republic through his patronage of Britannicus.*"

Thus ends the story of Aelia and the beginning of the history of Pallas ... but I have another story now to tell: this is of the meeting of the lady Finuviel with the great bard Abelard."

"Hush, my child" laughed Roaring Flamebringer. "One story each day is enough, my little queen. I am grateful and gratified by the story of Aelia but we both need our rest. I would have you refreshed for when you tell your next tale ... so lie down once more in the protection of my grasp and sleep.

Later today when you are rested, we shall speak of your next story. Be assured I am curious to hear it! But not with you weaving through exhaustion and your eyes barely able to stay open. You are a child and need your rest. So sleep, little one, for we have plenty of time."

Ra'el needed little encouragement and, letting out an enormous yawn, lay back in the comforting clasp of his claws. Within seconds, she was fast asleep as if enchanted.

FINUVIEL

Ra'el awoke to look into the gently whirling eyes of the dragon, now golden in their warmth for her. His breathe caressed life's blood back into her sleeping limbs whilst of his charity she could see he had prepared breakfast to her liking: raisons, nuts and leaves for her to eat.

"It is time for your next story" whispered her captor being careful to allow the girl to ease back into the world of the living from the realms of dream for fear too harsh an awakening would cut the cord between the source of her stories and the reality of her prison in the cavern of his home.

"Fear not, my friend. I never forget a story. But your kindness in such a soft waking is much appreciated and inspires me to tell a story of hope where my stories thus far have been of sad yet noble death" and Ra'el smiled gratefully at him.

"I will still eat you" he replied "... eventually!" then laughingly sat back and continued:

"But not yet, my queen. For I confess I do love stories such as thine and I sense you have many yet to tell. Do not think that I do not know what you are about here: you seek to buy yourself life through your stories. Well I am content to play this game and whilst you entertain me I will care for you as the most precious part of my treasure. Whilst you are with me, you shall also benefit from my powers over age: you shall not grow old in my presence. But one day your well-spring of story shall dry up and then

I shall enjoy the delicacy of your fair hair and blue eyes for they are my favourite dish."

She nodded, understanding fully the bargain he now offered but also emboldened by his words. For Ra'el realised that, wise worm though he might be, he had only discerned part of her plan and she still had hope therefore to win freedom from the sleeping dragon.

"By your leave, Roaring Flamebringer, mightiest of dragons, I shall tell the Tale of Finuviel and her love for the gentle bard, Abelard."

Part One

Burning emeralds smouldering amidst the covering of the leaves
Green gleaming gems glistening as through the trees she weaves
Slender as the hazel, straight as any plane, hair silver as the birch
Winsome as the willow, her heart the mighty oak, her seat a lofty perch

The steel of her blades is tempered like her soul to honesty and truth
Courage is her bearing, charming and disarming, the arrogance of youth.
The winds of tempest tossing then tearing her tumbling treetop terraces
She reigns over rain, shadows silent sun, her kindred stars embraces.
Fallen petals of merle golden sweet, silken carpet for her delicate feet
Apple blossom crowns the noble bower of the elfin queen's royal seat.

Humbly bending before the burrowing breeze, he bears himself brittlely bland
A stranger to this lofty arbour'd place, his destiny lies in another far land;
Fate's prisoner that he should walk this day beneath the branches she holds sway
To become captive to her baleful intent, and with his love for her jesting pay!
Yet her heart is not stone but frost-like thaws and melting grants him safe entry
To mould as molten metal in the passion's fire kindled by her soft elfin beauty.

So fair forest-maid Finuviel finds her fate,
In the realms of human love is consummate
Whilst the woven wise words of a simple bard,
Bind her heart, mind and soul to Abelard.

Thus begins our tale of the meeting of steel,
That through kind words was taught to feel;
Of a sylvan queen of silvern crowned brow,
By her love for kindness was she brought low.

The soft rolling hills of Emilion eventually join the massed forest of the Onduril near where the foot hills of the mountains of Harroch meet the mighty rushing roar of the running waters of the river Sandrach. The sylvan kingdom of Onduril is light and sparsely populated with ash and beech trees at its southern entrance but as it progresses north it becomes darker - a lightless place of oaks and pines in the shadow of tall ice-capped crags. That is until one reaches a break in the mountains (the Pass of Feorn), through which the Sandrach thunders to create an enormous water fall.

To the north beyond the falls is then an uninterrupted sun-drenched view of the green sea. Either side of the river as it crashes through the pass are the rare and precious copses of the mallorn trees which are the home of the elfin kind in this secreted part of our world.

But recently born into this place of light and magical mystery was the new queen of her people, the youthful Finuviel. Tall, fair-haired, with the sparkling green eyes of her race, she was not yet two hundred years old and far from wisdom, though fully endowed in grace and courage, when the story of her love does begin.

Onduril was not a peaceful place. Already as the sovereign of this fair land she had led her armies in war with the wolf-packs that sought to terrorise her woodlands whilst defeating in single combat a sea serpent which had swam in hunger-induced exploration from the estuary of the Sandrach into the outskirts of her kingdom. With elfin blade she was unsurpassed in skill and temperament whilst also endowed with the courage and intelligence that made her a feared opponent.

Her parents had been taken and slain or were being held captive by the mountain giants to the far west of her lands and her intent was to one day mount an assault in revenge for that loss. But for now she bided her time, recognising that her own skill and that of her people would need to be much further advanced if she was to gain victory over the might of the tall folk with their *hammers of thunder* and *spells of confusion*.

Perhaps, the foresight of her people had granted her father some knowledge of his capture at the hands of the giant-folk for he had left his swords in his daughter's care on the day he was taken. This gave her the hope to seek her father out and rescue him: for why else would he have left such powerful weapons in her care?

The swords were both magical of course.

Enderion was a sword of healing and wisdom: returning strength when such had been lost in battle, restoring flesh or broken bones when forfeited in combat, even offering life briefly to those slain mortally whist also shining the pathway to the thing of most desire in its bearer's heart. Right now it shone brightly whenever she raised its tip and pointed it towards the north-west; sure sign in her mind that the father she loved was alive and waiting for her.

Carnoch was a sword of slaying: it weaved at speed and could sever iron, any armour or sinew in a single stroke; on occasions it would also send a force of lightning into the breast of an opponent and it had been just such a blast of energy that had allowed the queen to remove the threat to her people of the hungry sea serpent.

On the day our story begins, Finuviel was dancing from one mallorn branch to another, chasing a squirrel which had bravely stolen one of the hazels from her breakfast bowl. She was laughing gaily as she flew from tree to tree, landing soundlessly on the tips of branches which barely bent beneath her light frame.

She was bare foot and bare armed but her swords were with her as always and she wore the light silver coat of mithril mail that was her constant companion. It hung from shoulder to knee, moulded by elfin smiths to the narrow-waist of her female frame, encrusted with diamonds and pearls such that it shone like the stars in the heavens both in the day and at night, yet so closely knit were the rings that it was as silent as the elfin maid who wore it and impenetrable to all weapons save a blade of magic ... or the hammer of the giants.

Into her mind came the message from one of her scouts at the outer rim of Onduril - for her people had long possessed the wisdom of telepathy:

"A stranger has passed through the dark passages and is heading towards the Pass. A single human, unarmed. What is thy will, my lady?"

"Is he determined and unwavering or lost and faltering?" she asked as yet unconcerned.

"He does not look lost. He does not hesitate and his direction will take him straight to our capital in the trees, my lady" the scout observed and within her mind came the image of a man in humble attire, bowed under the weight of his backpack, hooded such that his features were invisible to her eye, but striding purposefully through the deep undergrowth.

With no path by which to travel, the stranger yet walked straight as if able to read the secret signs her people left as a guide to those with whom they traded.

"I shall join you now. Let him come and I shall find a suitable spot to meet this bold intruder!" the queen ordered and straightway set off south, running rapidly through the trees.

Part Two

Into the silence of her darkest forest,
The beauty of his music caressed
Ere she had seen his noble visage,
Her heart was captured by the bard
The birds were silenced by his voice
And fair Finuviel deprived of choice
Walked in amazement into the glade,
Where his songs he lovingly played
His melody filled a dark hole in her soul,

His words made her pure essence whole
Lost in the charm of his powerful grace,
Her every desire was that he she embrace
Time abandoned, she succumbed to his spell,
To his enchantments her innocence fell
Finding the courage to step out from the trees,
She knelt at his feet and offered her pleas:

'Fair bard, whose art has captured my heart,
I am at your command whomsover thou art
All that I am, I place before you to see,
All that I do shall be accomplished for thee
Treat me with kindness for I am your slave
Deal with me honourably is all that I crave
For I am the queen of these glades of Onduril
Enslaved by your magic that in me doth thrill'.

Finuviel stood on the topmost branch of a tall, ancient and gnarled pine tree, her eyes closing briefly to enjoy the piquancy of its sharp scent and the sweet bitter taste of the tree that hung in the air around her. Then she looked down on the man below as he struggled through the tangle of the undergrowth, brambles clutching at his cloak, roots looping out to catch his feet.

She smiled, for the forest was playing a game with this foolish stranger - yet she also noticed that the game was not distracting him from his purposeful stride towards the heart of her kingdom. Despite every twist and turn flung in his path by her beloved and loyal trees, he maintained his direction as if drawn by a magnet towards the royal seat of her demesne.

So she followed him, skipping from tree to tree above his head silently watching his progress and hoping for some clue as to his intent. She could not see his face, for the depth of the hood he wore was like a cowl, but she was nonetheless interested in this man. He showed great strength in his arms as he pushed back the branches that would slice at his eyes and his stride was youthful and powerful. Once, she was able to glimpse the contours of a muscular leg through his trous as he climbed over a fallen bark ... and blushed at the quickening of her heart that was the result.

As the noonday sun turned the glades beneath the elf to the same emerald green as her eyes, the stranger came to a halt, removed his pack from his back, and stood straight. He was tall, she immediately noticed, far taller than she had first thought. The bag he carried must be heavy to have so bent his back yet he must have great strength to have held it thus for so long. Now, she was intrigued: what was it that he carried? Some great treasure? But, despite her curiosity still she waited to see what the intruder would do ... and thus did her reticence betray her.

The man looked around him for somewhere comfortable to sit and set himself down in the contoured clasp of the roots of a great oak. Finuviel watched in glee as the tree roots quivered in eager anticipation of rending this upstart in their inescapable grip when suddenly she and the forest were silenced by a single note of pure pitch and considerable charm. The man was merely testing his tonsils, but to the creatures of the forest this was like some great and favourite overture to a long-awaited concerto. Every creature as far as Finuviel could see or hear had ceased to breathe for fear they might disturb or interrupt the music they hoped would follow. Into this hushed silence came the sound of the man opening his sack to remove ... a small journeyman's harp.

He played a single arpeggio that made the leaves and branches around her vibrate in joy, brought out the tuning key from where it hung around his neck and made a small adjustment to two of the strings (none but he had noticed anything amiss) then broke into song - and the forest came to life.

The wave of music struck Finuviel and flayed her. She was tossed as if by the most tempestuous of storms and the wildest of winds: her heart and pulse raced; her hair became alive; her body was on fire one moment and ice the next. She gripped the bark of the tree in which she stood for safe-keeping as her legs turned to water and all strength left her.

She clung desperately to the trunk for fear that she would fall yet also wishing with every sinew in her body to crash down to the ground before he whose music so enthralled her. Around her, she sensed the trees closing in on the singer in appreciation of his skill, her own command of them lost as they transferred their allegiance and came under the charm of his spell. The pine in which she clung so precariously was an old friend yet now it sought to fling her from its branches and thus free itself to listen to the blessings of the wonderful ballad being performed below.

Then his words found her:

"Fair lady I mean you no harm this day
I bring you my aid in your heart's quest
I hope you shall listen to all that I say
And follow my lead as we head west."

She fell from the tree, the branches catching her to slow her descent but still it was a crashing tumbling fall and only her instinct enabled her at the last moment to land on her feet or else she would have sprawled in an undignified heap before him.

She tried to stand regally and offer him a curtsey but his spell was still running through her and her knees buckled such that she collapsed forward - to be caught in his arms as he stood now in silence, releasing her from his charm as he ceased his music and instead holding her steady to allow her to regain her composure and control over her aberrant limbs.

"Who are you?" she gasped as she clung to him.

"My name is Abelard," he replied, his voice soft yet puissant binding her pulsing heart yet closer to him. Then he flung back his hood with a toss of his head to reveal the soft face of a kindly young man: no warrior's visage but rather the round open fresh-faced gaze of a poet and dreamer, a man at peace with nature, whose laughing blue eyes bubbled with humour and whose smile sent the lady near to swooning save for the strength of his grasp of her and the burning fire within her.

Then his face took on a more serious look as he revealed his purpose in venturing unbidden into her lands: "I bring word from your father, my lady Finuviel."

This time her heart stopped.

Part Three

He held her in grace
As stars their dance trace;
She followed his lead
As the moon governs seas.
They talked of her quest
Against the giants of the west.
Innocent plans of adventure;
Releasing her father from capture.

They talked of desire
Burning beyond measure:
Of passions and flame
And love without shame.
Blinded to the divide
As if their hearts defied;
The contrast in their race
A chasm to embrace.

The man had no intent
Save her mission supplement;
His surprise was humbler yet
To love so deeply when they met.
Her inner-fire came as snow:
A caress on her heated brow;
As natural as the mountain's flame
Enduring as her steel-like frame.

Their bond was adamant
Together they were defiant.
As one they were a world apart
Forged inseparable, a single heart!
They faced the world with joined intent
The strengths in each would compliment.
No far-off obstacle did they fear
Nor whispered warning did they hear.

The bard was much travelled, the elfin lady would soon learn. He journeyed to take the wonder of his music into the halls of every kingdom: this was his simple desire. Of no matter to him that his voice could charm an army and ensure the conquest of a world! He was a man of peace and his love was for the simple things that joyful hearts could bring. His meandering passage through the realms of this world had taken him eventually to the great halls of the Giant Lords in the West - to the *Hall of Berechnor* itself.

There he had sung ballads to entertain the great people and watched as they relaxed into sleep. In this state would he have left them content, for he was no thief, assassin or spy to take advantage of their repose, if he had not heard a ballad as beautiful as his own yet delivered with such pity that his heart wept and the strings of his harp cried in concert for the sadness of the song's rendition. He was entranced and sought out the singer.

Thus, he came to the dungeons of the Giants: a place of torment for the few captives they deemed worthy of their protracted "entertainment" (for most of their captives, indeed most of their guests, they preferred to eat). Amongst the sorry state of humanity he found imprisoned there (bereft of reason in the main and without hope in every case) he discovered the Elfin King of Onduril, sole survivor of the hunting party taken prisoner many years past, still mourning his own beloved wife, the details of whose grim death Abelard refused to divulge to Finuviel however hard she pressed him to do so.

The sight of the bard gave the king hope unsought for. He had believed himself forgotten and destined to die in the misery of the giants' malignant grasp but now he had the opportunity to send word of rescue to his people.

"My lady, his words were simple and they were addressed to you more than anyone else. I remember them precisely as he gave them to me and now it is my gift that I bestow them upon you.

'To my people, the noble elfin race of Onduril, greetings from your king in captivity yet still defiantly alive. I ask that you follow the lead of my daughter in the quest I shall grant her. For I live, but the nature of the hurt done me by the Giants is such I fear it shall not be my part to lead you again in battle nor sit again upon the feathered cathedra in the Hall of the Great Mallorn that is our royal citadel. I hereby resign my office and grant my kingdom to the courageous care of my daughter Finuviel.

To my daughter, I ask you rescue me. For the knowledge that you will find me one day has kept the coal-fires of life burning in my breast. I leave it to you to decide if you will risk the courage of my whole people in an assault on the Geant with the inevitable war that this shall bring or risk your own courage in a personal assault. I shall be proud of you whatever you shall decide, but of your honour ask you come in haste for the power of my mind fades through the horrors I must endure.

I am your loving father, Halduril.'"

And with these, her father's spoken words repeated as if from his very lips, the bard finally fell silent and Finuviel found she could breathe once more.

"We go and we go alone," she spoke unhesitatingly. "It is why my father gave me his swords: for he knew I would come for him. He knew!" and she smiled at the knowledge that her father had trusted her so much. "I shall not let him down but nor shall I jeopardise his people in a war we would likely lose against the Giant-folk. No, I have a better plan: one small elfin warrior, scarce noticed by the mighty Geant, shall breach their towers and slay them as they sleep from the charms of your songs, my love."

But Abelard shook his head: "I shall not aid you in Giants' death. I forbear and abjure the death of any creature. But the rescue of your father is a noble deed" he continued as she frowned at his words "and to help you bring your father to liberty, I will gladly sing anyone to sleep if you in turn will promise restraint when they are helpless in my power?"

The lady was shaken by his words as she had assumed that the absolute love for her he saw in his frank and admiring gaze would see him do her bidding without argument. But then she realised he offered her wise counsel; if the rescue could be accomplished with no harm to giant life then the chances of diplomacy holding peace between the two peoples afterwards would be much greater.

"I accept your kind offer of aid and the terms under which you offer that assistance" she replied.

Then she leant forward and kissed him full on the lips which silenced him as cleverly as any charm he himself possessed. "I have the mastery of you, my dear heart, it seems, as you have shown that you have the mastery of me. Let us journey together to the aid of my father in both peace and love."

To the scouts watching the remarkable conquest of their queen by this humble man, she spoke now through the melding of their minds:

"This man has brought news of my father. The king is alive and I go to seek his rescue. I do so alone, for otherwise I would throw my people into a war that would see our world destroyed in the tempest of destruction that the Geant would bring down of us.

I bid all of my people prepare for war, in case my mission should fail or the Geant-folk take exception to my deeds of rescue. I hope to achieve rescue of our king without war, but the nature of any reprisal is ultimately in the hands of the Geant. Be ready, therefore, for my return and that of our King. And keep watch for the doom of Geant."

Then she nodded to Abelard and said simply: "I am ready and have been every day since my parents were taken. Lead on and I will follow and together we shall give you new deeds of which to sing. We leave now! For already it is in my mind that I have left my father to suffer too long for my conscience to ever be calm again."

Part Four

They crossed the salamanders' home
And ran where wild horses roam;
Forded rivers of melting ice and snow
Stood beneath tall falls of water's flow.

In giants' footsteps dared to tred,
Caves of dragons became their bed!
Through forests cruel and mountains foul
Their bond held true to their avowal.

Ever westwards was their journey made
Accompanied by the music he played.
Her love grew deeper every day
Whilst her beauty his simple soul did flay.

Then stone carved passage entrance gave
To the deep dark hole of the giants' cave
Grim gateway to fathomless halls of hate
And terminal path for the desperate.

They came at last to Berechnor
Questing for her father held prisoner
In the deep dark dangerous confine
Of dungeons hidden beyond sign
That life love peace and thought of liberty
Survives in this pitiable place of cruelty.

Abelard brought his lady to the court
Where the King of Geant's evil wrought
The spell that held her father dear
As captive for entertainment sere.

He stood and made his humble plea:
"Release my sister in return for she
Who is the daughter of the elfin king

You hold as hostage in safekeeping!
Keep the bargain that you made:
One life exchanged for this elf-maid."

Finuviel sought to fight her way free
But the bard's spell held her rock-steady;
Ensorcelled she was his to barter
Knowing the Giants sought her slaughter.

She bowed her head in abject misery
Her heart had betrayed her totally:
Not seeing his manly charm was a lie
But her pride then held her head high!

She surrendered to the Geant's will
Her heart's flame now a source of chill,
Eyes glittered as the coldest stone
Their force of malice would rend bone
Had not sung magic held her at bay
Whose one object was the bard to slay.

They journeyed in delighted company of each other: Abelard would entertain them each evening with the originality of his stories and the beauty of his music, silencing all around him as the creatures of the forests, deserts and plains would creep slowly in wonder to gather as an impromptu audience whenever they would halt. The lady would find them food and shelter, her wood-craft such that she could locate fresh water-springs, caves of warm shelter, the wood needed for warming fire, and the nuts and berries needed to sustain them. She offered no harm to any creature when in the company of the bard out of respect for his wishes in that regard.

They slept apart. Both were still in awe at the suddenness of their love and need for each other and thus were weary of too rapid a consummation of that love. If truth be told, the elf-maid was frightened at the passions aroused within her by her gentle companion whilst the bard was afraid of the many stories told of men losing their minds under the enchantment of the women of the elf-world.

She understood his reticence and was saddened by it yet there was a kernel of truth in the legends told: for her kind had often led foolish men a merry dance in quest of fun and mischief and, until this moment, she had considered the mind of men beneath her consideration. Her heart now told her differently: her love for Abelard had awoken in Finuviel both understanding and respect for mankind neither of which emotions had previously troubled her.

Abelard knew the terrain across which they made their passage and would regale her with the legends of the local people: the story of the salamanders who learnt to speak so wisely that eventually they ignored all other races and retired into the desert plains to converse amongst themselves; the tale of the cave-dragons who tired of their dark, damp homes and decided instead to make their habitat the tallest pine trees, regrettably starting a fire in the process that destroyed the old forests but since had seen new life grow from the ashes; the nomads of the western deserts who would travel the circuit of the whole known world in every one hundred years, none of whom had ever seen their own birth-place save the day they had entered into this world as a screaming babe; the sea-faring elfs who had discovered the western isles and built havens of such beauty that none who came upon them had ever sought to return; the army of trolls defeated by the Geant who had agreed to build the unbreakable walls around Berechnor, the Geant's subterranean city, in return for their own liberty.

Of one thing only would Abelard not speak: he would not tell Finuviel of the fate of his own family. The lady, in her state of love, feared some terrible tragedy in his past and was filled with both pity and compassion but could not find the words to uncover the secrets of his past for fear she would inflict the pain of remembrance in so doing.

But more than stories did Abelard recount. His journeys had taken him to the great sights of the pre-civilised world and these he now revealed as one precious gift after another as they trod the many leagues to their final destination of the western mountains.

Finuviel stood atop the crashing waterfalls of Hendron held secure by the waist by Abelard as she placed her arms out wide and allowed the rising wind created by the force of the water striking the lake three leagues below to lift her off her feet - briefly she could feel herself flying.

Next she explored with him the ice caves of Furmoch with their gem-like structures formed over centuries of crystallisation to take on the form of serpents and chimera, dragons and gryffon, winged horses and evil night mares.

On the plains of Prydain, they summonsed a herd of Fellian: wild horses tamed rarely but made subservient through the gentle melody of Abelard's harp. Two hundred leagues they travelled in three days courtesy of the regal gift of the Fellian whose sure step crossed furrow, brook, hill and marsh with equal and secure abandon.

Eventually, they reached the outer perimeters of the Geant kingdom. In the foothills of the mountains that offered natural protection for the great walled city that was their destination, they encountered the first indications of the *Doom of Geant*: the ruins of a man-made city whose warriors had fought and lost in battle against the giant people. Finuviel wept: not at the sight of the destruction but at the sorry remains of the many children sacrificed to sate the appetite of the Geant-kind for human flesh. Charred remains so pitiful, her heart was near breaking at this sight and only Abelard's strong arms around her prevented her from collapsing in her distress.

"Did none survive?" she asked between great sobs.

"The fate of the survivors was more grim than this" replied the bard and could not be persuaded to say any more.

From this point onwards, they travelled in silence: the lady still in turmoil over the wanton devastation she would encounter and her swain in some inner conflict of grief over the past. Finuviel respected Abelard's silence for she believed that he had lost his family to giants and did not wish to render his grief naked until he was ready to share his pain with her. Meanwhile, Abelard was grateful for the silence of his love, for it helped him come to terms with what he soon must do.

On the second day in the mountains, Abelard pointed to the remains of a great arched bridge, derelict and clearly unsafe but marking some great road or pass through the crags and promontories ahead of them. The span of the bridge was enormous and very apparently the work of the Geant.

"Must we cross?" asked Finuviel, her first words spoken in days.

Abelard shook his head and then pointed to a crevasse at the end of a shallow and winding track that ran below the bridge:

"The bridge is a decoy for the un-wary: built to draw the ignorant away from the true entrance to the *Halls of Berechnor*. The small cave entrance below is where we now must head and from this point we must be careful. Any giant we see, I shall seek to charm until we have reached the Halls themselves. But my hope is that we shall be fortunate and catch the giants in repose: for they sleep in the afternoon and thus we may be able to gain the heart of their kingdom before any shall see us.

I ask, however, my lady, that you remain here for no more than an hour whilst I go into the cave and scout the way ahead. If I am satisfied we can enter without complete mishap I shall return for you. If I do not return then you must flee and not hazard this venture without further aid ... for I shall have been taken and be dead."

"You shall have to charm me beyond any reason or reasoning before I shalt agree to you jeopardising your life in this way" replied the lady with spirit and the fire enkindled in her green eyes.

"There is no jeopardy" smiled her love and from his pack he removed the tattered remains of an old cloak. "A gift from a grateful dragon" he laughed and then donning the cloak he looked at her complacently. She returned his look in some bemusement and then asked: "And what precisely is this wonderful gift meant to achieve? If it is a cloak of invisibility then you have been taken in by the dragon, my love, most mischievously."

But then she jumped as she felt his lips in a gentle kiss on her cheek ... and yet the bard had not moved from his place before her!

"It is a cloak of displacement" he explained laughingly. "It confuses the eye such that you see me where I am not."

"And do you often use this cloak to sneak up and kiss maidens unsuspectingly and without their permission?" replied Finuviel haughtily.

"Nay lass just elfin maids" the bard jested then continued: "Will you give me your permit to see the way ahead?"

Finuviel nodded her agreement, tempering it with her own admonishment: "Yes, my love, you have my leave to go. But if in one hour you have not returned then I shall come find you. I have no intention of returning to my home without you."

Her concerns were unnecessary, however, for less than half the sands of her timer had passed into the bottom chamber before Abelard was returned with news:

"All is as I suspected and hoped for. The Geant are asleep and we shall have access to the Halls themselves if we go quickly. Once within the Halls, we can expect the soldiery to be awake but I shall sing my charms and this shall take us through safely to before the Giant King, himself, in his ancient chamber. You must then let me address the King first, my lady, for thus we shall be able to win you passage to the dungeons and your father."

Such was the lady's joy that she hugged her guide and lover and could not resist kissing him full on the lips in gratitude: "You have done so much for me, I can never hope to repay you, my love," she whispered.

Then, drawing her two swords, she bowed and invited him to lead them into the cave ... and the dark pathway to the Geant kingdom.

The cave gave entrance to a short unlit tunnel but her sword *Enderion* lit their path briefly until they came to the first bend. From that point onwards, sconces lit their route through a labyrinth of criss-crossing passages leading unerringly down into the heart of the mountain. As they ventured deeper and deeper, Finuviel began to see the first signs of life from the carvings of fruit and mythical animals in the stone of the passage walls to the occasional statue or fountain in alcoves to either side of them; the size and scale of these monuments to Geant civilisation were chilling, however, reminding the lady that she faced foes many times her size and strength, fully capable of crushing her without batting an eyelid. Abelard had been right, though, for the passages were not guarded and there were no signs of waking giant.

A great, gothic-arched, granite-carved doorway marked the entrance to the City of Berechnor ahead of them. The gates were lit on either side by enormous braziers and guarded by the statues of two huge Geant warriors - former kings or champions no doubt thought the elf. There was no other bar to their entry and the gates themselves were wide open. Briefly stopping to admire the phenomenal masonry of the Trolls, who had built the huge eighty foot tall stone walls that protected the city, Finuviel followed Abelard as he marched confidently along the main street towards the Geant halls in the centre of Berechnor.

Finuviel was amazed for the city seemed deserted. Shutters and doors were closed firmly and there was absolute silence as they trod their path up giant steps, each of which she had to clamber over as they were up to her waist, towards the heights of the citadel. She had begun to wonder if perhaps they were in the wrong place altogether when finally they reached a second stone carved gothic archway that was the gateway to the Giant King's own Hall chamber. Standing in the gateway was a giant, armed with mail and a great mace who glared at them both and demanded:

"Who are you and what do you want?"

Abelard began to sing and Finuviel smiled as she watched for the giant to start to fall asleep. Alas, this was not to be! For as Abelard sung, she felt her own strength dissolve as she succumbed to the charm of his enchantments. Within moments, she was paralysed, whilst the giant looked on in laughter.

Then: "Don't forget her swords and follow me, you are expected" commanded the giant turning on his heels to lead Abelard into the citadel. Abelard looked briefly and apologetically at Finuviel then removed her swords and wrapped them carefully in his cloak before placing them in his pack. With a gesture of his hands, he took complete control of Finuviel's legs and forced the ensorcelled lady to walk as a marchionette in pursuit of the giant.

The chamber of the Giant King was that of a warrior-king: great stone arches held a high ceiling from which were suspended the captured banners of fallen cities and armies in a riot of colour. To left and right were the spoils of war - gilt and gold embossed suits of armour, crested helms, bejewelled swords, intricately woven mail. Then in two columns running down the centre of the chamber were the mounted pieces of armour of the King himself: numerous suits of plate armour of incredible size and delicate craftsmanship, heroically proportioned as befitted the greatest of giants.

The King rose from his marble throne as the bard and his captive approached. He stood, towering over them, twenty two feet tall, radiating suppressed violence and immeasurable strength but also unremitting delight and glee at what he saw:

"She fell for your charm, bard, I see! Thus, you have brought her to me as you promised" and the King laughed until the chamber shook.

But Abelard halted and confronted the giant: "You have made a bargain and I have honoured my part. Release my sister and the lady Finuviel is yours to do with as you will."

At this, and despite the power of his charm on her, Finuviel was still able to shed tears: of shame for believing in a mere mortal man; of grief that Abelard had been brought to betray her for the sake of a sister; and of rage that the giants had so seduced her love as to turn a noble man to such a despicable act. The King, however, merely nodded and then commanded one of his many sentries: "Go fetch the girl and allow both the sister and this traitor free passage from my lands - never to return in safety or face my wrath."

"But wait!" the giant continued. "You have not given me the swords. Without her father's swords then all that is done shall be in vain. Give them to me and our bargain is complete."

Abelard smiled and took the swords, still wrapped in his cloak, from his pack. He carefully un-wrapped the cloak and allowed the swords to drop to the ground:

"Heed my warning, o King. Any physical contact with these swords and it shall spell your end and that of your host of Giants. Even I must be careful not to touch the blades and thus have held them safely in this cloak."

Then he walked over to the stupefied and paralysed Finuviel and kissed her cold unwelcoming lips before saying mockingly:

"Allow me, my lady, to return this *your* cloak to you. It has served my purpose well and now I hope it will keep you warm in the cold of the dungeon that shall be your home for the rest of your stay here. I promised you safe passage to your father and it is with your father that you will spend your time as a prisoner of the Giants. Remember this cloak as a token of my true feelings. I return it to your keeping as I give you back everything that was yours."

"Be gone" commanded the King "and take your sister with you."

Then turning to his guards he ordered: "Secure the elf in chains and then remove her and fling her into the deepest and darkest cell you can find. Ensure she has no contact with her father. And have her eyes brought to me tonight for my supper but leave the rest of her alive to savour the blind folly with which she came into my demesne. She was blinded by love and now she shall be blinded by my will.

Leave the swords on the floor where they fell. They are just another trophy now and we are in no danger of their powers whilst they remain in this hall under my guard. This foolish elf has delivered to me the two things in this whole world that could have defeated the inexorable roll of the *Doom of Geant*. Let her think on that in the many years of blind despair that lie ahead of her!"

Roaring Flamebringer once more looked to the skies and saw dawn approaching. The ancient dragon smiled in admiration at the immaculate timing of the young story-teller before him. Yet again, he must wait until a new day for the end of her tale. He was content to do so as this was a trial of skill that he was enjoying greatly.

"I must eat, my queen" he whispered and allowed his warm breath to caress Ra'el gently. She smiled in return and then asked timidly:

"Would it be too much to ask but I have another favour?"

The dragon looked at her a little warily for already he had promised to forego eating human flesh for her benefit and she could see him thinking "What next?"

He was, of course, right to be anxious as what Ra'el next asked for nearly broke the bond between them ... but she had to venture on with her plan and the girl's request was necessary if she were to ever have hope of release from his hold on her:

"You know that I hold all creatures dear to my heart and that to see the death of any animal hurts me deeply. I am inspired to tell stories not just out of a wish to preserve my life but also out of respect for you and your beauty, great dragon. It is this respect that gives me the courage to ask if you could refrain from eating meat for me whilst I am your captive. I promise that such restraint on your part will deepen my love for you and ensure my stories are even more inspired to your liking."

The dragon roared in response and allowed a blast of flame to crash to the floor before her in his anger, driving the girl backwards against the rock-walls of the cavern where she stood defiantly nonetheless and showed him no fear, merely gentle entreaty. His eyes went black in his fury and briefly Ra'el thought she had risked too much too soon in her request ... but then his good humour returned and he began softly to laugh:

"Your absence of fear inspires me in return. What you ask is actually a small thing given that you offer me a lifetime of stories and your own life and flesh at the end of this. Forgive my anger ... but heed my warning also. I will not take kindly to a request such as this each and every morning.

Be careful what you ask for on the morrow. Today, I shall agree to what you request and seek out rocks and herbs instead of meat to fuel my inner fire ... in return I ask that you sleep and then complete your story of the elf and her traitorous lover."

He let her sleep in the safety of his claws as he had each day before and woke her with the gentle silken touch of his nose that afternoon:

"It is time, pretty one."

Ra'el nodded and sat once more with legs crossed to complete the story of Finuviel and the rescue of her father Halduril.

Part Five

Contained within a crystal cage
Captive of the cruellest rage
Finuviel waited for the chance
To lead the giants a merry dance
Her lover's trap she now did spring
To bring the Doom on all within
The once impregnable granite wall
Curved around the King's great hall
She broke her bonds in stealthy haste
Laid all around her to bloody waste
Until she gained the royal chamber
The place set for her final encounter.
The King was ready for her might
He had no plans for a fair fight:
For he threatened those she held dear
If she should dare to him draw near
Seeing her father and Abelard held
It was as though she had been felled.
She sank to her knees in flat despair
As love had frozen her heart with fear!

Finuviel was stripped and left naked in chains within a cage of glass in the very centre of the Geant dungeon. The giant intent was simple: she was to be tortured then left on permanent display for all to see the foolishness of elf-kind. Her belongings were piled on the ground beneath her as she was suspended by glass manacles from the crystal dome of a specially-made cell. Above its glass dome was a viewing gallery that led directly to the Giant King's royal chamber. She was become another spoil of his many wars to be admired and gloated upon at the King's leisure.

"Enjoy what moments of sight shall remain to you, my lady" mocked one of her guards. "For when I return, it shall be to cut out your eyes for my lord's supper."

Then the guards had left her to lonely despair. However, the moment the guards were out of sight, Finuviel called softly:

"Io genventi elcamel *Carnoch*!" and her sword of dancing had risen from its concealment within the cloak of displacement her lover had handed to her as he had given her his mocking kiss. Its mirror self still lay untouched within the halls of the Geant King above her head.

Her sword rose majestically and then in a flashing scything movement cut through the glass chains as if they were ice, dropping the lady to the ground. She broke the locks to the cage's door and then donned her mail hauberk and put on Abelard's cloak which instantly showed her still captive within the glass cell and would continue to do so as she sought out her father.

Then grasping *Enderion* in one hand to help restore her strength and light the path to Halduril's prison and *Carnoch* in the other to ward off any attempt to prevent her rescue of her kinsman, she whispered to herself: "So let us see what else my tricksy lover has planned!" and crept carefully through the passages of the dungeons.

As she tripped silently amidst the grim cells that held those the giant's kept for their seer entertainment or to punish through despair and loneliness, she felt the urge to release all of the sorry prisoners that she encountered.

But she knew in her heart that their rescue would be brief. Rather, she must defeat the Geant and to do that she needed the wisdom of her father. For Halduril had entrusted to her the swords she held for a reason whilst Abelard and the Giant King had both described her swords as holding some great menace for the Geant. If she had the means to destroy the Geant then she needed to know what the power was that she now held.

Above her, she heard celebrations and realised the Geant were in banquet in the chambers overhead. Complacent in their defeat of her, they ignored the elf-queen and had left their dungeons without sentries. Finuviel smiled: her enemy were in one place and this would make her assault on them that much easier once she had Halduril safe.

She came at last to her father's cell and used *Carnoch* once more to shear through the iron locks on his cell door. He was standing waiting for her and their minds melded briefly in love and relief:

"You came. I am so proud of you. Now we must finish this!" were Halduril's words of comfort and encouragement.

"What must I do?" his daughter asked dutifully but also still unsure of the route to Geant defeat.

"If Abelard's plan has worked then even now he is held by the Geant in the Halls above us being mocked by the King. He seeks to gain us the time to reach the King's chambers where you must assail the Geant with the might of *Enderion* and *Carnoch*."

"Do my swords hold so much power then?" Finuviel asked in wonder.

"Alas, my daughter, they have no more power than they have ever held. Abelard through his clever tongue has tricked the Geant into believing the weapons hold some doom for them. Nonetheless, I have foreseen that each will aid you to defeat the Geant."

The noise of the giants was near overpowering. They were as loud as their bodies mighty whilst ale had loosened tongues and made their manner most raucous. They sang and shouted at the very top of their huge voices until fine dust descended upon their heads shaken loose from the stone fortifications around them.

Into the din of their festivities stepped the elf-maid ... to look in hope and then in horror towards the throne of the King before which knelt her lover. Having ensured his sister was safe from harm, Abelard had allowed himself to be captured by the giants to see that he was in the Hall for the final denouement of the Geant. But whatever his intended plans may have been, for certain they were now thwarted by the cruelty of the Giant King. Taking no risk of further betrayal, the King had seen to it that Abelard's tongue had been cut out - the bard would never sing again!

Finuviel removed her cloak and marched into the chamber. The wall of silence that greeted her was immediate: amazement, anger, fear then menace as nearly a thousand giant warriors, the elite heroes of their kind, looked in disdain at a single young female elf striding forward boldly to confront their liege lord in the heart of his demesne. A nod by the King to the sentries by the entranceway to his Hall and Halduril was grasped on either side and held flat on the ground but Finuviel ignored this threat to her father and continued determinedly until she stood twenty paces from the King then spoke into the silence of his throne room:

"That man you hold in chains has betrayed me and I will have my revenge on him and then depart!" and she pointed in anger at Abelard whose head bowed in sorrow at her words.

The King could not contain his surprise and then delight at her words: "Forgive me, my lady. It seems I was mistaken in you. By all means slay this foolish man and then I will willingly let you go free and allow also the release of your father. I had thought you my enemy but see now that we have much in common: not least our common disdain for mankind, it would appear."

Finuviel bowed to the King in acknowledgement of his words whilst the giants in the room relaxed and then began slowly to laugh: for an alliance of giant and elf would spell the end for all of humanity. The elf-queen waited until her father had been released and allowed to join her then she hoisted her two swords and flung them, *Carnoch* first and then *Enderion* following, to spin in a dance of death towards the chained Abelard, with the giants watching in eager anticipation of his demise.

Carnoch sliced through Abelard's chains releasing him to stand and catch *Enderion* by the hilt in his right hand. The power of *Enderion* immediately healed his severed tongue and returned to him the gift of his voice to charm whilst *Carnoc*h continued its encircling dance to return to the waiting right hand of Finuviel. The Geant were slow to react, such was their astonishment, and thus were they defeated.

Abelard sang. He sang as if his whole heart and soul were released to walk the many corners of the chamber of the giants. His song conveyed love and pity, anger and dismay, his sense of loss, his longing for his lady-love, the agony of his disfigurement, the joy of the restoration of his skill. His song commanded the attention of every giant and mesmerised them. The first note had frozen them and bound them to his will. And as he sang, they began slowly to succumb to the underlying charm of his music, relaxing into peace and then into slumber.

Finuviel and Halduril were free of his spell and yet they were frozen nonetheless by the beauty of his melody and both wept unrestrainedly as they understood the mixture of desire and pathos that ruled the heart of this kind yet puissant man. In moments, the giants slept and were defenceless. Then Abelard turned to Finuviel and bowing to her asked:

"What is thy will, my lady? The giants sleep, and thus we can hope to release the many held captive here from the torment of years of torture. You once made me a promise that you would not harm the giants but I know that through my actions you may regard that promise as no longer binding. I do not hold you therefore to that promise: if you wish, you may slay the giants as they sleep and rid the world of a great evil ... or you may let them live in the hope that they will learn from the events of this day and seek peace in the world ahead. I will aid you in whatever your design for I still love you despite my treachery."

"Foolish man!" replied the queen "You never betrayed me. But I promise you this: if you trick me like that again then I will be even more angry than I am now at your idiotic suggestion that I would break faith with you. I love and honour you. Before my father I do solemnly declare it is my intent to live as your companion to the end of our days. Let the giants live in the hope that they find peace in their hearts ... as I have found love in my own heart through the songs of a gentle man."

At which they embraced whilst Halduril looked on in joy and quiet satisfaction: for the plan that he had hatched the day he had first met the bard had worked out far better than he had ever intended. Though Abelard knew it not, he was without doubt the most powerful force for war *or peace* in the land. To have the bard's will tethered in love to his own daughter gave the elf-king great hope for the safety and protection of his people. There would still be monsters to be slain by elfin heroes in defence of his lands but there would never again be risk of an army seeking the defeat of his realm, protected as it would be by the ballads of the consort of its young queen.

"Thus ends the story of Finvuiel and her meeting with the bard, Abelard but this doth remind me of the tale of the Sorcerer of Gaitan whose mighty conjuring brought him to the attention of an ancient Mayan Emperor. The Emperor hoped to rule the world through dark magic and the sorcerer risked the life of his only daughter as price for evil partnership. Her escape from the clutches of theurgy and the love that followed are my next story if you are interested, my serpentine friend?" and Ra'el looked up at Roaring Flamebringer in polite enquiry who nodded, eyes gleaming green with pleasure but then the dragon noticed the weariness showing in her eyes and replied:

"Sleep first, little one, and later tonight you can begin your new story."

THE SORCEROR OF GAITAN AND THE LOVE OF LI PAO

Ra'el awoke to stand upon the ceiling of the world.

"Welcome, little queen, to Perythduin, my mountain fastness" Roaring Flamebringer spoke laughingly as he saw her awe mingled with fear at the overwhelming majesty of their view and the sheer terrifying drop to the world of men below.

"Before you are the sister crags of Torrent and Beshame, to the north is the mighty Stormfrost, to the east Flametop, Caradoom and Meneister. These are the mountainous homes of my family, alas all long gone to the savagery of man. Here on Perythduin, itself, I mated with my queen many centuries ago now and we had our only child ... for my kind are destined to mate for life and to have only a single off-spring. Both mate and child, thus, are more precious to us for being so unique.

Below you at the foot of this hill are the burnt ruins of the castle of the lord who took the egg that was my child as some trophy for his mantelpiece. The glassy knoll above the ruin is where I buried my queen, slain by the arrows of the defenders of that castle as she flew to retrieve her child and thus was I bereft twice.

I come here for one reason ... to grieve."

Briefly, she watched as the dragon let a single tear drop to turn to diamond as it came in contact with the ice cap of his home and retreat.

He was seated upon the highest pinnacle of Perythduin, his tail wrapped around the rock to hold him firm, his long neck out-stretched to survey his mesne, one cupped claw holding her carefully, suspended, and gripped no longer by the terror of the great fall beneath her but rather by the panoramic scene of mountains, hills and rivers and rolling fields for many, many leagues in every direction ... and equally held by the sorrow in her captor's eyes.

"Why have you brought me here?" Ra'el asked gently but she half-convinced herself she already knew the answer.

"Little queen, you have nothing of which to be afraid of on my account. All evil intent of mine has long since departed. I have brought you here because for the first time in over a millennium, my heart has begun to beat again with the soft pulsation of love. I have brought you to my home to ask ... if you would stay with me?"

"Am I your prisoner still then?" she queried and then was rocked back in astonishment by his reply:

"You are free to go and I will return you to your home and your family forthwith the moment you say this is what you wish."

Her intent had thus worked but much faster than she could ever have thought possible. His interest in her stories had turned into friendship and from their companionship had come this offer of release. Ra'el's mind was overjoyed ... and yet her heart bled.

"Would you mind if I stayed, my friend?"

The dragon slowly shook his head and made every attempt to contain himself at her response but she could see by the way that the tip of his tail was dancing that he was happy at her answer:

"You are my new queen" he said simply "and I shall promise you your heart's desire in return for the gift you offer me of your company. What is it that I can grant you?"

Ra'el did not need to think long to respond for her heart's desire was in her every waking and sleeping thought:

"I seek to learn to *read and write* for this is something that I never learnt when I lived amongst the tribes of my childhood. But now my inability to do so has made me different in the eyes of those with whom I go to school. If it is within your gift to do so then let me read and write so that I am no longer apart from my peers."

Roaring Flamebringer shook his head in sadness once more:

"Alas, child, whilst I shalt happily teach you to read and write and grant you also knowledge and wisdom and the gift of language and such power over words that you shall never be without opinion and considered wise amongst those with whom you live yet never can I make it that you shall be accepted by them as being one of their kind. It is your destiny to be lonely and apart, to have tragic things happen to you ... and to die young. I cannot change any of these things. But I can make it that you shall always be happy despite this."

"I shall gladly exchange the gift of my stories for the gift of happiness" Ra'el smiled "but on one condition: that you also are happy with me!"

"Your wish has already come true" whispered her new-found friend and then wept tears of pain and concealed grief that washed clean the despite in his lonely soul to replace the sorrow of centuries with the promise of joy in each other's company. Ra'el stood up and kissed him on the tip of his nose then hugged his neck tight before finally he lowered his head to allow her to sit cross-legged once more at his feet. This time, the story she told was not for him ... it was for them BOTH.

"In the ancient land of Maya, there is a province called Gaitan where lived a young girl: the sole daughter of the provincial sorcerer and judge. Her name was Li Pao.

She was known amongst the people of her province as "*the blossom that rose in the well-spring of their hearts" or peracer tal mai* in the language of the time for her gentle wisdom, kindness and frail beauty.

Some minor magic was hers, though a small shadow of the great necromancy that was gifted to her father, but she could charm small animals, tend plants back to life … and she had learnt to fly.

Her father was a powerful sage and theumaturge with mastery and governance over a thousand people in the villages along the banks of the delta that gave life to Gaitan. He was also ambitious: his intent was to become an Imperial Seer but to do this he must remove an existing theurgist and thus take his place in the demonic ranks of the sorcerers at the Court of the Emperor.

One day, Li Pao was sat reading by the fountain at the heart of her private garden whilst listening to the cadenza of a kingfisher. It was the beginning of twilight when the stars first show their face to those whose love is their divination yet the sun still shines rose-coloured as a memory of another blessed day, and the moon shines tall, slender and silver in the heart of a pale blue sky.

"Lacerte! Pa mai tal!" whispered the lady and the sconces lit dimly to aid her study of the tablet that so engrossed her.

Into this tranquil scene stepped her father, silently watching his studious daughter, a faint smile on his lips to see her so wrapped up in the story that she read. Something however gave away his presence and she looked up – then seeing her father she dropped the scroll, rose in one fluid motion and walked into his arms with shining eyes and a delighted smile:

"Beloved, this day could not end better than to hold you in my arms" she whispered then kissed him tenderly before beginning to regale him of the story she was reading. He listened for a while but knew if he did not stop her she would talk all night and not even notice that she did so and thus eventually he brought himself to interrupt the gentle, light-humoured chatter of his daughter.

"Li Pao. I come with news of importance, my dear."

"Oh!" she exclaimed, but smiling as she did so then laughed at herself for her prattle before sitting before him attentively and dutifully.

"Tomorrow I am summonsed to attend before the Emperor and to learn if I am given permission to challenge one of the seers in the Imperial Court. I have done my research and there is one whom I deem weak and well within my abilities to overcome. Nonetheless, there will be risk … but if I am successful then our circumstances shall change immeasurably."

Li Pao sat thoughtfully for a few moments and then asked humbly:

"Father, you are wise and your wisdom has guided us both to prosperous and happily fulfilled lives. I will follow your wisdom therefore without exclamation or hesitation. But you have also taught me to test your wisdom through my own limited knowledge and thus I have the temerity to ask:

Are we not already happy? For if so, then this risk you take is unnecessary to my eyes and will see another's life taken."

The sorcerer looked down on his daughter and a flicker of anger shone briefly in his dark eyes before his natural good nature overcame it and made him remember it was indeed he who had taught her to challenge him. It was in equable temper therefore he gave her an honest and full reply.

"To be an Imperial Seer has been my dream since I was a young child. Daughter, what you say is true, of course! We have sufficient of life to be happy … but I shall not really be fulfilled unless I have this chance to make my life's dream come true. Not to make the attempt will see me ponder for the rest of my life on what might have been … and worse it will become the seed of resentment and thus undermine our happiness. Dreams must be tested or our lives become a shell."

Li Pao bowed her head in acknowledgement but, deep within her, her heart whispered that this dream would be their unwitting undoing. Yet, she let none of her inner disquiet show as she replied:

"Beloved, your wisdom outstrips mine as always. To see my father achieve his dream is my heart's first and only desire. I am content with this answer and also I shall pray with all the potency and love that is within me for your success. Whom is it that you must fight?"

Her father held her head in his two hands in gratitude, his eyes sparkling with joy in response to her own gleam of love. Then he sat next to her and gave her full response:

"I have chosen a young wizard whose professed power is obscure and thus of no great value or threat. He says he has the wisdom of Gathering (though he calls it "*Uchben Kaatik*"). This is not a system or discipline of magic with which I am acquainted and I have studied all of the High Art and the Dark Power. Clearly this young seer has made his name from the study of a minor branch of the Low Magic or even of the Aether and such sorcerers are easily overcome. Indeed, I am surprised that he has survived as long without some skill in one of the senior branches of theurgy."

"Yaakuntik taat" Li Pao smiled radiantly and kissed him again though every fibre of her body was now in fear. For the young sorcerer professed to have answered 'the oldest question' and whilst his magic might be minor (and thus more familiar to her own gentler and peaceful studies of the occult) there was only one question to which this could refer in Mayan culture and that was *the capture of souls.*

"We leave at the chumuk k'iin saamal, kiichpan."

Li Pao nodded then blushed at her father's compliment before setting about preparing herself mentally and spiritually for the challenge they would both face on the morrow. Her soul must be clean … if she was to sacrifice it to save her father from eternal torment at the hands of a 'soul gatherer'.

For those not familiar with ancient Mayan (the origins of the language of magic): Lacerte! Pa mai tal! ... Alight! Bring me blessings! Uchben Kaatik ... The ultimate question Yaakuntik taat ... I love you father chumuk k'iin saamal, kiichpan ... at noon tomorrow, beautiful one

Li Pao had barely a fraction of her father's skill in magic but she was attuned to the Aether in a way that secretly her sire both respected and envied. Thus, whilst he was required to summons a daemon serpent to act as his steed, Li Pao stood serenely in the centre of her garden and just enquired gently:

"Ychi tai. Embrace me within your comforting spirit and transport me life and soul, safe and hail to the Palace of my Lord."

With arms outstretched, she rose slowly into the air to follow her father and his dragon across the snow-capped mountains and dense forests towards the many pinnacles and minarets in the city in the far distance that was the glistening white marbled home of the Imperium.

She travelled by the power of her mind alone, no need to summons foul demons or to endanger her soul. Indeed, so attune was she with the single essence of all life that she had released the secret of travel through time and space. Only her own sense of integrity forbad her from its use: for Li Pao feared any use of powers that disturbed the equilibrium and equality she sought in life and love.

As was customary, they landed in the tented forum and caravanade by the west gate to the city to be greeted by the black armoured custodians of the Imperial Court. They were strangers to the city and since each mage or magician was known to the guardsmen by sight or by conjuration, their arrival caused a brief stir.

"Announce yourselves or face the full wrath of our Emperor and his Council!" the first of the young soldiers challenged them, his pikestaff lowered as a warning:

"I am Platarch, Judge of the Western province of Trace, summonsed by the Emperor to challenge one of the Council in conjuration" replied Li Pao's father and with a twist of his hand, he produced a piece of vellum with the imperial seal that floated in mid air before them. The guard stood silently for a moment as if listening and then replied:

"This has been confirmed but you must make demonstration of your magic before you are able to proceed. Many challenge but few are worthy to do so!"

The theurge frowned slightly at the discourtesy of the young man's address but then his good humour returned and he looked across to his demon dragon.

"Be gone!" and immediately a gateway to the pits of Hell from which it had come opened. The guards shrank back in horror from the terrifying sight of the millions in torment in its fires but the momentary vision was brief and soon had passed as the magician returned his daemon to its home.

With a gulp, the sentinel nodded. He at least was satisfied. But then he turned to Li Pao before asking the mage:

"Who is it you bring with you? She must also make demonstration!"

"This is my only daughter, Li Pao. She has no ability at conjuration but some affinity with the Aether."

"She cannot pass unless she can satisfy me she has the right to be here. This is not a place for women with no value."

Li Pao saw her father begin to bristle with anger again and gently placed her hand on his arm. *"Allow me?"* her mind whispered in his. Then she turned to the young soldier and said kindly:

"Your daughter is home."

The young man blinked and his face went ashen. His pike wavered before him but then he held it resolute and firm once more as he demanded:

"What do you know of her, witch?"

Li Pao held her hand upright in the universal sign of peace before them both and whispered:

"Of your graciousness and generosity, wait one moment," and then pointed to a hawk that was approaching from behind them and which flew straight to its master's outstretched hand. The soldier looked at it in hope and immediately saw the message tube was in use. Placing his pike carefully on the ground, he withdrew the small scrap of parchment placed there to read these hurriedly scribbled words:

"Husband, our daughter is safe and returned home. She speaks of being chased by a wolf and being saved by the wind. Whichever of the Gods has done this has my thanks."

"How did you know?" asked the soldier through tears of relief.

Li Pao stepped forward and gave him a distinctive scarf of yellow and blue silk: "Your daughter dropped this as she ran and now I return it to you both. I was 'the wind' that saved her. May I pass?"

The Judge Platarch headed under escort into the heart of the city bound for the Imperial Court Chamber where he would be received by the Emperor on the following day but Li Pao held back to speak with the young guard, who was more than willing to offer his aid.

"I seek a young wizard whose skill will be with the Aether, as is mine, and whose power is known as 'the Gathering'. Have you heard of such?"

The guard frowned briefly as he considered how best to help her then grinned. "I have it! There is such a young man who sits on the Council but he is no ordinary man. You speak of the Emperor's one and only son, Jeh'lad."

"*It is as I feared,*" thought Li Pao to herself. "*My father goes up against a mighty opponent and should he win, he earns the enmity of the Emperor;*

should he be defeated, he shall lose his soul! There is only one choice for me and that is I must challenge Jah'lad first."

"Can you take me to the quarters of Jah'lad? I seek to discuss the powers of Aether with him for I believe there is much we can learn from each other." The guard nodded and offered to escort her himself.

Jah'lad's pavilion was modest compared with the quarters of the other nobles. Li Pao had not expected such humility from the son of the Emperor and found herself warming to her opponent. If the aspect of his home was an indication of his demeanour and outlook towards life then she expected she was going to like him.

The welcome Li Pao received from Jah'lad's servants was also considered and thoughtful. They asked with concern over her journey and took her to one side to wash her feet and then allow her to change into the day robes that were customary for guests in a noble's home. They provided her with a choice of jewellery and silks from Jah'lad's own mother's warde-robe, and when she was suitably attired, helped complete her make-up and then offered her light refreshment.

"Do you treat every one of my lord Jah'lad's guests as I have been so regally treated?" Li Pao asked, overawed at their courtesy, to which the major domo replied kindly:

"My lady, Jah'lad welcomes all guests and we are honoured when he have people to entertain. Jah'lad himself is a young man who seeks to be part of his people despite the magick he bears. He will be delighted to meet you as we understand your father is also a conjurer and one who seeks a noble place on the Imperial Council."

Li Pao bowed to acknowledge her father's intent then stood at the entrance to the grand chamber at the heart of the pavilion where Jah'lad would receive her. The twin doors were opened from within and she made the traditional first bow of greeting knowing her host would also be doing the same. But then Jah'lad broke with tradition and before she could glide to the centre of the chamber to make the second obeisance, he strode towards her and took both of her hands in his as if greeting a sister:

"The news has already come! You are an *Aetheric* as I. You have power over the elements. We must talk!"

At this, Li Pao could not stop herself. She began quietly to chuckle at his enthusiasm, at first startling Jah'lad but then he realised why she was laughing and joined in: "Forgive me my poor manners, my lady" and he sketched the deepest of courtly bows for her pleasure.

That was it. Li Pao now had a fit of the giggles and in great good humour with the young man, allowed herself to be guided to a window seat ... where the view of a single magnolia tree in blossom finally silenced her.

"My lord, I can understand why you ignore the ceremony and traditions of our people, when you awake each morning to the beauty of such a tree. It is in my mind that you study the Aether because you love the natural over the supernatural."

"My lady, I seek the source of that beauty."

"And what will you do when you find the source?" Li Pao asked, her concern returning.

"Why are you here, Li Pao?" Jah'lad replied ignoring her question but now serious in his turn.

Li Pao took a deep breath. She would need all of her courage for what she must say next and feared that the good humour that already existed between the two young people would be shattered at her words. But she loved her father and would do anything to save him:

"I have discovered today that my father intends to challenge you in order to gain a place on the Council chamber. Alas, he only knows you by your magick and is unaware of your true position in court. He will either die or disgrace my family. I also know the source of your own magick and fear that my father's soul will be taken when impure. For you are a 'soul gatherer' and seek the ultimate power: "*Uchben Kaatik*".

So I am come to challenge you myself. I have little chance of winning but my soul is ready and I will sacrifice it for the sake of my father and my family honour."

"What challenge is this that you set, Li Pao? And forgive me, but your magick is indeed weak and I will crush you if you dare to challenge me. Why should one of such beauty seek her own certain death?"

"To live without honour is to be dead" replied the girl sadly, her head bowed down briefly but then her head lifted once more, her long hair fell back from her face and a fierce light shone in her eyes as she continued: "My challenge is the 'questioning game' of course!"

"And if I refuse your challenge?"

For the first time since she had looked on the tree, the young girl smiled:

"I can answer that question, my lord. You have already accepted my challenge by asking me a question. So, now it is my turn!"

"You ... witch!" Jah'lad exclaimed then once again his good humour got the better of him and he laughed. "If I answer incorrectly you have won the challenge and take my place on the Council. If you answer incorrectly, I take your soul ... have I the terms correctly?"

"You have, my lord. Now I have answered two of your questions you must answer two of mine."

Jah'lad went to protest then stopped realising each time he did so, he was stacking the odds up against himself. "This is a clever lady" he mused "and I must take this challenge more seriously!"

Li Pao stood in the traditional pose of the challenger as she had often seen her father practice, her left leg slightly in front of her right, both knees slightly bent, her left arm raised at shoulder height, her right arm held above her head. Jah'lad remained seating, enjoying the spectacle of the young girl pretending she could do sorcery. "I am ready," he said simply.

"What is your name?"

"Jah'lad" he replied without thinking, surprised at the question.

"What is your favourite thing?"

"The magnolia tree."

Again he was surprised at how easy the questions had been. Li Pao nodded satisfied and then beckoned with her left hand for Jah'lad to launch his question.

"What is the 'Uchben Kaatik'?" asked the young lord, guiltily as he knew this question would kill the girl but he also knew he could not afford to lose his position on the Council. There would be a time when his power needed to be available at his father's right hand else darkness would fall over all of Maya.

"It is the element of all elements" replied Li Pao without hesitation.

Jah'lad's jaw dropped open and he was rendered speechless. He tried to rise from the window seat but was briefly paralysed in his astonishment at the girl's answer. She just grinned and then waited for him to regain his composure. Then as his powers of speech returned he went to ask her a question but with a gentle gesture of her hand she silenced him once more.

"My turn!" she laughed and he glared at her then realised she clearly meant him no harm. Her intent was and always had been to lose this challenge, but at the same time she seemed to want to aid him in his quest for the ultimate power.

"Do you seek to find the defining and all answering element?" she asked.

"Yes" he replied simply. "Can you help me find it?"

"Yes!" She answered matching her tone to his own and the simplicity of his response.

"What will you do when you find the controlling element, the source of the beauty that is within your magnolia tree, my lord" she asked her original question again but this time knowing he must answer and could not avoid doing so.

"*She has tricked me after all into answering her original question*" Jah'lad realised *"but at cost of her life. Is my answer worth her death*?"

"I seek to protect it from dark sorcery. I have sensed its demise at the hands of foul magick. I myself have turned my back on all magick and sought instead the power of the Aether to combat the evil of theurgy. If I find the element I will give my life willingly to protect it and save it from harm."

Li Pao dropped her arms, stood straight and then walked across to him knelt down and gave him an enormous hug before sitting down beside him on the window seat again with his hands held firmly in her own for comfort.

"I am proud of you, my lord. Now ask your question and capture my soul. With my soul to guide you then you shall find the element."

"Can this challenge be ended without the capture of your soul?" asked Jah'lad.

"No" replied Li Pao sadly, her hands shaking briefly in his.

"I shall not kill you" the young man replied defiantly and then was astonished when Li Pao curled up with another fit of the giggles before uncurling again to embrace him. "I shall have a very long life then!" she whispered in his ear "provided I can always answer your questions, my lord. And since I am always honest and dutiful, this shall not be very hard if you will always ask the right questions!"

"Your turn to ask, my lady" replied the lord, shocked at what she had said but then growing in the realisation that there was hope after all.

"Can I stay in your company, my lord?" the fair lady asked "For I love the calm and peace of your pavilion and the welcome of your people and the beauty of your tree. I welcome also the hope of your protection for the element that is the source of all beauty ... for that element is part of me also."

Jah'lad's heart leapt with joy and such was his delight at this question that almost he forgot to give answer and thus came close to losing the challenge. He lifted her right hand to his lips and kissed each finger gently once then looking deep into her eyes, replied:

"This day I vow to be your constant and eternal companion ... and to always ask you questions of which you know the answer. What do you ask in return?"

"If my father should challenge you on the morrow then I ask you decline for the sake of his daughter. Until then, we should keep our vows secret for there will be those who will fear the coming together of the 'soul capturer' and another *Aetheric*. There are dark sorcerers who seek the destruction of the Aether for it constrains their magick just as we who love nature seek the destruction of sorcery for it is unnatural."

"I must find the element before they do!" and Jah'lad strode around the room thumping his right fist into his left hand in anxiety.

"If I tell you where the element you seek is, will you promise not to be angered at me, my lord?" Li Pao asked shyly at which Jah'lad blinked then nodded before asking:

"Where is the controlling element?"

"She is here!"

Jah'lad shook his head in frustration. "No, I do not need some philosophical answer. I know that the elements are everywhere. The element of beauty is in that tree and the fountain beyond it. It is in the sparkle in your eyes or the fine jewellery you wear that never looked so wonderful until this day. But I need to know its source such that I can protect it from attack!"

"She is here!"

"You stubborn girl, you are in danger of losing the challenge. We have just promised our lives together and yet you still seek to throw the contest. You do not answer my question" fumed Jah'lad, going red in the face with rage yet also holding Li Pao's hands once more in anxiety for her. She silenced his anger with her gentle response:

"The most powerful element is the element of beauty and serenity. It brings balance to the other elements. It seeks consensus and avoids conflict between them. It can be the strongest of all elements when it achieves harmony and peace but is otherwise also weak when alone or without aid or support. Like the other four elements it seeks those who are willing to be its bearer and dedicate their lives to its purpose – it and they become one. Unlike the other four elements, *it can assume the powers of any element*: thus it can be the wind, or the air, or fire, or earth. But only to do an act of kindness or to create a thing of beauty: the controlling element has no defence against or interest in aggression or war."

Jah'lad blinked then asked: "How do you know all of this?"

"It is not your turn to ask," replied Li Pao laughing. "She is here!"

"Very well, ask your own question" Jah'lad retorted in exasperation.

"Had I asked this question at the start then would the challenge have ended in your inevitable defeat. But now I can ask in the knowledge that you know enough to work the answer out. Who am I?"

Jah'lad went to answer and then stopped. This was not a simple question obviously else the girl would have asked it at the start. And what clues had she given? Her knowledge of the Aether and the elements told the young man that she was a powerful *Aetheric* in her own right. Then he remembered the story told of her test on arrival when she had said "I am the wind!" Was her soul perhaps the host for one of the elements? Was she the element of the wind and was this how she knew so much of the other elements? Finally, he recognised his stupidity and looked at the girl in awed silence: "She is here!"

"You are *Uchben Kaatik*!"

"Yes" replied a bashful Li Pao. "Also I am yours! You have found me" and she kissed him.

The following day, the High Council were gathered around their Emperor to receive the challenge of the Judge Platarch. The chamber in which they presided was ancient indeed, a place welded by the wielding of sorcery to unimaginable height, glistening in golden splendour, a pool of immeasurable depth and indescribable purity in its centre, around which the twelve councillors sat in contemplation of the necromancy that was their daily study and defining purpose. On a dais at the far end of the chamber sat the Emperor, the many gemstones of his marble throne reflected in the waters before him. Magick had made him ancient before his years, as he offered days of his life and a part of his soul each day in return for the power of the daemons he wouldst summons.

He was waiting in eager expectation for a death through conjuration. One of his Council or Platarch would see their souls ripped to shreds in demonic torment such was the fate whomsoever lost the challenge of the learned Judge could expect.

"Bring the challenger before us" he commanded.

The doors at the end of the chamber rolled gradually open and Platarch strode into the Council Hall to bow before the Emperor then waited for the Emperor to speak, for by tradition, the Emperor's words must always be heard first and last. On this day, however, there was no great didactic or philosophical converse; the Emperor was eager to see blood and spoke plainly and simply:

"Welcome Platarch. You have proven your skill in theurgy already. Name he whom you challenge."

Platarch bowed once more then replied:

"He whom I challenge is known amongst your people as the Quiet One (H'lum). He studies the Aether rather than theurgy and professes to know the way of the Gathering. I challenge this man to stand forth and contest with me his right to be on your Council. I do so in the belief that there is no place for *Aetherics* in a world of sorcelment."

For the first time in many years, the Emperor stood from his throne before the Council in anger and, red ire burning from his gaze, replied with force:

"You challenge my only son, Jah'lad. Then know this, should you win, I shall challenge you and see you defeated and with you I shall slay every living member of your family until you and your name are forgotten for all time. I shall hunt you in this world and the next and see you tormented in life and in death. For this challenge, Platarch, I curse you and your family."

Platarch reeled under the damning force of the Emperor's words, but, alas, his challenge was already made and he realised that with it he had ensured his death and the disgrace and torment of his family. He thought of Li Pao and tears fell from his eyes as he comprehended too late the wisdom of her words to him. His ambition had destroyed them.

Into the silence that followed the Emperor's outburst, Jah'lad stood calmly:

"Forgive me father, but I cannot accept this challenge. I am already pitted against another challenger and in honour must defeat them before I can take on this contest."

"Explain!" demanded his surprised father.

"Platarch's daughter Li Pao offered herself as a suitable challenge yesterday and seeks her own defeat to save my life and that of her father. She tricked me into accepting her challenge to the 'questioning game' and as yet I have been unable to ask a question that she cannot answer. If she wins then I lose my place in this Council but if she loses then she loses her soul to me. In either case, her challenge replaces that of her father, Platarch"

"Bring the girl here in chains!" roared the Emperor. Then turning to the rest of his Council, he set them a task: "We must find a question to which the girl cannot know an answer and thus see to it that the girl is slain."

To Platarch he then said simply: "You are dismissed from my sight. Your family and your honour live on because of the sacrifice of your daughter but her life is now mine and her soul shall be punished in your place and for all time."

The Judge bowed low then fled the chamber in tears of distress at what his arrogance had achieved. Only now, did he come to understand that his ambition for his daughter was of far greater import than his reputation as a necromancer. Her loss flayed him and he prayed to the Gods that time could return the sands to their chamber or turn the leaves of its much travelled tome backwards and thus unravel the harm that his actions had precipitated.

Word went out into the City that Li Pao was to be brought before the Emperor and the girl, fearing that risk or harm might be brought upon the household of Jah'lad, gave herself up immediately to the sentries at the entrance to her new lord's pavilion. They took her, stripped her, and lashed her before dragging her bleeding body half naked before the Emperor's ire.

At sight of her Jah'lad almost broke all resolve in his distress but his task was as the girl had determined as they had lain the night before in each other's arms and contemplated how to win through the day ahead with life and love intact. He stood as stone with only the slow clenching and unclenching of the young man's right hand showing the level of emotion that he did seek to contain.

The guards flung Li Pao at the feet of her challenger and only he saw the slow wink of encouragement from the girl, who otherwise lay motionless awaiting her fate. But that one gesture gave Jah'lad the courage to continue on the path they had set upon.

"The question?" snapped the Emperor at which the eldest of his Council stood before him and spoke carefully:

"The girl has not studied necromancy and so is unlikely to be able to answer questions on its most dark secrets. Jah'lad therefore must ask her for the name of the demon that guards the ring of ice at the centre of Hell."

"Even I do not know the answer" replied the Emperor in astonishment "and am amazed there are any amongst us should have this knowledge of the intimacies of the world of demon!"

"One of us has made this their lifetime study and he avows to the answer. We have tested him and he speaks true. The girl shall die if this question is therefore asked of her" the old mesatheurge responded, although he had likewise been both amazed and concerned that such knowledge should be held. To himself he had already decided that once this session of Council was ended, he would seek greater understanding of the commitments his fellow councillor had made to obtain such knowledge.

Jah'lad stood before Li Pao. He bowed down and gently raised her face so that he could look into her eyes as he asked the question:

"Promise me you are the Ultimate Answer" he whispered softly and when she nodded, he then posed the question:

"What is the name of the demon that guards the ring of ice?"

"The demon is already in this place" the girl replied and she pointed towards the councillors. "For only the demon knows its own name. But in this place he bears another name and that name shall be sufficient answer to your question, my lord. For it is still the name of the demon, just not its secret name."

Then bowing to the Councillor seated next to Jah'lad, she continued politely:

"Your name is Biel'aan and you are also a demon in our midst come to summons our people to worship evil magick before the beauty and majesty of God's nature. I name you demon."

Biel'aan nodded in acceptance of her words and then shrugged:

"Your people choose the power of demon-kind. I force them to do nothing they do not seek themselves."

"They do not know the risk they face" responded the girl her face alight with eagerness to meet this new challenge.

"And what is that risk?" commanded the Emperor but Li Pao shook her head, the first to ever defy the Emperor in this way in his presence, and then compounded her solecism by laughing as she did so. "Alas, my Emperor, it is my turn to ask the question and not yours!"

The chamber grew silent again as Li Pao stood carefully, hugging the remains of her clothes about her to maintain her modesty and being careful not to catch the newly forming scars on her back. She took one short breath for courage and then asked her lord:

"Am I to be your wife?"

Jah'lad nodded with delight and the Council Chamber erupted as the councillors exclaimed in horror or surprise or in some cases growing understanding. The girl would not threaten the life of the man it seemed but then for the contest to end Li Pao must be asked a question she could not hope to answer.

Biel'aan stepped forward before the Emperor. "Sire, this contest will continue indefinitely I fear. For you see before you the Ultimate Answer in Li Pao. Someone whom through her communion with the elements is able to seek and find the answer to any question we might ask. Therefore, to defeat her, we must not seek an answer she does not know but rather an answer she will not be prepared to give. We must ask her how the elements might be destroyed! For with their destruction we can release the full force of demonic power upon this world under your mastery and that of your Council. You and your Council will become unassailable."

The Council nodded. This of course made sense. It was why Uchben Kaatik was seen as the ultimate weapon as well as the ultimate answer. To destroy the Aether would release theurgy without any balancing counter force, to become the unique source of power and authority in this world. Either the girl must release that power into their hands or refuse to answer the question and forfeit the challenge.

"I am ready to ask my question" and Jah'lad stood before his father. "But know this, sire, Li Pao is and always will be my one true love and I am sworn to her protection."

Then before anyone could intervene he turned and asked her hurriedly:

"Why does Biel'aan seek the answer to his question?"

The demon screamed and began to materialise in its winged form, all the better to attack the girl before she could have hope of answer but Li Pao was already prepared and brought a gust of wind to blow the demon back into its chair.

"The world of demon seeks absolute dominion over man and this Council; only the power of the Aether can prevent this."

Then turning to the demon, she laughed gaily in its face. As she did so, a gentle breeze took the topmost blossoms from the magnolia tree in Jah'lad's garden and carried them as a gift to descend before the Emperor. In moments, the flagstones before him were covered with scent and colour. He looked with new wisdom and with the realisation that nature's beauty was far more fulfilling than the power of evil. The wind continued to curl around the chamber, parting the wall hangings to let in the sun, and allowing entry to the soft singing of the birds outside as they announced the arrival of another twilight chorus. The surface of the crystal clear water before the Council bubbled as the joyful carp broke surface to take ownership of their fresh waters once more.

As nature reclaimed this recess of dark sorcery, the demon shrank from Li Pao, seeking to distance itself as far as possible from her simple purity. But she was relentless. The pillars of the chamber began to transform into slender oaks, soft tufts of verdant grass broke through the flagstone floor at her feet, and roses crept from her toes to twine around the feet of the chairs on which the Council were seated. With a final heave, the wind grasped the domed-ceiling of the hall and it flew into the heavens to disappear as a distant speck, leaving a blue sky and clouds that were the mirror image of the blossom before them.

With one final defiant scream of rage, the demon departed, and with its departure, a great weight lifted from each of the wise men whose Council had been its play thing for these many years past. The Emperor sighed and then turned to his son, who now held Li Pao with pride, securely in his arms, their task fulfilled. For their vision had been of a great risk to mankind from the wrong of demonic dominance in this very Chamber and Jah'lad had needed the aid of his new wife to oust the demon whose plan had always been to rule the world through the evil of power and the power of evil.

"Father, may I present Li Pao to you formally as my future wife and partner. She has proven herself fitting to be your daughter I hope?"

"My son," replied a much wiser man "it shall take me a lifetime and beyond to prove I am worthy to be her father. I accept her gladly into our household if she is willing. But how shall her challenge of you end?"

Li Pao smiled up at her new father. "It can only end one way and I am ready," then turning to Jah'lad she asked her final question:

"Will you ask the only question that shall ensure my soul is captured by you and thus this contest shall be ended?"

"Yes," Jah'lad shouted with joy and before the assembled council said the words that sealed her fate:

"Will you be my wife and souls mate for all eternity?"

"Yes" answered Li Pao. For her heart and soul had already been captured by this man the night before and she had lost the contest when she had fallen so deeply in love with him and his burning desire to seek out and protect the source of all beauty. Such protective custody as this gentle and kind man offered was all her own gentle heart had ever desired and her surrender physically, mentally and metaphysically to him the night before had welded their souls as well as their bodies to become one.

Given the choice of a world dominated by man or a world enjoyed by mankind in communion with nature, on that day, the people of Maya turned their back on sorcery and sought instead to discover **the magic that is nature itself**. In their first faltering step, they were guided by Jah'lad and Li Pao but soon the awareness of beauty that is in the soul of every man and woman began to blossom – as the tree that had brought Li Pao and Jah'lad together continued to do each day as a gift for them until in death they were joined in the soft ground beneath its companionable branches."

Roaring Flamebringer gave a long deep and languorous sigh of contentment. Then suddenly a mischievous gleam came into his eyes.

"I think you speak of things you know not of?" he laughed at which Ra'el looked at him quizzically. "You talk of flying and I think it is about time you had your first flying lesson."

"Oh no," cried the girl hurriedly. "I really do not think I am ready. Please ..." and then screamed before gripping her dragon's neck in terror as he launched up into the sky. Her eyes were firmly shut for the first few moments until eventually she summonsed up enough courage to open one slightly and then wished she had not. The ground was already a speck beneath them and they were rapidly ascending into the heavens. Then she heard Flamebringer whisper:

"Do not worry, little one, I can catch you if you fall. Open your eyes and imagine you are Li Pao flying through the Aether. This is my way of saying thank you for your latest story, but also I have one more gift for you. For you to receive it, we must ascend."

Ra'el nodded bravely and decided to sit back and look around her. The first thing she noticed was that they were travelling at an incredible speed and then she stopped to listen in surprise.

"What is the music?" she lisped.

"It is the dance of the stars" and Flamebringer banked to a swift halt. Then hovering in mid-air in the upper most reaches of the earth's atmosphere, he stretched out both wings as far as they would go and they began to glide gently.

"Will you dance to the melodies of the stars, my queen?" asked the dragon carefully and yet in hope. Ra'el hugged him around the neck in gratitude and then stood, at first a little shakily, and then with growing confidence and began to dance to the strange pattern of our world's destiny that is written in the ancient score that holds the mastery of the stars. After a few minutes of pleasure, Ra'el turned to her companion, eyes shining with tears, to thank him.

"My friend, I have loved the stars since the first day my village elders told me that each was a story of courage and adventure. But to see the stars from your winged back is to awaken to them anew – for me it is like a new birth. I cannot thank you enough for this great gift!"

"Tell me another story, little one," asked the dragon, "and let us show these stars that they are not alone in telling tales of courage and adventure."

Ra'el laughed in pleasure at his retort and then fell silent for a few moments, a slight crease in her brow as she considered which story to tell next.

"I have one" finally she whispered with excitement. "I shall tell you of Selene who was mother of all of the rulers of the desert kingdoms. She won the heart of her husband through her courage and skill ... as perhaps I have won your heart?"

"It is fitting!" replied Roaring Flamebringer nodding then realising this had nearly broken Ra'el's tight clasp of his neck and sent her tumbling, he laughed in return at her brief moment of terror before scanning the horizon. "I shall find us a cloud or mountaintop to sit on and you can begin your tale in comfort and less trepidation."

THE LADY OF THE MIRAGE

"Those that live in the desert will often see the desert sands drift across the sky line making myriad shapes and, mingling with the breeze, to create a philtre for the terrible heat of the sun, refracting its brilliant white light like a prism to assemble a pool of colour - the mirages for which the desert is so renowned.

And so it was that a young traveller rode atop a great ship of the desert, a camel of immense age and wisdom, gifted to her by tribesmen for the important journey she must make. It was her great fortune that day, in her haste, to stumble across just such a mirage, to enter its portals …

… and to find herself seated cross-legged in the manner of the ancient poets and mystics by a bubbling pool in the shelter of a solitary palm tree, her camel tethered to a branch and toasting the falling sun in the cool clear water of life before her.

Whilst she looked to the gathering shadows and saw the night's sky darken then gleam with the silver jewels of the stars, into her new world walked a hero of the desert, his cloak covering his face so that only his dark eyes could she discern, but with strength in his purposeful stride that cut a clean path through the dunes.

She stood, her gown translucent in the silver-glow of the moon, naked to his eye yet still with the shadow of her maidenhood concealed, the wind blowing her hair into an aureole of gold.

"My lady!" His voice doth straightway her gentle attention to his will command. "I must have your camel."

"Then know, my lord, that I am a stranger to this place and that without my camel, I shall be left here to die."

"I understand. Yet my quest is urgent and I must be in Ceripah by the morning to bring news that shall save the lives of all in that fair city."

"The camel is yours then" she replied. "One life to save many is a small price to pay. I ask only this that you slay me now as I would not wish the lingering death of starvation that awaits me here."

The hero paused, his hesitation clearly writ across his face. It was not his wont or desire to slay a maid of whose generosity he was about to take advantage.

"I cannot slay you. You must hope your death is quick ... but it shall not be at my hands" said the hero guiltily and grasped the reins of the camel before the maid could protest.

But she did not argue; greeting instead his words with silence but no reproach. She could well understand why he should be reluctant – she herself could not have done as she had asked, nor kill herself it seemed. So the "dry death" was to be her fate.

She watched as he rode into the sands in great haste. Partly because of the urgency of his quest but she knew also he wished to put as much distance as he could between them ... and the pangs of conscience he felt at leaving her alone, without hope, in the desert. He had broken the travellers' code in his action and only his quest could justify what he now did!

She said no word ... and her silence had more effect on him than any angry outburst or a curse.

Her panniers were with the camel and so she was now without shelter, save the few branches of the tree, nor weapon to hold back the ravaging animals that would smell the water in the morning, nor tinder box as the means to make a fire. Her hero had ensured by taking her few supplies that she might not live long enough to starve. For first she had to live through the cold of the night and then the morning raids of water-crazed animals.

So she made her decision. Her flask was still with her and she filled it with the best part of two days' supply of water then left the mirage to head towards the shelter of a tall dune in the distance. The maid went downwind to avoid her scent carrying back to the mirage and moved fast as she wanted to make shelter before the cold of the night gripped her in its paralysing grasp.

The lady reached the dune within the hour and used her hands and a little of the water to dig a small *wadi* for shelter. Then she removed her gown to hang as shelter and as a protective curtain across the hole in which, near-naked, she slept. Her own body heat rapidly warmed the sand around her and this gave the lady comfort against the cold of the night which crept sinuously upon her.

Through courage and the power of her prayers, she survived the first night ...

... and was woken to the howls and angry thrashings of a battle at the mirage, where hyenas and lions had met in mighty conflict over the life-bringing water of its oasis. Two lionesses fought off the hyenas whilst their lord drank from the brook. One hyena was slain and his body stripped, cracked and broken bones left to dry in the sun. The bones were so mauled they could have been anything: buffalo, prairie dog, hyena ... or those of a girl.

The lady waited several hours until certain the pride had moved off and then broke camp. She needed to find better shelter as the dune was now already almost red hot to the touch and her skin would begin to burn if she remained in that place. She was not so foolish as to walk in the midday sun but knew rather that she had a few hours yet before she must find new shelter - and in that time she hoped also to find some outcrop of rock in whose shade she could hide.

The night before, the maid had used the stars to tell her which way was north (the way she must head to reach the mountains at the edge of her desert). She had marked the way with four small strips of her gown as an arrow. Dressed in the remains of her gown, she picked up her flask and headed into the desert, using the unique shapes of the dunes to keep her on a true bearing. Years in the desert and the lady knew the risk of going around in circles and also that it was a mistake to use the sun as a guide.

Two hours into her trek and she saw ... her camel, but rider-less!

Then great anxiety did grip the lady and she hurried across to her former companion. As the maid had feared, on reaching him, there were the clear signs of conflict in traces of blood on the camel's rear. She hugged the camel tightly for comfort then asked him to show her the way to where her hero must have been attacked.

The lady no longer cared about the heat of the sun, nor the damage it would do to her skin. She had a man to rescue from whatever adventure or danger the fates had cast him into and did not hesitate for a moment in pursuit of his release.

Dusk approached. Her camel was weary as she picked up the first traces of a large camp: evidence of kindling being gathered from broken branches on the dead stumps of the occasional tree and the removal of gorse which had been dragged through the sand. Soon she could smell the smoke of the fires, still a few miles off, and so tied up her faithful camel and from that point determined to approach the camp silently and on foot. The night would be her shield; the stars as always her guide.

She smelt the tribesmen long before she came into their sight: two guardsmen behind a small rock on the approach to the camp. Neither had washed for some time whereas she was always careful to leave no scent. The smell of their stale sweat was palpable from quarter of a mile away. And so she skirted to the east to arrive at the outcrop from the direction of the camp. An enormous camp fire was at its centre and if the guards looked that way, they would lose their night sight in its glare. But they did not look, and the small garrotte in her hair took the first whilst she used the knife hanging from his belt to slice the throat of his companion.

She ran briskly now as far as the outer circle of tents (for camps in these deserts were always constructed in three concentric circles of tents with the guards on the outside and the nobles or prisoners in the centre, closest to the safety and the warmth of the fire) and then she stooped to the ground to listen.

The lady could make out the sleeping breath of forty two men and the waking breath of two in the silence of the night. The two awake could not be smelt over the smoke of the camp fire, but she knew they would be patrolling the fire to keep it burning (as she had done many times in her own village or for her own tribe when on the move).

The maid stooped once more ... and heard what she hoped for: two slower, more laboured breathing patterns. One was clearly an old man - this would be the tribe's leader, a man of importance, and if she could slay him then this would grant her the confusion to make good an escape when her actions were detected in the morning. The second was a younger man, but injured and she suspected not able to breathe through his nose for the blood that was still there - this would be her hero.

First, to find where the tribesmen kept their camels! Then to remove the sentries! A simple task as they were standing with their backs to the fire watching the entrance to two tents. She circled the camp until she found the corral where the camels had been tethered then crept back to the two guards she had slain to take a spear and one of their cloaks.

Armed, she returned to the camp and crept silently amongst the shadow of the tents, knowing by instinct where the guides had been buried in the sand (all tribesmen set their tents the same way to avoid falling over the ropes in the night). Once in sight of the fire, she removed her gown and then, carrying the cloak and spear, crept to the far side of the fire from the two guards ...to run… then jump and throw the cloak on the fire ahead of her, creating a gap in the flames to leap over the fire and plunge her spear into the back of the first guard. The second guard turned and froze in astonishment, as he caught a glimpse of a naked young woman ... before losing his sight in the blaze of the fire behind her. He turned away to regain his sight; was calling for help when the spear took him in the throat. As he struggled on the end of its point, she swung him round by its tip and cast him into the fire, his silent screams ending as the flames plunged into his lungs.

Bending down to check the other guard would not disturb the night, the lady then removed his scimitar. "Now where next?" she mused. "My hero can wait" she decided. "After all, he was ready to leave me waiting at the mirage, so a few more minutes discomfort is surely his just desserts?"

The guards had been watching the entrances to two tents and it was to the larger of these that she went first. Cutting her way in through the rear of the tent, she followed the sound of heavy breathing in the pitch dark of the inside until she came to the small pavilion's centre, which was sectioned off by wall hangings and surrounded by braziers of scented oils, casting dim shadows on the ceiling. Lying on many cushions was the shape of a middle-aged man. Someone important indeed, she hazarded, and swung the scimitar, removing his head in a single blow.

The maid stooped once more. "Good," she thought, hearing forty one sleeping men breathing and no waking breath.

She carried one of the braziers carefully and placed it by the hole where she had entered the tent then climbed back through the hole and cut a new entrance into the adjoining tent.

Her hero had been badly beaten but was very much alive still. Moving quickly to his side, she kissed him on the lips to wake him. His eyes flicked open in surprise but her lips prevented him from speaking. Then she cut his bonds and signalled for him to follow her. They crawled out of the tent and at last she spoke:

"I will take you to my camel and you must ride on as before. I will cause a disturbance here which will ensure you are not followed for many hours and leave traces that will ensure that when the tribesmen wake, they follow me and not you."

The hero frowned and whispered fiercely: "I have already made the mistake of leaving you once, my lady, and will not make that mistake again. You come with me where I can ensure my people can protect you from the wrath of Baltaar. For when he wakes to find me gone, he will hunt us both down ... and if he finds you alone, your fate will be far worse than the fate to which I left you."

"Who is Baltaar, my lord?" his lady asked innocently suspecting that she had already removed one problem.

"He is my brother. He is also the king of my tribe and has brought his army to this place to destroy the people of the plains. This camp contains his advance guard and he will ride with them to the opened gates of Ceripah tomorrow unless I can get there first and warn them to bar the way."

"Then, my lord, you must ride. Let me be your decoy. But do not fear for me. Once you have reached Ceripah, send help back for me ... and I will promise you that I shall stay out of the clutches of Baltaar for at least the next two days. Now run ..." she cried and pushed him towards her camel then kicked over the brazier she had placed by the tent-side, sending burning oil spilling over the canvas to ignite in a roaring mass of flame.

Within moments, several tents were on fire, and screaming soldiers were running from them in panic or plunging towards the main tent, which was an inferno by now, to rescue their king. In the ensuing chaos, the lady crept as a shadow down to the corral where they had tethered their own camels and swinging a burning branch, scared them off into the desert ... all except one on whose back she rode off whooping into the night, making sure that the tribesmen should hear the direction in which she rode.

Within an hour, she could hear the sound of pursuit. One of hundreds and three score hooves - the whole camp! The rapidity of their pursuit told her that they had discovered Baltaar's headless body and also that his brother (her hero and clearly a prince) had escaped. It also meant that they believed she was the prince so her fate would not be a comfortable one if they caught up with her.

However, she also knew that if she could survive the heat of the desert for twenty hours until the next sunset, then her enemy would have to return to their camp: for she had slit the water flasks hanging on each camel in the corral and knew that their water would run dry in that time. No-one in the desert risks a journey across the heated sands without water.

Except, that is what she was intending to do for she had only enough water for two days, and so, if her lord did not send her help as she had asked, she was likely to die the "dry death of the desert" after all. "*How ironic,*" she thought to herself and smiled.

Her pursuers set a furious pace, clearly not yet aware that they were facing a shortage of water. Each time she stopped to listen for their pursuit, she could hear that they were closer. Briefly, they lost her in the dark of the night as she turned eastwards to avoid a group of hyenas ... and so she whooped once more to encourage them. On they came.

Then the sun came up and as dawn lit up the dunes, she could see her hunters by the dust clouds they were making. She had no more than three leagues distance on them and no chance of losing them in the vast wilderness until nightfall. Twelve hours and three leagues - this would be much closer than she had intended. In her favour, was that she had rested her camel as much as she could during the night. In their favour, she must tread the ground first and one stumble by her camel in a hidden sand hole, or should she get caught in a sand slip, and her enemy would be upon her.

But she had one further advantage over her pursuers - she knew her destination. For in all this vastness of desert, there was only one place she could be certain that her hero would find her. So she rode, like the wind, for the mirage where first they had met.

Her enemy drove their camels harder and harder ... soon she could see their terrified faces, sweat-flecked and driven beyond limit. Then the arrows began to fall. Fired from a league, they had little chance of striking the lady and were intended to distract her - but she knew that to hit her at that distance, they must stop and this would gain her valuable time and so she rode on.

The sun reached its zenith and pursued and pursuer slowed to a trot and then a walk. The lady dismounted and then screamed as her bare feet touched the heat of the sand. But she knew that to ride her camel in that heat would be its death and so she trod on, each step doing great damage to the soles of her bare feet and bringing almost unbearable pain. She let her mind hark back to the camp fires of her youth and the fire walkers of her tribe, hearing their gentle coaxing: "Look ahead, think only of the last step and not the next, the pain will not last ... but you will."

She said the prayer, over and over again, that all of the flame walkers in her tribe recited: "There is no pain except the absence of God and in your presence, as I am now, I remain safe" and gradually the burning sensation faded.

The camel offered her some shade as she walked in his shadow but now she knew her enemy would start to gain ... on the back of a camel, her stamina and lighter frame would bring her victory, but on foot through the dunes, strength and height were key. She must walk faster than she had ever walked for two hours in the burning heat of a midday sun through sands that often went above her thighs, knowing that to slow down spelt her death.

Then disaster struck as she became the first to hit a sand hole.

She heard the whoosh of the sand and felt her legs sucked from beneath her, barely having time to cling to the reins of the camel that through instinct began to back away, as a ton of sand fell into the hole beneath the surface of the dune. Briefly, the rushing sand buried her but she clung to those reins though her hands bled and blistered before the camel finally backed away far enough for her head and shoulders to come clear.

She could hear the shouts of the pursuing tribesmen. They had seen her plight and now this had strengthened them to make a dash to catch up whilst she was still buried in the sand.

Nothing for it! She knew it was not lady-like but desperation must. She spat at the camel and struck it right between the eyes. It flinched and backed further dragging her clear of the sand. She stood shakily, hugged the camel briefly and then mounted it as, despite the danger that a ride in the sun's heat would kill them both, the alternative was an equally certain death.

They rode for the tallest dunes knowing that their pursuers on foot would have to skirt these and lose valuable time. The lady also knew that their water shortage would mean they could not risk mounting to follow. This one hour in the saddle might gain the lady eight hours lead.

But her enemy were determined and a party of four mounted whilst twelve rode back to the camp, leaving some of their water for the four riders and the remainder pursued on foot. Thus, they would defeat her: on camel and on foot and by sharing their water carefully. She cursed them and rode on.

At the end of the hour, the four mounted tribesmen and the lady were many leagues ahead of the rest of the pursuit. But now she must dismount again and potentially face these men in combat. For, they would catch her long before she reached day's end.

She bad her camel rest and then took a bow and quiver from its saddle holster. She had not had time to check the bow before, when redeeming the camel from the corral, so it was with relief that she saw the string was tight and well-made, the bow was composite and had great carry, and the arrows were well-feathered and iron-tipped. This was the weapon of a skilled hunter and one of which even Gilgamesh would have been proud.

She knew she would have time to fire two arrows before her enemy came upon her. The easy shot would be to take the camels, and this would have been her choice if her own camel had been rested and ready for another ride. This was not the case, however, and therefore must she kill the four men and take their camels.

She was careful to place herself so that the sun was over her shoulder as she stood atop one of the dunes. She would have both the range on her enemy and also her arrows would come out of the sun and surprise them.

The lady stood still and prayed then extended her left arm and aimed along it at her first target. Her right hand grasped the first arrow over her shoulder by its fletching and spun it to rest tip first on her left hand where it clasped the bow firmly. She drew the string back holding her breath as she did so whilst standing totally still. Then as she released her breath slowly, she plucked the string like a harp, let her fingers go slack and drew her hand back the fraction of an inch needed to release the arrow.

It struck the first tribesman in the chest - a lung-shot she hoped and watched with glee as the soldiers responded as they had been trained whilst stringing a second arrow to her bow ready for release.

The moment the first tribesman had gone down, his nearest companion had reined in and dropped off his camel, bow in hand and knelt to take aim. He would look for a chance in the fight to follow to release an arrow and the maid could expect some injury at least from that quarter before being able to fire back and slay him. The other two riders came on towards the lady and she knew she had time to take one of them ... but not both. She left her shot until the last possible moment to ensure the rush of the second rider would protect her from an arrow from the archer below.

She released ... an eye shot. Then rolled beneath the hooves of the oncoming camels before grabbing the lance off the soldier she had blinded and driving it through his neck and out several inches on the other side. He fell from his camel dead, wrenching the lance from her grasp as he toppled backwards, just as the first arrow was fired from below and dropped short - an aiming shot, no more. She could expect the next shot to be much more carefully placed.

So now she stood alone on the dune, with an archer below her and a soldier with spear and shield in front of her. Her opponent had dismounted from his camel and approached her wearily using his spear to shepherd her towards the edge of the dune in order to give the archer an easy shot at her unprotected back.

She rolled and the spear swung, its tip catching her in the ribs - a long and ugly scratch, but not disabling. Nonetheless, she dropped her bow and curled up over the cut. Her foeman could see the blood running down her gown. "*A wounded and unarmed girl*" she could see him thinking. "*How easy does this get?*"

He advanced confidently. He even held his arms wide as if to say: "*Come on little girl, what are you going to do now?*" and her silver dagger dropped down her sleeve to land in her outstretched hand. He saw the knife; she saw the fear; then she heard him scream:

"Aiiiiiiiii. H'ash ..."

But the dagger was already through his throat and sticking out of the back of his neck. All tribesmen feared a dagger such as she had just used and *those that wielded them.*

She felt the air move and turned enough for an arrow from below to take her in the right shoulder rather than the neck as intended. She snapped the end off in her left hand then ran to pick up the spear and shield from the ground in front of her. She would return for her dagger later.

The archer was now worried. He had seen three of his companions go down, one mortally wounded, the other two clearly slain. He faced a solitary young girl but armed with spear and shield and with the advantage of the high ground. He considered firing another arrow and then chose instead to mount his camel and swung it round ready to ride off.

As he mounted, the lady threw.

"Winds of the east bear my spear true."

It took him between the shoulder blades, pinning him to the neck of his camel with its force. He screamed, and then begged for mercy but she had none in her now. She walked over to where she had cast down her bow and strung one last arrow. He looked up the hill of sand towards her, the shadow of his nemesis against the bright glare of the sun, and never saw the arrow until it took him in the throat.

Finally, she returned for her dagger and carefully ensured that her pursuers were dead, finishing off the first of her assailants who was drowning as his lungs filled with blood from the puncture from her first arrow. As was customary, she removed her foemen's ears and noses, to show their companions and her pursuers that their path was senseless, and then mounted up: with five camels now, she was rich! More importantly, she had the water she needed to survive the rest of her journey.

She still had half an arrow in her shoulder and a cut across her rib cage. The smell of blood would attract carrion-eaters for miles in this desert. She realised therefore what she must do to survive and stopped briefly to wash away the blood then steeled herself for removing the arrow.

The tip of the arrow had come clean through her shoulder beneath the collar bone and was protruding some three to four inches the other side. She had made a clean break of the fletched end of the arrow and covered the entry hole with cloth to stop both blood loss and infection. But she knew she must remove the rest of the arrow or risk it catching on something as she rode thus doing great damage to the delicate nerves that ran through her shoulder.

She had been taught the trick of this by her father and one-handed cast a loop in the garrotte string she carried always in her fair hair then cast that over the tip of the arrow and tied the other end to one of the camels. She turned her back to the camel then kicked it with a flick of her foot and it launched forward a few paces pulling the arrow clean and straight from her shoulder ... but not without an enormous wrench of pain.

About now, she finally fainted, remaining unconscious on the ground, surrounded and sheltered by the camels for almost an hour before the heat of the sands caused her to stir, to wake, and finally to mount and ride off towards the rendezvous with her hero.

The sun finally dipped behind a giant of a dune, the shape of the pillared temple of Petra and the colour of the golden belt of Belthesar, and the stars now guided her along the last few leagues to the solace and protection of her mirage. Yet she was so very weak and even the constant comfort of water could not take away the growing pain of the two wounds she still carried. The slice across her ribs would not heal, as the constant movement of her breast disturbed and re-opened the wound. She needed oil to aid the sealing of the cut, and regretted not bringing some with her from the braziers in Baltaar's tent.

She knew what she must soon do if she was not to fall asleep in the life-ending stupor that comes from loss of blood, but feared the scar this would leave ... for the lady valued her looks and had womanly pride in her appearance. "A beautiful corpse or a living woman with a scar?" she berated herself. The choice was simple and yet still she hesitated.

"Enough!" she cried to herself and dropped from the camel. Then she scoured the ground until she had found a small stone, stick and a piece of gorse. She unbound her garrotting rope once more and wound it around the stick and then placed it sharp end on the stone and began to twist back and forth until the friction of stick on stone generated heat, then a spark, and finally the gorse took light. Tearing a strip of sacking from the saddle bags on one of the camels, she wrapped this around a larger brand. Finally she set the brand to the gorse until the sacking had also caught light.

Now she gritted her teeth and brought the naked flame to touch her soft skin and the gaping wound left by the spear tip. She drove the burning brand determinedly into her flesh to rapidly seal the mouths of the cut in one cauterised mass of burnt and healing flesh, then flung the branch to the ground in the agony that followed. Pouring water on the newly formed scar, she then bound it tight to complete the healing and picked up the brand once more.

Ahead of her, a mere two hundred paces, she could make out the swirl of refractive sand that formed a dome over her mirage. The tree and bubbling brook were still there as she remembered them. And so she strode forward and passed beneath the crimson, blue and green beams of coruscating light ... to find herself returned to the camel trail she had left days before when first she had encountered the mirage.

She had lost her hero."

The dragon smiled for he could see Ra'el was already beginning to weave with exhaustion. "I forget sometimes that you are but a little one and needs must have your full quota of sleep. Come, for this has been a long and important day for us both and I would not have you fall off my back through sleep. Nay, I would have you rested that you can continue this tale to its conclusion. So, close your tired eyes, my queen, and I can wait until a new dawn for the ending of this story."

Ra'el needed no further encouragement but, grasping tightly to his warm neck for comfort, she curled up in the protective circle between his wings and fell rapidly into a deep slumber.

She woke to the familiar red glow of the cavern beneath her home. Before her was a breakfast of nuts and dry fruit, whilst her companion, out of delicacy and in keeping with his promises to her, was eating some tubers he had baked in the fire of his breath. She looked to the pool of water in the crevasse above him where earlier she had had her first experience of a shower warmed by Flamebringer's heat, and to her delight, the pool was already bubbling away.

"Thank you," she mouthed and stripped to plunge deep into the hot glow of its waters whilst once more her companion mused ruefully at the lack of any decent meat on the girl. Eventually she surfaced and blew a stream of water at the dragon, surprising him, before he retaliated and with a flick of his tail sent a wave of water over her head.

She came up once more, gasping, and raising her hands in surrender whilst he nodded with glee. But then, Ra'el looked forlornly across at her clothing.

"My love," she whispered, "my clothes really do smell. And I have nothing with which to clean them."

"Do not worry, little one! I have eaten many a princess in my time and I think you will find I have amassed a wardrobe that would satisfy even your wildest of wild imaginations." Then noticing that Ra'el had gone a little green at his offer, he continued kindly:

"And have no fear. I ate the bones and cleaned all the blood off. The dresses are as good as new."

Ra'el gulped. However, she did not wish to offend her friend when he clearly was in such a generous mood so stole herself to take a look at the dresses and not to think too deeply about what had happened to their previous owners.

Roaring Flamebringer had not exaggerated. A regular diet of princesses for several thousand years had left behind a wardrobe of which any queen would have been proud. Ra'el could easily have played with the many gowns, jewellery and headdresses for hours, but she could tell from the slight orange tinge in Flamebringer's eyes that he was growing impatient. So, she chose something relatively simple and practical. A silk and lace gown, embossed with pearls and cut with slits to allow her legs to sit tight across the back of her dragon when they might go flying again.

"Good choice" laughed the dragon. "That belonged to an elf and she could tell stories too. But alas she allowed her fear to become the better of her and thus she died. Had she possessed your courage then I would have let her live. Now, you have a story to finish and then I have a question to ask."

Ra'el's head went up in enquiry at his last remark but the dragon soothed her:

"Have no concern. My question is harmless but I will hear your story's end first."

So, once more the girl sat cross-legged before him to tell the end of the tale of Selene.

"The Prince made King by the death of his brother returned from the desert a broken man. He had found the mauled bones of his love, the Lady of the Mirage, besides the tree where first they had met, and known the darkest depths of despair. His men had escorted him home to Ceripah and his palace in the gardens of the city, which he had rode many leagues to warn of attack and to defend with his life.

The news had reached him on his arrival three days earlier that his brother the former king was dead, beheaded in his tent, by a spirit of the night who had fled into the desert, never to be seen again, but Hathesar had known immediately whom it was who had slain the tyrant and paved the way for the brother to now become king.

In his gratitude, and to keep his oath, he had ridden to the meeting place with the girl, intent to offer the Lady of the Mirage half his kingdom and his hand in marriage. He had arrived one day later than promised ... a life time too late for the girl-heroine of his dreams.

His steward caught his attention as he stood before him:

"My liege, there is a message from the Kingdom of the Plains: a message of peace and support for the new King of Ceripah. The messenger asks that the message be given in person before this hall if you shall permit?"

"Let the messenger be brought forth" replied the sad and grieving King.

The messenger wore a black gown and mask. The only adornment was a cunningly wrought bright silver dagger - the garb and weapon of the H'ashaashin. All in the royal chamber were amazed for rarely did the H'ashaashin go abroad and for many this was the first time they had seen sight of one of these fearsome warriors. The messenger was of medium height, and slim as a reed; yet all knew that if the dagger were ever drawn in anger, none in the hall would survive the berserker onslaught that would follow.

The messenger passed a scroll to the steward and whispered softly in his ear then stepped back with folded arms. The steward showed astonishment at the warrior's words but then unrolled the parchment and stood in the centre of the hall to proclaim the news from the Plains.

"The messenger has asked that I read this message to you all.

To the great people of Ceripah and its newly crowned King Hathesar, we send you greetings from the Fortress of H'ael in the plains of Belchol. We have long wearied of the tyranny of Baltaar and therefore seek to join our two kingdoms in a union of minds, hearts and bodies through a dynastic wedding.

We offer to you this day, our daughter and the well-spring of our people, the fair Selene, to be your queen, whose dowry shall be my kingdom on my death, for the delight of your heirs and their heirs after them.

Moreover, and as token of our love for Hathesar, and as sure sign that we speak true in our dealings with you, the messenger who stands before you has been sent with one mission and then to be thereafter at your command: this mission is to slay Baltaar and thus rid the deserts of a vermin whose existence has long threatened both our kingdoms.

This messenger is one of the holy H'ashaashin and this shall be the last mission given by me before this my most honoured warrior shall enter your life-long service ... I offer my messenger as a further gift, born of my love for you as my fellow King, and soon, I hope to be con-joined with me as part of the same family.

I thus pledge an eternal treaty between our people, sealed through the wedding of my daughter with yourself and by the death of Baltaar at this messenger's hand. My messenger will humbly and willingly receive your most honoured reply.

Writtyn this day, the fourth of the month of the eagle in the southern plains of the desert of Kings by King Mulsepah the second, Grand Vizier of Mirrim and ruler of the desert plains of Castillion."

Hathesar rose slowly and spoke then to the messenger in voice fair yet fey:

"Know that your mission is futile. My brother is already dead ... at the hand of a maiden of such courage that her deeds will be sung by my people for as long as we shall hold breath. Know also that it is my greatest wish and desire that the maiden should have become my queen. Be certain of this: all my desire to be wed has been taken from me in the heat of the desert now that the maiden is dead."

Then he lifted one small and gnarled bleached bone and pointed at the messenger:

"If the magic of which your people are so renowned can return the life into this bone and bring the maiden for whom I yearn back to health and happiness then I will willingly marry the fair Selene, in exchange of the life of my love, but my heart shall forever rest with the Lady of the Mirage."

At his words, the messenger removed her black mask and threw back the hood of her cloak to reveal her glowing golden hair. To his astonishment, the King saw before him the lost lady of his loving heart and was overwhelmed with joy.

"How can this be?" he asked her.

"The bone you hold is that of a hyena but if it is your wish that I bring it back to life so that you can love it forever, then I shall! But my bones are still within my body and my love for you is constant and unchanged. If you will marry me then I will be the happiest lady that ever lived. I hope that it is me that you love and not a wild dog of the prairies."

At this, the King laughed with mirth and joy and relief. Then asked his lady the question he had wanted to ask since first they met at her mirage:

"My lady, my sweet: I would know your name, my love."

"I am Selene, daughter of King Mulsepah the second, and the captain of his H'ashaanan also. But from today, I am at your service and I become yours to command as my father has asked."

"Then I command you to marry me" replied the King and dutifully she did.

From that day forwards, her hero ensured that she was never left alone again nor was ever short of food or water but cared for her constantly during their long lives. They were blessed with children and grandchildren and their descendants became the rulers of all the great kingdoms and tribes of the desert from that day to this."

Roaring Flamebringer's eyes whirled in pleasure as the story came to its end then he whispered to Ra'el: "I also promise never to let you go hungry my love. Thank you for this story, it is indeed satisfying to know how the great kingdoms of the desert came into being. But, permit me now to ask my question?"

Ra'el unfolded her legs and stood before him: "Ask your question. I am ready."

"When first we met, you talked of Artor and then told me the Tale of Oweine. You talked also of the Grael and your knowledge of its resting place. You hinted that this was in some way associated with Bedevere and his ancestors. My question is this: can you tell me more?"

Ra'el grinned at this and then, as her enthusiasm took over, she breathlessly replied:

"In your horde I can see the hilt of *Caelibann, Calibarnus* that is also known as *Caledfwlch, Escalibor* or *Excalibur*, once carried by Artor and Gawain then given to his brother Gareth and finally to his son, Bedevere. Upon its blade is woven by magic the story of each knight that has carried it. If you shalt let me hold that blade then I canst tell you the story of Bedevere and how his family came to wield the Spear or Lance that guards the Grael.

But of more import, I can tell you of the legend that is associated with the *Holy Grael* and the *Spear of Longinus.* For they are but two of the four artefacts given to man-kind by God and which if brought together have the power to heal the world.

For one thousand years, the Sword and the Spear gave Bedevere's family victory on the battlefields of Europe but when the last male descendant of his line died in 1703, alas the Sword's power for war ended. The Spear still has power but it heals harm, where once it was a talisman for war. Their final task still lies ahead of us.

Today, the Sword is believed to be buried beneath Bedevere's coat of arms in the tomb of his most honoured descendant, yet the legend of its burial in a magnificent tomb in the Abbey of Westminster is and always has been a ruse. The Sword has never gone out of sight of the Lake of Avalon, but rather it was placed to rest by the blessed body of the Magdalen in the caverns beneath her City of Vezelay, so that her tomb and the Sword might be guarded together.

At the same time, the Spear and Holy Grael lie hidden at the other end of the Oyster Trail, believed to be buried beneath the old entrance to the church that Bedevere's descendants built, below the oak carvings of Christ's cup, the Molet or Star of David and the Oyster shell of de Scale.

I have followed the 'Oyster Trail': from the Escutcheon of St Mark in the Imperial Palace of the former Byzantium; to St Mark's Square in Venice and the saint's quartered shield on the floor of the Palace of the Doge; through Italy and the monument in Florence to Bedevere's greatest mercenary Knight, leader of the White Company; to pilgrim centres in Spain and France, including my beloved Vezelay, Avallon and Fontenay (where the last Knights of the Court of King Artor are still to be found in the wild woods of D'Etapes on the banks of the Camut); and finally to its end in Albion, near the former capital of the Roman Empire.

At the end of the Trail, I found the oak carvings as foretold in my great, great grandfather's book and in their shadow, buried beneath the grass that brushes the ancient flint of the church tower, I found a wooden casket within which sat a potter's platter and simple cup and the rusted spear point from an old Roman pilum. Are these two of Christianity's greatest relics? Only the Sword can reveal this; for its blade is said to tell the legend of all of the Holy artefacts."

"Is this story or is this truth?" demanded the dragon.

"Entrust me with the Sword, which was placed here in safety by the heirs of Charlemagne himself and then I can confirm if what I have heard read to me in my great, great grandfather's library is truth or not."

"Tell me first how the sons and daughters of Charlemagne came to have Bedevere's Sword and how the Oyster Trail which is a pilgrim's trail is connected to Bedevere? I suspect a trick and that you seek the Sword for another purpose."

"It is the Spear that ultimately I seek." Ra'el replied but then sensing this would not satisfy her friend, the girl continued: "Charlemagne's and Bedevere's ancestors are one and the same. His family is related through Charlemagne's sister and the Oyster is displayed on the arms of their family (for they are also known as Scales or de Scales). But let me tell the tale of how the Spear came into the hands of my ancestors. This next story is my history. Then perhaps you will let me see *Calibarnus*? I would not wield it nor use it, merely try to read its blade with your aid."

Flamebringer nodded slowly. "Tell this story of the distant past. Tell the story of the *Spear of Longinus*. If I am convinced of its rightness then the Sword is yours to use as you wish. Forgive me for suspecting a trick as by now I should trust you. It is just the Sword is very powerful and dragons fear the might of such swords for they are often forged for our slaying."

Ra'el stood before the dragon proudly: "I will tell the story of the *Spear of Longinus*. For my grandmother was of the same line as Bedevere. It was she who told me the secret hiding place of my family's Grael and the Spear. The story I tell this time is about MY family's purpose here in this world."

THE SPEAR OF LONGINUS

The Crucifixion

The young Centurion awoke early that spring time morning. What little moisture there was in the otherwise arid air around him, was captured briefly in the mosquito netting that was his vain attempt to keep at bay the hundreds of insects that would otherwise have supped all night on his sweet blood.

He had been born in colder climates on the northern coast of the former Gallic kingdom of Norsemandia and then served his childhood in the warm climate of Hispania, with the cool and refreshing air from its mountains to the north and west. He retained his childhood colouring, with dark hair, green eyes, freckles, red-faced when he caught too much sun, standing out a mile and at least a foot taller than his peers: the fair-haired and tanned legionaries from Italy or the blonde long haired giants from north western Germania that he fought alongside and now commanded.

Before he was born, his grandfather, a young Gallic light cavalryman and exceptional scout, had faced a difficult choice: to fight at Alesia under the defiant prince and romantic hero, Vercingetorix; to flee and join the freedom fighters in the kingdoms of barbaric Britannia just across the Cold Sea, the Mare Britannia; or to throw in his lot to join the new power in this part of the world. For Gaul had fallen under the yolk of Rome just 90 years ago when Julius Caesar had crushed all local resistance; it had then seen a brief rebellion crushed ruthlessly by Germanicus and Tiberius just a couple of years before our story begins which had seen Longinus' father's village of birth burnt to the ground and every male child and man slain, the women taken into slavery.

His grandfather had seen the future and signed up as an Auxiliary in the Legio X, Ventorix, based in Gaul at the time his son was born. The regiment that was to become their second family had then moved to Lusitania where the son had married a graceful freedwoman from Caledonia and they had been gifted with a son they named Longinus.

The Centurion had been brought up as a child in a Roman garrison town called Castellum Brentoricum, before being moved again to Palestine by Sejanus, Commander of the Praetorian Guard and to be at the command of the Provincial Governor and Procurator in Judaea, a knight, praefect and an appointee of Aelius Sejanus, whose name was Pontius Pilate.

His grandfather had retired in honour and died a venerable old man. His father had died assassinated by a sicarius, a Judaic assassin, when on a mission in Nazareth to infiltrate the resistance under a religious leader called 'the Nazarene' and his son had honoured him by following his father into the Legion now known as X Fretensis. The son had then distinguished himself in action in Parthia and won his grass crown when standing over a wounded colleague. The Legion remembered the grandfather and father and now honoured the son with his appointment as primus pilum in the first cohort. One year later he had his appointment as Centurion of the second century in Legio X serving alongside a young officer from Spain called Vespasian, who was attached to Pilate's staff.

"Longinus. Get your big lazy lump out of bed: we have orders coming in, you red-faced barbarian you!" was the courteous greeting of his primus pilum with whom he shared a tent. The size of the garrison in Jerusalem had outgrown the Garrison Fortress and Citadel; it now sprawled across the hills as a City of Tents, laid out in an orderly grid, with wooden plaques showing the number of each Tent, acting as signposts; in some cases the Tents had been laid out along streets which had been named after their counterparts in sacred Rome. The City of Tents reached as far as the foothills of Golgotha.

Longinus stretched and rolled out of his camp blanket then reached immediately for his cuirass of scale armour and his red plumed helmet; times were 'troubled' in Ierusalem and Longinus always ensured his armour was to hand and it was the first thing he put on (even though he would later strip down to have a bath in the Bathhouse). But receiving their *Orders of the Day* came first and Longinus had no intention of falling victim to a stray arrow coming unbidden out of the half light of a new dawn or the chance throw of a dagger cast in hope as much as in anger that it hit a vulnerable target.

Times were 'troubled' because the young rebel called the Nazarene had spent the last three years gathering his supporters and he was now come to Ierusalem on the Sabbath in order to celebrate the Passover. On his arrival, he had been greeted on the main road to Ierusalem some three leagues outside the City and processed in honour as the whole City came out with palm leaves to proclaim him 'King of the Jews' (an act of open treason for which an arrest warrant had already been issued by Pontius Pilate leading to the man being hauled into custody the night before, when found in hiding in the Garden of Gethsemane).

On his second day in Ierusalem, the Nazarene had caused a riot in the Temple, sending the Sanhedrin's taxes and their payments to the Governor to cover their bi-annual tax return to Rome (which were being counted at the time), rolling across the floor of the Temple. Longinus' lips twitched at the thought of the chaos that must have caused. Nothing had been taken, but the disruption had meant the Procurator had been short of a payment to Rome and that could spell death in this time of Tiberius.

Then the Nazarene had held a huge gathering of his followers outside the City to which at least five thousand had attended, based on accounts of the food needed to feed the gathering. This was an unlawful assembly and to make matters worse, the Nazarene had then preached about the end of Kingdoms and the destruction of the Temple at Ierusalem. This was incitement to riot and another warrant had been issued, this time by King Herod and the Sanhedrin.

A young man, and one whom Longinus disliked on sight as the man was a sicariot, had offered to reveal the location of the Nazarene's hiding-place, and the following day the Nazarene had been arrested, together with a number of other sicariot betrayed by the man Iudas (including the leader of the assassins, a man named Barabbus). Barabbus and the Nazarene were to be tried this morning by Pilate.

It was now the day after the Passover and the City was full of Judaens; a huge crowd was milling around on the streets and in the empty Forum, with nothing to do as all shops, market stalls and public buildings were closed until dawn broke on the Sabbath. The crowd was becoming increasingly restless at the arrests made by the Roman Governor and the followers of Barabbus were inciting this anger, going around saying to the crowd that they should demand the release of Barabbus.

At the same time, the leader of the Sanhedrin Caiaphas and the former High Priest, Annias, had conspired to persuade Pilate of an 'ancient tradition' to release a prisoner on the day of the Sabbath after the Passover. No such tradition existed but Pilate was already in trouble with Tiberius in Rome over placing uncovered statues of the God Augustus in the Temple at Ierusalem and so did not want to breach any more of the local traditions in error or through his ignorance.

Given the growing discontent and the presence of large crowds in the City the presence of soldiers in the capital had been doubled with the arrival of centuries from Legio IV and V Syria. Then only the day before, a sicariot had murdered Pilate's only son and the Governor was wracked with grief, whilst his wife was terrified at further slaughter and sent word to her husband to wash his hands of any involvement in the trial of the Nazarene or Barabbus.

Longinus ducked under the awning that offered a brief moment of shade at the entrance to his Tent and stood out in the sun, then winced as his armour started to burn wherever it touched his skin. He muttered several oaths at his misfortune to have been born with such frail skin, and to have ended up in such a God-forsaken land (*except it was not 'God forsaken'* he thought, *far from it: it was more inspired by the Divine and more spiritually aware than anywhere else in the world he had been posted*). Still he would need to get to that Bathhouse fast and get some cream on his skin or he would roast in his tin suit.

He could not hide his pride though when he looked at his century, lined up immaculately, boot straps tied tight, helmet straps undone to allow the helmet to be pulled forward to protect eyes and offer shade, the small square of black leather attached to the rear of the helmet, protecting necks from sun-burn, and concealing their yellow silk scarves that stopped the sweat from pouring down inside the shining scales of their armour. They were as immaculately turned out as any young son of a Senator on their first campaign – except the sons of Senators were often too proud of their appearance and stood aloof: that is until they faced their first assault, and then they became immensely grateful when Longinus' veterans stepped in to save their arrogant posteriors.

It was the knowledgeable who would spot the subtle differences between the 'glory boys' as the young nobles were called and these experienced campaigners: first the belt, lower leg and upper arm holsters for the sharp throwing knives Longinus' men each wore was no part of any official manual; then the bags of iron stola for their slings gave away the fact that many of his legionaries had begun their careers as Auxiliaries or even as the enemies of Rome. On their sword belts were the campaign medals and coins awarded for distinguished conduct with a total of nine grass crown awards in this one century alone.

The century's standard then boasted over thirty campaign and seven battle honours dating back to the days of Marius and Sulla.

Longinus only knew about the garrotting ropes because he had seen them in action but could not see them now, concealed and tied in the legionaries' long fair Germanic hair. The two pilae each man carried glinted sharp and rust-free in the sun and he expected that his inspection would show every sword had been oiled and cleaned meticulously: you could shave face hair without cutting the skin, slice silk or plunge one of their gladius through a sack of tubers.

Martius, his primus pilum, stepped forward and presented Longinus with his short sword and sword belt then helped him to tie it on at just the correct angle to draw the sword fast yet display an arrogant disregard for the uniform he wore as befitted a veteran officer. The Centurion then went down the lines, looking each man in the eye as if they were not worth the bite of a flea before standing before them to open the sealed scroll that had been handed to Martius by a hassled looking messenger, a young officer and aide de camp in the command of Vespasian, currently a guest with Pilate in the Regional Governor's Palace in the Citadel at the centre of Ierusalem.

"Orders for Second Cohort, Legio X read as follows:

To offer protection to the troops detailed for the escort and execution of the criminals Barabbus I Sicariot, leader of the sicariot in Ierusalem, and Iesus Nazarene, who claims to be King of the Jews. Both are expected to be sentenced to torture and then death by crucifixion later today. Pilate."

Longinus then handed the scroll back to Martius who would secure it with the rest of the Century's important documents (one week's pay and payroll records, manifests and invoices, stock requisitions, the Centurion's personal record, daily orders, disciplinary records and any commendations), which were held in a fire-proof iron-clad steel former banking box, a sturdy trunk the size of a coffin, lockable by several bolts, chains and padlocks. As the Centurion handed the scroll to his friend, he muttered under his breath: "So much for Roman justice: these men are condemned before they are tried!"

But Martius replied, showing much insight: "These men are implicated in the death of Pilate's son. Do not expect reason or justice. Imagine how you might act if the assassin who slew your father came into your hands. Pilate is a grieving father: give him some slack!"

It was in reflective mood that Longinus dismissed his men for Martius had reminded the Centurion of a deep and enduring hurt: *'If anyone knew who had killed his father it would be Barabbus or the Nazarene. Could he get to the prisoners?'* he mused *'but then to what purpose if he did? Barabbus had not revealed the name of a single member of his rebellion despite being tortured. Why should he tell me anything?'*

Longinus and Martius were both in the Bathhouse, having a massage and preparing their skin with oil to protect them from the heat of the sun as they would soon be out in the thick of it; they were detailed for guard duty from morning to dusk.

Martius gave Longinus the unwelcome news.

"The Nazarene is to be taken to Herod for trial and we accompany him. Pilate ducked hearing the case on the advice of his wife apparently: fearful of further reprisals! Herod is to be Pilate's hatchet man, except I am hearing that Herod's hands are tied by his damned religion which does not allow him to take blood until the Sabbath after the Passover.

We need quick executions to avoid a riot on the streets as the followers of the Nazarene try and rescue him from the Mamertine here. One of his followers has already attacked one of our legionaries; our man was allocated to the party who made the arrest under Pilate's and Herod's warrants last night. The legionary lost an ear (except I cannot see any sign of a mark on him and he seems a bit vague about it).

By the look of things we will be marching and counter-marching between Herod's and Pilate's Palaces all day! And the roads between are rocky, hot and humid offering little protection against ambush as they have yet to be cleared properly. There are yards of thickset thorn bushes on either side that could hide an army. We will need cavalry as outriders, so need both auxiliaries and scouts with us. Three cohorts should be enough of an escort but let me pick men who can cope with the heat and stay alert. The opportunity to try and rescue the Nazarene is just too good to miss."

Longinus nodded, welcoming his colleague's advice and then asked the question that had been burning him up all morning:

"Do you think I can get to Barabbus? I need to know who killed my father and Barabbus must know. Will Barabbus be open to talking to me?"

"You aim at the Moon, my friend," Martius said gently, avoiding mocking the young man for he understood what drove him to ask even though his request was beyond anything either could do. "Your only chance to speak to Barabbus is when we will be escorting him to his own execution, carrying the cross piece of the crucifix on which he will be slain in terrible agony. I cannot see you being able to offer him any inducement when you are the man who will supervise him being tied to the cross to die. He is more likely to curse you. But ..." and Martius paused in thought then continued:

"The Nazarene is another matter or more precisely his followers. They left him in droves and have spent the last few hours denying ever knowing him. Any one of these 'disciples' or 'apostles' as those closest to the Nazarene are called might give you the information you need. I know one: his name is Lucius and he is a physician here at the Camp. Let us have a chat with him."

Pondering briefly at how had a follower of the Nazarene managed to infiltrate their Camp and more worryingly why was he known to Martius, who should have turned him in immediately the warrants for the arrest of the Nazarene had been issued (for this would automatically have included family, friends and followers), Longinus was also in two minds about meeting Lucius. '*But Martius was right: this was his only chance to learn about the world of the sicariot and to understand more about his father's death*' he realised.

The informer Iudas i Sicariot had already told his paymasters on the Sanhedrin all he knew: and so far he had denounced a family of fishermen, an Essene preacher, a tax collector, lawyer and a physician but none of these followers of the Nazarene had been men of violence, except for Iudas himself. It was worth talking to Lucius as this might lead deeper into the infrastructure of the Nazarene's following. Somewhere amongst the five thousand followers Iesus had gathered on the hills above this City must be the army that would win the Kingdom of Iudaea for 'the Messiah' as the Nazarene was now being called. That army would include Iudas' fellow sicariot and once he had those under arrest, then '*one must reveal the name of his father's killer surely?*'

The Mamertine in Ierusalem was nothing like the infamous prison in Rome. This was a conversion of the cellars of the Governor's Palace and extended underground to sit immediately below the rooms refurbished to become the Curia and the Law or Curiale Courts for the City. The jail was a dry place, well-lit, spacious and currently sparsely occupied, although that was expected to change if the City disrupted into riots. There were twelve single cells and then one long hall and finally two chambers that shared a single furnace, with wall chains and raised racks: these were the torture chambers at the farthest end.

The entrance to the courtrooms above took all prisoners past the torture chambers as an unsubtle reminder of what awaited those who did not cooperate fully with their interrogators. In the case of slaves, all evidence had to be taken under torture whether a slave cooperated or not so the chambers tended to see much use.

However, in deference to the Passover, and also in anticipation of a possible surge in demand for its facilities, Pilate had cleared out his prison by virtue of the mass execution of all male and female prisoners at the start of the week. It now hosted just two prisoners and Longinus was here to accompany one of them on a long march to Herod's newly-built Royal Palace at the port at Caesarea, the official capital for this sub province of Syria, some twenty leagues from Ierusalem.

The door to a cell halfway along on the right hand side was opened by two of Longinus' legionaries, whilst two more stepped in and kept careful watch as the gaoler took out his keys and began the laborious task of unbolting the long and heavy chains that bound the prisoner and only occupant to floor and wall. Longinus could not help himself but looked into the eyes of the man before him and saw total calm. '*Where does this man find the courage to face his terrible death with such serenity? Does he not realise his fate?'* And unable to stop himself, Longinus asked the prisoner:

"Have you been told what is happening?"

The Nazarene looked up at Longinus and his smile tore at the Centurion's heart but his words raised alarm bells in Longinus' mind as it was clear that someone had been talking to the Rabbi. The man's name was Iesus and his voice was soft and cultured. He spoke to Longinus in perfect Latin: "Whatever happens to me will be my Father's Will. But be gentle on Lucius, he is a man of peace."

Martius had selected his three cohorts carefully and they were the very best of Longinus' men. Martius also had Lucius assigned to the escort as the physician, together with eight scouts and two Waggoner – their covered wagons were to carry the troops' pilae, their water supply and food, camp bed rolls and to offer cover from the sun for any wounded or those affected by sun stroke. They were also helpful should the escort come under attack and need to hold ranks or seek cover.

The prisoner walked roped either side to two legionaries, with Longinus and his men divided equally front and rear. Martius as primus pilum led the escort from the front, the aquilifer or standard bearer at his side, the blazing Imperial Eagle of the Senate and the Republic of Rome, glistening gold. A timpanus just behind the aquilifer marked their time on his drum as they marched through the heat of the early-morning and still rising sun. Longinus was free to march alongside the troops and took this chance to interrogate Lucius, what he found surprised him.

At first, Lucius repeatedly denied any knowledge of the Nazarene and then both men had looked across at Iesus and seen the prisoner's tears at which Lucius had stumbled then turned and shocked Longinus with his next words: "Of course I knew him, know him. Yet still I have denied him who is the fulfilment of my every dream!"

"You dream of his kingdom here in Iudaea? You dream he is your Messiah?" Longinus asked in his naivety and ignorance and the young physician shook his head:

"I dream of a world at peace where all that are sick have been healed. My Master heals the sick from impossible afflictions. He makes the blind to see, the deaf to hear, casts lepers free. I dream of a world where all can do this in his name. What we do today is wrong. This is a man of peace we send to his death."

"Tell me who his followers are. Who were to be his generals; his sub-commanders; his assassins? Tell me this and I can ensure the pain he suffers is less, his death can be quick. I can see to that." Longinus begged but Lucius stuck to his ground and would not be moved from his claim that the Nazarene had no rebellious or political ambitions:

"You already know the names of most of us. There are seventy two of us, all preachers, teachers, professionals, civil servants, officials working for the state, but not one of us is a warrior. We were all shocked when the man among us, Petrus brother of Iacobus, brought a sword to the night that our Lord was arrested. Your men released us because he was the only man armed and because Iesus agreed to come without the need for force.

"Since our Lord's arrest, we have all denied we have known him and shut ourselves away in fear. We have shown through our cowardice that we are not warriors. As to the five thousand, wherever Iesus went, the local people would come out to greet him and yet I foretell that this day those same people will demand his death."

"Why?" asked Longinus confused.

"Because the Kingdom Iesus prepares is not in this world but is the world we shall find when we die. Iesus is preparing the way for this through the sacrifice of his own life. Only through his death can we all learn to have the same courage to die."

Longinus could see the Nazarene listening and so challenged him: "Is this true?"

"My father shall see this Temple destroyed and restore it in three days. For I am the Way, the Truth and the Life!" and Longinus could not persuade him to explain any further.

It was in deep frustration that Longinus arrived with his prisoner at the Royal Palace at Caesarea. Herod's City was very different from Ierusalem. The Capital City of the former Kingdom of Judea had sprawled across the hills and valleys that surrounded the original Citadel built by King Solomon. Sieges, capture, and changes in ruler had seen further fortifications and garrisons built up.

As it became a centre for commerce as well as the administrative and religious centre for the region, trading markets, shops, stalls, tentings and accommodation began to spread out, to capture the more fertile ground for crops, vines, fig, Cyprus and plane trees and olive groves.

Then the Romans arrived and brought irrigation to the region, allowing yet more expansion but also built their own Palaces, Temples and municipal buildings. Roman villas were built on the gentle slopes overlooking the City and around the Forum whilst an imposing Garrison Camp was built by the east gate with the City of Tents for the growing garrison beyond. Eventually they also built a Roman port at Caeserea that became the official capital.

One legion and two half legions now lived here in a Garrison Fort designed to house only five hundred legionaries. Once you added the families, their camp followers, artisans and auxiliaries: nearly seven thousand were based in Ierusalem organised in groups of three to four hundred under twenty Centurions and a staff of twenty officers (the sons of Knights and Senators looking for advancement through a successful military then legal and political career and usually a total menace to career professionals such as Longinus and Martius).

Caesarea by comparison was a modern and purpose-built Royal Seat and civic administrative centre, with what defences it offered being the natural terrain: a City built to show support for Roman occupation in partnership with Judaean leadership. It was vulgar to Roman eyes that detested kingship and despised by the Judaeans who hated all attempts at appeasement. It satisfied no-one except Herod who enjoyed the peace and quiet it offered and the opportunity to engage with other cultures.

Longinus liked it because, unlike Ierusalem where the irrigation system was constantly being sabotaged by the sicariot and the City was overflowing with people (indeed it was over-heating in every regard and rife with the diseases that go with over-crowding and poor water supply) in Caesarea, the water system worked and the air was made fresh by the breezes coming up from the Middle Sea. Every fifty paces was a sheltered courtyard with a fountain of clean and drinkable fresh water, shades to shelter from the sun, places to sit in the cool shadow of its tall beautifully built buildings and hardly a soul out of doors as the inhabitants took cover from the sun in their tall houses, each floor a palace of carved sandstone and mosaics, incense burning, perfumed oil in the wall lamps, coloured glass, and the cool of silk carpets on limestone floors.

Their prisoner had been with Herod barely ten minutes when word came out from Herod's major domo:

"Back to Pilate, I am afraid. The original warrant was issued by Pilate and the charge of unlawful assembly is the more heinous offence. Herod refuses jurisdiction."

'And here starts the fun and games' thought Longinus to himself. *'We could be at this all day … except Herod knows that the crowds that must be stilled are in Ierusalem and not Caesarea. Pilate needs a resolution more than Herod and the wily old Fox understands this!'*

It was approaching midday and Longinus, his cohorts and prisoner had been back and forth between Herod and Pilate several times even trying the Sanhedrin but the Priests in the Temple were still unclean from the blood of the sacrifices they had made on the Passover and refused to see anyone. In the end, Longinus managed to persuade one of the staff officers at the Governor's Palace to take a message to Pilate. The missive was short and blunt whereas Pilate favoured the more formal and descriptive style of the young Julius Caesar. Longinus' note had little to recommend itself to the Governor … and yet it showed courage and right now that was a rock that Pilate's shaking temperament needed dearly:

"Domine each time we take the Nazarene to Herod we increase the risk of ambush and Herod probably wants this. I strongly recommend you hear the case of Barabbus and the Nazarene and make the decision here in Ierusalem where we are ready for any riot or attempt at rescue that follows. Longinus, Centurion, X Legio."

Pilate was still in shock at the loss of his only son. It was this rather than fear for his safety that made him reluctant to hear any case. He was unsure in his own judgement; his self confidence overwhelmed with grief. So the fearlessness of the young man rang a chord where otherwise Pilate would have ignored the abruptness and brutality of Longinus' message with contempt; instead he showed curiosity and so asked for the Centurion to join him.

Longinus stood rigidly to attention before the Governor wondering why he had just put his career at risk over the case of a rebel leader with no followers whom no-one wanted to try yet everyone wanted to see dead. He waited for Pilate to speak first: it was a long wait as the Governor was himself unsure why he was even entertaining the advice of a young man from nowhere, the grandson of a Gallic rebel. Then he saw the medals and grass crown and knew this was a brave and loyal man indeed. Eventually, Pilate broke the silence to ask:

"How do I do what must be done without all of Ierusalem breaking out in riot?"

Longinus needed time to think and also to recover from the surprise of being asked for his advice. He had never met Pilate's son or else he would have realised the reason. Pilate's mother had been born in Perth in Caledonia and had been tall, prone to sun burn, with long flowing black hair and deep green eyes. Her looks she had passed on to her grandson.

And now Longinus stood before him, with his black hair, red face and green eyes. Pilate could not admonish this bold young man who reminded him of his own son, and whom he suddenly remembered had lost his father to the same sicariot that had assassinated the young Pontius Iulius.

"Domine, what is it that must be done?"

"I must sentence one of Barabbus or the Nazarene to death to appease my masters in Rome. Know this: that Sejanus, my patron, is dead and Pleitus Plautinus Marcellus has been sent to do an audit of my Governorship by the Emperor Tiberius. I am required to show the Might of Rome yet also to avoid another act of sacrilege as Tiberius seeks to establish religious tolerance within his Empire. Sejanus was alas terribly anti-semitic and the Emperor's newfound tolerance is a backlash against the policies of Sejanus. Herod Agrippa, adopted son of the great Agrippa of Arpinum whom Tiberius held in respect, is also pushing for my removal and I must show that I can balance the execution of a rebel leader and maintain a tradition of leniency at the time of the Passover. What shall I do Centurion?"

Longinus spoke without needing to think:

"The Nazarene has no following whereas Barabbus' followers are already in Ierusalem inciting the crowd to spring their leader out of the prison beneath our feet. Put the Nazarene on trial and make no finding then put the matter of which of the two men you release this Passover to the crowd to decide."

Pilate considered this advice carefully and the more he thought about it the more satisfied he was with Longinus' suggestion. He had one last question but was already putting the Centurion's plan into action in his own mind:

"Longinus. If this works, I want you on my staff here at the Palace. Can you be certain that the Nazarene has no following? All depends on this."

Again the Centurion did not hesitate: "I have met one of the followers and spoken also to the Nazarene. These are gentle and humble people, not warriors, who have fled in dismay and fear at the arrest of their leader.

There is no following. Try the man and test this yourself; you will see what I mean." But as he said this, one niggling concern gripped him. Martius, he was sure, was a follower of the Nazarene and if his legion were infiltrated then this was a far greater risk to the security of the Governor than any threat of sicariot rebellion.

Pilate clapped his hands then issued his instructions to Cornelius, the Commander and Decurion of his Praetorian. "Bring the Nazarene to me. I will see him in the Curia. Have him ready for me to see in five minutes." Then turning to Longinus, he said: "Will you join me? I would have you watch and give me further advice based on what you know of this man."

Longinus could hardly disagree and gulped then nodded, saying: "I am honoured Domine" though he felt far from that and his soul was sinking into his boots as he considered the risk of his own legion mutinying: this had not happened since the time of the civil war between Marcus Antonius and Octavian.

The Curiale Court was a stark chamber with long marble benches against two of its walls for the Council of Provincial Knights that were Pilate's political advisors and the Merchants or Chamber of Commerce for the Province, two rectangular marble tables with the seats for advocates, a square wooden dock and the stella or curule chair on a low podium on which Pontius Pilate was already seated when the Nazarene was brought in.

There were no advocates as Pilate was not only Procurator but also one of the City's magistrates and would prosecute and judge this case himself. Two clerks would record the judgement taking it in turn to record every word said.

Ten of Pilate's personal bodyguard stood around the chamber's walls, whilst ten members of the public had been dragged in to sit on the benches usually used by the Council. They were the witnesses required to see justice in action and had been paid to keep their mouths firmly shut. They had been standing outside as petitioners, not aware that the Court of Petitions was not open that day in deference to Pilate's recent bereavement.

The petitioners included an industrious yet humble, gentle, courteous and obsequious tax official, a lowly clerk in the Procurator's own administration and a man trusted by Cornelius, the young officer in charge of Pilate's protection that day. The clerk had come to petition against the wrongful arrest of his Rabbi, an inspiring teller of stories who had visited Cornelius' house and cured his daughter's sickness with an act of healing the young soldier could never forget. The clerk's name was Mateus.

The Nazarene stood silently before Pilate. He was not insolent or defiant, he did not show disinterest, rather he seemed alert to everything around him yet rose above it. He was wise to what fate he faced yet so calm and accepting of that fate that Pilate was struck momentarily dumb. How tell a man who seemed to accept everything that you must sentence him to death *for being followed*? Then the Nazarene spoke:

"You would have no jurisdiction over me if it was not that we do my Father's Will. Be not afraid."

"Who are you?" the Governor stuttered in shock at the man's words.

"I am the Way, the Truth and Eternal Life" said the Nazarene knowing that Pilate followed the path of Mithras and would recognise the sacred prayer of its High Priest: *'I am the Path to Eternal Life'*

"What is 'the Truth'?" Pilate asked in genuine confusion unsure of the significance of the addition of that wording to the well-known advocation of the soldier's faith.

"Be pure. Be consistent. Stay faithful. Do not stray from the path. Remember me for my words are the Truth."

"You are accused of seeking to become King. This is treason. What say you?" Pilate persisted and again his words were tossed back at him:

"It is you who say this. I have no interest in a kingdom on Earth; I offer a kingdom in heaven. My Father is King of all Kings and it is he who gives you jurisdiction over me."

'I cannot pass sentence on this man. Longinus is right' mused Pilate. *'The Nazarene is either deluded or if what he says is true he poses no threat in this world and I shall offer no judgement on what shall happen in the next'*. And so the Governor passed no sentence on the major offence but sentenced the man for the lesser offence of unlawful assembly:

"Take this man, beat him, scourge him then dress him in the purple of Kings and place a crown of thorns on his head before presenting him to the crowds. We offer them their King or Barabbus, a rebel leader and murderer. Let the people of Ierusalem decide who shall be released but I can find no guilty intent ('mens rea') in this man."

Longinus stood next to the Nazarene as the first lashes of the whip struck his bare back, the combination of iron stones (stola) and fish hooks, cutting the skin in places, bruising it in others, designed to inflict the maximum amount of pain for the minimum number of lashes. He saw the look of shock on the man's face as the first blow struck: a look of surprise that something so evil could be done by man on their fellow man. Then the Nazarene became tranquil once more drawing on mental reserves that Longinus could only admire. *'What a soldier this man would have made'* he thought in admiration. *'He fights us with no weapon save his character.'*

Longinus held Iesus as he stumbled. The Nazarene stood to nod gratefully before whispering conspiratorially: "I knew you care. Do nothing to put yourself at risk my friend; for me death was foretold at the beginning of time. Be true to yourself. Yet your act of kindness is the mirror and the antidote of the torment I have just suffered. It is why my Father offers us all the hope of his salvation."

"What is salvation?" the Centurion asked confused whilst fear gripped him once more. *'Did the man mean there was to be a rescue attempt? Was Martius about to charge through the door and take down the small bodyguard in the Curia?'*

"Not today but one day you will know. Then remember this, my dear friend. I will save you."

They stood on the first floor balcony overlooking the Forum, an enormous and angry crowd before them, three centuries of legionaries holding the gathering back from the wrought iron gates to the Curia. Pilate stood in the centre of the balcony, imperial and imperious in the white toga he was entitled to wear as a Senator of Rome, a single purple stripe showing his status as their appointed Procurator of one of the furthest outposts of the largest Empire in the world. To his right was a bearded man, covered in grime and blood from frequent beatings, missing the finger nails on his right hand, bloodied but unbowed and fighting against his bonds; in chains yet still resisting and having to be held steady by no less than four legionaries.

To his left was the Nazarene, dried blood on his head beneath the crown of two inch long thorns from the scrub bushes that could be found in every local mountain pass, used by shepherds to construct enclosures and fences for the protection of their herds. His purple robes torn and in tatters, showing the lash marks beneath. Yet still he was the calm before every storm and Longinus' heart went out to him. The young Centurion knew what was about to happen and suddenly the injustice of it all struck him deeply and he began to shake: *'should he intervene, some last act of madness to save this man from a fate he did not deserve?'* He looked again at the man's eyes and saw the slightest shake of the head. It was enough for Longinus to hesitate and then he was too late as Pilate spoke.

"Who should I free for you today?" Pilate shouted into the murmurs of the crowd at which there was silence as all turned to listen, many needing to wait for neighbours to translate for them. As the crowd paused, Pilate posed the question again:

"I am giving you the choice. You, the people of Ierusalem decide whom I shall release today. This is the justice of Rome. This is the justice of the Emperor Tiberius. Shall I release Barabbus, a convicted murderer OR Iesus of Nazareth, a Rabbi, and a man who says he is the King of the Jews?"

Whilst most of the crowd were waiting for their translation of Pilate's formal Latin, several of Barabbus' men had been primed for this moment and shouted:

"The Emperor Tiberius is our only Ruler. We have no Kings. Let this man live and you are the enemy of Caesar."

Pilate paused, feeling trapped now for they were of course right. Whilst he knew Iesus had never actually made the claim to be a King, nonetheless through his own words the Governor had cornered himself. He had one more go as he felt in all fairness that he owed the gentle man from the banks of the Sea of Galilee his one last chance:

"Would you have me kill your King?" and then he kicked himself for he had meant to say 'Messiah' and in the heat of the moment had used the wrong word. In such moments can the fate and future of the world be determined.

In one breath, the crowd began to chant: "Crucify him! Crucify him! Crucify him!"

"So be it" whispered the humbled Procurator. "Release Barabbus and have the man Iesus taken to Golgotha for execution. There are two robbers, a young man and woman already up there on their crosses after this week's clean out of the prisons. They can keep the Nazarene company. Longinus, I look to you to see the execution goes without incident. Do what you can for the man." Then the Governor was gone, leaving Longinus and the Nazarene alone on the balcony (if you ignored the celebrating crowd outside).

"Are you ready?" the Centurion asked and Iesus nodded. "For all time I have waited for this moment. If I show fear it is because despite all that will be said, I am human yet also I am one with my Father who is Divine. The humanity in me shall know pain, suffering and death and so knows fear, yet my Father's Will shall still be done."

"What Father could sacrifice his Son in this way?" Longinus challenged, thinking of the sacrifices his own father had made for him and his family, putting his wife and children first when food was scarce, when their tent was too small, when deciding on postings, in ensuring they were adopted by the Legion, in choosing impossible missions to obtain rapid recognition and freedom not just for himself but the whole of his family.

"Mine is a Father who loves his creation so much he would sacrifice his own Son that those he has made might have the lesson they need to serve him in Paradise."

"A lesson in murder, torture, torment, what lesson is this?"

"A lesson in love and above all it is lesson in Hope. Even out of this most terrible of sacrifices, my Father can bring Good out of Evil. My story does not end with my death. Come find me when I am dead, see to the safety of my burial and trust me when I say that my Father will destroy this Temple and rebuild it in three days. Be patient for a little longer and we can make the sacrifice of your and my fathers have meaning."

Longinus was defeated. The man's depth of purpose was such that he could rebuff every challenge with the certainty of his vision and mission. There was no space for doubt. He beckoned for his men to escort the Nazarene downstairs and then sent word to Martius.

"I want our whole Century and that of the third and fourth centuries turned out to do guard duty along the long winding road to Golgotha. Double ranked on both sides of the roads and covering 35 paces in both directions with an escort of 20 legionaries around the prisoner himself (three hundred men all told). They need to be here in fifteen minutes and we need the prisoner on his hill-top by just after the next watch. Too much time has already been lost playing charades over this man and by the look of things we have one almighty storm brewing. Just my luck as I am without a cloak" he added muttering at which one of Pilate's bodyguards laughed and said:

"You will be borrowing the prisoner's cloak soon. Where he is going he won't need it!"

As soon as Martius and the three centuries arrived, Longinus supervised Iesus' selection of the oaken cross piece he would carry up the hill and from which he would be suspended from one of the many uprights used each day by the Romans for public execution and left in the ground as a constant reminder of the 'rule of law' in Judaea.

Then Longinus issued his orders and the first ranks of the legionaries formed up in line as the gates to the Praetorium were opened out onto the street. Creating a shield wall, twenty legionaries punched a hole in the crowds, pushing them back left and right whilst their colleagues formed lines either side of the narrow road to allow Iesus and his escort to march unmolested. Iesus stumbled briefly, as his feet left the flat stones of the practise arena in the Praetorium and caught on the first cobbles of the street. Longinus was there to steady him and on they went.

On two occasions Iesus was stopped briefly by female members of his family and by three female followers. Longinus called a short halt on both occasions to allow the women to say their farewells and then they carried on. Longinus noticed they were still following them and so he turned to Martius:

"I need a word with you" he whispered to his friend. "Drop back where we cannot be overheard" and Martius looked surprised but did not argue. The moment they were out of earshot of Iesus' escort, Longinus rounded on the man and demanded:

"Tell me what you are. Admit you are a follower of this man. Tell me you are not here to betray me!"

Martius' reply was unashamed and without fear: "I believe this is a good and peaceful man. He has ordered me to be true and loyal *to you*. He knows he is going to his death and he is ready for this. If all he says is true, his death marks the beginning of a new world for all of us."

"A new world? Where? Judaea? Rome? Is this rebellion?" asked Longinus unable to hold back his scorn but also his fears for he remained loyal to Rome. Martius raised his eyebrows briefly then asked his friend and superior:

"Did the Nazarene ask you to do nothing that would put yourself at risk? To be true to your beliefs?" and as he saw the flicker of memory mingled with the confusion of surprise that Martius should know this turn the other man's eyes from bright green to black pools, Martius laughed softly not in scorn but in joy: "He has told me the same. I am more loyal to you now, given his words, than ever I was before. Tell me what I must do, my friend!"

"You can start by forgiving me for being such a young fool then I do have a task and one that can only be done by someone I can trust completely and explicitly."

Martius held the left arm of his friend, the soldier's sign that they were one with their colleague, from a time when you would hold the shield arm of the man next to you to stop your shield wall from being torn apart by the barbarian hordes before you: the ultimate sign of solidarity and appreciated by Longinus.

"Can you look after those ladies behind us? They mean to follow us to Golgotha. The crowds might get rough when they see the execution and our men might retaliate. I don't want the women harmed. Then when we get to Golgotha see they are away from us when we mount Iesus on the cross: it will be messy and not a sight I would wish any woman to see. The matron in the middle, not yet fifty and looks thirty, is the poor man's mother. Protect her from the worst and see she reaches the place of execution in safety."

Martius smiled and whispered back "We will make you a follower yet. But I have a better idea" and he beckoned over to a young man following the escort at a short distance, his cloak covering his head from the heat of the sun and his face from recognition, except for the briefest of moments when Longinus saw the signet ring on the man's left hand: a knight and a member of Pilate's praetorian.

"I think you know Cornelius?"

At which Longinus' mouth gaped wide open then he had to ask: "Are you about to tell me that with the exception of Pilate, Barabbus and myself, the whole court room back there was full of the Nazarene's followers!"

Martius creased over in uncontrollable mirth at that then apologised to his friend. "I did want to tell you but I needed you to meet Lucius first. He told me how you reacted to the Nazarene and from then we have been waiting. But no, there were four of us only in there, Cornelius and three of the petitioners. Cornelius is loyal to Pilate. Iesus made him promise to be true because one day he will do Iesus a great service. Not today but one day a time will come when the message of Iesus will be in danger of becoming lost and it will be Cornelius who will put things right."

"Cornelius is that important?"

Martius shook his head in silent desperation at his friend's total lack of understanding. Eventually, he stopped to explain the way the Nazarene worked and the denarius finally dropped for Longinus:

"The Master can see that every one of us will have a moment when our actions will further God's Will and the cause of Peace on Earth. He gives us the freedom to choose to do the right thing when that moment comes and leaves us to live so that we have that chance. This he calls 'Hope' and it is a gift given by God uniquely to man. Your time will come, and mine, the three petitioners will all write accounts of what they saw and will see and hear this day when their time comes, and Cornelius' time will come. Just as today it is the Nazarene's time to do God's Will."

The next moment a young man was thrown over the shield wall by some friends and ran to get a touch of Iesus' robe as he carried the cross, calling "Rabbi, Master" as he did so. The man was young, athletic and wore the white toga of a Roman knight or member of the Senator class. This caused the soldiers to pause briefly as it was an offence punishable by death for the whole of your cohort to lay hands on a Senator or his family.

"For the Gods' sake, don't just stand there!" screamed Longinus and several of the legionaries snapped back to attention then went to grab the young man, succeeding in catching him by the toga. But with a sudden twist he was out of their reach, leaving his toga in the hands of one of the soldiers, running naked into the crowds until he disappeared through a doorway that was slammed shut and bolted in the face of the chasing legionaries.

"Back in the ranks" shouted Martius and then for Longinus' benefit whispered:

"I heard you were without a cloak sir. Might have just the thing for you" and one of the men brought over the fugitive's toga which with a reciprocal grin and a muttered "If I ever find you staged that stunt I will stuff this robe down your laughing face" the Centurion folded the toga several times over his sword belt ready to put on once the storm that was still brewing should reach them.

When Iesus stumbled for the third time, Longinus halted and called out for some help. His own legionaries were already close to exhaustion. In full armour in the midday sun, they were in danger of collapse from the heat. He sent four to find some water and a kindly matron opened up her tenement to let them fill their helmets and that of their colleagues from her ground floor well. She refused any payment, instead telling the men of a story once told to her by the Nazarene of a good man from Samhiraya.

Meanwhile, a young man called Simon, a merchant from Cyrene on the north coast of Africa but here to celebrate the Passover, volunteered his help to Martius. He was strip-searched for weapons, especial attention being given to the long locks of his hair but he was found to be unarmed. He held one end of the cross-piece allowing Iesus to rest one shoulder at a time and to protect the scars and lash marks on each shoulder from re-opening under the friction and force of the roughly hewn oak.

From here-on, they began to make much better progress until finally ahead of him Longinus could make out three uprights on the very top of Golgotha. Two already had guests: one a young man, crying out in pain, begging for mercy, seeking water to quench his thirst, struggling to breathe, slowly and painfully drowning in the waters trapped at the base of his lungs; the second a young girl, fair once but she had been tortured and now faced the exhaustion that comes close before death. No energy left to even cry out.

Some attempt had been made to cover her and show her respect in death but she was near naked and no more than skin and bone. She was probably less than thirteen and had been used to pass through narrow windows to let her accomplice in to properties where he would then steal the contents. Kept near to starvation and tethered each day by her partner as if a dog on a leash, she had been allowed to roam the rooftops at night free and for this she had remained loyal and grateful for small mercies to her partner in crime. '*What a terrible life and now this desperate death*' Longinus reflected.

Then came the part he hated as two of the soldiers bound Iesus' arms to the cross piece then rammed nails through the bones of each wrist to hold the arms steady before hoisting the cross piece upright using pulleys, rope and tackle. Finally a nail was rammed through the bones of both ankles and into the post behind. Standing back, the legionaries admired their handy-work then sat down to roll dice for the man's robe. Despite its tattered state it was finest silk and purple and some of the material could be rescued to become a silk scarf for one of the many ladies in their camp.

Longinus just watched Iesus as the task of breathing became harder and harder and the sun beat down with such ferocity that soon all three being crucified were begging for water. The young robber cursed the Nazarene mocking him and saying: "I have heard of you. So much for all your vaunted powers! Where is your God now? Where are your followers? Who is there to rescue you now?"

"Hush" whispered the girl the other side of the Nazarene finding the strength to speak for the first time in hours. "This is a good man who does not deserve to be here" then turning to Iesus she said: "Wherever you go, take me with you. I have sinned but I shall not sin again."

To which Iesus replied: "Today you will walk with me through the Gateway to Paradise" and a few minutes later with a last almost silent gasp her head fell forward and she was dead.

About now Iesus' courage nearly failed as the pain was so great he began to ask "Why is this happening to me?" then once more he dragged up new reserves of courage to say more calmly. "Father, Thy Will Be Done!" Almost an hour later, he turned to his best friend, Iohannus, who was watching at the foot of the cross with growing despair in his eyes and asked the young apostle to look after his mother and take her into his home. Then having made provision for the living, he looked once to the skies and said his final words: "There! It is Done!" and his head fell forwards, his knees sagged, his rib cage collapsed and with a final gurgling cough he was silent.

It was three in the afternoon and as Iesus died the clouds cast their shadow over the hill, there was a crack of thunder and forks of lightning began to strike the tallest buildings in the Capital starting with the Temple, the Governor's Palace, the adjoining Curia and the Temple Palace. "This truly was the Son of God," Longinus shouted his voice lost in the wind. Then the rain fell for the briefest of moments before the storm passed over and the skies cleared.

One of Longinus' tasks was to break the legs of those being crucified to hurry along their deaths. He needed Golgotha cleared of any bodies before the Sabbath as otherwise this would see a highly charged complaint wend its way from the Temple Palace of the Sanhedrin to the Governor's Palace on the adjoining hill. The sight of the bodies on Golgotha as they looked out of their windows first thing in the morning might put the Priests off their breakfast as they came out of fasting.

The girl was clearly dead and he had her taken down carefully. "What do I do with her?" he muttered to Martius "She has no-one to look after her body or any tomb in which to rest her." Then without further thought Longinus took the toga off his belt and handed it to Martius. "Here use this" he muttered "and there is space in the catacomb which I had reserved for myself and my family but after this day I intend to ask for a transfer. A child such as this deserves better of us surely?"

Whilst the question was rhetorical still Martius felt he must make answer: "Leave it with me, my friend. She shall go with all the honours we would give to a Senator's daughter. Did you not hear the Master? She goes to Paradise, one of the first to join the Angels when the Rabbi opens the gates for us."

"How? What I have seen destroys my faith in God or Gods."

To which Martius replied: "Be patient. This is not the end but the beginning."

Now it was the turn of Iesus, but Longinus did not want to mutilate the body any further not least when he was pretty sure the Nazarene had stopped breathing some time ago. So he asked Martius if he could borrow a Spear and then plunged it into the lungs of the dead man. Water and a few spots of dried blood came out showing that the lungs were no longer working and that they were already filling with water as a consequence.

"Cut him down" ordered Longinus "and bring me his mother. Be gentle with her for she has just lost her only son."

Whilst they were lifting down the body of the Nazarene, Longinus approached the third of those being crucified whom from his curses was still very much alive. He took one of the metal hammers they had used to drive the nails into ankle and wrist joints then smashed both of the man's knee caps, ignoring the screams. Ten minutes later and the man could no longer bear the weight of his own diaphragm and began to drown in the waters trapped in his lungs unable to speak. Twenty minutes later, he was dead. Longinus used his spear once more just to be certain then turned to face a delegation of Maria, mother of the Nazarene, a man whom he recognised as Iesus' best friend Iohannus, Cornelius, Martius and a well-dressed and prosperous merchant or civil servant, from a distance Longinus could not be sure but he was certain they had never met before.

The stranger spoke first.

"Centurion, I am newly come from the Governor's Palace where I have successfully petitioned Pontius Pilate. I was only able to get to see the man through the good offices of the Princep's wife, another follower of the Rabbi you know as the 'Nazarene'. Here is my petition and the counter signature of the Governor is below" and he handed a scroll to Longinus which the soldier read hurriedly then re-read to make sure he understood it correctly.

"You are Iosephus of Arithamea in Syria? Can you prove this?" he asked. The man was a scholar, an antiquarian, lector at the University in Alexandria, a successful businessman and merchant, knighted for services to Rome and much travelled across Europa, North Africa and the Middle East. He always carried papers of identification with him and immediately took out letters of introduction from the curator of the famous library in Alexandria, from Germanicus Caesar nicknamed 'little boots' and his patron, from King Herod for whom he had done some secret service, from the Lady Antonia Caesar and from the former High Priest, Annias.

'*Impressive*' thought Longinus his face impassive but thinking that since the list of referees included the lady who had successfully warned Tiberius of the betrayal by his former best friend Aelius Sejanus, and also the person tipped to succeed Tiberius as Emperor, Pilate must have agreed to see this man in lightning speed.

"You are offering your tomb and to pay for funeral expenses. This is a generous offer and I can see why the Governor was grateful and able to accept. On behalf of Rome, I also thank you. Is there anything we can do to assist?"

Iosephus had brought three wagons: one for the body which Longinus and his men loaded with Iesus' corpse and two for the few mourners. With the exception of Mateus the tax official, Iohannus, Iosephus and Cornelius, the rest of the mourners were women and a young girl, come to express their grief but also to look after the Nazarene's mother, Maria, in her sorrow.

Finally, before Iosephus left, the equites asked one favour: "This will sound absurd and the folly of an old man, I know, but I ask you look after that Spear with care. It bears the blood of a man I loved with my whole heart, anima mea. Keep it for me that we may remember him through it. One day I may come back for it. But for now we wait!"

"What are we waiting for?"

"The third day, of course!" and Iosephus went to mount the wagon at which Longinus' suspicions were aroused once more and turning to Martius he instructed his friend:

"Clean up here. There is a pit we passed on the way up Golgotha where the criminals executed on Wednesday were flung. Add this man to the pile then pull down the uprights and brush over all traces of any crucifixions. Head back to Camp and don't forget the men!" that got a grin before Longinus continued and Martius knew when not to argue: "I will see you later. It won't be long."

Longinus accompanied Iosephus' party to the man's tomb set in the northern slopes of Golgotha, within a small walled and gated garden beautifully tended and tethered with the soothing sound of running water from bubbling brooks and refreshing rills beneath the shade of Cyprus and palm trees, the walls home to vines, honeysuckle, clematis and wisteria with raised beds of herbs: thyme, rosemary, fennel and mustard seed.

The Centurion watched closely and reverently as Iesus' wounds were cleaned of blood by the tears of the women and a young girl who prepared his body for burial, then the dead man was bound carefully to hide the scars. There was no sign of fresh blood for the man's heart had stopped many hours before. The body of Iesus was wrapped in a long binding sheet of finest linen, bathed in myrrh, the scent of frankincense drifting from thuribles hung from the cave's roof and as perfumed oil in the red glass hanging lamps set on the walls, gold coins were placed on his eyes, the parchment scrolls of the prayers of passing rolled and placed on his hands and by his feet.

Rose petals were placed upon the ground, strewn so that no-one could step on the floor of the tomb save that they left a clear path through the fresh blooms on the floor. Then a huge stone was rolled by the four men to cover the entrance before finally a plasterer, hired and paid for by Iosephus, sealed the stone to the surrounding rock face. In thirty minutes the plaster was dry and Longinus was content that the body was well and truly buried. To make certain, he would send a guard to look over this tomb starting at dawn the next day. The Centurion suspected some trick but also feared some act of sacrilege by those who were the enemies of the peace that the Rabbi had advocated.

There was one further thing he must do and so he asked Iosephus for another favour. The man was generous and at a signal one of his servants approached from where he had been watching the burial from a vantage point further up the hill. The man guided two horses, fully and expensively caparisoned, their harness gleaming, a sure sign of huge wealth.

"Take one" said the kindly knight. "You can return it whenever we meet again."

Borrowing a soft nosed, sure-footed Arab mare from Iosephus, Longinus rode into the City to arrive at the Governor's Palace just as dusk began to fall to make his report to Pilate. His luck was in as Cornelius was back in uniform and in charge of the guard detail for that night. The young officer let Longinus in and had word taken to Pilate who saw the Centurion immediately in his private vestibulum, a clerk on hand to take any notes.

"I wish to report that the execution went without hitch. One man did try and touch the Nazarene and escaped but was unarmed" at which Pilate laughed.

"Yes I heard about that. Got off scot free and clothes free as well by all accounts" and both men grinned before Longinus continued:

"One thing we must watch for, Domine. The followers may say the man did not die. To prevent this, I oversaw the sealing of the tomb and suggest a guard is put on that tomb until the Passover celebrations have ended and the City has calmed down. Three days should do it: starting at dawn tomorrow!"

Pilate nodded then it was his turn:

"This could have waited but I wished to say 'Well done' and that I meant what I said. I want you on my staff: you have impressed me today and I could do with your bluntness to advise me. I am not a monster and am always ready to listen. There is a place for you if you want it and a chance to have your own legion when either of the two assigned to Judaea comes up. That might be sooner than you think as Plautius is making a pig's ear of things in Northern Gaul and may get the young Vespasian on his staff to give him a bit of backbone as he prepares for the invasion of either North Germany or South Britannia. That would put you in line to take charge of the first Century as well as your current command. Good men are needed to keep the peace and your handling of this incident has brought you to the attention of many."

Longinus was clearly stunned and asked for the weekend to think about the offer and to talk it through with his family (he was not married and had no brothers or sisters but he loved his mother; and her sister also lived with them in the legion). Pilate was not in the least offended. If the man wanted to discuss it with his family then he was treating the offer as genuine and taking it seriously. Pilate could wait a few days.

The orders for Longinus' Century the next day were to spend a couple of hours in the Forum, outside the Temple, the Sanhedrin and the Governor's Palace: a show of force in key places where riots might be incited but otherwise to remain low key.

"Are we being stood down?" Longinus grumbled and his friend Martius once more surprised him with the news he was able to get from his network of drinking cronies:

"Have you not heard? Barabbus left town for Caesarea. He intends to concentrate his considerable malice on King Herod who is become the new target for his animosity. Herod will not be getting the quiet Passover he had planned after all. The risk level assessment in Ierusalem has been adjusted downwards whilst Pilate is taking his time in answering Herod's request for additional security details, saying he does not think he has the jurisdiction to interfere in what is a local matter between Jews after all."

Both men laughed as Pilate's revenge for Herod's earlier lack of cooperation in the trial of the Nazarene had now come full circle.

Longinus was never able to account for his actions the following day but something made him wake early in fact so early that he was up and checking the Camp perimeter with Martius still tossing in a deep sleep. In the five years both men had known each other and shared the same Tent this had not happened before. Longinus was a heavy sleeper and so was never the first to rise except on that fateful day. The feeling Longinus woke with, he had experienced before and on both occasions it had been when he was on the march and the prelude to an attack. Yet scanning the perimeter and checking in with the Guard details there was nothing amiss or in sight for three leagues in every direction.

Then *'Golgotha'* his mind screamed and without pause he headed for the tomb carved in the side of the hill, running and not stopping. With less than a quarter of a league to go, Longinus caught sight of the four legionaries he had detailed to stand guard from midnight, heading back towards Camp. It was now five in the morning and in the distance, the first cockrel had begun to crow as the dawning rays of the sun cast the hills in shadow.

"What are you doing?" he demanded, his face almost purple in rage.

"But sir, your orders were clear. They had your signature and everything: 'Return to Barracks immediately'" one of the men stuttered and the others nodded, one passing a scroll across for Longinus to inspect.

"Who showed you this piece of fiction and when?" And the four men gulped then pointed behind them and to the right. "Two minutes ago at most" they mumbled.

Longinus took off once more at a run but could see no sight of anyone and so carried on towards the tomb. With luck the tomb robbers, defilers or those seeking to make mischief from claiming Iesus still lived would not have had time to break the plaster seal. There would need to be at least three of them to roll away that stone and his men had only seen a solitary stranger. He might still be in time to nip whatever was planned in the bud.

He arrived at the tomb to see the stone was already rolled to one side and began to curse. Then, fearing the worst yet with his courage and breath returning, he walked to the entrance of the cave and immediately knew that nothing he could see made any sense.

First, he inspected the plaster seal. What he expected was to see that it had been chipped away to allow the despoilers of this tomb to get a grip on or levers beneath the stone and roll it to the left – a promontory of rock prevented it from being pushed to the right. Instead, the plaster seal had come away from the wall but remained intact and attached to the stone in one piece as if the stone had been pushed *from the inside* outwards. Moreover, there were no fresh marks in the grass from the stone having been rolled: it appeared to have moved through mid air!

Second, the rose petals had not been disturbed and yet he could see the lamps had been lit as had the scented incense in the thuribles and the air was not stale but smelt as clean and fresh as the first morning of Spring outside. The lamps were blazing away, the scent of perfumed oil wafted in every direction which brought Longinus to the third and final unwelcome discovery.

There were no shadows to hide the simple fact that the shroud and binding cloths in which Iesus had been buried had been unwound and stacked neatly and that the body of Iesus was gone.

And there was no way that any of this could have taken less than fifteen minutes and yet his men had said two minutes, add the two minutes at most it had taken him to run here and there just was nowhere near enough time!

Something made Longinus turn and briefly he was dazzled as his eyes passed from the comparative shade of the cave to bright daylight. Against that light he could make out the silhouette of a man dressed in white, a fellow mourner perhaps or briefly he thought the man might be a gardener or someone who helped those buried in this place. Out of the light came the words:

"Gaius Gallicus Longinus, you are close to the truth when you think that my job is to tend for the dead here. I am a shepherd for their souls. For today, the Gates of Paradise have been opened and all of God's Angels have come to summons the living and the dead to rejoice in this new beginning. I harvest the souls of this place but it is my Master who has made this possible."

"Are you a God?" Longinus asked confused, afraid yet curious.

"Fear Not. I am a created thing as are you. I serve the Lord my God as shall you. I am not dead nor am I a spirit. I do not possess the gifts of the Holy Spirit nor do I have a soul nor can I create new life and a new soul as can God, man and woman when you give birth to a new human child. Yet I am given the powers to move mountains, dry up the oceans, steal the air from the skies when I act in the service of God. My name is Gabri'el and I am an Angel. Today I bring news of great joy! For the Son of God, who is also God, has risen from the dead and opened the Gates of Paradise to all who believe he is the Way, the Truth and offers Eternal Life."

"Where is Iesus' body?" Longinus asked in exasperation not understanding as much as half of what the Angel had just said. The Angel laughed:

"He is alive as he foretold: for is not today the third day? You will see him walking and talking and breathing as you do. For now he remains in Ierusalem to complete his mission but soon he will send his Holy Spirit to breathe new life and new courage into all of his followers."

"How will I know it is he? What must I do?"

He will reveal himself in the breaking of the bread. Your friend Martius can explain. As for you, your task is two-fold. Bear witness to the Truth you have seen here and look after your Spear!"

Then the Angel was gone and Longinus was left to think he had dreamt the whole thing until he turned back to the empty cave and its mysteries that could not be explained. '*Martius has a lot of explaining to do*' he mused and it was in a thoughtful mood he walked slowly back to Camp, thus missing the arrival of the women of Ierusalem who had come to pray at the tomb and brought food for the guards.

"What trick is this?" shouted Martius who was standing and fuming at the entrance to the City of Tents. "Iacobus who is one of the Nazarene's followers just woke me to say the tomb has been raided. Is this some trick of Pilate's? Were you in on it? The guards are saying that you ordered them from their station and then were seen going towards the tomb. Why have you taken our Master's body and where is it?"

When Longinus had finally calmed his friend down, he told him everything as Gabri'el had said it and all that he had observed when he had discovered the empty sepulchre. It was only when Longinus referred to the 'breaking of the bread' that Martius began to believe him. "You could only know of this from a handful of people and from the Nazarene himself. It is a secret way he left us to remember him by on the night of his arrest. Already we do this in his memory."

"Do what?" Longinus asked in some pique.

"We take bread and wine, offer it to God and he turns it into his own body and blood. When we eat and drink this we remember all of his promises of living with him in Paradise when we are dead."

"Can I join you when you next do this?" Longinus asked nervously fearing his friend's rejection or suspicion. "I want to believe. For a few moments I glimpsed a whole new world when I met Gabri'el: one where life has far more value than Rome gives to it. For we toss away the beauty of God's creation and treat life far too cheaply. What we do is Evil and yet the sacrifice, the Nazarene's anamnesis that I have seen, has truly achieved Good from Evil as he foretold. I must see him again for he has one final task for me or so I believe."

"We meet tomorrow night. Join us then. We won't eat you and you might enjoy the company. You will relax and be at peace, of that I am certain."

The First Witnesses and their Persecution

As soon as word spread across Ierusalem that the body of the Nazarene had been taken, Pilate issued warrants for the arrest of all his followers. He summonsed Longinus to his Palace and without preamble ordered him to take charge of the search. "We must squash any suggestion of this man still being alive or the City will be up in arms."

Meanwhile, the Sanhedrin had sent their Palace Guards out into the City dressed in casual clothes to hunt down the disciples and any friends and family of Iesus. They found Iudas and hung him for no other reason than that they could not trust him.

Longinus sent Martius to get word to Iohannus to take the Nazarene's mother, Maria, the younger Maria, sister of Lazarus, Martha and Maria the Magdalan into hiding. "Tell him I will hold back my search until tomorrow, pleading honouring the Sabbath as my excuse" the Centurion whispered urgently. "I can give you a day to get his friends and family safe, but any open assembly I will have to disperse with force. I have my orders." And the two men embraced as Martius went into the City to find refuge for those closest to Iesus.

The Nazarene's followers elected Iacobus as their new leader, the owner of a fishing trawler and a moderately wealthy man as a consequence, who had been amongst the first to be called to follow Iesus; he had persuaded his brother Petrus to do so also. On discovering the empty tomb and fearful of arrest, Iacobus and Petrus had fled to Galilee where both had seen Iesus alive and preaching on the banks of the sea. "Cast again" their Master had said to them and their trawler had almost sunk under the weight of their fresh catch.

Iacobus had returned to Jerusalem filled with the Good News that the Master was still alive, only to be arrested and taken up before the Sanhedrin. He was now being held captive charged with sacrilege and blasphemy. His brother, Petrus, had fled Jerusalem for a second time, no one knew where? A few frightened and dispirited followers headed out towards Emmaus or towards their former safe haven of Nazareth. The rest gathered in fear in the attic rooms of the tenement buildings in the centre of Jerusalem, moving from one loft or roof-space to another as the hunt carried on beneath them.

A young man called Stephanus was elected on the Sabbath by the few apostles still in Ierusalem to join the small group of followers: he was to replace Iudas as one of the 'twelve'and they nicknamed him 'the oarsman', the 'diakonas', (for in life he was a ferryman on the Galilee). Others amongst the 'twelve' took nicknames also such as the 'Eagle', the 'Doctor' and the 'Stone' until such time as they were safe to make their mission public.

Alas, Stephanus was caught that night by the Temple Palace Guards who were dressed in mufti, their swords concealed beneath their robes, patrolling the City's public areas. They found the new apostle talking openly to a group of bystanders in the Forum about the 'risen Messiah'. Stephanus was dragged outside the City's walls and stoned to death just as the sun woke on the dawn of a new day.

Then Petrus returned to Ierusalem with more news of a fresh sighting: "I have seen Him," he cried. "He asked me 'Where was I going?' He asked me to 'Feed his sheep'. For each time that I denied him he gave me a new chance. Truly, He is alive and has forgiven me!"

Martius had brought Longinus along to the gathering the night they heard of Stephanus' martyrdom, which was closely followed by the news of the execution of their leader, Iacobus, brother of Petrus. The Centurion looked around at the assembled gathering. Not surprisingly he could see tears, fears, respectful and mournful silence but also a glimmer of something he had seen before when commanding his men to make yet another stand for the glory of Rome: self-pride and hope was in every eye. He recognised Lucius and Cornelius, Iohannus, Maria, mother of Iesus, the sisters, Maria and Martha, the young girl from Magdalo and Mateus. He was pleased to see Iosephus there also. The rest were strangers but all eager to hear from him.

A young man called Marcus was especially interested and kept scribbling on his tablet, taking notes. "You were at his trial?" he would ask in awe or "You are certain he died?"; "You saw him buried?"; "It was definitely 'Gabri'el' – that was the name?"

There was no jealousy or envy that Longinus should have been so involved in the Nazarene's last moments and have been amongst the first to be given the Good News of the resurrection. All were grateful to hear Longinus' words and his account, to listen to him bear witness to the Truth.

Then, as Martha and Maria were handing around the food, and Lazarus was telling Longinus of the Master's ministry in Galilee, two followers joined them from Emmaus buoyed up with excitement and news of yet another sighting:

"We did not recognise him at first and we were still stunned by Iesus' death and fearful, poor company! Yet we were joined by a stranger who told us to rejoice and began to explain to us how everything that happened from the moment Iesus came to Ierusalem to his return from the dead had all been foretold by the prophets. Then we stopped at a wayside tavern and he took bread and wine, broke it and shared it with us. In that moment we saw it was Iesus and the next moment he was gone."

When Longinus had a chance to extricate himself from the eager attentions of Marcus, he wandered over to join Martius and Cornelius. "How certain can we be of any of this?" the Centurion asked still doubtful. "I saw a man standing with the sun behind him and an empty tomb but it would have been so easy for someone to have bribed my guard detail and emptied that tomb that night; two men walk with someone they know for hours yet only recognise him when they stop to have a drink; and another claims to see him when he is feeling guilty about denying him and has run away. This is not convincing evidence!"

"Come" said Cornelius courteously. "I need you to meet some people."

First he brought Longinus over to meet the Magdalan. "Maria holds a very special place in the affections of the Nazarene. She has been his constant companion since his Ministry began, listened more than any other to his words of wisdom and wonderful stories, and was the first to whom the Nazarene showed himself when he returned from the dead."

Now that Longinus was in her presence, the first thing he noticed was how young she was: sixteen, possibly seventeen at most? She was just in the first blush of womanhood but without the self-confidence yet to know this. Next she spoke to him, and her quiet, lisping, stuttering voice came as a surprise. He had expected a voice full of vigour: for the person chosen by God to be the first witness to the resurrection of his Son to be a powerful orator, bearing witness in ringing and rousing tones. In contrast, he struggled to hear her softly spoken words, so quiet and shy was she … yet there was no question that every word she spoke rang true and that she exuded empathy and sympathy:

"I saw him. I did not deserve this but it was my Lord and Master. I shall always believe. He died and came back. Made Evil become Good. Forgive me, my words. I struggle with my tongue. I pray for the day we meet again!"

Then as Longinus thanked her for her words and told her he had understood everything she had said and believed her, the girl's whole face lit up with a smile of joy and without hesitation she bent forward and kissed him.

"She likes you" Cornelius whispered in his ear as the Centurion stood there in shock. Then Iosephus joined them both and as the knight spoke, Longinus began to get the first glimpse of the mission with which he was to be entrusted by the Nazarene:

"The Magdalan is our most important witness. Others will meet our Master, of that I am certain, but the girl's simple belief is our greatest asset. Anyone who meets her shall see she is telling the Truth. Alas, there are those who will wish to destroy or divert our faith and will seek out the girl to ruin her reputation, to punish or torture her then stone her to death or crucify her. So she must be protected."

Cornelius could not agree however: "She is too important to be hidden." Obviously this was a discussion both men had held before with ground firmly set and neither seeking to budge. Longinus looked to break the deadlock by turning to the Magdalan to ask:

"We all wish to protect you but we also all wish you to meet people. What is it that *you* want?"

First she corrected Cornelius: "I am not important" before dismissing the need for protection: "God will protect me so I need no protection." Finally, she answered Longinus' question: "My Master's ministry was to go out to the people and that is what we must do, surely? I would very much like to travel the world, not to hide but to open the Gates of Paradise to everyone in the world. Except I do not know how to do this!" she added hesitantly.

At that both Cornelius and Iosephus smiled. They could agree to that: a mission to bring the Good News to the world. "Let me take you!" said the old man gruffly.

"I would join you" muttered Cornelius "but I still have a task to perform here in Judaea I believe." Then both men turned to Longinus. They did not need to say anything; the plea was naked in their eyes and sat invitingly in the brief pause as they waited for the young Centurion's reply; an unspoken request as imperative as any order.

"No" he replied hastily in answer. "I am about to join the Governor's staff" then seeing the look of disappointment on the Magdalan's face his opposition collapsed before her silent entreaty. "What is involved?" he asked accepting the task and Maria's eyes shone. It was Iosephus who answered the young man his face filled with excitement:

"I am an immensely wealthy man with many connections and can get us around the world with no difficulty whatsoever. We take the Shroud in which he was buried, the stone Grael he used as his platter when he first broke the bread and your Spear which showed that he died and which has specks of his precious blood on its point. Martius has a piece of the purple Robe he won off one of your men. He also knows where he buried the cross-piece on which the Nazarene was hung. These are all important when we tell the story that must be told. As Maria has said, we must take the Good News '*to everyone in the world*'. Leave the itinerary to me."

"Come" said Cornelius "We have more people to meet" and he took the Centurion across the room to where a child was playing quietly with her wooden set of animals and an ark.

"My daughter" the Praetorian said with love and pride. "She was dead and brought back to life by the Nazarene. Lucius was our physician and had done all he could. She was already in her shroud when I returned from a campaign on the borders of Numidiia to learn that my only child was dead. I went out to find the Master; I had heard of his many acts of healing. I will never forget his words: '*Your faith has healed her*'! On my return to my house I was greeted with the news that my daughter lived. Whenever I see my daughter, I have no doubt but that Iesus is also alive."

This more than anything said that night shook Longinus to the core. He had sought out the Nazarene to discover the name of his father's assassin. '*Had he got it all wrong? Should he have been seeking out new life for his father? Could the Nazarene have brought his father back to life?*'

Next, Cornelius introduced Longinus to Bartimaeus. The man's eyes were white with the damage done by years of cataracts and to all appearances he seemed blind and yet he gazed into Longinus' eyes fearlessly as he told him: "I was captive to my blindness, forced to beg for my living and then the Nazarene gave me back my sight. Now I can see the glory of creation surrounding us and I can see the wonder of God's love within you. He told me that my faith had healed me. I have truly been saved."

The word for 'saved' he used was Greek and it meant to be released from prison, literally to be brought out into the light from darkness. It was the closest in Greek to the phrase in Hebrew used by Isaiah to describe the Messiah: "He shall set captives free, release them from their prison, save those who are oppressed". At last Longinus understood what the Nazarene had meant when first they had met and the Rabbi had said that one day he would 'save' the young officer. It was his destiny to find the light of the Nazarene's message coming out from the darkness of the cruelty and slavery of Rome. Good from Evil. He was to be enlightened.

"Lazarus you know of course" and Cornelius interrupted the young man's reflections to add another surprise to what had already been an evening full of surprises. "But did you know he had been dead three days and Iesus brought him back to life at the request of Maria and Martha, his sisters?"

What do you say to a man who has died and returned from the dead? Longinus was momentarily tongue-tied and Lazarus, used to the reaction broke the awkward silence:

"Returning from the dead is a great gift yet it is only worthwhile if you then do something special with the extra time you have been granted. I have no idea how long I have and so treat each second of life as special. I intend to spread the word just as Maria the Magdalan wishes to, for surely there can be no more fitting task?"

"Why then are we shut away in hiding in an attic if we should be out there bearing witness?" Longinus challenged him and Lazarus laughed then said: "Good for you. Is that what you plan to do? We are waiting for one last sign and then trust me we all shall be out there preaching the Good News."

At that, the room suddenly went silent. It started as a hushed gasp from the Magdalan and then rippled across the room as conversations stopped mid-sentence, mouths opened agape, eyes looked unblinking and there amongst them all was the final person that Cornelius had wanted Longinus to meet.

The Nazarene stood amongst them with a personal smile of greeting for every one of them: all responded in silent joy and grateful contemplation. There was no doubt that this was Iesus, that he was alive and not some ghost or spirit and that he was overjoyed to be in their company.

"Do not be afraid" he said simply and Maria the Magdalan ran into his arms whilst Petrus patted him on the back and others shook him by the hand or touched the hem of his robe. The Nazarene crossed the room to embrace his mother whose eyes shone with victory and vindication then took the time to speak to all of those gathered in hope to meet him. When he came to Longinus the Nazarene confirmed what Longinus already knew in his heart that he must do:

"Look after my Maria for me" he said and then he moved on.

"Although I know some of this story," Roaring Flamebringer interrupted his young friend, "yet I am intrigued that a follower of Islam should tell it and even more interested to know what happens next. I am a dragon and thus a convinced and committed Christian and old enough to have seen Christ die on the cross. Despite this, the story of Joseph of Arithamea's journey across Europe remains a mystery to me and I want to hear more … but in the morning, for still you are young and must sleep and once again you have timed the telling of your story to leave me with so many questions that I fear sleep shall be a distant dream for me!"

The girl laughed as she had not appreciated before that dragons were believers in Christ. Had she stopped to recall the *Revelation of St John* then she would not have made such an error, but her mind was elsewhere caught in the grip of her own story:

"The story of the spread of Christianity is one shared with Islam for it blazed the path for the teachings of Abraham and Isaiah to be accepted across the known world, one of the foundation stones on which my faith was then built. Tomorrow, I shall talk of the 'mission', the first use of the Spear and the forging of the Sword. But all of this is preparation for my story of the task given to my family in the years since the first conversions to Christianity."

Roaring Flamebringer grumbled: "Now there is even less chance that I shall sleep! I give you six hours and then we shall break our fast with the second part of your story. From here, we enter unfamiliar territory for me. I shall guard you as you sleep but confess I am VERY impatient to hear more!"

Ra'el hugged him briefly around the neck then yawned and slid slowly back to rest in the crook of his front leg, the warmth of his body staving off the cool of the mountain-side as she fell into a deep and contented sleep.

She woke to find that her dragon friend had found a blanket from somewhere (best not to ask too closely) and covered her gently in its soft folds. Roaring Flamebringer was watching her intently for the first flicker or indication that she was awake then as soon as she began to stretch, he nudged the bowl of cereal he had prepared for her with his nose and said a simple: "Eat!" His own hunger for the next instalment of her story was so apparent she had to chuckle then she ate fast not wishing to test his patience too closely. "You can wash later" he muttered and she did not argue but sat once more before him, her eyes open to the world of her imagination, took a deep breath and continued the tale:

"There were three important ministries in the first thirty years of the Christian Church: first that of Paulus, Timotheus and Bartholomeus to Greece, Cyprus, Malta, the Adriatic and the Middle East; second the arrival of Petrus in Rome; and third that of Iosephus and the Magdalan who journeyed to Western Europe and Britannia. At the same time, there were the persecutions of Claudius, Nero, the Sanhedrin, and the fall of Ierusalem and Medina.

Paulus' mission helped forge the Hellenistic Christian Church with its Coptic tradition, apocryphal Gospels, founded on the anamnesis and Eucharist, but also it was inherently misogynistic.

Petrus and Paulus fell to either Nero's or Domitian's persecutions in Rome but not before both had established the Church in Rome which under Constantine would sweep away all other traditions when its Synod met in Nicea.

Alas, when Rome fell to the pagan hordes in the seventh century, too many compromises were made and Christianity was paganised from within, leading to the Synod of Whitby which saw the virtual abolition of the Celtic Church traditions as founded by the Magdalan and led to the birth of Islam as the contra-pulsion to the Paganisation of the western church and Helenisation of the eastern church. The simplicity of the faith of the Magdalan sits at the heart of the new faith of Islam.

In the ninth century, the Magdalan's tomb was found by an explorer, monk and knight, St Badilo, and her body moved to Vezelay to be honoured in peace in the caves you now guard.

Then in 1200, the Christian Church changed direction once more. This was in part due to the discoveries made by the Crusaders in the Holy Lands about the earliest days of their faith and how the mysticism and simplicity of belief of the Magdalan had been subverted, her reputation sullied posthumously (as Iosephus had foretold it would) by Gothic, Frankish and Saxon Kings, and by the pagan Emperors and Bishops of Rome. Instead, from the start of the 13th Century the Christian Church began to teach once more about the faith of the earliest Celtic Christians. The mission of the Magdalen became part of the official teaching and tradition of the Church, its accepted history, and the basis for one of its most famous pilgrimage routes: the 'Oyster Trail'.

Even the name of the 'Oyster Trail' betrayed the ongoing confusion that remained at the heart of medieval Christianity. It was so named to allow the Church to adopt the Magdalan as its version of the Goddess Venus, so often shown as rising or being born from an oyster shell. But this was a ruse, just as the 'relocation' of the sepulchre of the Magdalan to St Maximins Chapel in Provence in the thirteenth century was a guise of war to avoid its capture by the invading Italians. The Magdalan's remains are kept safe in Vezelay, protected by the falsehood that she is buried and displayed elsewhere, guarded by stewards drawn from every Christian and Islamic nation and these faithful guardians included my parents and grandparents.

The use of the symbol of an oyster is actually a reference to the last of the Magdalan's descendants, whose name is de Scales or Oyster shell and who are part of both the de Clare family (the last of the Angoevins and Plantagenets) and Sir Bedevere's family, the keepers of the Spear of their ancestor, Gaius Gallicus Longinus that was placed in to the safekeeping of Sir Parsifal and then Sir Galahad. And so our story continues:

In the meantime back in Ierusalem, things were moving fast. There had been over a hundred sightings of the Rabbi, Iesus, preaching openly to large groups on hill-sides across Iudaea, not just limited to Ierusalem. Longinus' troops were soon stretched to the limit trying to disperse each gathering yet never knowing where the next one would pop up. The distances being travelled by the Nazarene were impossible; the stories of miraculous healing ran into their hundreds and, more worrying yet, many were witnessed by the very legionaries detailed to break up Iesus' peaceful meetings. Indeed, Longinus found that his own cohorts were in danger of becoming the most fertile recruiting ground for new followers of the man they were now calling 'Christos'. He reported all of this faithfully to Pilate.

"What shall we do?" the older man asked in exasperation.

"These groups are not violent. Their gatherings are peaceful. The followers of the Nazarene offer no political threat. But they do thrive on our attention. So let us leave them alone. The Nazarene is possibly the fifth or sixth to claim to be 'the Messiah' this twelve month and who can now remember any of their names? Allow this movement to fizzle out. I will leave a few informers in place just in case it suddenly begins to become organised as a movement or changes its message from advocating peace to promoting insurrection. But we are spread out too thinly and encouraging rebellion through our presence."

"Agreed" said Pilate in haste and relief. "I cannot see the attraction of this man, myself. He seemed mad to me. But he was clearly harmless. I regret his death. However, you speak as if he is alive. Do not ever forget we killed him: *you* killed him and you have his blood on your pilum to prove it!"

Longinus had another difficult meeting with Pilate two days later. He was about to throw away a promising career as a professional soldier and potentially antagonise the most powerful man in the region: one whom he was also about to ask for a favour.

Fortunately, he had some powerful matrons on his side to help him. His mother had gone first:

"You must go with the Magdalan" she had said "and follow your stars. Staying will just see you eaten up by the constant thought that your destiny lies elsewhere. I am encouraged that what you seek to do is honourable; you leave to protect someone who is vulnerable. So, I shall help: I have a niece who lives in Caledonia. I am sure she would welcome 'a visit' and you can say she is ill or getting married. I will cover for you."

"But what about you?" her son had asked out of love as much as duty.

"You will come back" she said with certainty "and I have the Legion as my family. Martius will see me right" and Longinus had nodded for his century would offer her their hearths in honour of his father and grandfather and (little did he know it) out of respect for him also.

Maria, sister of Lazarus was next. She arrived at the Camp, a far-away dream-like look in her eyes as always, and asked for Longinus but would not say 'Why?' Fortunately, Martius caught sight of her and acted as her escort, muttering the whole time that she must have taken leave of her senses to walk openly into a Roman military camp with a warrant for her arrest issued and nothing to protect her except her winsome smile.

She ignored him and her eyes remained in places far away, beyond the reach of living man, until that is that she came into the presence of the Centurion. Then her smile took on a much older look, her expression was appraising and appreciative; she spoke directly to him, her news was clearly spoken although at first Longinus could make no sense of her at all, whilst Martius' eyes lifted to the heavens as if to say *'She is always like this and I can neither make head nor tail of her either!'*

"I am to bring you to meet a friend of mine. She can help."

"Maria, sister of Lazarus. Good morning. Welcome. Will you join me and then you can explain yourself as I have not got a clue what you are talking about!"

Maria laughed then chided Longinus saying "You sound just like my sister, Martha. She is always so practical too. You could just trust me and come with me but I guess some explanation might help?"

"Unless you intend to tether me with a rope and drag me like an ass behind you then yes, indeed, *some* explanation would be a great help!"

Her eyes danced at the thought of this man having the knot tied between them and then she looked at him properly and what she saw made her become instantly serious.

"I love and honour our Master. I would do anything for him. I bathed his wounds with my tears yet glorify to see him alive. I filled his house once with the smell of the finest oils and perfumes and wish to do so every day of my eternal life. I honour the man because he is also God and the Son of God.

If I seem fey or nonsensical it is because what I have seen brooks no explanation. Rather, it is there for us to accept *on trust*. Iesus can do things I shall never do nor do I need to because the Master does them for me. So, forgive me if I shall always do what he asks without question or need for 'explanation'."

Then seeing his continued frustration but also that his inherent good manners were preventing him from arguing with her, she started to chuckle and decided to have mercy on him. Looking back, she could not be certain why she did so? Perhaps, because mere moments before she had fallen so totally and utterly in love with her green eyed, red faced barbarian that she felt she owed him at least this one courtesy? But he was going to have to take *her* on trust in future or he would be permanently frustrated and she would not be able to control the wonderful joy and laughter bubbling up inside her each time she saw the exasperated expression on his face!

"My friend is Cordelia Quirilia, daughter of Aemilius Sextus Quirilius, Senator and a former Consul of Rome, whose privilege it is to be married to one, Pontius Augustus Marcellus Pilatus, the appointed Procurator and Governor of Judaea! Coming?" She added with a grin and Martius snorted at his friend's discomfort then went to get the leather polish, the wire brush for his Centurion's helmet plumes and oil for his armour and weapons.

"What are you doing?" Longinus asked. "I am not courting the lady."

"Idiot!" his primus pilum replied as he began the task of unknotting the tangle his friend had left in the red dyed ostrich plumes, taking a quick look at Longinus' cloak and deciding there was just one hole or twenty too many to darn and throwing it back in the trunk then finding a boot lace missing, he began to hurriedly untie one of his own, talking to his friend the whole time as he did so:

"The lady will almost certainly get you an interview with her husband tomorrow and stay with you to offer you her support. Take your lead from her as the Lady Cordelia comes from a family with at least twenty generations in the Senate. She can handle Pilate. But you need to look your best if you are going in front of the Governor as he must not think you are surrendering your commission, but rather going on a mission of mercy. Let him see you are still a soldier of Rome but also one who values his duty as the pater familias and is going to the rescue of a distant niece with whom you shall return, of course!"

"I am lucky in my friends" was all the poor man could think to say and watched as Martius cleaned up his armour and weapons then listened as Maria stood by the awning of the tent entrance and sang softly to the rising of the sun.

"What do you sing?" he asked of her gently not wishing to disturb her music yet curious and appreciative.

"Just a few words" she replied: "Praise You! Rejoice in You! Thank You God!"

The Lady Cordelia was tall with a patrician face and long golden hair tied in a forbidding knot of ringlets that made her look like the Gorgon, Medusa – an imposing look she deliberately fostered because she was in reality a generous-hearted and gentle soul, easily persuaded to help the vulnerable and those in need, a welcome foil to her husband's austere and more heavy-handed handling of local affairs.

She was also much younger than her husband, married at fifteen when he was thirty three and had just entered the Senate. She had their only child at sixteen (Pontius Iulius) and now at only just thirty-four she was still a child at heart in many ways but a child whom had been brought up in one of the noblest, pious and most severe of the houses of the ancient Roman Republic.

She had become a follower of the Nazarene when he had attended to one of her maids, a slave whom she loved and cherished dearly and so had been grateful for the man's successful ministrations. Soon, she had begun to join her maid at the Nazarene's private gatherings in the homes of other followers or the hills above the town of Nazareth and particularly in the Magdalo Castle besides the Sea of Galilee owned by one of the Apostles. It was not long before she was caught up in the excitement and adventure of it all.

The death of her son at the hands of a Jewish assassin could have changed all of this: caused her to seek vengeance amongst the Jewish people. But she was wise enough to be able to differentiate between the large numbers of Jews flocking to hear the Nazarene offer peace and the handful of violent freedom fighters representing no-one but their own anger and hatred.

She was also well-informed and could see immediately that the followers of the Nazarene were being slain by the same assassins as had taken her son, even to the point of inciting the crowd in Ierusalem to have the Nazarene crucified at her husband's orders. She had understood the trap waiting for her husband and tried to warn him. She knew Longinus had done the same. Yet, the blood of the Nazarene would always be associated with the name of 'Pontius Pilate'. She had considered divorce when news of Iesus' execution reached her but then she recalled one of her many conversations with the carpenter's son from Nazareth:

"He will need your help if he is to be saved from the despair of what he will do" the Rabbi had said to her one day as he paid a visit to check on one of the many children at the Palace who had developed a fever. Only now did she realise that the 'He' referred to was her husband Pontius.

Finally, she was grateful for the message of hope that the Nazarene had given her on the news of her Son's death:

"You will meet him again in my Father's kingdom when the Gates of Paradise will open to all who believe in the Truth."

"What is Truth?" she had asked unconsciously reflecting her husband's question that he would ask at Iesus' trial a few days later.

"I am" Iesus had replied with utmost simplicity and speaking in Hebrew he had mirrored the same sacred word as Moses had heard when addressing the burning bush: "*hvh I*".

"Will my son truly be there to meet me?"

"Your prayers will save him."

"What should I say?" at which the Nazarene had smiled then chided her gently:

"Cordelia, my lady, there are no magic words. There is no formula like a spell. God hears the Truth in your heart. Say what you truly believe and God will listen."

So, she had prayed every day since and on each occasion her heart had asked that: "Thy Will Be Done!"

They met at the House of Lazarus that night in preparation for Longinus' meeting with Pilate the next day. Martha and Maria were staying with their brother as he had taken them both in, initially to be able to hide and protect them from the constant searches and arrests by the Temple Palace Guards but also because all knew in their hearts that the Nazarene had promised one final gift or sign to grant them the courage to go on their ultimate mission. Whatever that final sign was to be, Ierusalem was where this would happen and so they waited patiently.

The followers were still in danger despite Longinus' revised orders to leave their gatherings alone. The Sanhedrin had a different agenda and each day, the followers would gather to learn that one more of their number had been taken and stoned or hung by order of the High Priest for blasphemy. At the forefront of this purge was a Roman citizen, legal advocate and experienced mediator named Saul.

Lazarus greeted Longinus then updated him on the grim news:

"Yesterday, two of the apostles left for Damascus to see if they could persuade their City Elders to give us safe haven and to harbour us from the brutality of the Sanhedrin's persecution. Damascus is its own place and will listen and aid us if we are seen not to be trouble. Only two days ago, however, the Sanhedrin put Simon's sister to the rack then stoned her to death this morning. She was only twelve. We need somewhere safer than this City or we shall be exterminated. Alas, the news gets worse for Saul has left the City of Jerusalem to go to Damascus himself to plead the case that we be refused entry as blasphemers."

"Are we safe in this house? Should our meeting tonight be cancelled?" Longinus asked in genuine concern but Lazarus was able to reassure him:

"The Temple Palace Guards would not dare to assail the Procurator's wife and a Quirilius at that! We are safe until she leaves and then I suggest we use the lofts and exit several tenements down from here. But do not worry! Martius has men watching over us as does Cornelius. We will have plenty of warning of any raid. Now all we must do is wait for Maria who has left to fetch the honourable Roman matron."

They did not have to wait long. Ierusalem was currently under a curfew following the threatened riots at the Passover. The streets were deserted save for those with permits issued by Pilate's praetorian. This included the Governor's wife, under escort to make a house call to friends and acquaintance, guarded the whole way as she sat in comfort in her litter. Maria was walking alongside; the young girl's safety covered under the umbrella of the protection offered to the Roman matron. Their guards carried lanterns to light the way; the street lights had been extinguished as the last rays of a tired sun had disappeared to reveal a full Harvest moon in all its splendour. The narrow alleyways with their tall buildings on either side saw little moonlight and sat in sinister shadow. The escort brought their light with them, but it was Maria who ultimately led the way to her brother's house.

The House of Lazarus stood in the Merchant's Quarters of the City, a four storey tenement, each floor galleried around a single atrium that stretched from the ground floor-well to the roof-top garden. The house had been used by the Nazarene's followers from the moment that Iesus had reached Ierusalem for his triumph, trial execution and resurrection. It was large enough to house the handful of Apostles and disciples for the meetings that Iesus had held in the days after the riot at the Temple, when warrants for Iesus' arrest had been issued yet the man needed somewhere he could relax as he prepared to face the terrible ordeal ahead of him. It stood a few hundred yards from the Garden of Gethsemane whilst the windowless upper room hired by the disciples for the Passover celebration was on the same street, above a deserted warehouse formerly used to store dried figs.

Cordelia felt safe here as she had visited Maria and Martha often and sat in awe as the Rabbi had spoken of a world at peace where all were equal, without sickness, violence and oppression.

"We are all rich" he had said the day after he had processed into the City to be greeted as King. "Our fortune is the gift God has given us to one day be his guests in Paradise. We must all seek to claim this gift."

"How?" they had all whispered.

"By every good deed we do to our fellow man or woman." The Nazarene had replied and Cordelia had looked around at the inspiration this wise man's words had brought to the poor, the humble and the simple folk who listened so intently and understood the inherent power that he brought to every gathering. *'He speaks revolution'* she thought '*but not revolt. He offers us each a task within our abilities and talents but only if we choose to follow him. All is therefore possible!'* But she also realised that for those seeking a Messiah who would lead armies against the Might of Rome, the simplicity of this message would disappoint.

The challenge had come from Iudas: "Master, you know I will always follow you but surely there is no place for the world you describe when our every deed is stage-managed by the oppressors of Rome? They have defiled our holiest places; they hold us in prison in our own homes; and they worship false Gods and craven images. They burden us with taxes we cannot pay and grant our most lucrative merchant contracts to their own equites, leaving our people destitute. Surely we must fight?"

The Nazarene had turned to Cordelia, a silent look of courteous apology for the brashness of one of his disciples before meeting the sicariot's challenge.

"Yes we must fight. But whom? With what? For what? My father offers his gift to **all** men and women. Our weapons are his Word. Our cause is to bring the Good News to those who are sinners. Those who fight with the weapons of man must be defeated. Our victory shall come when we fight with the weapons of God."

"What are those weapons? Will God cast down the Romans as he did the walls of Jericho with trumpet blast?" at which Iesus laughed at Iudas' fighting talk then shook his head.

"Iudas, Iudas, Iudas. You forget what it is for which we fight! We seek a kingdom in the next world: in life after death. We have no ambitions for victory in this world" then pausing for effect the Nazarene continued: "Save this. Through our sacrifice we shall obtain victory over all death."

"Am I welcome here?" Cordelia had asked concerned at the sense of feeling, of anger and hatred of Romans she had seen underpinning Iudas' challenge.

"Yes" Iesus had replied without hesitation "For the day will come when the comfort of God's gift will be your refuge against much sorrow" and she recalled the briefest moment of sadness and the falling of a single tear from the corner of one of the Rabbi's eyes.

"Of course you are welcome here!" Maria interrupted them all, giving Cordelia a little hug of friendship then glaring at Iudas and all laughed as he fended off the imaginary daggers flung at him across the room from her fiery eyes.

There was a sharp rap on the door and Lazarus unbolted it then flung it open to be greeted by his sister who stepped into his arms. Then Maria looked quickly around before seeing Longinus. At sight of him, her head went down to hide behind her hair but not before he had seen the glimmer of delight there. Then Maria remembered her manners and turned to hand Cordelia into the Reception Hall. The lady could see many she knew but noted with sadness the absence of many that had already been taken under arrest or slain or had lost their faith and belief under the terror and threat of torture and death. This was a much smaller gathering than that she had been accustomed to on her previous visits, yet it had important tasks to complete for the Master.

"My lady" Longinus went to say, humbled by her presence, made awkward despite towering a whole foot taller above her head. She laughed and then chided him: "We are all equals here Gaius. Call me Cordelia and we shall be friends!"

Cornelius stuck his head in briefly to let them know that all was clear and that he would be outside with Martius. "Have we long?" Longinus asked him and Cornelius shook his head. There would be no time for a social gathering. The longer Cornelius and his guard were seen outside this house, the more suspicions might grow. The new arrivals headed up to the third floor where the shutters had been thrown open to bring air from the still and humid night outside into a large room the family used for meals and to entertain guests. The walls were plane and unadorned save for shelves of scrolls and parchments bearing the scriptures and their many commentaries.

Eleven were already seated around the room on cushions, food being served by Martha and Petronella, Petrus' daughter, onto long, low cedar-wood tables; the wall sconces had been lit, lamps and lanterns hung from the roof rafters. Conversation was muted, respectful, interspersed with the occasional impromptu prayer or a brief reflection on the scriptures. Martius and Mateus were sharing notes on the many things spoken of by the Nazarene and his memorable stories, Lucius was playing with the children of the house, and Iohannus was in silent reflection, some inner burning emotion or visionary insight had captured his loving heart. Bartimaeus was gazing out at the stars in joy.

Petrus was the group's newly elected leader and showed both his pride and trepidation. He had just lost his brother, the stalwart and the rock in the family and now must step up to replace him. Despite his moments of occasional bravado, he was a truly humble man and knew he was not ready for this task. Yet faith kept him going for *he had been forgiven.*

In the furthest corner, the Magdalan sat with eyes bright in gratitude at all that was being planned in the Master's name. Standing over her was Iosephus; he already had arranged passage for the small travelling party with his private yacht and two ships as escort from the sanded beaches of Antioch to the port of Heriklion and on to Valetta in Malta then Tarraco in Tarroconensis; from there by land through Celtica and Gallia and on to Britannia, landing in the west country (avoiding the war-like Iceni) then following the Severnus north then east, hugging the coast through Dacia and past Allan, across the Firth of the Forth to Perth and Fontainblas. After that he was in territory that was truly foreign and unknown to him with no charts to aid him. He would ensure Cordelia had the details before she left tonight as they would need papers of passage for most of their journey and these would carry most weight and see less enquiry or challenge if sealed in the name of Pilate.

Cordelia stepped in to the room and all stood to bow but she ignored them and instead brought the meeting to swift attention:

"To business" the Governor's wife spoke with determination and everyone turned to listen. "Maria tells me, Longinus, that you have offered to protect the Magdalan as she journeys across the Roman Empire and on to the lands of the barbarian. It is important the Magdalan is kept safe but just as important she is seen and heard. I can help.

Tomorrow, after the sixth hour, around the second watch, you must report to the Governor's Palace. I will have broken the news to my husband of your 'niece's illness' and that 'at your sacred and much-honoured mother's request' you go and bring her back here to the family of your Legion to be looked after. You will be taking a servant (the Magdalan) to act as your niece's chaperone for the return journey and will go in the company of a wealthy friend of mine (my husband need not know whom and will not ask). My task will be to ensure that the necessary papers you need to take leave of absence have been drafted and are ready for you to collect. Do not be late and turn out in full uniform."

"Yes ma'am" and Longinus grinned for he had clearly been given his marching orders and had every intention of obeying them to the letter. The honourable Cordelia might choose to come across as a meek and obedient wife but Longinus could see that she was a powerful lady who almost certainly ruled the Palace household and subtlely guided her husband's political ambitions. But she had not finished with him, however:

"I have one condition, a single requirement for my aid." which silenced all conversation around the room leaving only Longinus with the courage to say: "I will meet this if I can" yet he was fearful of what was to be asked for he was a poor soldier with little influence and could not think what he might be able to offer in recompense for this lady's support.

Cordelia's reply was laughingly spoken with a brief glimpse under her eye lashes towards her friend, Maria, sitting humming on one of the window sills, gazing longingly at the heavens: "Come back, Gaius. If not for the sake of your Legion, or my sake or yours or your mother's then do this for the sake of one whom I love very dearly."

Longinus nodded but it was the Magdalan who surprised them all with a question none of them could answer: "Must we begin with a lie? My ministry is important but my safety is not worth deceiving any one. Cordelia, cannot I meet your husband and tell him the truth that the Centurion looks after me?"

"My child, my husband would refuse to let Longinus go. The Centurion reminds him of our Son. You are very alike" she added as an aside to Longinus, before giving Magdalan some reassurance:

"The niece is real and Longinus will travel to meet with her and what better chaperone than you, my child? If we stick to the bare bones without embellishment then there is no lie. Longinus, the Magdalan is right. So we say 'you are asking for temporary leave for you, a servant and a wealthy merchant to travel to Caledonia.' If asked for more than that then it is also true that your mother has asked to see her niece" and Cordelia made a mental note to brief Martius on her way back to the Palace so that the ever-reliable primus pilum could ensure this was true before the morning with a letter from Longinus' mater to prove this "and the wealthy merchant is someone who wants to tour the world so has leapt at the chance to come with you."

The Magdalan shook her head sadly, her transparent face clearly saying to the world that she thought her way was better but no-one else could agree with her. Pilate would never have seen her and certainly would not have endorsed her mission. Iosephus whispered something in her ear and she laughed, all thought of what she feared was to be 'deception' forgotten as her innocent mind was transported to new delights elsewhere. This gave Longinus a chance to thank Cordelia which she ignored, instead adjuring him to take care.

"The Nazarene asked me to take care of his Maria. Did anyone ever tell you this?"

"Oh yes" replied the lady as the Centurion helped her back into her cloak, offering its warmth against the cold of a cloudless night, and then holding her hand as she stepped into her litter, waiting outside under the watchful gaze of Cornelius and a cohort of Praetorians "But which one?" She continued. "Which Maria needs your protection and which already has God's?" Then she was off into the dark of the night leaving one very baffled young man with a lot of thinking to do.

One of Martius' legionaries tapped him on the elbow as the Centurion was watching the litter with two lines of lanterns moving sedately along the narrow alleyways towards where the Merchants' Quarter joined the open spaces of the Forum and the steps up towards the Palace. Only once he had seen the lady gain the comparative safety of the Forum did the Centurion then turn and nod to the man.

"Sir" he whispered. "We have five minutes at most!"

"Is it a raid?" Longinus asked and got the briefest of nods then the soldier was gone, drifting into the shadows. Longinus bolted Lazarus' door and sprinted up the stairs to where the gathering was still talking about the Magdalan's mission.

"Visitors" he whispered urgently in Lazarus' ear and the man immediately signalled for quiet then began to issue urgent instructions: "Bring all sign of the meal but leave the shutters open and lamps lit for they will already have been noted. Then follow me!"

They went to the fourth floor and through a hatch onto the roof garden. The men helped the ladies and children, gathering the food, wine and water bottles, platters and glasses carefully and bundling them into baskets which they strung over their shoulders. Once on the roof, they avoided treading on the terracotta tiles and followed a narrow path used for maintenance that led onto the roof garden next door. "Keep going" Lazarus whispered as they went across three further roofs then dropped down through another hatch into an unlit and deserted building at the furthest end of the tenement block.

Once indoors and no longer audible to those about to raid Lazarus' house, the man turned to Longinus:

"You, the Magdalan and Iosephus must leave now. Go by the rear gate the moment you hear the Palace Guards break down my front door. The alley in front of this row of houses will be watched but the rear of this house gives onto a private courtyard from which you can make good your escape. I know you are not at risk yourself but it will endanger our mission if you, the Magdalan and Iosephus are found in each other's company. The rest of us will carry on our party in the cellars here. This is the house of a friend but one whom wisely has already left Jerusalem. Provided we leave no sign of light, those outside will believe this house is deserted. I will leave in the morning and take my sisters with me. We will head for Calpurnicum where my summer house can be found and where I first learnt to fish. Trust me, I will be fishing again soon" and Longinus looked at Lazarus quizzically not understanding why 'fishing' was so important.

Lazarus saw the other man's look of confusion and laughed then explained: "My friend, it is good to have you among us for it gives us a great excuse to tell the many stories we all have about the Nazarene. When Iesus recruited Iacobus and Petrus, he called them both 'fishers of men'. We are all such. If you need ever to leave a sign for a fellow follower, then draw the sign of a fish, but one standing on its tail" and Lazarus drew a mark in the dust at their feet with his toe then quickly scrubbed it out.

"That did not just look like a fish, it resembled lettering." Longinus observed and Lazarus smiled; the same smile of joy Longinus had often seen on the face of his sister. "You are, of course right. We have mentioned perhaps that we refer to Iesus as 'Christos' in Greek. The fish you saw is made up of the first two letters of Iesus' name: Chi and Rho." Then both looked round as they heard the distant breaking of glass and splintering of wood.

"The Raid?" Longinus asked and his companion nodded then guided him to the rear of the third floor and a wooden external staircase that dropped three storeys down onto a private walled ground floor courtyard that was unlit. Lazarus pointed to an archway on the far side through which Longinus could just make out the silver slender silhouette of a young girl standing in the light of the moon and the stooping grey shadow of an older man both waiting for someone.

"Go!" Lazarus hissed as he saw Longinus hesitate unsure what words to say to the man whose sister he intended one day to marry, if she would have him!

Longinus ran down the stairs, across the empty courtyard, under the archway and into the moonlight. Once he had joined the couple, it was Iosephus who took charge saying a simple "Come!" then he lead the girl and the soldier down steps, into dark courtyards, along narrow winding alleys, across private squares and cloisters, through empty buildings but never leaving the maze of the Merchants' Quarter. Suddenly and without warning he signalled for them to halt and be quiet. Before them was a wider section of cobbled street, partly lit by street lanterns above the entrances to four elegant Roman style villas.

"Mine" he whispered and pointed to the second domus in line. Then he pointed once more but this time to a cloaked man, barely visible, standing out of sight in the shadows of the entrance to the first villa. "Not mine!" Iosephus said grimly.

Longinus bent down and removed a knife where it was concealed in its ankle holster covered by his boot straps and military issue woollen socks; only for the Magdalan to grab his arms and hold them with a strength he would not have credited her with, her head shaking desperately. "Thou shalt not kill!" she lisped, pleading with him with her eyes to return the dagger to its sheath. The Centurion shrugged then did as asked before folding his arms resignedly. They were trapped unless they could get past that sentinel.

Before either man could stop her, the Magdalan ran. Not towards the villa but rather down the alley in full view of the look out. Without hesitation, the man took after her, leaving the way clear for Iosephus and Longinus to gain entrance to the knight's villa. But Longinus was all for following the girl until Iosephus whispered: "Trust her. She had a head start and knows the City well. Unless the man has help, she will lose him. You, however, need to get back to your Camp and the quickest route is through my villa which gives onto the Forum, the far side of which is the Garrison Citadel and your Camp. I will wait up for the girl but even if she is caught, surely none will harm her?"

Alas Longinus could not share the older man's confidence and with a heavy heart he trotted back to Camp, fears for the girl and for Lazarus and his family competing with his own concerns should Cordelia be unable to persuade Pilate to grant him leave of absence.

As he reached the outskirts of the Camp of Tents, he heard footsteps behind him. No-one was going to challenge him this close to Camp surely? And if they did, he had every right to be patrolling the perimeter whatever the time of day or night. He turned therefore to face his would be pursuer and his face broke into a smile of relief. It was Martius with a sack over his shoulder, clearly returning from another drinking bout with the veterans of his former cohort and with what looked like tomorrow's provisions for them both.

"What have you there?" Longinus asked at which Martius replied with a muffled oath as whatever it was kicked him awkwardly: "Found this! All yours Centurion" and dropped the sack on the ground.

"Ouch" it went then the Magdalan stuck her head out and grinning told him the good news: "I thought I might be safer here than with Iosephus. Martius has promised to make me breakfast and I can say prayers for the best outcome from your meeting with Pilate!"

"What about Iosephus? He will not sleep a wink worrying about you" and the girl's enthusiasm at her escape from her pursuers drained away in an instant as worry for her knight errant took over.

"Leave it with me. I can send two legionaries in uniform with a message. They won't be stopped" suggested Martius. "You two need to get better acquainted if you are going to spend the next few years together."

'Agreeing some ground rules for a start might be a good idea' thought Longinus for his task had been daunting enough when offering to protect the girl from others without the unwelcome discovery that the girl also needed to be protected from herself.

"Do not run off again" Longinus admonished her at which her expressive eyes began to fill with tears and he pranced off to go and find a tent pole or two he could kick down in his anger: he was angry at her, but also annoyed with himself for berating her when what she had done had been selfless and brave.

After a few minutes kicking his mess tin across the floor matting of his Tent, Longinus suddenly realised the girl had not followed him. He had assumed she would and in exasperation went to the entrance of his Tent to go in search of her. She was standing there, not daring to make a sound or disturb his anger let alone enter his Tent unbidden.

"Are you coming in?" he asked gruffly and she nodded then walked slowly towards the far corner of the Tent, curled up on the floor and lay perfectly still, her eyes black pools looking at him without blinking. His grandfather had kept a wolfhound and one day when bored it had eaten the ostrich feathers on the old man's best helmet. His grandfather had shouted at the dog but not touched it. The poor dog had lain on the floor, not daring to come close, with the same lost look in its eyes as the Magdalan, until his grandfather had clicked his fingers once and all had been forgiven. Except Longinus knew it could not be that simple with this girl.

"Can I be forgiven?" he asked tentatively to which she replied: "Yes but you must want this."

Then when he continued to remain stubbornly silent glaring at her, she continued in a whisper: "I am sorry I worried you and that I made you angry but I can make no promise that I will not do something like this again. Iosephus had put himself in danger for me and I had to rescue him."

This was the most he had ever heard the girl say. He could see he was going to have his hands full with her as she had no concept of self-preservation or indeed self anything. She had also posed him a difficult question that he was struggling to answer. Did he want to ask for forgiveness? Self-pride made him want to say 'No' he had nothing for which he need ask to be forgiven. Yet he wanted to see the girl happy again and it was a small price to pay surely? Except she would see the lie in that! "Drat the girl" he muttered at which he saw the twitch of a laugh on her lips and asked her outright: "Are you teasing me?"

"Testing you rather" she replied and she rolled over with her back to him so he could no longer tell if she were sleeping, laughing or crying. She was doing none of those: instead she was praying that Longinus would get a good night's rest in preparation for his meeting with Pilate.

Pilate met Longinus in his scriborium, his private study where he would spend an enjoyable hour or two away from the constant drag of the administration of his Province, his nose buried in his favourite Histories and Philosophies. He welcomed the formal prose of Caesar but also enjoyed

Virgil in preference to Lucretius, Cicero or Livy, and read Catullus rather than Horace. In the case of Catullus, it was because the events told through the poems reminded him of his father's first years in the Senate when he had sat through the attempted Catalline insurrection undone through the power of Cicero's oratory in the trial of Milo. The elder Pilate had backed the Julians and seen advancement for his family as a consequence.

He reflected how things had turned full circle since his father had supported a young and ambitious Octavian against the older, better connected and more experienced Antonius. The death of his beloved Julius Caesar, Pilate had named his only son after him, had brought Caesar's nephew, Octavian, to the forefront of politics. The Antonines had then been crushed to pave the way for Octavian to become the First Man in Rome: the 'Princeps'; the 'God Augustus'.

Augustus' wife Livia wiped out a generation of Julians, Claudians and Antonines to put her son Tiberius on the curule chair as Emperor. Sejanus had been Tiberius' appointment as Commander of the Praetorian Guard and used his rank and influence as well as his close friendship with Tiberius to build up a network of Senators in powerful positions and who owed him favours, including Pilate.

Then Sejanus, Pilate's patron and sponsor, had made an attempt at the bigger game, marrying one of the last remaining Antonines as a prelude to an attempted coup that had seen his entire family wiped out when Tiberius had heard about it. Now, anyone appointed by Sejanus was at risk of removal and being returned to Rome in disgrace.

Pilate needed good and loyal men around him who would therefore speak well of him during any Audit. Except Pilate suspected he was already damaged goods and any offer he might make of patronage would be hard to realise in reality. A letter of commendation from Pontius Pilate might have the reverse affect from that intended in the not so distant future.

It was with some anger and a sense of betrayal, therefore, but also a sense of the pragmatic that Pilate listened to Cordelia as she broke the news to him that he was about to lose a good staff officer.

"I know Longinus' mother well. We often visit the City's markets together. It was from her that I heard her niece is in trouble. The details do not matter but what does is that she has asked her only son to go and fetch the girl back from Outer Caledonia (almost as far as Ultima Thule) to join the Legion where she can be looked after. Her son wants to take up your offer of coming onto your staff but is loyal to his mother. I suggested he see you today and ask for a temporary leave of absence. He is not looking for another posting so clearly wants to return. Timing could have been better but that is outside his control.

If you agree, I can get the necessary papers made up for him and his two companions: the first is a friend of mine who has agreed as a favour to bankroll the whole expedition and is heading to Caledonia on business; the second is a servant he is taking to act a chaperone for the niece. If he has all the right documentation and your seal on it he will get there and back much more smoothly and much quicker."

"I wish you would not get dragged into this sort of thing!" Pontius muttered but Cordelia would have none of it:

"Gaius Gallicus Longinus is well-respected and held in high regard within the Xth Legion. Treat one of their own well and should you ever need the Legion for something *personal* then they will treat you well in return. You have an Audit coming up and this is the sort of thing that can help make or break a reputation. Tiberius is strong on family values so supporting a young officer who needs some leave to assist a relative in trouble is going to get you lots of positive feedback from the Legion when Marcellus talks to them. Right now you need to be stacking up as many favourable reports as you can get."

'*Cordelia is right of course*' he mused. '*I will make sure the young man is coming back and also that he knows who to thank for helping him on his way then wave him off. I have nineteen other Centurions who can step into his shoes. Indeed, I ought to spend more time with the junior officers: if things heat up in this Province then it will be the Centurions who see me through and not the officers in my staff who are almost all still wet behind the ears.*'

Thus it was that Pontius Pilate agreed to see Longinus in his private study at the sixth hour precisely. Longinus stood nervously rigged out as if parading for the Emperor himself but with a tell-tale twitch of his right eyebrow a sign of the tension he felt. Pilate saw the twitch and recognised it. He was pleased: had the young man shown over-confidence then he would have stamped on him and his pretensions. As it was, the man was seeking a favour from his Governor and was unsure of the outcome yet still prepared to brave the lion in his den. '*First for some fun*' thought Pilate.

"Do you know my wife well Centurion?"

"Sir, my mother has been fortunate to both be befriended by and aided by the Lady Cordelia."

"You are surrounded by well-meaning women it seems!"

Fortunately, Longinus realised the statement was rhetorical and held his peace. If the Governor saw him as facing insurmountable odds then he was not going to argue. Pilate continued after a brief pause:

"Coming back?"

"Yes sir. This regiment is my true family and I like this posting. I also have someone I think I would like to come back to if she will have me."

That brought a raised eyebrow but Pilate on reflection could only see a good outcome in this. Longinus was asking for leave for one personal mission to rescue a relative then planning to return to the Legion to settle down.

"What do you need?"

"Thank you sir" Longinus said with relief and heartfelt gratitude. "I need temporary leave of absence plus papers providing myself, my servant and a friend of my mother's with safe passage through Roman provinces and to the borders of Britannia and Caledonia."

Pilate smiled then took the wind out of Longinus' sails as he told him: "The papers are already written up. Just give the Clerk in the ante-room next door the names to insert and you have permission to leave immediately. I have given you two years leave. I do not expect you to take anything like that long but the seas are unpredictable and kept even the great Julius Caesar waiting for six months. Good luck!" And Pilate smiled at him genuinely wishing him well then escorted him to the doorway to the ante-chamber, opened the curtain and stuck his head into the Clerk's office next door to say: "Here is Gaius. See to it those papers are completed immediately then bring them into me and I will seal them."

As Longinus dictated the three names he began to panic inside. When planning this with Cordelia, he could not remember if they had wanted to risk Pilate knowing that Iosephus of Arithamea was the third name on the manifests or not? Iosephus' name had appeared on some of the arrest warrants when Pilate had first sought to take into custody those responsible for desecrating the tomb of the Nazarene. The equites was an obvious suspect in any foul play as the tomb belonged to him and he had the largesse to bribe any guards. Now, it was too late. Longinus would have to hope that either Pilate did not check the papers or that the name did not trigger a memory.

"Done" said the Clerk "Back in a moment" and he knocked on the lintel to the archway into Pilate's study then walked silently into the scriborium holding three sets of travel documents in triplicate, the ink still drying and three copies of the absence with leave orders (one for the Governor's records, one for the Legion's records and one for Longinus). Pilate was at his seat but as he went to seal the first of the documents, Cordelia entered. The Clerk bowed and left them alone.

"Busy?" she asked. Pilate sat back and laughed then explained what he was doing: "Just about to seal the travel papers for our friend, Longinus. The young man was nervous and very grateful. Your advice was sound as ever."

"Good! In which case you can reward me! Cancel all of your meetings; complete all this boring paperwork and bureaucracy in the next minute;

and take me out for the day. The Passover has seen us trapped in this Palace as if it were our prison. Give me this one day, please Pontius."

He could not refuse. His sealing wax was already melted kept permanently bubbling in its brass crucible. He plunged his signet ring in on the end of its wooden holder and affixed it a total of twenty one times in rapid succession not even looking at what he was signing then said. "Facit!"

Next he called for the Clerk and his appointments secretary. To the Clerk he said:

"These are for Longinus. Extract the copies for the records here and the Legion's records and give the rest to the Centurion. No more paperwork until tomorrow. Is that understood?" and the Clerk nodded already working out in his own mind whom he could get to sign the urgent documents in Pilate's place. There was no deputy Governor as such but a lot of the post could be handled by Pilate's staff or one of the other magistrates in the Curiale Court.

Then Pilate directed his appointment secretary to clear his diary for the day. Finally, he turned to Cordelia to ask "Where shall we go?"

"Surprise me" was her delighted reply whilst in the ante-chamber Longinus was thanking his lucky stars and the Lady Cordelia.

Longinus waited a fortnight in Ierusalem to give Iosephus' staff the time to reserve their chambers at the Inns and Taverna along the route they would be taking through Syria and Jordan to the Middle Sea. Iosephus had asked for staging posts and changes of horses to be booked at local Inns every four hours. "We ride fast!" the knight said excited at the prospect of the journey ahead but Longinus could not see the pleasure of eight to twelve hours in the saddle and was even more concerned at how the young Magdalan would cope.

"Why Syria?" Longinus asked thinking that to go west to the coast then travel by sea from Caeserea (the nearest port) or Tyre or to go South to Egypt and Ramses would be far more comfortable for them all. Iosephus explained: "I want to go by land to the Middle Sea as the seas on the west coast can be dangerous, unpredictable and changeable during the middle and end of the Spring months. The land route is much quicker and I have three ships already docked and provisioned waiting for us at Antioch. They could come south to Tyre in the time it will take us to ride north but not further south without yet more delay. Antioch will be unexpected should anyone pursue us."

The Magdalan was in no hurry to leave, however. "We must wait here" she said turned stubborn for the first time either had known her.

"Why?" Longinus asked pulling at his hair in frustration and even Lazarus' sister, Maria began to become impatient but all The Magdalan would say is "We Wait!"

They were dining in the house of Iohannus when news reached them of events in Damascus. Teleus, another follower and one of Iosephus' many servants, had gone ahead to Damascus to prepare the way for his master. He returned with mixed and confusing news:

"Remember the man Saul? The advocate and lawyer sent by the Sanhedrin to Damascus to ask the City Elders to reject the pleas of we persecuted Christians. On his way to the City, he had a fall from his horse bashed his head and was temporarily blinded. On reaching Damascus, one of our disciples, Ananias offered his help and a miracle occurred: the man was healed of his blindness. Saul now calls himself 'Paulus' in honour of his rebirth and is zealously preaching the Good News of the risen Christos."

"This is glad tidings surely?" Longinus asked but Teleus shook his head grimly before continuing:

"Paulus began to preach about our Master being the Messiah. His words were powerful, electrifying and he soon drew big crowds. Alas, he came rapidly to the attention of the Jewish community in Damascus and they sought his arrest, trial and execution. Paulus escaped, lowered over the walls at the dead of night in a basket hidden beneath a covering of grapes. We have a new and powerful missionary but the gates of Damascus are closed to us. We shall need a new route."

"Can we trust this convert? He was responsible for the deaths of many of our followers. Surely he is sent to create mischief?" Longinus asked suspiciously and Iosephus nodded in agreement but the Magdalan surprised them all with her words:

"Paulus brings the Good News to the Eastern world. We must rejoice in his wonderful mission. Is this not another example of Good brought from Evil? Have no fear for us in Damascus. We are in God's hands and so safe from all harm!"

"We can leave then?" Longinus asked hopefully and bashed his head slowly against the wall as the Magdalan said "We wait!"

The Ascension and the Paraclete

The next morning the Magdalan woke the whole household at dawn. Lazarus, Maria and Martha, Petrus, Petronella, Iohannus, Mateus, Simon, Bartimaeus, Marcus and Lucius, Martius, Longinus and Iosephus had all stayed over at the House of Zachariah, brother of Zebedee, father of Iacobus and Petrus. "What is it?" muttered Longinus never at his best when woken early. "We go" said the girl. "The Master!"

They broke their fast together in companionable silence, around one large circular table, looked over by an increasingly impatient Magdalan. Finally, when all had eaten and the dishes had been cleared away they turned to the Magdalan. She pointed to the hills to the east and south of the City towards Rach'el and Bethlehem. They could see even from this distance that huge crowds were gathering, with pilgrims snaking in long lines along the winding paths from Ierusalem through the rolling hills towards the summit of a solitary mount called Elohim, meaning 'the place of God', that sat between the village that God loved ('Rach'el') and the birthplace of King David and the Nazarene at Bethlehem.

"What is it?" Petrus asked and the Magdalan replied simply: "The Master."

In haste they headed to the hill of Elohim to see and hear the Nazarene, in awe at the size of the gathering as tens of thousands had taken to the mountain tracks to get a sighting of the Rabbi. Then suddenly he was standing amongst them and had begun to preach:

"I give you a new commandment!" at which words silence gripped all who had come to see the miracle of the man who had died and risen from the dead. "Love your God and love one another as I have loved you. I go now to join my *Father in Heaven*. Together as One we have prepared for each of you a place in Paradise. Eternal life will be yours if you follow my teachings. Remember me in the breaking of the bread."

As he said these words those watching saw him gradually fade away as if rising like white smoke into the heavens. The Magdalan wept openly as she watched her dearest friend leave her at last, whilst the rest of his followers looked upon the empty space where moments before their Master and Teacher had spoken to them, alive and vibrant, now as ethereal and untouchable as air.

Then fear gripped the crowds and they ran in hysteria, not knowing where they were headed, scattering to the four winds. Petrus summonsed his friends and together they sought out the upper room in the City where they had held the Passover meal; they barred and bolted the doors, hiding from they knew not what.

As the dust of the many feet in flight settled, one lonely forlorn girl knelt in prayer on the hill and waited still. As dusk turned to dark, the girl's head fell forward in human frailty and she was half asleep and shivering with the cold of night when the Angel found her.

"He has not left you" the Angel said, his words of comfort cutting through her drowsiness and bringing her head up in joy. "Look to your heart and you will find him still there. Wait but a little longer for The Comforter is coming and then you shall never be parted."

So the Angel kept her company that night; they talked of the prophesies; the Angel explained the scriptures; preparing the young girl for her new mission and ministry; offering her the warmth of its love; keeping vigil with her until the dawn.

As the sun broke through the shadow of the hills to announce another new day, the bars and bolts on the entrances to the upper room in which Petrus and the disciples were hiding burst open, the heavy oak doors were flung to the ground and the air caught fire. Tongues of flame appeared before their eyes but instead of fear, each of the followers felt renewed strength and purpose.

Longinus and Iosephus turned to each other and said simply: "Now we know for what we waited!" Some of those in the room found that they had the gift to be able to speak in tongues, some that they could understand or interpret the languages of other people and places, some were granted the ability to heal, yet others could see the future and help mould or change it. All were granted a gift and every one of them felt reborn as Paulus had on his way to Damascus.

They ran out into the streets and in their excitement began to preach the Good News to those who had woken early to find the best bargains in the markets of the Forum. People stopped to listen but also to laugh, accusing the followers of being drunk. But then to their astonishment they noticed that the disciples were conversing in many languages, not just their native Aramaic.

"It is far too early for us to be drunk!" Petrus called above the noise of the growing crowd and they laughed at his good humoured banter then became attentive as Petrus spoke of the gifts of the Spirit.

"You know that we are the followers of the Nazarene. Many have seen him on his ministry and can attest to his continued life after his execution by Rome and his burial in the tomb of Iosephus. The Centurion Longinus is here and he saw the Nazarene die and supervised his burial then saw him alive three days later.

Today, the Nazarene sent us a gift. The gift of his Spirit that we might be reborn: a new birth in preparation for a new life after death in the company of God and the Angels.

The miracle is this: the gift of the Spirit can be *yours* if you believe in God and his son, who has risen from the dead to show us the true way to Eternal Life."

The crowd were restless at first. Petrus' words sounded blasphemous; he seemed to be speaking of more than one God. But then some of the disciples began to lay their hands on the few crippled and disabled beggars who had set up their pathetic stalls, poorly written signs on pieces of driftwood or the inside of the bark from palm trees telling sad stories of ailment and injury, taking up the length of one whole side of the Forum. As those who were blind or had been lame stood to rejoice, Lucius wept at the sight of so much healing, his own personal dream come true, whilst the crowds demanded: "Show us! Show us how to become disciples."

From deep within, Petrus found the courage to hold out a shaking hand and lay it gently on the first to seek the Master's gift. A young woman whose smile as the Spirit entered her was enough to encourage the whole crowd to surge forward. Soon, it was in danger of becoming a riot and Longinus sent Martius back to the Camp to bring aid whilst he pulled his cloak over Petrus' head to hide him and whisked the fisherman through the first doorway he could find, bolting it behind them both as they hid in the deserted courtyard beyond.

On the hill where the Nazarene had made his last appearance as man, a thunderous storm was raging yet so charged was the Magdalan with the gift of the Spirit that she shone bright silver like a star come to Earth defying the rage of the tempest.

The Angel looked upon her in awe then said: "Now you understand all of God's purpose" at which she nodded, unable to speak for fear she scream from the mountain-tops in her joy whilst the Angel shouted over the roaring winds that surrounded them: "Go tell the world that the gifts of the Spirit are there for anyone who believes and is willing to be reborn" at which, filled with such energy she could do none other, the girl ran as if she had swallowed the wind and sang as if her heart was bursting in joyful communion with her Master.

The Mission. Welcome in Damascus

The historian, Pilate, took his name from the Eastern Orthodox tradition but at a time when the schism in the Church, East and West, had yet to occur. Pilate was writing at a time when the Roman Empire had come together under the Constantines and had adopted a new faith. Millions were eager and hungry to hear of the history of their new Church. In the East, both Pontius Pilate and his wife, Cordelia were canonised. Pilate the historian was writing in the 4th Century about the early Christian Church in Europe:

"Mary Magdalan and Joseph of Arithenea came to Damascus from which Paul had been earlier ejected. Mary was tried by their Sanhedrin and soon after left for the coast at Antioch (Lattakea) in Mesopotamia." (Pilate, 4th Century AD)

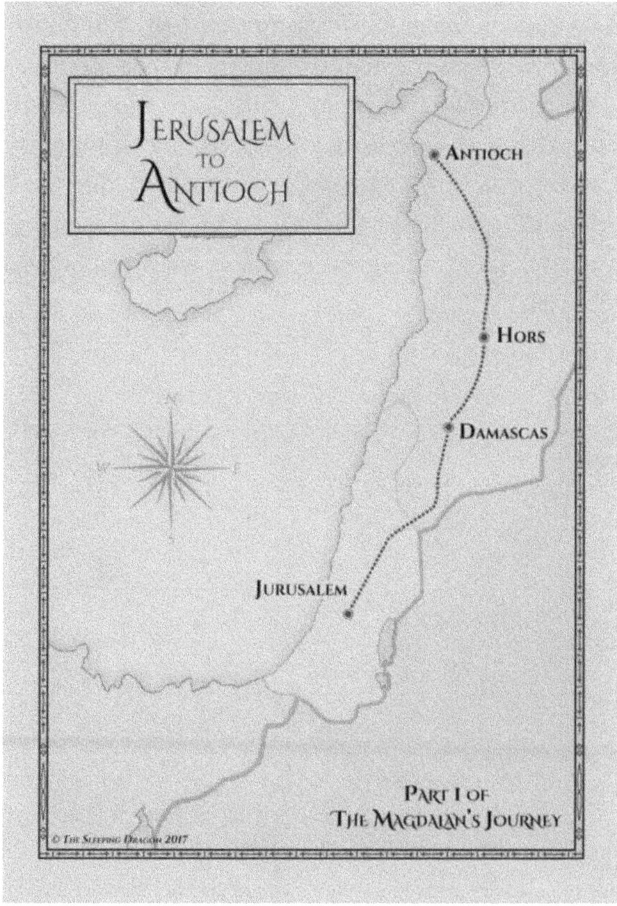

They said their farewells on the road to Amman, heading north out of the City towards Tyre. It was a small gathering, not wishing to attract unnecessary attention. Petrus, Lazarus and Maria had come to send the three missionaries and their small escort on their way with prayers.

Longinus had learnt to ride as a child and begun his military career as a mounted scout. He was secure in the saddle and admired Iosephus' selection of horses. He chose a fiery black Arab stallion that would need a tight rein but could carry the Centurion's weight and was bred for speed and endurance. Iosephus had over three hundred horses in stables across Judaea, Syria and the shores of the Middle Sea. The knight was an experienced and exceptional rider and had placed all of his riding stock at their disposal. The old man was shorter and much lighter-framed than his Gallic companion and had chosen a sure-footed mare that would outrun Longinus' stallion but did not have its height or stamina.

Martius had been worried stiff at the idea of his Centurion heading off without a bodyguard or armed escort into the wilds of Britannia. He had tried to foist a cohort on Longinus but the young officer knew that this would see them challenged every step of their journey and need a lot more paperwork. In the end, they compromised and Martius selected a legionary who was also a convert to the new faith and who had family in Transalpine Gaul. His name was Perseus but he was far from being a demi-God: short, stocky with a pock-marked face and possessing very little conversation. He made up for his physical shortcomings and lack of intelligence by being a genius with the slingshot and the throwing knife.

The Magdalan liked him on sight and surprised him, as she had Longinus, with a kiss of welcome and a shy grin. At which he had fallen in love with her so comprehensively that he was prepared to sacrifice his life for her if the need arose, except she promised to herself that she would do all she could to never let this happen.

The final two members of the party were servants of Iosephus: husband and wife. The couple's names were Annanias and Cerestile. She would be both chaperone and maid for the Magdalan whilst he would liaise with the rest of Iosephus' staff who had already based themselves at the staging posts on the long road between Ierusalem and the sandy beaches of Lattakea (Antioch).

Maria had ridden on the back of an ass once but that was the sum total of her experience on 'horse-back'. She looked at the huge flank of her magnificent Arabian mare in momentary trepidation and confusion then made a hushed and stuttering confession to the Centurion.

"What do you mean, you cannot ride?" Longinus exclaimed in dismay. Then he watched in astonishment as the girl whispered hesitantly in the mare's ear and it knelt slowly before her, allowing her to mount on its back carefully before standing upright again, the girl clinging on to the cropper to avoid being shaken off.

"I did not say 'I cannot ride'. I said 'I have never ridden'. Not the same at all" and she laughed at the dumbfounded expression on the Centurion's face.

The journey to Damascus would take six days. They made good time on the first day, riding at a steady fifteen leagues each hour and covered one hundred and fifty leagues. It took its toll, though, as both Longinus and Iosephus bemoaned their saddle sores then the Centurion just managed to catch Maria as the Magdalan keeled over in exhaustion and fell from her horse.

"We wait for almost seven weeks twiddling our thumbs and now she wants to be everywhere by yesterday!" Longinus muttered but he could not be angry with the girl for she had been vindicated by the Master's gifts of the Spirit. He had seen the Master alive twice now and watched him ascend into the heavens. He would bear witness all his life and attest to these miraculous events. And it was all thanks to this young waif of a girl who had stubbornly told him 'to wait'. Yet she would kill herself if she insisted on going at their current reckless pace!

"Leave it with me" Iosephus said conspiratorially once Longinus had shared his concerns then the equable equites staggered wincing as he tried to walk to the stables without rubbing his saddle sores to issue new orders for the morning to Annanias, who was in the stables checking over the fresh horses for the next stage of their journey. He left the girl fast asleep in the crook of the Centurion's arm.

Iosephus returned after fifteen minutes with the news that he had changed the staging posts and sent out two of his servants to book some new accommodation for them all. "Six hours each day in two three hour stages doing sixty leagues per day: it is much slower than I would have liked but we still reach Damascus in six days' time and Antioch in twelve: my ships will wait for us!"

Somehow word had spread of the Magdalan's mission and that she carried with her physical evidence that the Nazarene was genuine, had died and risen. As they approached Amman the next morning, a crowd had already gathered by the road wanting to hear Maria. At the front was a man paralysed by a fall when plastering a building for a wealthy client. His whole family had brought him because they had heard of the followers of the Nazarene and that they could heal through 'the laying on of hands'.

His wife spoke for them all: "He is a good husband and father and he is also the person who puts the food on our tables through his hard work. Now he will not work again and we all shall suffer as a consequence."

"Do you love him?" The Magdalan asked fearing the lady was bemoaning the loss of her household's income rather than showing compassion for her husband and then the girl saw the tears being held back bravely and had her answer. She turned to Longinus and asked:

"Can I hold the Spear?"

Longinus was surprised but could not refuse her and so strode across to his saddle bag and removed a rolled piece of cloth, covered in oil and within the folds of which was the point of his pilum. He handed it to the girl and she laid it gently the length of the injured man's sternum then said: "Thy Will Be Done!" at which the crowd gasped as the spear-point began to glow bright burnished gold. Next came the distinctive scent of rose petals and, as they watched, the man opened his eyes, sat up then stood and embraced his sobbing wife.

The Magdalan indicated that she would like to say a few words but alas she was so petite that she was lost to sight in the crowd, her words muffled by those surrounding her. Iosephus came to the rescue, pointing to a milestone by the roadside then helping the girl to stand on it, a little shakily at first but growing in confidence as she spoke:

"I come with Good News. My Master has died and been born again so that we **all** may be reborn: a new birth in which we shall be bathed with God's Spirit. I have seen my Master alive and I have been filled with his Spirit.

I am a simple girl. I am not clever or wise. I do not deserve this great gift from God. Yet I have received this gift because, despite my sins and failings, God loves everyone including me. You can receive his gift as I have done if you believe."

The questions began immediately but they were not challenging, rather gently spoken because all could see that this was 'a simple girl' as she had described herself and not some Pharisee or Sadducee so wrapped up in the intricacies of their arguments that they missed the fundamental simplicity that sat at the heart of their faith: Love and Hope.

"When you saw the Nazarene was it a dream?"

"He held me in his arms. I felt his strength" and Maria smiled briefly at the memory.

"What is it that we must believe?"

Maria had no difficulty answering that for she had been coached by an Angel:

"Believe in God. In his Son who has risen from the dead. In Love. In the Commandments. And that there is life in Paradise after death."

Meanwhile, as the gentle questioning continued, Longinus stood holding his spear-point in his hands, looking at it in awe, not daring to cover it; indeed unsure what to do with it. Iosephus saw the man's hesitancy and rightly guessing what was the cause, came over to whisper in his ear:

"The Spear is not magical. The miracle you saw was an act of compassionate healing by God. Maria's prayer and the Spear were symbols of the importance of the prayer but God could just as easily answered Maria's prayer had she just asked him. What we do know is that the Spear was a weapon of war and is now made an instrument for healing by God. Once more *Good* comes from *Evil*."

Many families within the crowd invited Maria and her companions to join them in their homes for the midday meal but Iosephus was insistent that they must push on. For he guessed, rightly, that this would not be the last crowd they would meet between Amman and Damascus that would want to hear Maria speak. His worry was that either Maria would tire under the constant barrage of questions, however well-intentioned, or that the crowds would attract those seeking the Magdalan's arrest and death as a means of preventing the spread of the Good News.

Maria could gladly have spoken to the crowd for days without ceasing. In the end, Longinus hoisted her from her perch on the milestone, and carrying her over one shoulder *still talking to the crowd behind them* he deposited her on the back of her horse then turned to the crowd:

"We will be returning this way again when our mission has been accomplished. Look out for us then" and with a wave the party rode north, leaving many converts behind them who decided en masse to go south to Ierusalem. They wanted to see the places where the momentous events that Maria had described had taken place: the Tomb, Golgotha, the Procurator's Palace and the Way of the Cross as it had been carried by Iesus.

That evening the party came to a small Inn at the entrance to the village of Pereiston on the road to Damascus. The village sat on a hill in front of the remains of a Phoenecian fort that had long ago been pulled down to be used as foundation stones for the handful of houses in this lonely spot.

The Inn was made from bricks of dried mud since bleached pale cream by the sun. Its forecourt was covered by a gazebo made from Ash and which was the home for an enormous grape vine in burgundy and green. As they dismounted, Annanias rushed forwards, eager to tell them his news:

"Paulus is here! Well to be precise he is staying in a Taverna in Caiaphon which is the next village but I am certain he would welcome joining us for supper" and was rewarded with a beaming smile of pleasure and delight at the prospect from the Magdalan. Iosephus, however, could see his carefully planned itinerary going out of the window not least if Paulus persuaded Maria to join him.

The sun was just starting to dip behind the hills to their west, its long shadows cast over the still sea visible in the far distance turned red in its light. The half moon had risen to stand proudly in the dusk of the twilight; the stars still slept as it was not yet dark enough for their brilliance. Maria stood in prayer at the edge of the desert, listening to the birdsong and the howls of the prairie dogs as they offered their praise for the passing gift of another glorious day.

The men-folk were seated on cushions around a low table in the shade of the gazebo; the table was groaning under the weight of freshly cured meats, nuts, olives and fruit. They were talking of their plans, not noticing the girl had wandered off to offer her own gratitude to the Master for all he had created and to thank God that He continued to offer her new adventures.

Paulus had arrived an hour earlier, bringing his follower and scribe Timotheus with him and both men had been greeted with joy and honour by the Magdalan, and with suspicion by Longinus and Iosephus. Paulus had seen their mistrust and shrugged his shoulders now used to the fact that the earliest followers would always remember him for his part in their persecution. He had been more surprised by the innocence and genuine affection in Maria's greeting. That had been unexpected and welcome.

As the men relaxed over supper, Paulus spoke for the first time of his own mission, returning openly and without rancour to their suspicion of his motives and actions:

"I am not welcome in Ierusalem" he explained. "I am seen as a traitor by the Sanhedrin and as a murderer by my fellow followers. Even you are suspicious of me. But this does not matter. My mission is to take the teachings of our Master to the peoples of the Middle Sea, in particular the Gentiles of Asia, Media, Cyprus, Crete, Malita, Greece and the coast of the Adriatic. I am no longer Saul but have taken a new name: Paulus as a sign of the change in me that God has made possible."

Iosephus nodded then spoke sagely of their own mission:

"We must cross many of the lands of which you speak and the risk is that we duplicate our efforts or worse confuse those whom we meet. You are as I: brought up to analyse our actions, to describe them in legalistic language, to interpret our Master's words literally, to set rules based on our interpretations. The Magdalan is different. She sees things teleologically. She is inspired by the spirit, and is hesitant when trying to put her thoughts into words. The Master still lives IN HER. She is an empty vessel filled with his simple wisdom. Her presence and not her words will convert thousands to follow the Master. Our mission is not as yours, therefore. You shall convince the pagan world *through your arguments*; we offer the chance to see the Nazarene alive and doing good deeds *by the power of his Spirit in action* through the medium of the Magdalan. She is like Longinus' Spear: an Instrument of God."

"What shall we do then?" asked Longinus, "We are already on the road and to turn back to Ierusalem now will raise suspicion over our original intent."

Iosephus had already thought this through and his answer was welcomed by all four men:

"Paulus and Timotheus must carry on their mission as they have already planned. If Maria were here she would say their purpose is 'God-gifted'. We shall travel fast through the Middle Sea and head for Hispania, Gaul and Britannia returning via Helvetica, northern Italia, Byzantion and the Black Sea. In this way we split the task of spreading the word across the known world between us."

"What about Roma and the rest of Italia?" Longinus asked and Paulus nodded in agreement with the Centurion. Both men knew that Rome was the key that would unlock the civilised world.

"Roma will summons us when the time is right" said Iosephus sadly at which Maria joined them and added her contribution as a question:

"The people in Roma will welcome us. But what is 'Rome'?"

They invited her to join them and she perched down briefly, sitting between Timotheus, whose arm she hugged tight, and Perseus whom she greeted with a shy smile, then asked Paulus eager to know: "What do you tell people when you meet them?"

"I speak of a new covenant between God and man: of Faith, Hope and Love; I talk of the great Power of prayer. I prepare people for the Master's return in glory." Maria nodded at his words, her eyes shining in response but she still felt the need to correct Paulus in one important regard:

"The Master never left us. This is the mistake I made on the mount of Elohim. He has already returned in glory when he rose from the dead. I can feel He is still here within and around me. His Spirit fills me such that when I breathe it is the Master that breathes and when my heart beats it is his heart that pounds. Do not seek a 'second coming' when the Master is already with us. Rather help us to find the Master today in each of us and not in some distant future."

"Do you not think that the end of the world, the Armageddon, is approaching as foretold by the Prophets? Is this not part of our faith?" Paulus challenged her but Maria laughed then explained herself in ways that Paulus and Iosephus struggled to understand yet the simpler-minded and more straight-forward thinking Longinus and Perseus were able to grasp and they were inspired by her words:

"It does not matter if the world is about to end or not. We are taught to spend every day as if it was our last but this does not mean the end of the world is upon us. Rather it means we could die and be judged at any moment and so must do good things at all times."

"What do you mean when you say: 'good things'?" asked Paulus intrigued.

"Good things are acts of healing, kindness and charity especially to prisoners, captives and those who are oppressed, prayer and fasting; spreading the Good News; praise and rejoicing in all of God's creation. Now excuse me as I wish to sing to the glory of the stars and they will be awake now" then with a bow, she stood and walked a little way into the dark silence of the desert to watch the heavens. A few moments later and the men could hear the lilting sound of her softly sung prayers.

Paulus left that night to begin the mission that would see the Eastern Church emerge as the bedrock (the 'petra') of Christianity for the next three centuries. Then one day a Roman Emperor had a vision on the Malvern Bridge when about to do battle and dedicated the victory that brought him the Imperium to the God Christos. His mother, St Helena, was a Christian and he honoured her during his life. Helena would influence her son's eventual conversion and that of the whole Empire.

Helena, the Emperor's mother, was a British Princess brought up in the traditions of the Christian settlements established by the Magdalan in Britannia, Caledonia, Gallia and Hispania including the former lands of the Trinovantes, Col's Caister or Colcaister where Helena was born. One of those traditions was the location of the cross-piece hidden in Judaea by Martius and which Helena found when on pilgrimage.

Sadly, the Roman Emperor needed a faith to bind his legions to support their new Imperial family and so the more gentle faith left by the Magdalan was crushed, many references to female disciples, apostles and deacons over-written and many of the Gospels shelved to be forgotten for centuries, including the *Gospel according to Maria the Magdalan* and the *Diaries of Joseph of Arithamea*. The historian, Pilate's account and that of Nicodemus writing a century later would also be shelved.

It was only nine hundred years after Nicaea that the story of the early Church was told by Menessier, de Boron and Phillip of Flanders: the mission of Joseph of Arimathea and the Magdalan's to Gaul and Britannia became accepted as the official history of the founding of the Churches in Europe. By then, the Church had already split between paganised west and helenistic east and was at war with the energetic and unifying force of Islam.

Iosephus was proven right and the party made slow progress, having to stop every two to three hours to allow Maria to greet the crowds gathered at the roadside to hear her gentle words. The girl never had a moment's rest and would fall from her horse each night in total exhaustion, to collapse into the deep sleep of the truly fatigued, being caught by the ever watchful Longinus and carried to her room to rest. The Centurion was become increasingly worried as the girl had been light-weight before but this journey was taking a huge toll on her frail frame and she was now so thin and fragile she was no burden at all.

"Will we lose her?" he asked Iosephus in the agony of his concern for her. Iosephus shook his head before answering:

"It is not our decision in the end but God's. She does God's Will and she lives for as long as she is needed to do so."

"She is almost a ghost. I swear I can see through her at times. Is she dying?"

"She has already died and been reborn. She is almost pure Spirit now. Ask her how she feels about this. I can offer you no reassurance but she will know the right thing to say to give you calm."

Longinus had a sleepless night, watching over the girl in fear that the Master would take her in the night. She muttered silent prayers in her sleep amidst the occasional chuckle at some delightful memory and her smile at all that she had seen that day. Perseus would pop his head in occasionally sharing his commanding officer's concerns for Maria and praying every day that she be given the strength to complete her mission. She woke to the sight of two very tired and anxious young men and was quick to reassure them:

"I am alright. I am human so tired but also filled with the Spirit so restless to do God's wish. My Master and his Angels are my constant companions, I can see them now all around us and they populate my dreams with their wonderful wisdom. I have you to protect me as I am frail and the Angels protect me from the forces of Evil that would seek to tempt me to sin. With all of this protection surely I am safe?"

"What sin could you ever do?" asked Perseus in awe and surprised confusion, unable to believe the Magdalan could ever commit a sin.

"I could surrender to the pain and weakness of my human frailty. Instead I let God take me to where I must go. I have surrendered to God." Then she paused before continuing with a grin of pure mischief: "I admit also to a terrible sense of humour that means I take too much pleasure in 'surprising' Longinus." Then turning to the Centurion she silenced him with her simple apology: "Forgive me for testing you when we first met. I had no right to do so."

Teleus greeted them on the sixth day as they came in sight of Damascus. Alas he had only bad tidings: "Warrants have been issued for the arrest of the Magdalan in the name of King Herod the Fox. If she enters Damascus she will be taken, tried and executed for blasphemy. Go past. You are not safe here."

"Is the Magdalan the only person to have a warrant issued?" Longinus asked and Teleus nodded. "Then take me to the Legate here. Syria is the official province of Rome and Judea is only a satellite; the City Elders will not wish to countermand a pass issued by the Procurator of the nearest Roman Fortified City commanding nearly two full strength legions which pass is on behalf of someone under the protection of a Roman Centurion. Two Legions can be here within the week if I send word."

Teleus smiled for the first time then said "Follow me." It was left to Perseus to point out the flaw in Longinus' plan:

"Sir! I think I can see Maria riding towards the City" and in the distance they could see the dust sent up by her mare as she galloped towards the tall gates of Damascus and the stone archway at its entrance.

They watched in horror as she surrendered herself to the guards at the gate and was escorted into the City. She was soon out of sight. "Let us hope we are in time" Longinus whispered in fear for the girl and then followed Teleus as he led them to the Citadel where the City Elders sat each day in conference. Iosephus left them at this stage to go and find the Court of the local Jewish community where Maria would be tried.

The Court rooms adjoined the Temple at Damascus with three High Priests sitting in judgement, Pharisees acted as both prosecuting and defence counsel; scribes maintained a record and the Temple Palace Guards would bring in the prisoners from the lock ups below. The public were allowed entry to a viewing gallery: a mezzanine floor above the three judges and facing the gated enclosure where the accused would stand to face trial.

Iosephus had to wait several hours, sitting through trials for petty theft, burglary, embezzlement, two minor instances of blasphemy and one of adultery. Except for the two minor cases of blasphemy and that of embezzlement, the rest were sentenced to be stoned immediately and taken outside the walls of the City for their sentence of death to be carried out.

"The next case is that of the blasphemer, Maria the Magdalan of Magdalo who surrendered at the gates of the City this morning and has pleaded not guilty, refusing to give evidence when under torture." The judges nodded and the girl was carried into the dock, unable to stand on legs where the calves had been broken by the rack and on the soles of feet burnt and blackened by the poker's fire. Still she smiled by way of greeting then her face lit up with joy at the sight of Iosephus. The old knight could not restrain the tears as he looked down on the broken girl yet still she was unbowed.

"You are accused of blasphemy. How plead you?" said one of the Pharisees acting as the Clerk of the Court that day.

"Excuse me sir but who accuses me?" The girl replied fearlessly.

"The Sanhedrin in Ierusalem has issued a warrant as has King Herod" but the girl persevered with her objections:

"Sir, forgive my ignorance but their jurisdiction is Judaea and not Syria. Neither Herod nor the High Priests in Ierusalem are here to prosecute me. How is this trial to proceed?"

The Pharisee was an honest man and turned to the three judges to advise them: "The girl is right. Syria is its own Province and superior to Judea in its authority. Rome and the Legate do not recognise a 'kingdom' of Judea. It is for you to decide if there has been blasphemy."

"Did torture reveal anything?" one of the judges asked and the Clerk shook his head at which another of the judges could be heard to mutter: "Stone the torturer, the useless good for nothing oaf."

"Very well. We will examine the accused" the chairman of the bench determined and then turned to Maria:

"You were heard to say there is more than one God, is this true?"

"No, Sir. I have always and still do believe there is only one God."

"And Iesus of Nazareth, who or what is he?"

"He is the Messiah!"

"Do you believe the Messiah is God?"

"Isaiah teaches us that the Messiah is the Son of God and thus also one with God. I am a simple girl and will not challenge the Prophets though I admit to not understanding what they say sometimes. God does not ask for my understanding, however. God asks for my devotion and acceptance of the wisdom of the Prophets."

The whole bench had sat back at this. They were all men appointed for their integrity and wisdom. Yet they had to admit there was much in the scriptures they had to take on trust and could not explain. The girl had highlighted the first principle of faith: she believed in things that were inexplicable. Still they tested her but they had already concluded she was honest. The question remained whether she had said anything that was contrary to the teachings of God and the Prophets. The youngest of the Priests on the bench, in his mid twenties and highly intelligent but also adamantly supportive of Damascus' independence from the sapiential authority exercised from Ierusalem, posed the next question:

"You talk of rebirth. What blasphemy is this?"

"No blasphemy good sirs. It is similar to the preaching of the Essenes who are well-established in your proud City. A baptism that opens our eyes to a greater understanding of the scriptures and our hearts to God's love and God's will."

"What then are the gifts of the Spirit of which you speak?"

"The gifts of God are to allow us to ask him to do wonderful things. He listens to our requests: to heal, to speak in other languages; to see the future; to have Hope. God uses us as his instrument to do God's wish."

"No magic?" the Priest persisted.

"No magic, sirs! God's Will"

"And what is this 'Hope' of which you speak? Is this to be revolution?"

Maria's response was long and detailed as she explained the greatest gift of God to the High Priests of the Jewish community in Damascus. These men had tried Paulus and sentenced him for blasphemy despite his skills as an advocate and mediator. Maria could never compete with the use of language, understanding of the law and the logic of Paulus; instead she let her heart speak. The three wise men on the bench could sense the truth in her words and continued to thaw towards her as she described the guiding principle of her new life.

"Hope is the most powerful gift from God and the thing that makes us different from animals, demons and Angels. They have **instruction** but we are given the **ability to choose** how we shall meet the wonderful adventures set by God. When we choose we hope we do the right thing. When our choices lead us into danger or towards death it is hope that keeps us still believing in God and continuing to make the right choice.

I chose to come before you because I believe I have done nothing wrong and that you are entitled to hear the Good News of the life and words of the Nazarene. The Sanhedrin in Ierusalem would deny you that opportunity; that choice. I offer you the choice. This is my Hope, sirs."

After the shortest of discussions, the chairman pronounced his sentence and that of his colleagues:

"We are unanimous. We wish to hear more of this Iesus of Nazareth. We seek to have the 'choice'; to be offered Hope where others who do not have the best interests of Syria in their hearts would seek to deny us that hope. Maria the Magdalan, you are free to enter our City in peace. God go with you."

To their amazement, the chamber was suddenly cast into bright sunlight. They looked to the row of circular windows just beneath the roof rafters but could see only the dullness of dusk. Then they looked towards the girl as directed by their clerk; he was pointing in awe towards her. Maria shone suffused in the joy of their judgement and they were left in no doubt of the right and justice of their decision but also that the young girl was full of the Spirit of God. Her emotions were transparently genuine and she exuded faith and truth from every pore and corpuscle.

The spectators in the gallery cheered and the Guards helped Maria out from the dock and carried her to where the knight, Iosephus was waiting to hold her gently in his arms and bear her to the Guest House which he had hired for them to stay at. Outside crowds had already gathered at news of the judgement, wanting to hear the Magdalan or just to see her, to touch her to be part of her world of Hope. As Iosephus held her close,

Longinus and Perseus arrived with the promise of Amnesty from the City Elders who had no desire to create a breach with Rome over one young simple-minded girl.

The crowd guided Iosephus to the steps of the Palace where Maria sat half way up them, resting her legs and feet, facing the crowd, visible to all, and spoke for their benefit:

"The Messiah has come. He has fulfilled the words and prophecy of Isaiah. He has risen from the dead, set captives free from prison, and remains alive in anyone who follows him. He has given us a new commandment: to love God and to love each other. He has given us great gifts: to heal; to speak foreign languages; to see the future; and to have Hope. I bring you that Hope: that if we believe in my Master we can all be reborn and have the Spirit of God in our hearts, minds and souls."

"Teach us how" they all asked. "Grant us hope."

To which she replied:

"Listen and I shall tell you about the life, death and resurrection of my Master" and into the hushed silence that followed she spoke for hours. All were attentive, none left that gathering, each would recall her every word and would tell others the following day.

They stayed for three days by the end of which all in Damascus had asked her for the laying on of hands. Maria knew this was beyond her ability for tens of thousands had gathered that morning to listen to her and so she decided to send for help, addressing the crowd that morning saying:

"I will send word to Petrus, the leader of our faith, and ask him to come to Damascus with the disciples. They will welcome being amongst those who respect them and they can cope with the huge numbers who wish to be baptised in the Spirit. But I must go on. My ministry is to spread the Word and it has only just begun."

Longinus just shook his head in disbelief. Over one hundred thousand lived in Damascus and the whole City was seeking to become followers. If Maria could convert the people of Damascus then he had great hopes for the future but she took such terrible risks.

Maria could not agree with him: "There is no risk if we do the right thing surely?" And Longinus pulled at his hair in frustration at her constant innocent naivety and absolute certainty that she was doing the right thing.

"But what if you are wrong?" He finally managed to ask and her reply silenced him completely.

"How can God do wrong? I do God's will after all."

The journey to Antioch followed the same pattern as that between Amman and Damascus. The crowds had soon worked out where Iosephus had booked accommodation for midday and suppertime and were waiting, sometimes in small groups of less than thirty but on other occasions the local villages would journey to a rally-point and gather in their thousands. All were attentive, gently questioning this simple girl who clearly told the Truth. None were left in any doubt of what she had seen and it was their amazement at her witness that converted them to believe in her message. As Iosephus had said: "*When they see her then they will believe her and believe the message she bears*!"

Each day she became more and more exhausted, collapsing as night fell and the crowds finally released her, often falling asleep without having eaten. She was so painfully thin and her wounds from her torture were taking a long time to heal, despite her youth. She needed rest and was getting none. Iosephus rode with her set before him, holding onto the cropper, drifting in and out of sleep but even this concession by her did not alter the fact that she was shattered each night and at risk of total collapse.

"All will be well at Antioch" she whispered between yawns '*but that was still days away*' thought Longinus and he spoke across the sleeping girl to

Iosephus. "Have your ships come to Tyre. We approach Homs and we can reach Tyre in one day's ride if we go fast to the coast as opposed to the three to four days we will take to reach Antioch. Once the girl is on board your yacht she will finally have the chance to recover."

Iosephus agreed immediately and beckonsed for Annanias then briefed his maitre domo on the change in plans. They reached the outskirts of Homs that evening and ten thousand were there to listen to Maria, waiting on the road south of the City in an enormous valley through which the Road to Damascus trod in a steady line south and north.

Maria spoke for four hours under the stars which were out in force. She would have continued in the moonlight but the crowds needed to find their way home and so the gathering broke up. But not before she had converted another ten thousand to belief in the Nazarene. Everyone in the crowd trusted and was inspired by her; all vowed to journey to Ierusalem to see the place of the death and resurrection of the Nazarene.

The crowd's questions were innocent and at their heart was the genuine desire to recall every detail of Iesus' last moments and his ministry:

"How many times did he fall when he carried the cross?"

"Three times: this was seen by me and by Longinus also."

"What was the Temple his Father destroyed and rebuilt in three days?"

"He was referring to his body as the Temple for his soul and his spirit (anima and animus). He died and then his body was restored three days later."

"What is the Messiah?"

"The Messiah is the Son of God offered as a sacrifice to show God's love who by his death allows sins to be forgiven, the lame to walk, prisoners to be set free, ends oppression and opens the Gates to Paradise for those who believe."

And so the questions went on, never challenging, gently and courteously delivered and all of her answers were received in silent awe and then total acceptance. She did not force belief upon them but left no place either for doubt in her words. They *chose* to follow her Master freely and thus their faith was stronger.

The following morning they went to head west from Homs towards Tyre and a fearsome sandstorm arose in the desert before them. They watched as it tore towards them from the west fuelled by a savage tempest over the sea. The road to their north was clear. Maria had not been told of their change in plan so asked in all innocence: "Why do we not head for Hamah through the north gate? The storm is to our west but if we head north we may be able to go round it or get ahead of it."

"Seems someone wants us to go to Hamah" muttered Longinus. "Can we get word to your ships Iosephus?" The knight nodded. "I will send riders through the storm. It will be great peril but it must be done."

The Magdalan had overheard and asked both men outright to explain themselves which they did rather sheepishly, expecting her anger. But she laughed gaily, reminded them she was never angry, especially with friends then said:

"I can solve this. We head to Hamah. Delay your servants riding to Tyre until we are at least an hour on the road north. Then I promise that the storm will die down and your servants will be safe. As for us, we did one hundred and fifty leagues in a day once, let us do so again and then we shall reach Antioch in less than three days."

"It will kill you" Longinus spoke in distress.

"No. I am not to die yet" and her self-confidence raised the spirits of all of them. *'We can at least try'* thought Longinus with hope restored. They reached Hamah in time for a late lunch and were greeted by another huge crowd. Maria straightaway warned them she had two hours only then spoke from her heart for an hour and answered their many questions for the second hour.

Hamah was a great trading post and included traders in spices and herbs from the Far East, Africa, the Middle Sea, Media, across the Arabian desert, Persia and Parthia, as far as Gallia. A merchant from Luguidenum would take her words back to his home City and when a few weeks later she came to Luguidenum, it was to find the start of an active Christian community already established. The first Christian community in India was also founded by a merchant passing through Hamah and who was struck by the memory of the soft-spoken words of the girl filled with the Spirit of God and talking of things beyond imagination or explanation yet clearly truly spoken.

From Hamah they rode due west through the mountains on unmade tracks often disappearing beneath the cover of gorse towards the peninsula on which the ancient port of Antioch sat. They had a hundred leagues to cover over rough ground uninhabited except for the occasional nomadic tribe, the risk being they were taken captive for their horses and for the price the two women would bring in the slave markets of Kahramanmoraq and Aleppo. But God protected them and they had no serious fall nor rode into an ambush by any of the tribes of that place.

They stayed steady without deviation on the tortuous route they had chosen and were rewarded by sight of the most beautiful mountain ranges in the world, rising out of the sands as ice-topped giants. *'You can understand why so many believe God inhabits the tops of mountains for they are glorious.'* Longinus mused whilst Maria sang quietly rejoicing in the sight of an act of creation so wonderful yet approachable. "It is there for us to enjoy, blessed be God" she whispered and Longinus hearing her nodded in agreement.

Antioch was in a peninsula which jutted out into the Middle Sea, the closest mainland port to Cyprus which was their first stop, where they would take refuge briefly in the small harbour at Limassol, south of

Nicosia before making the journey to Heraklion on Crete in the Greek Islands. They would then sail to Tunis and on to Pollenca in Mallorca before crossing the Balearicum Sea to their final destination of Torrenco (Valencia). The peninsula on which Antioch sat had three sea-facing coves, one carved out of volcanic rock and used as the harbour for large draught vessels then the other two coves were shallow sand and allowed small fishing trawlers and triremes to be pulled onto the beaches for safety and shelter from the occasional storms.

The seas near Antioch were generally mild as the sea was fairly shallow; the coastline was the farthest from the rage of Charybdis where the docile Middle Sea met the anger of the Atlantic. The beaches were soft strands of warm sand, except where there had been volcanic action such as off the eastern coast of Cyprus: believed to be where the Minoan Empire had sunk beneath the Seas following an eruption on the bed of the Middle Sea.

Longinus entertained Maria with the legend of Atlantis that had been lost to a similar disaster but had sat much further to the west and in all likelihood had sunk at the same time as the Po burst its banks and the Mare Britannia was formed c 8000BC. Atlantis was often also referred to as the 'Western Isles' and in all probability it now lay beneath the Atlantic west of either Lusitania or Hibernia. Some of its legend suggested the ancient Empire was warm all year around and that therefore its climate was influenced by the Gulf Stream, which changed direction as a result of the same seismic disaster that caused the tsunami which destroyed Atlantis. This could place Atlantis at the mouth of the Charybdis but on the Atlantic side.

Maria was fascinated with the stories of the most ancient of civilisations and Longinus kept the girl quietly entertained with accounts of the art and architecture, culture, strange creatures and heroes of the lost cities of Atlantis, Crete and Minoa, as they rode through rough terrain under the heat of an unforgiving sun.

The fury of Charybdis had heavily influenced the kindly and sage knight's choice of land and sea route, sticking to the mild-mannered Middle and Balearicum Seas and crossing Hispania by land. The party could have sailed into Marsela but Iosephus felt that Hispania would offer fertile ground for Maria's simple faith. It had a tradition of both rebelliousness and producing leaders who would punch above their weight, whereas Gallia was still recovering from the defeats at Gergovia and Alesia, ninety years earlier. The faith of the Nazarene would need powerful supporters when they came to tackle Roma. For as Maria had so wisely observed, they might persuade the people in Roma to join them but 'What was Rome?'

Longinus stopped to consider Maria's question, unsure he could answer it but recognising that an answer was needed. Roma was a City influenced by a handful of powerful families whose institutions and people would defer to the desires or needs of the 'State of Rome' over the preferences of the people in Roma. On the few occasions when Roman leaders had tried to place the People of Roma before the State of Rome they had been ruthlessly exterminated as rebels: the Gracchi and Marius in his seventh consulship came to mind. The Senate was where the power-base lay in Roma or more accurately in the power held by the informal title of Princeps in the Senate, a title reserved to the head of a handful of families that had inter-married, amassed and inherited huge wealth and held half of the provinces of the Roman Empire. Those families (the Julii, Claudii and Antonii) were currently headed up by Tiberius.

For once, it was Iosephus pushing the company on. They had arrived in sight of the southern harbour at Antioch as night fell but the old man's ships were moored in the northernmost cove and he wanted them camped besides his ships ready to sail at dawn next day.

"One hour more is all I ask" he pleaded and they agreed but with Longinus and Perseus taking it in turns to bear Maria before them as the girl was already weaving in weariness at twelve solid hours in the saddle on uneven and treacherous ground in the heat of the desert and the cold of mountain tracks and valleys. She needed a warm bath then to sleep for a week but had not complained once, merely fallen off her horse twice without word or warning when too exhausted to continue. Fortunately she had landed in gorse and thorn bushes both times so had a relatively soft landing with only scratches as any indication of her falls.

Iosephus' private yacht was a long-draught flat-bottomed trireme with a large covered canvas cabin to the rear, a top and fore sail, both square but with the latter allowing some ability to tack. It was slim and made for speed with a crew of 184 oarsmen or diakonae, eighteen crew including helmsmen and riggers, six galley staff (cooks and cabin servants) and six mercenaries. Iosephus had freed his oarsmen and they rowed for good pay and fought for him also should they encounter pirates. The total ship's compliment, including the party (who had the freedom of the ship but would sleep in the comfort and privacy of the rear cabin) was 220 souls.

The two ships that were coming as escort were not as fast but had the advantage over the yacht of a larger draught and four banks of oars. Again these were manned by freedmen, in this case all mercenary soldiers, hoplites or former Roman Auxiliaries, armed with shield and short sword but half were also archers. Each ship carried an armed crew of three hundred and if any pirate encountered this little company they were in for an incredible surprise as pirate ships would typically boast at most a company of fifty fighting men. Even a fleet of pirates would struggle against eight hundred experienced marines. Iosephus was taking no chances with his charges but once again Maria wrong-footed them all.

"I want everyone to throw their weapons into the sea or I refuse to get on board" she said sleepily, her eyes barely open, just avoiding an enormous yawn then getting the hiccoughs and a fit of the giggles at her attempts to hold the yawn back.

"You should be asleep" growled Longinus whilst Iosephus refused point blank to order any such thing. For a start the men would refuse as these waters were dangerous.

"God will protect us. Trust in him" the girl replied then her head dropped forward and she was fast asleep in Longinus' arms. "Now what?" he muttered and Iosephus shook his head not knowing how to answer the girl.

"Perhaps we could disarm the ship Maria travels in? She won't see the other ships that close and what you don't see you cannot worry about" suggested Perseus and his Centurion had to laugh.

"That might work you know" and Iosephus perked up considerably. "We can suggest a compromise and that the weapons on my yacht are locked away in bankers' boxes with Maria holding the key. The other two ships can throw a few lumps of rusty metal into the sea far enough out of sight for Maria not to know the difference. I will see if my servants can find a scrap yard and buy up enough odds and ends to look like 600 weapons being dropped overboard."

It was Cerestile who interrupted her master's plans and stopped them in their tracks:

"Forgive me, domine, but why are we seeking to trick the girl? Surely she deserves better of us than this? If we think she is wrong then we must persuade her. If she is right then we must trust her. But all this effort because we will not talk to a young, lonely and frightened girl who has this wonderful and naïf faith and trust in God just seems cowardly and deceitful."

Iosephus' head rocked back and he laughed until tears streamed down his cheeks then turned to Cerestile and said: "Bless you. This is why I asked you and Annanias to join me for you are absolutely right and I needed your good sense to tell me I was about to get things very wrong indeed. I will talk to the girl in the morning and let us hope she is not stubborn."

Perseus then surprised and stunned them into silence: "Perhaps it is not that she is stubborn. She could be right you know."

Annanias had spread a large canvas awning from the rudder at the rear of the knight's yacht and pulled it taught across five oars rammed into the sand and acting as impromptu upright tent poles. He had then tied two oars to make a ridge and roped the whole structure up, securing it with guide ropes into the sand using marlinspikes as tent pegs until it was secure. Then he hung two tapestries as partitions to separate off the sleeping accommodation for Maria and Cerestile.

There was plenty of room and the warm sand made an ideal mattress whilst Longinus covered the sleeping girl in a silk rug and passed round bed rolls and blankets for the rest of the company. Soon five were asleep, Longinus and Perseus taking it in turns to sit at the entrance to the canvas tenting guarding against any night birds but in the knowledge that within the three ships were eight hundred men they could call on for aid.

"How are you going to protect eight hundred men?" The discussion over breakfast had rapidly disintegrated into a heated argument; well the three men sitting opposite one young girl were getting very heated but she was serenity itself.

"There is no need to get cross as you know that just makes me giggle!" Maria replied and Longinus nearly choked! Iosephus tried reasoning with her: "If we agree only to use the weapons if we are attacked and to store them away otherwise, how can that hurt your principles?"

"It is not **my** principle. We are commanded by God: 'Thou shalt not kill'"

"If we promise not to kill anyone and just to threaten them a bit; how about that for a plan?" Perseus joined the fray and then ignored his commander's muttered "What a hare-brained idea! How about we tie her to the mast and ignore her like Odysseus and the Sirens." Then he glared at Maria who had started to chuckle and that just made her laugh even more.

"Surely it is for the men to choose? You said you would not impose your beliefs on anyone. How about you ask the men?" At last Iosephus had found an argument Maria could not resist and so she grinned and agreed to address the men.

"Line them up then carry me out to meet them. It shall be their choice. We are all agreed?" and the three men nodded; they had won and were prepared to be gracious in their victory.

"Maria we will do our best to avoid any trouble so your concern at the use of weapons should never arise." Longinus reassured her and she just smiled.

They had argued for the best part of an hour, good sailing time lost and the crew were impatient to be on their way. This showed as they lined up to listen to their paymaster and the girl they were there to protect. Longinus held the crippled girl in his strong arms and Maria did not keep the crew waiting long:

"My brothers, thank you for offering me your protection. I am humbled and grateful. In return I offer you my protection. For our journey my prayers shall be constant that every one of us shall reach our destination safe and unharmed. I carry God within me and know that we shall be protected by he who controls the wind and the waves. I ask one favour in return: that you also pray. For if eight hundred prayers are heard rather than the quiet voice of one girl, surely God and his Angels will hear us?"

"Teach us how to pray" one of the marines shouted out and all showed their assent to the question.

"You must prepare and then speak the words you will find in your heart."

"How do we prepare?" another marine asked her.

"Cast aside all anger, violence or thought of war, terror and harm. Fill your hearts with love, peace and happiness. As you rejoice so your soul will fill your hearts and your minds with God's will" then Maria closed her eyes and the power of the Spirit filled her and began to spread out to those before her. There was no need for her to lay her hands upon them for the men were already receptive and wanting to have God's greatest gift. The Spirit found them eagerly, almost greedily.

No-one could remember who was the first but within moments Longinus and Iosephus looked on in astonishment and dismay then utter defeat as one after another the diakonae and mercenaries threw down their weapons and knelt in prayer.

"Now we are safe" said Maria turning her head towards her two friends with such a grin of mischief on her elfin face that Longinus came close to bursting a blood vessel or several in his pent up fury and nearly dropped the girl until suddenly he saw the funny side. Yet again the girl had done the unexpected: her faith was astounding and he had a sneaking feeling Perseus might have been right. She was not stubborn; she was being driven to do the right thing and teaching him a lesson in humility in the process. He remembered the question he had never been able to answer: '*you must want to be forgiven in order to be forgiven*'. So it was that finally he had the courage and humility to say:

"I want to be forgiven. Will you forgive me?"

"Yes with all my heart, soul and mind" she replied and stretched forwards out of his clasp to kiss him in gratitude for his act of contrition.

"So let me get this right. I am paying an extortionate price per day, 'top whack' I would have you know, for a bunch of mercenaries who are going to *pray* all the way from here to Hispania? Alright" and Iosephus turned to his helmsmen "you see another sail then you head off as fast as the winds and oars will take us in the opposite direction. God just might decide it's the pirates' turn to win for a change and I am taking no chances" and he strode off in a huff to load his kit onto the trireme.

"Best get you settled" said Longinus gently. "And for the record, I personally think that you and the Master can do anything you put your minds to. I am privileged to be in your company."

"Don't leave me" said Maria surprising him once more "I am lonely when you are not with me" and Longinus smiled for he had no intention of leaving the girl until her mission was accomplished and she was returned safely home. Then a random thought struck him: "Where or what is home for you? Do you have a family?"

Maria was thoughtful, a rare moment of reflection and then Longinus recognised that his question was giving her pain and the silence was her coming to terms with some ancient grief. He cursed himself for hurting her. Finally, she answered him, truthful as always despite the pain it clearly caused:

"I am an orphan. My parents got ill and I was too young, we were too poor to get help or medicines. I was an only child and had no knowledge of uncles or aunts. My parents had moved to Nazareth from Magdalo. I never knew why they had come. The Nazarene found me on the streets of the town. I had not yet come so low as to beg and was too young, just, to sell myself for men's pleasure but I was being used as a look out for a pick pocket and thief. It was my first hour on my first day and already I hated it and was ashamed of what I did. The Master saw me and I followed him without hesitation. The thief I worked with was caught the following day and lost both of his hands. I am a sinner therefore and so what has happened since is all the more glorious."

"Did the Master forgive you?"

"No" she replied smiling. "He offered to but I asked to **earn** my forgiveness and so he gave me this mission. We are all moulded by the choices we make but also by the things we ask God for. It would have been easy for me to have asked for the slate to be wiped clean but I think I owe God far more than that and am blessed by the joy of this mission, the adventure, the challenge. To think I could have missed all of this if I had asked for forgiveness. I definitely made the right choice and have no regrets even if it takes me a hundred years in this world and a thousand in the next to make amends for my sins still I made the right choice."

"Your choices are always surprising yet they are always right. I learn so much in your company you need never fear I shall leave you alone. But right now there is something important you must do for me."

"What is it?" she asked her eyebrows rising in gentle enquiry.

"I need you to rest. We shall be many days at sea and I want your feet and calves to be well on the mend by then. Your mission needs you to be able to walk and ride for we shall be covering many leagues when we reach land."

"Alright, I promise to rest. I shall pray and that will take my mind off the pain."

"Can you not heal yourself?"

"Oh no, that would not be right at all" and Longinus knew she was right yet being right seemed a far harder path than doing the selfish thing; and thus he learnt his second valuable lesson of the day.

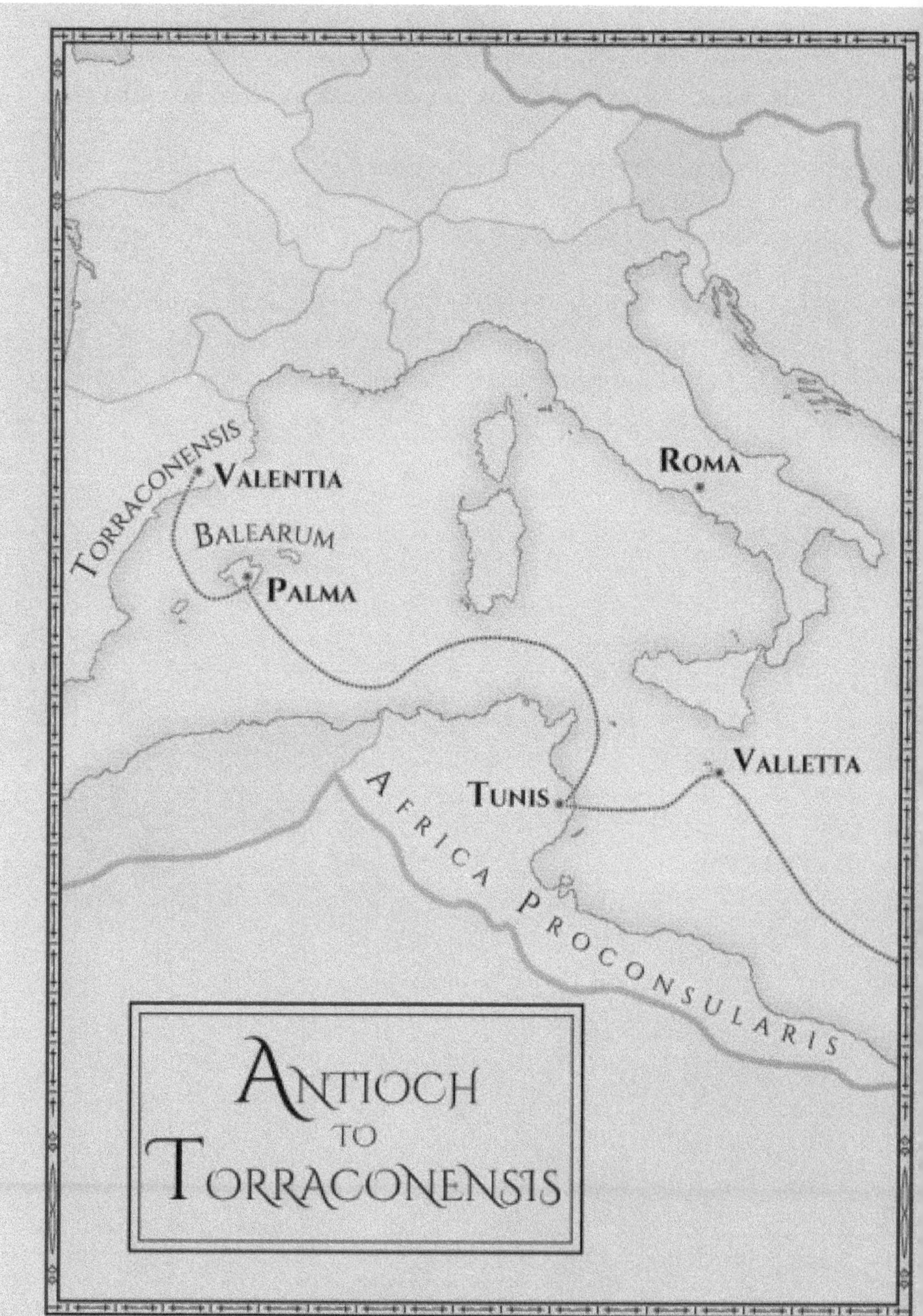
Torraconensis
Valentia
Balearum
Palma
Roma
Tunis
Valletta
Africa Proconsularis
Antioch
to
Torraconensis

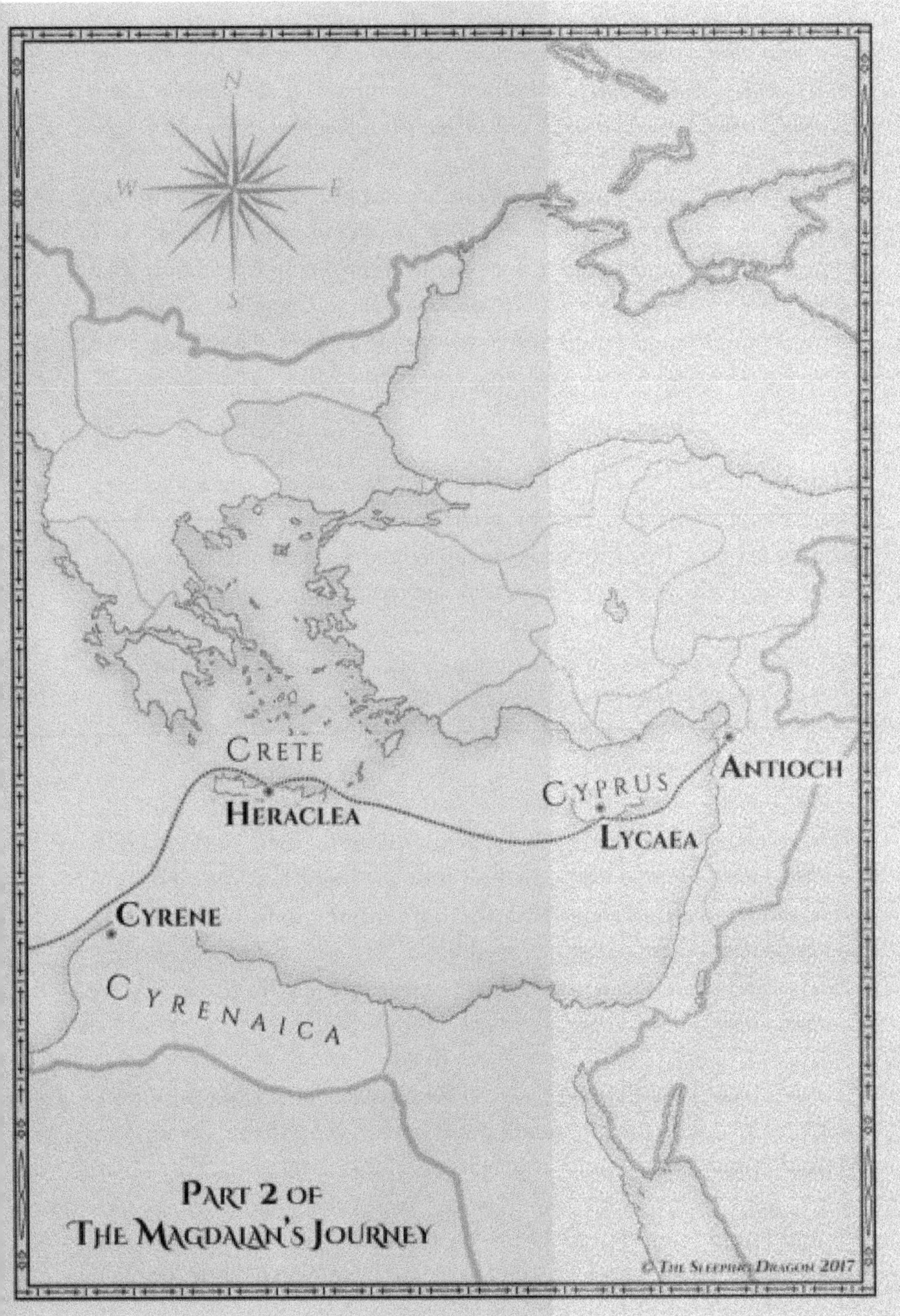
N
W
E
S
CRETE
HERACLEA
CYPRUS
LYCAEA
ANTIOCH
CYRENE
CYRENAICA
PART 2 OF
THE MAGDALAN'S JOURNEY

The other important historian to write of the missions to establish the early Christian Church was Nicodemus, writing in the 5th Century and drawing from Pilate (4th Century AD), Eusebius (3RD Century AD), the Gospel of Mary the Magdalan (2nd Century AD) and the Letters of Josephus (1st Century AD).

"The Magdalan sailed from Antioch to Cyprus, Crete and the south Isthmus of Greece, North Africa, the Balearic Islands and Torraconensis. She addressed both Jews and Gentiles at each, with many converting to Christianity as a result. Paul would later find Christian communities along the Adriatic in Greece and Maleta during his own mission, all of which had been established following Mary Magdalan preaching the word of God." (Nicodemus, 5th Century AD)

They set sail on the seventh hour in the morning on the Syrian Sea and were in sight of Cyprus by midday, going south around the long promontory past Rizorjapasso, Famagusta and Larnaca and then as the sun was directly over their heads they sighted their first stop at Limaea. Iosephus had considered stopping at Pathos but was fearful of the crowds and so had chosen the smaller fishing village. The sea had been as calm as any lake and green in the shallows but deep blue once they had left the coast of northern Syria behind them.

The girl slept: indeed her sleep was so deep that she slept through the ships mooring up and taking on fresh provisions for their journey. They cast off late afternoon and sailed on into the night heading west-nor-west under a moonlit night with the stars shining so brightly you felt you could hold them in your cupped hand. Still Maria slept, recovering the strength she had sacrificed during their journey from Amman to Hamah.

As dawn broke, Antalaea was just visible to their north from the crow's nest but Heraklion, their destination was beyond the horizon. Finally, the Magdalan woke.

"Where are we?" Maria asked in some confusion, sticking her head out from beneath the canvas of her cabin to see the helmsman holding the tiller on the poop deck above her. She looked to port and starboard and could only see sea in every direction.

"We are a day and a night from our destination of Heraklion, ma'am" the helmsman replied. "We will moor up and stay a day there, give our legs a chance to remember what land feels like. Then we have a difficult time going through the Greek Isles on the Aegean and Messenian seas. Winds are too changeable so we will use our oars and that takes time and energy. It is then three days with a reasonable wind to Valetta in Malita, two days to Tunis north of Thapsus in Tunisia near the ruins of Carthage and a further three days to Polenca in Mallorca. Then two days to Torrenco. Allowing for overnight stops in Valetta, Tunis and Polenca, we will take fifteen days from when we leave Heraklion to arrive in Hispania."

"That is much faster than had we gone by land."

"Indeed yes" the helmsman replied proud of his ship's speed "for we can do a steady fifteen nautical leagues each hour and sail continuously without the need for a break. The winds are favourable at this time of year and unless there is a storm then we should be able to catch a cyclone in the Middle Sea that will sweep us to Tunis and Polenca from Valetta at three hundred and fifty to four hundred leagues each day."

Maria gasped then looking around her asked: "Kind sir, do you know where the rest of my company have gone?"

"The Centurion and the legionary are at the prow being sick over the side as neither have much experience of the sea. The owner is talking to the captain of the crew down below. Can you manage steps?"

"Alas no, my legs are still too harmed to bear me. I can wait here in the shade and I thank you for your courtesy."

"Pray for me" the helmsman replied and that earned him a glowing smile of joy from the girl that raised the spirit within him to rejoice at the task he had been given. Maria went back to her prayers and in no time the gentle movement of the ship had sent her into a deep sleep once more.

She did not wake again until she heard the noise on deck of the crew preparing to moor up. It was dawn of the following day and they had arrived at Heraklion a few hours early. Two stone pillars denoted the entrance to a huge sea harbour designed to take merchant and war galleys of all sizes with the quays for over fifty ships to dock at once. Derricks, cranes and cross beams with pulleys could be seen on one side with the warehouses and silos for storing goods and provisions behind, whilst private and non-commercial mooring was on the other side of an enormous sea wall.

Although Iosephus intended to re-provision here, he preferred to purchase goods from the markets inland as the prices were often better than he could get from the sellers who had won the contracts to monopolise the sale of goods in the ports (which whilst often duty free also tended to have a huge mark up) plus he preferred to use the tackle on his ships and his own crew as stevedores as he had had some poor experiences of using both the equipment and the portering staff in other ports.

The port was on the north-western edge of the City and had been built with a huge buttress of stone to protect the northern approach, the harbour entrance being from the east with storms usually rising from the west. The harbour walls were vaguely lambda shaped. This was a busy harbour with trade to and from Athens and Corinth, the Adriatic coast line of Italy, Sicilia, Sardinia, Marsela, Cyprus, Malita, Aegyptia and Syria, Iordan and Iudaea, through the Dardanelles and Byzantion to Media, Mesopotamia and southern Russia, and northern Africa through Tunis and Thapsus.

As soon as they docked a customs official jumped aboard and asked for their papers. He glanced briefly at the manifest but was more interested in the travel documents and especially to see Pilate's seal on them.

"An important mission?" He asked Longinus but the young man shook his head then told him the truth: "Pilate wants us back fast so prepared the documentation to expedite things."

The man nodded in understanding then asked: "I can see only some of you. Where is the girl referred to in the papers?"

"Follow me" Longinus replied affably. "She had a fall on deck and is resting to allow her injuries to heal" then he took the clerk to where Maria could be seen sitting and chatting with the helmsman. One look and the clerk was satisfied: a simple country girl and he could see from how she was seated that she carried some form of injury.

"Best have those legs seen to by a physician. They are not healing straight" he said solicitously then returned the travel documents to Longinus saluted the Centurion and said: "Welcome to Heraklion" before jumping back down onto the wooden planking of the quayside.

Seeing Longinus, Maria waved the young man over then asked him: "Am I allowed ashore?"

"No" the Centurion replied without pause and without any threat of contradiction. "Crete is part of Paulus' ministry. Your job is to get better for when we reach Hispania. Until then you stay on this ship."

Then he went in search of Iosephus: they needed a good surgeon or physician to look at the girl's legs and he had been remiss in not doing so earlier. She had been tortured over a week before and heaven knows the infection that could have got into her wounds or the distortion in broken bones that had not been splinted. She had even ridden with those injuries and must have been in terrible pain. Once Longinus had shared his thoughts with the kindly old man Iosephus was mortified: "Fine protection we are proving to be. Leave this with me and I will find the best healer in Heraklion."

That evening the knight returned with a man even older and more wizened than he but who exuded charm and compassion. He took one look at

Maria and smiling said: "I bet you are a real handful but I can see you are a very special person too. May I look at your legs and feet?"

Recognising a kindred spirit, Maria was shy for the first time since Longinus had known her. She was also agreeable to any and everything the kindly doctor asked. His examination did not take long. He gave the girl an avuncular kiss on the cheek and a gentle pat on the head that brought tears to her eyes as she imagined him as the father she had lost and could not remember.

Then the doctor took Longinus to one side and suddenly he was very serious. "I am afraid there is no question but that infection has got into both the burns she received and the broken bones. She must have both legs removed from just below the knee and we must hope the infection has not spread further. She will be crippled alas for the rest of her life but unless I operate within the next day she will not have a life beyond this Sabbath. I would not plan to leave this port until we are certain there is no further infection."

"Can you repeat what you have said to her other guardian? I am afraid the shock of what you have just told me will see me break down in tears if I am asked to tell anyone else."

"Of course" and Longinus sent for Iosephus and Perseus then held onto the rigging in despair as the doctor told them both the terrible news being as clinically neutral as possible. 'How could God do this?' Longinus asked himself, a burning rage inside him as much guilt that they had not seen to the girl's injuries before this as dismay that their mission should end in this way.

"You need time to take this all in" the kindly doctor advised them. "I will come again tomorrow morning and be ready to do the operation then. I would strongly recommend no further delay. In the meantime I will clean up her wounds as best I can and that will remove some of her pain."

"Is there anything we can do?" Iosephus asked almost pleading for some scrap of comfort.

"A miracle might help" and then the physician was gone, striding across the deck and down the gangplank, leaving a desert in the souls of all three men until Perseus said in all innocence: "Can we do miracles? I have never tried but perhaps we should?"

Longinus looked at his legionary in exasperation then slowly he saw the light of hope: the moment of his mind's release from the darkness of its captivity. "Do you think you could do miracles?" he asked Perseus direct.

"Not I! But I think God wants us to learn a lesson here."

"Go on" Longinus encouraged him whilst Iosephus remained confused still.

"We are each Instruments of God. Maria told us that. But only if we have faith."

"How do we suddenly get that amount of faith?" the old knight grumbled. "I am too set in my ways. You, Longinus, have too many fears and suspicions ..."

"... which leaves you, Perseus. Do you believe you can heal Maria?"

"I want to very much but I have no talents, no special gift."

"Could you use my Spear?" And at his words suddenly the light of hope lit in Perseus' eyes and his face was made beautifully fair.

"I could heal her with the Spear" the young man said without fear or hesitation. "It will give me the talent that I lack. It is special and I am steadfast. Together we can become the Instrument needed to heal the girl."

At last Iosephus understood. "You both believe that the artefacts we carry are not instruments in themselves but rather they give us the faith we need so that we become Instruments of God."

"Yes" Longinus replied "but Perseus is right too. It is a merger: a mixture of artefact and someone open to faith which ingredients together become a new compound in the sight of God."

Then turning to Perseus he said: "I will fetch the Spear but it is my belief that it is yours to keep and not mine. Use it wisely" at which the young man's face fell in despair as he admitted reluctantly but truthfully and humbly as always:

"Alas I am not wise."

Iosephus shook his head at that: "Today, you have outshone me in wisdom who is considered one of the wisest men at the University of Alexandria. You are wise when it matters!"

Longinus returned holding the Spear reverently then the three men returned to where Maria was sleeping, the pain of having her wounds cleansed had sent her into a faint and from there into a deep sleep. "It is for the best" whispered Longinus. "I am in no doubt the girl would say she 'was not worthy' to be the subject of a miracle but this is about us learning a lesson in faith as much as Maria being healed."

"What should I do?" asked a nervous Perseus.

"Pray for God's help, take the Spear and place it across Maria's legs and feet then put your trust in God."

Perseus did not hesitate. Once he had committed himself, he was fully determined to go through with this. He knelt in prayer and never had he looked so lovely as when blessed with the beatific beauty of his communion with God. Both of the men watching were astonished for neither had appreciated before the pure spirit that resided in their companion. They had taken him for granted, believed him to be of little account and yet his faith shone so brightly when in prayer that they were dazzled.

Then he took the Spear and almost it sung to him, an Angelic choir echoing just beyond their full reckoning on the very edge of perception, burning gold as it had once before. Longinus and Iosephus felt that they were the privileged audience to an act of grace that was beyond their understanding, little people in the presence of Titans, mice standing before the ferocious might of lions, spectators watching the union of mighty monarchs.

As the Spear touched the girl, a golden thread weaved in a spiral around her legs and sank beneath the skin. Her legs shivered and shimmered then turned gold, reflecting the colour of the Spear. The healing was instantaneous as it had been with the paralysed plasterer. One moment Maria was asleep with the pain of her breaks, burns and infection, the next the burns were healed, the bones made whole and were no longer crooked and the sickly sweet smell of her infection had been replaced with the pungent fair scent of rose petals.

Her eyes sprang open and her first words were "I rejoice in my saviour who has healed me."

Then she looked to where Perseus was standing unable to take his eyes off the Spear and afraid of the act of healing he had just witnessed: he was fearful of this gift he had been granted for he was too self-deprecating to believe he could do such things. Maria understood immediately the self-doubt he felt for she had been to that dark place once also and her words restored his faith and rescued him from the doubts he had begun to experience:

"Dear heart, I thank you for your faith. Your faith has healed me and I shall love you all the days of my life for this gift of thine. I would be honoured if you would pray with me." Then together they prayed, rejoicing in song one moment; in silent communion the next in joyful company with each other and the Angels.

From that day to this, the story of the Spear will always be associated with the name of Perseus (Peridor, Sir Percy or Parsifal).

The physician came next morning but by then Maria had already been to the Forum in Heraklion and proclaimed the Good News to a crowd approaching forty thousand including merchants who would take word of her simple faith to the Black Sea, North Africa and Western Europa. The small community in Marsela (Maria later discovered) was founded by a Genoan merchant in Heraklion who heard the Magdalan proclaim the news of the Nazarene: "For my Master loves me, he has risen from the dead and embraced me; he has rescued me from captivity, and healed me when I was lame. He is the Messiah of that I have no doubt."

Then Maria had led all present in the 'breaking of the bread' and by some miracle everyone present was able to take the bread and drink the wine; there was enough for all.

"Do this in memory of me" she whispered into the absolute silence of the gathered thousands and they all shouted "Amen." Each one of them would return to their families in their home communities and break the bread in memory of the Eucharistic feast in Heraklion, remembering as they did so the sacrifice (anamnesis) of the carpenter's son from Nazareth.

The physician looked at the girl's legs and feet then shut his bag theatrically and with a laugh in genuine relief said: "I will not be needing this then! How you have been healed is a miracle but there is no doubt that you are healed. I wish I could take the credit but this is God's work and not mine."

Maria took his hand and held it to her lips then still holding it in her lap for her comfort softly said: "You saved my life. Had you not diagnosed my harm when you did then I would have descended into a coma never to have recovered. Take the credit that is due: for you share this miracle with God in equal measure."

"Bless you my child" and then he was gone to go to heal others but always mindful that sometimes not everything could be healed by his surgeon's skill or his bag of herbs and medicines. From that day, prayer also had its place in his almanac: if prayer was the only answer, he would never be reluctant again to seek or suggest a miracle. If just one patient lived who would otherwise have died because he paused to say a prayer then that was worth the effort in his mind.

In the end, they stayed two additional days in Heraklion not because of the need to care for Maria but because the whole island was receptive to her simple message, the breaking of the bread, her acts of healing and her gift of tongues. Merchants from across the world stayed over to hear her preach and the port was soon bursting at the seams. When she announced she was leaving nearly one hundred thousand came to her final Eucharistic feast and all sought baptism in the spirit. She prayed for some means of offering them the gifts without the laying on of hands for there were too many to do so and the Angels came to her in her dreams:

"The Eucharist is ultimately the cornerstone of the new covenant with God not baptism or the laying on of hands for it is new and it is universal. Receive the Eucharist and the gifts of God's Spirit will come to those who have faith. Each time you break the bread you are reborn."

"Thank you, thank you, thank you" she whispered in relief at the elegance and simplicity of their answer and wondered why she had not seen this. Her sermon on the last day was almost entirely about the Eucharist, therefore:

"When we receive the Eucharist it is another example of the Trinity that is at the heart of all of God's creation. We believe in one God who is Father, Son and Spirit, who rose from the dead after three days. We believe that we, mankind, have the unique ability to create souls through the union of man, woman and God. Then, at the moment we receive his body and blood, the God in the bread or wine recognises the God in he or she who leads us in the breaking of the bread, and the God in every one of us.

'The Eucharist' as we call this wonderful moment is not only God's gift to us by which we remember him but also it renews us: each time we shall break the bread we open our souls to the gifts of the Spirit and we are reborn.

We are all encouraged to break the bread: for Iesus told the disciples that when two or more are gathered together then he will join us in the breaking of the bread. Go and do likewise and remember the Nazarene as you do this.

You do not need to be priests or disciples. You do not need me to show you anymore. Already many of you are breaking the bread in the comfort of your homes in the company of your families. This is truly wonderful. You do not need my permission to do this. All of you can do the same. The words are simple for a good reason; to be copied. The actions are those you would do when offering up any meal to God. The important part is that you remember God as you do this and you open your hearts and minds to receive God's Spirit. If you have faith then My Master will come.

I leave you with God's new commandments:

Love God and Love Each Other.

Keep Faith and Hope that one day God's gift of the Spirit will flood into you as it has in me, undeserving as I am. Yet all are deserving in God's eyes.

Amen."

Having never intended to get off the yacht at Heraklion, news of the Magdalan's sermons there spread across the world and the company began to get invites from communities who had heard Maria's inspiring words but were now encountering questions on detail or were trying to fill in gaps in their understanding and being caught up in the wrong sort of detail. Paulus would encounter some of the communities formed in Greece on the back of the Sermon at Heraklion and was able to set rules that ensured consistency across the rapidly expanding early Christian Church. Maria took a different approach and encouraged communities to seek their own answer in prayer and in their hearts: "For I am no more privy to God's knowledge than anyone who has an open mind, a loving heart, a pure soul and who prays."

Without intending to do so, both Paulus and the Madgalan now found themselves in conflict over their visions for their faith. Not the important parts (or so Maria thought) but the sort of detail that Paulus as a lawyer regarded as important and Maria as a young girl who struggled with words or complex ideas found irrelevant.

Maria's response was to be more disciplined about where she preached and to avoid going onto Paulus' patch in future. Paulus' response was to promote the female deacons and overseers he encountered and appointed in the east and to reinterate the equality of men and women in leading the faithful as teachers of Christianity.

Alas over the next eight decades slowly but surely the early Church fathers would wipe out all references to the important role that Maria and other key women had played in the establishment of the early Christian Church; in particular they played down the important part played by the four Marias, Martha and Petronella as well as two of the first four deacons. They discouraged the appointment of female priests and restricted the breaking of the bread to an exclusively male priesthood.

A rift was beginning to appear, therefore, between those who followed the Magdalan and were guided by the Spirit and those who would follow 'Pauline' theodicy and looked towards the hierarchy of a priesthood 'like Melchisedech of old'.

The company left Heraklion and headed for the Corinthian Straits. Rowing carefully through the southern Greek Isles on the Ionian and Aegean seas was stressful for everyone. It was hot work down in the guts of the ship, the oarsmen were soon tired and the crew and passengers bored at the constant sight of bleached rocks and not a lot else in this lifeless, uninhabited and deserted stretch of the Middle Sea. Maria decided to seek out Decius the helmsman and ask him why they had not headed out into the more open Aegyptian and Libyan seas.

"The winds and currents are all wrong had we gone south of the Greek Isles. This way two days of hard slog and then we pop out into a current that will sweep us straight into the harbour of Valetta. But you can see why Sparta produced terrifying warriors and not a lot else!" and he pointed north to the barren desert lands of the former Greek kingdom, made famous when its King Leonidas had held the straits of Thermopylae against the Might of Persia.

Decius had explained all of this to Maria who had been curious at the choice of route. He was a former legionary who had been promoted to be in charge of his cohort and then retired after fifteen years service to work freelance as a mercenary and paid crew. He bemoaned his quiet life:

"Our boss is kind and wants us more for show than to actually *do* anything. I have not seen a single bit of action in the three years I have worked for him, begging your pardon, miss, as I knows you don't like that sort of thing."

"I am surprised, given how hard this stretch of the Middle Sea is to navigate, that Heraklion does so well as a port." Maria observed then grinned as she realised she had sub consciously ducked discussing Decius' new and 'quiet' life. The older man had deep reserves of patience, needed to helm any ship with a crew of over two hundred, and enjoyed talking to the girl as she was always so positive and interested in all that the experienced helmsman did, if totally barking mad in his opinion. He also knew this coastline intimately and had a map of the Islands permanently stored in his memory so had no difficulty answering her questions.

"That is easy. Heraklion is less than a day from Athena, two days from Cyprus and three days onto the Black Sea. Almost everything going to Athena or Corinth from Iudaea, Aegyptia, Media, Syria, Persia or Parthia will drop off at Heraklion and let the local fleet do the last tricky bit around the Isthmus to Athena."

On the second day, Maria took to reading and singing to the oarsmen who were hot and close to exhaustion, rowing thirty minutes on and thirty minutes off in every hour. The girl's gentle singing voice and softly spoken reading voice helped them relax and she also reminded many of a daughter or younger sister left behind in Syria, Iordan, Iudaea and Aegypt from which provinces they had been recruited.

Maria tried to raise their strength and restore their stamina through her prayers but soon discovered that it was her talent for singing and playing music that most inspired them. Someone found an old lyre battered but not unbowed and after thirty minutes she had restrung and tuned it and began to play the shepherds' songs of her youth and King David's settings of the psalms.

The oarsmen were renewed in spirit and rowed harder for her entertaining them in this way. The yacht was a trireme and so technically had only three quarters of the oar power of its two sister ships but it was lighter weight, designed for speed and with the inspiration of the Magdalan it began to draw away from the other two ships.

Needless to say that sparked off the competitiveness of the other two crews and soon the three vessels were in a race, the tempo increasing, down-time reducing to fifteen minutes in the hour then ten then five. The ships were now doing more than twice their earlier speed and after three hours they burst out of the channel they had been in and waved goodbye to Kallithea and Argos to their north, whilst before them was Sicilia and the port of Syracusea (but they would avoid any part of Italia until they were ready to take on Rome). Instead just south of Sicilia was Malita, their next destination.

A north easterly wind took hold of their sails almost immediately whilst there was a powerful current sucking them south of Sicilia. In five minutes their speed had lifted to just under thirty knots. At this rate they would cover over seven hundred and fifty leagues in a day and reach Valetta by mid morning the following day.

Iosephus finally caught up with Maria who had climbed up the rigging to sit in the crow's nest. Longinus had gone green with worry and was back to his spot on the prow where he could retch into the sea without the spray from his vomit flying back to land on the banks of oarsmen now getting a well-earned rest. Iosephus had no intention of joining the girl in her lofty perch but rather he stood at the base of the mast and shouted:

"At this speed we could just carry on to the Punic Sea and Tunis. We would be there in three days and it would save us having to land at Valetta. You would have to stay on board if we docked at Valetta as Malita is part of Paulus' planned mission. What do you think?"

"Tunis" she shouted back then stood on the narrow rails of the crow's nest and flung her arms out wide shouting: "This is how I imagine flying must feel like."

"Come down right now" roared the knight so incensed his face had gone bright purple in anger. Maria sniffed then swung down beneath the crow's nest until she could wrap her feet around the mast and slid all the way down using it like a giant pole. "Why are you cross?" she asked innocently as her feet touched the safety of the deck.

"Have you seen the state Longinus is in? Do you care that your antics are making your friends ill?" At which her head went down in shame and she replied contritely:

"I did not know but I do now. I will not do anything like that again. Why were they scared?"

"All it takes is a single sudden lurch of the boat, a freak wave or gust of wind and you would have been flung to the deck and slain instantly."

"Forgive me, my friend but who controls the wind and the waves?"

"I know that God does but do not be arrogant. Do not test God's powers by endangering yourself unnecessarily. Remember the temptation of Iesus in the desert when the devil sought to see him fling himself from the cliff tops to be saved by Angels. God might throw you to the winds to teach you a final lesson in humility."

"I am rightly chastised. I shall sit in the cabin and not move from there until we reach Tunis."

"I had better warn Decius then as he will get a real ear-bashing with you sitting under his nose for three days!"

"Does he mind?" the girl asked suddenly worried that she had distracted or upset the helmsman and Iosephus laughed. "I am only teasing you, my dear. All of the crew enjoy talking to you and every one of them is frightened when you do something that is reckless."

"I promise to be good" she answered truly penitent and Iosephus sighed in relief.

The three days at sea passed quickly for Maria as the oarsmen took it in turns to chat to her in her cabin, realising that her stunt in the crow's nest had been born out of boredom. Instead they told her stories of incredible monsters they had seen at sea and she spoke of the parables, the prophecies and the miracles of her Master. They had many favourite stories that they would ask her to tell again and again: the good Samarhiyan, the son that was prodigal with his inheritance, the steward who buried his master's money, the rich man who could not give his money away, the poor lady who gave her last penny to the poor, the feeding of five thousand, the wedding where water was made into rich wine.

Next they asked about Iesus' ministry: his baptism by John, the meeting with Elijah on the mountain, the sermon on the Mount, his fast in the desert and his temptation, his procession into Ierusalem, the riot in the Temple, the Passover meal and the breaking of bread, his arrest in Gethsemane, his trial, crucifixion, death and burial; the day he rose; his ministry when reborn and his ascension. Finally, the coming of his Spirit: The Comforter.

Then they asked about his miracles of healing: the blind made to see, those brought back to life, the crippled that could now walk and the lepers who were cured.

When they finally landed in Hispania, there were eight hundred diakonae or deacons all experts in the life and the teachings of Iesus: they became the foundation of the Church in the west born through the enthusiasm of the men hired by Iosephus to offer protection to the Magdalan but who threw away their weapons in order to pray with her and to be ready to receive the gifts of the Spirit.

Tunis was the largest port that they had visited thus far. It was a deep water port built in stone and had been used by Rome ever since their destruction of Carthage at the end of the third Punic War. The whole City was designed as a grid with the municipal buildings you would find in any romance City: the amphitheatre and circus, Forum and Curia, Governor's residence and Courts, Baths and Praetorium, to which had been added a dry and wet dock, warehousing, the administrative building for the port authority, and three deep draught harbours. Tunis could take a hundred ships within its harbours with ease and then had long sandy beaches to the north where triremes could be pulled up to lie in safe haven from the tides and most storms.

Iosephus had hired private mooring in the port for all three ships, his quad rimes having a relatively deep draught and being totally unsuitable for the sandy beaches whilst Iosephus did not want the additional half a leagues walk necessitated by mooring up on the beaches so had hired a spot for his yacht right by the harbour master's gate to the City. It had cost a fair denarii and a bribe on top but there was no point having money if you did not use it and at the time, Maria had been unable to walk so being close to the City entrance had seemed sensible. Longinus laughed as they drew up, having a shrewd idea of how much the knight must have paid for this prime spot.

"How many days have we?"

"I booked us in for the week but suggest we leave the evening of day three or the morning of day four" the equites replied and Longinus shrugged his shoulders then said: "It will not be up to us. Let us see what sort of reception Maria gets from the citizens here. Many are from Roma so it will give us our first indication of whether we can influence the Roman establishment as well as its people."

But first, Iosephus had arranged for them to stay with a wealthy banker from Alexandria, who had agreed to let Iosephus use his house then subsequently arranged to do some business in Tunis so that he could meet Maria. Longinus, Perseus, Iosephus and Decius were talking this through. Decius had tagged along as he wanted to know the route from here and also if they intended to stay for any time or set sail as soon as possible.

Iosephus spoke of his friend and colleague: "I have known Hanafa since childhood and we both lived on the same street in Alexandria. He is a very old friend and a respected member of the Jewish community both here and in Cyrene. He is also open-minded and prepared to make no judgement until he has met us. He has invited us all to share a meal with him tonight. In particular, he wants to meet Maria as he has heard a lot about her. Not all good I am afraid as already the Sanhedrin is seeking to attack her reputation."

"What could they possibly accuse the girl of having done?" asked Longinus in shock.

"They accuse her of adultery for no better reason than that she is a young girl on her own." Decius broke the stunned silence that followed Iosephus' news to say in anger and outrage: "The poor girl must never know" and all four men agreed.

Hanafa's house sat on the sanded banks of a secluded cove with piers into a calm green sea and palm trees offering shade on the beach. They came in a small skiff, steered by the muscular Decius, Maria so excited that she held Decius' arm the whole journey. Hanafa was waiting for them by the sea, his wife and three daughters around him, the youngest of whom was Maria's age, the eldest just married and had brought her husband, who was busy supervising the servants as they laid out the meal on a long table beneath a silk pavilion in blues and creams that had been set out on the beach.

The house behind the family was whitewashed stone with a front terrace, central courtyard and atrium and four tall minarets: circular towers that each held a guest bedroom and sitting room with a semi-circular balcony giving on to sea views.

"Iosephus, welcome to my house" said Hanafa affably and the two men embraced. Then having made their introductions, Hanafa's wife, Anees, showed the four men and Maria to their chambers. "Iosephus! You are in the guest room in the main house, the rest get a Tower Room each" Hanafa shouted over the noise as his daughters were all talking at once and then the girls grabbed Maria by the hand and took her off to have a good gossip.

"Peace at last!" muttered Hanafa but with a twinkle in his eye and then he dodged Anees as she went to swat him with her apron. Hanafa invited the men to sit down whilst his wife and son in law continued to serve food onto the table and started to light the candles in lanterns hanging from the poles of the pavilion.

"It is for the best" said Hanafa. "I can ask you questions without offending the girl. But I will start by saying that the accusations of adultery are clearly absurd. The girl is no more than a child." And the four men sat back in relief but then Hanafa continued: "But is what she says true? Children live in a world of imagination. Can we be certain that she has not invented her story of seeing the Nazarene alive?"

"Hers was not the only sighting of the Nazarene alive. Hundreds of people saw him." Iosephus argued but Hanafa was persistent: "Maria was the first. Others may have followed her lead and many who saw 'the risen Messiah' may not have seen him before so he could easily have been an imposter."

Longinus could not contain himself any longer and red in the face he gave witness to what he had seen on Golgotha and in Jerusalem: "I was in charge of the cohorts detailed to oversee Iesus' execution, I thrust my Spear into his side then saw him buried. Days later, I saw him alive and he spoke to me. I did not follow anyone's lead. But I suggest you meet Maria."

"Why?" asked Hanafa, "A young girl with a delusion. How will that change anything?" and then he held up his hand as Longinus had leapt out of his chair. "Forgive me my friend. I can see you believe this girl. Very well! I will see her" and he sent his son in law to fetch Maria. She came down and straightaway went up to Hanafa and kissed him saying impulsively: "My bedroom is the nicest I have ever been in and has wonderful views of sea, forest and mountains. Thank you for this magnificent and generous gift."

"Ha! You are just saying that to get onto my good side" the old man said laughing yet they could see he was touched by her words.

"Oh, no. I always tell the truth" Maria replied innocently and Hanafa blinked then looked more closely at the girl before asking her: "Tell me about Iesus of Nazareth."

Maria took a deep breath then sat on the floor in the corner of the gazebo, opposite where Hanafa was seated whilst the rest of the men swung round in their chairs to listen to her:

"I have been told things about his birth and childhood but it is best that others tell you what they saw. I first met Iesus three years ago when I was just thirteen. I followed him without question."

He would do such wonderful things: he healed people; he told us how to live our lives; he made us happy; one day he walked across the water; another he fed five thousand people from five loaves and two fish. He told wonderful stories in which the people seemed real and did real things but his life was just as wonderful.

Then he came to Ierusalem and the people proclaimed him King. But they took him, they lashed him and mocked him; they made him carry a heavy cross and they crucified him. We buried him with tears. That was the worst day of my life, worse even than when my parents died.

So when I saw him alive I did not believe it at first. Then he held me in his arms and I wept and laughed and realised how stupid I had been. You see he had told us he was going to die and that he would rise from the dead and we had not understood. Then he went again, this time into the clouds and once more I wept. It took an Angel to tell me I had it wrong and that Iesus would always be with me. Then the Comforter came and I was filled with the Spirit of God and granted the gift of healing. Now I can feel Iesus is always with me to help me show others the way to Eternal Life."

She had spoken in a hushed and breathless voice, but with a gleam of excitement in her eyes, and when she spoke of the moment she had held Iesus in her arms, they could see her heart pounding at the joy of that memory. As always, what came across was her sincerity. Hanafa had watched the girl carefully and as he did so the other men could see his resistance being beaten down not by the force of her argument or by the strength of her evidence but rather by the clarity of her conviction and the transparency of her honesty. Her eyes and face shouted: 'This is Truth' and yet her delivery lacked confidence and her demeanour was bashful and reticent.

Then Hanafa's daughters joined them, dancing around the table, giving their father a hug before Rachel, the eldest, said:

"You men are all looking too serious. And father, you are not to bully Maria. We have all decided that she is very special."

Hanafa blinked then laughed before showing due penitence: "I do agree. Maria is very special" then turning to Iosephus he continued: "There are people I must see tomorrow morning but after that I would like to take Maria to meet the Council of Elders in the City. Although the Jewish community is small, we are very influential and we can ensure that Maria is seen and heard. Whether she shall be believed is another matter. But I believe her" at which Maria stood, walked to the table and knelt at the old man's feet saying:

"I honour you, father" after which she was silent for the rest of the evening until Longinus asked if she were tired.

"No. Did I yawn?" she said apologetically and everyone laughed at her embarrassment before Longinus put her out of her misery as he told her why they were all worried: "You have said hardly a word all evening!"

"I was remembering the day I met the Master."

Hanafa's son in law was called Ioshua and was a port official at Tunis, working directly to the Praetor and City Prefect. A young man, proud of his work, supportive of the Roman administration that had appointed him, he now took the opportunity to challenge his father in law's guests: "Why are you come to Tunis? We are not looking for a Messiah. We are certainly not looking to take our lead from a sixteen year old girl. You should leave."

Hanafa went to stand in anger but stopped as Maria rested her head in his lap to gain his attention then as he looked down she shook her head before standing and turning in one fluid motion to meet Ioshua's challenge: "I am not a leader and Iesus was more than the Messiah. We have come to Tunis to tell all of its citizens about his vision for how we can live our lives and about his gift of life after death. We do not seek to change your politics or administration or trade but we ask that there also be a place here for faith, hope, love and charity."

"What makes you think these need a place and that we do not already know everything we need to know about 'faith, hope, love and charity'?"

"I do not know" admitted Maria humbly. "Sometimes I come to a village or town or even a great City and am greeted by a handful who wish to hear me and yet the next day, just a few miles further on I might be greeted by thousands. I offer people the chance to hear about the Master. I do not presume they need to know about him but nor do I deny them the chance to hear of him if they want to."

"So there are places you have been to where you have not been made welcome? Where you have failed?"

"I may have failed everywhere. I am not the Master and know that I am inadequate to the task I have been given. But if even just one person listens to my account of the Master then that is also a success."

"You call one person a success?" and now Ioshua was incredulous. Maria turned towards Hanafa:

"Good sir, forgive me. It is wrong for a guest to argue with the son of the host or for me to monopolise the conversation. Ioshua and I can continue our discussion elsewhere if you all wish."

"No" interrupted Anees and Hanafa's daughters, Rachel, Rebecca and Raphael in unison. "Maria, we want to hear you" Rachel explained and Hanafa shrugged whilst gesturing to Ioshua to wrap up the discussion.

"Very well" continued Maria. "My Master once said that there is rejoicing in heaven if one sinner is saved. For that one person who listens if it means they gain eternal life then 'Yes' it is a success. Of course I want more than one person to attend but I would welcome one person as dearly as one hundred."

"You would not last one day working for me with such low ambitions!"

Maria nodded her head: "I am not clever and so do agree with you. The job you do would defeat me."

"Why should anyone listen to you?"

"They do not come to listen to me. They come to learn about the Master, his life and death, his parables and miracles."

"Tell us one of his parables please" said Raphael and there were nods around the table so for the next hour Maria told them some of her favourite stories as originally told by the Master. She started as always with the story of the good man from Samarhiya then she told them of Iesus' birth and childhood then she spoke of the start of his ministry and finally she finished with her eye witness account of his death, resurrection and ascension. They sat spellbound, even Ioshua was a willing listener.

Maria closed her eyes and there was the Master smiling at her, reminding her of all she had seen so vividly she could speak of his life with clarity, awe, love and affection. For he had entered the vast chamber of her heart and taken permanent residence there, never to be forgotten, eternally loved by this simple but generous-spirited soul. The rest could hear the love, the anguish and the final rejoicing in her joyous tale and in the timbre of her voice.

It was Anees who finally brought the stories to an end saying: "Child, you have not eaten. Eat! We are blessed by your company but I will not have it said of my household that we starve our guests. You are so thin I suspect you never eat but here you must do so or we shall be insulted."

Maria blushed and mouthed 'Sorry' at which Anees laughed then chided her: "I am teasing you. But even so, you must eat."

Meanwhile, Hanafa had taken Iosephus to one side and asked him as a friend: "Do you believe this girl?"

"You forget, I also saw Iesus dead then buried then alive again. But had I not, still I would trust and believe Maria. She speaks of things that are beyond explanation but clearly they are truth."

"Is she mad perhaps?"

Iosephus gave that question very careful consideration but before he could answer, Ioshua was standing and proposing a toast: "I wish to toast Maria" at which the girl blushed, Raphael and Rebecca booed and Rachel glared at her husband. "Listen please. Listen" he said taking their less than enthusiastic reaction in good part. "I just wanted to say to Maria I can guarantee you will have at least one person listening to you tomorrow … and that will be me!" at which he sat down to stunned silence and then Rachel leant into him and squeezed his arm affectionately.

"Perhaps it is I who am mad, my friend?" said Hanafa "But I do believe my son in law just apologised for the first time in his life!"

The girls went down to play in the sea under the stars. The water was still warm, the sand still hot under foot, enough to keep at bay the sudden chill in the air as the sun dipped beneath the far horizon, dropping behind the mountains behind them and leaving the moon to shine in its silver glory, lighting up their pavilion, turning its cream silk to gleaming gold. The men lit the wood burning braziers to throw warmth and light onto the sands then lay down to watch the horse play of the girls. Eventually, Hanafa turned to Longinus and asked:

"Did you really see this Nazarene alive?"

"Yes" answered the Centurion. "He spoke to me also, words for me alone to hear."

"You saw him that close?"

"As close as you are now to me but in a well-lit room."

"What did he say to you?"

"He asked me to look after Maria. For no other task would I have taken leave of absence from my Legion."

That night, Maria added Hanafa and his family to the long list of names on her prayer cycle as she knelt at the end of her bed to softly sing the psalms and rejoice in the beauty of the day granted to her. Hanafa and Anees listened to her gentle voice transfixed as they lay in the bed chamber below Maria's Tower Room. Finally, the old man rolled over to kiss his wife and say: "This is indeed a special guest we have with us. Forgive me my earlier doubt." Anees smiled and forgave him instantly: "I hear this new God has an especial love for the converted!"

As Maria slept, God's work continued to be done; eight hundred oarsmen launched into the City in search of revelry. As they drank so their tongues loosened and inevitably they began to talk of their mission: of the young girl who spoke the Truth and the crucified man who had risen from the dead. Word spread from Taverna to Taverna and soon spilled out onto the squares beyond: "She speaks of wonderful things; she will speak to all of us tomorrow."

The next day, Maria was accompanied by Hanafa, Ioshua, Iosephus and Longinus to the Curiale Court where the Council of Elders held their weekly meeting. Maria was to present to the Council and ask permission to hold two public gatherings. Three Council members were elders from the Jewish community who were likely to be the only opposition. Except Hanafa had spoken to all three the night before and they had agreed to go into the meeting with 'an open mind'. "It was the best I could do" said Hanafa crestfallen but Maria had hugged him in joy then said:

"No-one should ever be forced to believe in the Master; everyone must have a choice. An open mind is all I ask for!" and then she kissed him to make her point before skipping off down the cobbled street leaving the four men considering whether it was worth chasing after her and deciding it was beneath their considerable dignity to do so.

Meanwhile, Perseus and Decius had headed back to the ships to check on the crew (or rather to see how many of the crew had made it back from the night before). Perseus had only been to sea on troop carriers before so had no real idea what to expect of marines and guessed that at least half the crew would have returned to their hammocks. Decius gave the young legionary an odd look, wondered what sort of life they lived in his Legion and went for a more precise estimate of four. In the end, Decius was closest: it was five.

"Where are they all?" asked Perseus in all innocence. Decius woke up one of the five crew members and asked him a few questions: "How many Taverns in Tunis?"

"Seventy six"

"How many barmaids?"

"Hundreds!"

"There is your answer, Perseus, now put your boots back on and we are going to find every one of those Taverns and throw our men out of every barmaid's bed we can then find."

"So how come these five ..." and Perseus nodded in the direction of the five crew having breakfast on deck and then raised his eye brows before going red in the face and continuing in embarrassment: "Why aren't they, well, somewhere else?"

"Three are happily married and intend to stay that way and the other two have been known to get lost trying to find the way out of their own hammock. Probably took a wrong turning and lost the rest of the party they were with. When that happens, homing instinct takes over and they head back to ship."

So whilst Perseus and Decius had an enjoyable three hours scouring every Taverna in Tunis, Maria was standing before the Council of Elders so frightened she was visibly shaking as she addressed them. The Council were sitting in a long row the far side of a rectangular table in a room with no windows, pictures or wall hangings but it did have two rows of wall sconces with crooked candles that were smoking and had blackened the whitewash of the walls and ceiling above. The Elders were (as the name would suggest) old men with the exception of the representative of the Suderan community, newly established and who had elected their young tribal leader. Maria was standing before them her hands clasped before her, looking nervously along their ranks whilst behind her, Iosephus had bagged four seats for himself, Hanafa, Ioshua and Longinus. Maria gulped then introduced herself and her purpose:

"Sirs, my name is Maria called 'the Magdalan' and I am honoured to be allowed to speak to this august Council. I am a humble girl from the small town of Nazareth in Iudaea with no parents or status. I am come to Tunis because I have been given a message of hope for all mankind and one I would wish to share with your permission. The message is a peaceful one. Elsewhere that I have spoken, this message has brought joy and happiness.

I am asking therefore to speak in public to any of the people of Tunis who wish to listen to me. I am asking your permission as I respect this Council and its achievements for the greater good of Tunis and would seek to go out and meet your people with this Council's endorsement."

The chairman of the Council looked left and right for questions and unsurprisingly the first came from one of the three representatives of the Jewish community:

"Maria. What is this message? I had heard that you shall announce the Jewish Messiah has been born, died and has risen from the dead. Is this true?"

"Yes sir" and Maria bowed her head in acknowledgement of the question and questioner. "It is true that I shall announce it, true that I have seen it and true that it has happened. However, it is my belief that the Messiah has come for all mankind and so I am come to bring word of my Master's message not just to Jews but to Gentiles also."

The next question came from the second of the Elders from the Jewish community:

"Do you seek to persuade Jews to follow you rather than the faith they have respected for thousands of years?"

"I do not seek for anyone to follow *me* and my Master's message is the fulfilment of the prophets. He said often that we are to follow the laws of Deuteronomy and Leviticus and to obey the Ten Commandments. He added a new commandment: To Love God and Each Other; and he repeatedly encouraged those who were wealthy to give their riches to the poor. There are two new messages: that with the Coming of the Son of Man the Gates of Paradise have now been opened; and we can all be baptised in the Spirit of God, receiving gifts such as the ability to heal."

The third of the Elders from the Jewish community was so eager to ask his question that he did so before the chairman had invited him:

"Can you heal?" he asked.

"No" Maria replied "But I can ask God and God can heal" at which the Elder looked triumphant and then turned to his colleagues on the Council. "My eldest daughter is sick. I brought her here hoping perhaps that she might be healed. Let us put this lady to the test" and the rest of the Council nodded: most wanting to see a miracle in the same way as they would have greeted some clever trick of magic; the minority hoping Maria would fail and thus be uncovered as a charlatan. One of the scribes was acting also as the Clerk to the Council that day and at a signal from the chairman, he rushed out and a few moments later was followed into the court room by a lady in her mid twenties and in terrible distress, moaning and complaining of a fever.

Maria asked Longinus for his pilum which Perseus had returned to the Centurion in case Maria might need it. She un-wrapped it from its cloth and held it with reverence and care then looked towards the lady. The next moment, Maria frowned and whispered to herself: "Something is not right." Suddenly her eyes opened wide with the clarity of insight and she looked first at the lady and then at the Elder, before turning to the chairman:

"Might I have a private word with the Council member who asked me to heal his daughter? It might be a good idea if the daughter joined us."

"This is most irregular. Why should we do this?"

"I ask for an adjournment for a few minutes no more. It will help your deliberations." Maria was insistent and with poor grace the chairman gave her the adjournment. As the girl headed to join the couple in an adjoining Committee Room she whispered to Longinus: "Get me a doctor" and he nodded then had a hurried word with Ioshua who sprinted out of the double doors that gave onto the steps to the Curia and kept going, headed for where the physicians kept shop near the herbologists and astrologists.

As soon as Maria entered the Committee Room, she turned to the Elder to ask: "Honoured sir, do you know why your daughter has a fever?"

"She is sick. That is obvious" he said looking confused.

"How would your household treat a daughter who was unmarried and with child? Would you help the daughter? What would you do to the child?"

Suddenly, all in the room went still. The Elder turned slowly not daring to believe then when he saw the guilt, not detectable by any other save himself as her father, he turned back to Maria not in anger but in joy: "My wife died in childbirth and this is my only daughter. I would treat my daughter and my grandchild as the most precious things to me in the world."

Then Maria turned to the daughter and said: "It is not too late for me to save the child" at which the daughter burst into tears to be held in the embrace of her father. Looking up and seeing pride in his face where she had expected anger, she said to the Magdalan:

"Undo what I have done please I beg of you."

"Very well but you will need to lie down."

The daughter lay on the ground, her father offering the comfort of his cloak for her to lie on then holding her left hand in his right as he knelt beside her and kissed her once. Then Maria placed the pilum across her belly and said the simplest of prayers: "Save this child but Thy Will Be Done" at which the spear-point glowed golden as did the young lady's whole body as the power of Maria's prayer invited God to remove all traces of the poison the lady had self-administered in her attempt at an abortion. Within moments, the lady began to moan and then suddenly the bottom half of the Elder's cloak was drenched with amniotic fluid as her waters broke.

"Where is that doctor?" Maria muttered then went to cradle the head of the child that was desperately seeking its own birth and to encourage the young mother to push with all her might. Without warning, Maria found she was looking into the widest largest blue eyes she had ever seen, holding the newborn child in her lap and thinking how wonderful God is to make such things possible. Just in time the physician arrived to cut the cord, remove the placenta and clean up the mother.

"Good clean birth, no tearing of the mother or sign of internal bleeding and the baby looks incredibly healthy. Councillor, you have a grandson" the physician whispered to the Elder whilst Maria helped the mother latch the child on and begin breast-feeding her child. Then catching the Elder's attention, Maria whispered: "We should return if only so that you can excuse yourself to be with your daughter and grandson."

Returning to the court room there were many raised eyebrows. The Council had seen and recognised the local physician as he had arrived and assumed the worst namely that whatever magic the girl used had gone horribly wrong and necessitated proper medical attention. The girl was clearly a charlatan. The chairman said one word directed at Maria "Well?" but it was the Elder who answered him:

"By a miracle, my only daughter has given birth to a son. Without this girl's prayers both my daughter and my grandson would now be dead. I am certain that she does God's Will."

The Council were stunned. There was a hurried conference between the three Elders from the Jewish community before the most venerable stood and said:

"First, I would like to record that the Jewish community has no objection to the young girl called the Magdalan speaking to the people of Tunis and second, I ask your leave on behalf of my colleague who would like to be in the company of his daughter and newborn grandson at this time."

The chairman nodded then asked the rest of the Council of Elders: "Has anyone any objection to this girl's request?" There was none and Maria had her endorsement. She got as far as the front row of the stalls set out for the public and then was embraced by a jubilant Iosephus, Longinus, Ioshua and Hanafa.

Taking advantage of the longer days in North Africa, Iosephus suggested that they set out for the Forum around the sixth hour after noon when the cool of the evening would begin to draw in and most of the market stalls would be packing up: "We will have more space, less distraction and will not antagonise the traders who might otherwise see us as competing with their business" he explained for Maria's benefit and she nodded, already nervous enough as it was; she did not want to antagonise anyone.

"But no-one will come" she said sadly finally letting her fears surface.

"We will just have to see won't we" Hanafa said but he was quietly confident they would see good numbers for he had taken a walk after they had all eaten a light lunch at a souk overlooking the Forum and in every square or Bar he had visited there had been only one topic: "The Magdalan is here tonight". Eight hundred diakonae had successfully spread the word in every Bar, Inn and Tavern reinforced when the Elders got back into their communities to say: "This is the real thing. She can do miracles. She speaks Truth."

Maria arrived with thirty minutes still to go. Ioshua and Hanafa had organised for a podium to be erected with an awning so that the girl did not get sun stroke and set the stand up near the steps to the Praetor's Court which housed the port administration where Ioshua worked. "See that balcony there" and Ioshua had turned Maria gently by the waist and pointed above her head: "That is my office. I could watch you from there … but I am not going to. Instead I will be right at the front with Rachel, Rebecca and Raphael. Hanafa and Anees will be with Iosephus on the far left and Longinus will be on the far right to be joined later by Decius and Perseus."

"Where are they?" Maria asked in momentary alarm.

"Do not worry. They are just hunting down the last of Iosephus' crew. They will be here!"

Then the crowds began to arrive. Small groups at first: family parties and groups of friends. But soon whole tenements or streets began to arrive, most bringing food, drink, tables and cushions, preparing for an enjoyable evening out, a social gathering with Maria as the entertainment. Ioshua mixed amongst the crowds and asked a few tactful questions to gauge their temperament; the crowd were not here to challenge but rather had all heard good things about Maria and wanted to be part of this new movement they had labelled 'Christianity'.

Perseus and Decius arrived with a few minutes to go and with eight hundred oarsmen in tow. They both looked at the crowds already assembled and realised they need not have worried about numbers for over seventy thousand were gathered, and more would come the following evening.

A single bell chimed the hour and Maria stepped up onto her podium. She looked around, making brief eye contact with hundreds ensuring she was visible to everyone and then she spoke in a whisper that carried like mist on the wind so that all who would listen could hear. She spoke in tongues though she did not know this, such that everyone would understand her and people from darkest Africa or the furthest Far East or the most barbaric Britannia, trading through Tunis would hear her words in their own language and take her words back home with them.

"I am here to bring you the word of God" and her words were greeted with absolute silence.

"God sent his only Son to live amongst us as one of us. The Son spoke of peace, of freedom, of the end of all sins and he promised us Eternal Life with God if we followed him.

He gave us a new commandment: to love God and each other

He gave us a new covenant: each time we take bread and wine and do this in memory of him then we are refreshed with the Spirit of God and God will be present. He has promised us this.

He sent us the gifts of his Spirit: to help us heal, speak in many tongues, to see the future and to have hope.

God's Son died and then rose from the dead to show that we can all do the same.

His name was Iesus of Nazareth and he was my best friend.

I saw him die, I helped bury him, I was the first to see him alive again, I saw him ascend into the skies and I have received his Spirit.

Iesus is my Master and has been for over two years now. My Master remains with me and in me, guiding me to do good things.

So today, I have come before you to say that you too can be filled with God's Spirit, you too can feel the presence of God in the breaking of bread and you too can have Eternal Life after death in the presence of God.

All you need do is to believe and when your heart and mind is open, God will fill them with his wisdom and love."

There were questions, so many at first that Longinus had the oarsmen line the questioners up in eight rows two at front, back and both sides. Each row typically had five or six people in it waiting for their turn to ask a question. Maria answered them all with humble courtesy, drawing on something the Master had said or done to illustrate a point. She answered over three hundred questions in the four hours she stood before them and when finally she admitted it was 'well past my bedtime' she was greeted with a loud cheer and the crowd surged forwards to touch her and to thank her. Longinus stepped up to the podium taking hold of her as her exhaustion caught up with her and she stumbled and would have fallen beneath the feet of the crowd had not the Centurion been there with his firm arms to steady her then lift her and carry her to the safety of Ioshua's offices.

"Is there a back way out?" Longinus asked and Ioshua nodded. "Can you have a litter there in five minutes?" again Ioshua signalled in the affirmative and then went to find one, pointing Longinus towards the rear of the building. The exit was well sign-posted and Longinus had no trouble finding it as he walked along wide straight corridors through the occasional set of double doors that demarcated the different departments and then down a single flight of stairs to arrive at the barred and bolted rear entrance. A quick look through the viewing hatch next to the door and he could see the rear of the building was deserted. He would need to wait for Ioshua.

A couple of minutes later there was a sharp tap on the door. Longinus looked out and could see Ioshua with a litter behind him. The young Roman unbolted the door one-handed, his right arm still cradling a sleeping Magdalan, and then he pulled the metal bar across and was able to heave open the left door. Moments later, Maria was lying in the litter with the curtains drawn shut on her way to Hanafa's house with Longinus and Ioshua as escort. Perseus and Decius had gone ahead with Hanafa and the rest of his family.

The next day the attendance was even greater and questions took longer as a consequence. Maria had a brainwave as she came to the end of questions:

"The opportunity to receive God's greatest gift is not to be missed. 'Yet how do I grasp this single chance in a lifetime?' I hear you ask. Tomorrow I leave for new lands but before I go, I will be breaking bread with as many of you as can make it. Through the breaking of the bread you will know God and God will know you. Please come if that is your wish for any and everyone will be welcome."

The records show that one hundred and thirty thousand attended the second of Maria's talks and that '*almost two hundred thousand were converted to Christianity in Tunis at a single service of the Eucharist on her final day at the City*'. (Nicodemus writing in the 5th Century AD)

She cried non stop as she said farewell to Hanifa and his delightful family. Only her surprise then joy when Ioshua gently kissed her on both cheeks stopped the flood. "We will never forget you" he whispered in her ear whilst Hanifa roared "Come again! Soon! If you can make Ioshua human then there is nothing you cannot do" at which Maria stood before Hanifa and defied him and thanked him all in one breath:

"You must know I have done nothing. Ioshua is lovely so don't bully him" at which everyone even Ioshua laughed for no-one could ever bully him whilst Maria continued as a whisper heard by Hanifa and Anees alone: "I came an orphan without a home. Now I am blessed by parents, a family and a place I can always remember as my domus. I will presume on your generosity and return. I promise."

Polenca in Balearicum

The crowds were already gathered on the beaches and out into the sea as Iosephus' flotilla came into the Bay at Polenca. Word had gone fast across the entire coast of the eastern Mediterranean and the oppressed, the poor, the frail, the ill and the humble as well as the rich and the noble gathered in hope watching the still seas for the three ships to come sailing in. It was fast approaching midsummer and the days were still growing longer.

Maria stayed on board, sitting on the lower deck with her feet dangling in the cool of the blue waters of the sheltered bay and looked at the tens of thousands gathered to hear her. Many had waded in to the shallow sea and stood just feet from her vantage point. She held up a hand hesitantly and the crowd grew still respecting her wish for silence.

"The Son of God, Iesus of Nazareth is alive and with us today when we break the bread in his memory. He stands at our shoulders, he sits in our hearts, he is there in each of us, for we all have been made in God's image, and he is present in the bread we share at our Eucharistic feast."

Then she spoke for an hour and answered their questions far more than before as the question and answer session had increasingly become the tradition wherever she went. She finished by leading them in the celebration of the Eucharist and to her intense joy the Spirit descended on some of the faithful and before the crowd's eyes an act of healing occurred.

A young man, crippled as a child and whose legs had grown crooked after an accident, flung down his crutches as his mother prayed that he be healed. She had watched in amazement as her son's legs had straightened, the bones re-knitting, and then he had found the strength to stand. They embraced before the cheering crowd and Maria gave thanks to God on their collective behalf. From that act of healing began the early Christian community in Mallorca, founded around a small community of faith healers.

Then Maria jumped down into the water and walked amongst the crowd greeting as many as she could with her shy smile. They surged forwards to surround her and guide her to the shore then sat at her feet as she spoke once more:

"Today is the beginning. But it is up to you to create a place for God here. You must be true to his way, pure in heart and mind, and seek forgiveness for your sins." Then raising her hands, she asked:

"Master, hear my prayer I plead. Forgive those here who have sinned, take away their fears and guilt and leave them cleansed to receive your Spirit." Before turning back to the crowd and saying: "For those wishing to be forgiven, your sins are forgiven."

"Teach us how to forgive others as you have" asked one of the crowd and Maria replied:

"Once my Master was asked by a Sadducee 'How can *you* forgive sins?' Iesus replied: 'It is God who forgives sins. If you ask God then he will forgive you. Would you rather I had said 'God has forgiven you.' Then my Master turned to those he had forgiven and said 'God has forgiven you' and they went away cleansed of their sins.

So it is with us today. If we pray then we can obtain God's forgiveness especially if we do this when Iesus is present in the breaking of the bread. I encourage you to seek forgiveness through prayer and penitence, and that those who lead your community in the Eucharistic celebration include an act of penitence or contrition, offering forgiveness as I have done through the medium of prayer."

"Can anyone forgive another?" another in the crowd asked.

"Anyone can ask God to forgive another just as anyone can be forgiven by God themselves" and from there developed the penitential rite that became the first part of the celebration of the Eucharist and a hundred years later was an established prayer and intercession said each day by the developing priesthood of the early Christian Church. The early Church fathers would later turn this personal act of contrition Maria established into an institution that could only be performed by the sacerdotal orders of the church.

Maria's vision never foresaw a need for ordination and the ordained. Rather she envisaged communities selecting their faith leaders from within and looked to their communion with God to ensure consistency and avoid heresy. She thought everyone would be able to be as close to God as she had become and never appreciated that she was in a special position: the disciple that Iesus loved above all others, his first apostle and the one with whom he remained both before and after her death.

It was this difference in Maria's vision of a Church guided by the Spirit, the personal communion we each can accomplish with God and the Angels and Paulus' vision of a Church led by appointed leaders that would see Constantine the Great, who followed Pauline theodicy, have removed almost all references to Maria the Magdalan and her ministry from the histories and the Acts of the Apostles.

Maria was back up in the crow's nest looking west in hope of sight of the eastern coast of Tarraconensis and shouted in delight as she caught her first glimpse of the waves crashing against the cliffs some thirty leagues distance.

"Three to four hours yet to go: we have come a little south and will follow the coast from here. Wind is southerly and will help us but we will need to row the last hour as we manoeuvre into the harbour at Valentia which is not intended for large ships like ours." Decius shouted up to the girl who nodded to show she understood and then indicated she intended to stay up top and watch the coast from the height of the mast.

"She will be safe?" Longinus whispered, anxious as ever at the risks the girl took without thinking. Decius reassured the Centurion: "She has no fear and her sense of balance is better than any of my crew. A sudden gust of wind might blow her away as she is so thin and frail but other than that and she is no more at risk than if standing on deck."

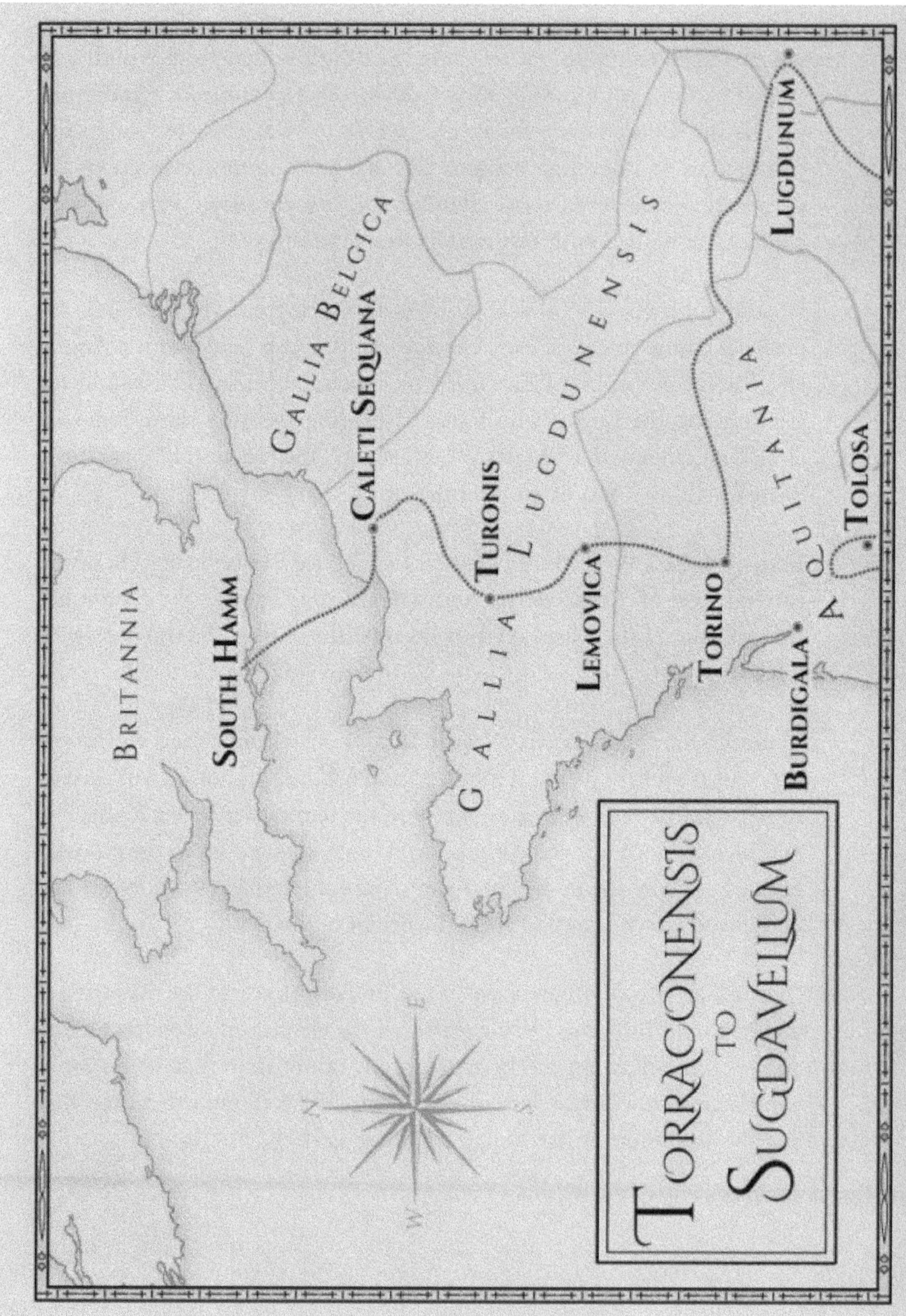
Torraconensis
to
Sugdavellum
Britannia
South Hamm
Gallia Belgica
Caleti Sequana
Turonis
Gallia Lugdunensis
Lemovica
Torino
Aquitania
Burdigala
Tolosa
Lugdunum

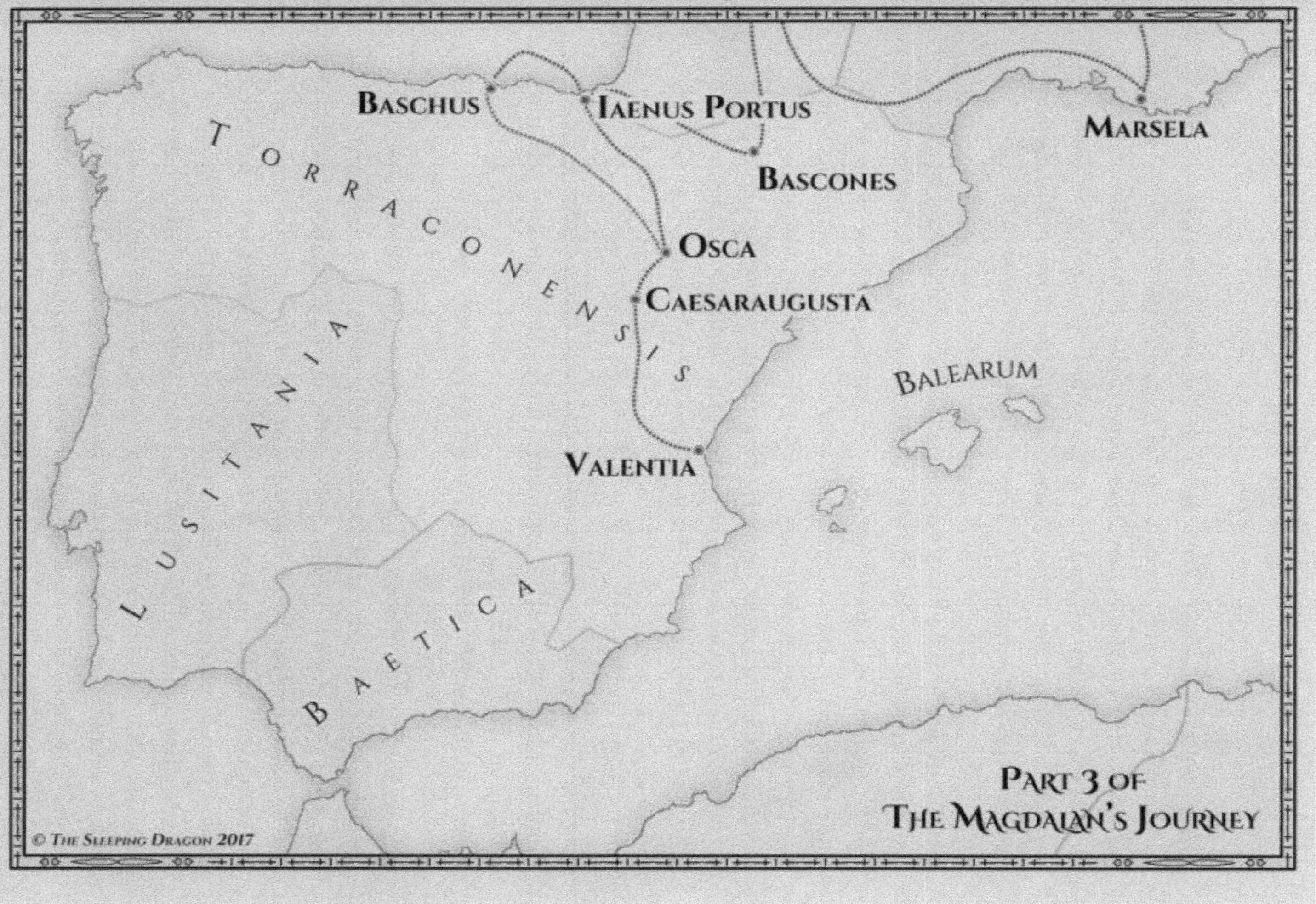
Baschus
Iaenus Portus
Marsela
Bascones
Torraconensis
Osca
Caesaraugusta
Lusitania
Balearum
Valentia
Baetica
Part 3 of
The Magdalan's Journey
© The Sleeping Dragon 2017

The historian Pilate continues his account of the mission of Joseph of Arithamea and Mary Magdalan:

"Mary landed at Valentia (Valencia) in the Province of Tarraconensis, the east coast being the most populous part of Hispania and travelled to Osca (Zaragosa), through Basschus and on to Iaenus Portus (Bilbao) before crossing the Pyranees at Pampano and into Cisalpine Gaul near Torbelli. At Iaenus, she addressed people from across Hispania including the desert lands of Baetica and the mountainous passes of Lusitania." (Pilate, 4th Century AD)

This stretch of the Mare Balearicum was sheltered by land south, west and east and so avoided storms; the only disturbance was the waves as they struck the coast and the only rough water was the rare occasion that an anti-cyclone hit the shores of southern Gallia and eastern Hispania: usually accompanying the infamous 'sirocco' whose fiery ferocity would turn the marshes of the Camargue into a flaming fire pit before discharging its energy into the narrow stretch of sea between Mallorca and the ancient kingdoms of La Mancha and Aragon (home of the Ceratani beneath the Pyrenees).

South of Valentia was an enormous park and forest surrounding the Aqua Albufera. Maria was lost in admiration of the flamingos and pelicans floating on the lake and laughed with joy and child-like delight as they made mad riot in the water in their attempt to get airborne.

The harbour at Valentia itself was a few leagues north of the City and lay facing east-west with protective stone walls to the south and north. It comprised a dry dock for repairs and smaller ships with shallow draughts and a deeper dock for larger shipping that would just take the length of the two quadrime. The trireme was directed further north to a sanded and shallow cove. Decius called to Maria to descend from her perch then once she was safely on deck and both sails had been gathered in, he beached the prow, the ship shook at the impact sending Maria tumbling over on the deck to be caught by Perseus and then the crew dropped down the sides of the ship into the shallows and hauled the ship beyond the high watermark using two long ropes that wove in and out of the channels for the oars.

Valentia was typical of romance cities, a rectangular and precisely laid out grid of shops and housing with the Forum, Curia and courts at the centre, to the north was a strand of grass and parkland and the south boundary was the Fluvia Turia which was navigable almost as far as Caesaraguntum. As Maria slept, Iosephus, Longinus, Perseus, Decius and the ship's captain Metellus met on the beach with the maps set around them held flat by stones and looked at their options. Metellus set the scene:

"We can go to Osca and Pampano by road then cross into Gaul north of Pampano and head for Torbelli. We will need horses and the journey will take five or six days. Alternatively, we can take the Fluvia Turia to just south of Caesaraguntum: it will be slow and steady, travelling under the speed of our oars and doing forty leagues per day at best. We get within twenty leagues of Caesaraguntum and then transfer to horses for the rest of the journey. Or we can follow the coast to Narbo and Arcolate and head directly to Luguidenum from there avoiding the difficult roads east from Torbelli."

Iosephus was adamant that Maria must be seen by the people in Hispania. He also felt that the river route would leave them most vulnerable as only the trireme could navigate the whole stretch of the river which was shallow and silted up in many places. They would be rowing against the flow of the river and the oarsmen would need to rest. Twenty leagues each day was far more likely than forty. Road represented the best route and they could send out the diakonae to sort out accommodation and hire horses at the staging posts along the road they would be taking.

"How long will it take for us to be ready?" Longinus asked and Decius had the answer:

"Five days to sort out the horses and accommodation. We can send men south and west to spread word of Maria's arrival and ministry. The men know what to say having spent the last few weeks listening to the girl's every word. Each one of them could tell the story of the Master without prompting. Best to keep them busy and this is a task they will welcome. Most will ask Iosephus to be released permanently as they believe they have a new ministry to spread the Good News to the people of Hispania and Cesalpine Gaul."

"Could we not go straight to Gallia then and leave Hispania to Maria's diakonae?" Longinus asked thinking that the rest would do Maria good. She was starting to look translucent again and had lost more weight, he could not think from where but when he had last caught her as she collapsed at the end of another late evening Maria had been so light he could have easily held her under one arm. She slept whenever she was not telling the oarsmen stories or singing to them.

Iosephus shook his head then reminded them: "Word has already gone ahead that Maria is coming to Hispania. If it were to become known that she had landed in Hispania and sailed on then we would lose all chance of the people here joining us as followers rather we would incur their justifiable anger. Also, if Maria can publicly endorse the ministry of her diakonae then it will make their task immeasurably easier."

Decius had been reflecting on all that had been said and proffered his own advice: "Going by river is too slow and by sea would see us only able to spread the word along the coast. The big centres are on the east coast but still we would do more harm than good if we did not go inland, avoiding the purpose of our mission which is to spread our Master's word. The only reason to set sail once more would be if we were to land in Beatica and northern Africa, then brave the Charybdis to visit Scalabis, Tangeris or drop down to the western coast of Africa but that would take some explaining to any customs or port official as our manifest shows our route and that our destination lies north not south. I suggest a compromise: head for Iaenus across land. If we can add Lucitania and the west coast to the places Maria speaks at then we have a good chance of taking the Good News of the risen Christ to the whole of Hispania. Let it be known that Maria is to speak in Iaenus in a week's time and people will travel to hear her."

But Longinus could not agree to that and reminded them: "The crowds that Maria attracts are 'unlawful assemblies' and we are now in a Roman Province and one of the oldest. If we give advance notice then it will be Roman legionaries with a warrant for her arrest that will be waiting for her when we get to Iaenus."

"As ever it will be Maria who decides" and Iosephus brought the discussion to a close:

"We are agreed that we will not need the ships from here. I will hire a new crew for them and they can take on provisions and return to Iudaea via Alexandria. I do need to make some trade profit from this exhibition after all. I will hire ships in Sargoventum (Soragoventum) for the short journey by sea to Britannia but do not wish to risk our current ships on the Atlantic so they go home.

As to our route by land, let us head to Osca in five days time and spend the next five days in the best Taverna we can find in Valentia resting but also giving Maria a chance to speak to the locals. We can still go to Iaenus from Osca but deciding the first stage of our route now is important as I need to arrange accommodation and staging posts before we can leave Valentia. The longer we delay a decision on the next stage, the longer we remain in Valentia and each night Maria speaks to the locals here we put her at risk of her arrest."

Before they sent the diakonae out on their mission, Decius had one final task for them. First they cut down several of the oak and palm trees that offered shelter on the beach where they had landed. These were trimmed of branches and bark until smooth then lain as rollers behind the bow end of the ship. With ropes tied to the sides of the trireme, the men divided into two teams. Once Decius had an offshore wind, he set the crew to pulling the trireme until its bow was in the water then set his two sails and let the wind do the rest, running the hull of his ship carefully over the rollers until with a huge splash the prow was floating in the sea. Then turning to port he brought his ship in line with the coast and anchored her. Finally, he shouted across to Iosephus:

"We can drop Maria off each evening along the coast, a different location each night or use the Fluvia Turia to go inland … but key is that she will be kept moving and thus we reduce the risk of her arrest, especially if she stays on the ship as she did at Pollenca."

Longinus could see the sense of this immediately and Iosephus was pleased as he enjoyed the comfort of his private yacht. They asked for fifty men to volunteer to continue to be their crew and when all eight hundred did so, they selected the strongest but also the most courteous as they would be acting as ushers at any gatherings to celebrate the Eucharist with Maria. Then, just as they were proposing to waken Maria to ask her where she would like to set down first, a messenger on horseback rode into the cove where they had beached. His message was from the Council of Elders of the Jewish community at Valentia asking Maria to attend a meeting that evening.

Maria woke to the unwelcome sound of four men arguing and cut across their raised voices with a simple: "I rejoice in God for each new day and every adventure that comes with the rising of the sun."

They turned to her, shame-faced at being caught in argument and then Longinus explained: "You are summonsed by the Elders of the Jewish community. It is not a warrant for your arrest nor are you on trial but we suspect a trap."

"Get me there safely and God will do the rest. I go alone as I will not risk any of you if it does prove to be a trap. But have no fear for me. My mission doth not end in Hispania; here is where it begins." Thus Maria silenced their arguments with her softly spoken words, her conviction and her courage. Longinus was insistent on one amendment to her proposal: "Not only will I take you there but I go in with you for the Master told me to look after you." Maria bowed her head acknowledging that she could not contradict the Master's will. Then Perseus said: "I am coming too!"

"No" said Maria, "I would be worried for your safety and have no need of your protection." But Perseus laughed before trumping her with his new-found wisdom: "I shall not be going to protect you; it is Longinus that I am commissioned to protect, my lady."

The diakonae spent the rest of the day touring the City visiting its many markets, souks, bars and Taverna, spreading the word that Maria was seeking permission to speak to the people of Valentia, directing them to meet outside the Temple Palace where the Elders were to meet under the chairmanship of the High Priest of the Temple here. Meanwhile, Longinus went to present their travel documents to the Praetor, who asked to see him in person and the Centurion was ushered into his triclinarium. Gaius Severus Tartellus, Procurator of Tarraconensis and Port Administrator at Valentia and Marcus Suevus Semillus Antonius, City Prefect at Valentia, were already reclining on their triclinium and beckoned for Longinus to join them. Tartellus explained their interest:

"Have no worries Centurion, we have already approved your papers and added our own seals. Provided your party causes no disturbance you have free passage within Tarraco, Tarraconensis, Valentia and on to Osca as well as through the sub province of Articolate (Aragon). We are after gossip; especially about the equites, Pilate."

Longinus sat opposite them and tried one of the olives which was sweet, soft and succulent. Eating it carefully to avoid the juices staining his toga also gave him important thinking time:

"Sirs. I can say very little as I was about to be appointed on his staff when this mission came up but I will tell you what I can. I found Pilate receptive to advice and anxious to be seen to administer his sub-province well. He is honest and pious. His wife is well-liked by the Jewish community. Pilate is, however, despised by the Sanhedrin and King Herod both of whom seek his removal but would react the same way to any appointee as Provincial Governor. Pilate is grieving over the loss of his only Son and is the last of his line. Therefore he wants to impress as a consequence so that his family name might be remembered with honour.

Although he was loyal to Aelius Sejanus as his patron, at no time were the legions in his province sounded out to mutiny. I genuinely believe that the treachery of Sejanus came as a surprise to Pilate: not least as Pilate's family and his personal loyalty was to the Julian line and this would have made it extremely unlikely that he would have backed Sejanus against Tiberius Caesar.

I enjoyed my posting and intend to return once I have collected my niece from Britannia. I could work with Pilate but equally I could work just as well with his replacement if he is to be summonsed back to Roma. My first loyalty is and always will be to the Senate and Republic of Rome then its Princeps, Tiberius Caesar, then my Legion then my family and finally myself."

"Your loyalty to your master is commendable" Antonius spoke smoothly, smiling to take away any hint of sarcasm before breaking the bad news: "Alas, word in Roma is that Pilate's recall is inevitable. Iudea is strategically important to defend Aegyptia and Syria which both produce huge quantities of wheat. It is too important and a region we can ill afford to see rebel again. The release of the man Barabbus has resulted in an official complaint by Herod to the Emperor. You do well to be travelling at this time. Come back as soon as you hear of a new appointment. Good men such as yourself will be needed when the new Procurator selects his staff."

Tartellus had one last question before they dismissed him: "Tell us more about the young girl, the Magdalan. Why do you travel with her?"

"I can answer the second part of your question most easily: I swore to my mother I would look after Maria as a favour. Alas, I am still a mother's boy at times. My mother brought in some massive reinforcements when the Governor's wife, the Lady Cordelia, added her request I look after the girl to my mother's. I was out-numbered and out-manoeuvred: my surrender was pitiful" and all three men laughed.

"The girl is very young, often a child, simple-minded and innocent but she also has wisdom beyond her years. She preaches a message of peace and offers no threat to Rome. She spends most of the time in dream or visions of the world after this, life beyond death. But she also offers healing and some of her actions seem miraculous, certainly are hard to explain. She insists this is not magic nor her doing but God's will. She sees herself as an empty vessel to be filled with God's Spirit and as an Instrument of God's compassion and healing love."

"Does she blaspheme?" Antonius asked still absorbing Longinus' description.

"She is from the Jewish faith so believes in one God only. Her faith is different from the many Gods we honour in Roma. The Emperor tolerates the Jewish faith so she does not blaspheme. However, if an Emperor were ever to require the Jews to relinquish their faith and to believe in the Gods of Rome then her faith would be in conflict with ours and her teaching would then become blasphemous."

Finally, Tartellus drew the discussion to a close with a surprise request issued more as an instruction:

"We would like to meet the girl. Can she join us for supper tomorrow? We will invite a select group but we would like to see this simple girl from Nazareth. For when she speaks, thousands flock to hear her yet she does not incite rebellion, rather sends them home to their families and communities to be 'good people'. She is an enigma and I shall reserve any judgement of her until we have met."

Longinus gulped then bowed in acquiescence. The meeting now over, he found a steward at his right elbow who escorted him to the Clerk of Transits office where the Centurion collected three sets of freshly sealed papers and then went on his way back to find Decius.

The helmsman had moored up at the Pontus Virillis. The bridge spanned the Turia with moorings either side and for many paces in all directions along the river's wide banks. The bridge was wide enough to be the home for two rows of shops either side of a cobbled road on which four rows of wagons were moving sedately nose to tail. In several places, the two rows of buildings had joined to form covered archways above which were tenements of apartments with stunning views of the river.

Maria was waiting for Longinus, a cream lace shawl covered her head, her stola was chiffon in rusts and reds over a white linen chiton and peplos. She could not hide the fact that she was a child still, not yet become a woman and her clothing clung on to her thin and frail frame. She looked as if she was half-starved and Longinus promised himself that he would take her out to eat at the best Inns and Taverna in the City until he had fattened the poor girl up. She looked like an abandoned waif and Longinus feared that the Council of Elders would gobble her up in one mouthful for their supper.

"Come" said Maria nervously. "It is a good walk and I do not wish to be late." Then she held Perseus in one arm and Longinus in the other and they headed towards the Curia.

The Xirivella was behind them, the Mislata was to their north west, and the Roman City of Valentia was dead ahead to their east, surrounded on two sides by the Turia, and a long strip of emerald green public gardens, parkland and avenues of Cyprus and palm trees that provided the north west and north east boundaries. The southern and far eastern boundary of the City was its magnificent port, with tall masts and proud prows clearly visible, lanterns hanging from every bow spit, and tied to the rigging, providing a tessarae of coloured glass and flickering light, the sound of creaking beams, hulls contracting and expanding in the heat, the constant chatter of the crews and stevedores as they unloaded their wares or guided their long barges into safe haven.

Although it was strictly out of their way, yet Maria guided the two men down onto the quayside and was greeted by many of her diakonae, already mingling with their peers on other ships, exchanging stories, myths mainly about sea serpents and pirates, but stopping mid-sentence to wish the young girl 'Good Fortune', offering her their prayers then telling those around them that this thin slip of a girl, with head downturned in embarrassment, was 'the Magdalan'.

"She is normal; one of us!" one of the stevedores exclaimed in surprise in Metellus' hearing and the ship's captain agreed: "And that is part of her magic. She could be a sister, a daughter of any of us yet God has chosen her. If God can choose a simple girl from Nazareth then any of us can be chosen by God."

Soon a large crowd were following the girl and her two escorts as they headed across the Via Augustus and on past the monuments to the Pompeii and the Marii. Before them were the Temples to Mars Ultima and Jove Omnipotens, the Palazzo Agrippina and the Temple to Castor and Pollux.

The Statue of Athena looked down the colonnade that was the entrance to the Forum to where the Praetor's Palace, the Curia and the Curiale Court were approached by a huge colonnaded curved expanse of marble stairs, rising seventy steps above them, between each column of marble was a silver birch, its bark indistinguishable to Maria to the columns either side. She stopped and stood jaw dropping at the foot of the first tree then touched its straight trunk tentatively and in awe. It was only as she looked up and saw the brightest of green leaves that she finally accepted that this statue of nature was really a tree. In the end Longinus, nervous of the crowd surrounding them, dragged her away whilst reminding the girl that it was she who had said they must not be late.

"It is a *silver* tree" Maria said to Longinus slowly, looking over her shoulder and he laughed.

Their destination was in the older part of the Forum through the covered markets and auction houses, the slave market, which saw Maria shudder in distress and pull out her money bag impulsively to offer to bid for two young children and buy their freedom. She was soon outbid and Longinus pulled her away: "You cannot hope to buy every slave in this market and what would we have done with two children?"

"I would look after them" she pleaded but Longinus shook his head: "You would not be allowed to. You have no status yourself and those poor children would grow up with no home, no employment and no self-respect. If you wish to end slavery then Roma is where you need to begin and the Emperor is who you need to convince."

"Take me there! Take me to Roma."

Longinus laughed then seeing her deflate and the look of utter defeat on her transparent face, he took pity on her saying: "One day, perhaps, we shall go to Roma. But right now, Rome is so powerful it would crush us without pause for thought" then he wiped the tears from her eyes for all Maria could do is imagine herself as one of those children.

The Jewish Temple had been built sixty years before the Romans had set out the layout for this City and was timber-framed with stuccoed walls and tall arched windows. It was now hidden away, surrounded on all sides and over-shadowed by the much newer stone clad Temple Palace, the home for the High Priest which also housed the meeting rooms for the Council of Elders and the administrative centre for the Jewish community's many trades and their banks. The Jewish community in Valentia was proud of its independence and had grown rapidly in size and wealth over the last fifty years as the City's Port had thrived, opening up its great sea gates to trade with Tarraco, Granada and Beatica in southern Hispania, Marsela and Palma Beaticorum, and then further afield to Salermo and Tangeris.

The Council of Elders had already heard of Maria's ministry from their counterparts in Tunis and Heraklion. They intended to make up their own mind and to take Maria as they found her. There were sixteen on the Council, chaired by Demetrius, the High Priest at the Temple, and they had taken evidence from merchants who had been at Tunis and Heraklion. The High Priest was astonished as he listened to six different sets of testimony from those who had witnessed the Magdalan speak. He summed up what they had all heard:

"The testimony is universally positive. The girl is young, honest, speaks from her heart and believes all that she says is truth. She has been responsible for at least one miraculous case of healing and those who follow her teaching have healed many others. What no-one has asked the Magdalan is 'where does she see the Jewish faith of Abraham and the Prophets going?' Is our faith about to be left behind or is the man from Nazareth truly our Messiah and the fulfilment of all of our prophecies?"

The Elders were all in agreement: the Magdalan must be tested on her vision for the new faith she was promoting. They would be gentle though, for the girl was clearly benign; but was she misguided? Young minds could easily be distracted; to turn away from the faith of their fathers only to return when they became wise in later years.

One of the Temple servants entered and walked across to where Demetrius was seated, stooping to whisper in the High Priest's ear: "She is here and slightly early. A huge crowd has followed her. For no other reason than they are curious to know what will happen to her. She has not spoken to them nor does she intend to do so unless granted permission by this Council. She is very nervous and very young!"

"Are we ready?" Demetrius asked his fellow Council members and seeing that they were, he asked the servant to usher the girl in. "Has she companions?" he asked and when the servant nodded then indicated two, the High Priest continued: "Have them wait outside."

Maria walked with in, her fair hair and head covered beneath her mantilla, humbled in the presence of these wise men, her hands clasped nervously before her, then looking around hesitantly wondering if she should be seated or stand before them. She bowed to the High Priest and all sixteen Councillors then stood in silence, waiting for the High Priest to make her welcome or at least hoping that he would.

At a signal from the High Priest another of the Temple servants carried in a chair and placed it facing the long table at which the seventeen men were seated. The High Priest beckoned to the chair and indicated that Maria should sit, thus it was that the girl broke the silence as she said impulsively:

"Thank you sirs for letting me sit. Thank you also for seeing me. I am here to answer your questions as fully as I am able" and then she sat, her feet dangling just above the stone floor of the Grand Hall in the Temple Palace, rocking left then right then left again, a habit from childhood when nervous and totally sub-conscious but she could never be still, her hands were gripped tightly in her lap, her head was bowed humbly, she was seated in silence as she waited to be spoken to.

"Are you Maria the Magdalan?" Demetrius asked by way of ice-breaker, seeking to let the girl build up her confidence through answering questions about herself.

"Yes that is my name."

"Tell us about your childhood and your life before you met the man you call your Master" one of the Elders asked and Maria smiled to herself briefly then grinned openly as she recognised the compassion behind the question.

"Forgive me that I smile but I was a happy child and my parents loved me. I am remembering a time of great joy when I smile. My parents and I had five years of happiness living together in their Castle of Magdalo by the Sea of Galilee before they became ill and I could not help them. Not one of the many physicians that tried to help us had the cure they needed and I did not know enough to be able to nurse them myself. I learnt that wealth is not the answer to disease or corruption. I watched helplessly as they died within hours of each other" at which she paused and they watched the pang of sad memory cross her young face, her eyes cast down to try and avoid them seeing her brief moment of dismay; but they saw her sadness and understood. One deep breath and then she continued:

"I gave away all of the great treasure my family had amassed over centuries and the Elders of the nearby town took me in as an orphan. I was given work for which I was grateful. Then at thirteen, I was told I must find my own way in life. I had no idea what to do as I had no particular skills or talents. Into that dark moment stepped my Master. He asked me to follow him and I did so without hesitating."

The Council were silent, each recognising the vulnerability of the girl before them, most having grand-daughters the same age as Maria and thinking how terrible her life had been in comparison with the protected and pampered lives of the girls in their own households. Then they remembered that they had an important task: their faith and that of their fathers and those who had gone before them was under possible threat from this innocent-looking young orphan and they could not afford to show her sympathy if what she preached was heresy or blasphemy. Demetrius invited the Elders to continue their questions and several put their hands up at once. The High Priest invited each in order of age, respecting the venerability of the Council, giving precedence to the wisdom gained through old age.

"Young lady, your Master told many stories as if they were true yet they were intended to offer guidance only. How certain can you be that the whole of your Master's ministry was not one long story – helpful as we consider how to worship God but fundamentally not real?"

Maria looked the Elder in his eyes, her own clear crystal blue orbs opening wide at the suggestion that all she had encountered was an invention. Yet she understood also that the question must be asked. So she went back into herself to uncover the memories of what she had seen: not the stories told but the miracles to which she had born witness.

"Noble and honoured sir, I saw Iesus die on the cross, I helped bury him and then I saw him alive again. These are not stories told to me but things I have seen with my own eyes. I was there when he changed water to wine; I offered my own tent to him when he stood on the mountain with Elijah; I saw him cure the blind and help cripples to walk again. Sir, it was as real as I am and that is why I follow him still."

Now the questions began to come thick and fast, Maria treating each with courtesy, turning to face the questioner, standing her ground when important to do so, but never getting angry: for she appreciated that these questions must be asked.

"What is the breaking of the bread and why is it so important to you?"

"On the night my Master was arrested, he had supper with all of the disciples and I was one of the many who sat at his table. During the meal, he took up a loaf of bread, broke it and passed it around until we each had a piece. Then he said: "This is me! Whenever you break the bread and pass it around as I have just done then you will remember me and I will be with you once more." It is important because Iesus also said we would recognise him in the breaking of the bread."

"What do you mean 'recognise him'?"

"He is still alive and lives amongst us. The breaking of the bread is his sign to us that he is present."

"Surely you would recognise him?" and briefly Maria recalled the moments she had seen him alive but also when she thought she had lost him only to find he was still resident in her heart. She did not realise it but her face had lit up at the memory for all in the chamber to see.

"Two of our disciples travelled nearly twelve leagues in his company but did not recognise my Master until they broke bread together. I cannot explain that however.

You see my own experience has been different in that I have always recognised my Master. He has never left me from the day he rose from the dead and is still with me now. He is here as we speak.

My ministry, however, is not just to those who have already met my Master. Most people have never met Iesus of Nazareth and yet they will come to meet him through the breaking of the bread."

"I do not understand" said several of the Elders at once and Demetrius invited Maria to explain herself. Her reply surprised them.

"I do not understand either. I 'accept' that through some miracle I am filled with the Spirit of God, can feel my Master within me and can see my Master before me … but I can offer no explanation. What I can say is that I have seen the Spirit of God come down on my companions when we have come together to break bread."

"Do you speak Truth? Are we really to believe you?" one Elder asked his frustration showing.

"I speak Truth. But what we each shall believe depends really."

Demetrius leant forward at this to demand of her: "Maria, on what does this all depend?"

"I am a girl who has been given sight of the most wonderful things. Alas, I lack the ability to describe all that I have seen properly. Had one of you, great sirs, seen what I have seen then your questions could all have been answered in a way we could all have come to understand. Instead, the most important message of our lives, the Good News that my Master has died and is risen to give each of us Eternal Life, has been entrusted into my faltering hands: to be carried forward by the stumbling and hesitant words of a humble young girl from Magdalo then Nazareth with no family and of no status. So it depends on me really but the message would be in much safer hands if it depended on each of you."

All on the Council sat back at that. They had expected a visionary, zealous in her new faith and someone who saw herself as the new leader of that faith. Instead, they saw someone who was held captive by a holy message and felt inadequate to the task of taking that message forwards. They had heard Maria was honest and now they were encountering her humility. Both won them over yet they still had the key question to ask. It was left to Demetrius to do so:

"What happens to the Jewish faith if we all convert to follow this new faith of yours?"

Maria suddenly could not contain her tears as she recalled her Master's ministry, his torture and death. She let her hair cover her face and her mantilla covered both whilst she raised her hands in gentle supplication and apology. After a few moments, she was able to collect her thoughts sufficiently to speak with quivering voice and her eyes remained covered as she did so:

"When my Master died, we disciples all thought that was the end of our faith. Many ran away or denied they had known Iesus. So I can appreciate why you are concerned that this is a new faith come to take Jews away from the beliefs to which they have been loyal for centuries. You must fear the same desolation we felt.

When my Master returned to us alive, he held me in his arms then he talked of our faith being 'refreshed' and we were each to be 'reborn'. There was no talk of conversion from the Jewish faith to a new faith. My Master's faith and my faith and the Jewish faith are the same but with the Jewish faith being given fresh energy and wonderful new gifts: that we can see

Iesus alive and with us again in the breaking of the bread; we can be filled with the Spirit of God to do God's Will; and that we can live with God eternally in Paradise.

One day, when asked 'How can we gain the kingdom of heaven?' my Master replied: 'Observe the ten commandments and the law as found in the Books of Deuteronomy and Leviticus.' Good sirs, my Master was offering us the same faith we have professed our whole lives but with the added help of God's Son and his Spirit.

It is with some trepidation that I come before you to ask your permission to offer the people of Valentia and Tarraconensis the chance to receive these new gifts from God. Every one of you would be so much better than I at spreading the Good News of my Master. I ask one thing therefore: Do not let my inability to pose or respond to an argument, my lack of knowledge and understanding of the scriptures, my absence of wisdom, my youth and immaturity see my Master's message become lost due to the failings of its messenger! I know I lack a fraction even of your knowledge and wisdom … but I have seen wonderful things and wish to share what I have seen with others."

Demetrius was still seeking answers but most of the Elders were happy with what they had heard. Out of courtesy, they let the High Priest ask Maria several questions before the most venerable of the Elders whispered to the young man that they were not here to *interrogate* the girl.

"Was Iesus of Nazareth the Messiah?"

Maria answered that without hesitating: "Yes he *is* the Messiah"

"You say you are a Jew?"

"Yes. I observe the commandments and the law. I read the scriptures each day and believe in the Prophets. There is only one God, the God of Abraham and Moses. To show my commitment to my faith, I pray, fast, give the little money or possessions I have to the poor, I am pure in spirit and chaste in my life."

"Then why do we need to listen to you and the words of your Master if we already have the faith we need?"

At that, Maria grinned then had to apologise to the Elders:

"Forgive me sirs. I could not help but laugh at the idea of anyone needing to 'listen to me'. My Master's words: now that is another matter.

My Master once told the story of a rich man and a beggar. The beggar would ask for the scraps of food from the rich man's table but the rich man refused. One day they both died and the beggar was greeted by God and his Angels in Paradise; the rich man went to Hell to be tormented. There was a place where those in Paradise and Hell could see each other. The rich man saw the beggar there and called out saying 'Save me and I will never sin again but be generous with all that I shall have.'

So the beggar asked God 'what can be done to save this man?' God replied: 'Did not the rich man have the scriptures and the prophets to guide him? If they would not teach him to repent then how can we trust his word now?'

My Master was clear that the scriptures and the prophets should be enough to ensure our salvation but also that He is the culmination of all that the prophets foresaw. My Master's life, ministry, torture, death and resurrection were all foretold by prophets such as Isaiah, Ezekiel and in our Books of Daniel, Tobit and Maccabees.

The Jewish faith we profess is all we need provided we realise that Iesus is the be all and end all of our faith. If we ignore the ministry of Iesus then we are as the rich man: surrounded by the scriptures and the prophets but ignoring their message."

The Elders were growing restless at their colleague's relentless questions and whilst their most respected Councillor was having a whispered word with Demetrius, the youngest of the sixteen jumped in to ask:

"Maria. We have done nothing but asked you questions all evening yet some of us also wish to offer our aid. At risk of prolonging the ordeal for you, can I ask: what is it we can do for you?"

Maria's surprise then childlike delight at that question reinforced her age and as she grinned back at the questioner, the other Council members wondered if they had been unfair on her. Maria took away any concerns they may have had as she responded:

"Good sirs, this has not been an ordeal. I welcome the chance to talk of my Master's ministry. I will gladly talk of him for days on end and my companions must often drag me away when I do so. As to what I would welcome: your permission to speak of what I have seen; and if I might do so in the Temple one evening then I would be most honoured."

The Council sat back, talking over each other's shoulders as they discussed Maria's two requests, the majority already having reached a decision. Demetrius was soon in danger of becoming a minority of one. In the end, it was what Maria had said about her faith being the same as his but with new energy that persuaded the High Priest to support her: for he was fully conscious that he was in danger of losing the young generation in Valentia to the call of Rome and its Pantheon of Gods. An energetic and revitalised faith with a sixteen year old role model might just turn around the current Exodus towards the pagan religion of the world's capital City.

It was Demetrius as Chair of the Council, as well as High Priest, who announced the decision of the Elders to Maria who had decided to stand to hear the result of their deliberations.

"Our decision is unanimous on both requests. This Council grants its permission for you to hold public assemblies in the City of Valentia in order to spread the Good News of Iesus of Nazareth and we give permission for as many of these meetings as necessary to be held within the safety and security of our Temple."

Maria stood like a statue, at first unsure she had heard correctly, convinced by the questioning that the Council were against her but also not sure she had answered their questions particularly well! Then as the decision began to sink in, her face broke into the widest smile of pure joy.

She had a sudden urge to embrace someone, to say thank you in the only way she ever could or would. Demetrius had stepped around the table to congratulate her and so she hugged him with all of her pent up energy and anxiety. Her head rested sideways on his chest, her arms encircled him beneath his priestly chasuble. The High Priest thought perhaps he should be shocked or take offence but her affection was so genuine yet innocent that he decided to return the embrace. With a delighted grin, she looked up at him and said: "This means a lot to me and I thank you, therefore."

Longinus was hardly able to speak as he whispered in hushed and awed tones: "You gave the High Priest a hug?"

Maria had just regaled them with the highlights of the meeting and the glad tidings that they had permission to hold assemblies and to speak in the Temple. The girl was baffled as to why Longinus should be so thrown by her embrace of Demetrius and so told the Centurion that the High Priest had hugged her back so it must have been alright. Longinus was not sure whether to tell Maria that she was too young or too old to go around hugging High Priests and concluded that there was not a right age to do so. Finally, he was able to admonish her saying: "Hugs and High Priests are off the Agenda. Do you understand?"

"Not a word" and Maria turned her back on him and walked off into the crowd outside the Temple complex. It was already dusk and Maria made her way back to Pontus Virillis, Perseus and Longinus eventually catching her up and a large crowd of several thousand following, carrying torches, candles and lanterns. As soon as they reached Iosephus' trireme, some of the crowd called out for Maria to say something and so she mounted onto the ship's deck and stood facing this sea of faces lit by candlelight and by the waning moon above them.

"I am tired and so I shall say a few words now and invite you all to hear me in The Ancient Synagogue at noon tomorrow.

Someone asked me recently if they must convert from the Jewish faith to the new faith of my Master. Another asked me how do I join your faith? What is the rite of passage I must go through?

I went through no rite of passage. I was *called* and I *followed*. So it is now for you: if you want to follow my Master then follow him.

How do I follow my Master?

I listen to my Master's wishes which resonate in my heart and visit him where he resides in me. I pray, praising him, thanking him and asking for his help. He guides and helps me.

There are many things I believe in and over which there is no compromise. Taken together, if we believe in the following things openly then we are become followers without the need for any rite of passage:

I believe in God the Father and his Angels;
God the Son, his ministry, death and resurrection;
God the Spirit, The Comforter;
the ten commandments plus a new commandment to love one another;
the breaking of the bread; the gifts of the Spirit;
and life after death."

Maria had intended to speak for a few minutes but as the stars came out in the dark blue sky above her, she lifted her face towards their radiance and sang a song of praise then led the crowd in a prayer of thanksgiving that lasted an hour but passed as if it were mere moments.

When finally, her eyes came to rest on the crowd and her communion with the Angels was ended, she shivered, appreciating for the first time the cold of the night then she broke bread with those gathered around the trireme and the Spirit came upon them, crackling like the fire of Archimedes.

Three sets of parents were ushered to the front bearing their children: one was unable to walk, the second was blind and the third was said to be possessed by a devil, and would thrash out uncontrollably whilst screaming in a harsh and foreign language.

Perseus handed Maria the Spear and then lifted her down so that she could stand in the shallows. As she looked at the children, she wept to see their discomfort and misery. Then the blind child held out her hand and Maria allowed the young girl to touch her face. As the blind girl did so, her face broke open into a smile of joyful recognition: "You are Maria" she said falteringly and the Magdalan sobbed.

"Master, please help me" she pleaded between her tears and laid her hands gently on the blind girl's eyes. Then she touched the lame girl's legs with the Spear. Finally, she came to the boy who was said to be 'possessed'. Turning to his parents she offered them consolation and the benefit of her insight. "Your son has no demon in him. He has no evil in his heart. But to be healed, heart, soul *and mind* must all be healthy. I will try and heal his mind and remove the constant rage he feels."

Then she approached the child and as he thrashed out seeking to harm her, she took his blows and ignoring them, placed her hands slowly and carefully on his head:

"Master, bring this child peace."

At her words, the child's violence ceased and he turned his head towards his parents and said a single word: "Love" then the blind child cried out in ecstasy as she looked for the first time upon the stars whilst the lame child stood carefully then began to wade in the shallows delighting in the touch and feel of the cold water. The crowd erupted in songs of praise and would have mobbed Maria save she had walked into the shadows for a private moment of prayer in thanksgiving to her Master. "I love you" she said simply before Longinus and Perseus found her and hauled her back on deck.

The Synagogue was full and over-brimming at noon the following day with thousands in the cloisters of the Temple Palace that surrounded the timber-framed Temple and tens of thousands gathered on the steps and the colonnaded square beyond. The High Priest, Demetrius, was in raptures for he had dreamt of the day that the people of Valentia, Gentile and Jew, would unite in prayer. In just one day, the Magdalan had achieved his dream.

As she arrived, her lace shawl covering her hair, her eyes downcast, made timid before the eagerness of the crowds, the High Priest came forward and embraced her, publicly acknowledging his support of her, at which she lifted her head, her eyes alight with gratitude, her good humour returning, a shy grin on her face as she pondered on what Longinus would say. Longinus was a few steps away and was in no doubt that the High Priest and the Magdalan were doing the right thing to embrace: for at Valentia, the Jewish faith and that of Christians first joined as one as was and is God's desire.

Her *Message to the Valentians* as later reported in the writings of both Pilate and Nicodemus was simple: "We are united in our belief in one God. There are many paths but one way to Eternal Life. Whether we call ourselves 'Christian', 'Jew', 'Roman' or profess to no faith at all, if we live by the commandments and break bread in memory of Iesus then we are promised life after death."

When Nicodemus wrote of her Ministry in the fifth century, his account included Maria's Ministry at Valentia and her belief that all who believed in one God could find salvation. Alas, those who came after her had a different vision and it was not until the seventh century that in exasperation at the conflicts between faiths that broadly believed the same thing, the Holy Prophet would be granted his vision by God and found Islam on the basis that all of 'The Book' should one day be united. Nearly two thousand years later, a Pope would talk of belief in the Holy Spirit uniting "All of the same Book" in his Penticostal message. A long journey to knit back together that which had been torn apart by man took one more bold step forwards.

That evening, Maria was dressed in silks for her stola and chiton, with the finest Aegyptian linen for her peplon, all borrowed from Celestile. She wore strings of pearls as a choker, a gold amulet and sapphire ring, again borrowed but this time from Iosephus and worn originally by his wife who had died many years ago when young. Iosephus still grieved for her but his generous heart saw him come to the girl's rescue as all of the company knew her meal that evening at the Praetor's Palace would be one of her most important trials. Her hair, usually a riot of tangles and knots, was groomed until straight and shining, her eyebrows had been carefully curved and highlighted, she was wearing make up for the first time in her life and hated it, although Iosephus, Longinus, Perseus and Decius all approved: she did not look half-starved for a change.

Longinus was wearing his best toga made of the finest wool from Roma, with the red stripe that denoted his status as an officer in the army of Rome and as holding the rare honour of having been awarded the grass crown, with its entitlement to enter the Senate and to become a civil servant or part of the judiciary on retiring from military life provided he could meet the land holding requirement. As Maria and the young soldier walked from their latest mooring point along the Via Caecis through the Gardens of Suetovia towards the Praetor's Palace and the Novum Forum, she could see his tell-tale twitch of nervousness above his left eye and impulsively she gave his arm a squeeze then whispered:

"It will be alright. I am only one young girl and pose them no threat. They are interested to hear me and want to be able to say they have met me. I am no more than a trophy or a prize to them. Enjoy the meal and promise me you will stay calm whatever they might say."

They reached the Palace and were greeted by two of the Praetorian Guard, their red cloaks and jet black plumes showing their status. The couple presented their papers with the Praetor's and City Praefect's seals alongside that of the Provincial Governor and Procurator of Iudaea. Whilst they kept their faces appropriately devoid of any emotion, the two Guards were impressed and showed this by the way they immediately showed the couple to the Praetor's private quarters.

The triclinarium had been set out with six couches (besilliae) for the guests and a low table (mensilla) set between them for their supper. The room had a mosaic floor of intricate design showing one of the many naval victories of the first Antonines. The walls were stuccoed and painted with woodland scenes and mock arched doorways and windows; an early example of tromp d'oeil which would become the height of fashion in the reign of Nero. The ceiling was a painting in honour of the God Augustus, depicted sitting in state as Iupiter Omnipotens. The ceiling painting would be the subject of the second challenge that Maria would meet that evening; the first would be the height of her besillium.

The couple were shown to the vestibularum where both had their feet washed as a sign of welcome and two house slaves touched up Maria's make up and straightened the folds on Longinus' toga. This gave Tartellus' steward the chance to announce the arrival of two of the guests to the Praetor.

As Maria and Longinus returned to the triclinarium, Tartellus and Antonius were there to greet them and show them to their seats. The three men lay on their right hand side on their besilliae but Maria sat upright, her hands in her lap, feet dangling and swinging from left to right and back again as they had when before the City Elders. She gulped at how high the seats were, fearing she would fall or roll off if she dared to make the attempt to recline as the men-folk were. They had barely made formal introductions when the steward announced the arrival of the last two guests.

First was Statius Gemellus Gracchus, City Praefect at Larida, which lay just north of the future home and birthplace of the famous El Cid. Gemellus was in his twenties and already destined for the highest honours after a successful posting on the staff of the elder Germanicus Caesar, now dead, poisoned by the Pisonis. Gemellus had a new patron in the younger Germanicus Caesar, nicknamed 'little boots' or Caligula.

The second guest was Varus Marus Caecius Fluvius, Admiral of the Roman fleet that patrolled the Hispanic coast, whose responsibility included protecting these shores against pirates and escorting the grain supply for Roma from northern Africa. Varus Caecius had come from Tunis with news of 'The Magdalan' and had leapt at the opportunity to meet her.

Their food was brought to the table on long dishes of silver, embossed with the reliefs of the most famous victories of Rome, mythical creatures and the legends of Roman Gods and demi-Gods. Each dish had already been prepared in portions the right size to be held in fingers and eaten without staining pristine white togas or ruining the silk of any lady guest. Some of the dishes had wooden skewers with which to hold them and all were accompanied by sauces in which they could be dipped, ranging from steaming oil, kept bubbling by burners beneath the crucible in which it was served, to spiced chilli and ginger.

Set before them was carp and turbot, thin slices of cured beef, ham and roast belly of pork, rolled eel and oysters, peppers stuffed with soft cheese, olives stuffed with tomato, small pies and pasties filled with dormice and pigeon marinated in red wine, olive bread, a puree of pork, fig and apricot, fresh figs and pears, sliced melons and oranges, a salad of couscous and lime, vine leaves wrapped around grilled goat's stomach in a cherry sauce, lamb with mint kofta, the braised head of a stag, sheep's eyes and the breast of a peacock, its tail plumes and magnificent head and crown adorning the dish, adding colour to a table that groaned with magnificent food sourced from across the Empire. The meal was accompanied by wine from Baeatica, Roicaea and Reita, watered down to reduce their potency.

Maria ate a small piece of olive bread and drank water, not daring to try the rich assortment of dishes before her. In contrast, the five men ate and drank liberally and as they did so their questioning of the girl became more and more challenging until they ran out of wine.

Tartellus started the questions:

"Maria, we welcome you and are astonished at your youth. If you had any rebellious intentions, your following would already run in the millions and you would represent a greater threat to Rome than Spartacus or Vercingetorix. Yet you say that you pose no threat. How is this?"

Maria replied carefully, taking time over each word to avoid stuttering or stumbling, rather speaking in perfect Lingua Romanorum, of purity found usually only in the oratory of the Courts or Senate. Yet her words were gently spoken, heartfelt and sincere.

"I understand that there are many things in this world that can be resolved by the violence of war and rebellion but I believe that this resolves nothing in the next world. Every person is a creation of God and if I harm another person then I harm God. So I advocate peace and peaceful solutions."

Antonius went next intrigued at her response seeking to test her further:

"What do you mean by 'peaceful solutions'?"

"To reach agreement or a consensus in preference to going to war; to ask for concessions and freedoms in response for greater loyalty in preference to the division of rebellion; to sacrifice oneself in preference to harming another."

This silenced the men briefly as each had chosen a military career and so facing Maria's devout pacifism, they were doubtful, felt she was being naïf. Yet a part of them bemoaned the loss of colleagues, peers, family and friends to the indiscriminate hunger of war. They welcomed the current peace within the Empire's boundaries after almost a century of civil wars and conflicts: Marius and Sulla, the Italian Wars, Spartacus' rebellion, Julius Caesar and Pompeius, Octavian and Antonius. Almost fifty years of peace within its boundaries was welcome to those Romans who sought family life but provided limited opportunities for those with ambition in public life.

After a brief silence, Tartellus brought Maria's attention to the ceiling and its depiction of the God Augustus as Jupiter Omnipotens:

"What do you believe about the divinity of Augustus? For you challenge Rome if you say that Caesar is not divine."

"Perhaps I challenge Rome but if so my challenge is very small and woefully weak, so insignificant that surely mighty Roma will just ignore me? But what do I believe?

First, I think your ceiling is very beautiful and I am at risk of just sitting here and staring at the wonderful sky and the enticement of the distant mountains that an unknown artist has painted with love and pride in his work. I am bewitched by its breathtaking realism, transported to places of excitement and adventure through one man's artistry, desiring to meet him and thank him for his great gift.

Second, I think the Roman world has honoured the Emperor Augustus by saying that through his great achievements he now sits in glory with the Gods. I am happy to share the view that this great man may well now sit in Paradise.

However, your faith does not say that the great Augustus was the creator of the stars, our land, skies and seas, of the animals and fishes and of man. Augustus is not God the Creator, whom my faith teaches me is the only God.

The difference between my faith and yours looks to be very minor: I believe in one God with many facets, attributes and powers and you believe in many Gods each with a single facet, attribute or power.

I believe that those who do God's Will earn the right to live with God. You believe that such men or women sit as a God in the company of Gods. These differences are surely not worthy to be called a 'challenge'? At a time of religious tolerance can we not accept such differences provided they do not lead to impiety or rebellion?

I promise that I shall not decry the faith of Rome for it is not in my nature to be critical. I am pure in my faith and chaste in my life and offer my piety as an example for others. I will always be positive about the good I find in people whatever their faith for I believe that all good things are God's Will."

The five men were stunned because this time Maria had unconsciously spoken in the purest Latina, her words resonating like the finest oratory of Cicero and with the fluency of Julius Caesar. Her answer had also rocked them for it was clear there was a difference between their views of divinity yet they could also see that the difference need not prevent each belief set to be tolerant of the other. But her response had also raised one fundamental question. Gemellus took on the challenge:

"What do you mean by 'good things'?"

"Not everything I shall say is certain and some things are the beatings and promptings of my heart rather than the teachings of my faith. My Master was never asked the question you have posed of me yet some of the things he said guide my heart and so I believe the following are good things:

- to come to the relief of another who has been harmed even if a stranger;
- to forgive a child or a friend when they return seeking our aid;
- to die to save another;
- to heal the lame and the blind;
- to offer comfort to prisoners and those who are oppressed;
- to give your last penny to the poor;
- to be open to the needs and desires of children;
- to never harm or hurt a child;
- to pray for others; and
- to show your love to strangers and foreigners.

Each of these was praised by my Master during his ministry. I would then add: to praise the meek and humble; to glorify and rejoice in God's creation and to honour an enemy rather than assail them. For my Master once said 'Blessed are the peacemakers for theirs shall be the Kingdom of God'."

"You ask so much" Tartellus said in hushed tones, not wishing to challenge anything that she had said for in his heart he agreed with every word. Varus, however, had yet to ask a question and now did so:

"Why do you seek to go to Caledonia?"

Maria blushed then looked at Longinus in apology for she could not and would not lie even for a friend:

"We told Pilate we were seeking to aid Longinus' niece in Caledonia otherwise we would not have got Pilate's permission for Longinus to be my escort. The real reason is that I am asked by my Master to take word of his life and ministry to all peoples in the world. Others will bring the

Good News to the world of the Roman Empire whilst my mission is to bring the same message to the world of the barbarian."

Antonius could not help himself but, showing genuine concern for the girl, said:

"If you go with an escort of four or five only then you go to your certain death. The barbarians slaughter strangers and are intolerant of the faiths of foreigners. You will be sacrificed and die a terrible and horrifying death. Gemellus will tell you that when serving with Germanicus, what they found in the forests of the Ardaenum and Teutobriges was human sacrifice, the victims mainly being young girls slain in the most gruesome manner, sickening soldiers who had believed they were inured to death."

Gemellus nodded recalling those who had been slain by the torture called 'The Raven' and others blinded and left to be eaten by rats caged in helmets placed over the girls' faces. "Life is held as cheap by the barbarian hordes" he muttered and Longinus went pale for he could not bear to see his charge harmed. Yet the girl was fearless:

"If I am to die in the lands of the Briton, the Celt, the Germanii, Alemani, Burgundi, Franci, the Caledonii, Gael or Pict then so be it. There is no alternative surely if those who live in Britannia and Gallia are to hear the Good News and be given a chance to follow my Master? My Master was tortured and slain in agony. Why should my fate be any different?"

Tartellus stood, a little unsteady from the drink he had consumed, but he wished to honour his guest and so standing straight he asked his fellow guests to join him in a toast. Then he noticed he was out of wine and tendered his cup towards the steward. The steward bent forward and whispered: "We are out of the Raetan. I can offer the white grape from Beatica?"

Tartellus shuddered and shook his head for he had been drinking red all evening and knew that mixing colours would play havoc on his constitution. He realised he faced ridicule if he had to admit he had run out of the Raetan and looked across the chamber to Maria, without intending to do so yet a silent plea in his eyes.

Maria signalled to the steward then asked him quietly, whispering in his ear, to bring her two amphora of spring water. Next she prayed silently to herself: "Once you turned water to the finest wine at the request of your mother and to save the wedding party of a friend from embarrassment. I seek to save my newfound friend Tartellus from the same embarrassment and so ask for the special gift of your miracle."

The steward's jaw dropped as he watched the clear liquid dull and change colour to a deep red. It was part of his responsibilities to taste any wine served and handing one of the two amphora to a fellow servant, the steward took a fresh cup and poured a small gout which he tasted then gasped. This was the finest Raetan he had ever tasted, so smooth it would not require watering down yet so deep and full of flavours that it would ignite any palette. He made an announcement:

"Gentleman, my Master has asked that I serve his best wine for the toast that he wishes to propose" and began to fill their wine cups with the new wine. When he came last to Tartellus, the host whispered: "Where did you find it?" And the steward nodded towards Maria then said simply: "The girl prayed for it." With their cups full and each man enjoying the distinctive nez du vin of the best Raetan any of them had ever sampled, Tartellus spoke with genuine feeling:

"I offer you our praise for a brave young girl whose vision of peaceful unity may seem fanciful yet she can do wonderful things that none of us can explain. Maria, you are under my protection for as long as you shall be in Valentia, the Province of Tarraconensis and Upper Hispania."

The men all stood and raised their wine cups whilst Maria blushed bright crimson, then Varus offered his protection for her ships should she travel on the Balearicum and western Middle Seas and Gemellus joined in, offering free passage to Osca and Pampona.

The conversation moved to gossip about events in Roma where Tiberius' ousting of Sejanus and his followers was still the talk of the City. Power had temporarily moved to the Island of Capri as the Emperor had gathered his immediate family to avoid their assassination or his family members becoming a front for others who sought to rule the Empire. He had also summonsed his administration, trusting freedmen such as Pallas, who had carried the message of warning from his mistress, the Lady Antonia Caesar, over Senators and other appointments amongst the nobility.

What was about to follow was a period of terror and tyranny that would see any powerful family in Rome or provincial appointee under suspicion of supporting rebellion hauled before the Curiale Court and executed, their family inheritance being added to the growing coffers of Tiberius' Exchequer. "Tiberius will not last long" muttered Gemellus. "Hush" was Tartellus' response. "Such talk is treasonous." Then Antonius broke the silence that had followed Gemellus' *faut pas*, saying with a laugh:

"Pilate will be recalled long before the Emperor passes on. You do well Longinus to have found a mission that keeps you away from politics for the next two years. The young Germanicus is an even worse prospect as Emperor than the 'old man'."

"I pray for Pontius Pilate for the sake of his wife. I pray for Tiberius for the tolerance he has shown to my faith. I pray that Germanicus will make a good Emperor when his time comes" was Maria's solitary contribution to their conversation and all five men laughed.

"Alas, my dear, even your prayers cannot change the madness that has gripped our City of Roma since Sejanus' fall" Tartellus interrupted her good naturedly. "But we love you for your constant good will."

The conversation continued for many hours and what emerged was a union that would ultimately see the assassination of Germanicus and his replacement with the feeble but proficient Claudius. When six years later, the Procurator of Lusitania joined with the four conspirators, four legions and half the navy of the Roman Empire were ready to invade Roma.

Three Senators in Roma and the Praetorian Guard would remove the need for them to do so when they assassinated Caligula as he took the private passage from "The Bedroom" as the canopied private seating area at the old Coliseum was known towards his refurbished Imperial Palace at the end of a gladiatorial contest. It was another just under thirty years before the legions in Hispania would rise to place Galba on the curule chair as one of the shortest-lived Emperors. By the time of the Year of the Four Emperors, the four legions in Hispania were down to three (they had lost the Ninth in the northern lands of Britannia), discipline in the remaining legions in Hispania had deteriorated (as they had remained inactive on home duty for longer than any other legions), and their short-lived attempt to place one of their own on the throne of the civilised world was easily crushed by Vitellius' legions from Gaul.

As the night drew on, Tartellus noticed Maria's head nod and her eye lids become increasingly heavy. "I had forgotten she is still a child" he whispered over his shoulder to Longinus, who looked across the room then stood hurriedly and just reached her as she collapsed forwards in sleep. Lifting her easily in his arms, he asked his host permission to retire and take the girl back to their ship as it was long past the time she usually slept.

But Tartellus surprised him by refusing. Instead he offered them both the comfort of the guest cubilla in his personal chambers in the Palace and to send word to Iosephus such that the elderly knight would not worry when neither of them returned. "Maria is welcome to stay here for as long as she is in Valentia" he offered surprising all of his guests. "This way it will be known she speaks with my full blessing."

The conversion of both Tartellus and Demetrius saw the Good News of the Nazarene spread rapidly throughout Tarraconensis to the provincial capital of Caesaragumptum. Tartellus was summoned by the Provincial Governor and Legate of Lusitania, Senator Aurus Fabian Scarius, and convinced his fellow Governor that the teachings of this new faith were harmless, even beneficial given its strong commitment to peace.

Any Governor feared riot and rebellion but welcomed peaceful tranquillity and stability. *'A leader who advocated celebrating a new faith in the home and who was against any form of war or violence is a new concept'* Scarius pondered and the more he thought about it, the more he could see only good coming from supporting the Magdalan's mission. So Tartellus returned to keep a watchful eye on this new movement but agreeing with Scarius not to interfere with its peaceful intent.

Maria stayed six days in Valentia and then accepted an offer to stay with Gemellus at his villa in Larida, one day's ride from the City and half way to the City of Orsa. In that time she preached every day at the Temple and twice in the Forum, drawing crowds of thousands, praying to the Angels each night to offer her guidance then explaining part of the scriptures each day, showing how the Nazarene's ministry had been foretold and fulfilled the prophecy of the Coming of the Messiah.

"The Messiah has come already and now is dead?" one of the crowd asked and Maria laughed gaily then replied:

"My laughter is not at you but in delight at the memory of what my Master has achieved. In Isaiah, in the 64th verse, the death of the Messiah is foretold but also we are told that *he will rise.* My Master died but also then rose from the dead and is still alive, seen by thousands to whom he preached after his death, and continuing to live in me and in tens of thousands who have joined him in the breaking of the bread. I have seen him and felt his arms surround me.

The Messiah is not dead. He resides in me, heart and soul, his tent upon the sanded beaches of my heart, a pavilion that I visit each waking moment to learn of his intent for the world. My Master *is* the Messiah. There is no past tense, only the glory of him alive in the present. I rejoice and am glad!"

Tartellus was genuinely saddened to lose the good company of the young girl whose courage and fearlessness in the face of the challenges she would meet in barbarian lands had touched his soldier's heart. Her miracle had not only saved him from embarrassment before his friends but also sealed his trust in the truth of Maria's account. He believed she had seen 'wonderful things' and he hoped for this world of peaceful unity she foresaw. "I would keep you here" he whispered to her "if it were not that you go to stay with Gemellus and I know you will be safe there. Go in God's grace" and he rode with her as far as the outskirts of his City before finally waving her on.

Metellus and Decius had sailed for Alexandria that morning and so the company were back to their original six, but left behind over one hundred thousand who would break the bread in communion with each other and in memory of the Nazarene. Iosephus had organised staging posts once more and taken the opportunity to buy some fine Arab mares and stallions at the auction and horse fair in Valentia. He was able to offer a change of horses between Valentia and Larika, then fresh horses and a further change between Larika and Orsa. Orsa to Iaenus Portus would take four days and then a further two to three days ride from the northern port to where they intended to cross into Aquitainia and Narbonnensis via Pampona.

Maria spoke once at the Synagogue at Larika, to a crowd of over one thousand but spent the best part of two days relaxing and using the piscina in Gemellus' villa which had the attraction of real carp swimming in its waters; she fell in love with the swimming pool and swam with the fish for hours, feeding them from her gentle hands. Gemellus was a genial host, as convinced as Tartellus that Maria was honest and spoke the truth about what she had seen and he was excited by all he had heard her say but unable yet to commit to turning his back on his household Gods and the Gods of his ancestors.

The company arrived in Osca to huge crowds already waiting for them at the gates to the City. Maria was delighted when Teleus rode out to greet them and as he dismounted she leapt from her horse and ran into his arms to welcome him. "Come" he said radiating happiness. "The City Elders have already offered you their welcome and the City Praefect, Servius Sextus Flavius has made it clear that you are to be offered every courtesy. This is so different from the welcome we received at Damascus."

"You are silly" Maria replied. "I am much more interested that you are here. Tell me everything of your travels" and for the next hour Teleus spoke of his journey across land through the Macedonian mountains, the Alpes and the Pyrenees before dropping south from Tolosa to Osca.

"If I see another mountain as long as I shall live …" he moaned then laughed in delight at being with them all again. Iosephus and Annanias took Teleus to one side to brief him on the slight change in plans and the detour to Iaenus Portus.

Teleus, in turn, was able to reassure the equites that accommodation had been booked in Tolosa, Narbo, Marsela, Aix, Arilate, Valentum, Vienna and Lugdubellum (Luguidenum), following the valley of the Rhone from Marsela. The route from Luguidenum depended very much on their reception as they went through the Roman Province of Celtica to its borders with the Parisii. They could go east across the Massif Central and northern Alpes to Helvetica, or follow the Saone north to the City of Lusitania or branch off the Saone going west from Carbillonum, skirting the capital of Gaul, heading to Allanum, Bibanari, Torino, Bibracte, Rocca and Sugdavellum.

"We will need to ride fast for we can expect a reception party at every stop from hereon. Word is spreading fast and people want to hear what the excitement is all about. There is no hope of secrecy now. We must hope we are well-received and trust in Maria's obvious harmlessness to protect us all."

Perseus surprised them all with his observation as he corrected Iosephus: "It is her prayers that protect us. We are in God's hands."

Maria spoke outside the City walls at Osca and then entered the City to stay at a small family-run Taverna on the banks of the River Ebro, in the gardens of the Ribera passage by Pontus Almodarus. Her brief time crossing the Middle Sea had taught her to love water, its gentle lapping against the wooden piles of the quayside or the rage of its tempests as the winds tore at the ship's sails or storms tossed up heavy winds and mountainous waves to crash against the sanded shores. Her chambers looked out to the stars above and the river beneath her balcony, both heartening her and offering her solace and inspiration for the journey ahead.

They rode in haste for Iaenus Portus, aware it was a detour yet wishing to give the people of Baetica and Lucitania a chance to hear the Word. They stopped briefly at Tudela and Calaharra before making their night stop at the City of Legrano in the region of Bascchia (Basconis). To their north was the country of the Bascones, who had fought for their independence in the time of Marius and Sulla, been offered such by Julius Caesar in return for their support in his civil war against Pompeius Magnus and been betrayed by Octavian who had refused to honour his uncle's promises.

Longinus warned Maria: "Our travel documents are meaningless until we reach Iaenus Portus. There is no administration of the Basschia or Bascones region to whom we can apply for safe passage. We must hope we can avoid being taken as captives to be held hostage. We stick to the main roads and travel with the first caravanade to leave Legrano, praying that its numbers and escort will deter any bandits. If we are taken, best is to plead poverty and hope for our release. Iosephus, you need to go south with Teleus and join us at Iaenus Portus by sea but if you come with us then we will all be held until you can sort out a ransom."

So the company split, promising to meet up in five to seven days time. "Why so long?" Perseus asked and Longinus explained that Iosephus must go many leagues out of his way to skirt around Bascones country and then must sail along the coast for at least two days to reach Iaenus Portus. Their own journey would be slow as they were part of a wagon and caravan train that would trudge along the tortuous mountain tracks and occasional stretch of Roman road at a fraction of the speed they could do on their Arab horses.

On the second night, disaster struck.

Maria had taken to telling the children with the caravanade stories as night fell, to give them courage and welcome dreams but also because some had heard her singing to the stars and asked her to tell them about the concerto of the cosmos. Soon the parents began to listen in and when it became known that this was 'La Magdalena', the whole wagon and caravan train would stop at night to hear Maria's stories, join her as she broke the bread with them and listen to her sing quietly in praise.

Then a horse had stumbled and broken a calf. The poor family who owned the horse had no spare and knew that not only must they put the horse down as its life would be pitiful on three legs but also with only one horse they would no longer be able to keep up. They did not ask for help but rather the Wagoner took out his Ferrier's hammer and made ready to slay the horse with a single blow behind its ear.

"Stop!" Maria tried to shout but it came out as a gasp and so she ran and flung her arms around the horse's neck.

"We have no choice" the poor man pleaded and so Maria prayed and as she did so she asked the Wagoner to join her in prayer. He shrugged his shoulders but seeing the naked plea in the girl's eyes he followed her as she asked:

"Save this horse from an unkind death and grant it health and that it be healed of its injury. Do this I ask out of love for me and for the family whose horse this is."

Then to everyone's astonishment, the crooked calf straightened and the horse was able to put its weight on it again. The horse knew what had happened and who was responsible and swung its head round to nuzzle in Maria's hair whilst the Wagoner knelt in tears to give praise.

The parents of the children were not the only ones watching the Camp each night and when her celebration of the Eucharist with the people of the caravanade was ended, Maria walked off into the darkness to have a few moments alone to sing a song of rejoicing and thanksgiving before she retired to her camp bed. Longinus could hear her soft voice coming out of the shadows and was reassured … then suddenly the singing was cut off abruptly.

The Centurion ran to where he had last heard her voice a lit brand in his left hand but he could find no traces of the girl save two drops of blood on the ground that made his heart churn within his chest in an agony of fear for her.

As the sun came up to announce the red dawn of a new day, the caravanade moved on. They could not delay in order to search for a girl taken by bandits. Longinus must hope for her release. The Centurion ordered Perseus to stay with the caravanade in case Maria by some miracle was able to rejoin them whilst he waited with a spare horse in the hope that the girl might be released or escape and make her way back to where she had last been with friends. He knew the girl had nothing to offer: no money or jewellery. He hoped the bandits who had taken her would see her innocence and set her free yet he feared that more likely they would blind her or kill her to prevent her revealing the secret of their hideout.

He had waited two anxious days when on the third night as his head was nodding in drowsiness before the embers of a fire he had lit to keep him warm and scare away any wild animal, he heard a whispered "Domine" and then a sack was flung into the light of his camp fire, rolling to stop at his feet. He looked into the dark but could see no movement and so stooped to open the sack.

To his delight, inside was a sleeping Maria, with the small scar of a recently healed cut on her fragile throat where a knife had been held to silence her but otherwise no other sign of her being mal-treated. Longinus stroked her hair and cheek to wake her and she stretched, yawned and opened one eye then bent forward and wrapped both arms around Longinus' neck with a beaming smile.

"What happened?" the young man asked and Maria allowed him to lift her onto her feet before saying: "We have free passage through the land of Basschia. The chief of all of the Bascones tribes has granted us this and I know he keeps his word because he also promised to let me go and he has done so. I trust him!"

"Yes but what happened?" repeated Longinus persistently and Maria grinned in mischief as she could still frustrate the young soldier and he was absolutely adorable when his green eyes were blazing with fury … and she should not be thinking such thoughts as he was destined for her best friend after the Master, but she had danced the flamenco and her blood was still racing from the experience.

"I was kidnapped to order. I was not your typical ransom captive but taken prisoner to be brought before the Chief of all the tribes of the Bascones and the only person who can bind all of the Bandits to a single command.

One day he will lead his people in revolt but he waits until Roma is weak and will wait as long as is necessary for that moment when his countrymen can claim their rightful independence."

"Maria, unless you tell me what happened I will put you back in your sack and leave you with a note saying 'Keep Her!'"

"Do not be mean. I am telling you but you keep interrupting. Well they held a sharp knife to my neck, shone a torch to light up my face said 'Yes this is the girl' then tapped me on the head and I collapsed and did not come around until something sickly sweet but pungent was held to my nose and woke me with a start.

The bandits all had their faces covered with masks or scarves wrapped around their heads to conceal all but their eyes. One of the men spoke Latin and asked me to mount a horse they offered: a mare in reasonably good condition, bred for the uneven tracks to be found in the mountains and tethered to the saddle of the bandit who was to be my escort. I knew I had no choice so did as they asked without argument.

We rode for a day and a night through beautiful country and across the western edge of the Pyrenees, with views out towards the Atlantic, the Middle Sea, the central plains of Hispania and the south and west coastlines of Gaul. We rode into valleys comprising a single glacial lake or green forests stretching in all directions or the softest of grass-lands with villages and towns hidden as they formed part of the rock of the mountains or where we walked through labyrinths of caves made by water and lime to create subterranean seas and statues of mythical creatures and monsters.

On the second night, that would be yesterday night, I came at last to the camp of the bandit chief. I had been looked after well up until then, fed and treated with respect, allowed to say my prayers and encouraged to sing which the men seemed to appreciate and enjoy despite my voice being so weak. The bandit chief took one look at me and asked: "Are we certain? This is just a common girl."

I surprised him by replying in his own native tongue: "My name is Maria also known as the Magdalan. Yes I am an ordinary girl of no status and no wealth."

"If you have nothing to offer us then we will slay you" replied the bandit chief angry at my words. My reply made him even angrier until his wife stepped in to whisper in his ear as I said: "I will not lie to you to save my life. I am not special nor do I have any talent."

Whatever his wife had said washed away his anger and left him with the naked emotion of despair writ across his face and in the sag of his proud shoulders. Finally, he asked but fearful of my response: "Can you heal?"

"Who am I to heal? Take me now" was my reply and his face came alive again, hope rekindled as he whispered: "Then you are She!"

I had been taken captive to bring healing to his only son, you see. His men had watched my healing of the merchant's horse then heard accounts of my healing of three children at Valentia, already a story told around camp fires across the plains of Hispania. The chief had sent out bandits to take me and bring me to where his son lay in a fever and an affliction which his physicians feared would see his son's death. Their medicines had not worked and now they had turned to me.

The boy was unconscious, so wrapped up in the fever was the child that he was no longer responding to any attempt to wake him. I knelt by him and kissed his brow then washed the sweat away with my tears and dried his forehead with my hair before saying in humble prayer: "Master, if it is Thy Will then heal this child."

We all watched in anticipation then dawning hope and finally joyful astonishment as the boy's fever broke, he yawned, woke and seeing the worried look on his parent's faces said: "I feel hungry."

The camp broke into celebration, from everywhere came drums and musical instruments, lyres and harps and reed pipes of every size and instrument. The music they played was a riot of sound, fiery, emotive and passionate. And then they danced and before I knew it I had been whisked off my knees and was being taught the steps of the flamenco, the twists and turns, how to be held as if flying or swooping to lie vulnerable and on the ground, to fall to leap, clap and turn my shoulder in disdain, to flirt and take flight. We danced until the embers of the fire began to recede then sat around the fire on logs and poked the fire until it caught once more and then I sang.

The chief bandit came to the fire's edge and stood before me and his people then he lifted me as if I was made of feathers and holding me high above his head said: "This girl has saved my Son. She is to be granted whatever she wants."

"Good sir" I had asked in reply "Can I celebrate the breaking of the bread with you all? And then I would ask for safe passage through your lands for myself and anyone under my protection."

"You have your safe passage but what is the 'breaking of the bread'?"

"My Master whose power of healing I invoked through my prayer, once broke a simple loaf of bread and passed it around so that everyone who supped with him had a piece. Then we ate it and he told us that each time we did the same we would remember him and he would return to be with us."

"Your Master healed my son?" the chief asked and I nodded in confirmation. "Then I would wish to remember him with honour. Show me the way of this 'breaking of the bread' that I might remember him every day."

So with the chief's permission, I led them in the Eucharist feast, showing them how simple it was and that it only needed two or more when gathered together. As we prayed in thanksgiving for the miracle of healing, the Spirit came down on several of the bandits and they began to speak in different languages to the amazement of their peers.

"What is this?" the chief asked me but humbly for now he understood what drove me and could see that the Master lived within me. So I told him about the gifts of the Spirit and then I told him of the greatest gift of all: the promise of Eternal Life.

"How can I gain this gift?" and I could see the naked hunger for a life in Paradise in his eyes.

"It will be hard for you yet call me if you need help and I will come. You must obey the Ten Commandments and continue to break the bread as I have shown you."

He knew of our commandments for he was well-read and said: "No killing, no stealing and no running after other people's goods or wives. This is hard for a bandit but what you offer us is riches greater than anything we might gain through banditry. Maria, my lady, I must think on this and I must persuade my tribes that your way is the right way. I promise to try. But now we must return you and we will ride both night and day to take you back to where we found you. One of your companions is keeping a lonely vigil waiting for you there. My people watch him and are amazed at his courage to stand alone in that deserted place. He is protected by his courage and by your own free passage. We take you to him now."

I am afraid that soon after that I fell asleep and have no recollection of being put in the sack, just of looking up and seeing the security of your wonderful face looking down at me" then before Longinus could say or do anything, Maria kissed him on the lips then hung her head shyly. "That is for waiting for me" she whispered then mounted her horse and together they rode for Iaenus arriving just after dawn.

Iaenus Portus was a repeat of Valentia. First Maria spoke to the City Elders to thank them for the permission they had granted her. Then she met the Praetor and City Praefect who were both on good terms with Tartellus and happy to grant Maria the chance to speak in both the Forum and the Port, providing her with a sealed document giving her right of assembly.

Iaenus Portus was the second largest port they had visited so far on their travels, its docks providing safe haven for several fleets of ships trading with the west coasts of Hispania, Gallia and western Africa as far as Dakar and the Bay of Guinea, as well as Tunis and the north coast of Africa, Hibernia and Britannia but also the port saw several adventurous ships that would brave the Charybdis to sail via Baetica and on to Bibralta, Tangeris or Aligeris and then return.

They spent two days in Iaenus Portus and on both Maria spoke to huge crowds drawn from all of Lusitania and Baetica. Nearly one hundred thousand joined her in the breaking of the bread across the two days. Two of the diakonae brought back to sight men suffering from blindness due to their cataracts and other acts of healing were performed by people within the crowd celebrating the Eucharist who had been filled with the Spirit.

Maria's *Message to the People of Iaenus Portus in Lusitania* (as summarised in Pilate's 4th Century account of her mission) was: "My Master brings you the gift of 'Hope' through me and through the breaking of the bread. Remember him but also remember that he came back from the dead to show us that we can do the same. It is the hope of *life after death* that drives me when I follow my Master. To serve him faithfully in this life so that I can do so eternally in the next."

Iosephus joined them on the sixth day since they had left Legrano and the party were now complete. Teleus was sent on by ship to Budigala then on to Sugdavellum to ensure they had a ship waiting to take them to Britannia. The company rode fast on the narrow mountain tracks across the Pyrenees and into Pampona which was their last stop in Hispania to meet the growing crowds eager to listen to the inspiration of Maria but starting to ask more and more questions about the new faith. In Pampona, Maria spoke for only a short time and the Eucharistic celebrations were also short-lived as some instinct told her that the crowd was impatient to ask questions of her.

Inadvertently, in answer to one of the questions, she declared a position in opposition to Paulus' teaching. He would not forget and from the moment he heard her words, worked to undermine her vision setting the path for the divisions that would continue until the birth of Islam and the Synod of Whitby.

"I have a rich neighbour who is a follower. Should I denounce him?"

"Our Master said it is hard to cross into Paradise if burdened with riches. He did not say it is impossible. You say you seek to denounce your neighbour. To whom and for what would you denounce him? Rather pray for your neighbour that he may gain the wisdom to give his money to the poor and follow my Master."

"Teach me how to pray as you do."

"Find your heart and speak the words you find there even if they make no sense."

"What is our soul?"

"I do not know but I can say what it does. But I cannot locate it or describe it. My soul is the home for my conscience and for my inspiration to follow God. It is the home for God's Spirit in me and ultimately the part of me that will live with God until we are told on the Day of Judgement who will be those fortunate enough to be judged worthy of Paradise: they will see the return of their mortal bodies."

"You speak of the return or resurrection of our bodies: will we return as children, adults or as we were when we died? What shall we look like?"

"It is my hope that we shall return as we looked at the moment of our greatest love and greatest good. We will be seen at our very best. My Master returned as he looked when he sacrificed himself for us, his greatest moment in life, but with the difference that his pain had been replaced with joy."

"When Iesus returned from the dead did he still have the wounds he received?"

"Yes and he was bleeding from them. His blood went on my clothes as I hugged him."

"Paulus is also of this new faith and speaks of the need to be baptised. Must we go through such an initiation?"

"I have never been baptised and yet am filled by the Spirit. Baptism is there for those who need it and feel it is helpful. But if we believe in one God, break the bread and follow the commandments then my Master has promised us Eternal Life. This is the new covenant of which he speaks: a promise that cannot be broken by adding new requirements."

"Petrus is a leader in your faith. He does not yet preach but he does set the rules for those he leads in faith. Should we follow these rules? One is that we must be circumcised. Is this true?"

"Petrus once asked me to tell him about the visions I had received from my Master. When I had done so he then wanted to cast me out but my Master came to him and protected me as did some of the other Apostles accusing Petrus of 'being a bully'. Then one day a man called Cornelius had the same vision as I had once had and Petrus was converted. He accepted that we must preach to the Gentiles as well as the Jews and that there is no need for circumcision" then Maria added with a grin of mischief: "That was a close call!"

"Who is the leader of our faith? Is it you or Paulus or I hear of the man Petrus in Ierusalem, is it him?"

"My Master leads our faith."

"If I am asked to swear an oath to Rome, what shall I do?"

"Unless your oath says you cannot believe in one God, Iesus and the Spirit then to swear an oath of loyalty to Rome is no sin. Rome offers much that is good and should not be written off for the oppression done in its name. Rome does not oppress, it is men who oppress just as Rome is not 'Evil' but evil deeds have been done in its name. Be careful whom or what we condemn and remember that we are encouraged to forgive, to turn the other cheek when struck."

"You say your Master, Iesus, is 'within you'. Is this as a growth or are you with child?"

"No, I do not have a growth and alas I am too young to be bearing his or any child. My Master has filled me with his essence, his Spirit, and all that he is without bodily form. I can see him and that he is alive just as on occasions I am guided by his Angels and can see them. But most of the time my Master speaks to my heart and helps me better understand my faith."

"Describe Paradise to us."

"I can only say what my Master has said and will not attempt to guess. It is the place where God resides, timeless. A place has been prepared for each of us: often described as a tent ready for us to occupy but also as a place in 'his Father's house'. We are free to walk the boundaries of Paradise but may not cross into Hades. It is a place where we serve God but willingly doing work that we enjoy. We take no possessions into Paradise and go before God naked.

I believe more than that but my beliefs are personal and carry no weight for I am a simple girl, granted the wisdom to speak the words of my Master but without the wisdom to permit my own ideas to be heard."

"Will you return to Hispania?"

"One day I shall if I am permitted to do so by my Master and by you and I live long enough."

Gallia (Narbonnensis and Celtica)

The early Church historians Eusebius and Nicodemus talk of the establishment of the early Christian Church communities, practising in hiding in caves, catacombs, deserted groves and ruined Temples with 'christians' surviving persecutions under Domitian in the first century AD and the second Domitian in the second century AD.

Nicodemus wrote as follows:

"Joseph of Arithamea took Mary Magdalan through Gaul on their way to Britannia establishing new communities of Christians in Luguidenum and Sugdavellum … Mary journeyed from Tolosa to Marsela then Torino before leaving Gaul to take ship for Britannia from Sugdavellum." (Nicodemus, 5th Century AD)

The Celtic legend of Parsifor (Sir Percy of the Round Table) and the Legend of 'The Grael' also touch in passing on Mary Magdalan's mission to Gaul in both the 'Lay of Parsifor' and the Ballad 'Parsifor the Perfect Knight' (both date back to the 10th Century and possibly date from the same time as the Legend of Orlando). The first written and illuminated versions date to the early 13th Century and will have changed dramamatically from the original versions under the influence of Phillip of Flanders account of the Grael legend:

The second section of the Lay of Parsifor: Parsifor the Grael Knight.

"Parsifor held before him the sacred Spear
His foe was too fearful to his puissance dare
Before them he knelt devoutly in prayer
The Sacred Grael securely gript in his care

Facing many assaults from the pagan hordes
His holy blade withheld their lethal swords
Stood statues stilled by softly spoken words
Angelic choirs sung the sweet song of birds …"

The third section of the Lay of Parsifor: the Lady of the Lake.

"Her Master has made her heart his home
And loves her eternally as She has become
A vision of faith for the questing soul
To guard The Grael is her divine role
She took God's message to the pagan world
Offered the choice to follow his holy word ..."

The second section of the Ballad of Parsifor the Perfect Knight: Sir Parsifor's Tomb

"As stone they gazed glass upon the vision of the Grael
The legend of its bounty at the heart of many a Tale
Quest to foreign lands by seas the young knight sail
On God-sent Path, the Way and Truth that never fail

A vision of peaceful unity across a distant tranquil land
In his heart God stands upon the soothing shifting sand
Guided by the wisdom of the loving God once made man
In communion with his lady, adoring his soul shall bind

Heart following the gentle and loving purest maid
Hope beyond the grave in his tower honourably laid
A knight so perfect with her tears was by her buried
Forever she guards him: by their bonds of love are tied

She lies in grace her elfin face watches her lake and City
Where waters of Avalon meet the crystal caves of Vezelay
Her sepulchre in state circled by Angel's prayers continually
Her spirit transforms it to a place of richest beauty

Fighting for the lady: honoured for his sacrificial death
Granted by comrades the request of his final breath
Buried in full view of the lady of the lake's grace
Her loving companion forever in this holy place

Where she healed the sick and cured the lost and lame
Fair hair and childlike eyes earning her eternal fame
By the purity of her heart giving without sin or shame
In hushed reverence of the lady: Magdalan is her name ..."

The road from Pampona to Tarbelli, Tannia and Tolosa was well-trod, wide yet winding as it touched the steep sides of mountains. For much of its passage it was carved through ancient gullies, a small stream running on natural cobbles on one side of the pathway that once had been a river of such fury it had cut through the granite of the proud mountains that loomed over their heads to create the tall cliffs and banks that shaped the valley that was become their treacherous path. Between the cobbles were growing edible herbs and fungi, a gardener's paradise had they the time to enjoy it but they did not stop to inspect the plant life in constant fear of a rockfall from overhead.

They struggled to find a camp-site; pebbles and stones were constantly under foot and kept them awake as they tried to get comfortable. Halfway through the night it began to rain with water pouring down the steep sides of the gulley and the stream at the bottom overflowing its banks. They had been used to the arid heat on the plains and dressed accordingly so were caught out by the change in weather, rapidly being drenched and shivering in the cold.

Then the winds blew along the gulley preventing the company from erecting the tents they had brought and dousing their fire which crackled, hissed then went out. They squatted in the wet and dark, woollen blankets held over their heads to offer some shelter but rapidly the ground began to fill with water, huge puddles joining to become a fast-flowing river in which they were sat and soon there was no part that any of them could call dry. In the end, when it became apparent that none of them was going to get any sleep, they led their horses along the water-logged tracks and walked through the night and into the sun of a new day's dawn.

Tarnosi in Aquitania was still a day's ride ahead of them but to ride in damp clothing with harness that was dripping wet would see all of the party become ill through their efforts. Instead they headed for the first farm house they could see, sitting just off the cobbled Roman road, a villa with terraces of grape vines on the hills beyond. They hoped for a warm welcome and were not disappointed when the lady of the house came out to greet them and took one look at the bedraggled state that Maria was in and invited them indoors to sit by the stove in the culinarium, calling for the house slaves to bring warm towels and fresh robes and toga.

Iosephus introduced the company to the lady whose husband was out tending the vines and being helped by their two sons. The lady insisted they stay the day and the night that would follow. She had never been graced with the gift of a daughter and had taken to Maria, but also could see the girl was in danger of going down with a cold, was close to tears through lack of sleep, and her hair was a tangled and an anarchic mess. A cup of hot broth later, sitting cross-legged before the hot hypocaust with the doors open and with the warmth and comfort of a fresh woollen robe, Maria began to feel human once more. As she thawed out, she began to chatter, conversing with their hostess as if they were life-long friends. The lady was touched by the girl's innocence and introduced herself:

"My name is Caeloreth and my family have worked these vines for over one hundred years. I am the last of my line and my kin. I have been married for twenty years to a wonderful man called Tartuff whom you will meet when the sun goes down but I have already sent word to him that we have guests. He will want you to eat with us. My sons will join us also. I suspect they will fall hopelessly in love with you, Maria, but ignore them; they are still young and it will do them good to be rebuffed! Now what brings you here in such a sorry state?"

Maria answered overwhelmed at the welcome and their rescue from the bitter weather outside:

"We travel to Britannia which I have heard is even colder and wetter than the mountain pass we have just travelled through. I bring news of my Master, a teacher and preacher. I wish to share what I have seen with as many people as possible for the words of my Master offer hope."

"You are terribly young to take on such a mission and Britannia is not a welcoming place. The great Julius Caesar was flung back by an alliance of Kings and he took eight legions with him. You seek to conquer Britannia with just six of you! My dear child, you will be harmed I fear and I could not bear that."

Maria held her hand briefly offering what reassurance she could as she said:

"I do not seek to conquer anyone. I offer the words of my Master for anyone to choose to follow or dismiss. If I am seen as any sort of threat then that is very sad as I could not intimidate a mouse!"

Then Maria began to talk of her Master's ministry, her voice a sing-song lilting melody, full of the joy she felt at each memory, bringing to life Iesus' stories, seeing the man alive before her, eyes brimming with tears as she felt the warmth of his embrace, and Caeloreth was stunned into silence, listening intently, understanding why this frail child should wish to share the chariot journey of her life with the barbarians to their north, entwined as her short life was with the Good News of the Son of God.

"You journey to Marsela and Luguidenum?" Caeloreth's question was rhetorical but still Longinus merited it with an answer: "Yes but after Luguidenum we are unsure of our route. Maria would like to preach in Burdigala, Marsela, Viena and Luguidenum also Torino. Alas, even with fast horses we will take seven days to reach Marsela and another se'ennight to reach Luguidenum."

"Can I see you speak in Burdigala?" Caeloreth asked nervously and Maria's response was immediate and impulsive, embracing the lady and nodding vigorously.

Burdigala was in the separate Province of Celtica north of Tarraconensis that was administered by the friends Maria had made in Hispania. Word had come north of a new Rabbi and faith healer but details were sparse. Maria's company were ushered in through the gates to the citadel, their travel papers were impressive but they would still need Longinus to report to the City Praefect's office. He did so immediately to be greeted by the son of a senator, Lucius Gaius Veres in his twenties and serving his first administrative posting. Of more importance, he was on good terms with Antonius and seeing his fellow City Praefect's seal was delighted to issue fresh documents to cover the journey from Tolosa and Burdigala to Marsela together with a message for the Praetor at the City's Port.

"Marsela is probably the largest port on the Middle Sea and the Praetor, Glaucus, is an old friend. This epistle will see you through Marsela and asks you are given leave to travel to Luguidenum. I leave the route you take to you, Centurion" and then with a cheery wave he dismissed Longinus to go and find the rest of his company, sitting in trepidation in the ante-chamber to the Curiale offices where Lucius ran the City.

"Where next?" Longinus asked thrown by the lack of crowds to greet them but Maria's confidence could not be dented:

"I will speak at the Synagogue. Even if I am alone, still I would wish to pray for the people of Tolosa."

Longinus need not have worried for Maria was going to draw crowds the moment it was known she planned to speak. Crowds gathered ready for prayers that evening and the new Synagogue was full as Maria was invited by the High Priest to lead those gathered in a discussion of the scriptures.

"We must always be ready for each day might be our last" and Maria spoke of her vision of Paradise and what she meant by being prepared: "through prayer, fasting and charitable work and deed; above all through the purity of our faith."

Caeloreth hugged her when she had finished, so proud to be part of Maria's mission, whilst Maria's head fell forwards on her shoulder in gratitude at all the lady had done for them. "I promise to return" she whispered.

Their reception at Narbo in Narbonnensis was very different again. This time the City knew to expect the Magdalan and so had gathered in huge numbers by the four gates into the City and along the Via Porta. The cheering began the moment the small party came in sight at the approach to the north gate. Maria remained outside of the City walls until Longinus had presented their manifests at the Praetor's office, this time talking to the crowds about her mission:

"It would be easy to reserve the Messiah's message to the many Jews around the world. For our reward for years of following God was to be the *first* to hear the words of his son. But God created every man, woman and child in this beautiful world of ours and the Good News that his son has died and is risen from the dead belongs to all of God's creation. I take this message of hope to all, whether civilised Roman or barbaric Briton as equals in God's eyes."

They rode through the walled City of Aribates and then headed south to the complex of estuaries, lagoons, deep basins and lakes and the series of small ports and havens that sat on the delta of the Rhone. The City of Marsela itself was at the southern-most point of the Rhone delta with its man-made port facing due west, a three league long sea wall protecting one large deep water quay and over twenty smaller docks. The City was built around the Old Port with the Palace and Gardens of Pharo, the large amphitheatre and circus, the Forum and Curia all on the south banks of the Old Port, the Praetor's Palace, City Praefect's Palace, Praetorium, Curiale Courts, Temples to Jupiter, Neptune, Mercury and Athena, the Synagogue, Temple to Isis, Court of Petitions, Port Administration and Garrison Fort to the north, with the Military Camp beyond the north walls. Nearly three million people resided or traded in the City and its many ports, home to Rome's largest fleet.

Maria was frightened for the first time. As they rode towards the City Centre it took over nine hours to traverse the many quays and docks to the north of the City which stretched almost as far as the outskirts of Narbo. Every road, street or alley way was crammed full of people, the quaysides heaving with stevedore and marines, the Forums and Auction Houses were a riot of noise as traders negotiated fiercely for the best bargains and outbid each other in a frenzy of purchasing. The numbers petrified her. She could not see how she could possibly be heard by so many and they did not seem remotely interested in anything other than business or trade.

Their party were waved through the north gate without their papers being checked by guards overwhelmed by sheer numbers. The approach to the Praetor's Palace up a flight of seventy marble steps, was nine long snaking queues of those seeking to have their permits, manifests or visa approved by the Praetor's administration.

"How long have you been waiting?" Longinus asked a man ten places on in the queue that he and his party had just joined.

"Six hours but there are others who have slept over from yesterday!"

"Go find where we are booked in to stay and I will keep our place in the queue" Longinus suggested and Iosephus quickly took charge of the party, heading towards the Gardens of Pharo, to the west of which was the guest house where they would be staying. He made haste wishing to get Maria out of the crowds as quickly as possible as she was now shaking visibly at the onset of agoraphobia.

It took a further hour to negotiate the crowds milling around the port, come to collect a friend or family member or to board one of the many ships bound for all parts of the Middle Sea, Black Sea and Atlantic. At last they gained entry to the relative peace and tranquillity of the Gardens and walked along its main avenue, tall Cedar trees on either side, to arrive at their lodging, a villa that had been carefully converted to be a place to eat, with a bathhouse and guest accommodation. It had a reputation for being exclusive and quiet, offering magnificent sea views to the west and views of the Gardens from its balconies at the front. Iosephus had booked out an entire floor of six chambers or cubilla, two vestibulare and two triclinarium with a central atrium and cloister. The party would be staying in comfort and would have food served in their private rooms and not the public rooms below. They also had their own private staircase to the bathhouse, piscina and frigidarium.

Maria went straight to her chamber and pulled the curtain shut behind her, seeking the privacy of her own company, not wishing the rest of the party to see her so over-wrought. But her friends knew her too well and she had been unable to hide her feelings from them. Hesitantly, Iosephus asked if he might come in and then listened to the choked sob and almost inaudible 'Yes'.

The knight did not give Maria a chance to speak but came straight to the point: "The numbers we will find here can be frightening at first. But you have to remember that to God everyone is important. We are here for three days and in that time we might touch the lives of less than one in ten of the people here. But it was you who said to change just one person's view of God is a victory. I happen to think you will do better than that but to convert all of those we have just seen is not your task but belongs to others. You need to start the process … then let go so that others can also do God's Will, God's Work."

"I am frightened they will crush me under foot."

"Speak in places where your audience will show their respect. Stick to Temples and the Synagogue and avoid the Forum and Curia. This way the crowd will regulate itself. It is your best hope."

Longinus staggered in at the second hour, the stars were out and it was the middle of a bitterly cold cloudless night. He left Maria asleep but woke Iosephus instead and did not wait for the old man to get out of bed but began to talk the moment Iosephus had stirred: "Nice rooms! We have travel passes to Luguidenum and a permit to hold a public assembly. The civil servant I saw (fat chance of seeing the Praetor when it was gone midnight before my turn came up) did not even look at my papers but said: 'What do you want?' Then he drew out a scroll that already had the Praetor's seal on it, filled in the blanks and handed it over to me. Five hour wait for a sixty second appointment with a freedman. Heavens only knows how long the wait is to see the Praetor? Anyways, we have all the documents we need. As long as we avoid a riot, we should be alright. How is Maria?"

"She is frightened of the numbers. She has never seen so many people in one place before. Torture and a horrible death at the hands of the barbarian hordes she can cope with. Heckling or worse no-one listening to her and she is in a right mess."

Longinus spoke softly at the entrance to her chamber: "Are you awake?" then hearing the muffled 'No. I want to be alone' he ignored her and stepped through the curtain to see the girl standing on her balcony looking out at the many lights on the ships in the harbour, so many it was impossible to tell how many masts and ships they belonged to. "It is all too much" she whispered then turned quickly and launched herself in tears into the young man's arms. He held her tight not sure what to say let alone do with this child who had taken the dream of a dead man and made it become the new reality for so much of the Roman world.

"Why are you frightened?" he asked conscious of the total inadequacy of his question yet needing to hear her speak. She shook her head then admitted: "I wish I knew. I have followed my Master's lead and not once stopped to ask how I, me, Maria truly felt. Now I know. I am scared. Sooner or later I will be murdered: by barbarians or Rome or the Sanhedrin in Jerusalem or some zealot who takes exception to my Master's message of peace. The knife that will kill me could be in the hands of any one of those millions of people out there. What should I do?"

"You could stop. Already there are communities of followers in Damascus, Heraklion, Tunis, Valentia, Iaenus Portus, Tolosa and Narbo because of your mission. Indeed most of Hispania has communities that now follow the Master's teachings. We could call it a day?"

"No" she said determinedly then more quietly "No, my friend. Forgive me. I just need comforting. I hate being an orphan as right now I want the reassurance of my mother." And she hugged Longinus more tightly then asked him: "Will you stay with me tonight? I need your protection from the nightmares, from the childish fears."

Longinus went to lay out a bed roll on the floor at the foot of her bed but Maria shook her head. "Hold me" she whispered and lay on her bed then folded back the sheets. The young man blushed unsure he wanted to do this; afraid of too much intimacy, recalling he was promised to another.

"Just hold me, nothing more" the girl pleaded and so he got into the bed then pulled her across so that her head rested on his chest his left arm holding her tightly, gently stroking her hair with his right hand. In seconds, she was asleep leaving Longinus unsure of his feelings for her but knowing that at that moment what he wanted to do more than anything else was to kiss her.

He woke first to find Maria sprawled half across him and half with her feet dangling off the side of the bed. He was a restful sleeper, hardly moving in the night but the girl slept like the child she was, taking up the whole of the bed and unable to get still, yet dead to the world for all of her restlessness. He carefully untangled himself from the knot she had cast around him and left her hugging a pillow and lying diagonally across the bed.

He could not resist a smile as he looked at her then noticed the bruises from the blows she had received from the boy she had cured from 'possession' and how frail her arms and legs were. She was so terribly thin, how she had the energy to go on, he just did not know? They had a journey of five to six thousand leagues ahead of them mainly on horse-back and surely this would kill her?

Suddenly Maria woke up and realised that Longinus was no longer in bed with her. She threw the pillow away in disgust then looked around in panic until she saw the Centurion standing at the window watching her. She was out of bed in a moment and across the room to rest against him, lifting his arms to hold her once more. Longinus gave her a quick squeeze but then stepped back leaving her looking at him in deserted dismay.

"Come, we must get ready for you to lead us in the Eucharist at the Temple of Jupiter Omnipotens. We have permission for you to do so and it can take a few thousand with ease, with space in the Forum outside for many tens of thousands. Are you ready?"

"Have I upset you?" she asked at a tangent but showing what she saw as most important to her. Longinus shook his head then bowing he left her, desolate and not understanding that he loved her too much to let her become distracted from her mission. "Lead us not into temptation" he muttered to himself remembering the words of the Master as he had led them all in prayer in the loft at Lazarus' house and went to find his own chamber then headed for the frigarium. Iosephus was already relaxing in its cold water and asked him how Maria was.

"No longer upset by the large numbers of people here. I think she is now upset with me!" and he told the old man about how he had spent the night with the girl. "Nothing happened" he pleaded, begging the equites to believe him and Iosephus did: "She is looking for a father figure" he explained "and I am more of an ancient uncle but I think she has chosen you to fill the gap left by the death of her father."

"Then I am a fool and must hope she can forgive me. I just walked away from her when all she wanted was my company" and Longinus plunged his head into the water to shake the cobwebs out of his head. Just then two of the female guests joined them, both in excellent shape and as was typical of women in Roman society not at all ashamed of their naked bodies. Iosephus enjoyed the spectacle of both women trying to flirt with the Centurion whilst the poor man was preoccupied with thoughts of Maria. In the end, the women gave up and headed for a massage whilst Iosephus chuckled and Longinus looked at his friend, his expressive face saying "What are you laughing at?"

Then Maria joined them from her bathe in the piscina, just a short linen slip to cover her modesty and which clung to her frail frame as she plunged into the frigarium. Her head came up and she blushed bright red as she realised both men were naked as was the custom in Roman baths but this was her first time in one. Then she grinned at Longinus and said: "Let me do the talking" which effectively shut him up as she explained her needs to him:

"I love you and I need a shoulder to cry on right now and strong arms to hold me when I get frightened and I hope that can be you. I understand why you walked away from me and if in the future you think things are becoming too intense between us you have my permission to do so again. I am not ready for an intimate relationship; I need your hugs and your kisses and to be held when I am asleep and someone to listen to me when I say ridiculous things like now but which come from my heart. Can you be the person who holds me, kisses me, hugs me and listens to me?"

Longinus laughed then said: "Of course. Forgive me that I mis-read your intent. I was also unsure of my own feelings for you or rather I feared I wanted more than you were offering and needed time to understand my own feelings better."

Maria blushed once more then held out her hand keeping her eyes firmly fixed on his, whilst Longinus took her hand and kissed it then turned and climbed out of the water giving Maria a shock as she saw far more of him than she had ever intended and she rapidly averted her eyes whilst he placed a towel strategically over his manhood and asked her: "Coming for a massage?"

She shook her head vigorously avoiding looking in either his or Iosephus' direction then began to reverse out of the frigarium, holding her slip by the hem to try and cover her face and block her view of both men yet also covering her modesty and discovered to her dismay it was too short to do both. She stepped behind a tall pot plant and swore never to go into a Roman Bathhouse again.

Maria was far more confident as she later joined Longinus, Perseus and Iosephus walking across the Forum towards the square on which sat the Temple of Jupiter. The High Priest of the Temple was a Roman knight, elevated to become High Priest and in the process of looking for a suitable bride. His name was Caius Ventullus Secundus, whose father had been a successful merchant and adopted by the Ventullus family when they needed a wealthy son to carry on the name and fund the dowries of three handsome but impoverished daughters.

The elder Ventullus had married the youngest of the daughters, taking advantage of the reform of the Oppian Law and saving himself the cost of a dowry. Caius had been born one year later; Ventellus Primus dying during the protracted celebrations that followed this happy event when, the worst for drink, he had fallen off the quayside into the sea and drowned.

Caius was delighted that Maria was to use the Temple of Jupiter to host her Eucharistic feast and had put several notices up regarding the celebration of the Eucharist to be held that evening. The notices were prominent and the conversation in the Forum was all about the service to be held later that day. Tens of thousands visited the Forum and spread the word to the many ports and docks in the City. Caius was also delighted in Maria, herself, and could see her as a more than suitable High Priestess and one moreover who would bring people in huge numbers to worship at his Temple. Maria laughed at the interplay as Caius flirted outrageously with her and Longinus was gripped by an excess of protectiveness bordering on outright jealousy. Maria had just enough common sense to know that this was one High Priest she had better not hug.

The assembly at Marsela took on a different format but one which by the time Maria reached Luguidenum had become so accepted that when a century later the Bishop of Lyon wrote of the early Church and its ceremonies, the Eucharistic service followed the tradition that Maria established. She began with a welcome and then asked for the forgiveness of sins for those present. Then she read from the scriptures: on this occasion the reading was about Daniel and the Lion. Into the silence that followed her hushed, humble and faltering reading from the Book of Daniel she posed the following question:

"We are gathered here today because my Master's sacrifice offers to each of us the choice to change. But who changed in the story I just read?

For this is a story about resurrection and our ability to change through being reborn. This is first a story about the rebirth of the Lion! Daniel's act of kindness did not change Daniel: it was the Lion whose nature was changed from a man-killer to become a loving friend.

My Master has offered us the ultimate act of kindness. He died for all of us so that we might each be reborn. His nature did not change. He was God made man and returned to life as God made man. My Master is Daniel in the story.

Whereas, in many regards *we* are the Lion: it is our nature that shall change if we accept my Master's act of kindness. We are reborn filled with the Spirit to love one another, to heal, to seek peace, to forgive each other, to pray, to fast, to be charitable, to speak in tongues and to prophesy.

And so, as we prepare to break the bread, remembering my Master's life, death and resurrection, becoming filled with God's Spirit, seeing my Master amongst us and within us as he promised, let us open our hearts, minds and souls to be changed; to be 'reborn' to lead new lives following the Way, the Path that Iesus of Nazareth set us.

But my Master is also the Lion. If we change then just as Daniel was given the gift of life by the Lion so shall we be given the gift of life after death by my Master.

And so we learn that most important lesson of all. God, my Master, can be found in every living thing and in everyone. He is always with us and surrounds us right now!"

She went to take questions, looking into the sea of faces that stretched beyond the Temple's doors to the Forum and the colonnaded squares outside the other Temples in the Citadel. Nearly two hundred thousand had gathered to hear Maria speak and more would join as those come to the Forum to buy or sell their wares stopped to listen. To Maria's amazement there was not a single question. Rather all waited for the breaking of the bread in the hope that this would change their lives.

She did not disappoint but moved smoothly on to break bread and say the words her Master had spoken at his last Passover meal, assisted by the Temple servants, they distributed the bread and at a signal to confirm that all had a piece, she said: "Take this and eat it. This is me, the Son of God. Never forget me." And then she ate the bread and all watching her did the same.

As they did so, many saw a vision of tongues of flame above their heads bringing the gifts of the Spirit. Some sang songs and the psalms, others spoke of new worlds, new lands and strange places to be converted; some lay their hands on their neighbours: healing aches, pains and minor ailments; one man went across to a blind beggar at the side of the Palace steps and as he gently caressed his eyes, the man leapt for joy as his sight returned.

But Maria did not notice for as she had spoken the words in his memory, the Nazarene had stood before her in reality.

She knelt in tears, her head bowed and she kissed his feet then stood and kissed the scars on his hands and wiped the blood from his brow. But he looked at her sternly and said: "Am I not always with you?" She looked at her feet in shame at which he took her face in both hands, lifted her head so that she must look him straight in the eyes and said: "What you have done for me is truly wonderful. Yet you must find the courage to continue no matter how great the numbers or the challenge."

"Where shall I find such courage?" she asked and the Nazarene replied: "It is already within you. If you are ever frightened again, seek me in your heart and I will succour you."

Then she was alone once more but she could never be truly alone for she carried her Master with her at all times and was filled with the Spirit, The Comforter. She turned to all gathered at the Temple and thanked them, saying:

"You have each become this day a follower of Iesus of Nazareth through the breaking of the bread. Go back to your homes, your communities, your workplace and spread the Good News that my Master is risen so that we may earn Eternal Life. Break the bread, pray to God, seek the forgiveness of sins, remember the life and ministry of my Master and help others to be changed that we may all be reborn!"

At the end of the service, she hunted for Longinus and found him recruiting volunteers as ushers for the service next day. "Did you see him?" she said excitedly. Longinus looked at her and said with perhaps the smallest indication of impatience creeping into his voice:

"One Maria who speaks utter and baffling nonsense and in riddles is bad enough. Two of you are too much! Explain yourself!" and Maria laughed then did as she were told: "Did you see the Nazarene at the breaking of bread?"

"No" said Longinus without thought then seeing the look of disappointment on the girl's face he added: "But you did, I take it. You do have a special relationship with the Master so this is bound to happen. Do not worry if others do not see him. He is real and alive but clearly is choosing to be seen by you but not by me. I am not upset or jealous. I saw him twice alive when he should have been dead and that is enough for me to believe in him and follow him. I follow you too by the way because I can see you are honest ... if maddening!" he added.

The hug she gave him took his breath away.

The next two days the numbers attending the Service of the Eucharist grew. The distribution of bread would have become a problem except there were hundreds of volunteers who broke the bread in unison with Maria and who helped distribute pieces of their loaves. Maria was clear: anyone who had the confidence to say the words of consecration and whose heart was open to God's Will could break the bread. Every volunteer was accepted and when those gathered saw how easy it was to participate in the breaking of bread, many more came forward. Maria was questioned on this at her service on the third day.

"What training or what permission must I have to break the bread with my family and friends?"

"The disciples received no training or permission. We were shown and we do what we saw. So it is now. I have shown you what to do so now it is up to you. There is one thing I do ask but it is not a requirement merely my own request and something I have personally found helpful: Look to your heart and ask 'Am I in the right frame of mind to do this?' If you are then you already have permission from God; you need not wait for anything more."

"What is 'the right frame of mind'?"

"You might be thinking any or all of the following: I wish to do this for others. I wish to come closer to God by doing this. I remember Iesus, his life, death and resurrection through doing this. I welcome the Spirit of God by doing this. I believe in One God and this is my proof."

On the third evening they had a surprise visitor. Caius had come to the Inn in the Gardens of Pharo with two lictors in attendance in order to wish Maria good fortune on her journey and to ask a question. They met in one of the two private triclinarium that formed part of the suite of rooms hired by Iosephus. Longinus joined them both as chaperone doing a wonderful impersonation of a gooseberry as Maria unkindly teased him later. Caius spoke admiringly of the huge numbers breaking bread and offering healing and the forgiveness of sins. To avoid prosecution under the laws against unlawful assembly, the Eucharist was being celebrated by families in their home by small groups of three or four and in hiding in the hypocausts and catacombs of the City. Caius knew and was turning a blind eye. Suddenly, he could contain himself no longer and blurted out:

"Would you marry me?"

Maria blinked in surprise but did not laugh and taking the request seriously she let him down gently: "You are very handsome, rich and well-connected. Alas, I have dedicated my life to my mission of bringing the Good News to the world. I am also in my view too young and too immature to be thinking of marriage. Caius, you can do so much better than me. I decline your wonderful offer but ask: Can we be friends instead?"

"Gladly" the young man replied "but I shall keep asking you just in case you change your mind. There is one thing I ask as a favour."

"What is it? Provided it harms neither my faith nor my honour then I would do anything for a friend."

Then Caius shocked them both:

"I want to become a follower of the Nazarene. My Temple comes alive when you celebrate the Eucharist and lies silent and empty at other times. How can I do this and yet still remain High Priest of my Temple?"

"You could offer yourself as the High Priest for the other followers of my Master and hold daily services of the breaking of the bread in your Temple, inviting anyone to attend. You can still undertake the rituals and ceremonies of the Temple but dedicate them in your heart to Iesus and not Jupiter. For it is what is in your heart that God sees. If it is belief in my Master that God sees then you are his follower."

"Are you happy that I become a follower? Do you require any further test of me?"

"Do you believe in one God who sacrificed his son that we might have eternal life and whose Spirit fills us in the breaking of the bread?"

"Yes"

"Then I welcome you as my brother in faith."

They left for Luguidenum at dawn the following day, heading out of the north gate and backtracking slightly as they took the road to Aix with its massive perimeter wall and Viena with its two bridges of stone and from there headed north following the path of the Rhone towards Luguidenum.

They reached Tartelum just after noon and Longinus presented their papers to the praetorship there. Veres', Tartellus' and Pilate's seals were still sufficiently impressive to ensure Longinus was interviewed by the freedman, Decarion, who was administering and clerking for the praetorship. Decarion added two additional visas to the large terrier Longinus had already accumulated: one for the sub province and region of Tartelum that covered Mons Limarus and Valentum, the second was a pass issued in the Governor's name and using a copy of his seal that would get them into and out of Luguidenum.

"You should make Valentum tonight and Luguidenum tomorrow. The roads are excellent from here northwards" the clerk advised Longinus who was genuinely grateful.

Iosephus and Longinus were doing all they could to keep the company moving. Their fear was that they might be pursued as they were now in territory that was potentially hostile towards the faith of the Nazarene. They had been fortunate in the Governors, Praetors and City Praefects they had met thus far but they could easily be followed by a sicariot or arrested at any time under warrant for inciting an unlawful assembly or riot.

Maria was the problem as she would seek to meet people whenever they stopped. The compromise was that she promised not to give a sermon beyond ten minutes as part of the Service of the Eucharist. This kept the service to thirty minutes and they were delayed by no more than half an hour at places such as Aix, Viena, Tartenum, Mons Serpentum, Mons Limarus and Astera but seeing more than twenty thousand attend services and convert to becoming followers of the Nazarene. These fledgling Christian communities would become the foundation or cornerstone of the second diocese in Gaul centred around Luguidenum (Lyons).

Because the first ever history of the early Christian church was written by one of the first bishops of Luguidenum, the Christian community founded there takes on a much greater significance than perhaps is merited with as large if not larger communities centred around Marsela, Tunis, Valentia, Torino, Iaenus Portus and Baetica. However, this diocese includes where the Magdalan was finally laid to rest after her sepulchre was found in the Holy Land. Vedselae was the place the Magdalan chose herself for her final resting place, although it was seven to eight centuries before her wish finally became true.

Luguidenum is a City built around two rivers which divide to form a long thin island: the rivers Saone and the Rhone. The Romans saw the strategic significance of Luguidenum and the military advantages created by the natural defence offered by the two rivers and so built a simple grid of buildings on the island between the two rivers, served by stone bridges and with a fortified wall and Garrison camp to the north of the City. Gallia and Helvetica had been in rebellion only 90 years earlier and the Romans had fortified key places to ensure that they could protect Gallia without tying down huge numbers of troops. Luguidenum was one of those places established to hold the borders with Helvetica and southern Alemania as well as Gergovia, Burgundia and the Rhone valley.

They were met at the southern barbican on the Pontus Confluentia which crossed the Saone from the Ars Mulaterra to the watermill where the two rivers split. The smaller Pontus Pastora was to their right and had been closed off. Longinus presented their travel papers to the Decurion in charge of the three cohorts holding the southern gate and was immediately taken under escort to see the City Praefect.

Maria was placed under arrest and sat on a hay bail chatting to the two Praetorians who were assigned to guard her whilst Perseus, Iosephus and his two servants were allowed into the City on condition they report to the Praetorium before the curfew at the eighth hour. "What will happen to the girl?" Iosephus asked the Decurion in genuine concern. The officer shrugged his shoulders then mimed strangulation before pointing into the centre of the City and moving them on: "Get on your way or you will find yourself in the same trouble."

The City Praefect did not keep Longinus waiting long. "My name is Cordelius Sestus Amarillus and I have come from Rome. Pontius Pilate has just been recalled to Rome and his seal no longer provides you with any authority. How close were you to the man and did you know Aelius Sejanus?"

"I had been offered a position on Pilate's staff and had to deal with a difficult situation over the Passover that could have seen an uprising but which, in the end, went peacefully. My mother knows and respects the Lady Cordelia. I never met, knew or had any dealings with Sejanus but he was responsible for my father's posting to the Xth and I am a Centurion so my loyalties were and are to my Legion, the Tenth."

Amarillus watched Longinus carefully for any sign the man was hiding something but concluded this was an honest soldier. "Several commendations and the grass crown I note" and Longinus nodded. "Alright" said the City Praefect perking up and having reached a decision about Longinus "I could use you right now and you are going to be here for a few days which will help me, whilst we decide what to do with the girl you are escorting."

"She is harmless sir."

"This is a military base first and foremost with Teutoni, Suevi and Helvetii less than two day's march to our east. I cannot afford any large gatherings however peaceful as they offer a means for the enemies of Rome to hide in our midst. If the girl can be persuaded to behave then she lives but for now I intend to lock her away and it has even been suggested that we remove her tongue."

"Sir" said Longinus alarmed at the Praefect's threat. "Maria is young, honest and has never been anything but a friend to Rome. If you allow me to explain your concerns to her I can stand as guarantor that she will not hold any public meetings unless authorised by yourself. She will ask to observe the Sabbath at the local Synagogue."

"Not going to happen. By my order, all public services including religious have been suspended until I can be certain that sufficient safeguards are in place to ensure these services are not being infiltrated by the barbarians at our gates."

"I understand sir and will vouch for the girl even if I must tie her up myself to prevent her doing something stupid. You mentioned some way in which I can help you?"

"She stays as a guest in the cells beneath us but I will keep any torture to a minimum."

"Sir she does not deserve this."

Amarillus stood up and started to pace up and down in the scriborium in which they were having this meeting, one of his Praetorian standing at the door. He nodded to the soldier who stepped out of the room to leave the two men alone. Only when Amarillus was certain they were alone did he brief Longinus.

"It is important that I am seen to have placed the girl under arrest as what I am about to ask involves her also. I need to know what is happening across the borders to our North in Britannia. I was hoping you might be persuaded to send information from your mission to Caledonia. This request comes from Rome. I can have one of my staff brief you on what we know already, a few names of possible leaders, a couple of tribal capitals but the reality is we are woefully short on intelligence and your mission is too good an opportunity to miss. When word gets out that Maria has been arrested and imprisoned by Rome then this should bring Maria to the attention of the tribal leaders and elders across our borders. I need to know what defence they could offer against possible invasion and also who are the allies and potential client kingdoms when we do cross the Mare Britannia again?"

"We are going back then?" Longinus had to ask excited and Amarillus nodded then expanded:

"Tiberius won't commit. His successor will attack Germania first in memory of his dead father. But Britannia will see us invade in the next decade. Julius Caesar failed because he relied on Commius' intelligence and the man was a traitor, his descendants no better. We need a reliable source and the view in Roma is that is you, Centurion. Pull this off and you get your own Legion before you make twenty five!"

"I cannot tell Maria this as she would never agree but I am loyal to Rome and promise you a full report on the social, political and military set up, strengths and weaknesses we find. If any hint that I am spying for you gets into the hands of the tribes in Britannia then both Maria and I are dead."

Amarillus nodded then offered Longinus his hand: "Do this for me and it will make your career and ensure Maria's safe conduct." The Centurion took the hand cementing the agreement between the two men then sat silently as the Praefect gave orders for Maria to be brought before him.

Maria was escorted by two Praetorians and gaily chatted to them asking about their families and hobbies, had they any injuries, what would they do when their service with their legion came to an end? The men had tried ignoring her but that just encouraged her to ask more questions so in the end they talked about the different places to which they had been posted, delighting her with tales of elephants and giraffes. She was laughing at the description of a giraffe as she came before Amarillus and unintentionally he became the next victim to her guileless charm.

"Maria known as the Magdalan, you are charged with unlawful assembly in Marsela, Vienna and Tolino. How do you plead?"

"I plead 'Guilty', sir, but it was never my intent to create any disturbance and everyone seemed very happy."

"Alas the offence is strict liability and your intent is immaterial." Maria just looked at Amarillus her head on one side in total confusion and the Praefect decided to have mercy on her: "What I mean is that it is enough to have been part of the assembly to be found guilty even if you intended no harm."

"Don't you think that is a bit harsh?" Maria asked innocently and Amarillus laughed then admitted: "I do not make the laws merely apply them" before continuing to the girl's dismay: "I sentence you to custody of course but also you must be either tortured or scourged. What have you to say?"

"Please sir. I am not very good at torture or at being lashed and think I would not enjoy either. Could we skip that bit?"

"Have you an alternative suggestion?" the Praefect asked bemused and bewitched by the girl.

"I could sing for you."

Amarillus sat back in his chair and pondered on what he could do. The prospect of an evening in the company of this beguiling yet innocent young lady was so tempting he was more than happy to throw the law book out of the proverbial window yet he also knew that some punishment was necessary for Maria to be accepted by any barbarians she should meet in Britannia and Caledonia.

Finally, he ruled: "Maria, it is the sentence of this Court that you be placed under the custody of Gaius Longinus and that you sing for the City Prefect Sestus Amarillus. You are to receive a single lash being the minimum sentence this Court can give and I do so because I accept that there was no harm intended by your actions."

"Does the lash hurt?" Maria whispered in Longinus' ear and he replied: "No! The shock obscures the pain for few seconds."

"But how?" she asked frightened by the prospect of both her solitude and impending torture.

"You will soon know" Longinus replied sadly and Maria realised she was trapped and must face her punishment she hoped with the same courage as her Master. Still she had one more thing to ask for:

"I have one final request. This stola and the peplos beneath are both borrowed from Celestile. I would ask they are removed with care and that there be no blood on them to ruin the silk and chiffon from which they are woven."

Amarillus nodded and issued instructions to her escort. "Take her to the cloister and have her whipped in the atrium there. She is to be naked to protect her clothing and advise the executioner that he is to apply a single lash and if he leaves even the smallest scar then I will have his lash turned on him!"

Longinus whispered in her ear as she walked past him to find the atrium: "Be brave and it will soon be over. You cannot be tried a second time for these offences and have got off lightly" then seeing the indignant look on her face he continued hurriedly "though I wish this could have ended without such torture."

"Let us get it over with. Want to watch?" The Prefect asked and when Longinus shook his head, the Governor continued: "Me neither" and they watched the girl walk bravely between her two escort, whispering "I forgive you. You have been merciful and I am grateful" then turning to one of the soldiers asked in a stutter:

"Please hold me if I should feel weak and talk to me of wonderful things that my mind can be elsewhere when I am struck."

Then the two men waited in silence for what seemed an age before they heard a single scream of pain followed by total silence. One of the Praetorians that had been her escort returned to the Amarillus' scriborium to report: "The sentence has been carried out. The girl has fainted. Her back is bruised from the marks of the iron stolae but the skin has not been broken. What is to be done with her?"

Longinus followed the soldier down to the courtyard at the centre of the Praefect's Palace, surrounded by a covered cloister, with ancient hop vines and wisteria twisting as columns and pillars around the stone arches of the palazzo, a marble fountain and pool full of carp at the centre and by which lay the girl, still naked, a trail of blood from where she had bitten her tongue, her eyes staring unblinkingly into some distant place, not moving, so child-like and so wrong to have had this pain inflicted on her.

He asked for something to cover her and one of the Praefect's slaves ran to fetch some linen cloth and a blanket, her cloths were neatly folded and were untouched as she had asked. Longinus rolled her gently in the linen then covered her in the blanket, making a hood to cover her head then lifted her limp body and carried her to the large Reception Hall where petitioners were still queuing to see the Praefect. Amarillus joined them and asked "Where will you stay?" and when Longinus admitted he did not know, impulsively offered them the use of the guest cubilla at his Palace.

Maria woke to find she was lying on her side and before her was a floor to ceiling archway that gave onto a balcony and through which she could see the City of Luguidenum stretching north before her. Unlike Marsela which was given over to sea trade, this was a City made over for war with a walled central Citadel (Caister) and barbicans at each of the six bridges plus a City of Tents (Campanum) a full league square and a timber and brick Castellum with moat and draw bridges north and south. In places the City walls were ten paces high with a deep motte before them and wooden spikes at the base.

There were four tall square wooden towers used as observation posts and the Garrison Fort was also heavily defended with a wooden palisade reinforced in brick in places and holding one of the six Legions that rotated through the City. Finally at the southern end of the City, where the Forum, Curia and Curiale Courts sat, was The Praetorium.

The City was currently home for three legions (VIth, XIIth and XIVth) and one thousand Praetorians plus the same of cavalry. Taking families, auxiliaries and scouts, artillery, armourers, carpenters, blacksmiths and medics into account, there were over sixteen thousand based in Luguidenum who counted their Legion as their family and home.

Maria rolled gingerly onto her back and nearly fainted once more at the spike of pain. She could feel no blood as she ran her hands gently as far as she could reach but could feel the weals that were the marks of the lash. The whip used had over thirty strands of leather each with a round iron ball fixed at the end and designed to bruise. The pain was greater even than that from when her legs had been broken on the rack. Then she noticed she was naked beneath the sheets on the bed on which she lay and she was still clueless as to where she was; there was no picture or ornament in the room to offer her any indication of her location and no landmark outside to help her.

'Best wait' she thought then saw a small bell by her bedside and decided to test it out and see if it would bring her help or summons her gaoler. A young girl, her age, a slave and servant at the Palace entered, smiled and offered to fetch her clothes and food to break her fast. "Yes please" she said to both returning the servant's smile.

The clothes were made of the finest Parthian silk, in mauves and crimsons to contrast with her sapphire blue eyes. The choker, broach and amulets that were brought with them were the finest white gold and silver she had ever seen and belonged to Amarillus' mother, long dead but still remembered with love. All three were inlaid with lapus lazuli, aquamarine and sapphires.

The servant had also brought some salve and carefully ministered to Maria's bruises before helping her pull the silk peplos over her head and straightening it carefully over her back. Maria was embarrassed at having layers of silk only to cover her modesty and still felt naked but the servant was complimentary and fetched some mascara and rouge to apply the minimum amount of make up to the girl's elfin face. As Maria stood, the sun shone into the room and lit her up so that the servant could see how shapely yet frail and thin the girl was. "You are beautiful" the servant said involuntarily and kissed Maria on the lips. Maria blushed.

"Do you like?" the servant asked and Maria nodded slowly but said: "I welcome the hugs and kisses of friends but have no wish for any more intimacy than that."

"I understand" replied the servant. "There are many of the matrons who come here who are the same. If you need companionship then ask for me but now unless you have any more questions I am to take you to my Master."

"I have one" admitted Maria sheepishly. "Where am I?"

"You are in the Praefect's Palace as the honoured guest of my master, Amarillus, although that is a secret entrusted to only a handful of people. Officially, you are held captive in custody for offences against the state. Unofficially, you are to be pampered and offered every courtesy but must remain within the walls of the Palace. Your escort, Gaius Longinus is also a guest and you will see him when you meet the Praefect. He has asked to see you as soon as you have broken your fast."

"Why the secrecy? I do not like deceit."

"My master will explain but nothing but good is intended. My master likes you."

Maria joined Amarillus in the enormous State Chamber, a triclinarium at one end and the benches for his privy council at the other. This was where the Praefect conducted his most private business. Longinus was already reclining on his besillium and at his signal, the three of them: Amarillus, Longinus and Maria were left alone.

Maria lowered herself gingerly onto her besillium, in part afraid that her clothing was revealing too much but also to avoid catching her bruises. She sat upright as always, her back ram-rod straight. Longinus caught her eye, asking silently if she was alright after her ordeal and she smiled to show all was well. Amarillus saw the smile and began to explain why her punishment was necessary.

"Forgive me your brief pain. I am told that all will heal and the worst may be a few marks of the lash will still show but these can be covered by make-up. Your punishment was necessary for two reasons: you now no longer face charges for 'unlawful assembly' at the places within the Empire you have visited for you have been found guilty and punished. In Roman law you cannot be tried a second time for an offence for which you have already been punished. Later today, I will provide you with papers that give you free passage to the port of Sugdavellum (Sargovellum) and permission to hold religious services in your own designated Temple or any Temple in Roman territory. This will protect you from further charges whenever you hold the celebration of the Eucharist."

Maria's eyes lit up with gratitude at that and momentarily her beauty stunned the two men, silencing them. With an audible gulp which Amarillus attempted to disguise as an unconvincing cough the Praefect came to the much harder part of his apologeia:

"There is a second reason why your punishment was necessary. We think that when it is heard that you have been punished by Rome and your lash marks are seen by the barbarians you seek to convert, they will be much more open and receptive to meeting and listening to you. A 'necessary evil'."

"If this evil can be turned to good then I shall be satisfied. I need no apology for what was done. You applied the law with mercy and compassion and I am grateful.

Alas I am also human and weak, with no experience of physical pain until I was tortured in Damascus and now I have been scourged. My experience is nothing compared to the pain my Master suffered for my sake. Ignore me if I wince therefore for I must learn to be more stoical and courageous.

One day I will face an ordeal far worse than what I have already suffered even unto my own death. I must be ready for that moment and face my end fearlessly or undo all the good of my Master's sacrifice."

Amarillus looked at Maria in admiration whilst Longinus vowed privately that he would never let Maria come to harm again even at cost of his own life. The Praefect let the girl know his feelings:

"You are more courageous than you give yourself credit for. I will not be the only one that hopes that you can avoid the premature death you foresee. Your faith has already seen the sacrifice of your Master. You need to balance this with an example of a leader of your faith living happily surrounded by the love of his or her family. You will see the number of your followers tail off dramatically if all you offer as role models is martyrs.

The majority of your followers will never be martyrs but will live in peace in the comfort of their family. You should value their contribution as of equal worth to those who sacrifice themselves. Give them hope also. Surely, you will achieve as much if you marry and have children as if you die a lonely and savage death? Seek life not death. I for one would curse any God that allowed you to die without experiencing the joy of growing old gracefully and much-loved."

Maria was blushing deep purple, her cheeks burning and her head shaking for she felt this praise was too much. "I am only a simple girl" she whispered. "You place me on a pedestal from which I must fall. I am not this person you describe but just someone lucky to have been the first to see my Master alive."

"O Maria" Amarillus exclaimed in exasperation. "You are a fool. You are far more than I have described and have no idea of the charm you cast over all whom you meet. Nearly two millions follow your Master because they have met *you.*"

"It is my Master they must follow and not me" and she would not be moved from her view that she was not important, becoming unusually stubborn.

In the days that followed, Amarillus played constant court on Maria, treating her as a princess, adorning her with the finest jewellery and silks, instructing his servants to oil and massage her frail skin, to bathe her and wash her in the finest perfumes and ass' milk, to trim her eyebrows and groom the tangles in her hair. She would join Longinus and the Prefect for supper each evening, and was regaled with stories of the myths and legends of ancient Roma and Graecia. She responded with child-like delight yet her grooming showed the womanhood that was waiting to burst forth and when it did, she would break hearts and turn heads: indeed she already was.

On her first day, Longinus sent word to Iosephus to come and join them at the Praefect's Palace where Amarillus had offered them accommodation in his extensive guest quarters. Iosephus brought Perseus who carried the Spear and sent word to his servants that they would decide their route from Luguidenum soon so they must be on standby to ride north or west when told.

At night, Maria would occasionally have nightmares and then she would take up her bedside candle stick and go in search of Longinus' room and sit in the chair in his room watching him or if he were awake, she would clamber in bed with him just to be held in the security of his strong arms. One day when both Amarillus and Longinus were absent, she went in search of the female servant, Delpha, and took solace in her company as she kissed Maria then held her in her arms and gently rocked her to sleep.

On the third day, Amarillus gave Maria permission to hold a Eucharistic service in the Temple of Mars and had his Praetorian Guard put up notices across Luguidenum. Interest was huge especially amongst the legionaries who were already aware of the Praefect's admiration for this slip of a girl who chatted with her captors, faced torture and being scourged with courage, and who had forgiven those who harmed her without any rancour. They wanted to know more and so the legionaries came en masse and the service over-flowed with more than sixty thousands within the dark of the Temple and sitting in the comfort of a sunny day, many bringing picnics and using this as a family occasion, on the banks of seating of the Circus, Stadium, Arena and the Amphitheatre or the steps of the Forum.

"Today we learn about the mission of a man sent to die that all of us might be enlightened." Maria began and then spoke of her Master's ministry as she welcomed them to each part of the service. She began with his teachings on the forgiveness of sins: "If you are penitent and join in the breaking of the bread then God will forgive you because you have God's Son as your advocate, your lawyer, defending you."

Then she introduced the scriptures and told the story of Petrus in the Garden of Gethsemane. "Petrus struck off the ear of one of the legionaries in my friend, Longinus' century. My Master told Petrus to put away his sword then healed the man's ear before saying 'those who live by the sword will die by the sword'. My Master invites us to 'turn the other cheek', to be ready to be harmed again rather than offer harm to others. I ask that we each learn that prayer can be the mightiest of weapons, peace the strongest of shields and that when we use weapons to kill another we risk doing damage to our own soul, no matter that our actions are honourable."

Her sermon was on the nature of war: "Many present with us today are mighty warriors who fight to protect us from the terrible savagery of those who would invade our lands if it were not for the heroism of these men. Yet my Master says we should not kill. How do we reconcile these apparently conflicting views?

My Master wants peace and blesses all peacemakers. If peace can be attained through peaceful means then we should do so. But the evil of this world is that there are those who do not value life and as a consequence will kill the innocent and the vulnerable for no better reason than that they can.

We are fortunate therefore that there are those who are prepared to give their lives to protect the vulnerable. My Master recognised this when he said: 'No greater love hath man than to lay down his life for another.'

So, if we seek peace but protect the vulnerable when they are threatened, both are lauded by the Angels and will earn us the love of God and his gift of Eternal Life.

Do not decry those who go and meet the barbarian seeking peace and prepared to die if the barbarian does not listen. Equally, show respect for those who fight to save our lives and risk their own to do so. Both are welcome in my Master's house in Paradise: for God will find us on whatever path we take provided we believe in Him, love Him and love each other: for He is the Path, the True Way to Eternal Life."

As they broke the bread Maria spoke of the last days of her Master's life and then his rising from death and meeting the disciples fleeing to Emmaus. When they came to the breaking of the bread she invited the many who had brought food hampers to break bread with her and thus they were commissioned as Ministers of the Eucharist, the legionaries acted as her ushers ensuring all had a piece of bread as she said the words: "This is me!"

Finally, she said goodbye to them, inviting them to remember her Master and invite him into their homes, their family and their community or legion by continuing to break the bread together. As she walked back through the Forum towards the Prefect's Palace, the Praetorian Guard formed an impromptu escort for her and in her happiness and gratitude she began to sing. It was a psalm set to music by King David and known by the Jewish community many of whom joined in and also helped their neighbours with the words and the tune. Soon thousands were rejoicing in song.

Maria had long been considering how the newly formed communities of Christians could avoid their leaders being arrested for unlawful assembly. Something Amarillus had said gave her the idea that would mark out the community of Luguidenum and protect it from the persecution of the second Domitian in the third century AD. Her permit from the Prefect included any area she 'dedicated' as her Temple.

Some of the community at Luguidenum asked Amarillus if they could meet Maria as they had some questions to put to her. "We are talking about four of the Elders of the community here, no more than that" they said. The Praefect was happy to agree especially if it kept the girl longer in the City for he was smitten and considering everything from adoption to betrothal. She knew nothing of this and compounded things by laughing in delight at his stories, offering her natural wisdom when he put questions before her, always seeing the good in people and the positive in any situation. He was in danger of falling in love who until this week had always believed his love of the army would never be challenged.

The Elders met Maria over lunch and immediately asked if she would consider leading the community in Luguidenum in a Eucharistic service set in the catacombs. "We have used the tunnels beneath our City for secret meetings for years" they said at which, Maria had her brainwave. "Why do I not dedicate the catacombs as my new Temple as then we can use them for religious services and will be covered by the permit the Praefect has issued?"

Thus it was that Maria went to Amarillus and asked if she could visit the catacombs that night.

"Why?" asked the Praefect in surprise and so Maria told him as she would never lie, especially to someone she liked and respected. Amarillus said 'Yes' without needing to think about it whilst making a mental note to have his spies take a look at the catacombs. If this is where 'secret meetings' were happening then this might include more than Maria's religious meetings and unwittingly, the girl may have uncovered the headquarters of any rebellion and insurrection in the City. She surprised him by standing on tip toe and kissing him in gratitude leaving him in silent reflection before issuing his instructions not only that the catacombs should be watched twenty four hours each day but also that he wanted Maria watched over and protected.

That night Maria dedicated the catacombs and in the process founded the principle of dedicating churches for local communities, moving the faith of the Nazarene from services conducted in homes, synagogues and existing social centres to purpose-built and re-dedicated facilities and institutions. Soon, the communities she had founded were building their own Temples, seminaries and monasteries.

In the morning, she met with Iosephus and Longinus over breakfast and proposed they went north to Suevum then by-pass Lusitania by going west to Viena, Osere, Augis and Taurentium then north to Carterum, Derum, Enterum and Rona then west once more to Sugdavellum.

"It is at least one day's ride to Viena, another to Taurentium, another to Carterum then Rona in a day and Sugdavellum completes the week" muttered Iosephus preferring to go north to Lusitania but Maria was worried that whilst her travel documents would impress the Praetors at the small centres such as Viena and Enterum, even Rona, Lusitania might easily see her run foul of its Procurator or City Prefect, only this time he might not be as kind, forgiving or accommodating as Amarillus.

She parted from Amarillus with a kiss of genuine pleasure, hugging her new-found friend and promised to see him soon, whilst he prayed devoutly for her safe return. He had just briefed Longinus with some disquietening news. One of the many spies asked to keep an eye on Maria had reported back that Amarillus' men were not the only ones watching Maria's movements.

"Bandits?" Longinus had asked fearing another kidnapping attempt but Amarillus had shaken his head before continuing: "We brought the man watching Maria in to be interrogated. He has said nothing under torture but we found this on him" and Amarillus produced a wicked looking, deadly sharp and curved knife with a steel blade embossed in silver and a black onyx handle.

"A sicarius" hissed Longinus and the other man nodded then begged the Centurion: "Please be very careful and look after Maria for me" the Praefect asked "for the hunt is on."

Longinus decided to try and throw any pursuit off by leaving Luguidenum at midnight and crossing the Pontus Aquafera which was still technically closed for repairs but not if you had a permit from the City Praefect and were escorted by a cohort of Praetorians, wearing black cloaks to prevent the crescent moon that night from glinting on their armour. The company would join the road to Tarterum just north of Luguidenum but anyone trying to follow them would head east in the first instance thinking they were heading for the Alpes, Geneva, skirting south of the lake and into Turino in northern Italia.

Longinus and Perseus would take it in turns to drop back, watching from the shadows for any pursuit but they saw none and as dawn arrived the party had skirted around Maconum and entered Bomaris which was to be their first stop. There were a number of Taverna around the Central Square and Iosephus had booked them into a tall timber framed plastered building, part of a row of tenements of different heights and styles, painted in vivid creams, ochre, reds and navy blue, with the rooms Iosephus had chosen looking out onto the square and its market stalls in the centre. Bomaris was quiet with a Temple and small infirmary to the north of the square.

For once Maria was wide awake and as the others slept, she put on her cloak and slipped out into the cold of the morning's first light, heading for the Temple. The High Priest was a local man and fast asleep, his role as High Priest comprising looking after the 'sacred goat', a badly behaved animal that had become sanctified when it had head-butted the leader of a local tribe of bandits from the foothills of the Massif. The bandits had proceeded to pillage the village and taken several of the girls in the village hostage in their anger at this insult but the goat was still honoured for its courage.

The goat had died the following year but the High Priest knew a soft living when he was granted one and found a substitute that was equally evil-tempered. Alas, whilst he slept, his goat met the good-natured Maria and became a changed animal arousing the suspicions of the good people of Bomanis and leading to the priest's eventual removal.

As Maria explored the deserted Temple, its altar bare of any donations, no votive candles lit and its statues of Jupiter, Mars and Athena bare-headed and without the customary adornment of flowers, she tried a solid oak-planked door near the far end of the sanctuary on the presbyter. She had expected this to lead to the priest's vestibular but instead it led to a narrow spiral staircase and short tunnel that gave on to a series of inter-connected caves (now the cellars for some of the best wines in the Burgundy region beneath the Convent and the famous Hospital at Beaumes).

The caves looked ideal as a safe place for services of the Eucharist to be held without arousing the suspicion of the local praetorship, which was administered by two clerks in the middle rank and whom Maria would later go to see. But first, as she wondered once more through the caves which formed a circle that would bring her back to the spiral staircase, she heard the soft tread of footsteps in the shallow and fine sand on the ground of the caves: someone was behind her and following her. Aware of her vulnerability, she turned and smiled fearlessly at her pursuer, to be welcomed by the High Priest in imperfect Latin and then his native Gallic. Praising the Spirit of God for her gift of tongues, Maria replied to his enquiry:

"I am Maria the Magdalan and have been granted permission by the City Praefects of Tolosa, Marsela and Luguidenum to hold religious services in any Temple of my choosing and to dedicate any new or existing building for Eucharistic services. I want to dedicate your caves if I may?"

The Priest had no objection, especially if the religious services brought a new congregation to his Temple, last visited by tourists six weeks ago. His reply was typically avaricious: "I get fifty per cent of all donations; I mean the Temple gets half not me personally, of course!"

Maria nodded not expecting any donations then asked if the High Priest would post some notices announcing that a '*Service of the Eucharist celebrating the life of Iesus of Nazareth would be held at noon at the new Temple dedicated to 'The Risen Christos' in the caves beneath the Temple of Olympus.*'

"Who's he?" the High Priest asked having never heard of Iesus or Christos.

"Best you come and find out. Now please direct me to the sacristy, some candles, candelabra and altar clothes."

As noon approached, Maria stood outside the Temple doors and waited to greet the first arrivals to ask if they would act as ushers, directing people to the caves below and explaining how the breaking of the bread would need them to distribute the bread they would break into pieces when she did then pass them around. She had sent the High Priest shopping and he had bought over one hundred loaves which were left for volunteers to take as long as they were happy to break and share each loaf.

By noon, three thousand had gathered. Most had heard of Maria and some had come north from Maconum and even from Luguidenum and Marsela, a small troop of volunteers and disciples following her. Others were curious and had come in response to the High Priest's Notices, seen as they were shopping at the colourful market stalls in the Forum.

Maria welcomed them all from a small altar table set in the furthest cave, explained the meaning of the breaking of the bread then reading from Isaiah she spoke of his prophecy of the Coming of a Messiah, then told them of the day of his ascension:

"Almost everyone was frightened as our best friend suddenly rose into the sky and vanished. We thought he had finally left us. I was left alone on that mountain as everyone else ran away until I was greeted by an Angel who told me to look in my heart. As I did so, then I saw that Iesus was still with me and would be forever.

I asked how others could also find Iesus in their hearts and was reminded by the Angel of Iesus' own words: *'I will be with you once more in the breaking of the bread'.* And so, when we break the bread we become open to Iesus being present within us and to the Spirit of God coming down on us and granting us his gifts."

The volunteers who had followed Maria from Marsela and Luguidenum plus hundreds of new disciples helped distribute the bread and then all said together: "This is Iesus of Nazareth. Eat this bread and remember me" as they did so several gasped as the Spirit entered them and granted them wonderful gifts: of healing, foresight, to speak in many languages and to hope. Then all knelt in thanksgiving and the service ended with Maria's simple words of dedication: "Let these humble caves be the safe home for any who wish to celebrate the breaking of the bread. Go now and pray to Iesus for he welcomes all of our prayers."

Maria saw the two clerks of the praetorship at Bomeris and it was a simple matter to have a copy drafted of Amarillus' permit which became the official dedication document for the new Church in Bomeris with the two clerks acting as witnesses and adding their own seals to both the copy and the original. "You will need several copies for your journey to Sugdavellum" one of the clerks observed and set his scribes the task of making ten copies, each of which he witnessed.

The community in Bomeris would celebrate the Eucharist in the Temple of Olympus and in the caves that were the *Temple to the Risen Christ* in their thousands the following day and had the confidence to continue to celebrate without Maria. Later their descendants would survive the persecution of the second Domitian in the third century AD to be proud when their faith became that adopted by the entire Roman world in the fourth century AD.

Soon after the second hour in the afternoon, the party left Bomeris headed due north, following the path of the Rhone until that evening they reached Tarterum but word had gone ahead and over thirty thousand were waiting with lit lanterns to greet them near where an old warehouse stood half on land and the other half into the river.

"It is a miracle it is still standing" muttered Longinus as he stooped beneath a collapsed and rotten door lintel to see that someone had been very busy. An odd assortment of seating ranging from benches and dining to casual to office chairs filled three quarters of the warehouse with a raised platform, solitary chair and a tall and narrow console table set with a white linen cloth and two candles denoting the sanctuary.

Maria did not wait but welcomed them all and led them in a prayer asking for God's forgiveness then found the scripture of Moses being blessed with bread and manna from heaven. "We are also blessed in that as we break this bread the Spirit of God will come down from heaven and fill us" so they broke the bread, many having brought bread with them and who now passed it around.

The Good News spread and the next day, even though Maria had left Tarterum for Osere (or Auserum) in the half light early that morning, over three hundred set out to follow Maria as her disciples. Self selected or selected by the Spirit of God, they would offer help with the huge numbers at the Services of the Eucharist. When Maria saw them, she rode back to greet them and called them her 'diakonae' in honour of Stephanus and the oarsmen who had so faithfully supported her on her journey across the Middle Sea and through Hispania.

They travelled west to the Desert of the Tuilii and then headed north-west to Equillae, Normia, Chacaeni, Sauvinae, riding past each, or stopping briefly to invite those gathered to follow them on to Avallonae, then they followed the meandering Fluvius Saerena to Monitus before going north from Pressae to Avallonae. At Avallonae, Maria said a short service for the hundreds who had followed her on the road from Bomeris then the company stood on Avallonae's famous hill and looked as the last rays of the sun pointed to the confluence of the rivers Camut and Lot then shone on the lake formed by the meeting of these two great rivers. The still waters were turned burnished red gold by the dying light of a sinking sun which then pointed a single beam like a finger at the isolated hill-top many leagues away on opposite side of the valley where the first settlers had established a camp and named their place 'Vedselae'.

"Can we reach Vedselae in safety for surely the sun has given us a sign?"

"Alas, my lady" it was the wise knight who answered "The light will not hold and this road is treacherous with what looks like the sweep of a forest between this hill-top and the one you would have us gain. I suggest we settle and make camp here. We had accommodation in Auserum many leagues to our rear and in Carterum many leagues to our north. Neither is any longer within safe reach tonight."

"Very well" replied Maria "We sleep here. Can you arrange with Longinus, Perseus, Annanias and yourself the rota to stand guard as our numbers make us vulnerable to assault? Yet above us is a deserted Roman Keep overlooking Avallonae, built by Julius Caesar to survive the attack of hundreds by the rebel prince, Vercingetorix and to keep constant guard over the ruins of Gergovia. We shall be safe there."

Longinus and Iosephus were to take the first watch, holding the narrow entrance to the Keep and the first floor window that was no more than an arrow slit. The two ladies slept on the third floor and could retreat through a hatch onto the roof of the Keep for their last defence whilst Perseus and Annanias slept on the second floor and were to hold it if awakened or come to the aid of their comrades in arms on the ground and first floor.

Three hours into the night and just as Iosephus was entering the second floor to waken Perseus and Annanias for their turn at watch duty, there was a rustle in the trees, no more than that and then an arrow bounced off the stone of the door lintel, inches from where Longinus' hand had been resting. The Centurion drew his sword and whispered for his comrades to join him. Ten men armed with swords and sharp curved knives stepped out of the forest that surrounded the Hill of Avallonae on which the Roman Castle was perched. Annanias and Iosephus joined Longinus, both carrying a spear and a legionary's rectangular and slightly concave shield. They were ready to aid Longinus as he held the entrance to the Keep.

"Where is Perseus?" whispered Longinus as he moved his head to let another arrow go sailing by them.

"'Getting ready' is what he said. He has 'had an idea'!" Annanias replied somewhat taken aback at his colleague's actions.

"He is not meant to have ideas!" The Centurion growled. "Very well ten against three and we must watch out for the archer in the woods also."

The ten ran at the doorway, forming into a wedge as they charged. The first man thrust with his sword, easily parried by Longinus and he fell to two spear thrusts. But now Longinus must meet the assault of two men who both swung with sword and knife simultaneously. Annanias met the sword of one with his shield then thrust with his spear forcing the man to step back. Iosephus froze paralysed with indecision. Meanwhile Longinus had ducked under the attacks of the second assailant and thrust his sword into the man's groin.

His screams cut through the quiet of the night, wakening those sleeping in Avallonae who straightway picked up pitchforks, hammers and staves to be born as make-shift weapons and headed for where they could hear a battle in progress. The scream had also woken the ladies. Celestile did as ordered by Longinus and opened the hatch to the roof and hauled herself up through it. Maria ran towards the scream to see what healing she could do.

Three men now assailed Longinus and he was forced to step back, grabbing Iosephus' right shoulder with his left hand to bring him back from the paralysis of fear, parrying two thrusts whilst Annanias held off a third thrust and Iosephus, now back with them, two more. A slice of a dagger however penetrated Longinus' guard and blood appeared from a fine slice along his left thigh. Not debilitating yet but blood loss would take its toll. By stepping back, Longinus had allowed two of their assailants to step through the archway whilst two more were pressing hard behind them.

Longinus knew they must repulse this attack or they would be overwhelmed.

Then suddenly, there was a great commotion outside and the men before Longinus were momentarily distracted, turning their heads in alarm at an assault from their rear. Longinus did not hesitate but thrust and took the man in front of him in the heart whilst Annanias thrust forwards with his shield and sent a man tumbling backwards and then Longinus heard a gasp and glancing to his right saw Annanias toppling backwards an arrow through the right eye.

"Keep your shield up" Longinus growled at Iosephus whilst stepping into the hole in the enemy ranks that Annanias had created and thrusting again at an opponent's vulnerable legs. The assailants fell back to reform and Longinus ducked just in time to allow an arrow to pass harmlessly over his head. When he stood up, he had Annanias' shield for protection and could feel cold hands touching his wounded thigh and heard the sound of softly spoken prayers.

"What are you doing here?" he shouted and Maria replied: "You know that you getting cross with me just makes me want to laugh. Now stand still and let me see what I can do to try and heal this." As she spoke her soft and delicate hands passed gently over the cut and the skin knitted together whole and hale once more.

There was a brief pause as the enemy regrouped. Longinus' eyes became accustomed to the dark and he could see why the enemy had been distracted. Perseus was mounted on one of Iosephus' finest stallions which was kicking out at the ranks of their attackers, whilst Perseus held a shield to protect his left flank and was using the Spear of Longinus as a lance.

It shone bright gold and had already taken three men in the shoulder with thrusts that wounded and disarmed them but the Spear could not slay an opponent. In addition to the three men all clutching their right shoulders, his horse had taken down a fourth man with a blow from a flailing hoof to the head, whilst Longinus had slain one and seriously wounded a second and Annanias and Iosephus had slain another. Three men remained standing and were struggling to get past the shield and the defence of Perseus using his lance, tipped by the point of Longinus' spear, as a stave to hold off all attacks.

Then Perseus disengaged to sit low in his saddle, lance pointed steadily before him and charged the line of three men. Their courage gave and they scattered giving Perseus an easy target as he thrust his lance into the posterior of one of the fleeing men and he fell to the ground, unable to walk. Perseus turned to see the other two men running for the cover of the trees and hoisted his lance then turned to smile at Longinus just as the arrow took him in the heart.

"No" screamed Longinus and ran towards the fallen knight, Maria running at his side. He knelt and held the man's head whilst she took the Spear and prayed through her tears and then held the lance tip to his bloodied breast whilst slowly withdrawing the arrow. Iosephus was by them and was trying to say something but Maria could not hear him through her sobs whilst Longinus was trying to hear Perseus' last words.

"I go to a better place" Perseus whispered. "Let me go" and he smiled as the flame of triumph in his eyes slowly faded and departed. Finally, Longinus could hear the words of the old equites: "The Grael, the Shroud and the Robe. They can grant us far more healing power than the Spear alone." But Longinus shook his head then lifted Perseus in his arms and turned towards the tearful Maria. "He wanted to die protecting you" he said to her "and he has gone on to prepare a place for us all in Paradise. We must not be sad surely?"

The girl sniffed and then wiped her nose down her sleeve as a child would do before stuttering as she then said: "Could we not have tried?"

"He did not wish for us to do so. You once said you would never force your faith on others. Can you not see that to force Perseus to live beyond the time determined by God would be a sin?" And Maria's head bowed in shame for indeed her wish had been to challenge the gift of a good death that had always been Perseus' dream and God's destiny for him.

"He was a true knight and I shall remember him all my life in my prayers. Bury him here at this place of his greatest triumph and when I shall die bury me across the hill in the place named Vedselae that he might look over me and protect me in death as he has done in life. In death I shall tend the lake, the green rolling grasslands and the forests of the valley between us that this land shall always be blessed by those who shall do good deeds and that Perseus' view in death shall always be beautiful."

"Come, we need to get under cover for there is an archer and three assassins still out there in the dark" Longinus muttered and they headed back to be under safe cover of the Keep. Without warning, Maria stepped into the shadows to kneel and tend to the wounded groin of the assassin downed by Longinus. Her healing was almost instant and brought the man back from the brink of painful death through blood loss. He stared at her in amazement and asked: "Why have you done this thing? How have you done this?"

"Who am I to decide who shall have the benefit of God's healing and who should not? I have not healed you. You are created by God as am I. God did the healing and my prayer was the means by which God's healing power was focused on you."

The sicariot was amazed and swore: "I cannot seek your death when you heal your enemies as well as your friends. You could not do such healing if your words were heresy or blasphemy. Take me with you."

Gently, Maria laid her hands on the man's head and as she did so his eyes came alight with the power of the Spirit and he spoke in prophecy for the first time:

"All we believe is accomplished by the resurrection of Iesus of Nazareth."

Then he looked at Maria and spoke with certainty as the power of prophecy continued to flood within him: "You need not face a sad death. You can choose another way and still do God's will. Whatever choice you make, I offer you my protection. My name is Galahaidra."

They buried Perseus beneath the archway that was the entrance to the Keep, standing tall in death as he had stood to meet the attacks of their enemies in life. He held the lance, with the spear-point removed, his Shield in his left hand; he wore his helmet and looked proud, the smile on his lips brought fresh tears to all of their eyes. Though dead, his face was full of life and there was no sign of the rigor of death. His body did not smell of decay but of the freshness of newly cut rose petals. Maria wanted to bury the Spear with the dead knight but Longinus persuaded her that they would still need its powers to convert the barbarians. "The Celts, Britons, Gauls, Gaels, Caledonii and Picts all believe their weapons are magical and so will welcome you for the magic of the religious artefacts you carry."

"I will return one day" she promised as she stood and watched them lay a stone over Perseus' resting place then cover it with turfs.

They laid Annanias next to him; the arrow removed carefully and his eye lids shut to hide the sad damage done to one orb by the arrow's path. Annanias was dressed in Iosephus' finest robe and with the knight's best rings on his fingers.

Both men had died bravely defending those they loved. They were still burying the two men as the rescue party from the village of Avallonae at the bottom of the hill finally arrived. The villagers carried with them a prisoner: one of the sicariot who had slain two of their comrades and who now glared at the rest of the party through red-rimmed eyes of fury. He was not yet eighteen but already a killer. When he saw Maria he spat in her face, catching all by surprise.

"No" she cried as those holding him went to cut him down. "Can you let this man live for he is young with so much life still ahead of him?"

The leader of the war party from the village shook his head as he said: "This young man cut down two of my best friends. But watch …" and he asked the sicariot: "What will you do if I let you go?"

"Hunt down the adulterous witch called the Magdalan and slay her then throw her body into the Sea that her soul may never find succour, cursing her every minute of my life in the hope that she will burn for an eternity in Hell."

Nearly in tears again, Maria asked: "What have I done that you hate me as you do?"

"You are alive. That is enough. You shall not permit a witch to live!" and he went to spit at Maria once more but this time they were ready and wrenched his head back.

Maria walked away, her shoulders sagging under the weight of all that hate. Longinus went up to her and held her then whispered in her ear: "What he says is madness and evil but you must never think it is truth nor think his evil words will convince anyone about the real you. Once someone has seen you they will attest to your goodness as so many do already."

She leant into him, grateful for his strength and comfort then said:

"Now we know why I was directed to this place for it is far from the most direct route. Perseus was destined to die here and so am I. It is a beautiful place and I am content. But now we must push on with our mission. We go north except I have no idea where. We need Iosephus."

The old man was doubly upset at the loss of both Annanias and Perseus but when Maria broached the subject of where they headed next he laughed at the girl's total absence of any sense of direction: "We need to go west not north. We must get to Torino and then it is a straight road through Carbillonum, skirting the capital of Gaul, heading to Allanum, Bibanari, Torino, Bibracte, Rocca and Sugdavellum. But to get to Torino we head to Carbillonum and Bibinari. If we can do Bibinari in a single day then we shall make Sugdavellum in three days."

That was a huge incentive and knowing it was her frailty that was holding the two men back she told them: "I am feeling much stronger than I did when we were riding north through Syria so have no fear for me and go for it!"

The road to Tartellum was tortuous: Roman cobbles in places, tracks and paths across the tops of hills in other places, non-existent, not even a track to follow, around the settlements at Vedselae and Petron as they rode from the spring at the base of the hill on which Vedselae stood and went south towards the Font Aeneas where they had to push through the dense undergrowth of the Forest of Aepas with no path at all save the shadows left by the sun to give them direction in order to find the Roman road to Tartellum from Avallonae. Eventually, they broke clear of the Forest to find the flagstone-paved, straight road to Carbillonum from Auserum.

From the City of Carbillonum, which they reached after the City Gates had been shut and bolted and so were waved on by the sentries there, the road to Torino continued as flat paving stones and the company made much better time, riding at sixteen leagues each hour, whereas to reach Carbillonum had taken fifteen hours at a tenth of that speed. They rode in the dark but the moon was waxing, a half crescent, and bright offering its silver light to show them the way. Heading south west, they reached Bibinari in five hours. It was nearly dawn and the company had ridden the whole day and night without rest. In the last hour Longinus and Galahaidra had taken it in turns to carry Maria on their saddles before them as the girl had fallen from her horse several times weary to the point that she kept falling asleep.

Bibinari was a town with a well-established Gallic farming community and recently-built municipal buildings in the local stone: this included an Arena and Forum built by the Romans as well as several large villas that had been built on the slopes of the hills around Bibinari. There was no defensive wall and no garrison to defend the town which had no strategic value and relied on its trade in wine and commodities and its location as a stop on the roads from Lusitania and Luguidenum to Torino for its income. Bibinari had three Inns all outside the circuit of the town but Iosephus' servants had booked them into a guest house besides the Forum. Hop and grape vines covered all of the hills approaching and surrounding this small farming settlement with dense oak forests beyond.

There was no praetor's office and also no Temple. Rather there was a stone circle which still had the signs of the human sacrifice offered at the summer solstice and a sacred grove of oak trees where the druids held their secret gatherings. Longinus shuddered and refused to go near either, casting the sign of the 'evil eye'.

The welcome at the guest house was warm, kind and generous-hearted with the lady of the house washing and clothing Maria as she slept, covering her in silk sheets and opening the window shutters to give the girl the benefit of the cool morning breeze. She popped her head in every hour to check that the girl still slept whilst making breakfast for the three men.

Celestile had retired to her room to weep. For twenty years she had lived in the warm companionship of Annanias who had worshipped the ground on which she trod and done little things for her every day that she now noticed and missed for the first time when he was gone. He had died fighting to protect the vulnerable including herself and he had earned a hero's death. She could think of nothing less likely to have happened but was proud of her dead husband. The couple had two children, both being looked after by their aunt, and whom she would ensure knew how bravely their father had died … if she could ever stop the tears from falling. Suddenly,

Celestile knew she should be with her family and so built up the courage to go and see Iosephus.

The equites was also in mourning for Annanias and welcomed Celestile with a warm embrace and a moment when they both wept. Then he spoke of his many fond memories of the man who had organised his life so well for nearly two decades.

"I have made a bequest" he told the poor widow and named a sum so vast that Celestile gasped.

"It is too much" she finally was able to say but Iosephus shook his head and persuaded her to accept his generosity, saying:

"Think also of your children. They will need to be set up in trade or business or will need a dowry to ensure they can marry the right person. I will see your Son gets a good apprenticeship and sponsor and pay separately for his knighthood. I wish to give your daughter away and to stand good for her dowry when the time comes as well. You have made my life comfortable for almost twenty years and now I wish to make your life comfortable. It will never be enough."

"I want to go home, Domine" she asked fearful of his reaction but Iosephus nodded before saying:

"Celestile, you go with my blessing. You must ride to Burdigala from Torino. I will provide you with an escort and send word to Decius to bring my yacht to the City for your use. We will get you home as soon as possible."

Maria woke whilst the men in the company were in the market, buying provisions for the ride to Torino then the City of Bibracte. If they left early enough taking advantage of the longer days in the month of Julius then the City of Bibracte was possible in a day and Sugdavellum the following day. So Maria left them to it and headed instead for the small Taverna near the Forum to ask boldly about the local druids. The servant behind the bar looked at Maria and seeing her youth and innocence he told her paternally:

"You would make a good sacrifice. A young girl on her own with the rarity of blue eyes and fair hair, sticking her nose into things best left to her elders. Have you a death wish, child?"

"I want to know where I can hold a service of prayer to my God and ensure I do so without unintentionally insulting the ceremonies and services of other faiths here."

The servant was thoughtful. He did not want Maria to come to any harm but understood why she would wish to be careful. Finally, he compromised: "There is a house on the Via Apulia which sits next to the Bathhouse. It has an oak door painted black and a ram's head with curling horns over the door. Knock twice then once" and he went to serve another customer.

She did as suggested and a house servant came to the door unable to make eye contact, head bowed looking at the ground, mumbling: "The Master is not here, go away!"

"When your Master finds out that I knocked and sought to meet him and you sent me away then he will be furious. I have no wish to see you in trouble so will write a note." The servant nodded and stayed with the door still half open, waiting for her scribbled note. She wrote carefully and legibly (for once):

I am the Magdalan. I am come to preach to the people of Bibinari but I have no wish to offend. Can we meet?

Then she handed him the missive whilst he pointed to the curtain that opened onto the atrium where Maria sat on the marble surround to a fountain of a hydra and dangled her feet, playing with the gold fish in the water as they nibbled her bare toes.

A tall man, with a long black beard, wearing a black gown and robe with a single silver star on his right shoulder, entered the chamber silently and stood facing the girl. He dismissed her immediately as of no consequence and seeing his look of disdain she accepted his verdict without hesitation. She had no wish to be seen as of substance and would rather be invisible than hold the attention of those in any room. She looked at the man and introduced herself humbly and hesitantly:

"I am Maria and am seeking to lead a few of my followers in a service of prayer and dedication. I do not wish to accidentally interrupt a service being run by those of other faiths and religions. I am come to seek your advice."

"Leave!" he said and turned intending to return to his studies.

"I saw a nice grove of oaks to the north of the town. I shall use that."

The druid stopped in his tracks, turned to look at the girl properly, saw the stubbornness and the courage then sensed the power of her prayers and the grace given to her by the Spirit. He looked briefly into the future and what he saw shocked him. Finally, he offered the girl a chair and then sat opposite her and spoke softly and carefully:

"I am not often wrong when I judge people but you have hidden depths that I missed. There is no common ground between our faiths yet you offer a chance for mutual tolerance that I would be foolish to ignore. If you can find a space for those who worship the natural world and the power of the spirits that inhabit our trees, rivers and mountains, then we have much that is in common. Your God created everything both seen and *unseen*. Please leave a place for the worship of the 'unseen' in your ministry."

Maria smiled and offered what reassurance she could: "My Master taught me to hold all that has been created in awe and wonder including trees, forests, rivers, lakes and mountains. Angels are my companions and are often unseen although they are not of the spirit world. Perhaps there are more similarities between us than I had realised?" then returning to her subject, persisted in her request:

"May I use your grove? Advise me on what I can and cannot do to avoid sacrilege."

"Yes you may use it. Do nothing to dedicate it to a new God or faith. Ensure all that you do is true and do nothing that my God might see as blasphemous."

Maria could sense that the druid before her was hungry to learn more about Iesus' ministry and so she obliged, answering some of his questions then sitting back, she closed her eyes and talked about the earliest days beginning with Canaa and the banks of Galilee when Iesus began to recruit his disciples but also of Tyre, Sinon and Nazareth where he first met Lazarus, Martha and Maria and Maria the Magdalan. Then she spoke of the miracles and the druid could not contain his eagerness to hear more:

"Maria, I have no name, I should perhaps have explained this earlier as I must have come across as impolite for not introducing myself. I am also not the Chief Druid in this region but carry a lot of influence so you have come to the right place to ask about the grove. I must ask though: your Master, he could do magic?"

"My Master's miracles are not magic. He is God and thus all of creation is here by his power. He commands the natural world. We are also his creation and we respond to his power. All he does is done with compassion and love. He is the God of love."

"You speak of your Master as if he is alive?" the druid asked confused.

"He died and returned to life. The Centurion who executed him is one of his followers now, having seen my Master alive when before he was dead and buried. I buried my Master with tears and was the first to see him alive three days later. His healing power continues and he comes to us in the breaking of the bread which will be the service I propose to hold at the grove."

"Your Master has conquered death?" the druid asked in amazement for this was the magic that every druid sought through human sacrifice.

"Yes and he also offers his followers life after death, to live eternally in Paradise with him. He prepares a place in his Father's house for all of us."

The druid sat back in thought then clapped his hands and two servants, who scared the living daylights out of Maria and whose gaze at the girl was pure menace and malice, entered the atrium and stood either side of where she still sat by the fountain. She gulped.

"I would very much like you to be my guest" said the druid smiling and for once Maria did not return the smile. "You offer such potential through your knowledge of your Master's magic and once I have extracted that from you as painfully as possible then I propose to sacrifice you so that I can claim your essence to add to the powers I already possess."

Maria found that her mouth had gone dry and began to realise how foolish she had been to come out alone. The barman at the local Taverna had warned her to be careful and she had ignored that advice; more fool her! She went to speak and one of the men clamped a hand over her mouth whilst the other lifted her like a feather and they carried her into the basement where the iron doors to the oven of hypocaust sat open, a fire raging. Fearing that her fate was to be incinerated, she fainted. Opposite the oven was an archway that led to a dark cell where they chained the Magdalan, awaiting their master's pleasure. She woke a few moments later and wondered if she felt more relieved that she was still alive or should be worried at the prospect of torture followed by human sacrifice in the oak grove later that night.

Maria began to pray: "Thy Will Be Done. If I am to die grant me your courage to face my death knowing that we shall meet again in Paradise. If it is Thine Will I live then rescue me from my prison as foretold by Isaiah. Whatever is Thy Will: Give me the strength to follow you no matter what evil I shall face. For I believe and trust in you."

Then her prayers turned to rejoicing at all she had seen and heard in her short life. She felt a sense of gratitude that she had experienced God's creation and been present during his Son's ministry. Whatever her fate, the wonder of all she had already seen could never be taken from her. Her's had been a good life she decided and one for which she would be eternally grateful. If it ended now then so be it.

Longinus, Iosephus and Galahaidra returned to the guest house at which they were staying to discover Maria had gone 'exploring'. The Centurion cursed away, appreciated by Iosephus for his colourful use of several languages but shocking the innocent Galahaidra. "Where will she have gone?" the young sicariot asked and Longinus' expressive eyes suggested that he neither knew nor cared particularly.

"If found by my compatriots she will already be dead!" the former assassin muttered in dismay but Iosephus was more hopeful as he pointed out of the window by the table they had sat at, hoping for breakfast. The shutters were already drawn and the window looked onto the Forum. There were several men watching the entrance to the guest house, sitting on stools dotted around the terraces protected by the shade of pergola and gazeboes or lazing in the shelter of the entrance doorways to villas.

"Mine or Amarillus'!" and the old man grinned. "We are being watched and with luck, one of those men will know where the girl has gone. Stay here!" and the knight rose from their table and stepped across the cobbled street outside to talk to a tall man leaning against the wall of the tenement opposite them. He was back after a couple of minutes: "Via Apulia. There is a house there that has the reputation for being the last place young girls see in this life."

"Why in God's teeth would Maria go there?" Longinus asked despairing at the girl's latest folly. "Best go there and find out" replied Iosephus affably then more for the other men's benefit he added: "We will need to go armed."

They obtained directions from the lady of the house, who assumed they sought the Bathhouse. "Not to the same standard as you will have found in your travels" she mentioned in passing "but it has some good staff who are always helpful. The solarium has a copula with a view of the entire town, done with mirrors and glass whilst the piscina has some rare green tench and golden carp. The owner loves the sea and his villa has a huge collection of ornamental fish, squid and octopod."

The three men headed briskly for the bathhouse in order to reconnoitre the villa further down on the Via Apulia. They were surprised therefore to discover that the house they were seeking was next door to the bathhouse. The ram's head told them all they needed to know and feared. This was the house of a druid and one who was so powerful and well-connected that he could declare himself publicly above his front door without fear of prosecution or reprisal.

"The house will be protected. Best we stake it out from the bathhouse and enter tonight" whispered Iosephus but Longinus was unsure: "Druids hold their services including sacrifices in the middle of the night. During the day is our best bet to rescue the girl."

"In which case we need a ruse or some reason to gain entry for we will be out-numbered by the druid's staff." Iosephus advised and headed for the bathhouse.

The bathhouse's attendants were very helpful as Iosephus talked about their travels across the Middle Sea. Then the old man mentioned that he was a collector of rare fish from the coral reefs around the Aegean, Ionian and Aegyptian seas and asked if there were any fellow collectors. "I have heard that this bathhouse has an exceptionally fine collection of rare fish. Would it be possible to see them?"

The attendants were delighted to talk about the fish and one of the staff took him to view several aquaria housed in the walls of the piscina. As Iosephus got chatting, they mentioned that the owner kept the prize species of his collection in his own villa. "He has far more space to house and display the fish. Perhaps, he might welcome a visit from a fellow collector?"

Iosephus began to decline, only really having discussed the fish as an excuse to look around the bathhouse in order to see if the three men could access the house next door from the baths. He started to make his apologies when the maitre domo joined them and said: "It is no problem really. The owner lives next door. I will go and ask if he can see you then show you through to his house if you would be willing? There is a connecting corridor." Iosephus had no difficulty agreeing and asked if his two companions could join them. "They do not have the same interest as me in fish but I would not want to lose them!"

The maitre domo at the bathhouse was back in a few minutes with a beaming smile. "The owner has a spare half of an hour and would be delighted to talk about his collection and also your own. My Master is not much travelled so has acquired his many and varied fish and sea monsters through agents. If you have any rare species you might consider selling you would make him immensely happy?"

"This is fortunate indeed" replied Iosephus. "Alas, I am moving from the country into the centre of Alexandria and will have much less space in my new town house so must sell part of my collection: mainly the larger species, many of which are also the rarest."

"What are we doing?" whispered Longinus and Iosephus chortled then said "Do keep up Centurion! As soon as you get close enough, Galahaidra and you need to threaten the owner. But wait for my signal."

"Have you suddenly developed a hatred for fish owners?" the Centurion asked exasperated and Iosephus nearly choked on his laughter, just about disguising his mirth as an unconvincing cough.

They were taken into the maitre's office and he pushed on a panel, the depiction of an enormous octopod holding a fisherman beneath the waters in its tentacles, which panel sprang open on hinges to reveal a dark corridor at the end of which they could see the light of an atrium and a magnificent multi-tiered marble fountain depicting a hydra.

"It is by Phideas and I have seen the companion piece which is of a sea serpent" Iosephus exclaimed in genuine delight. The far side of the atrium was an archway towards the owner's private rooms; it was clear that someone had been listening to their conversation for at Iosephus' delight on seeing the fountain, a tall man stepped into the atrium to greet them.

"I would pay any price for that piece" he said eagerly. "To have two such pieces in one collection would be a life's dream" and then, remembering his manners, he introduced himself:

"I am the owner of the bathhouse here in Bibinari. It is a relatively humble facility in a humble town but the aquaria and copula attract connoisseurs and both are amongst the finest examples of their type. I am fortunate indeed to have amassed my collection but am always looking for yet more rare breeds. I am sorry to hear that your own collection is to be split up but if I show you around you will see that your fish and sea creatures will be finding an excellent home and I can assure you of the best prices for any species you sell to me!"

"Are there any breed of fish that might interest you? I may have what you seek. I would welcome seeing your collection. It is a hard wrench to see my own being broken up but to know it goes to the best home will make it much easier for me."

"Come then! This house wraps around the bathhouse next door and I have enlarged it extensively, with pools, piscina and aquaria. My largest species is an 'Aenean Octopod' and I also have a 'Nautillus'."

"You test me I see" replied the old man. "I have heard of the *Aegean* Octopod but never of the Virgilian variety" and there was a laugh behind them as a tall patrician-looking man of indescribable and indeterminate age, with a trimmed black beard, dressed in a dark robe and a silver star on his right shoulder joined them.

"I have to be certain" the druid explained, dismissing his servant with a twirling wave of his right hand. "So many people seek to take my life accusing me of the most despicable things, none of which are true. But I choose not to give their accusations the credit of my defending myself against them. I am gladdened to meet a genuine collector. Please follow me" and he pushed the top right hand corner of another panel with a tessarae of fish of all species caught in a net.

Lighting a sconce immediately beyond the doorway, they entered a huge circular chamber lit by a skylight and before them the four men could see an enormous water tank, the contents of which were the genuine article: an Aegean Octopod. It was devouring the last remains of a young girl or so they hazarded a guess from the remains of fair hair, legs, an arm and clothing, one blue eyeball resting on the tank's pebbled floor. Longinus doubled over, being sick at the sight of the last sorry remnants of Maria being eaten by the sea monster and Iosephus went pale then looked away. It was Galahaidra who had the sense to draw his curved silver sicarius and place the blade at the druid's throat. "Who was she?" he asked barely able to speak and afraid of the answer.

"A slave I bought just for this purpose. She had no life ahead of her and the Octopod's poison was quick" the druid replied. "Now who are you? You have no hope of leaving this house alive without my permission. Explain yourselves and I might let you live."

The next moment, Galahaidra and Iosephus were desperately trying to pull Longinus off the druid as in a red rage the young officer's hands gripped the man by the throat. The druid fought desperately but Longinus was too strong. In the end, Galahaidra stepped back and then swung the pommel of his dagger at the back of the officer's head and the Centurion dropped onto his knees. The druid gasped but after a few moments was able to recover his breath sufficiently to mutter: "Keep him from me" but Iosephus shook his head.

"We are here to collect a friend and then we depart. But unless you take us to where we can find her, I will unleash Longinus on you."

"You are companions of the Magdalan?" The druid asked with understanding dawning then observed in surprise: "I had been told your sect were not violent. So much for the reliability of my sources" and he rubbed his red raw neck ruefully. "Very well, follow me to the basement. The stairs are hidden in this section of the house and very rarely visited except by a select number of staff. It is where I keep my special guests: those who are to be the victims of human sacrifice. Maria is a guest at the moment. She did walk in of her own accord. I cannot really be blamed for taking advantage of her folly!"

"We will be the judge of that" snarled Longinus and the four men headed for the far end of the druid's aquatic collection where a staircase from the water sluice descended to the furnaces for the hypocaust. "Through there" and the druid pointed towards the cell they could see beyond the archway.

Longinus ran into the cell to be greeted by chains on the walls and floor but no girl. He would have murdered the druid there and then if he had not seen the man's genuine look of astonishment. Instead, he muttered: "Now what?"

The druid was genuinely puzzled and stooped to inspect the chains and locks. "These locks have been opened rather than picked. I have the only keys as I do not trust my servants with my guests. Her escape is impossible. The girl should still be here."

"Trust me" Longinus replied. "Nothing that girl does ever surprises me. Now show us out and we let you live." The druid nodded, totally bemused by what had happened and more than convinced that the Magdalan was a mage of great proficiency. He had no wish to earn the enmity of such a powerful sorceress and so willingly showed the three men to his front door.

As soon as they were out of sight, Longinus said: "I am going to find the Praefecture or magistracy here. There must be some representation of the Procurator, Praetor or Praefecture's office. You go and find Maria who I am betting is asleep back in her chambers by now with no idea of the fright she has given us all."

In the end, Longinus found a helpful barman and learnt that law enforcement and policing was the role of the magistrate sitting in the Curiale Court and supported by two lictors. "We don't get much crime" admitted the bar keeper and Longinus thought *'Just how wrong can you be'*!

It was approaching evening by now and Longinus wanted to see the magistrate whilst he could still take action that day. He ran to the Magistrate's Court which, he discovered, doubled up as both the Court of Petitions and Pleas and Curiale Court: all three were chaired by the same freedman, Caius Gallicus Pellastus. Longinus used his travel papers and Letters of Introduction to impress the Usher and jump the queue to see the young magistrate. This was Gallicus' first posting and he was bored to tears with the petty thefts and minor contract breaches he spent all day dealing with.

"Have you noticed how many young girls keep disappearing in your town, magistrate?" Longinus asked without preamble as he marched into the virtually empty court room. Gallicus rocked back in surprise at this interruption to another dreary day then stopped to think about what had been said and slowly nodded his head. He could think of at least five cases in the last three months and as he turned to his clerk who was also his personal secretary and scribe, he asked the man what the records showed. The clerk knew the records off by heart and did not need to refer to them: "Twenty four in twelve months" he said without blinking.

"Want to make a name for yourself and get out of this dead posting?" Longinus then asked and Gallicus almost bit his hand off.

"I do not know the man's name but the owner of the bathhouse is a mass murderer and also a druid into human sacrifice."

Gallicus slumped at his desk then explained why his reaction was less than enthusiastic: "That man has been accused before and is called Daedlus. He has a lot of support in the town, to such an extent that he is untouchable unless I can catch him in the act with evidence."

"Take your lictors now. Go to the man's house. In his atrium you will find a secret panel in the form of a mosaic of fish in a net. Beyond it is an Octopus and the remains of the girl slave it has eaten."

"By Jove! I will go now" and the young man left with his lictors, a dazzling career in the law ahead of him.

By the time, Longinus had returned to the guest lodge by the Forum, Iosephus and Galahaidra had found Maria precisely where the Centurion had predicted, fast asleep in her chamber, as if nothing amiss had happened to her.

"Fetch a bowl of ice-cold water from the frigarium" muttered the Centurion. "Make it as cold as possible." A few minutes later, they had handed Longinus the water basin, with splinters of ice broken from one of the large blocks that were used to keep food cold and fresh in the cold room or frigarium and the Centurion did not pause but threw it over the girl then watched as she spluttered and woke up with a start before saying to her: "That is for worrying us sick. Now what happened?"

Maria leapt up and gave each of them a hug in joy at being reunited. She did not mind the dousing for she had feared much worse at the House of Daedlus and knew she had been foolish to go on her own. Inviting them to sit on the rug on her floor, she folded her legs beneath her and told them of what had happened to her.

"You know that I had been taken and was to be sacrificed by the druid in the House of Daedlus where you searched for me. I am not sure what torture was to precede my sacrifice nor how I was to be slain" and Longinus made a mental note never to tell the girl that she was to have been the meal of a giant octopus "but I began to pray with all my heart that I be rescued but also to thank God for all he had done for me in my life.

What happened next I cannot explain yet I will try! Suddenly I was no longer alone. Before me stood my Master and he said to me: 'You have still to finish your mission'. Then I walked with him through this tunnel of light and each step we took, he would explain to me the meaning of the scriptures, of his own miracles and the things he had achieved and then he foretold how our faith will grow to one day be that of the whole of the Roman Empire. I saw a vision of our 'Church', a single powerful faith that will replace the Pagan Gods of Rome with one God.

But more did I see. In the future, there will come a time when the following of Christ will be threatened by the invasion of new pagans from the North. A king will stand up against the Pagans and he will unite Gaul and Britannia, resisting those from northern Germania and the Saxon kingdoms on the Bight of Heligos. To keep his kingdom united, the wise King will set a quest for his many knights to seek the Spear, Grael, Shroud and Robe. He will found a new kingdom on Earth: one where Right is considered more worthy than Might, based at his capital city called Camelot, sitting at the confluence of the rivers Camut and Lot overlooking the lake of Avallonae.

Our mission is not only to bring the faith of my Master to Gaul or Gallia, Britannia and Caledonia but also to leave a trail which the most worthy warriors of a future generation will follow in quest of the most sacred symbols of our faith.

Finally, I came to the end of the tunnel and turned to say goodbye to the Master but he was no longer besides me yet I could still feel his presence. I blinked in the bright sunshine and found I was back at the guest lodge and it was late afternoon. I asked where you had gone and the lady here did not know whilst Celestile had already left for Burdigala. So I decided to have a lie down and the next thing I knew you were all here with me!"

"You are very lucky!" Longinus exclaimed. "If it had not been druids it could easily have been some of Galahaidra's former companions. You are being pursued by assassins and have now added druids to the list of those hunting for you."

Maria tried to look downcast at her telling off, but she could not; she was just too happy to see them all again and nothing would distract her from that. Instead, she said: "I am not sure I want to stay in Bibinari beyond tonight. Can we leave early tomorrow and head for Torino then on to Bibracte? If we leave at dawn then we can reach Torino by noon."

The girl was asleep once more and the three men were sipping the local wine, drunk ice cold, whilst watching the townsfolk making their way home through the Forum. They were just considering turning in for the night when one of Iosephus' men came over and spoke to the knight: "We have unwelcome guests" the man whispered from the shadows behind them then walked on ensuring he was not seen talking to them.

Galahaidra looked around the Forum with its tables set out for people to drink at in the warmth of the midsummer evening. He did not recognise anyone but then he knew his former comrades would already be aware by now that he was guarding the girl and thus would have kept anyone he had known out of his sight. So, instead of looking for familiar faces, he looked for the signs of someone watching them. He dropped his napkin clumsily and bent down slowly to pick it up then sat back quickly and 'Yes' he just caught one man hurriedly turning his head away.

"I have one" he muttered under his breath to Longinus whilst the Centurion had marked two more based on where they had seated themselves. "Table to your far right" he whispered and Galahaidra pushed his chair back so that he could glimpse that table in the reflection of the brass water pitcher on the next table then he nodded slowly confirming that Longinus was right. There was nothing to give the men away … save that they were located such that they could see both entrances to the guest house and Maria's balcony window. *'Too much of a coincidence'* thought the former assassin.

"How would you have done this?" Longinus asked interested in how the sicariot would approach Maria's assassination. Galahaidra closed his eyes for a moment then slowly went through the options:

"We prefer a dagger's thrust at close quarters in a crowd and then to move on. Sometimes, we will take a victim in their sleep, hand over their mouth, throat slit in which case we go in and out through the window. Tonight, I would climb the wisteria on the outside walls of the guest house, enter via the balcony window, slit throat and disappear. Tomorrow would be to use the hustle and bustle of the Forum, attract Maria to look at some ware or another or come to someone's aid get her on her own briefly then quick stab of the knife to the heart or the back.

The attack at Avallonae was not our usual tactics and we only launched that attack because we were over-confident: we were not expecting the valiance of Perseus' defence. My former comrades will not make the same mistake again."

"Which?" asked Longinus "Or must we defend against both?"

"Both but separating the girl from us is the easiest method as she keeps wandering off anyway. Those who hunt us will have seen her go out alone this afternoon and will be waiting for the next time she does the same. Forgive me but does she not understand how much at risk she is? These three are the 'advance guard'; there will be at least another eight or nine including the archer, who may try a shot at us as we ride by, possibly forcing us to stop for something so that he gets a clear shot. They will have enough assassins to mount all three assaults. I expect an attack tonight and another on the road from Bibinari to Torino then a third when we reach Torino or Bibracte."

"So glad I asked" and the Centurion grinned to take the sting out of his words.

As soon as it was dark, Longinus and Galahaidra made their plans. Iosephus was told what his role was to be and at first was hard to persuade but eventually the equites saw the sense in what was being asked of him. Longinus ensured the window shutters to Maria's chamber were wide open to allow some air into the room as it was a still night. He lit the lantern by her bed but shut most of its shutters so that it gave only a dim light, enough for the girl to find her way around the room should she wake, but not enough to disturb her deep sleep.

Then Galahaidra and he waited. Fortune favoured them as the sky was clouded and the moonlight shone only briefly but otherwise the moon and stars were hidden. It was around the third hour when they heard the crunch as the first wave of assassins trod on the broken terracotta tile they had left by the window balcony.

Longinus flung back the shutters on the lantern, blinding the four men that had climbed through the window and Galahaidra took one out with a slash across his throat. One man stumbled, still blinded by the lantern, but the other two launched themselves at Maria's bed, slicing through the silk sheets to the girl beneath … only to see feathers go flying everywhere. Galahaidra took out the second assassin with a blow to his heart. Then the last two sicariot tried to back away from the young man only to have burning oil from the lantern flung over their heads by Longinus. They screamed as their hair and clothing caught fire. Two thrusts from Longinus with his short sword and it was all over.

"Stay clear of the window" Longinus hissed as Galahaidra went to check whether anyone else was shinning up the wisteria on the front of the house. The former sicariot stepped back just in time as an arrow flew through the window to bed itself in the wall opposite. Longinus carefully pushed the shutters closed with the tip of his sword, keeping clear of the windows then turned to Galahaidra:

"Go check on Iosephus. I will keep vigil here but I think we will not see another attack tonight."

Iosephus was standing guard over Maria, whom Longinus had carried whilst asleep and put in the old man's bed then substituted two bolsters to look as if the girl slept in her own bed. The equites had a short sword and opened the door to Galahaidra with shaking hand. The young man grinned: "Do not worry. They have gone for the night but, just in case, Longinus has sent me to guard you both."

"The girl could sleep through the end of the world" the old man muttered "whereas I cannot sleep a wink."

"Try and get some sleep" Galahaidra suggested "as we will be leaving at first light in two hours' time."

Maria was furious that she had slept through the excitement but Longinus disabused her of any idea that she would have enjoyed the attack: "Had you been there they would have killed you and as it is, we killed four of them."

"Oh" she exclaimed. "I thought you had just scared them away. Must we keep killing them? I am sure my Master would have found another way!"

Longinus just looked at the ceiling in exasperation whilst Iosephus suggested she eat her breakfast and pack then be ready downstairs in five minutes. Once the girl was upstairs the three men discussed where the next attack would come from.

"Ambush will be next" Galahaidra reminded them. "If we see anything intended to stop us, we ride straight through. Longinus, grab Maria's reins if that happens as it will be something designed to make her stop."

It was in the half light just before dawn that they left Bibinari and headed towards Torino. Maria had embraced the lady who owned the guest house and whom had became another who had rapidly adopted the young girl; Maria promised to return not least as the town would be both safer and begin to prosper following the arrest of the druid and the collapse of the druid's circle. A number of leading merchants were arrested as Gallicus uncovered records of the sacrificial victims at druidical meetings and evidence of illegal trafficking in slaves as well as money laundering and the running of brothels. He was later rewarded by a promotion and a larger staff to assist him in his investigation as he went about cleaning up the town.

The company rode fast, covering twenty leagues in each hour, exchanging horses every three hours and approaching the outskirts of Torino just after the tenth hour in the morning. Maria was a much more confident and proficient rider now and only fell off once. She had also learnt to fall much better with less risk of injury and got straight back on without a murmur of a complaint when she did fall, although Longinus spotted some nasty cuts and bruising when the girl went to wash the dust of the road off her in a river at their mid-morning stop.

There was a huge queue to get through the City barbican at Torino and the guards posted at the East Gate were struggling to cope. Worried that they might be left out in the open for a good hour if they joined the queue, the party rode over the Pontus Laurus towards the lesser-used North Eastern Gate. As they did so, they heard a cry of fear from within one of the small round timber-framed and mud-walled huts by the roadside. Instinctively, Maria reined in and turned towards the sound of the cry.

"No" screamed Galahaidra turning to place himself between the hut and the girl whilst Longinus, recognising the danger, grabbed the girl's reins and yanked her horse's head around to follow him. Alas, Maria had not been ready for this and toppled sideways to land with a crunch in a thorn bush, which cut her badly but prevented any broken bones. The next moment an arrow took her in the right upper arm and she fainted in pain and shock.

Galahaidra had dropped from his horse and was standing over her faster than Longinus could blink, holding his mount one-handed and placing it between the girl, himself and the archer. The next moment, he had lifted Maria onto his shoulder then shown amazing athleticism as he vaulted back into the saddle before holding the girl across his pommel. "Ride!" he shouted and the three men took off, leaving Maria's horse behind in their haste. Another arrow flew over Galahaidra's shoulder as he stooped in his saddle to protect the unconscious Maria.

"Is she badly hurt?" shouted Longinus and Galahaidra shook his head before shouting in his turn: "It looks a clean wound. We will need to stop soon so that I can remove the arrow and bandage up the wound but unless the arrow has been poisoned, there is no risk of long-lasting harm."

"What now?" asked Iosephus. "We dare not go back and we are currently riding north and away from Torino. We have missed one of our staging posts and must ride these horses for twice as long. We cannot keep up this speed for long especially when Galahaidra's horse is carrying two riders. And we must stop soon or Maria will be at risk of bleeding to death."

Longinus stood tall in his horse and looked north, east and west then pointed to their east. "There is a rock formation over there that will provide us with natural defences against any attack and where we can rest our horses and give aid to Maria. The road we are to take branches off this road soon and heads north-west to Bibracte whereas the road we are currently on is the Roman road from Torino to Lusitania. Our pursuers will not expect us to go due east as that takes us back almost the way we have come."

Galahaidra could see the sense in this not least as it would also give them the chance to watch out for their pursuit. "We must hide our tracks carefully" he suggested.

Galahaidra with Maria before him still and Iosephus rode for the rock formation, known as the 'Rock of Daniel'. On reaching it, Iosephus slowly lifted down the girl from Galahaidra's horse and then Galahaidra took out his knife and carefully cut the shaft of the arrow as close to her skin as he could without the shaft vibrating. Even so, the girl let out a moan and beads of sweat appeared on her brow. Then with the barbed tip removed, he pulled the shaft of the arrow clean through her arm whilst the old man clasped some gauze to the wound to try and stop the bleeding.

"It missed the artery thank goodness" Galahaidra whispered then helped Iosephus bind the wound tightly. Once done, Galahaidra left Maria with Iosephus and went up to watch the approaches from the top of the Rock.

Meanwhile, Longinus had found a gorse bush and pulled it clean out of the arid ground and then used it to sweep over their tracks. He walked backwards as he did so and would have been spotted by their pursuit had not Galahaidra whistled. Then as the Centurion looked up, the young man had pointed to the south. The Centurion rapidly looked for cover and saw a rain ditch. He pulled on the reins of his horse until it was lying down in the ditch and then he lay flat besides it.

Their pursuers were coming fast and rode past Longinus; they also missed the company's tracks. Galahaidra watched as they got to the junction of the roads to Bibracte and Lusitania and smiled as the party split, four going north-east and three going north-west. He waited until they were out of sight and hearing then whistled once more and Longinus stood up, guiding his horse towards the Rock.

"Maria will need a couple of hours of rest" Galahaidra advised his companion "and we have only three sicariot chasing us now, except they are ahead of us so we can expect another ambush. The good news is the archer went towards Lusitania."

Just after noon, Maria woke and immediately berated herself. "You warned me and still my instincts took over. I deserve the pain of my wound. I won't lose my arm, will I?"

Galahaidra laughed then reassured her: “It is the smallest scratch. But it will hurt and that will remind you to do as you are told in future.”

“You are as bad as Longinus” she retorted and then she grinned before saying: “I am lucky to have so many men to protect me!”

They mounted up with Maria before Galahaidra as before. She weighed hardly anything and he was fit, lithe, light-framed and athletic. Longinus on the other hand was tall and heavily-built whilst Iosephus carried the weight of many years’ good-living and the girth to go with it. Placing Maria in front of Galahaidra made sense as all three horses were carrying about the same weight. As an added precaution, one of Iosephus or Longinus took it in turns to ride one hundred paces ahead of the other two horses, to scout ahead for any ambush or sign of the sicariot.

They made good time on rested horses and were soon within an hour of Canomacus when Longinus called a halt. “We have to assume that there is an ambush between here and our staging post at Bibracte. Three men will not attempt another night attack at our stopover point but they may try and draw Maria away from the rest of us again or at the very least separate Galahaidra and Maria.”

Iosephus paused in thought as he recalled his earlier visit to the City then he smiled:

“We will be expected to come in to the City via the South Gate. But the guest house I have booked us into is actually on the west side of the Sequera so we could enter Bibracte from the settlements at Auvinus and Rosillius and come in through the West Gate. It adds one hour to our journey but we will be at less risk and still arrive before night falls. Our foe cannot watch all of the gates or hunt us down in every Taverna and Inn.”

All could see the sense in the knight’s suggestion and so they headed north-west along old tracks once used by the local Gallic farmers but disused since the Romans had built their roads. One ancient track took them through valleys, dense forests of oak trees lining either side, having to cut through boughs that had fallen across their way, fearing ambush at any moment, the ghosts of fallen warriors from the time of Julius Caesar, or evil spirits haunting Longinus who jumped at every movement, on one occasion being spooked by a flesh-eating monster that turned out to be a squirrel.

Maria was dismissive of both ghosts and spirits, laughing as Longinus admitted to his fears then saying: "How can you fear ghosts and spirits? Either they do not exist or they are created by God and to be held in awe and wonder for that reason."

"Bet you would be afraid of a crocodile if you met one" he retorted and she smiled and said "No, I have never met one" then asked him in eager excitement to tell her what they looked like.

"They have an enormous mouth with long rows of sharp teeth that can bite a man in half and they have plates of armour all over them and a tail that can knock a head off a man and they can walk on land, run or swim in water and they are bright green and pretend to smile then eat you or pretend to sleep then attack you."

"Now you are teasing me" and she went off to talk to Galahaidra whilst Iosephus burst out laughing at the look of stunned shock on the Centurion's face.

"Sometimes truth can be less believable than fantasy" the older man said sagely.

They finally pushed through one last dense bush of brambles and suddenly before them was the valley of Rosillius, a series of rolling green hills and wooded copses, Cities and fortified towns, villages and hamlets, stretching west to east from Osis and Renum on the furthest north-westerly tip of Gallia to Bibracte, Rocca and Lusitania.

They had cut through the thickset undergrowth and trod carefully through the tortuous tracks, uneven ground and tree roots looking to trip the unwary for three hours which had taken a lot longer than they had originally envisaged. They were all shattered. Now it was beginning to get dark.

"The road from here is too dangerous for us to ride in anything other than daylight. We will have to camp out in the open and ride for Bibracte or Sugdavellum on the morrow" Longinus advised them all but Iosephus was deeply concerned at yet another stage missed: "Our horses will soon be blown even though we rest them over night. If we must miss Bibracte then we should also ride a lot slower tomorrow until we reach our staging post half way between Sugdavellum and Bibracte!"

"Another early start" muttered Galahaidra and Maria gave his arm a squeeze before saying: "Is this not fun though? We have no idea where we are going really. My only sadness is that those chasing us have successfully distracted us from our mission. I will not hide again when we get to Sugdavellum and you are not to kill anyone else by the way. Thou shalt not kill!"

Longinus decided they could risk a fire as the nights were getting cold the further north they travelled. They were leagues away from where the three sicariot would be looking for them; indeed they were in the middle of nowhere. *'Anything that found them would either be wild, barbaric or up to no good and probably all three'* the Roman mused. The fire would keep any wild animals at bay as well as offering warmth though he decided not to tell the girl that for fear he might give her nightmares.

Galahaidra had scouted the area and was able to direct Maria to a river and spring where she could wash. She took herself off, delighted at the opportunity to clean the dirt of the horses from her clothes and her legs, the dust from her face, eyes, hands and arms and generally to freshen up in the cold of the river. She took off her clothes and dived in enjoying swimming in the moonlight under the stars. The water was clean, crystal clear and ice-cold. As she finally got out, she had to hunt for a few moments in the dark for where she had left her clothing … and that is when she saw the wild boar.

It ran at her, its tusks down seeking to gore her and she turned tail and dived straight back into the water. Then she stood with the water up to her neck and glared back at it. It was not budging and knew it had her trapped: slowly but surely her teeth began to chatter and she started to shiver with the cold.

At a loss as to what to do, she began to sing. The wild boar snorted then crouched down. Unsure what to do next, she sang some more. The wild boar rolled onto its back then stood upright again and gave its head a shake. "Are you cross with me or do you like my singing?" she asked more to herself than the boar but it gave a high pitched squeal and for a moment she thought that it might be friendly. So she started to walk out of the water towards it holding her hands at her side. Its head went down, tusks aimed right at her and she dived straight back into the water, right up to her neck again.

She sang again and the boar quietened down once more but as soon as she tried to leave the water it got angry and would go for her. Then she tried singing whilst she was walking out of the water and for a moment the boar put its head on one side to listen, but just as her left foot cleared the water the wild boar went to bite it. Splash! She was right back where she had started.

Then the wild boar must have smelt her clothing for it suddenly went into a frenzy, tearing her simple linen stola and peplos to shreds in seconds. Now she had no clothing and would have to find a way of getting back to the camp without being spotted, always assuming she could get past the wild boar whom she was rapidly going off.

"I have never eaten meat, always respecting all of God's creatures and especially I have never eaten pork as this is forbidden by the laws of my faith … but I am willing to make one exception in your case, you horrid little beast" she muttered and then shivered again as the cold water of the river was slowly turning her skin blue.

She decided there was nothing for it and called out: "Help!"

To her utter astonishment, four striped piglets ran up to see what their father was doing having been attracted by her call. Now she understood why the boar was so cross. He was protecting his family. She forgave him immediately but this still did not resolve how she was going to get out of the river and find some clothing. In the dark, she tried to make out the far bank of the river but could not. Beginning to become frightened for the first time, genuinely believing she might die of exposure, she started to hum through gritted teeth. At which the piglets began to dance in time with her music. 'No' she said to herself scarcely believing her eyes then she laughed; a sound so out of keeping with this place yet so joyful and catching that the piglets and the boar all squealed in unison.

"I will sing to you if you let me out of the water" she promised and started to climb out of the river. The boar charged her and splashed into the river a few feet but she was able to back pedal quickly enough to stay out of his range. Now she was desperate to get warm and then she realised her own stupidity.

"Master" she said. "You made heaven and earth and all of the creatures on land, in the sky and the seas. I have no wish to harm these pigs or be harmed by them. I will happily sing to these pigs if you will grant that they let me go free."

This time as she sang, she felt the comforting warmth of her Master rise within her and watched as the piglets and the boar bowed their heads then parted to let her through. Then they followed her, which was not what she expected and she grew concerned: "Little ones you must run away. Those with whom I travel may seek to slay you and eat you" but the family of wild pigs ignored her, except to grunt occasionally whenever she stopped singing.

She got to the edge of the camp and could see the three men sitting around the fire whilst tethered to her left were their three horses. She headed towards the horses to check out the saddle bags for a change of clothing, followed by the family of wild boar who were quite tame and content now, then as she reached the horses she realised that her saddle bag was still on her horse back where they had left it at the ambush outside of Torino. She had no clothes and no blanket and had been adopted by a family of wild pigs. This night was going to take some explaining!

She stood behind the three horses and then cried out in a small voice: "Help!"

All three men's heads went up in unison and Galahaidra stood. They were blinded however by the light of their fire and none of them had yet to gain their night sight. So, whilst Longinus and Iosephus asked: "Who is it?" Galahaidra began to step away from the fire and then circle towards where the voice had come from.

"It is me" said Maria "and please do not come any closer."

She could see the relief on the men's faces and then when the oddity of her request sank in, Longinus asked reasonably: "How can we help you if we cannot come any closer?"

"It is a very long story" and the girl sniffed "but essentially I have lost my clothes. All of them!"

The men laughed which Maria thought was decidedly cruel and thoughtless of them as she was shivering, in all likelihood dying of cold, and all they could do was laugh at her discomfort.

"I also have adopted a family of wild boar and you are not to kill them or eat them" she added through gritted and chattering teeth before continuing: "and I am very cold and need a blanket or I will turn into ice!"

"Come and warm yourself by the fire then" said Galahaidra with a grin but she shook her head then realising they could not see her head shaking, she said with some asperity: "I have no intention of anyone seeing me naked!"

"Have to sleep with the horses then" and all three men turned away from her and ignored her. She considered crying, she did feel pretty miserable. But she remembered her Master had rescued her and tamed the wild boar so she should be rejoicing; just she had failed to ask him about clothing. Finally, her good humour returned. She quietly un-tethered one of the horses then started to lead it back into the woods to find somewhere to sleep. She intended to use its warmth and share its blanket during the night then ride off before first light in the morning and the others had woken. Except Galahaidra heard the three horses whinny and saw the shadow of one of them being led away. "No you don't" he muttered then nudged Longinus and whispered: "She is taking one of the horses."

Swearing under his breath, the Centurion stood up then set off after the girl. She was leading a horse, trying also to keep the family of wild boar close as she did not want to lose one to the men; she was barefoot; in unfamiliar woods; still cold and now very tired. He caught her up in moments and grabbed the reins off her at which she shrank away ashamed of her nakedness and then began to cry.

"Here" he said and opened the saddle bag of the horse she had been leading to pull out one of Galahaidra's robes and a belt. "Put it over your head and tuck the waist in to the belt or you will trip over the hem. I cannot see you in the dark so you have nothing to be embarrassed about. Once you are dressed, come back to the fire to get warm – we have spare blankets."

"And the wild boar?" she asked.

"Best let them go. You cannot bring them with us in the morning. They live here and will be happiest if you leave them. Say goodbye to them now then join me at the campfire."

A few minutes later, one tearful, wet, cold, bedraggled and almost blue, embarrassed young girl in a robe several sizes too large for her with a belt she had knotted twice around her waist finally returned to the campfire she had left nearly two hours earlier.

"I suppose I have missed supper" she asked in a small voice and all three men nodded before passing her a bowl of broth and a lump of bread at which her eyes lit up. "Next time" she said. "Can one of you come with me to guard my clothing?"

They joined the road to Sugdavellum approximately six leagues north of Bibracte and hopeful that any pursuit was still waiting to ambush them to their south. From Bibracte there could be any number of coastal ports that might be their destination including Osis, Malum, Aquasequerum, Cerborum, Portius Itius and Quintinus. Sugdavellum was not an obvious choice as it was in-land, the sea accessed by a ten league stretch of river and a cutting: a man-made canal. Yet that was why Iosephus had chosen it not only in order to throw off any pursuit but also because it was the largest City at that time in northern or furthest Gaul.

Except any and all plans to throw their pursuers off their scent had not taken Maria into account. First, she refused to travel any further in Galahaidra's dirty robe insisting that they find somewhere where she could buy some clothes for her. This would see them stop at every village, town and crossroads to ask for a dressmaker, costumier or seamstress leaving a trail of breadcrumbs that even the blindest of blackbirds could follow. She eventually found a dressmaker outside Maconum and spent an hour and a half trying on clothes whilst all three men stood outside wringing their hands in dismay.

Second, on arriving at Sugdavellum whilst Longinus was presenting their documentation to the Praetor and confirming they were on the manifest for the four ships hired by Iosephus that were due to leave the following day then adding Galahaidra to all of the relevant documents, Maria went to the Temple where the High Priest was gracious and happy to give his consent to her celebrating the Service of the Eucharist. He had heard of her from those who had seen her in Luguidenum and Tartellum and immediately had Notices sent around the City to welcome people to the Eucharist.

"You have done what?" Longinus stormed when the girl told him.

"We must not hide our ministry or let those who seek to prevent it from doing so through our own fear." Maria replied grandly then spoiled the effect by sticking her tongue out at him and then getting a fit of the giggles when he went red in the face with anger.

"Do you think that anyone north of Thesus does not know where Maria is going to be tonight?" Galahaidra asked and Iosephus shook his head glumly before adding: "I think she must do it deliberately. I mean no-one could be *that* stupid, could they?" Galahaidra laughed but then offered a crumb of comfort: "I saw the three men on the road from Torino and would recognise them if I saw them again. Now we cannot hide from them let us set an ambush for them instead!"

So whilst Maria went to the markets and to the fishing quays, looking for volunteers to help her with the breaking of the bread that evening, Galahaidra and Longinus hid amongst the crowds looking for anyone following the girl, whilst Iosephus sat at tables never more than fifty paces from the girl reading the scriptures, sipping wine and people watching.

As he watched, Iosephus saw the girl walk into the crowd, closely followed by a young man, whose robe was hooded, hiding his face and whose right hand was sitting within the folds of his left sleeve. The man was wearing too much clothing for the heat of the market. As the equites watched, he started to push through the crowds and was less than ten paces from Maria, getting closer as Iosephus stood in dismay.

The equites' sudden movement attracted both Longinus' and Galahaidra's attention. They both reacted in different ways. Longinus ran towards Maria barging people to left and right then seeing the flash of a blade at which he screamed "Maria" and she half-turned to look into the eyes of her would-be assassin. He hesitated briefly as she looked fearlessly at him, perhaps struck by her blue eyes or just her obvious youth, and his hesitation was just long enough for Longinus to run smack into him, knocking the man over and sending his knife flying through the air to land a few feet away. The Centurion drew his own dagger from its ankle pouch, knelt on the man's chest and holding the man's head on the ground with his left arm he went to slice his throat.

"No" commanded Maria. "Release him!"

Longinus looked up at her in confusion. Then seeing she was serious, he stood slowly and let the man go. The sicariot stumbled to his feet then ran into the crowd and was gone.

As Longinus had looked to rescue Maria, Galahaidra had put himself in line with Maria then span round quickly with his back to the direction she had been walking in. As he looked into the crowd behind Maria, two heads dropped down involuntarily.

The young man dropped to his knees obscured by the crowds briefly then circled quickly keeping out of sight until he was able to get alongside the first of the men trailing Maria to say: "I saw you the other day just north of Torino."

Galahaidra never gave the man a chance to answer as his silver sicarius sunk into the other man's heart and came away swiftly, too fast to leave any sign of blood but fast enough to dispatch the man instantly. He held the man up, waited for the right moment then dropped him under the hooves of a horse trotting by and moved on whilst all attention was diverted by a horse rearing and unhorsing its rider; another man lay insensible at the horse's feet. The first woman screamed a few moments later but Galahaidra was already lost in the crowd.

He looked around but at first there was no sign of the other two assassins. Both had been uncovered and one was without a knife. To some degree the ambush had worked. But the assassins would regroup and next time they would work in darkness. Then, the young man recognised a face and slowly approached a bar at the north end of the Forum outside of which one of the would-be assassins was now sitting at a table with a half finished goblet of wine in front of him. Galahaidra turned away, not needing to get any closer to know that the man was dead from the dull, staring and unblinking eyes. Amarillus' men must have been watching over all of them and the assassin had run straight into them.

Maria went over to where Iosephus was sitting recovering from the shock of the attempted assassination of his charge, and she kissed him to thank him for saving her life. "Did we get them?" he asked and she shook her head silencing him completely as she mentioned that she had told Longinus to let one of the assassins go. "You are not making this easy" he grumbled and she gave him a hug not in the least bit contrite.

The Synagogue at Sugdavellum could take a thousand at a pinch, the City had a population of thirty thousand but on that evening word had got out that the Magdalan had come on her mission to the City and people travelled from across Celtica some as far as fifty leagues in every direction to come and listen to her words. Many had heard her speak before and when they arrived volunteered to administer the Eucharist or to act as ushers. Most would hear her for the first time and like those before would be thrown by her youth, naturalness and humility. No great religious lawyer or philosopher but a girl who spoke from her heart about what she had seen.

She started by explaining the origins of the breaking of the bread and its importance as for most this would be their first experience of the Eucharistic service. Because the majority present could not fit into the Synagogue, she waited for people to convey or translate her message to the tens of thousands standing in the square outside.

Then she spoke to the scriptures. Choosing a passage from Genesis, she talked of the flood, a story that would resonate with the people of a City that had been flooded several times by the Mare Britannia and the Sequera, each an event that had left a shadow of sorry memory.

"How sad" she said "that we should so anger God that he struck so many of us down with his flood. Yet God promised he would never again slay us indiscriminately if we should anger him. If God needed to send us a sign that we must change then next time he would find a way other than a flood. God has kept that promise. When a new covenant was needed, rather than destroy us, he sent his only Son to live with us, teach us, heal us and then to die for us."

When it came to the breaking of the bread, she moved amongst the huge gathering, perhaps as many as one hundred thousand, and embraced many, concentrating especially on the infirm, disabled and the children. Many who were lame, blind, deaf or infirm through disease were healed that evening as they received the bread and with it were filled with the Spirit. Longinus and Iosephus walked at Maria's shoulders as her acolytes whilst Galahaidra watched the crowds for one face he would recognise. *'He is not here'* he finally realised *'which either means he will make the attempt tomorrow or he is calling in additional help and will try and assassinate Maria when she is in Britannia'.*

They would be sailing from Sugdavellum to the Mare Britannia and then crossing to the Aer Weiht which they would navigate going east to arrive in the ancient Celtic kingdom of the Atrebates (Wyncaister, South Hamm, Sales and Dunroaving). The journey would take two and a half hours up the canal from the Sequera and the Sedus to the Mare Britannia and then twelve hours to cross the sea. Iosephus was taking no chances and had hired four ships booking them on the manifest of all four.

Whilst the old knight would be sailing on a ferry boat which would take as many as thirty passengers as a decoy, Longinus, Galahaidra and Maria would be the only passengers on a merchant's ship. "The one risk is from the crew and the Captain will tell you which if any he hired in Sugdavellum in the last twenty four hours. Galahaidra can look them over and if any are the assassin then we leave him behind." Iosephus explained.

The quayside at Sugdavellum ran along the Rivers Sequera and Canum and the cutting that ran parallel with the rivers to the sea. The canal cutting had been dug by the Romans as the estuary at the mouth of the Canum had begun to silt up. Vessels of all types and sizes from quadrimes, triremes and barges to skiffs and tubs lined the banks on both sides of the canal, including fishing trawlers and merchant ships.

The port was not military and its administration came under the City Prefect, boasting two magistrates, one dealing with civil matters and the second criminal in the Praefecture and the Curiale Court respectively. The Prefect's Palace was sited at the confluence of the river and canal, adjoining the Courts, the Curia and the chamber of commerce for the City.

Set at the highest point of Sugdavellum, steps descended from the complex of the Praefect's Palace, Courts and the four Temples to Jove Almighty, Juno the Mother of Rome, Romulus and Remus and Mars to the new Forum, a square paved terrazzo with a covered market at the far end and a colonnade of statues of local dignitaries and the Julians: Julius Caesar, the God Augustus and the Emperor Tiberius. The older Forum was now a cattle market and auction house. A fish market was located along the west bank of the river Sequera, a series of covered stalls with brightly coloured awnings and tentings, and hundreds of baskets of fresh fish on display.

The Crossing of the Mare Britannia

Pilate's account of the Magdalan's mission continues:

"Joseph of Arathamea brought Mary Magdalan to Briton to the Hall of Godric Bann Caedric, Prince of the Atrebates, Lord of Salesbrey and Hammshire, crossing the Britannic Sea. A storm saw their ship separated from the others in their fleet and sink, with all hands rescued by God's miracle." (Pilate, 4th Century AD)

The four ships hired by Iosephus were all triremes, flat-bottomed barges with a main sail and fore sail. The ship that was to carry Maria, Longinus and Galahaidra was called 'The Valiant' and had been equipped with a fo'castle, a crenulated raised platform with a trebuchet mounted to fire to port and starboard. There was a front cabin beneath, which was allotted to Maria, and the standard rear cabin made from a piece of sail canvas stretched across the bow of the ship. Iosephus had hired thirty mercenary soldiers to guard Maria. Thirty minutes after Maria had stepped onto the deck of 'The Valiant', all of the mercenaries had thrown their weapons overboard. Iosephus cried in despair but the girl would not budge. "There has already been too much killing" she said stubborn once more.

"Throw her overboard next time!" Longinus muttered and the old man grinned.

The ships embarked at the seventh hour, the delay was whilst Iosephus took on the provisions and merchandise which he intended to trade at the coastal town of South Hamm at the mouth of The Solent's estuary. The journey up the Sequara was quiet, uninterrupted by anything more alarming than disturbing a family of heron; their progress was slow as they rowed at a steady three to four leagues each hour. The view either side of the river was of quays, docks and piers with small vessels and private yachts moored up besides the villas of the wealthiest knights in Sugdavellum.

After two hours, they had their first view of the mouth of the Sequera, where its smooth waters met the contained fury of the channel, cliffs holding back the sea from eroding the land beyond, sandy beaches beneath the cliffs, glistening gold when the tide was low, covered over when the sea was launching itself at the tall white chalk cliffs.

Iosephus' ship, 'The Rose', pulled alongside 'The Valiant' and the knight signalled that he would come aboard. A derrick with a wooden stage, planks held together by iron cross pieces then roped at the corners to the crane above, was used to swing the old man across from the deck of one ship to the other. As soon as the equites' feet hit the deck, he rushed over to Longinus and broke his news.

"There are high winds and fog predicted. These seas may become dangerous. What would you do?"

The skipper of 'The Valiant' interrupted: "These seas are always unpredictable. The fog could just as easily blow over or we could hit a freak wave in calm waters and capsize. We can sit in Sugdavellum for the next year or take the risk. This is summer and our best chance to find calm waters is this time of year."

"Absolutely no point in asking Maria as she will just say we are in God's hands" muttered Longinus and the other two men laughed resignedly. Iosephus reflected for a few moments before advising them all: "We should let the crew of each ship decide and be guided by the four skippers. If they are content to proceed then we should be the same."

Twenty minutes later the four barges hit the rough waters of the Channel, the prows on each rising six to twelve feet as they hit the crest of the incoming waves and then began to cut through the sea, settling as the wind caught in their sails to drive them forward. Maria had been asleep on a bunk bed in the Captain's cabin, and was thrown into the air then covered with water as the sea entered through every hole and gap between the planking and the small arched oriel windows that faced forward. She picked herself up off the floor and reached for a bucket to start bailing out but the sea-water was already finding its way back to the sea. Shaking her head to free the water in her ears and hair, she looked for a change of clothing and saw in dismay that all of her luggage was now drenched. She laughed and decided the best course of action was to go up on deck and let the sun and wind dry her.

It was still morning, between the tenth and eleventh hour, and the sun was not yet fully arisen, but it was warm and the wind was refreshing. She saw Galahaidra and called across to him in joy: "We are at sea. I love the sea." Alas her young hero was looking very green and had already decided that in the future he would stay firmly on terra firma.

Longinus pointed into the far distance where they could just make out the thin white line of the white horses breaking on the cliffs of the Aer Weiht: "Maria, you should get a much better view from the crows' nest. Feel free to take a look whilst the waters are calm."

"Calm?!" growled Galahaidra and retched over the side once more.

First, Maria dropped down to the banks of diakonae and sang for them. As she did so, they relaxed into a steady rhythm; with a following wind, their role was to keep the prow lined up with the direction of the waves. The Mare Britannia was dangerous because the waves could come at you from any direction, with cross winds and under-currents making sailing without a keel, a constant challenge. The helmsman was kept busy and had the aid of two other crew men as they fought with the rudder against the grip of the oncoming waves.

"'Ware!" shouted the lookout on the fo'castle and a wave broke over the ship, filling the banks for the oarsmen then draining away in seconds. Maria was completely drenched once more and understood why the crew went bare-chested as there was little point in wearing clothing save to cover one's modesty.

Perhaps it was the constant danger or Longinus would later suggest teasingly, perhaps it was that with the oarsmen chained to their banks, Maria had a captive audience, but something prompted her to tell the crew of the life of her Master and his gift of life after death. The diakonae were slaves and life expectancy ran in months for oarsmen on the galleys and barges of the Roman world. The prospect of life in Paradise was attractive and they were eager to hear more. "We seek to be free" they said simply: "Will we still be slaves?"

"My Master came to save us from oppression, to free captives and slaves. In the Kingdom of my Master all are equal before God. We shall stand side by side with Angels, Emperors and Kings. All of us embraced in God's compassionate hands."

"I have heard of the Messiah. Is your Master the Messiah as foretold?" one of the diakona asked and Maria replied without hesitating: "He is."

"Will he lead his army to defeat Rome?"

"I have been asked this question often and once asked my Master. He is a man of Peace and also a compassionate God. His kingdom waits for us when we die. He does not seek a kingdom on Earth until God shall come in judgement on the Last Day. Do not look for armies or revolution. Peace and love is his message."

"Why must we suffer here on Earth?" another of the oarsmen asked.

"Our reward shall be the same as if we were wealthy" and many of the oarsmen dropped their heads in disappointment "… but it will be easier for us who are poor to earn the reward of Eternal Life. The wealthy must give away their riches as well as believe and follow the commandments. The rich must become poor, meek and humble in the sight of God. For those already poor, it is enough that we believe and have hope and that we never envy the riches of others. For wealth is transitory and has no value in my Master's kingdom."

At her words, their eyes shone once more. As she looked, tears sprang into her eyes at the hope that she could see around her. So she led them in the breaking of the bread and they felt renewed strength and stamina returning, to brave the seas with new-found courage and the knowledge that though they shall die, the Master had conquered death and opened the way for them to Eternal Life.

From her vantage point in the crows' nest with the company of a young urchin, Felstum, from the shipyards at Malo, Maria could see both the Aer Weiht with its long line of cliffs leading to The Needles which sat proudly to their west, and then beyond the young ships-mate pointed out to her the coast of the Kingdom of Roavia, Dunrovia, the land of the Atrebates and the estuary of The Solent, with long wide beaches of the softest sand topped by the finest stone beneath turfs of the purest, green wild grasses. From a distance and in this rare moment of sunshine, Britannia looked idyllic. But Felstum warned the girl:

"Do not trust all that you see. Britannia is many kingdoms ruled by warrior Kings, all savage barbarians, and the land is more commonly cold and wet with constant rain. They will happily trade with their fellow Celts and Britons but despise Romans and Rome and recently sent aid to the revolt that was crushed by Germanicus. Rome remembers and will invade Britannia once more in revenge. But the great Julius Caesar himself may have won battles here yet was still defeated by this miserable country: more by the weather I believe than any skills in warfare."

Then Felstum pointed to the sky to their east and muttered: "That does not look good" as the couple could see dark clouds gathering and the occasional flash of lightning heading in their direction. Within minutes the first of the rolling waves driven by the winds of the storm struck 'The Valiant' and sent the prow twenty feet into the air. Maria and Felstum clung on desperately then the young lad signalled that Maria should descend using the rigging. His shout was carried away in the winds.

Maria started to descend, watching as 'The Rose' and the other two ships turned to the west to run before the storm. But the skipper of 'The Valiant' would not be defeated by "a derisory squall" and headed south-east, putting his prow at an angle to the waves and using his fore sail to give him momentum as he sailed into the wind. The beat of the drums marking time for the oarsmen was doubled in its frequency. "Row!" roared the helmsman as the current tore at his rudder looking to send it flat against the bow.

Maria was still twenty feet above the deck when the two waves struck. The first crested at thirty feet and struck the prow, sending the ship bucking up and then forwards into thin air. As it descended, the second wave came from the starboard side, again at least thirty feet tall, and struck the exposed hull of the ship broadside on, turning it over. Maria was flung clear and landed in the sea just missing being caught by the main mast and rigging as these snapped and floated as jetsom in the waves. She looked towards 'The Valiant' and all she could see was its upturned hull and the banks of oars, many broken or entangled. But she could see none of her companions or the crew.

Rising and falling with the height of the waves, the girl dived beneath the tempestuous sea and swam under the hull to come first to the helmsman at the bow. He was dead, struck by the mast as it had toppled over; a deep cut in his skull. He was still holding the rudder, dedicated to his final task, seeking beyond hope and life to save his ship. On his belt were the keys to the banks of oars and she grabbed these then swam to where the oarsmen were trapped in their rimes, partly submerged as water gradually filled the upturned hull. She quickly unlocked the first few banks of diakonae and then breathed the last of her air into one of the oarsmen, handed him the keys, indicated he should continue to unlock the chains and headed back to the surface.

She took a hurried breath and dived back under the water a second time to search for Longinus and Galahaidra, watching as she did so as the freed ranks of oarsmen began to swim for the surface. She found Longinus first, caught by the ankle in the rigging of the fore sail and she pulled out his ankle knife then cut him free. He swam immediately to the surface, short of air, his head spinning but still alive and able to follow the path of the strike of a lightning fork to the surface.

Galahaidra was drifting in the currents and she saw him by chance as she had looked for him in increasing desperation in the dim light of the sea. He was no longer breathing but he had been in the water for five minutes at most. She knew from the many stories she had been told by the crews of the ships with which she had sailed that she could still bring him back to life as long as he had been in the water for only a few minutes and swam to him then gripped his mouth with hers and began to breathe the promise of life back into him. Then she held his head under the chin and swam with her legs to the surface.

As she finally broke through the waves and swam beneath the dark sky of the storm, she saw that Longinus was twenty paces away and called for him desperately. He swam over to her at which she handed him the unconscious Galahaidra and said to the Centurion:

"Breathe air into his lungs then let him cough up the water. I have more to do" and before he could argue, she dived back beneath the waves.

Now she was looking for any more crew members. She saw with sadness the fifteen diakonae that had not been able to be released in time, still chained to their oars. Then she spotted the Captain, swam to him and felt for a pulse, opening his eyes to see if there was any flicker of life. When his eyes contracted, she was overjoyed and breathed air into his lungs then caught him around the chest and expelled water from his lungs. Fixing her mouth onto his once again, she returned to the surface. As they reached the dim light of a clouded black and troubled sky, the skipper spluttered, coughed and his eyes sprang open.

'One last task' thought the girl handing the Captain into the hands of two of the oarsmen, the rest were already grabbing the debris and detritus from the broken ship: if it floated then it would save their lives.

Maria headed for the fo'castle and the prow cabin. She was after one thing: the Spear that had been left in the Captain's locker. The hull was still floating and part of the cabin had trapped air within it. She took a quick breath to test the air and was relieved to discover it was not yet stale. Filling her lungs, she swam to where the locker now sat on the ceiling of her upside-down world. It was clasped shut but not locked and she was able to open it and take out the precious relic. Then she swam through the bay window of the cabin and reached the surface once more.

Several of the crew saw her and reached to haul her to the comparative safety of the upturned hull. To her delight, one of those who had pulled her to the relative safety of the hull was Felstum.

"You made it!" she stuttered, the cold of the water eating at her and then she gave him a hug. As she looked around, to her delight she could see that most of the crew had made it to the surface and prayed to her Master in gratitude.

"We are still in trouble, Domina" Felcum warned her as he pointed to the huge waves still running before the winds of a ferocious thunder storm. "We must avoid being capsized and stay clear of the strikes of lightning. But if we can live through the next ten minutes, this storm will clear the skies and in its wake will come the flattest of seas."

Maria pointed to the many oars still attached to the hull and asked: "Can they be used to stabilise us?" and Felstum nodded then crawled along the planking of the hull to talk to the Captain. In moments the crew were working on the oars to rope them to the sides and level them up into a single bank on either side of the hull, providing massive additional decking should anyone fall overboard and preventing their impromptu ship from rolling in the waves.

The Captain returned with Felstum, Longinus and a weak but very much alive, Galahaidra. As the skipper got within earshot of the girl he said simply: "We all owe you our lives. We shall survive to grant your heroism meaning but are grateful to you whatever shall be the outcome."

"Hold me" replied the girl "because I was never more frightened in my life than when I was alone in the sea and thought you all drowned."

Longinus took her into his arms immediately noticing how cold she was and wrapped her in his cloak of wool which got warmer as it got wetter.

Then the waves struck once more but this time the remains of the ship carried them as three crewmen used oars at the bow as a temporary rudder to steer the prow into the waves. The banks of oars to port and starboard prevented them from rolling and they fought clear of each wave. Alas four of the crew were dragged from their holds on the hull and taken by the waves.

Before anyone could stop her, Maria had grabbed a rope, thrust one end into Felstum's hands and dived into the sea. Three of the men were beyond her reach and that of the rope but one man, floundering and beginning to sink as the cold cut into his flesh and burrowed beneath his skin, was just within her grasp. As he went under, she dove and caught him by the hair then dragged him to the surface before being hauled in by Felstum. The man was still breathing and clung to her with all his strength and hope. They were lifted back onto the hull as another wave struck, sending Maria spinning and she would have been lost to the waves but for the rope that Felstum continued to hold tenaciously and defiantly.

Longinus was livid with the girl for taking such risks but could not berate her for secretly he was also proud of her exploits. The crew left him in no doubt how they felt, jeering as their temporary vessel successfully mounted each swell and then pointing and laughing as the lightning struck the waves expelling its energy harmlessly into the water. They sang Maria's praises and already the story they would regale when they reached port had started to take shape.

Maria had no time for that nonsense, however, and led them instead in prayer for their continued safety. As she said: "Gaudete …" the winds finally died back; the tempest tore past them and was gone; blue skies and calm grey green seas surrounded them; and the diakonae raised a huge cheer then prayed with all their might: "Rejoice and Give thanks for the Lord our God is our Saviour."

"Thank you Master" Maria whispered then leant into Longinus' arms, closed her eyes and let the fatigue finally take over.

There was hardly any wind but even had there been, there were no masts to capture it. So the diakonae untied a third of the oars on either side and made makeshift rawlins with rope from the rigging tied to the sides of the hull. Soon they were able to get up to speeds of three leagues each hour and started to head for shore, some seven or eight hours away at their current speed. Now Maria was praying for the safety of 'The Rose' and its two companion ships but also she hoped that they would come and rescue them.

In the end, they were rescued by two merchant ships coming out of the port at the mouth of the Pleides and sailing for Portius Itius. Seeing the capsized crew, one of the merchant ships stopped and took the men on board then tied the hull of 'The Valiant' to their bow and headed for the Solent with it in tow. 'The Valiant' would make a fine prize as salvage and be more than enough compensation for the merchant's loss of one trip's trade to Portius Itius.

The crew now found that they were free, their slavery ended with the change in ownership of 'The Valiant'. They were immediately re-engaged being offered their former jobs crewing 'The Valiant' once repaired but now as paid freemen. They could not believe their good fortune and all looked to Maria in gratitude then followed her lead in praying for their dead comrades. "For surely they are in Paradise" said the girl with a smile.

They reached the port of the South Hamm by the fifth hour after noon, the crew of the merchant ship lending the rescued company blankets and seating them on the deck to warm themselves in the sun that was beating down on them through a clear and cloudless sky. Longinus held the girl carefully for fear he disturb her fragile sleep; nothing could tear her from his grasp, such was the gratitude he felt for her rescue of him. Yet also he held her tight for fear that one day she would throw herself into a situation that even her prayers could not master.

Galahaidra stood over them both. He no longer felt sick and had found his sea legs. More than that, for the second time in the space of a few days this frail young girl at his feet, barely older than a child and still childlike in the awe and wonder with which she greeted the world had saved him miraculously and at risk of her own life. He was bonded to her in a way only those who have lived by an oath of self-sacrifice would understand. So convinced was he in the rightness of The Magdalan that he had assumed a new mission in life: to bring to their senses his fellow sicariot. For Maria was a cause worthy of their extravagant sacrifice.

She woke to a new world and whispered "Britannia" in awe as she looked at the chalk hills of the Downs rolling to her east and west, with settlements dotted across the slopes of these graceful hills and the long white line of The Ridgeway crowning each hill. She ran as soon as her feet touched the ground in order to mount the first of the hills but had under-estimated its height and over-estimated her own strength and stamina. She hardly got beyond the sand and grasses of the dunes she found at the cove where they were put ashore by the merchant ship than she folded over, her hands on her knees, gasping for breath. Longinus caught up with her on horseback.

He laughed at the sight of her then teased her: "It will be a lot quicker on horseback" and he nodded towards a second horse he was leading, already saddled up for her and with women's clothing he must have either bought or borrowed rolled neatly in the saddle bags.

"Beast" she laughed. "Where did you get the horses?"

"All arranged by Iosephus whose man was waiting for us on the beach where we landed. But you will insist on running off …" and she grinned apologetically but this one reverse was not going to stop the habit of her short lifetime. As a child she had jumped into every puddle, clambered through the darkness of every cave, climbed each rocking tree, scampered over the falling tiles of every unsafe rooftop, welcomed every wild dog or hungry lion, had been first to brave any adventure and last to give in to impossible odds or surrender her implausible dreams. She would be no different now she had grown up: except only Maria thought that she had 'grown up'. The rest of the world knew that she remained a child in thought and deed.

By horseback she was able to head towards the Downs and rode to their summit; once sitting proudly at the nearest high point she could look beneath her to the valley that shone gold in the sun with its lines of white horses and large figures of giants cut in the chalk of the hills. To her west were the stone circles of her dreams, huge grey menhirs standing proudly around altars to an old and forgotten religion, set to show the message in the stars and which granite Temples were now the home for druids and sun worshippers where once they had celebrated the creation of the Universe by a benign and sage Godhead.

Maria pointed to where a shaft of the sun shone on one of thirteen such circles, the largest of which sat in isolation on the flattest of plains, land that once had rested six feet beneath the ocean's bed near the warmth of the west African coast but now stood proudly surrounded by the Downs and the Mendips. The other twelve circles had settlements around them and individual stones that all singularly and collectively pointed to this thirteenth altar, the relic of an earlier time. They had been erected before the Mare Britannia had existed, when Gallia and Britannia had been one and so were connected with similar rings or circles of stone in farthest Gallia.

"Longinus, my brave love. We go there!"

"Not tonight" he replied: "For our accommodation has been booked by Iosephus with the Lord of this kingdom in South Hamm where I have left Galahaidra and Felstum. Iosephus' ship is safe and has made harbour in South Hamm just after we made land. They outran the storm but it was a terrifying moment for them. I have hired a young Briton as your chaperone by the way. You will be talked about and I would not have your reputation sullied because people take your natural affection to be more than it is."

"Thank you" the girl whispered and turned the head of her horse to follow the Centurion into the valley where the large settlement of South Hamm sprawled across the estuary of The Solent.

The Mission to Britannia: the kingdom of the Atrebates, the South Hamm and The Summoning Circle in the land of the Durotriges

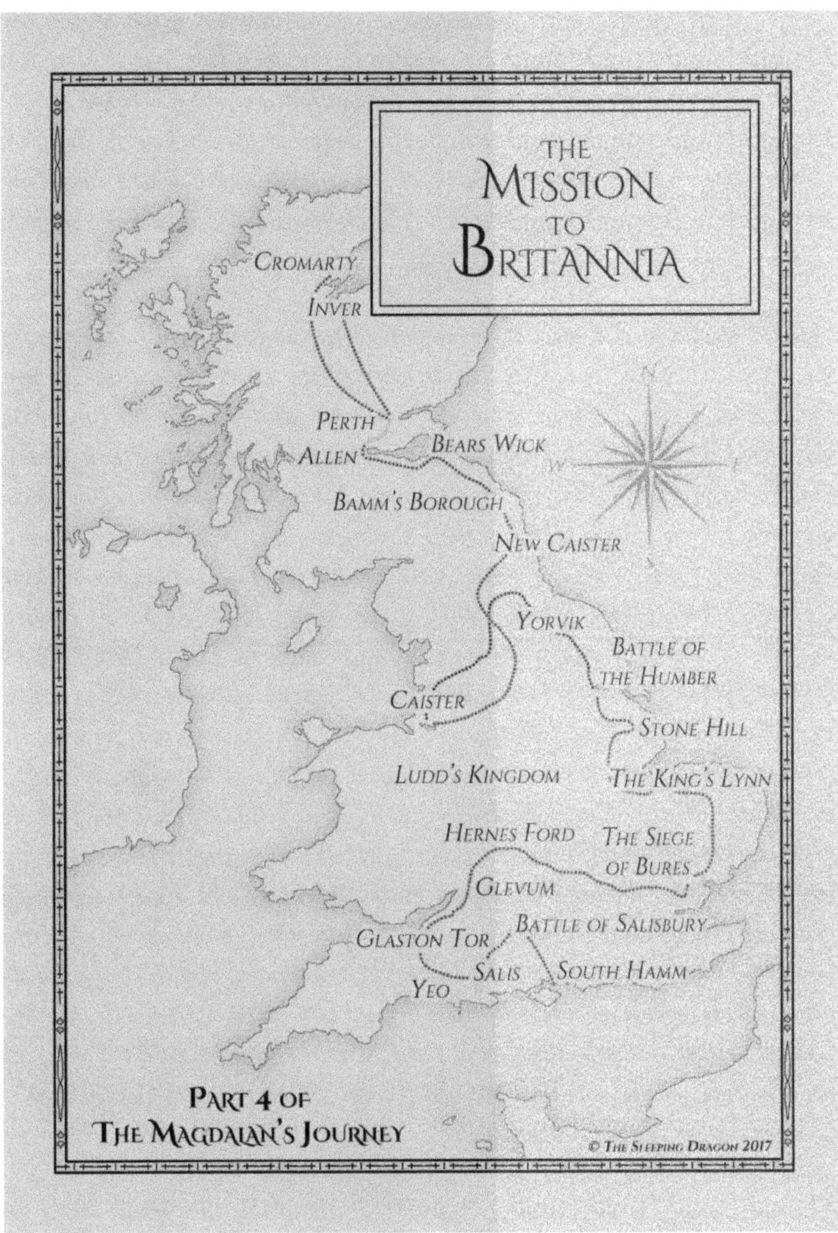

Pilate and Nicodemus both tell of the journey to Glastonbury and its famous Tor in the Mendips, bearing The Grael, Spear of Longinus and Christ's Robe and Shroud, also the secret of the location of the Cross.

"Joseph came before Prince Godric and the smith Macsen by whose skill was Calibarnus forged. The Spear became the Lance born by the first Christian Knight and the Robe was formed to be the Standard of the Christian Armies that would ally with the moor to defeat the pagan in the dark years. With the Centurion Longinus, they did battle at Stonehenge and defeated two Kings then came to Glastonbury where Mary Magdalan did dedicate the chapel." (Pilate, 4th Century AD)

"Mary Magdalan did address the pagans at the Sudh Hamm in the land of the Atrebates, Stone hynge in the kingdom of the Durobriges and Glevum, the capital of the Dobunni and Catuvellauni, and many were converted, turning their backs on the conjurations and foul simoncy of their past. Prince Godric Bann Caedic Wulfridson did adopt Mary Magdalan as his daughter and sole heir to the kingdoms of the Durotriges and Atrebates, the Camps of Saeles Bray, Colis Saelis and Saeles Vale, the kingdom of Dunroavin, Milton, Chard, Stour, Basing and the Vale of the White Horse as far as Devizes and the Hundred of Marl; the ports of Sudh Hamm, Lyme, Hestin, Mare Pevens, Lymin, Rottin and the mouth of the Bourne; the castles of Col Arun's Dell, Lewes Caister and Dor Caister; the New Forest, the Sudh Downs, the Nordowns, the Hogs Back, Rayling Isle and the ford at Gwuilde. Hereafter she became the first Christian princess and her descendants included Princess Helena, the mother of Constantine the Great. At Stone hynge, Mary did return to life Craedech Prince of the Catuvellauni, Dubonni and Cornovii whom she did marry to create the largest kingdom in Britannia on the deaths of Prince Godric, Prince Wulfrid and King Caractacus. Dobunni was the largest of the western kingdoms and stretched from Stroud to Chipen, Ciren, Glevum, the Hills of Tewle, the Malverns, Herns Ford, Worces Caister, Kenill's Wood, and the Ham of Eves and into the Celtic Kingdoms of Cumrovi and Catuvellauni." (Nicodemus, 5th Century AD)

They drew up at the timber-framed King's Hall, the Moot Hall sat opposite, and entered its massive structure, a fire ablaze in the centre, smoke drifting through a hole in the straw thatched roof. The Hall was lit by candles and lanterns but otherwise was lightless with no windows and the door covered by a huge black and white leather hide taken from one of the local cow herds. Around the fire lay several wolfhounds which stood at Maria's entrance and mobbed her. She showed no fear as one of them led her with her hand in its soft mouth to meet the Master of this Hall and the tribe that lived in a circle of mud huts around them.

"I am the Prince, Carl Godric Bann Caedric, Lord of Hammshire and the Prince of the Durotriges, Atrebates, Belgae and Regni, the Aer Weiht, Sales Bray and Dunroavin, and I rule this land from South Hamm and the mouth of the Bourn to the town of Salesbray and east to Hastin and the kingdom of Lewes. Mine is the largest of the southern kingdoms of Britannia. Why are you come?"

Iosephus had earlier shown Maria a rough map of Britannia on the back of a hide. This land was divided into numerous small kingdoms but many had merged to form larger realms namely: Cantiaci, the southern kingdoms, the western kingdoms, the middle kingdoms of the Cantevellauni, the kingdoms of the Trinovantes, the Angles of Deci and Deva, the Iceni and Coritani, the kingdom of Dacia incorporating the Parisi, Brigantes, Selgovae and Votagini, and the tribes of Caledonia.

Maria was hesitant, not through fear or the importance of this first meeting but because she had no idea of local politics and whether Godric's claim to so many of the smaller kingdoms was genuine. She chose to believe him but reserved judgement in her heart:

"My Prince, Lord Godric Bann Caedic of the Durotriges and Atrebates, the Belgae and Regni, of Salesbray and Hammshire, grandson of Prince Commius of the Atrebates, I am here to bring word of my Master who was executed by the Romans, was buried, yet returned to life to bring all of us the gift of eternal life."

"You are Roman?" He asked, a storm brewing on his forehead and in the fury of his eyes. One of his councillors interjected and the Prince sat back then said: "Show me!" and two of his warriors stepped forward turned

Maria roughly around, removed her stola and tore the back of her peplos. Longinus lurched forward in anger to be met by two crossed spears and Maria's gentle: "I am alright, dear heart, but thank you."

Clear for all to see were the remains of the lash marks from Maria's sentence for the crime of unlawful assembly. Godric nodded and smiled:

"You are not Roman. Tell me more of your mission."

Maria carefully tied the stola and the shoulder of her peplos so that it did not fall forwards and continued to cover her then smiled at the Prince.

"I am here to tell anyone who will listen about my Master. His gift of eternal life is there for any and everyone who listens."

"I already have the promise of eternal life if I die with a sword in my hand" Lord Bann replied dismissively.

"Great lord and Prince. Perhaps not all whom you rule are a warrior or even own a sword? Might they not also wish for the reward of life after death?"

"Only women, the young and the old have no sword" and Maria remained silent letting the lord's own words sink in before finally Godric continued reflectively: "A wise lord thinks not only of his warriors but also of those who are vulnerable. We fight to protect them. There are many amongst the old, the infirm, children and our women that I would welcome being with me in the Hallowed Halls of those Fallen in Battle. If we are to celebrate eternal life without our family then what joy is in that?"

As she nodded in agreement, for the first time his ferocious face broke into a smile and he welcomed her:

"You are Maria known as The Magdalan and I know of you. Already my people talk of your rescue of the crew of your ship. I bet you do not have a sword yet you should have one for you have the courage of our greatest heroes."

Then turning to his steward he commanded:

"Seek out Macsen son of Mauwen, our greatest swordsmith and ask him to make a sword suitable to be carried by a young female hero. Name it the gift of the Lord Bann: *Cael I Bann* in Celtic that shall be '*Calibarnus*' in Latin and '*Ex Carl I Bann*' or '*Ex Carl I Bur*' in Briton. Let it be forged with gold, silver, bronze and iron and dragon's fire is to burn as it shimmers, the name of the heroes who bear it to appear as runes on its blade and the message shall say '*She who bears this sword bears no fear.*' Let the magic of this sword see its bearer win any battle. My lady, will you accept my gift?"

"Yes my lord" replied the girl kneeling on one knee to honour him "But I ask one thing."

"Ask but be careful for what you ask" the Prince said frowning.

"I ask that this great gift, this sword of might may also be geased that '*Any who bear it shall bring Peace to this land*'".

The Prince smiled then rose from his great cathedra and offered the girl his hand, raising her to her feet and then addressing the warriors gathered in his Hall.

"What this girl asks for is noble and gladly do I grant her request. Know this, that the Lady Maria has my protection and is welcome in all of the lands South of the Hamm as far as Sales Bray and Hastin, Gwuildesford, Basing and Dor Caister" then he bent forward and kissed her at which she blushed then grinned shyly, mouthing 'thank you'.

The Prince roared with laughter and pointed to some cushions by the fire. "You are still cold from your swim. Sit close to the fire and eat with us" to which Maria replied:

"The greatest honour that those of my faith can give is that we break bread together. Would you join me in so doing?" and Maria had spoken in Celtic to the surprise and delight of the Lord. He agreed eagerly, as if truth be told he was fascinated by the girl. Alas too young to be his wife but already he had adopted her in his heart as a daughter to be cherished and one of whom he could be proud. The following day he would send her and her companions to his armoury and kit them out in his best armour, helmets and shields.

Maria spoke softly and told the tale of her Master's ministry as a story, a legend of a special hero destined to sacrifice his own life to free them all from death. The stories of the son who had gone off with his inheritance, the man going to the aid of a stranger and the water turned to wine, resonated with their culture and all identified with the Samarhiyan, the father of the son who was prodigal and the wedding party. '*We have all been there'* they thought.

Then as she told the story of the Master's final hours they all said in unison: "This was supreme courage." The story of the tomb astounded them and when Longinus and Iosephus added their witness to Maria's account of his death, burial and resurrection, they gasped then applauded. Finally, Maria explained the significance of the breaking of the bread and she took a loaf, broke it and offered it around. As they ate it, she beckoned and Felstum led an old man to her; he was crippled and using two crutches with a bandage over one eye where an old battle scar had disfigured his face.

"Welcome Prince Wulfrid father of Godric Bann Caedic, former Prince of the Atrebates and Hamm" said Lord Godric Bann and bowed to the man who was clearly held in honour for some feat of arms, but whose courage had left him disabled. Then turning to Maria, Godric asked: "What is it we do here? For this is my father and I honour him greatly."

Maria had not known of the relationship between the two men, merely singled out Wulfrid because of his disability. Still she persevered with her intent saying to the Hall at large in a voice like a whisper yet heard by every ear:

"My Master is not a God of War although I have foreseen a time when to follow him will bring victory to those who fight in his name. My Master is however the one God, creator of everything and thus has the power to heal."

Then she took out the spear-point from its oiled cloth now in the custody of Galahaidra and handed to her as Felstum had fetched Wulfrid. She guided the crippled man's hand to the spear and he grasped it, his grip still powerful. Then she prayed:

"Master! Heal this man as I love him and his son. I honour them both for their courage."

All in the Hall gasped as the spear shone bright gold and then the crutches and the eye patch glowed. Wulfrid lifted the patch from his eye and threw it to the ground then smiled at his son as his ruined sight returned. Next his crutches fell to the ground and he stumbled forwards then as all watched his legs straightened and he walked with confidence into his son's embrace.

"My son" said Wulfrid. "I honour you and thank you for the care you have given me. No longer am I a burden to you. Suffer me to join you as one of your housecarls, loyal to your name, constant in your service, fighting at your side."

"My heart rejoices to have you at my right arm, father" then turning to Maria, Lord Godric Bann said: "I name you shield maiden, protector of our tribe and willingly will I break bread in your memory."

"My lord" Maria replied "I welcome it that you honour me. However, I ask that rather than we break bread in my memory we do so remembering my Master."

The Prince laughed then chided Maria gently: "You are like a daughter: when granted a wish you cannot resist asking for more! Yet I am so in charity with you and that which you ask for continues to show your nobility that I happily agree to your request."

Then he took a closer look at her and said: "You need to eat. You are a half-starved rat! I can almost see right through you!" and he broke a haunch off the deer being roasted slowly on the spit over the fire then tossed it across the room to her. She caught it, imagining the shame had she not then took a small bite. It was delicious and yet her own creed determined that she not eat meat for all animals were created by God and to be honoured. Iosephus saw her hesitation and rightly guessing the cause whispered "Book of Genesis" then briefly her Master appeared before her to chide her once more.

"The natural world is made for you to care for but also to succour you. By all means do not eat meat in excess but equally to eat the gift of this good lord furthers my message." The Master told her and as she looked around they were in a room of light, the mirror of the Hall of Godric, but they were alone and everything was gleaming white without shadows.

"Is it not a compromise to eat meat for this reason?" The girl asked timorously, afraid of her Master's anger but he laughed. "Maria" he said "I doubt anything you could ever do will anger me. But some things are not part of my message. People may wish to make further commitments than that which I ask but we should never make the mistake of seeing such as having the same weight as my teachings. Over the centuries there will be those who add to our message for personal or political reasons. Ignore them and never fall into the same error yourself."

"I do not understand" the girl asked her head spinning and the Master held her head gently and kissed her on the forehead. As he did so, insight filled her: *'I am asked to eat meat to cement a friendship that will open the way for thousands to hear your message OR to refuse meat because of my personal creed but which is not part of your message. I do wrong if I refuse for then I put my personal beliefs before your message.'* she thought and then apologised to her Master: "Forgive me, Master, for I have sinned."

Again she felt the touch of his lips and heard him say: "Your sins are so easy to forgive for they are never very serious. Remember once I told you always to forgive children their sins. My rules also govern me. How could I not forgive you, my child?" and then he was gone and with her eyes blazing blue Maria stood once more in the Hall. She held the haunch with care and then took a deep bite and smiled then laughed at herself as the juices of the meat dribbled down her chin. The warriors watching burst into joyful laughter with her then toasted her Master as she had wished.

She spent that night in the Prince's Hall sharing the heat of the same fire, having to endure the constant attention of his wolfhounds which were smitten with her and kept licking her face for attention. Longinus was growled at and backed off quickly to join Galahaidra who was sitting with a group of Godric's bodyguard and swapping stories of their adventures and challenges. Longinus sat down on the log they were using as a bench and was initially greeted with suspicion but they warmed to him as he described his many campaigns in Germania, Africa, Media, Parthia and Persia.

"Your tactics are very different" one observed "You make more use of your shield for example." Longinus nodded then added:

"We moved from an oval and round shield to a rectangular shield for our legionaries for two reasons. First, it locks better with your right hand man so that both shields offer protection with no gap for arrow, sword or spear to penetrate. One of our battle formations is known as 'the tortoise' and sees us covered front, top, side and rear by our own shield and that of others in our legion.

Second, a rectangular shield gives a better cutting edge so the shield also becomes a weapon to cut neck, chin or calf and shin."

The following morning, the Prince took them to meet Macsen. His smith had two forges, two ovens and two smelting fires with several moulds to provide the shape for blade or hilt. Macsen had already begun the process of smelting, forging and forming the blade for Maria using two more ancient blades that had belonged to heroes sung of by Celtic bards but the full story of whom had been lost in the mists of time. One blade had never been broken; the other had never been defeated. "Give me a year" the smith muttered "as this sword has a lot of magic to go into it."

"Is it truly magic or is it God's Will you forge?" Maria tested him.

Macsen smiled then said "Now that for a girl is quite an intelligent question. This blade is a prayer as you suggest. We ask God: 'Is the wielder worthy in the eyes of God and if so will they bring 'victory in war' or 'slay an opponent' or in your case 'heal a kingdom' and 'bring peace to that kingdom'? If in your hands, it will do as asked but not everyone will be as deserving as you."

"Forgive me great smith but I am not as deserving as you suggest and I can see many others more worthy than I" at which the smith laughed so much his hands began to shake and the shaft of the blade he was merging and moulding dropped by accident into the smelting pot for bronze and iron. When he removed it, the blade was slim, perfectly formed for a lady with a light blue sheen, the colour of her eyes.

"I shall work on this one" he muttered and threw the thirty other attempts he had started on back into the flames of the furnace. For an hour he heated the blade and added a fragment of gold or silver or copper, smelted them together then hammered it until he could see the twisting flames of dragon fire then repeated the whole process again gradually building up layers of metal on the blade that he would finally polish back so that each shone through.

When this stage of forging the blade was finished it had over fifty layers of metal as composites, each providing a swirl of colour but from a distance it shone with the distinctive blue light that had first attracted him to it. Yet the blade was still to be finely polished over manymonths so that it would cut silk and drive through a tree stump, light as the spoon from a table, four foot long with a hilt that could be held two handed by Maria and one handed by Longinus.

Before Maria left, Macsen had one further task and some gifts from the Prince for them. First, he looked again at Maria's eyes then opened a cedar box on a shelf above his work station and removed nine sapphires: one 24 carat 18 oz gem stone for the pommel, and eight half cut sapphires each 18 carat and 12 oz for the crux of the hilt and the end of each of the two guards. Each stone flamed bright blue as the girl's eyes had done the night before.

Then he went to his store room and returned with the finest steel chain mail: Maria's hauberk was four foot six long, slit from the waist at back and front to allow her to ride and with flowing bell-shaped sleeves of chain, the waist woven to follow the contours of a lady, nipped in, slender at hip and shoulder with a V cut in the back that was lined and edged with leather to allow it to pass over her head and to prevent her hair catching in the links as it did so. It was tied with leather laces at both sides and had a white-gold leaf and silk collar around the leather at the neck. The steel of the chainmail had been polished to shine silver and white. With it he gave her a steel gorget that sat on top of the hauberk, protecting her slender neck and shoulders, and including a chin guard.

Next he passed around five round shields each with a prancing horse on a green background and five horned and winged steel helmets, one a grand helm with eye and cheek guards and the carved wings of a dragon cast in white gold for Maria so richly adorned with sapphires and diamonds that it clearly had been made for a prince (and indeed had been the Godric's own as a child but Macsen had remoulded it for the more slender elfin face of the lady). It gleamed in gold and silver on a conical frame of steel, but was smaller than the other four helmets.

Then he gave them five long swords, each of which had been made by Macsen for the way they caught alight in the fire of the furnace, all with emeralds to match the shields, save one that was finer and lighter than the others ("A sword for a heroine" said the smith) and this final sword had a single large sapphire on its pommel the twin of that which the smith had chosen for the sword 'Calibarnus'.

The smith handed round the leather under garments that would protect them from arrows and stop oil getting on any clothing beneath and helped them into their mail then strapped on their black leather belts and scabbards (dyed white in Maria's case) finally handing around the sharp scutae or daggers that they would use for hunting, eating and silent killing. Longinus and Galahaidra also kept their own weapons, using the back, ankle and upper arm holsters they wore all the time, but the others had no weapons and so, with the exception of Maria, welcomed the Prince's gift.

They left the smithy to be greeted by the Prince and his warriors and a great mass of people who had gathered around the Hall of their overlord to send Maria safely on her way. "Will you break bread with me?" Maria asked softly and the lord nodded in delight then showed her the many loaves he had brought in case.

"I can show your people how to do this and they can break bread when I am gone." Maria offered.

"You will anoint them as priests?" the lord asked amazed and grateful and Maria nodded but added: "Anyone can break the bread once they have been shown. Those I show today can show others."

Godric smiled and thought '*This is power indeed*' then asked "Will you do others the same favour?"

"Only if their welcome is as yours but nothing will take away the fact that you are the first" Maria reassured him at which Godric embraced Maria and whispered in her ear: "Come back and tell me of all of your adventures. Remember your new sword waits for you here."

The company rode west for nearly a whole day but none challenged them. The four men (Longinus, Galahaidra, Felstum and Iosephus) were armed as the Housecarls of a princess (Maria). The prancing pony on their shields marked them out as warriors from the Kingdom of The Ridgeway 'Via Roa' or 'Dum Ro Via', later to be called 'Dunrovia'. Lord Godric's seal was on the single parchment giving the party permission to ride these lands but the shields were their true passports. The chaperone Iosephus hired (her name was Haladriel) was as good a rider as the equites and a Celt from a local tribe: she was wearing a blue girtle and a gold band on her head and gold and sapphire bracelets on her arms; she looked every part the princess accompanying Maria in disguise as her escort.

Maria's disguise was genius and no-one could see her long fair hair, hidden beneath her helmet, whilst her blue eyes were now in dark shadow. Haladriel, riding with them was much taller and had dark hair and green eyes. She would never be mistaken for Maria. Finally, they were now six when before they had been four. Should their pursuers ask after them then: 'Have you seen a party of four, one girl with fair hair and blue eyes?' would illicit no other response than 'No'.

They stopped twice. First to visit a secluded lake known as the secret or hidden pool, a circular stretch of shallow black water reputed to be magical. Maria stood before the waters and was greeted by silence. Then as she went to walk away from the water, she turned to see another wild boar. "No" she said "I am not going to run away or take my clothes off and sing to you" the girl whispered and Felstum looked at her as if she had gone completely mad! The boar put down its head and Maria sang at which it rolled over on its back made a grunting sound and at its signal two piglets ran up.

"Please" begged the girl looking at Longinus who surrendered without attempting to resist or argue and walking over to the family of wild boar, tried to persuade them to get into a sack. The next moment he was running for cover as they chased him, Galahaidra and Felstum soon following suit, Iosephus and Haladriel wisely staying out of things.

"Goodness me" exclaimed Maria at all the fuss, clicked her fingers and the mother boar leapt into her arms and then supervised with squeals and more grunts as her two offspring were sat one in each saddle bag, heads sticking out to see where they were going.

"What is it with you and wild boars?" Longinus asked and she replied: "They like me! Anyway, the Gallic word for wild boar is Verres and the Latin for the Truth is Veres. It is a sign." Longinus' look of total incredulity pretty much summed up what all four men thought but Haladriel was supportive: "The Wild Boar is feared across Briton and when it is known that our lady has tamed wild boar it will enhance her reputation."

Their second stop was at the head of the Stour valley to admire the views of rolling hills, forests and secluded lakes and to let the family of wild boar have a run. They terrorised a local family of rats, chased a ferule cat that had made the mistake of hissing at them then put a roosting partridge up into the air.

As the sun went down, they arrived at the enormous stone circle that was their destination. It was deserted and so the company set up camp outside of the circle, not through superstition but because they were worried that the cross pieces might fall, such was the angle at which some of the stones now stood.

"Why are we here?" Longinus asked and Maria took them all to stand by the altar then took off her helmet, gorget and chin guard to stand waiting. After just under half an hour she looked up and set herself to face the North Star as it sat below the handle of the Sickle.

"North" she said and pointed to the stone above which they could see the north or pole star. Then she pointed to some of the twelve signs of the zodiac, the Archer, the Scales, the Fish, the Water Holder, the Crab, the Twins, the Lion, the Virgin, the Bull, the Goat, the Ram and the Scorpion. As she did so she named them in their original Arabic rather than their newer Latin names and pointed to one of the stones which marked each sign then explained:

"Six of the signs are below the horizon and can only be seen when we go to the far south of Africa. But by lining up the six signs we can see, the stones will then tell us where the six signs we cannot see lie."

"That leaves some stones unaccounted for" Longinus queried.

"The two facing the altar line up with the sun on the summer solstice, the two behind us line up with the sun on the winter solstice then you have the Moon, Jupiter, Venus, Mars and Saturn."

"But why are we here?" Longinus persisted.

"My Master has taught us to love his Father's creation, to explore it, discover it and admire it. Here we have the first example of man's discovery and understanding of how the star's move in our skies. Note the Earth is not central and the circle shows an understanding of the differences between the north and south hemispheres moreover those who designed this celebration of the stars knew our world is spherical like an orange and not flat like a platter. We come to acknowledge that science is at the heart of faith and to embrace science as the true journey of discovery of God's creation."

"Why is this important?"

"Because God's gift to me includes the gift of prophecy and I can see a time when religion will attempt to depress science, limit it, even call it heresy and science will then seek to discredit religion, describing it as irrelevant and as mythical. Then one day it will become necessary for science and religion to join to meet a common threat but the centuries of division will prevent this and our world will fall to an evil that is to come.

Yet here, in this place, we see hope. Here magic, faith, religion and science once were joined and can be so again. So we leave a trail of crumbs for all to find in the centuries to come where both the journey (the Quest) and the items found at the end of the Quest (Grael, Spear, Sword, Shroud and Robe) will teach a lesson of hope that will allow us to unite in the face of an enemy we shall all share."

They looked around then asked her: "How will we make this place known?" at which Maria laughed then still chuckling explained herself further: "This place will never be forgotten but our task is to ensure it is remembered for the right reason. So tomorrow we shall invite the locals to a service amongst the stones and then here is where we shall one day bury the Robe: to be found when it shall be needed."

Maria was the only one of them to get any sleep. Haladriel dreamt of being sacrificed by druids and kept waking up in a sweat, Galahaidra feared the stones were giant trolls come to eat them all, Longinus was spooked every time he opened an eye and saw the stars and kept making the sign of the evil eye to fend off the mythical creatures that had become constellations and would come down from the heavens to assail him, Iosephus kept hearing the wild boars grunting in their sleep and feared he was unclean for eating pork himself so dreamt of washing himself repeatedly, and Felstum had been at sea most of his life so found the noises of the many animals that forage at night deeply disturbing and leapt out of his bed roll when he heard an owl hoot, waking the others with his startled scream except for Maria who slept through it all.

The following morning, Maria stood in the circle to greet the Dawn Star, Venus, with a prayer of rejoicing. Longinus started to cook them breakfast and did for a moment consider rashers of bacon taken from the wild boar but knew Maria would be upset so stuck to barley, milk, walnuts and hazelnuts for Maria then went foraging and returned with three fish and five eggs which he fried up on his small field stove with some bread for the men and Haladriel.

With breakfast out of the way, Maria took them back to the stone circle. She pointed once again to those menhir or standing stones indicating the twelve signs of the zodiac. "Twelve is important" she said cryptically and then she marked out twelve paths for them to follow. She did this by laying a line of white pebbles from the centre of the altar to each of the twelve menhirs then carrying the same line beyond the circle.

"Where we are is The Summoning Circle. There are twelve more stone circles and each has a settlement" she said. "We follow these lines to find those other settlements and summons their people to meet us here or, for those unable to join us, to simultaneously break the bread in their own stone circle."

They rode to the first of the settlements and were met by the Elders there. The Elders and the settlements warriors were impressed by the arms of the companions but even more so at the wild boar the girl carried. "Wild boar are protected by our people and believed to be the spirits of former warriors" they explained. Needless to say that spooked everyone in the company except Maria.

Maria explained what she intended to do that evening and the Elders promised in their turn to send word out to the surrounding villages. Prince Godric Bann Caedic had sent word out already not only to those in his lands but also he had wanted to ensure his neighbouring Kings and Lords were aware that Maria was under his protection. As a consequence, Maria could expect to be welcomed and feted at each of the twelve settlements.

The Prince Godric was proving a far better friend than Maria had realised and she promised to herself she would definitely return to see him, whatever the outcome of her mission, short of her own death.

They met the same welcome at the other eleven villages and returned to The Summoning Circle with their mission completed by noon of the following day, where Maria stood once more by the altar surrounded by the stones, briefly in thought. Then she turned to speak to Longinus: "Tonight something remarkable, wonderful will happen. So much so that it will change the future and see Good triumph over Evil. Alas, if I were a servant of Evil, all my efforts would go into preventing what we now plan. The enemy of Good will now know what we intend and indeed may have learnt when my good lord Godric Bann Caedic sent word of our presence. Given the short notice, what might a foe do to prevent tonight's service?"

Longinus thought long and hard, sharing Maria's concerns with the others in their party. Galahaidra was the most helpful as he talked through the possible tactics an enemy might adopt:

"Maria, the enemy, whomsoever they are, has a number of options:

First, they can prevent the service tonight by destroying the circle here. But then we might rebuild it or even it might be enough that the shadows of the standing stones still exist. Many stones have already toppled and still I can sense the power here, so destroying the circle is unlikely to be achieved by tonight;

Second, they can attack the other settlements but they will be defended and the same applies as here: is there really enough time to remove all sign of a circle's existence?

Third, and most likely, they attack our greatest vulnerability and that, Maria, is you. They launch an attack here hoping to find and capture (unlikely) or slay you (most likely);

Fourth, they set up in competition with you, inviting the Druids or some other faith of the Celts or Britons to announce a meeting tonight."

It was Longinus who broke the bad news to Maria: "There is only one option really. The enemy will strike here seeking to hunt you down and kill you and if they fail in that then they will damage the Circle or try and defend it against those who come. Alas, those from the other settlements will come believing they attend a peaceful service so they will probably be lightly armed and thus walk or ride into a massacre."

"We must defend the Circle then" Maria replied to which Iosephus added "And we must send for help. Send Haladriel to the Hall of Godric and let us hope his war party can make quicker time than our foes."

All agreed to this and Haladriel was sent with a hastily scribbled note from Maria and the girl's sincerest prayers for her safe deliverance. Meanwhile, Longinus took Galahaidra to one side to ask: "How many will we face?"

"My best case is that they only discover our intent this morning and that they send one or two lords' war parties from outside the area we have visited. Perhaps from the far reaches of the Severnus and Glevum or the Hill of Eves; then there are the Mendae Hills and the Tor of Glaston even Sulis lies within a half day's ride. This would see either one or two war parties of thirty to forty attack us four hours from now. They may bring archers but mounted archers are rarely seen outside of Arabia, Parthia and Persia so expect cavalry only.

If they discovered our intent yesterday then we face an army of hundreds and our extermination so there is little point dwelling on that scenario."

Longinus nodded then said: "So we must do as before and lay a trap and an ambush."

"What have you in mind, my friend?"

"The only cover is the stone circle so our enemy must ride across open ground to get to us. We do four things: set Iosephus and Maria the task of making bows and arrows for two of us; you and I set trip wires and sunken posts to unhorse our enemy on the open ground before us; set Felstum to make traps that maim or kill with sharpened posts that are held on taut ropes, man pits and concealed nets in the entrances between the stones (I will show him how); and have you and I on horse-back in hiding in order to mount an ambush, coming from where we see the enemy has the least view of us and to attack where the enemy has the least men."

"Can I use the spear?" Galahaidra asked and when Longinus nodded then he said with a smile: "I am very much liking this plan. Maria, Iosephus and Felstum can hold the gap between the stones that mark the winter solstice to the south of the circle. Two could hold ten there indefinitely. But will Maria fight?"

Longinus shook his head before admitting: "If we become so desperate that the girl must fight then we have already been defeated. It will take a minor miracle that she let the rest of us do so."

But he was surprised when she agreed to his plan. "Just do not kill anyone and then I can heal those you wound and put everything right again."

"Has she any idea what she is doing?" Galahaidra muttered and Longinus snorted then took what he could out of Maria's muddled thinking: "I think she said 'Yes' so if later she kicks up a fuss about the death toll we will just have to say she confused us."

"Trust me" laughed Galahaidra "That is truer than you think."

Three hours later they were ready so Longinus set Galahaidra as look out for the northern and eastern approaches and Iosephus to watch the approach from the west. Meanwhile, Felstum helped the Centurion add another man pit and they used some of their arrows as a row of pointed spikes at the base.

"How long until the service begins?" Longinus asked Maria and she checked with the sun and the small stone at the centre of the circle that acted as a sun and moon dial.

"Two hours but we may see arrivals from the other settlements before then."

Then they heard Galahaidra's whistle and saw Iosephus running back to camp in response. Maria picked up hands full of arrows and stepped behind the altar, placing her helmet and gorget on, her sword in its scabbard, her shield by her side. She would keep Iosephus and Felstum fully supplied whilst they fired their arrows.

Galahaidra leapt over a number of the traps and made it back to the Circle where they all lay low, hiding behind the stones, watching for the enemy's advance.

"How many?" Longinus whispered. "Forty" Galahaidra replied. "Armed but they are tired. No archers."

Longinus checked everyone was in position including their horses hidden within the ring of stones then as he looked north again, he saw the party on the furthest slope, perhaps four leagues away. They would do that in a quarter of an hour; more if they tried a flanking attack but at the moment they were coming in stupidly, one large group and no scouts.

"They cannot see us" Galahaidra hissed. "Our ambush will do much damage."

"It is too early to tell, be patient."

As the enemy war party reached the flat plain on which the stone circle stood, they spread out into a long line seeking to encircle their enemy but still they could see no-one and came on fast, intending to confirm the circle was empty then look for their prey's tracks.

"Arrows to fire at flanks" Longinus whispered then held his hand aloft. Suddenly two horses stumbled, flinging their riders to the ground and hobbling as they had each trod on spikes planted in concealed traps dug into the ground. Then two riders trotted into the trip wires: panels of sharpened staves, held under tension by ropes, were released to spring forward and maim both riders and their horses. The riders fell and lay still, bleeding to death and stunned by the man traps but not yet dead. Two riders were down, wounded and two more unhorsed.

The captain of the war party called his troop to a halt and Longinus called "Archers" at which Felstum and Iosephus launched five arrows in a minute at the enemy troop. As the first arrows landed by the riders' feet, spooking their horses, the second volley of arrows had been released and one struck a rider, wounding him in his sword arm. He fell back, looking to repair the damage whilst the captain ordered his party to split in three, seven going left and eight to the right, twenty to stay in reserve but falling back out of range of the arrows.

Longinus signalled for the Archers to fire to the left, the direction the captain had gone in, whilst Longinus and Galahaidra mounted up and prepared to take the party going right in the rear. "Fire" shouted Longinus and at the much shorter range the two men were able to get six arrows into the air before their enemy could take evasive action. Two arrows struck their target, one bouncing off a shield but the second struck one of the horses in the rump and it bucked, sending its rider to the ground to break his neck from the fall. He took several minutes to die during which Maria wept as Iosephus clung on to her, not letting her go to the man's rescue.

The captain had pulled the rest of his party back out of range and from his new vantage point was able to see Longinus and Galahaidra, mounted on their Arab war stallions, charge into the party to the right. He was too far away to go to their aid and watched in dismay the massacre that followed as the Roman Centurion and the former sicariot launched into the rear of the small party of warriors at speed and with surprise on their side.

Galahaidra's lance (the spear point had been lashed tightly onto a long pole made from freshly cut and stripped ash) took one of the rider's in the right shoulder and unhorsed him then as another turned it took him in the stomach, again unhorsing him and leaving him to bleed slowly to death unless attended to. The third rider met the lance with his shield but the spear point cut through the wood of the shield and unhorsed him also, with a deep wound in his left breast, penetrating his lungs and just missing his heart.

Meanwhile, Longinus had charged with his long sword held straight before him and his powerful thrust had gone through the spine of the first rider he met, killing him almost instantly. The next man had hardly turned when Longinus' sword went through the second rider's heart then his stallion reared and crushed the skull of the third rider. The last rider swung at Longinus to meet a parry from his sword and then Longinus swiped at him with his shield, his stallion reared and attacked with both hooves and as the rider dodged these attacks, Galahaidra took the last rider out with a strike to his groin. The attack had lasted less than a minute with nowhere near enough time for the captain on the far side of the stone circle to send help. Longinus then swung his horse round and rode down all four wounded men. There were no survivors.

The enemy captain now took stock. He had lost thirteen men so far but he still had twenty six uninjured. He signalled for his entire troop to move to the west of the camp and as they did so they came under fire once more and one warrior was hit in the face, screaming in pain and retreating out of range. A second was hit in the eye and fell dead. The remaining six arrows missed any target.

Longinus and Galahaidra had ridden once more for the protection of the stone circle and were ready this time to attack the enemy's right flank. The captain sounded the charge and four horses hit the trip wires at speed, lost their front calves and flung their riders, three were stunned and one rider fractured his hip and was unable to stand. Two more men went down to eye shots and then the troop reached the stone circle where they were funnelled between the stones only for two to fall into man pits and be killed instantly, one more assailant was impaled by a trap and died slowly and another was flung into the air trapped in a net. Then Longinus and Galahaidra charged unhorsing two men who had trampled over their dead comrades to gain entry to the stone circle.

At last, the captain had gained the circle and he and his men began to surround Galahaidra and Longinus.

As they were both encircled, everyone paused at the sound of a hoot of childlike laughter followed by the singing of psalms. Into the battle came Maria leading Iosephus and Felstum all riding in full armour with winged helmets and embossed shields to charge at the rear of the enemy … and that had been part of nobody's plan. Maria's sword shone and wove bright circles of light that dazzled her opponents before her blade disarmed them. She had commanded her sciartum *to defeat but not harm her enemy* and this was a sword made by Macsen with powers that could only be unleashed by the worthy. Maria's worth was so great that the sword was bursting with energy.

At the same time she called on the Spirit of God and within her saddle bag The Grael began to glow, its power to inflict un-healable wounds on the unworthy was unleashed on her enemy, a power that would later wound the Fisher King for having impure thoughts.

Behind Maria, Iosephus and Felstum were also armed with blades forged by Macsen and these twisted and twirled in the air before them. Five of their foemen went down in Maria's first attack and five more took wounds from The Grael and fell to the ground. Two riders struck at the girl but their blows were deflected by her helmet and shield.

Longinus took advantage of the war party's distraction to thrust home with his long sword slaying two more with fatal blows to the heart. Galahaidra's lance unhorsed another of the riders and then spun before him making an impenetrable defence. A few seconds later and Maria had taken down three more riders, Felstum and Iosephus had slain three of the unhorsed riders and three more had sustained wounds from The Grael.

The captain surrendered: with twenty three wounded including himself and unable to fight again without the aid of a healer, fourteen men slain, two unhorsed and at some distance from the battlefield and one trapped and hanging in the net overhead, he had no choice.

"I am the King Casterix of the Durobriges in the Tor of Glaston" the war band's captain said "and I surrender to your commander."

Longinus stepped forward and took the King's sword then said: "We wish to tend to your wounded. Have we your word that you shall not harm us as we do so?"

"You have my word as King of the Tor at Glaston" and Longinus nodded to Maria who ran to aid the wounded starting with the man with a face wound then the one left with a wound to the abdomen whom she found in tears and then finally using the spear to counter the harm done by The Grael. Next she helped the warriors from Glaston with the burial of their dead before the rest of their troop, including the man released from the net, was sent on their way north. Just as they were departing the first of the followers for the service that night began to arrive in their hundreds. Maria met them on the plains whilst the others in the company tidied away or covered and made safe the traps they had lain down and buried in and around the circle.

It was half an hour to go to the service when the second enemy war party from the City of Glevum arrived and this war party was fifty strong. But already one thousand participants for the service had reached The Summoning Stones and then a fighting mad Prince Godric, Haladriel at his side, reached the stone circle with three hundred of his best warriors.

Prince Godric took one look at the King of the Dobunni and Catuvellauni, who was leading his war party of fifty Housecarls, already turning in flight at the sight of a superior foe, and charged after him. Maria caught up with the Godric as much to try and restrain his ire as to fight at his side and rode at his left flank; Prince Wulfrid was at his right hand. In their first charge, Maria took down eleven warriors, all with minor wounds and unhorsed and captured by those following her, Prince Godric Bann and Wulfrid slew six of the enemy warriors between them whilst sixteen were unhorsed and captured with terrible wounds through the power of The Grael.

The enemy captain this time was Caractacus, King of the western Catuvellauni, the Dobunnii and Corvinii; he surrendered when the Prince, his only son, was unhorsed and slain by Godric. He wept as he held the young man's body and in his grief promised never to return to Godric's lands. Maria's grief was equally great and Godric held her in her distress, looking at his father, Wulfrid, in hope of some answer to alleviate the tears but the girl herself knew there was only one answer. Taking the spear-point from Galahaidra once more, she sliced her own hand so that her blood and the blood of the Master which her faith taught her resided still within her could mingle with the Spear and the blood of the dying Iesus. The Spear shone bright silver rather than its usual gold of healing.

This time she touched the young man's cold body gently, the lightest of kisses of sorrow upon his forehead then prayed:

"As you brought Lazarus and Cornelius' daughter to life grant me the gift of this man's life also."

With shock and amazement Caractacus watched as his son took a long deep breath then sat up, no sign of the deep wound in his chest visible, waking as if from a deep slumber to the shouts of acclamation from the rest of the captured war party. Thirty three had been taken captive, four had fled and thirteen were dead. Yet with the resurrection of the King's son such was Caractacus' joy that peace was secured, the captives healed through prayer and released whilst Maria was invited to join the King of the Catuvellauni at dinner the next night.

"I will come" she said simply then turned and rode across to lean in her saddle and embrace Godric. "You came to my rescue. How can I thank you?"

He laughed then said "What I hear is that you fought like a demon and used powers that disarmed and disabled half of both armies that attacked you. You had already won one battle before we reached this circle. Your whole company are heroes in my eyes and those of all who will praise you and your Master this night. I honour you and ask 'What can I do for you?'"

"There is one thing: I ask that you honour my Master tonight rather than honour me. All I have done has been his doing" and the Prince of the Atrebates nodded expecting the girl to say nothing different for he knew she would ask for no honour for herself yet he would still honour her in private: for no-one else could have done as she had achieved that day. The tale of her victories would be told throughout the lands of the Celts and Britons, growing with each telling, ensuring her a welcome from those eager to hear of such heroics and waiting for a new leader to defy the oppression of Rome.

"There is one thing you can find out from your new-found friend, the King of the Castavellauni" Prince Godric offered her by way of advice "Ask him 'Who commanded him to slay you? Who is your true enemy?'"

By the eighth hour in the evening nearly three thousand were gathered at The Summoning Stones to watch as the last light of the day and the first gleam of moonlight shone red and white gold upon the altar where one young girl stood wearing the armour given to her by the Lord Prince Godric Bann Caedic, son of Wulfrid, son of Commius son of Cedric son of Garaec half-son of the God Wodin, Prince of the Durotriges, Atribates, Beglae, Regni and Dunroavin, Salesbray and South Hammshire and made by the great sword smith and armourer, Macsen son of Mauwen.

On the stone altar before her was: The Shroud with its marks of the passion of her Master to be seen clearly as a spectral shadow; the Robe, pieces of purple silk cloth with the remains of a gold fringe and the blood stains from where the young girl's Master had been beaten then lashed by Romans as she herself had been; the Spear, the metal point of a pilum, gleaming iron kept well-oiled to prevent rust and with four specks of dried blood being the precious blood of her Master; the Grael, a stone platter on which her Master had first broken bread, a simple piece of clay pottery, tableware that could be found in any humble home; and her Sword, made by Macsen with the power to disarm but not harm any enemy, a vorpal blade and holy sword which did divine will if in the hands of someone worthy.

Each of these holy relics contained the power to heal, the power to speak in any language and thus be understood, the power to craft the future and the power to offer hope. They magnified the gifts of the Spirit and responded to the prayers of a supplicant. Together, they contained one further power that would be demonstrated that evening; the power to heal the natural world from the damage done by mankind or indeed from those who sought the end of the home of humanity.

In twelve settlements lying across the Vale of the White Horse, ranging from Glevum and Glaston to the north, the Cities of Salesbray and South Hamm to the south, Sulis to their west and the outcrop of rock that was The Carrock, Malverns and Chiltons to the east, with the River Thamis snaking as a blue and silver line along the base of the golden valley and the ancient path of The Ridgeway in white chalk linking one hill top to the next, thousands more people had gathered to simultaneously break the bread in union with Maria, following her lead as they collectively honoured her Master.

From this evening would the early Christian Church in Britain be born to continue until it was crushed by the Synod of Whitby in the seventh century, and to become part of the rich mix of former faiths that is part of the colourful tapestry known as Islam, and whose first Muslim knights would one day serve alongside their Christian cousins, seated at the same Round Table, guided by the King Artor, sharing the same common enemy: the invading pagans from Danemark and the Heligoland Bight.

"We are come to celebrate the life, death and rebirth of my Master, Iesus of Nazareth, known also as The Christ or Christos, the Messiah as foretold by the prophet Isaiah.

We have fought the enemies of peace and won victory. My Master has defeated death and the enemies of peace to bring us hope: Hope that we will be granted the gifts of the Spirit in this life; Hope that we will be granted eternal life in the presence of God in paradise in the next life; Hope that is the 'special gift' given only to mankind.

Today we follow his new command: to remember and honour Iesus, my Master, in the breaking of bread. We will together, ask for the forgiveness of our sins. We will reflect on the scriptures and a reading from the Book of Kings about the powers of the Gifts of the Spirit. We will offer ourselves to my Master as a living sacrifice and then we shall break the bread and each of us will hold a piece as we invite my Master to join us, granting us a new birth filled with God's Spirit and the power of his love."

As Maria said these words, in the twelve sister stone circles the volunteers amongst the village Elders, guided to the precise time of consecration by the position of Jupiter, led their own communities in prayer, introducing the breaking of the bread as Maria had described it to them when she had visited each settlement, enthusiastic, eager to learn, excited to discover what new power they were to be entrusted with through God's generosity.

Together, they came to the moment when tens of thousands across the kingdoms of the Durotriges, Atribates, Dunroavin, Dobunni, Corvonii and Catuvellauni united in breaking the bread, sharing it with their neighbour then holding it aloft said: "This is me. We do this to remember Iesus of Nazareth."

As they honoured his name, a bright light came down as tongues of silver flames to cover the altar at The Summoning Stones then guided by the placing of each of the standing stones, giants set for an ancient purpose, fingers of pure light crossed the Vale of the White Horse in search of the twelve other circles.

When all were ignited as a giant ring around The Summoning Stones, a powerful beam of energy, drawing its strength from all of the circles and the prayers of the thousands gathered at each, launched into the sky, cutting through the clouds, outshining the brightest star, a coruscation that sent a wave of healing: storm damage to trees was repaired, crops, fruit and vines become ready before their time, water was cleansed so that the beds of rivers showed as if covered with the clarity of crystal, the smoke of fires in the air was removed to leave it fresh and scented with the blossom of cherries and the ripeness of blackberries.

"It is done" whispered Maria in awe, unintentionally repeating her Master's words at the end of his ministry and all stood in silence as the light gradually faded, their act of healing accomplished. Into the silence, Maria sent them on to their new ministry to break the bread in communion with their fellow Celt and Briton with these words of hope: "There will come a moment in our future when we shall need to heal a harm done to our world. Until then, guard these relics and the knowledge of this gift of the God's Spirit until our time shall come."

Maria and her company were escorted to South Hamm by Prince Godric Bann and his war band to stay that night in the security of the Carl's Great Hall. She slept soundly, watched over by her own company and the many warriors of the Prince of the Atrebates, all eager to have sight of the heroine who rode under the sign of the prancing pony yet preached peace and forgiveness, and healed her enemy of their wounds. What they saw was a frail and woefully thin young girl, more a child than a warrior, and their respect for her Master grew. How else could this child have defeated the war parties of two great Kings if not supported and under the protection of a great God?

Glastonbury Tor and Glevum

"After the Battle at Stone hynge, Joseph took Mary to the Tor at Glastonbury. On the way she tamed a family of wild boar. She converted many pagans in the land of the Durotriges and on the shores of the Severnus as far as Glevum in the land of the Catuvellauni. Joseph then led the way to the Mendae Hills and north to the Malvern Hills in the lands of the Dobunni and Cornovii before heading east through the middle kingdoms of the Catuvellauni to the kingdom of King Col of the Trinovantes, establishing Christian shrines at Evesham, Waltham and Burntwood." (Nicodemus 5th Century AD)

In the morning she came to say goodbye to Prince Godric and could not stop her tears. "I promise to return" she kept saying. A huge crowd had turned out to see her on the road, hundreds more lined the Ridgeway which would be her road until she reached the Mendae Hills and rode through the Kingdom of Durotriges to locate the Vale of the Fluvius Severnus then crossed the borders of the Catuvellauni riding on to the City of Glevum. There were shorter routes but this way would allow her party to ride fast and allow for a change in their mounts at Glaston's Tor. Word had already been sent to King Casterix who had guaranteed their safe passage and to provide fresh horses in return for Maria addressing his warriors.

Maria had wanted to change into fresh clothing but Longinus insisted she wear her armour and helm, supported in this by Godric: "You risk an arrow from someone laying in wait whereas your armour will protect you."

"My Master protects me and I shall melt" she retorted but Godric could be far more stubborn than she and in the end she gave in with a smile, whilst Longinus made a mental note that threatening the girl with the Lord Godric Bann's displeasure might bring her to heel in future.

They left mid morning and arrived at Glaston's Tor by mid afternoon with a long ride still ahead of them. The welcome they received was gracious in defeat, noble in honouring the companions' victory and eager as the youngest warriors saw a kindred spirit in the young girl who had so comprehensively defeated the veterans of their tribe yet healed the wounded of their terrible harm.

When they saw the family of wild boar walking at her heel, they were even more excited at the prospect of meeting the girl and hearing her words. One of the King's wolfhounds made the mistake of taking too much interest in the mother and fled in dismay as its tusks went down and it charged. The King and his company cried with laughter and the ice was truly broken. Maria then knelt before the King in greeting and he raised her by one hand then introduced her to his wife, sons and daughters. All were amazed at her youth.

Finally, she stood in his Great Hall and Moot Chamber, far taller and larger than the Hall of Godric, with several fires lit and tall forged iron candelabra standing every five paces, wall hangings and woollen rugs hung from the timber-frame of the walls, showing great wealth and depicting a history of victories against those to their west from across in the land of the Situres and to their south from the Land of the Dumnonii.

Five hundred stood before the raised dais on which the King's seat and table were placed to listen to the gentle voice of the girl of the prancing pony, who honoured them by speaking in both Celt and Briton.

"I wish to be your friend" she began humbly "and to learn from you about all of the wonderful history of your kingdom. I have come not to bring war but to seek peace. That we have fought amazes me given your gracious and courteous welcome. I hope this marks the beginning of a long-term relationship founded on Truth and mutual Trust and I promise you my aid in your future endeavours.

I have come from far away, lands at the far end of the Middle Sea. Where I was born is occupied by Rome and alas I have been tortured and whipped for the message that I bring from those lands, yet also there are many Romans who respect my message and whom I love.

The message I bring is from my Master who was slain by the order of Rome yet returned to life to leave us his Good News: a place in Paradise in God's house awaits all of us if we follow him.

I am on a mission therefore: a quest, an adventure, a challenge: to bring my message before all who will listen. I shall not foist it upon anyone but I will offer anyone who wishes to hear about my Master, his life and teachings, the chance to listen or not to do so. I make no claims that my Master is mightier than other leaders or Gods but I believe my Master offers me happiness in this world and the next and I rejoice that he found me and has let me follow him."

As she finished, several of the warriors, both the veterans and those newly come to be counted as part of their King's war band asked: "How do we follow him, your Master? Tell us more!"

"My Master asks that we remember him in the breaking of the bread" and then without pause Longinus fetched a loaf from Maria's saddle bag and she passed pieces of bread around to those willing to try this new venture. "My Master took simple bread then said 'This is me' and asked us to remember him each time we did the same. When we do so and if we believe in him then he will come and offer us his comfort and aid. My Master is my constant companion: always present to advise me and he offers me his strength when I am in danger or need help."

"Was it your Master that defeated us?"

"Yes" she replied without hesitating. "For all can see that I am weak!"

Conscious that they still had a long journey ahead of them and would not wish to be late, Longinus signalled to Maria that they must leave. She took the bread and ate it and watched as all in the Hall did the same, eyes shining in the belief that they now had the 'power' of a warrior heroine and shield maiden: for not one of them believed she was 'weak'.

As she went to leave, hundreds flocked around her to touch her shield or helmet, to look into her eyes and see the blue blaze that was hidden within, and sense her fearlessness. They had all seen such before when in the heat of battle and knew this was the mark of the bravest of warriors. Maria would have been amazed had she known what they were thinking and regarded her own courage as wafer thin.

Casterix stood and waved them on their way shouting: "Come back when you can" and then they were on the road north, not going as far as Sulis but rather heading east through the Kingdom of the Dubonni. South of the Wolds they came to Stow, Miserden and the gorge of Birdlip, the former a large settlement that hung precariously from the local hills and sat sprawling in the sun in a deep valley like a crucible.

The gorge at Birdlip was breathtakingly beautiful, a wonderful act of creation more exciting than anything Maria had seen before and more lush than she had yet to encounter having travelled through deserts, lands made arid through lack of rain, large fields of dust and barren vines on the plains of Celtica and Tarraconensis, cold and treacherous mountains or dense deciduous forests that sat in shadow. So enthralled and enraptured was she with the peacefulness, tranquillity and serenity of the deep gorge of Birdlip that Longinus had to grasp her reins and drag her away.

"Promise me we will come back" she whispered in awe "for this is heaven on earth."

They had considered crossing the Sunbury and fording the Severnus at Upton but decided instead to brave the wooden bridge that crossed the Severnus where it had split to circumvent a natural island and the locals had built a bridge of two spans at the entrance to Glevum. Glevum sat to the south of the river but had two long quays that ran along both banks and offered a safe haven for merchant and fishing vessels that traded with the land of the Hibernans and the Dumnonii of Kernow, and with Roman settlements in Lesser Britannia and Lusitania in Hispania through the large City port on the Estuary of the Rivers Avonis and Severnus at the Gorge of Berista.

They dismounted and led their horses not daring to risk the vibration if they had ridden. The waters below them roared between the uprights, ancient logs that had been driven into the mud of the river bed to hold the bridge and that now lent at an odd angle, propped up downstream by rocks but vulnerable to each high tide and the four to five foot tall tidal wave or bore that would sweep down the Severnus. Maria was not at all worried but Haladriel nearly refused and Galahaidra felt sea-sick just looking at the broiling water. Longinus hurried them across, wary of falling in such deep water with their armour.

There was a guard post at the far side of the bridge with a wooden palisade and two watch towers either side of tall oak gates. The walls of Glevum were rectangular and set on a mound with a motte surrounding them into which the river had been diverted. The company was challenged the moment they stepped off the bridge and Longinus announced that they were the guests of King Caractacus.

"Which of you is the heroine, the Magdalan?" the officer in charge of the guard detail asked and Maria slowly removed her winged helmet. As with the warriors at Glaston, the guards were thrown by the girl's obvious youth and their leader asked: "Can you prove who you are?"

Maria shook her head then replied thoughtfully: "Your King will recognise me but easier might be to find one of your warriors that fought at The Summoning Circle in the Vale of Sales. I healed many and hopefully they will recall me." The guardsman nodded as this was a sensible request and sent word into the City.

Within minutes there was a commotion at the Gate and then the young Prince she had brought back to life was there and without pause welcomed her with an embrace and kissed her on each cheek. "My name is Craedech and I am mortified that you were kept waiting" he said but the girl would have none of it: "Prince Craedech, your men guard you well. There is nothing but honour in their actions and I am not offended, just gratified and indeed overwhelmed at your own wonderful welcome."

"Come" he said "There are so many who wish to see you". As she stepped through the Gates, Maria was greeted by long streets of timber framed halls, mud huts and outbuildings around a central, covered square with large iron vats for weighing and measuring grain. As far as she could see, the streets were lined with people all of whom had come to see the foreign princess with golden hair and blue eyes; the girl warrior who had defeated their King in battle then saved the life of their Prince. She heard the whispers become murmurs as they saw her, carrying her shield and helmet, her sword at her waist, her chainmail hanging almost to her feet and shining silver in the sun.

"She is a child" they whispered but then the warriors who had fought her replied: "And she defeated fifty of us almost single handed."

Caractacus came to the entrance of his Hall to welcome her: his Hall house was even larger and grander than that of Casterix with each of the Kings seeming to vie for the honour of having the largest home. She knew her Master would have made a story of this for, despite the size of their Halls, in his Father's house they would all be equal. She was ushered towards the top table but noticed the queue of poor at the far end of the large vaulted oak-ceilinged chamber, hopeful for scraps from each table, and remembered her Master's story of the rich man and the beggar.

"Noble King, set me a table at the foot of your Hall and invite those who are begging at your door to join me. For I am poor and not a princess so am not deserving of the honour of being placed at your top table."

The King was stunned. He considered being angry for the insult done to his hospitality then saw from the girl's eyes that she meant what she said but also that she was pleading with him for his understanding. "I seek to honour you" he said and Maria replied: "I am already honoured. Your invitation and your welcome have been truly magnificent. But I would see these poor people fed and would feel guilty if I was to eat when they starve."

The King's son came to their rescue. "This is easily sorted. Set up an extra Table as the lady suggests and I shall be its host. Let the lady and the beggars eat with their Prince. But on one condition: that when we shall dance and sing at the meal's end, the lady must dance with you first and then me and must sing for us both."

Maria blushed but the King was highly satisfied with this arrangement, whilst the Prince was delighted that he had successfully managed to ensure he had the exclusive attention of this young, mysterious, magical and beautiful heroine from distant foreign lands who had already won his heart.

The beggars were tongue-tied at first but Maria spoke of the stories of her Master, tales in which all were equal, and they listened attentively, in awe, as she spoke about the strange lands from which these stories came and the miraculous events of her Master's ministry. The young Prince sat back and watched as these simple and humble people unfurled, gaining in confidence in her company. They ate as if this was to be their last meal, heaping food high on their platters, whereas she ate little and did so with care; always ensuring others were satisfied before she served herself.

Then suddenly there was a high-pitched squeal and the head cook came charging into the Hall with a cleaver in pursuit of the piglet of a wild boar. "There goes our supper" roared the King in laughter as it shot under a table. A few moments later and all were scratching their heads for they could not find any sign of it. Eventually, the cook gave up and headed back to the kitchens to prepare an alternative dish to the suckling pig intended for their main course. Longinus looked across the Hall from the top table where the rest of the company were guests of the King and caught Maria's eye then stifled a laugh, whilst the girl reached down and stroked the piglet's ears to keep him quiet as he hid beneath her long chainmail hauberk.

The Prince asked her about her travels, was shocked to hear of her being lashed and her torture at Damascus, was amazed at the places she had visited, proud of her when she talked of her rescue of The Valiant's crew, and then she spoke of the gifts of the Spirit. "I know that you can heal for you healed me" he encouraged her "but are there other gifts?"

She nodded then spoke of the gift of tongues, ability to prophecy and to bring hope.

"You possess all of these?"

Again she confirmed that she did but was then dismissive saying that she had only been given these gifts to aid her in her ministry. "If it were not for my ministry then I would be unknown, have had no adventures, never travelled from Iudaea, would probably be a beggar or perhaps worse, certainly would not have come to Britannia and met you. All has happened because of my mission and I am nothing when you take that away."

The Prince would have none of this: "Maria, my lady, fair one. Have you never stopped to ask why your Master chose you?" and the girl had just looked at him, confused by the question. And so the Prince told her how he felt:

"Even had you not done all these wonderful things yet still would you have conquered my heart. As it is, your Master chose you because you are the right person for your mission and so never doubt your talents for they are real. You are loved and always will be by anyone who meets you."

Then the music started up and the Prince made his apologies to the rest of his table guests who were quite content to continue eating, and held out his hand to claim Maria. "My lady, you are to dance" he said then added kindly "I will cut in after a few moments and promise that the dance steps are very simple." But Maria was briefly in a panic before deciding she must come clean:

"My Prince, can I ask you for the most enormous favour?"

"My lady, as long as it is honourable I would do anything for you" and that brought a smile to her lips and a gleam to her eyes before she said:

"Can you hide this?" at which she reached beneath their table and held up the piglet. The Prince could not stop himself but laughed with joy then beckoned for a servant to join them. "No-one is to know. You are to take this piglet, feed it and then have it delivered to my lady's chamber in the Bower after she has retired for the evening. Above all, make sure the Head Cook never finds out!"

She danced with the King and found that the steps were similar to those she had been taught as a child around the camp fires of the caravanades that would visit Nazareth by Galilee, whose nomads had been so colourful, their tales of the mythical, magical and mysterious had gripped her young heart, whose music had caused her feet to dance and fingers to tap, from whom she had learnt to dance with Kings, her courtly manners and table etiquette as every nomad had been the King or Queen of *somewhere.*

Then she danced with the Prince not once but repeatedly, yet she did not notice that he monopolised her as she laughed in his company, was swung through the air, glided across the wooden floor, gazed into his eyes and lost herself in the delight of his company.

"Must you go?" the Prince asked wishing the evening would never end but alas she nodded for she had made too many promises to stop now. "I shall come back though" and with that the Prince had to be content though he was sorely tempted to follow her on the morrow. Then she kept the other half of her promise to the King and sat before him to sing: two songs from the Duovo of the desert, of love, passion, adventure and the beating of young hearts, whispered, sung breathlessly, then beautifully like the song of the lark in the morning, listened to avidly, heart rending and delightful, a distant echo of souls' searching.

The evening was still young in the Prince's eyes when Maria with a gay laugh admitted that it was already much later than she was used to and would he mind if she retired to bed. "This has been a magical evening and you have been the best company but I am already asleep on my feet and fear I shall collapse. Can you show me to my chamber and then I shall hope to see you tomorrow."

"Where will you go?"

"North then east" she replied "but where? That is for God to decide."

As soon as Maria had retired, and the Prince had only just stopped himself from kissing the girl as she had opened her mouth, yawned and blushed in embarrassment then apologised profusely, the young man went in search of Longinus. First, he asked the Roman to tell him all about the girl and was even more amazed at her adventures and yet so young. Then he asked the burning question: "Where are you heading?"

"Ultimately we are aiming for the farthest reaches of Caledonia as I have a niece to find and persuade to return with me but the route there really does depend as we are being hunted."

"Who hunts you and why?"

"Someone hunts us to slay Maria because they wish to prevent her ministry, her mission from being accomplished. Who? The same people who asked that *you* slay her." And the Prince had the good grace to blush then said: "I do not know who asked my father to attack you but I shall find out. Promise me you will bring her back safe!"

"Why are you so interested in a poor waif from the desert lands of Iudaea?"

The Prince spoke from the heart: "She is not poor but rather she is rich with so many gifts and talents. Wherever she comes from she must be considered a princess amongst her people as she is amongst mine. She has won the hearts of the lords of the Catuvellauni, Dubonni, Corvinii, Atrebates, Durobriges, Belgae, Regni, Hamm, Sales, Glaston and Glevum which together are the largest kingdoms in Britannia, greater even than the peoples of Cantiaci, the Angles of Decea, the Dacian, Trinovantes and the Iceni. I would be held in great respect to win the heart and hand of the lady Maria but that is not why I seek her out. It must be obvious that I love her."

Longinus smiled then replied: "Yes it is obvious yet still it is important to hear you say it. I will bring her back but whether she will accept you or not I cannot tell. Her nature is so giving and loving it is impossible to tell what her heart's feeling is for she is constantly putting her mission above her own desires. Remember also she is still a child" and then the Centurion left the Prince to go in search of Maria. The girl was still awake, the excitement of the evening spinning in her head and she gladly opened her door to her best friend.

"What is it with you and pigs?" he hissed then they both laughed before she showed him how the rescued piglet had fitted in to its new family. "Where do we go next?" he asked her bluntly and she paused then answered reticently to begin with: "I am not sure what I am doing but think we should try and convert the largest kingdoms first. So I am not going further west. Instead I suggest I go east then north. I have heard of the Trinovantes and the Iceni so thought of them next."

"And have you thought of what you will do when your mission is over? Settle down maybe? Marry perhaps?" he tested her but she already had her answer and it left him no more the wiser.

"Oh yes. I thought I might breed wild pigs!"

Longinus and the Prince caught up whilst Maria and the rest of the company were breaking their fast the following morning. The Prince had news and it was not good.

"Maria has made enemies amongst the druid community for turning in one of their brethren in a small town called Bibinari. The man was a sadistic animal and was executed by strangulation yesterday but Maria is blamed for his capture. The druids are powerful in Britannia but the Kings are not frightened of them and now so many hold Maria in such high regard, any risk will be from a curse or assassination.

However, there is another dark force at work. My father had considerable pressure put on him by someone and will not even tell me who it is!"

"It is not Rome, they have already declared their hand, the Emperor is tolerant of all religions; Herod and the Sanhedrin in Ierusalem have no power here, the sicariot likewise; the druids we know about, who else do we face?" the Centurion asked deeply concerned that yet another enemy of the obvious good in Maria's mission had now surfaced. The Prince shared his concern and then let his own fears be known:

"Who or what, they have power and influence and feel threatened. Maria's message challenges all who live by sorcery and magic. We have many mages and theurgists in Britannia, Caledonia, Helvetica, Suevia, Belgica, Francia, Burgundia, Allemandia and Germania. I have heard it said that the warlocks and wizards of this world have a secret order led by their most powerful sorcerers. I fear the world of magic."

Longinus was reflective; if such an order of powerful magicians existed and ruled the barbaric kingdoms from the shadows then Maria's faith and teaching would pose a serious challenge, offering gifts of great power through prayer and attainable by all, not limited to an elite few, but also her faith led people out of the shadows of deceit and into the light of truth. In Maria's world there would be no place for sorcery to hide. Then the answer came to him but alas he knew he could not get Maria to agree. The solution lay before him:

"My Prince, Maria teaches us that magic does not exist that rather we see things we cannot explain and ascribe them to sorcery. She believes that man will one day find a reason for the inexplicable through science. Yet much that her Master does seems magical to my eyes. I struggle often to see the difference! It is important we bring these men of sorcery out of the shadows in which they hide into the light where we may meet their challenge. There is one person who can help us but alas Maria is determined to go north then east and north so I must ask you a favour. Will you go where I cannot?"

"Who is this person?" said the Prince with determination.

"As you love Maria, I know that you will be welcomed with open arms by this man. He must have been approached by the sorcerers and rejected them but he will know who they are. I talk of Prince Godric Bann Caedric Wulfridson, Lord Bann of Salesbray and Hammshire, Prince of the Atrebates."

The Prince gulped then reminded the Roman: "In case you have forgotten, last time we met he chopped me to pieces and slew me. Are you sure my welcome will be warm?"

Longinus grinned then clapping the Prince on the back said: "Welcome to Maria's world. Best get used to the constant uncertainty and never-ending adventure. Prince Godric also loves Maria and has adopted her as his daughter. She wept inconsolably in his arms when she saw you dead. He will not hurt her again like that."

"She wept for me?"

"Don't get your hopes up too high. She would probably weep for your horse too."

The Prince snorted then asked: "Where do you go?"

"We ride for the lands of the Iceni and of King Col and Colin of the Trinovantes to our north and east. We travel north by the Malvern Hills then east by the Hill of Eves, then on to the Chiltons, the How of Marlyn and the Hill of Abin through the middle kingdoms of the Catuvellauni where we will seek the goodwill of the settlements there before heading into the Forests of Wolt and Watha's Ham, Eppen, the Broad Oak and the Burntwood. King Col's kingdom lies beyond Onga's Hall, Dodding, the ford of the Chelmer and Haeddingen. Then the land of the Iceni lies further north still amongst the Fens and around The Wash."

"Wear your armour" the Prince advised. "The roads and tracks you will be using provide many opportunities for ambush. See the lady who is Maria's companion is also protected with a shield and helm at least. The Iceni are the strongest of all tribes south of the Tees and Tyne but they love horses. So take some of your Arab horses with you as gifts and wear your shields where they will be obvious. For the emblem of the prancing pony is respected especially by the Iceni."

Longinus looked next to their arrangements for the long journey ahead. Iosephus had arranged for transport by sea back from the furthest reaches of Caledonia but had made no arrangements for staging posts and accommodation for the journey north from the moment they left South Hamm. The wise and kindly knight had always assumed that once they got to Britannia their route would depend on their reception and had been proven right. Instead, Iosephus had brought sixty horses over by ship and stabled them just north of South Hamm. Six were war horses (just in case). The Centurion had the knight send for six more Arabs to be brought to Glevum and then he went in search of armour for Haladriel.

Maria was all for setting off immediately but was persuaded to wait until the evening when they should be joined by the spare horses, one to be led by each member of the company. Haladriel took one look at the armour and reminded Longinus that she had signed up to be a chaperone for a young girl and not a mercenary soldier fighting for a half-crazed shield maiden out of Celtic legend. "Knew you would be pleased" was Longinus' reply and he walked off leaving her to change.

With a few more precious hours in her company, the Prince took the lady of his love to the Moot Hall and the Map Room there. "My father is one of the few to possess and understand maps. But here, let me show you the secret of this thing" the Prince explained.

Then before her eyes and to her delight, he retraced her journey from Ierusalem to Glevum, the places she had been to, the seas she had crossed and then showed her the vast lands of the northern kingdom of Dacia, the mountainous realm of the western kingdoms of the Situres, Demetae and Ordovicii, the eastern kingdoms of the Trinovantes and the Iceni and the north west kingdom of the Angles. All these things came to life on the battered parchments and the painted clay diaroma on the table before them and Maria was truly grateful. She now also saw the enormity of the distances they must still travel.

As afternoon became evening, they walked the streets of his City and she asked of his ambitions for his lands. She held his arm without thinking, bent near to hear him speak, stopped to talk to any child, taking interest in their lives and their activities, learning how so much of the life of Glevum was taken up with the River: fishing, trading, clearing the banks, maintaining the quays and weirs. All of the children could swim from the earliest age and became excited when Maria spoke of her own journeys across the seas.

The Prince, as was becoming his custom, would watch as his young companion and gentle lady made those around her comfortable in her company. He was imagining her as the future Queen of this land and already he could see that she would be much-loved by the poor, the humble, the warrior and the noble, and accepted by each as one of their own: a leader in both war and peace.

Yet he could see no indication that she loved him anymore than the love she felt for the children or her family of wild boar. He realised he was still to win the heart of this child from Iudaea and one who had no interest in the kingdoms of this world or worldly wealth, already living in the world beyond death, her mind elsewhere. It would take a supreme act of love and self-sacrifice to win his lady love and he started from the weak position that when they first had met, he was seeking to slay her! Surely not something destined to endear him to her? Yet she had forgiven him and wept for him.

Finally, he came to the great square at the centre of the City in which was the covered area that was the epicentre of trade and commerce in his kingdom. A large open timber-framed structure was protected by a straw-thatched roof held aloft by proud upright beams of oak and a huge vaulted ceiling. The sides were deliberately left open as a statement: what went on under that roof was laid bare for all to see. The covered area was paved and accessed by giant steps from all four sides. In the middle of this immense space were the measuring vats that regulated weights and measures for the whole kingdom as well as the acid vats, smelts and long trestle tables with their sets of balances and scales where the quality and value of coinage was determined and new coinage minted.

This was the true centre of government for the Kingdom of Glevum, far more so than the law courts in the Moot Hall or the King's Seat on its dais in the King's Hall: all the more remarkable because it was done in full view of the City's populace. The Prince explained:

"It is essential that our people trust each other when they talk of the value of a coin or the weight of an ounce of grain. Here we set the standard for each."

Maria could see the sense in this and married what the Prince was saying up with her own Master's message: "Your people are never short-changed just as we must never short-change God in our love and devotion to him" she whispered and the Prince looked down into her eyes and said: "You understand so much." But she shook her head at that. The world and the Universe were made never to be fully understood because this way mankind would always seek to discover more and never stop seeking the adventures set by God. "How boring the world would be without adventure" she murmured at a tangent and the Prince had to laugh for only the young at heart would think this.

Although only seven years' older than the girl, Craedech had already seen enough of adventure to welcome a pause, a period of calm, a time to settle down. Yet he felt that there was one more conflict still to be fought in his country as the many kingdoms in Britannia jockeyed for ultimate authority whilst he could sense that Rome was preparing to return and this time they would conquer, where before they had sought peace at their borders whilst they resolved a terrible civil war back at home. What irony it was that his greatest ally in the conquest of the lady of his love should be a Roman Centurion?

King Col and the Mission to the Kingdom of the Trinovantes

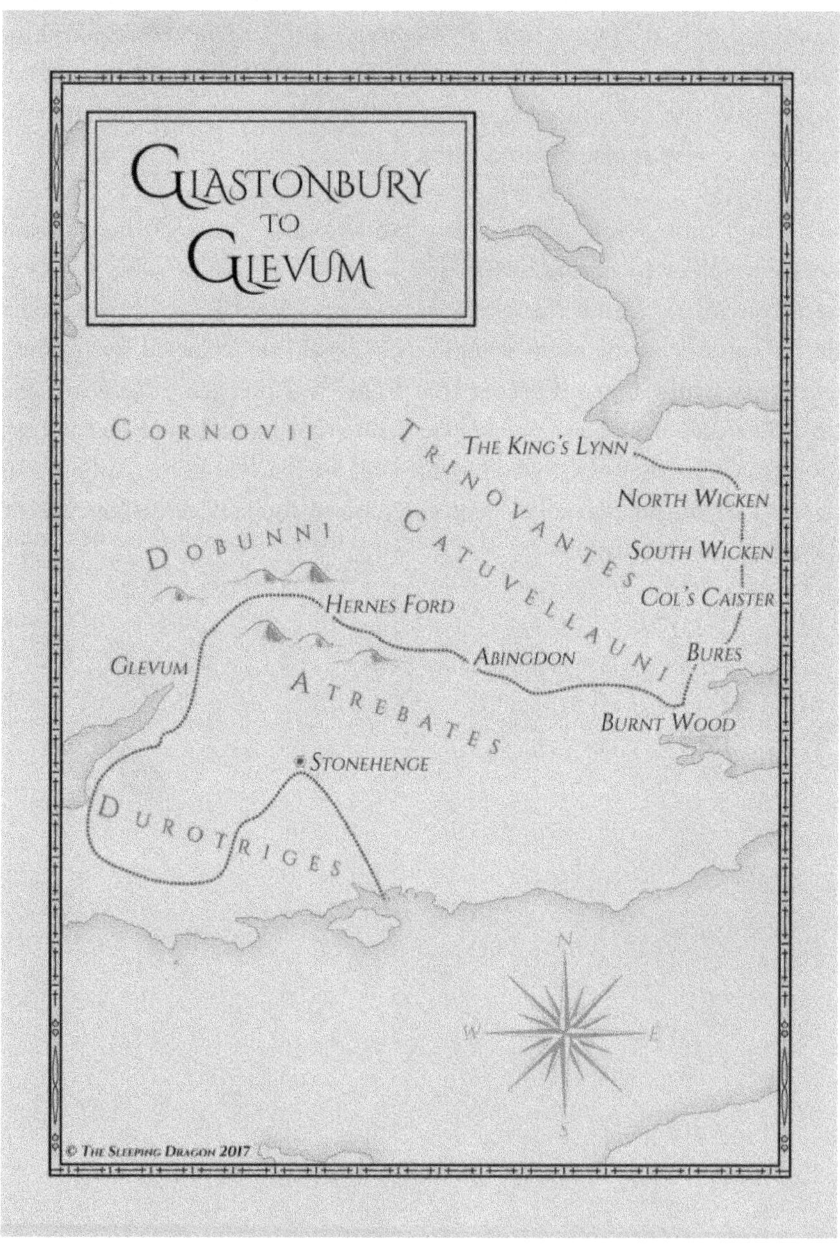

From Glastonbury and Glevum, Maria headed north to Hernes Ford then East towards the Middle Kingdoms of Britannia. King Col had just inherited the whole of the kingdom of the Trinovantes on the death of his brother Colin. He was at constant war with the Iceni. His recent victories had pushed the Iceni out of their homelands around the North Wicken, the rivers Waveney and Yare and the Ouse now formed the new boundary between the two tribes. The Iceni had, in turn, pushed the Dacians back as far as the Humber.

King Col's capital was the fortified camp at Colcaister (Camulodenum) but his largest population centres were Ips or South Wicken on the Or and Deben and North Wicken on the Yare and Waveney.

"Mary converted King Col and his whole kingdom foreswore their pagan Gods and sorcery." (Gallas 7th Century AD)

At last, and with an aching heart, Prince Craedach sent his heroine north along the banks of the Severnus and towards the Malvern Hills where his people had settled on its southern slopes and would welcome the company that night. He knew that when she woke and saw the views to east and west her heart would be won, at least to the unique beauty of this land if not yet to the man who would one day rule them.

Indeed nothing could have more certainly conquered her frail senses and sensitive heart than the stunning panoramic views of the Wolds, Malvern and Chilton Hills, the forests of Abin and Eppen and the west coastline of Britannia, countryside that was both exciting and inviting, unspoilt, full of natural beauty, with rivers and waterfalls, lakes and pools, woodland and forests, fields that were a chequered tapestry of colours bathed in sunlight.

That night they were met by the Lord Herne of Hern's Ford, his stag's head helmet frightening Maria for a moment as she was worried he might be another druid and truth be told it was a frightening mask. But Lord Herne explained that the stag was the symbol of 'Hern', a spirit of the woods, trees and rivers whose ford had become his settlement. He wore the stag's head to honour the past and the legend of his people but he had no connection with druids.

"Come" he said. "Prince Craedech, my brother in law has bid me make you most welcome. We are also great friends and he trusts me more than anyone else. I am to guard you with my life and treat you as a queen: to regard you as more precious than anything else in his kingdom. I have set aside a place for all of you by the fires in my Hall" and he showed her to his Great Hall, not as large as Lord Godric's but it could easily sleep a hundred in comfort and thirty warriors slept in the Hall beneath the south gable to guard them.

Maria was to sleep with Herne's wife in the Bower behind the dais, under the north gable. Herne's wife was in her mid twenties, the family resemblance to her younger brother was uncanny. She was tall, long auburn hair, the same patrician nose and strong chin with high cheekbones and the soft but kindly smile; Maria liked her on sight.

"My wife, the Princess Egtheghbreda" said the Lord Herne proudly and the lady saw straightaway that Maria was almost dead on her feet with fatigue. "Away with you" she scolded her husband taking charge of the girl and helping Maria take off her heavy armour and prepare for bed. Maria was so grateful when she saw the cushions, rugs and silks laid out for her repose that she kissed the Lord Herne on the cheek and then let his wife strip off her armour and leather undershirt, before clambering under a single silk sheet in her linen slip and seconds later was fast asleep.

Longinus apologised: "My lord and lady, forgive her that she lacks conversation and has not shown her gratitude for your hospitality with the courtesy of telling you of her endeavours. She is a child and easily tired. The rest of us, however, are wide awake and more than happy to exchange news and talk of our ventures."

Lord Herne smiled and then admitted: "I was hopeful of some news as what I have heard is confusing and that is putting it mildly. Let us leave the ladies to settle down for the night and talk about my brother in law. The Prince is smitten who has staved off the advances of every princess in over twenty kingdoms until now. I confess that I am bursting with curiosity so ask: what can you tell me?"

Longinus laughed then said: "If your men would like to hear also, I would be happy to tell our tale and answer all questions." Lord Herne was pleased at this and the men gathered around the roaring fire at the south end of the Hall with ale and food being served constantly as they sat in a circle to listen to Longinus, leaving the girl to sleep, Egtheghbreda, her lady in waiting, Haladriel and the family of wild boars as her company, safe beneath the Hall's north gable.

Longinus spoke of their mission and travels, the girl's courage in the face of torture at Damascus and being lashed by the Romans, her rescue of the ship's crew, her constant acts of healing, and the two battles in which she had fought. It was Herne who asked: "Is it true she healed the Prince?"

"The Prince was part of a war party sent to slay her which she defeated in battle and then brought the Prince back to life from the dead after he had been slain by Prince Godric Bann."

"Is she a witch then and has she bewitched my friend?" Herne now asked standing in anger, his hand reaching for his sword but Longinus shook his head and held up his hand asking for peace: "She has no power other than that of prayer. She prays and God often answers her prayers. Not magic but faith in God is what she possesses. When you meet her properly you will see she is an innocent and no more than a child. She would not seek to bewitch anyone yet there is no doubt your Prince loves her."

"Does she plan to take advantage of this?" Herne asked slightly mollified but still seeking to protect his brother in law.

Longinus laughed: "She has not even noticed that he loves her!" at which Herne whistled then grinned suddenly before asking: "At long last a girl Craedech must fight to win when so many have just swooned into his arms. Will she lead him a merry dance?"

"Not intentionally. She loves the Prince but she loves many people and I would say he is currently above a complete stranger but below her family of wild boar in the pecking order of her affections."

"What must he do to win her?" and then grinning to himelf Herne muttered "The poor sap. It will do him good to be humbled" but Longinus corrected him: "Maria would never humiliate the Prince and she likes him. He needs to let her grow up as she currently has no plans to settle down. But once her mission is out of the way then things will be different."

Herne nodded then changed topic adroitly. "All of the kingdoms in the south fear a Roman invasion and see it coming soon and yet we are too divided to be able to resist. When do you think an invasion will happen?"

"Not in Tiberius' reign but that is coming to an end soon. Germanicus will be Emperor next and he will want to attack across the Rhine and the Danube given his name. I would give it no longer than ten years as there is much for which Rome wants revenge."

"Will we hold you off as we did with Julius Caesar or are we too divided as I fear?"

"I think that the western and southern kingdoms are too divided and your war bands are very small compared to the size of a Legion. You count in tens and hundreds where Rome counts in thousands. What you also lack is a leader to unite behind."

"Do not laugh but there is one name already spoken of as a leader under whom all of the West Country and the South would unite."

Longinus looked at Herne puzzled and then replied in his confusion: "I would take such a leader very seriously and as no laughing matter. But who is this King? I have seen no sign of such an alliance between the kingdoms."

"I have said too much" Herne admitted "and will say no more. I express the hopes of those who are more optimistic than perhaps they should be, reading too much into recent events."

Longinus just shook his head even more confused now as he struggled to follow where Herne was taking him. He knew little of the leaders of the various kingdoms and so was in no position to comment on one that might unite the rest: "I am probably too tired but do not understand you at all, my Lord. I can think of no one who would bring the kingdoms together but then I have only met four of your leaders thus far" then he turned to Iosephus and Galahaidra to see if they were any the wiser only to discover that they had both fallen asleep.

"Just us it seems" said Herne with a laugh. "Tell me who you think is chasing Maria?"

Longinus was grateful for the change in subject as he was on slightly more solid ground now and he had given this a lot of thought: "Starting with the obvious: the Sanhedrin in Ierusalem have persuaded the sicariot to put a contract out on Maria; the druids in central Gallia seek revenge on the girl for something I did and she knows nothing about; the Roman authorities have prosecuted her for unlawful assembly but still could charge her with incitement through to insurrection but they tend not to hunt people down, just wait for them to cross a border or enter a town or City that they occupy. Then we have the unknown: the 'someone' who put pressure on Casterix and Caractacus and had to be very powerful to do so."

"Why those two do you think?"

"Godric had warned off many of the smaller kingdoms. The two to send war parties against Maria were the nearest not afraid of the Prince of the Atrebates."

"Which says a lot about Godric's influence. It also suggests that Godric knows who the 'someone' is."

Longinus nodded but there was something still niggling him: "The thing is it was Godric who suggested Maria ask Caractacus who had sent him. If Godric already knew then why send the girl on what has turned out to be a fool's errand?"

With both men scratching their heads over that one, Longinus made his apologies as he was due up at dawn for an early start as they headed for the Hills of Eves and Marlyn's How.

"Do you want an escort?" Herne asked showing his concern. "You have at least three parties out there looking for you and your lady is being very open about her itinerary. You will have crowds the whole way wishing to meet Maria and the chances of another assassination attempt must be high."

"Four men a couple of leagues ahead and four the same behind would be gratefully received" and Herne nodded. He would arrange things in the morning and knew whom he could trust but he had one final request: "Don't leave too early as I have still to meet the Magdalan properly!"

Princess Egtheghbreda and Maria spent an hour before joining the men at breakfast getting to know each other. The girl was incredibly flattered and humbled by the attentions of the princess and loved her on sight: she was so beautiful and regal and all that Maria had ever considered a princess should be like. Maria admired the way she dressed, her jewellery, her demeanour, her manners, her poise, elegance and serenity. She devoutly hoped she could one day learn to hold herself with the calm confidence of this beautiful princess.

Meanwhile Egtheghbreda was gently probing Maria to find out her true feelings towards her brother. She had received a note from Craedech *'who had got himself into a right state'* she mused advising her that he was in love but he needed help as he was not sure the girl he had fallen for loved him.

What she found to her delight was an unaffected and innocent child who was affectionate, kind and loving to everyone, amazingly brave, and driven by a mission that seemed overwhelming yet Maria somehow took in her stride. So different from the pampered and image conscious would be brides Craedech had brought home at the rate of one per month for two years to the dismay of his sister. *'Did Maria love her brother?'* In the end, the princess decided to ask Maria as the girl was always honest.

"Oh yes I love him. He is very nice to me" Maria had replied "and it was truly unbelievable when my Master brought him back to life."

"Yes but … but" and Egtheghbreda did not know what to say next. Maria clearly liked her brother but love was usually a little more *passionate*. Except I keep forgetting she is so young. There were two things she did say to her brother when she next met him: first, she would be very happy to have Maria as a sister in law; and second, if he hurt this child then she would never forgive him.

"What do you think?" Lord Herne asked his wife as they headed to the covered market to break their fast over the open hearth in the main square. It was too hot to eat indoors except in the cool of the evenings so everyone ate outside. Breakfast was hot bread, cereal, milk and honey. Lord Herne took the chance to talk to his wife as they headed across from the Great Hall to sit at the large trestle table that had been laid out for the Lord, his lady and their six guests.

"Probably the most truthful person we shall ever meet and she has been involved in the most wonderful adventures but she is not old enough yet to know her own feelings."

"Would she lead us against the Romans? She already has eleven of the kingdoms prepared to back her?"

"She is so totally against the idea of war that I cannot see any way she could be persuaded to lead us. She is not a rebel and despite her treatment by Rome, I could not draw her to be critical of them. Mind you, I do not think she is critical of anyone or anything. And there is the problem: she is not at all aggressive or angry or resentful so has no urge to rebel against Roma or anyone else."

"And your brother?"

"She is a good choice. I shall be frank: she is so much better than the other girls he has looked at. But she has yet to think about men. She says she loves my brother but in the same way as she might love a pet cat!"

"Introduce me please" and she did. Fifteen minutes later, listening carefully to her quiet voice that was almost a whisper and yet was telling him of the most amazing miracles, events that were world changing, feats of heroism that would be the subject of bard's ballads for centuries, a vision so intense her eyes blazed with the honesty of it, Lord Herne was enthralled. When he had a moment, he turned to Egtheghbreda and whispered: "This one is special. Your brother must tred with care but if he wins the hand of this lady he will be the second luckiest man in the world."

"And the luckiest?" his princess asked with a raised eyebrow.

"Why me of course!" and he kissed her hand.

The middle kingdoms of Britannia were much smaller than in the rest of the country and had resisted the temptation to come together, being proud of their history and independence. The Vale of Eves and the Forests of Abing, Waltha's Ham and Eppen saw dense woodland stretch from the Severnus where the river looped around the moated settlement of Eves across to the Chilton Hills which stood proudly as a natural wall marking the divide between the west and the east of Britannia. The forests then ran north uninterrupted until they reached Sutton on the north banks of the river Deben.

Occasionally, as at Marl's or Marlyn's How, Abin, Dodding, Waltha's Ham, Haeddingen or Bures, a hill-top settlement had been cut from the woodlands that surrounded it, standing tall to look down on a sea of emerald green: oaks, elms and sycamore. In other places such as The Burntwood or Onga's Hall, the settlements were at the edge of woodland and forest marking the beginning of fields for grazing. Then there was the settlement by the fords over the rivers Chelmer and Stour, and the pallisaded Fort built by King Col on the estuary of the river to which he had given his name.

Maria would visit all of these, with the largest settlement being the Fort at Colcaister; with nearly twelve thousand residents whereas the other settlements typically boasted one to two thousands. These were much smaller numbers than she had encountered in Gallia, Hispania, Africa and along the coast of the Middle Sea but with the densest population being on the south east coast in the land of the Cantiani, and around the Wash and the Humber which Maria had yet to visit.

Her journey took eleven days, taking in two settlements each day. Whilst she did not convert as many to the message as she had on the mainland of Europa, what she found was that the spirituality of the people in Britannia was far greater than she had previously experienced with her first encounter with both mystics and contemplative prayer helping her to develop a wider understanding of her own faith; she rapidly found herself as the pupil where before she had been the teacher.

Again she found her message was developing new depth in response to questions but also because she was no longer alone in being in communion with Iesus. Others were sharing her experience and able to spread the word much wider. In Waltha's Ham she met Giselda who was a mystic.

One day she was talking to her Master and Giselda asked to 'join her'. Maria was startled but then Giselda said: "Close your eyes!" and suddenly as Maria spoke to Iesus, Giselda became part of the same conversation.

"Today we take your ministry along another and deeper path" said her Master and Giselda then explained: "I can see your thoughts but also your prophecies. The gift I have been given is to interpret your dreams for you. The message we must give is that through prayer and dedication we can reach a level of communion with God and with our fellow followers. This is still the gift of prophecy but that gift has always needed those who dream and those who understand dreams."

"Think of Pharoah and Ioseph" Iesus explained. "Pharoah dreamt but Ioseph translated the dreams to give them meaning. Both had the gift of prophecy but each had a different aspect of that gift" and Maria did understand.

"So I am Pharaoh and Giselda is Ioseph?" she asked just to be sure.

"Yes" said her Master and Giselda in unison.

"But didn't Pharaoh come to a sticky end or was it a watery grave? Typical! I end up with the bad guy" and she got a fit of the giggles as she said this effectively ending her contact with both Iesus and Giselda.

Giselda had been a seer as part of the druidical circle to which she had belonged before her conversion. Her years of contemplation of the mysteries of nature had developed to become contemplative prayer and she began a whole tradition of mysticism captured as poetry, song, visions and allegories. She found a monastical society at Broad Oak, another at Burntwood and a third she would found at Aeoisyth in each case taking men and women who wished to explore the meaning of their dreams of the Divine and to develop their ability to pray.

Maria was unsure of this development. She welcomed the need to establish more places to celebrate the Eucharist and she herself founded chapels at Marlyn's How, Abin, Dodding and Waltha's Ham as well as endorsing the early contemplative houses at Broad Oak and Burntwood and the large pilgrimage centre at Cressing but she felt that the direction Giselda was taking many followers was more complicated than it need be and offered less to the poor, lame, prisoners and the oppressed whom they had come to save in Iesus' name.

It was Iosephus who reminded Maria of the occasion when Lazarus'sister, Maria, had bathed Iesus in perfumed oil and his other sister, Martha, had said the money was better spent on the poor. "Our service of the Master and his Father must include a place for both praising and conversing with God. Prayer must not just be a constant barrage of petitions." Iosephus explained. "It should not be all about the ministry of healing."

Maria felt suitably chastened yet still she struggled to understand how contemplative prayer was any different from her just talking to her Master?

"Let go!" said Iosephus and the denarius dropped. She had been forcing her faith on others again. Giselda had found a different path … but it was still a path to God just not one Maria was equipped mentally to follow.

What Christianity achieved in the early days as it spread rapidly across the west country and south eastern kingdoms was a level of *unity* that began to give Britannia's war leaders hope as they thought of the Might of Rome on their doorstep. National pride and retaining their independence may not be sufficient incentives for the dozens of small Celtic and Briton kingdoms to come together in mutual defence, but defending a new faith against the paganism of Rome looked to be achieving the unity needed to withstand the invasion when it would come.

There were no attempts at assassination: the sicariot appeared to be waiting for Maria's return to Gallia, not worried if she converted barbarians from paganism to Judo-chistianity. The threat the Sanhedrin had always feared was a massive conversion of Jews to the new faith and that had not happened … or not yet.

The druids had decided that Daedlus had been a bad lot: feeding human sacrifices to octopods was not part of their ritual and as the details of the psycopath's life became public, the Druid Council beat a hasty retreat disowning the mass murderer.

Rome had no interest in a sect of peace-loving religeuse who had no rebellious intent and whose leaders had already been punished. This would change in a few years' time but for now, Maria was still protected by Tiberius' policy of religious tolerance.

Which left?

Craedech had met with Godric and when he explained why he had come the laird had given him an enormous bear hug: "If I were your age I would have married her. I love that girl. As it is, I shall be giving her hand away instead. She is the child I never had and a daughter to make any man proud. She gets the lands of the Atrebates, Durobriges, Belgae and Regni, the shires of Hamm and Salisbrey, and Aer Weight when I die. Now who is after her?"

"I do not know and my father will not say" the Prince answered in deep concern. "Longinus and I hoped you might know."

Godric thought long and hard. He suspected that had he not already sent out his missive to the neighbouring kingdoms placing Maria under his protection, then he would have been the first to be approached.

"There is no-one could put that much pressure on me to do as they wanted. The threat must be specific to the two kingdoms. We had thought they were chosen because they were nearest but there is someone and something else connects these two kingdoms."

Craedech nodded in understanding. This made sense yet still left him in the dark.

From Burntwood, the company headed to Onga, Dodding then Greeting, Inga's Hall, forded the Chelmer and carried on for Witon and Cressing before turning north-west to Haeddingen and finally arriving at their destination of Bures in the kingdom of the Trinovantes.

One thing came to light that sent Longinus into hoots of laughter. On the second day of their travels, Lord Herne sent a message via Hosta, one of the eight men watching over the company and their captain.

'There are no less than four, possibly five different sets of riders following you. All were spotted when my men laid a trap. None of the groups seems to know about the others! Our men will pick up a hostage from each tomorrow and brief you on what we find out.'

The following day, Herne's men picked up five riders who had been following Maria for days: one was employed by Iosephus; another by Tartellus; a third by Amarillus; a fourth by Godric and the last by Craedech. "So now we know" laughed Longinus. "There are no less than six different groups protecting us and none of them knew about the others! It is like a farce out of a Sophocles Play."

They crossed the ford over the Chelmer and headed towards the Royal Seat at Bures where King Col's Hall had been built. To their north east was the Witon and the village of Cressing where Maria dedicated six huge timber-framed buildings that became the religious centre for the large settlements at Greeting, Inga's Hall, Burntwood, Chelm, and Witon as Nicodemus would later write in his history: *'Over ten thousand gathered for a Service of the Eucharist at Cressing.'* Many of the centres and shrines opened by Maria during her first ministry would in later years be re-opened by the Templars in her memory including 'Cressing Temple'.

King Col greeted Maria with fifty of his warriors armed and at his side. He came to meet her on the track from Weiht Col'neii (or Colne) as it climbed the hill through the forests to his Great Hall, a timber-framed rectangular thatched building standing on top of a bailey with watt and dauble walls, plastered over and painted in bulls' blood turning deep purple in the sun. Haeddingen was to the south and the crossing over the Rivers Stour and Brett lay to the north and east. In later years this crossing would be the site of Maria's descendant's flint and brick Castle and also host the first Friary and one of the oldest hospitals in England, opening in 1253.

Longinus was unsure of their welcome as King Col was the most powerful monarch they were to meet thus far on their journeys, with reputedly as many as six to ten thousand warriors at his command. His lands were said to be greater even than those of Caractacus or Godric through his expansion into the lands of the Iceni and Parisi.

As Longinus hesitated, Maria kept walking and thus approached King Col on her own with no escort. She knelt then sat back on her haunches, drew her sword and laid it across her lap. Next she looked unblinkingly into the King's eyes, her fearless blue eyes shining brightly, before carefully removing her helmet and shaking her hair free. It shone as the sun came out from behind a cloud to place its warm benison directly on her head and the King's warriors were dazzled by her visage.

She waited.

After a pause of no more than half a minute, the King stepped forward and offered the young heroine his hand. She rose slowly then kissed him on both cheeks as befitted the greeting of one monarch to another. He laughed then shouted aloud for all to hear: "This lady has no fear. I welcome her with all my heart as a fellow warrior. She preaches peace yet has the courage of the noblest warrior. I would know more of this lady." At which his escort cheered and King Col guided Maria by the hand towards the entrance of his Great Hall.

The Hall was typical of those she had found in most settlements, a tall vaulted ceiling with wall hangings and tapestries on the walls, rugs on the earth floor and several fires beneath holes in the roof. Around the fires were benches of seating or cushions and blankets for bedding. There was a raised dais at the far end of the Hall and Col signalled for a second carver to be placed alongside his own throne then honoured Maria by having her sit at his side. As his warriors lined the walls, Longinus and the rest of the company were shown to the benches around one of the fires.

Col leaned across to Maria and asked her: "Is it true that you defeated the armies of two Kings in two battles on the same day?"

"My Master did this, yes" she replied and he paused in thought before asking: "And it was your Master that brought Prince Craedech back to life from the dead?"

"Yes" and she smiled in acknowledgement.

"Would you fight for me?"

"My lord King, it depends for what it is that you fight. If you seek to save lives and if you will make every effort to avoid harming your foe then I would willingly fight. But I shall not kill."

The King roared with laughter. "You will fight for me but we must both fight with our hands tied behind our backs! How shall we win?"

"We will not win … but God will" and that silenced the King. Eventually he was able to ask: "Is your faith in your God that strong?"

"I do not mind if I die for my God as long as I do the right thing."

Finally, the King began to thaw. He could see her courage and now he understood what drove her. He knew she could fight and that she could heal as well. She would be a worthy addition to any war band, yet she refused to fight except on her terms. He was not surprised at her youth as he had been warned to expect this but her beauty had come as a shock and he recalled how she had dazzled his men. "Why have you come?" he asked at long last.

"I ask permission to speak to your people: to share with them a message of hope and a gift from God. I will force nothing on them and I am no witch to enchant them; rather I offer them a chance to choose to follow my Master or not."

"Your Master defeated two Kings then brought a Prince back to life?"

"Yes."

"Then I would be a fool not to let you talk to my men. If they also have the power of your Master then we will win more battles. But I wish to be certain that your Master will obey me."

"My Master obeys no-one but his father" Maria contradicted the King, standing up for her faith "and is unlikely to lend you aid if victory in battle is your only aim."

But the King had thought of this. At a signal, twenty of his men surrounded her companions. "Do not worry" the King said to her calmly "your friends will not come to any harm and will be sent on their way shortly. They are to be held in my custody to stop them interfering with what I am about to do next."

"Which is?" the girl asked with her chin raised defiantly towards him although she knew that what she was about to face would test her resolve to the limit.

"Why, my dear, you are to be my prisoner for as long as it takes until I can do your magic and if I must hurry you along a bit then I shall torture you in whatever manner it takes as painfully as it must be. Take her away!" and twenty more of his warriors took her by both arms and then dragged her so that her feet trailed on the ground until they had taken her to a cage outside, open to the heat of the day and the cold of the night. They stripped her of her armour and the linen shift she wore beneath then chained her by arms and legs so that she hung suspended, in tears at her nakedness, open to the ravages of the elements. "Seven days in here for a start without food or drink" one of her captors said unkindly.

To her right was a second cage, in which hung the naked body of another girl not much older than Maria, carrying the cuts and bruises from the many beatings she had received. "Be brave" she said to Maria "for when this ordeal is over surely only good awaits us in the next life?"

"Where I go, you go" Maria replied and began to pray. Instantly, her Master was with her. "Help me Lord" she asked "and help my companion also" and she turned her head to indicate her fellow prisoner. "I pray for her soul and that her sins shalt be forgiven."

Her Master replied: "She will be with the Angels within the hour but what is it that *you* wish? You could die and join me for eternity, your mission completed through the faithful communities you have left across Africa, Hispania, Gallia and Britannia. You could live and face the torment of King Col, teaching him through your defiance that your faith is stronger than his evil. Or I can release you as I did once before."

Maria did not hesitate: "Grant me the courage to face this torment" at which the Master smiled then gave her back her resolve with his words. "Maria, my dearest delight, you already carry the courage of mountains when they defy the terror of the mightiest storms. I have no need to grant you courage, for you out-surpass even me in that regard. It is why I chose you. Your ability to hope can defy any evil. Find the courage within you and I promise I will stand by you."

As the first hour passed, Maria heard the last gasp of pain from the poor girl kept captive alongside her and said prayers for her departure, watching and guiding her cleansed soul into the arms of the Angels waiting for her. "Go in peace" she whispered and now she was alone.

Longinus met the Yeorl Corin of Prydain in the forests south of the Stour along the Colne Valley. The Yeorl had been sent by Prince Godric to watch over Maria with twelve warriors and had already sent word of the girl's imprisonment to his lord in his mesne in South Hamm. "Four days and he will be here with an army. Word has also gone to Glaston, Sulis, Glevum, Abin and Waltha's Ham. The Kings of each will come.

Daecus Septimus and Felix Secundus Barius reported in next. Daecus spoke for them both: "Amarillus and Tartellus are too far away to send aid but we are sixteen legionaries between us and at your service Centurion." Longinus smiled for the first time since Maria's capture.

Finally Eorl Hosta, the leader of Lord Herne's escort of eight warriors briefed Longinus: "Lord Herne will hear tomorrow of Maria's capture and give him another day to muster then he will be here as will Prince Craedech in six days' time."

Then Longinus turned to Iosephus. "How many mercenaries can you muster?"

"I have four ships' crews in South Hamm and will send word now. Twenty have been acting as our escort since we left the safety of the Malvern Hills."

"So we have over sixty men at present. How many has Col brought with him?" Longinus asked all of his captains and Galahaidra replied to that:

"He had fifty with him when he met with Maria and I counted another fifty at least at his Royal Seat. If we attack now we face a century at least but when Col gets word that Godric marches this will rise to thousands and may see Maria moved to his Fortified Camp at Colcaister. Once there, we will not see her alive again."

"Can we ambush them on the move?" Longinus asked all of them and from the nods he received in return, this seemed to be their best plan. Hosta added yet more good news: "We can also look to draw on support from Onga, Dodding, Finching, Witon and Cressing within the next two days. Small numbers perhaps one to two hands from each but we may outnumber Col by the time he sets out for his capital."

"Why has Col so few here?" Longinus asked puzzled and the Yeorl had the answer to that: "Although this is his Royal Seat, Bures is not easy to defend and the small settlements around here could not hope to victual a larger army. He brings his best warriors but also in a number that the local populace can feed and not go without themselves. All of the Lords do the same save those whose Royal Seat is also their capital such as the King of the Dobunni at Glevum."

Over the next hour, his captains sent word for their men to gather at Longinus' camp site but to be wary of any scouts sent by Col to watch over them. Craedech's men brought word of the Prince. "Alas he could not keep away and has news from my Lord the Prince Godric that he wished Maria to hear. He will be with us on the morrow with his escort of one hundred of the best warriors from Glevum."

"We have The Spear and The Grael" Galahaidra added. "We can defeat Col if we attack tomorrow night with Creadech's aid."

Longinus agreed then asked his companion: "Can you get into Col's camp and stand guard over wherever she is held? I fear they shall slay her the moment we attack."

Galahaidra's smile told the Centurion all he needed to know. Next Longinus turned to the Yeorl Corin and asked about the defences at Bures.

"We face a wooden palisade atop a steep eight foot tall mound or bailey. There are two watch towers both by the barbican at the south entrance to the Royal Seat. The northern side is partly protected by a loop of the River Stour but the river is shallow in summer and so can be waded through. Oak trees have been allowed to grow by the northern wall to provide shade but they can also be climbed.

I have archers with me and we can take out any guards on the north wall from the safety of the trees then drop down the far side of the wall. We can lower ropes from the top of the north wall and will be inside their camp before our enemy can do anything about it. We will be on foot and face cavalry so our first objective must be to take and hold the enemy's enclosure where they stable their horses. Then we will be mounted and have the advantage."

"Do we know where their horses are held and where Maria is being kept?" the Centurion asked next and Galahaidra then Hosta were able to brief him: "I saw the cages where they keep their prisoners. It is at the furthest point from the entrance to the Royal Seat, behind the Great Hall *and besides the north wall.*"

Hosta went next: "Their horses are kept in an enclosure under the shelter of the same oak trees we will use to gain access to the camp. Within the first minute we will have gained the north wall, horses' enclosure and the cage where Maria is held. Of equal importance is that the Moon shall be full on the night of the morrow. All we need is a clear and cloudless sky and we will have the light we need to find our way whilst our foe sleeps."

Longinus summed up the situation: "All depends then on the Prince's arrival" before turning to Hosta to ask him to ensure that the Prince's troop gained Longinus' camp without being seen by Col's scouts.

As the sun began to dip behind the tallest of the oak trees to her left, Maria sang in praise and thanks for the wonder of another day of life. She had survived the cold of one night, shivering as she prayed for the warmth of her Master's love to hold her, then faced the heat of the sun, burning her frail and fair skin, yet her hair still shone and her eyes blazed clear crystal blue with the love she held for her Master's creation. Her guards left her alone as they could not look upon her, glowing bright gold like a lantern.

At noon, the King approached her accompanied by an old and wizened man with long white hair, wearing a navy blue gown covered in silver stars and the symbol of the crescent moon. He carried a staff with a shrunken head attached at its point, a sharp blade at its base: a weapon as well as a symbol of the magic by which he swore. Col turned and bowed to the man indicating that the warlock had the king's permission to question the girl.

"You have brought the Prince of the Catuvellauni and the Dobunni back to life demonstrating the greatest powers of magic and sorcery. Tell me how you did this and you shall live. Otherwise, your death will be protracted and painful; you will watch your own heart beat as you hold it in your hands; your entrails shall be dragged through your broken rib cage to become bloodied wings upon your back. The drugs I shall force down your mouth shall give you nightmares when you are awake as well as when you sleep. They will keep you alive to bear yet more pain. Ravens shall peck at your eyes and cheeks so that your last moments shall be lived blind and disfigured. There is no hope of escape for you. Your allies are days away, your companions too few to mount any hope of rescue. Tell me all you know and you can avoid all of this pain. You shall still die but painlessly and quickly."

Maria laughed much to the surprise of both men and then explained herself: "Great King and noble Sorcerer, my greatest wish is to tell everyone I meet all about the miracles of my Master. I will gladly tell you all I know whether you torture me or not. Alas it may not be what you seek to hear but it shall be the Truth."

The King looked at the Sorcerer his expression posing the question whether this was enough or must they put the girl to the rack and burn away her fair looks with hot pokers? He confessed to himself that he half wished the girl would resist more and thus he could have the pleasure of inflicting pain on her. The Sorcerer however indicated that they should let Maria speak by the faintest of shakes of his head before turning to the girl and saying:

"Tell us the Truth!"

"My Master is the one and only God, the creator of all things whose powers include the ability to raise the dead to life and to offer the dead eternal life in Paradise. He can heal and he can defeat the armies that are the enemies of Good. To those that believe in him, he gives them the gifts of his Spirit, powers that enhance our ability to pray to God for God's aid. My party of companions carry with us great artefacts that can also enhance our prayers.

In battle on the Vale of Sales I prayed for victory and to disarm but not slay my enemy. With the weapons given to me by God and through my prayers, I defeated two armies. Then I prayed that my Prince should be brought back to life and was granted my wish because my Master could see what I could not until just now: that I love my Prince with all of my human heart."

The Sorcerer was angry at this and threatened the girl once more: "I will render you with such torment and pain that you will wish you had never been born. Do you insist that all is done through prayer? If I prayed would my wish become true?"

Maria could not help herself but started to laugh uncontrollably, the Sorcerer's question showed just how far away he was from understanding the Truth. Eventually, she was able to answer him without choking up with laughter but the tears still streamed down from her eyes as she spoke in a whisper of joy:

"God sees the prayer in our hearts and not the words from our lips. If we act out of love and ask for something that is good and if God can see that we love God, worship him, trust him, believe in him and have faith that he will do as asked then God will listen. But whether God acts is God's decision. Not all prayers are answered but still it is worthwhile to pray. If you pray for personal aggrandisement then God will ignore you. If you pray to harm others then God is more likely to harm you. My prayers are answered by God because I ask for things that God would wish for. I pray that people are safe, not harmed, for peace, and occasionally for my own release."

The Sorcerer laughed in return then turned to Col and said: "Do your worst to this stupid girl but she has nothing to offer us. Her 'powers' are just the workings of the Goddess Fortuna: the turn of the wheel of chance favoured her in two battles. Another time, she would be defeated. If she had any powers then why is she still here as our captive? Surely her God would have rescued such a devout disciple? Grant her pain then kill her. She is to become carrion to be fed to your dogs."

Col did not wait but signalled to two of his men who approached carrying handfuls of hazel branches, stripped but still with thorns attached. Each bundle had been tied such that they could be held two handed and used as a flail. The cage door was opened, and Maria swung round on her chains until her back faced them. The first man struck and the branches whipped across her back and the sides of her exposed ribs leaving a trail of blood where the thorns had pierced her skin and great weals where the branches had flayed her fragile skin. Maria's back arched and the iron bands at her ankles and wrists dug in cutting her deeply.

She bit her lip but that did not prevent a whimper of shock and pain from escaping. And then the second man struck her and she screamed. Already her back was a bloody mess of scratches and scars but the agony would be much greater as the two men struck again, digging deep into the layers of flesh beneath the skin that were vulnerable to such a beating and more painful for the loss of the protection of the outer layer of skin.

At the fifth blow her head fell forward as she fainted and Col called a halt to her beating:

"Give her the drugs then when she wakes begin again. Call me when she begs for my mercy" and then the King and the Sorcerer walked off whilst one of the warriors took a small amphora full of a black liquid that smelt of rotting offal and opening her mouth forced a quarter down her throat. Maria's eyes sprang open and she screamed once more, this time in terror.

Maria found herself standing in the fires of Hell, demons mocking her nakednesss and pinching her, making her twist and turn as her skin began to curl away from the bone as burning flesh. Her eyes boiled to colourless white orbs, yet somehow she could still see as her Master was suddenly with her and held out his hand. She took it asking as she did so:

"How are you here my Lord? I am taught that you cannot enter Hell."

The smile he gave was brighter than the fires around her and she glowed in response driving the demons away and squashing the fires that spluttered and died. He answered her: "This is a dream but I am here to protect you from the horrors of your own imagination. Be brave and all will go away."

At which she woke and smiled at her tormentors before saying: "I forgive you for everything you have done and will do. Do not fear for me!" at which they looked at each other then stepped back afraid, not understanding why the drugs were not working, frightened that she was casting a spell on them. Indeed such was their fear that they dropped the amphora, its contents spilling out onto the ground as they did so, and ran for the protection of the Sorcerer. Meanwhile, Maria sang with joy, for the moment the pain of her back injuries forgotten as she rejoiced in the continuing love of her Master.

The girl was left alone to suffer the cold of another night. None of Col's warriors would go near her whilst the Sorcerer was exasperated with their superstition and kept saying: "She has no powers!" but he could not convince Col's warriors for they had seen the fearlessness in her eyes and knew it showed an inner strength which terrified them.

As the sun finally disappeared, the cold struck the sorry remains of the skin on her back that had been flayed so deeply her ribs showed through in places. The bitter cold bit into her exposed flesh as deadly daggers digging deep. She tried to pray but the tears of pain drowned out her words of praise. "O Lord" she finally whispered "let the pain not hide my love for you" and then she fainted once more to be taken to a place where her Master's Angels could care for her as she suffered.

The shadows guarded her as she slept, the sentries on the northern wall staying clear of her, granting her peace from their fear of her. There were four on the northern wall and one guarding the enclosure below. None saw Galahaidra, his face was blackened, his garb was black and he wore a black hood. He reached the north wall and climbed up the palisade silently using iron hooks mounted on his black gloves and leather boots to gain purchase.

He reached the top just as one of the guards looked over the wall. A quick blow with his sharp sicarius, a clean thrust through chin to brain and then he had flung the man over his shoulder to land in the mud of the ditch below him. The dull thud did not carry beyond the bailey but was the signal for the archers who sent four arrows at each of the remaining sentries on the north wall's ramparts.

They all fell and as they did so, Galahaidra vaulted over the wall and dropped feet first to land on the guard in front of the enclosure. One swift blow with his dagger and the man fell without a sound; the horse enclosure was his.

He looked around and no-one had seen the assault as yet. Then looking up to the trees above the north wall he saw the first four warriors drop down on ropes tied to the braches of oak trees, covered by twelve archers who had already scaled the wall and were instructed to take out any warrior that moved towards either the horse enclosure or the north wall.

Galahaidra walked into the enclosure, stroking the horses to avoid spooking them and selected a large war horse, a stallion standing at nineteen hands with a proud Roman nose and wild eyes. He led the horse out of the enclosure, took the Spear shaft and shield from the sentry he had slain and removed the spear-point from Longinus' pilum from the straps on his back then rammed one sharp end into the shaft and held it as a lance. Then resting both the Lance and his shield against the enclosure fence, he mounted the horse before picking up the Lance and shield once more. Now he was ready and he rode to where he could see Maria hanging by her chains within the cage that was her prison, her bloodied and naked back towards him.

Such was his anger at the sight that the Spear of Longinus came to life at the point of his Holy Lance to burn fiery red as dragon's flame. The sight of the fire from the Lance woke the whole camp and the warriors standing on sentry duty at the barbican and on the east and west walls sounded the alarm. But they were too late for already twenty of Craedech's men headed by the Prince and Longinus were at the enclosure and choosing horses to saddle up and mount.

King Col burst out of his Hall to see his camp was assailed. As yet unsure who and how many, he called his warriors to hold the Hall whilst summoning more aid from those who slept. But each minute that he wasted mustering gave Craedech and Longinus the time to bring their own troops over the northern wall.

"Slay the girl" screamed the Sorcerer and at his command ten men ran to do his bidding only to be confronted by the ire of Galahaidra. He did not wait but charged and as he did so his lance sent out flames from the fires of the final judgement, brimstone that stuck to their faces and burnt them to the bone whilst sending shards of flame to burn away their lungs. All ten fell and the rest of those mustering saw this and cried in terror, many running towards the barbican seeking to escape through the gates, only to be beaten down and slain by the sentries.

The Sorcerer looked to cast a spell. Before this night, the sight of this had so frightened his foes that they would run at the sight of his conjuration; fear doing the work of magic. He cast flames from his fingers and pointed his fire at Galahaidra but the young sicariot did not believe in simoncy for he held the real thing in his own hands. He charged and slew five more warriors before towering over the terrified Sorcerer.

"Your life is saved because I need to know whom is your master" the young champion said to the Sorcerer and then he plunged the lance into the warlock's gut who fell fainting from the pain of a wound to his stomach but not yet dead. The warriors around him scattered only to fall foul of a cavalry charge from Prince Craedech in whose eyes only the fury of death could be seen. The Prince had also seen Maria hanging as if dead and fearing the worst now sought death for all in Col's camp. He would leave the King until last but Col would die.

Longinus and Iosephus lifted Maria down from her chains and lowered her gently to lie on her side on the ground then covered her quickly to protect her modesty and save her from the cold of the night. The old equites wept at the sight of her deep cuts to her back, ankles and feet. Yet still she lived.

"We can heal her" Longinus reassured the old man and gripped the knight's hand to show the sincerity of his belief that they could aid the girl. The knight nodded then replied: "Whilst she sleeps let us take our revenge for if she were awake she would never approve of the slaughter we shall commit."

The King stood before his Hall his best and bravest warriors around him yet already they were afraid at what they had seen and they had not yet met a fraction of the strength that Craedech was now about to throw at them. Only the news that Maria lived would temper the anger of the Prince of Glevum. He was still seeking vengeance as were all of those who stood with him.

Col's war band was down to just under sixty warriors all on foot; he faced one hundred and sixty including cavalry and archers. He also faced the magic of The Spear and The Grael. Then, just as the Prince was about to sound the charge that would have seen the massacre of Col and his men, one small girl, wearing a blanket to cover her nakedness, wincing when it rubbed against the wounds on her back, walked between both armies and whispered as the wind: "Stop!"

All stood in silence at her almost silent command and slowly weapons were lowered.

"What is your will?" the Prince asked both joyful to see her alive yet how he wished to hold her and smooth away the harm done to her with his gentle kisses and caresses.

"I forgive these people for the harm done to me. I came to give them the chance to listen but it was never my will that we defeat or conquer them."

"They took you captive and tortured you" Longinus shouted at her unable to believe she could still forgive them but she turned and blew him a kiss then said:

"And they were defeated when they did so. They turned to the forces of Evil and they hoped thus to conquer Good. Yet still I defied them and would have done even until my death. I thank you for rescuing me but ask that you forego any vengeance on my behalf. I do not deserve this whom am but a simple girl. If we slay them now not only are their souls lost forever to the chance of redemption but we will have turned an act of Good into an Evil memory."

"What then shall we do?" asked her Prince looking at Longinus as he did so in confusion and watching as the young man unhelpfully shrugged his shoulders, equally clueless. Maria answered them both:

"We should ask King Col what he wants. We have shown that his Sorcerer has no power when facing the forces of Good. The King can still follow the evil in his heart or he can take this chance to choose the good in his soul."

"How?" asked Col in wonder at what was happening but also in admiration at the resilience of this girl whom he had flayed almost to death yet still she forgave him. This was real power and he craved it.

"Let me speak to your people: in your capital and the surrounding settlements. And in years to come let the name of 'King Col' conjure up the memory of a man who did good deeds, who succoured the poor, healed the lame and the crippled, kept no-one as captive, tortured no-one, and was admired and loved by all."

"Your magic can do this?" he asked lips quivering at the thought.

"No" she replied "but the magic already inside you can. My Master can awaken the good in all of us."

"How?" he asked once more.

"Through the breaking of the bread" she replied without hesitation. "If all will lay down their arms then I will show you now" and slowly a few did do so, dropping on one knee, almost in genuflection, to place their weapons on the ground. The cavalry dismounted and suddenly there was a rush as all placed their weapons on the ground before them eager to see this new 'magic'.

"I need some bread" Maria asked quietly her request falling falteringly onto the dark shadows of the night to be answered by several who had bread either in their saddle bags found as they had saddled up their horses or remembered as leavings from supper and still sitting waiting on the trestle tables in the Great Hall. Soon a great pile of bread was before Maria. She took one piece then said:

"This is not magic but rather a promise made by God to each of us. On the day my Master was taken prisoner, he took some bread, gave all of those at supper with him a piece" and she broke the bread and passed it around then lifting her piece and inviting them all to do the same said: "Repeat his words after me: 'This is me. Take my bread and break it and when you do so, remember me.' If we do this then you, Master, will come to us as you promised."

Out of the dark of the night, a comet descended and the light of Jupiter shone brightly high above their heads as a shard of silver to turn Maria's hair into a beacon of starlight. The Spear glistened gold in Galahaidra's hand, the stone of The Grael glowed cream and mauve as Iosephus took it out of the cedar box he had commissioned especially for it and placed it humbly at Maria's feet.

Then the light of the Spirit came down on her and her hands were alight with tongues of fire, her eyes blazed the blue of a summer's sky as she saw the future and gasped then spoke and all understood her whether they heard in their native Celtic, Briton or Latin.

"One day a Roman Emperor will be born in Col's castle of Colcaister and his mother shall be a British princess and he will turn all of the Roman Empire to follow the Christ, Christos, who is Iesus of Nazareth and my Master" she prophesied then collapsed as the flames of the Spirit burnt through her leaving her translucent, her skin so thin and frail that Longinus who was first to get to her feared she was gone. "She breathes" he said in relief to Craedech, Col and Galahaidra who stood over them both. It was Col who spoke next:

"She has seen a vision of my descendants ruling the Roman Empire. To make that dream come true I will gladly follow her Master. Teach us how to 'break the bread' and we will do it in her honour and that of her Master. She need fear us no longer for she has given me far more than I had ever asked for. She has given me the future."

Craedech carried Maria to where Iosephus now held The Shroud and The Robe. The knight spoke first: "The Spear and The Grael are needed also but wrap the girl in The Shroud, cover her in The Robe then call on all of these good people to join in a prayer for her healing."

"Who shall lead us in that prayer?" Longinus asked and it was Galahaidra who answered: "The person who must most want her to be healed. Prince, you must lead us" and the Prince's eyes shone at the honour and the chance to repay Maria for her own healing of himself.

They wound The Shroud around her, lay her head on The Grael as if it was her pillow, placed The Robe over her and the Spear in her hands. Then the Prince invited all to bow their heads in prayer and was gratified as without asking all knelt in honour of what they sought to achieve.

"My lord and master, my God, here is your daughter, loyal to you even at the risk of her life, harmed when she stood up for her belief in you, forgiving those whom harmed her. We are come to ask for the power of your healing that she may continue in her ministry and to be loved by those around her."

As he prayed, the four artefacts from the last moments of Iesus' life came alight once more and the golden thread of God's healing grace wove a net around the girl. The broken skin on her back, around her wrists and ankles was healed without sign or risk of infection. The pain receded to nothingness. Her eyes opened and into the silent anticipation of the many united in prayer she whispered for all to hear: "This is God's peace: that those who were once foes now are united in prayer. Thank you God for this the greatest of your miracles."

The Prince held her in his arms, his tears drenching her yet she did not mind for she had discovered the secret in her own heart: she loved this man beyond all other riches on Earth. Hesitantly, Craedech went to kiss her on the lips but she could not wait and opening her own mouth bent forward and met him on equal terms as it would always be for the rest of their lives. "I thank God for this miracle also" the Prince whispered for her ears only and she blushed.

The Prince lifted Maria, bemoaning briefly how feather-light she had become, and carried her to his horse. Sitting her in the saddle he then led her back to his camp, escorted by his warriors and those of his companions, leaving Col to honour his own dead and send messages to Colcaister to be ready to receive the Lady Maria the following evening.

When he arrived at the camp where Longinus and Hosta had first planned Maria's rescue, he had a campfire lit then carried Maria as if a child to lie down by the fire, wrapping her in blankets to be warmed through after her two nights naked and in the cold. He lay down besides her but could not sleep for fear that somehow he lose her again. One hundred and sixty warriors camped down around them, each also guarding the girl with their lives.

And Maria fell immediately into sleep and as she did so, she dreamt, but no longer the drug induced nightmares but rather of her Master alive, smiling at the peace he had achieved through her healing whilst she was secretly proud of herself that she had made the right decision when offered the chance to be rescued and refusing. "Well done" said her Master and he granted her one final gift of that day: as she fell into the deep and dreamless sleep she needed to recover from the terrors of torture.

As soon as the girl was asleep, the Prince, Galahaidra, Longinus and Hosta had their prisoner brought forward. The Sorcerer had been roughly treated by his escort, all of whom had seen Maria as she had hung in chains, her back stripped of flesh, a mass of blood and torn sinew. They were still angered at the memory of the torture to which the girl had been subjected and had worked out that anger on the warlock. He had few visible bruises to show from their assaults but he carried himself carefully and struggled to stand straight. He was subdued and wary, frightened even when he saw the Prince remembering the anger in his eyes. He also knew Galahaidra was quite prepared to kill him and so began with a request:

"I will tell you all that I know if you will promise me that you will let me live."

The Prince looked at the others and especially at Galahaidra. Eventually all, including the young assassin had indicated their agreement and the Prince was able to say: "You have our word that you will not be slain if you answer our questions truthfully and comprehensibly to the best of your knowledge. I do so swear!"

The Sorcerer nodded, smiled even, and said: "I am satisfied. Ask your questions" and Longinus led off:

"There are a number of enemies of Maria seeking her life: the Sanhedrin in Ierusalem; the Druid's Council and the Roman authorities. But we think that there is one other party seeking her death. Would you know who that is?"

"Yes"

"Did this party put pressure on the Kings of the Durotriges and Castuvellauni?"

"Yes"

"Who put pressure on these Kings and how were they able to do so?"

"There is a Supreme Council for all who profess to do conjuration or magic whether they be druid, shaman, wizard, witch or warlock. There are seven circles for those who do magic ranging from the outer rim to the innermost circle of the Supreme Council. The seventh circle is for those who are apprentices, adepts or do little magic such as the monks of some orders and bards when they seek to motivate other warriors through their singing. The sixth circle requires the conjurer or magician to go through an initiation ceremony and from that point the sorcerer knows of the existence of the Circles and either dies with that knowledge or swears an *unbreakable oath* to keep its existence a secret.

To progress through the circles one must earn promotion through demonstrating the power of our magic but also the influence that one can exert on the politics of the day. So we have two of our innermost Circle currently advising the Roman Emperor on astrology and divination, another interpreting the Emperor's dreams. I was advising King Col and two of my brethren were advising Kings Caractacus and Casterix.

Maria is seen as a threat: she is the most powerful mage we have encountered yet she is not part of our Circles. Or maybe she is not a magician but rather is genuine in her belief in God. As people turn towards religion they will turn their back on our magic and see through our signs and symbols as the tricks they really are.

Therefore we sentenced her to death and sent two Kings to slay her which should have been enough as she had little escort. How wrong we were! Next she falls into our hands at King Col's Royal Seat at Bures. Again we underestimated the support she now has and we were defeated."

"Where can we find the Supreme Council?" and this time it was the Prince's turn to ask.

"We meet all around the country but always the same day: the first day of the New Moon. Our next meeting is to be at the 'seven oaks' in one weeks' time. There will be eleven only unless you release me to be the twelf?"

"Take him away" countered Longinus. "He has told us enough for one night. There will be other nights and other questions so make the most of your time here with us" at which the Sorcerer was returned to his cell in the cage that had originally been used for Maria's safe passage but Maria had insisted she would prefer to ride with the Prince.

They set off early for Colcaister seeking the road north to the Hill of Assin and the Vale of Nay's land then east to Colcaister. They sent word to the Lords Herne and Prince Godric Bann Caedic who were due to arrive in two days' time to head north to Colcaister. Prince Craedech had heard his father was coming from Glevum to the lands of the Trinovantes and pleaded with him to stay at Marlyn's How to await events there.

He also sent a private letter to his sister with news he knew would delight her yet given the importance of that which he sought, he must still take the utmost care. He was aiming for the greatest treasure in the world and he feared a happy ending. *'Such happy endings only happen in legends'* he mused *'real life can not be so kind surely?'* Then he remembered that his best friend and brother in law would be joining them soon and laughed. *'Ha'* he thought *'I may have won the lady after all; despite all your pessimism!'*

As they were about to depart, word came that King Caelderac of the hill fort at Abin, together with war bands from Marlyn's How, Eppen, Waltha's Ham, Onga, Dodding, Finching, the Broad Oak and Burntwood, supported by King Ingen of the fort at the ford of the Chelmer with war bands from Witon, Margreeting, Inga's Hall and Cressing were just two hours away.

"Send them word to ride north to Colcaister. They will come from the south just as we come from the west. We are no more than twenty five leagues away to the west of Col's capital and they are just thirty leagues to the south. We will both arrive around the tenth hour."

"Where do we go from Colcaister?" Galahaidra asked once he had got Longinus, Felstum and Iosephus to one side. Haladriel was riding with the Prince and Maria and at the moment nothing was going to separate the Prince from his prize. He was sitting there transfixed as the girl told him of her mission, the new shrines and places of worship she had established, her capture and torture then her rescue and all spoken of with the charm and wide-eyed excitement of a child when talking about her latest toy or a visit to see the animals in their cages at the Coliseum or the circus entertainers in the Arena. He listened to every word, his pride in his future wife, or so he hoped, growing as he did so.

Iosephus had traded along this coastline and knew it well so talked as they rode, impressing them with his knowledge but also helping the time pass by as they headed east.

"Col's kingdom now stretches north into the lands of the Iceni and west into the lands of the Catuvellauni. The East Lands as his kingdom is sometimes known start really at his Royal Seat here in Bures then used to reach as far north as The Waveney but now reach The Wash. He has four large settlements and then lots of minor settlements clustered half to one day's ride from trading ports and river crossings. The main settlements are the two 'Wicken' or 'Wich' (meeting places and places of government, originally places for an assembly hence the name and once kingdoms in their own right before falling to the Iceni and most recently to the

Trinovantes). One is known as South Wicken or Aeps Wicken and the other as North Wicken or Nor Wicken.

Then Col has built his main garrison fort at Col Caister, Col's Castle or Colcaister, making a third large settlement except it has never been a centre for government, just a military base and trading post, so has not earned the title of 'Wicken'.

The fourth large settlement and the point furthest to the north of Col's kingdom is the settlement of Col's Lynn, sometimes called LynCol or Lincol, at the far end of the river Lynn with his largest trading port being his Royal Seat at the mouth of the Lynn known as King's Lynn. Both are in the very heart of Iceni territory but Col has recently defeated the Iceni in battle twice and won territory as a consequence.

He fears to lose Lincol as it is surrounded by the Shere Forest and isolated from friendly neighbours, the nearest being at the settlement at the ford of the Stam almost a day's ride away and also taken from the Iceni. Lincol costs Col more to defend than he can ever gain by holding it and he may yet surrender it.

The King's Lynn at the mouth of the Lynn is another matter being a very successful and prosperous port and destined to grow in trade and prestige. That he will fight to keep.

When you look at any map, and we should get Prince Craedech to show us a map from his father's collection one day, these territories are huge and the biggest threat Col faces is from the north and west. This is another reason why Col was not escorted by thousands when we met him at Bures. His army will be patrolling his borders with the Iceni so will be in the Fens and around The Wash or several days' ride to our north.

Where then might we go next? First, there are settlements to our east at Mal's Hill, the Leas of West and East Merse, along the banks of the Blackwater, at the mouth of the rivers Roe and Cole, then out to the Place of Frin, Walta's Ham and the Naze or north to the Vale of Otley and the Isle of Shote as far as Deben's estuary and the ford of the Or. We can ford the Deben inland near the settlement at Bran's Hill or take the ferry to the Royal Seat of Aeps Wicken (Aepswich) is just twenty leagues north of Col's fort here at Colcaister then head for Sudh Hill and The Hoo that sticks out into the mud and sand flats along that coastline.

Then we head either north along the coast: to the Wolds, the Ness and Alde, the Wick, north mouth or lowest end of the Orf, Reedham, the mouth of the Yare, the lea of Mundes, Crom's Mare, and west towards the Royal Seat at the mouth of the Lynn then into Iceni country and The Wash.

The alternative is to go directly north: there are many small settlements on the road north from here to Diss and North Wicken. We can go inland to the market by the river Stowe then to the ford of the river Yox or north east to the settlement at Diss and on to the large settlement where the Yare and the Waveney meet at Norwicken from where the road goes west to the Bay of Wiss and north around The Wash, fording the Stam, towards the Shere Forest and King Col's furthest northern settlements on the far reaches of the river Lynn. We can even go west then north to Thwaite's ford, the Isle of Ely, Dere and then King' Lynn. It is Iceni country from the moment we leave Norwicken or King's Lynn and head towards Wiss.

I think Maria will want to see all of these places but we can visit much of the coastline on our way back from Caledonia when we will be travelling by sea anyway. I vote we go north by land by the quickest route as we need to meet the Iceni, the Angles of Deca and the Dacians. Maria should ask some of her many followers to do the coastal route and prepare the way for her return by sea at a later date. If she can do Colcaister and Norwicken then that will have been a huge achievement in itself as the two cities represent half of Col's populace."

"Why are the numbers we have met so small?" Longinus asked wondering if they were missing some large population centre. He expanded on his concern: "Col's kingdom represents one of the largest kingdoms in Britannia yet the number of warriors he can raise is six possibly as much as ten thousand and his subjects, including his slaves, is perhaps one hundred thousand at most. We saw twice that in Damascus and Marsela's population was in the millions. Have we missed somewhere important or will we see larger numbers as we go further north?"

"The total population in the whole of Britannia is less than that of the City of Roma" Iosephus replied which stunned Longinus into silence for the rest of their ride.

Soon after this, the company had their first sight of Colcaister. They had seen much larger cities in their journeys around The Middle Sea but in the context of the small villages and cities they had seen elsewhere in Britannia, this was both the largest settlement and the largest defensive feature they had come across.

The City was defended by a twenty foot tall wooden palisade with four huge defensive towers at each corner and four gatehouses facing east, west, south and north. There were also three river gates for the Rivers Roe, Col and Lea. The palisade was square and each wall was one league in length. In the centre was a steep hill on which the citadel had been built, a smaller stone and flint Keep surrounded by a motte and a second ditch, around which a mound had been built with pointed stakes facing outwards. A narrow path, three men wide, snaked around these obstacles, crossed the motte by a wooden bridge before reaching the arched gateway to the Keep at the top.

One thousand men could hold the mound, one hundred was the maximum capacity of the Keep and four thousand men could man the walls at any time, another fifteen hundred were needed for the four towers, four gatehouses and three river gates. There were enough timber-framed halls and wooden huts within the fort for fifteen thousand residents. Including the four to five thousand warriors stationed at the fort and their families who shared their posting the resident population was currently around twelve thousand but with five to six thousand either trading and at sea or on defensive duties elsewhere at any time.

The City boasted a vibrant market dealing in silver, silk and fish especially oysters so many of its residents spent much of their time fishing at sea or in the mud of the Colnei estuary or on the mainland trading silver for other precious goods and commodities. Britannia would earn a reputation for its silver that was at odds with what the Romans would actually find when they invaded and the traders along the east coast were mainly responsible for Britannia's wealth in precious metal being embellished and exaggerated.

As they went to descend from Nacta's Hill towards the west gate, they also caught sight of the Army of the two Kings approaching the south gate. "Best we join up" Longinus suggested to the Prince whom as the most senior noble was technically in charge but everyone looked to Longinus for their orders. The Prince nodded then sent one of his outriders to speak with the two Kings whilst he directed his own troop to circle south then east to join up with Kings Caelderac and Ingen.

Half an hour later Prince Craedech was leading a war band of five hundred and twenty, on his left hand side was the Yeorl Corin of Prydain and the Princess Maria the Magdalan in her chain hauberk, helmet and carrying her shield once more, having been gifted her armour back by King Col, her sword was in its scabbard and she held the Holy Lance on which was the spear point from the pilum of Longinus, with The Robe as her banneret, The Grael and Shroud in her saddle bags, her eyes blazing bright blue with joy. On his right hand side were the Catuvellaunian Kings Caelderac and Ingen and behind him rode Longinus, Galahaidra, Felstum, Iosephus and Eorl Hosta.

The south gate was opened without hesitation and the company rode into the City of Colcaister to be greeted in the small square behind the Gate by King Col, alone without escort but bravely showing that his intent was peaceful and honourable. To his intense surprise and great joy, Maria leapt off her horse turned and handed her lance, shield and helmet to Galahaidra and Hosta to hold, then ran into Col's arms and hugged him.

"Thank you" she whispered so that only he could hear then holding his hand asked him: "Show me this City and let me meet your people" which he was more than happy to do.

Huge crowds began to gather whilst Col and Maria walked through the maze of the City's streets: not laid out as a square grid as she had seen in the romance cities on the mainland but curved around natural features and with extensions built to house growing families or wealth. Narrow streets and big wide open spaces for the cattle auctions plus three rivers to navigate and which had led to a network of canals and bridges that had been turned into houses sitting on the waterways. It was chaotic yet homely and at the end of her hour's tour, Maria was in love with Col's castle and could not wait to meet its people.

Ten thousand came to see her in the large assembly place, a square with covered seating at one end but able to take the numbers if all stood. Maria spoke for half an hour of the life of her Master and the events leading up to then after the breaking of the bread. Next she led them in a short service of forgiveness followed by the Eucharist and finishing with her prayer of blessing.

As they had walked around the City she had noticed that there were no beggars and asked Col directly 'why not?' He had explained that the blind, lame and crippled were looked after by their families or if not by their war band if they had fought or been part of the King's army and if without family and not been a soldier then his administration ran Houses of Healing. At her request, Col took Maria to one of the Houses of Healing and she was impressed with the caring attitude of the staff and the cleanliness of these places of care and nursing.

She asked the staff to come and to bring those they cared for to the service at noon also. Twenty-two blind, lame and crippled residents were brought by their carers and at the end of the service Maria invited them to the front of the gathering. Several of the soldiers Craedech had brought with him had been at Maria's service at Glevum and three had been filled with the Spirit and granted the gift of healing as had the Prince himself and Galahaidra but in the latter cases they had needed the Spear of Longinus to give them sufficient confidence to make the attempt.

So Maria took Craedech's and Galahaidra's hands then leading them both towards those who had been brought from the House of Healing she said to the two men:

"It is important these good people see that there are healers other than just me. This way those filled with the Spirit and granted the gift of healing will be willing to pray to God for his healing without my presence. They need to be directly in communion with God rather than make that contact through me."

Then she lifted their hands and lowered them so that they were each touching the head of one of the infirm. Maria prayed for the gifts of the Spirit to come down on the whole community and both men suddenly stood straight, their backs arching as if struck by a bolt of lightning, tongues of fire on their foreheads and flames of white light coming from their fingers to trigger the healing in the old man and young woman before them.

The old man had been crippled since birth but now his legs were seen to straighten and he stood steadily on both feet without any aid whilst the young woman had been blind from birth and now gasped as she could see saying:

"It is nothing like how I imagined it; so much more complex. Colour! I now understand the wonder of colour and it is all so bright it dazzles."

Twenty-two were healed, three by Maria but the rest by five 'helpers' including Galahaidra and the Prince. The person moved the most by all of this was Craedech who enthused as he asked Maria: "I begin to understand you more each day but this … how wonderful to be able to heal and how humble it makes me to realise God's infinite power compared with the little I can achieve without him and the great things I can achieve with his aid. How do you remain so calm with all this energy flooding through you?"

Maria laughed then confessed: "The first time I was filled with the Spirit I ran up and down three mountains and could not stop shouting with joy and singing but fortunately it was a windy day so no-one saw me and my words were blown away!"

Then they both laughed and she leant into him as he held her close. Looking up briefly she whispered for him only to hear: "I am glad of today. I want you to understand me better and I think you now do. Be patient with me, my love, for I cannot explain things well so need you to bear with me."

He whispered back: "I already love *everything* about you. You have nothing you need explain. I will love you whatever you say or do. I am happy to learn more about you but you need never fear if you cannot explain something for I am in awe and wonder at all you do!" and they kissed, at which the crowd of ten thousand who had been watching as they healed the blind, lame and crippled, cheered at the Prince's kiss and the girl's subsequent embarrassed blushing.

Heading North for the lands of the Iceni

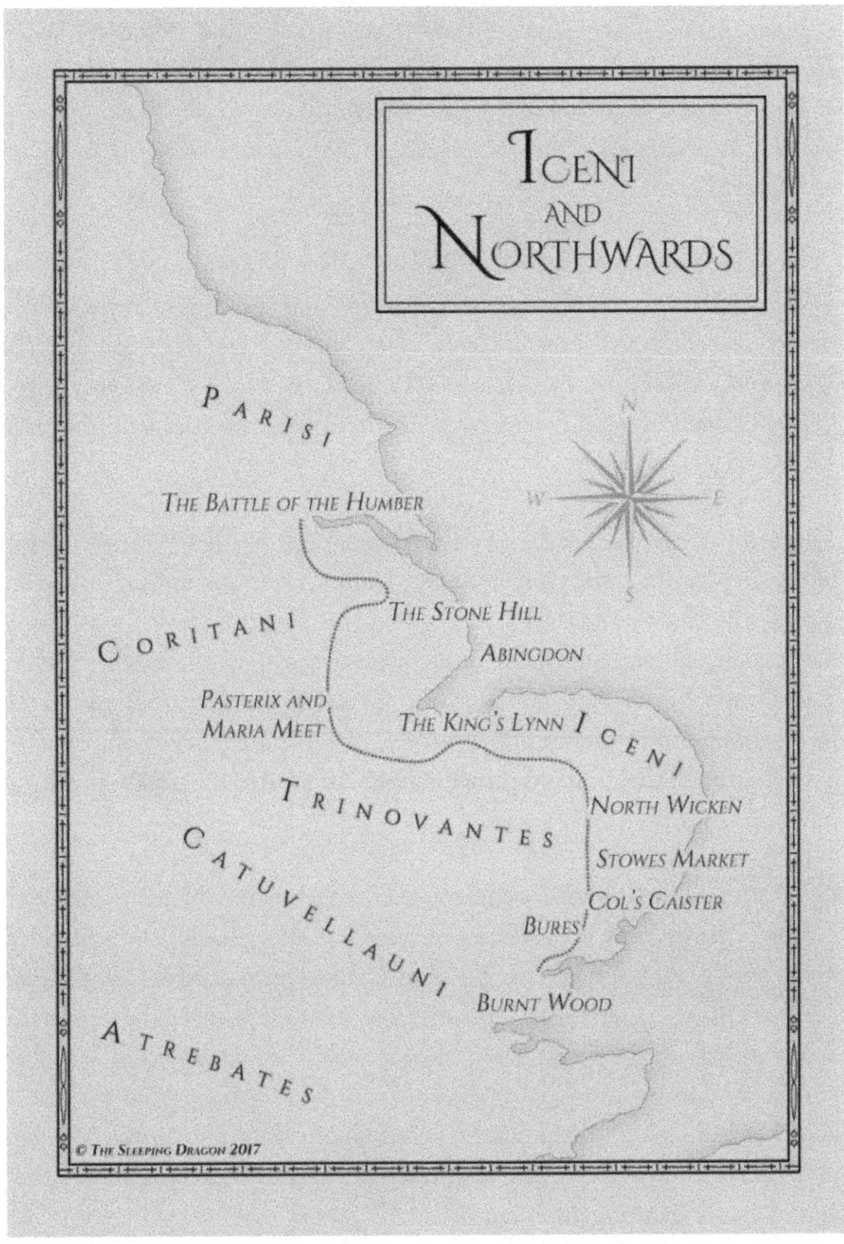

The Iceni under their young and energetic King Pasterix and his ambitious Queen, Guidevere, had defeated the Coritani, forcing them north of the Humber and pushed the Trinovantes out of their homeland around the Wash. However, not all had gone their way and two defeats in battle at the hands of King Col had seen them lose their hold on East Anglia, the Ouse becoming the new boundary with them also holding the Northern Wash as far as the coastline at Boston.

"The newly converted Christian Kings brought together a mighty army, the first to ride under the banner of 'Christian' and the largest army seen in Briton since the defeat of Julius Caesar. The army marched north towards The Wash and the Iceni, ready to do war if the Iceni, and their King Pasterix and Queen Guidevere, would not permit Mary to address their people." (Pilate 4th Century AD)

The company left Colcaister mid afternoon and headed for the crossing of the Deben; they had converted the whole City to the message of peace brought by the Master and as celebrated through the breaking of bread. The people of Colcaister spoke of the healing they had seen but also of the Prince's kiss. 'The Magdalan has fallen for a *British* prince' they would tell all who came to trade with them or visit the fort and they were proud of his conquest of this 'foreign princess from the sanded deserts of Arabia' as much as anything else.

Longinus and the Prince decided to ford the Deben inland at either Bram's hill or to go even as far as Blundes but they also needed to decide how many they would take north. The two Catuvellaunian Kings asked leave to return to their territories and this was granted with Maria especially showing her gratitude for they had come to rescue her. She asked to personally address those who had followed the two Kings and they were happy she did so. She spoke a few words about their part in the Master's mission then prayed for their continued safety and their eyes shone; they would gladly come again at her call.

But that still left them one hundred and sixty strong and this would attract attention wherever they went. Yet the Prince was adamant that Maria should have a proper escort whilst those sent by others to watch over the girl had no intention of returning to their masters until their mission was complete. Iosephus released his mercenaries with thanks and a bonus and they went away happy as they had another victory in battle to add to their chariot race of life.

In the end they decided to ford the Deben at Blundes and then head north towards Ston Ham and Deaesch (Diss). The road was relatively well constructed, not a Roman road with paving stones and deep ditches either side but much better than the tracks they had followed cut through forests but still dark and often overgrown. The road north was through arable fields and grazing, few if any trees except as part of the occasional hedgerow to mark a boundary. They were able to make good speed with little danger for their outriders to report and few villages. They stopped at the settlements of Mendel and Eye but met only a few dozens at each before making Deaesch just before nightfall.

They were put up at an Inn just outside the settlement but which had large stables in which to house their horses and the troops that came with them. There were ten rooms in the Inn and two went to Maria and Haladriel, one each to the Prince and the Yeorl Corin and the rest had to fight for the six remaining rooms or to sleep with their horses. Longinus and Galahaidra agreed to share a room, Iosephus and Felstum another. Hosta decided to sleep with his troops as did the two Decurions so the remaining four rooms were allocated to troops to act as bodyguards for Maria with four men in each, eight on duty guarding the corridors, doors and windows and eight sleeping at any time.

"We stay here a full day at least" said Maria between yawns as her Prince lifted her down from her horse and carried her towards her chamber. "Longinus" and she waved her hand until he held it "Can you see if there is a large place of assembly, a Moot Hall or similar and send the troops out to the surrounding settlements with word that I shall be celebrating a service tomorrow evening" and with that her head fell forwards onto Craedech's chest and she was asleep.

The local Karl came to the Inn to greet the distinguished party. The Prince of the Dobunni was held in much honour as the only heir to the largest kingdom in the West Country and it was already known by proclamation that the Lord Prince Godric Bann Caedic had made Maria his sole heir to the largest kingdom in the south. When word began to spread that the Princess Maria and Prince Craedech were considering marriage then this created a kingdom capable of challenging any other in Britannia. It also made both very important guests and the Karl of Daeasch and the surrounding country intended to make them welcome.

The Prince was immediately apologetic: "I am afraid that Maria is asleep. She has ridden all day and is still recovering from being starved, beaten and tortured only two to three days ago. She is also young and looks half-starved at the best of times so has little stamina to draw on. Today's ride will have left her exhausted but she did ask if we can stay all of tomorrow and leave the day after and also if there is any large meeting place where she can hold a religious service to which everyone is welcome? Can we stay and is there any large meeting place we can use?"

Karl Cedric Ghast, Lord of Daeasch, Scole and Bressing held three settlements from King Col. Col was his overlord and had already sent messages ahead that Maria was to be offered every courtesy. Cedric was ambitious and intended to demonstrate to his King that he could hold more lands. He already had his eye on Mendel, Ston Ham and Eye as well as Soham, Fraemlin's Ham and the strategic settlement at the ford of the Yox. He immediately agreed to the request that Maria and her company stay two days rather than the original overnight stay, and there was an enormous park in the centre of the settlement at Daeasch which would be ideal for any large gathering. He offered to send word out inviting people to the service and the Prince was happy to agree inviting the Karl in return to join them for supper.

Over supper, the Karl could not help asking about Maria for rumours were rife that she was an enchanteresss or some sort of witch, able to turn the minds of the Prince and the King or had charmed them to do her will. Craedech laughed then decided to explain himself for the Karl was looking offended.

"Maria is young and fervent about her faith in God. The reason why she is getting so much support is that it is abundantly clear that she is honest and that those who oppose her are not. Do not conclude anything about her until you have met and then come and talk to me again and I will tell you of her amazing adventures; so amazing that you will not know what to believe. As for me: no, I have not been put under a spell by her but still she has charmed me beyond all reason and I am very much in love with her."

Cedric promised to return at breakfast the next day to meet Maria and also to discuss in detail what they would need for the service. He was anxious to ensure that all went well yet not sure what this would entail. "Will you need seating? An altar? Candles?" he asked and in the end Longinus went to reassure him saying good-humouredly: "Go home. The girl can answer your questions tomorrow."

Cedric arrived just after dawn to hear Maria accompanying the birds as they sang to greet the morning sun. He approached her nervously and she turned towards him, welcoming him with a shy smile yet not sure who this reticent stranger was. Seeing that her bodyguard were not worried, she took comfort from that.

"My name is Maria" she whispered in her gentle voice and Cedric nodded then explained: "I am the lord of this settlement and am come to see what you might need for your service this evening." Maria's face lit with joy and she became excited at his kind offer of help. She asked for a podium and a trestle table for an altar. "I am so small people often cannot see me and, oh yes, is there a baker as I will need bread?"

They soon got chatting as he relaxed in her company and he could see all that the Prince had told him; the girl was no magician or enchanteress but rather a child given an important message to take out into the savage adult world. He feared that she would never survive but rather be crushed yet she had many powerful friends and allies who were offering her their protection. "Join us for breakfast" she asked and he nodded saying he would be delighted.

Over breakfast Longinus, Galahaidra and Hosta led the discussion on where they should go next. Maria was clear: "We must find the Iceni and share the message with them" but the rest were concerned as they would be coming from the lands of King Col and it would be known that they had finished on good terms with the old King. The Iceni had suffered defeats at his hands and there was no love lost between the Iceni and the Trinovantes: more likely is that they would slay her on sight.

"We must have faith" was Maria's reply and she became stubborn once more.

"In which case we would do well not to give the Iceni a reason to feel threatened by us" Longinus added thoughtfully. "Riding into their homelands with over one hundred armed warriors will provoke them to commit slaughter. We should go as a small party, bringing the horses we have captured but also those that Iosephus has provided us with as a gift and token of our peaceful intent. We should leave our escort behind. We will be shadowed by the Iceni from the King's seat at the mouth of the Lynn so that is where we should separate from our escort."

"Who forms this 'small party'?" Craedech asked alarmed at Maria entering the hunting grounds of the Iceni with only a token escort. Maria replied to that: "I ask Galahaidra and Longinus to join me if they are willing. Iosephus also for his wisdom and guidance but also because he can have ships follow us up the coast to provide us with our means of escape. I would be afeared for Haladriel and so ask that she remain here under your protection Cedric until my return. Felstum can you stay here and look after Haladriel?" And the young man nodded.

"Is that it?" asked the Prince. "Am I not to join you?"

"No, my Prince. You are too important to risk capture by the Iceni. I ask that if you love me, you obey me in this and remain here."

"NO" Craedech shouted. "I forbid it" at which Maria got a fit of the giggles and through her laughter said: "You and Longinus are so alike. He gets cross with me too and all it does is make me laugh. If I am to die then that is my fate. Longinus, Iosephus and Galahaidra are tied to my own fate, joined by the artefacts we bear. But you my Prince have the future of your people in the lands of the Catuvellauni, Dobunni and Corvinii to consider and must not allow yourself to be distracted from your destiny by a simple country girl from Iudaea. I am nothing and nobody when all is said and done. If I return then we can think about what I might become if I grow up but if I die then forget me."

"I have never heard such rubbish in my life!" and the Prince was so angry he could barely say more, spluttering about young girls who were a danger to themselves and had no idea about love and who were so stubborn that he was likely to explode. Maria just grinned enjoying every moment of his rant.

"When do we go?" Longinus asked and Maria was clear on that also: "We go straightaway before Prince Godric Bann catches up with us as he will stop me going." And a gleam came into the Prince's eyes. If he could hurry Godric along to reach the King's Seat at the mouth of the Lynn before Maria reached it then Godric was perhaps the only person who could control Maria's pig-headedness.

They rode north after breakfast, knowing they had three days hard riding before they would reach the coastline of The Wash. Once they reached Norwicken then they would be heading north-west through the mesne of Dere and skirting the Forest of Elves with stops every two hours to rest their horses. Except Maria became increasingly frustrated believing that the stops were to delay their progress and give Prince Godric and Eorl Herne the chance to catch her up.

"Please hurry" she kept pleading with her companions but it had no impact.

For once she did not seek to stop at every settlement they came to but pushed on towards the Norwicken where she was committed to spending at least one day in celebration of the Eucharist with the people she found there but knowing that was yet another day in which Godric could catch her up. They reached Norwicken as the sun had begun to dip beneath the trees in the forests to their west. The City was reputed to be the largest settlement in Britannia, a fortified citadel on the banks of the Waveney and the Yare where those living in and around had dug out salt for export, leaving a network of pools and interconnected canals and cuttings which laced across the flat northen lands of Col's kingdom and had filled with water from the rivers Waveney, Chet, Reed and Yare to create a haven for fish and birdlife, later to be known as 'The Broads'.

The Prince ignored Maria as they dismounted and went to find accommodation; he was still furious with her and not likely to forgive her for some time. Unable to stop herself, Maria found a dark corner to sit in away from the rest of her companions and began slowly but surely to weep, silently so that she would not disturb anyone but her tears flowed stubbornly as her heart was set on going into Iceni territory alone. She was not missed, everyone assuming she had retired to bed to sleep and so she was left alone: she felt lonely and abandonned in her self-imposed solitude. She had hoped someone would come and search for her, find her and comfort her and yet she had chosen to hide from everyone.

It was in this confused state of mind and unable to pray in her sorrow that she suddenly decided to go and find some horses. Picking three that were sure-footed and fast, she led them carefully and quietly away from the Inn that Iosephus had found for their accommodation, being careful not to be seen by Craedech's guards who were stationed around the sleeping quarters but were not visible near the stables. She waited until she was certain she was out of hearing of anyone at the Inn then mounted up and left the City to ride north-west. She would return one day to Norwicken but right now the Iceni beckoned.

Fortunately or unfortunately depending on your perspective, Maria was spotted by one of the guards watching over the company who had been assigned to keep an eye on the stables. He reported to the Yeorl of Prydain who woke the Prince of the Catuvellauni with the news that Maria had left on horseback headed for Iceni territory. The Prince leapt out of bed cursing then marched into Longinus' room disturbing both the Centurion and Galahaidra who were billeted together once more. Without preamble he said: "She has gone!"

That woke up both men. "Did anyone see her go to bed?" Galahaidra asked and when they each had to admit they had not then it was Longinus who accepted on their collective behalves that they had not offered the girl the support she needed:

"I am guessing she needed someone to talk to and feels pretty lonely as we all seem to have deserted her. Usually she would seek comfort from her Master but she knows he would not approve of what she is doing so she has deliberately shut herself off from her main source of comfort. I also fear that she has decided to go alone to meet the Iceni because she does not want to risk the lives of any of those she loves."

Craedech was almost spitting with rage as he asked: "Does she really think any of us would let her go into Iceni territory without our support at her side?"

Longinus suddenly had this terrible urge to laugh and feared that Maria had become a corrupting influence on him. Unable to hide the twitch of his lips he answered the Prince's question: "Yes" at which the Prince's mouth fell open and briefly he looked like a stranded fish before his good humour finally returned and he admitted to all of them:

"I have been harsh in my treatment of her. What she wants to do is noble – it is also misguided and mistaken but she is a child and I should have made allowances for her lack of self and her willingness to sacrifice herself. She needed us all to be good friends this night and we have not been. What now must we do?"

"I will find her" Galahaidra replied "but we must not try to cage her or bring her back here. When she is found then you, Prince, must talk to her."

Maria rode as if the Furies assailed her, changing her mount every hour, riding the fastest horses she had found in the stables at the Inn and with the advantage of carrying little weight, her hauberk so well-made it clung on her and weighed a few pounds compared to the heavier armour of those she had left behind.

Except Galahaidra wore no armour and so weighed no more than she; also he was a better and more experienced horseman and able to track her path from the broken branches and occasional hoof-print in the dust of the roads she used or the mud of the banks where she forded the streams and rivers that crossed her way. She headed north guided by the sun, taking the shortest route whether a road, path or track, recklessly leaping any obstacle.

Her Prince followed the trail left by the young sicariot but no-one could keep up with his relentless pace. Maria had half an hour's lead on Galahaidra when he left the Inn that morning around the sixth hour but he was gaining five to ten minutes on her in each hour. Still she rode recklessly flying through the trees, their branches lashing against her armour and helmet, leaping over rocks and the fallen trunks of trees struck by lightning in the spring and still blocking the way north that she followed.

As the noonday sun beat down on the girl in her steel armour, she began to glow with the heat, puffing out her cheeks to try and cool down. Little did she know that Galahaidra could now see her and he pushed on, closing the distance between them with each stride. She was coming up to the hour when she would change mounts and started to rein in, looking for a good place where she could use a tree stump or rock as a mounting block. And then she saw Galahaidra only a few hundred paces to her rear and took off once more.

For the first time she turned to her Comforter and prayed to her Master for deliverance but "Thy Will Be Done" she finished at which her horse reared and she fell into an enormous brook, to stand with mud dripping from her hair, her eyes, her hands and mouth and every inch of her armour. She took off her helmet, tried to wipe the mud out of her eyes but succeeded in smearing it all over her face then looked up at Galahaidra who had reined in and whose face was showing concern at her fall.

She could not help herself but began to laugh then after a few minutes was able to say a few words without breaking out into more laughter: "What a fool I have made of myself!" at which Galahaidra grinned then nodded before offering her some reassurance: "None of us will come out of this smelling of roses."

"Take me back" Maria said humbly and contritely. "My Master made it pretty clear that what I have done was selfish and unthinking. I will be asking for forgiveness for years!"

Galahaidra led her horse by the reins; the girl was so dejected she sat in sorry silence thinking of what she would say by way of apology and what should be her penance. She asked Galahaidra one question and then was silent for the two hours it took Galahaidra to locate Longinus and the Prince with twenty warriors as his escort and in case the girl had run into trouble.

"Was the Prince very angry?" were the only words she would speak during the whole two hour journey and Galahaidra had nodded at which Maria's head went down in dismay.

Longinus took one look at all the mud and laughed but the Prince could not see any mud, just the safe return of the girl he loved and had nearly been driven away by his anger. He dismounted and ran to where she sat astride her horse and straightaway lifted her down and kissed her despite the mud and grime. "Never leave me" he pleaded and she promised in a voice made small through her shame that she would never do something as foolish again.

"That I sincerely doubt" muttered Longinus as they rode back towards Norwicken to arrive at the Inn at dusk. Haladriel was waiting for the girl and poured Maria a hot bath then sat with her as she gradually unwound. Maria had been lonely when she had needed comfort yet had forgotten the promise the Master had made that he would always be there to comfort her in need.

So now she prayed in earnest and her Master stood in her presence, stern in his condemnation of her actions yet she hoped for forgiveness. The Master could see the guilt writ across her face but the girl must learn a lesson from this and so the Master was careful to ensure the girl saw no sign of his forgiveness until he could be certain she was genuinely penitent. He loved her but she was a child and still learning.

"Help me" she finally begged him.

"Help you to do what?"

"Master, I cannot put those I love at risk for the sake of my mission. Myself, yes, but the others are all good men and I fear they will be taken and killed."

But the Master remained stern and apparently unforgiving as he replied:

"It is not *your* mission and nor is it for you to decide whether your friends risk their lives for the sake of *my* mission or not."

"Oh dear. Everything I have done this day has been wrong! What must I do to put things right?"

"Let your friends decide for themselves what risks they will take for me and for you. Be humble and be contrite and who knows perhaps in a thousand years I will forgive you for forgetting to pray to me at your moment of despair?"

"A thousand years sounds a bit harsh!"

"Are you arguing with your God?"

"I seem to recall Abraham once haggling over the number of good souls he must find in Sodom and Gomorrah. Call it 'negotiation'!"

"Are you daring to tease me?" said the Omnipotent Godhead.

"Oh yes" and she grinned at which she felt the warmth of her Master's laughter and thanked him for his forgiveness and understanding. "Dumping me in that brook was a nice touch" she added.

Refreshed she went out to face the music and the condemnation of her friends. Instead, as she looked around their faces all she could see was concern for her and that nearly set her to weeping. Pulling herself together, she made an announcement:

"I have prayed about things and my Master is clear: it is not for me to make the decision about who comes with me to meet the Iceni. That is a decision we must each make for ourselves. Forgive me therefore for my sin of hubris: my belief that through my actions I could protect you. It took a bath in a muddy brook to bring me back to my senses but I am now in a much more sensible place. I shall leave for the land of the Iceni the day after tomorrow and welcome anyone willing to join me."

Her companions were stunned both at her contrition but also her acceptance at whatever they should decide. Her words prompted an immediate discussion but Maria would no longer be drawn, genuinely sitting back and accepting of whatever they might determine amongst themselves. They asked her a few questions but her answers were so non-committal that they rapidly realised she was genuine when she spoke of the decision being their's.

"How large an escort will you need?" Galahaidra asked Maria but she replied: "This is my Master's mission and he will make any number we take become the right number."

"Can I come?" the Prince asked in hope and she replied: "Of course. I was wrong to ever have tried to protect you in the way I did. God and my prayers will protect you but I want you at my side … always."

The following day they spent exploring the great City of Norwicken, a port, military base and centre for government and administration. Nearly one hundred thousand were resident within its palisaded walls, with an enormous motte and bailey sitting at the centre and streets weaving between the two rivers both of which were navigable to the east coast and the sea. There were three markets, one covered with awnings and tentings and the others housing the cattle auctions and horse fairs. People were genuinely excited to hear more about the Master and almost all of those they met committed to coming to hear the girl speak of the Master's life at noon the following day in the cattle market.

As the companions sat down for supper, suddenly the peace of their evening was disturbed by a loud commotion and then a roar of "Where is she?"

Maria gulped and went to hide but Craedech held her hand and would not let her pull away. Instead, the Prince went in search of the loud voice and within moments Godric Bann Caedic was standing at the doorway to the dining hall of the Inn and then he strode down its length, reached where Maria was sitting, and lifted her high into the air above his head whilst shouting: "Is it true that Col had you flayed?"

"Yes sir" Maria stuttered "but I am alright now."

"Nonsense you barely weigh as much as a baby lamb. So now what is your plan?"

"I go north."

"Iceni are next I take it. You will need me with you then!"

"My lord, you will be most welcome" Maria replied then gasped for air as Godric gave her a huge hug genuinely pleased to see her. Turning back to Craedech, the Prince of the Atrebates asked: "How many had you planned to take with you as escort?" Then when he heard that it was less than two hundred horses he wheezed with laughter and said: "It is just as well I saw your father then. He has sent help as has Casterix of the Durobriges. I left them all back on the road, making camp."

"When you say 'all' sir, how many do you mean?" Maria asked bravely fearing the answer but wondering how the Prince, her adopted father, would react to hearing she had tried to go up against the Iceni on her own. When Godric did find that out the following day, he gave her a right royal ticking off.

"At least fifteen thousand cavalry" the Prince replied and Longinus choked on his soup, Galahaidra looked totally stunned and Craedech was left speechless. Maria however, clung to Godric's neck and kissed him to the old man's delight. He whispered in her ear: "Did they hurt you when they lashed you? Do you still have scars?" and Maria shook her head. "All are almost healed" she whispered back then pulled up a seat so that Godric could sit next to her. He promptly piled her platter high with food and she looked at the mountain of meats and tubers in horror!

Minutes later there was another commotion at the door and Eorl Herne joined them. Craedech launched out of his chair to embrace his best friend and Herne laughed then asked with such a lack of tact that his wife ignored him for a whole day when she found out but then forgave him when he told her Maria's answer: "You and that girl from Judaea hitched yet?" which rendered Craedech speechless in shock once more but Maria laughed then said: "When my mission is over then I very much hope we shall be!" whilst dumping most of her food onto a plate for Herne to eat when Godric was looking the other way.

At noon, the following day nearly thirty thousand met in the cattle market to hear Maria talk about her Master's ministry from the day of his baptism by his cousin, Iohannus to his death on the cross. Then they joined her in the Service of the Eucharist and she spoke about the resurrection and ascension: how her Master had conquered death.

As they shared the bread she felt once more the communion with her Master and his Angels. She had been afraid that her love of the Prince and her folly at seeking to go alone to meet the Iceni might have changed her special relationship with the Master. Instead, he stood before her and said: "You are growing up and soon will be a woman whom has been a child since the day we first met. Will we change because of that? If your faith is that of a child's, innocent and pure, then we shall always be close. You can still be a woman just never lose the innocence you have always had as a child!"

As evening came, Maria had one further surprise. The Karl Hendrix, Lord of Norwicken came to visit her as she was preparing to depart with a message from King Col. "My liege lord has heard you ride for Iceni lands with an army and wishes to add his own support. If you can achieve peace with the Iceni then it will save many lives he will otherwise lose defending his north and west boundaries. He has three thousand cavalry at his Royal Seat of King's Lynn that he has placed at your disposal. You will launch into the lands of the Iceni with an army larger than any seen since we fought as one against Julius Caesar nearly ninety years ago."

"Which is dreadfully ironic" Maria would later say to Longinus as they sat on the banks of the River Yare drinking (wine for him and water for her) whilst watching the sun set and the moorhens fighting or tucking their heads under their wings "as I will never let them attack anyone and am on a peace mission. Trying to persuade the Iceni that I mean them no harm with nearly twenty thousand cavalry behind me is going to be a bit of a challenge!"

"It will need tact and diplomacy" Craedech interrupted, joining them both and puffing his chest out to indicate that he was their man if it needed a wordsmith to persuade the Iceni that their intentions were peaceful. "Oh, you mean like Lord Herne?" and the Prince had the good grace to blush as he recalled his friend's terrible faut pas! "Or Prince Godric?" suggested Longinus and all three of them paused for a moment then burst into laughter at the terrifying thought of those two lords leading the negotiation. "Best leave it to me?" Maria suggested in a whisper and was surprised when both men readily agreed, but they knew that any commitment Maria made to peace would bind the Kingdoms of the Catuvellauni, Trinovantes, Durobriges, Dobunni and Corvinii and was most likely to be accepted by the Iceni.

They rode north that night for the coast and the estuary of the Lynn where it joined The Wash, their army spreading over eight leagues as it snaked through forests and along ancient roads and tracks that had been poorly kept and maintained. They risked ambush at any point along their long line and so outriders scoured the trees brambles and hedgerows on their flanks. Maria insisted on riding at the front, bearing The Robe once more as her banneret but The Grael in its box was held by Longinus, whilst Galahaidra held The Spear set as the point of his lance and Iosephus bore The Shroud.

Lord Hendrix had ridden on to King's Lynn to make ready the three thousand cavalry that would join them; Prince Godric led nine thousand; Craedech Prince of the Catuvellauni led five thousand of his father's best cavalry; Eorl Herne had four thousand and Longinus had been given charge of the one thousand archers sent by Casterix of the Durobriges.

Galahaidra rode at Maria's right side with Felstum on her left whilst Iosephus had elected to ride with Longinus.

They navigated by the light of the moon and it was almost noon of the next day when they stood atop the hills that were the source of the Lynn and looked down towards the port. The road into Iceni territory lay south of the port and Lord Hendrix had brought his cavalry out to meet Maria. At a salute from the girl his men formed up behind Lord Herne and they headed west then north.

Almost immediately, their outriders picked up the signs of Iceni scouts from the occasional crushed leaf and snapped branch or part of a foot print in the mud, but though they watched the trees overhead and the brambles either side, they saw no other indication of the silent and almost invisible warriors wearing wode and become one with the woods around them. They sensed their presence, eyes watching out of the shadows of the forest and heard the occasional call, strange cries that cut across the silence of the day, as they rode through an emerald world, the sun hidden behind the canopy of the branches that were knotted above them. Faces turned ghastly green they began to bunch up, seeking succour in the company of their comrades. As the first day in the dense woodlands of the Shere Forest came to an end in this place of darkness and shadows, with the occasional beam of silver or golden light cutting through the greenery and both day and night were equally grim, Prince Godric called the army to a halt and summonsed the captains to meet with him.

"My fear is that we will be ambushed. The road ahead of us drops into a long ditch with steep banks and is a perfect spot to assail our flanks. The Iceni can also attack our rear at any moment and this is poor terrain for cavalry. We need to get out of these forests and our scouts tell me that there are plains and rolling hills ideal for cavalry to both our east and west. The Iceni use horses and chariots in battle so it is no surprise that much of their territory is ideal country for cavalry. I suggest that we head west moving with a much broader front and less vulnerable to surprise attack. We will be slowed up by the dense undergrowth but once we break out from under this tree cover we should get our first sight of the Iceni and some of their settlements."

They sent Hosta to scout the way ahead, using their swords to cut a path in a swathe through the bushes that had grown up around the large oaks, elms and sycamores that formed a natural palisade, slowing progress to a walking pace. Ditches, springs and brooks added to the natural obstacles they faced until they finally came to the roaring waters of the River Nene, where they split to ride north and south in search of a ford. Just over a league to the north, they came across a rocky gorge where the river narrowed before cascading down a steep bank as a waterfall at the base of which was a lake of clear water and a natural ford where the river continued its path across the silt and pebbles thrown up by the erosion of the fall and making a natural dam that held the lake waters in place.

A few hundred paces beyond the river crossing and they came to the edge of the forest. As Hosta and his party rode from under the cover of the trees into the bright sunlight, there ahead of them was a huge host of the Iceni; at least ten war parties had gathered to meet the warriors from the southern kingdoms. An arrow struck the ground before Hosta's feet and his scouts fell back to within the trees. It had been a warning shot but still Hosta needed to bring word that they had a road out of the forest and of the war parties mustered to meet them.

"They are curious" Col said on hearing word from Hosta. "If they sought battle then they would have set an ambush as we crossed the river and placed war parties on our flanks as well as across our path. Instead, they offer a show of strength but are letting us make the first move."

"Then I shall go and speak to them and will do so alone so that they do not feel threatened." Maria spoke up and then cowered as Godric roared so loudly that she had to cover her ears as he reminded her of the telling off she had received the day before when her father had first heard that she had ridden off on her own to meet the Iceni.

"Archers in the tree line, firing from cover. Lord Hendrix form up on our left flank; Lord Herne on the right. Prince Godric Bann will take the centre with Prince Craedech in reserve. Hosta, take the legionaries and a company of one hundred horses and hold the river crossing for us. If you see any sign of the Iceni looking to attack as we cross the Nene then send word" Longinus commanded and the two Princes, two Eorls and Hosta nodded in agreement and went to put his orders into action.

Maria sat thoughtfully then prayed and as she did so, her Master joined her. She asked: "What shall we do?" and he replied: "Those who live by the sword die by the sword. Offer the Iceni something they want and they will listen to you. There is no need for battle but much to be gained by seeking Peace."

"Thank you" Maria whispered then returning to the here and now she turned to Longinus and pleaded: "When we reach the Iceni do nothing however much we may be provoked. Make sure that all of our lords take instruction from you."

It took over two hours for their many companies to reach the river crossing and the forest's edge. It was dark when they first broke clear of the cover of the trees to stand beneath the gentle caress of the light of the moon, their armour and faces turned silver in its glow.

Before them stood the Iceni, dark statues with horned and winged helmets, the whitened skulls of animals, ferocious masks and blue war paint in swirls or daubed on their cheeks and across their bare chests and arms. They stood like an army of the undead, ghostly spectres lit by the stars. Over six thousand cavalry and the same of men and women on foot had gathered to the muster of their King. Those on foot were armed with cleavers, axes and wide bladed swords for they would hack their enemy to pieces showing no mercy for the wounded; there were a hundred archers but archery was not their strength, rather they would throw spears in volleys at their foes.

The heart of their army and their strength was their cavalry, with fiercesome war stallions, bearing long spears and attacking with drug-induced berserker strength and fury. At their front were their Shaman; High Priests of their worship of The Goddess Epona, whose concoction of herbs and hallucinatory drugs would give their warriors strength and courage beyond anything rational. The priesthood of the Iceni had come to take the measure of this new force called The Magdalan and, if needed, condemn or accept the sorceress depending on whether her magic was accepted by Epona.

Longinus ensured his army was in position, his flanking forces sat beyond the ranks of his opponents. The Iceni were lined up in two battles, their infantry at the front, their cavalry to the rear, with their archers in amongst their foot rather than as a separate company for they would take individual shots rather than send down the devastating volleys that Longinus' legion of archers could launch.

For a moment both armies glared at each other then Maria dismounted and led two horses as she walked towards the Iceni's ranks. "Where is she going?" muttered Godric and went to ride after her but much to his astonishment his horse refused.

The King of the Iceni saw the pony on her shield first and nodded in honour of the people of the White Horses whose chalk drawings of Epona pleased the Goddess greatly. Then he watched as the girl removed her helmet and her great mane of silver and golden hair fell down her back whilst her blue eyes shone with the clarity of her honesty. She spoke in his native tongue, her gentle voice carrying to his furthest ranks:

"Great King, I bring you a gift" and she released the reins of Iosephus' finest stallion and whispered to the horse then stood back as it reared then charged towards the King to stand fiercely and fearlessly proud before him. He dismounted and hesitantly held his hand out to take the reins then stroked the flank of its neck feeling its strength. This was a mighty war horse and a mount worthy of the greatest of Kings. Eyes gleaming in delight, he mounted and then let the reins go slack before hooting with joy as the horse launched into a gallop. Riding before his ranks, his warriors raised their weapons and cheered in his honour. Finally, he rode up to where the girl stood alone, her head bare, her eyes showing no fear.

"Are you not afraid to die?" the King asked in amazement. He had not intended to do so but what he saw in her eyes had startled him. Then regaining his composure and before she should answer, he asked the question he had intended to pose:

"What is it that you want?"

"Great King, I ask to speak to your people, not just your warriors but all who live under your authority and mercy. I ask to visit a few of your largest settlements and tell your people of my Master. I seek your permission and will go with only a handful of my closest companions. Then I go north."

"We fight the people of Dacia. You will not be welcomed by them if coming from our lands."

Maria stood in silence for a few moments seeking the advice of her Master and the Angels and their words bolstered her courage: "The Dacians will see me out of curiosity. I do not know if they will then let me live but that does not matter."

"Why the large army if you only wish to speak to us?" the King then asked seeing the emblems of the Catuvellauni, Dobunni, Atrebates, Durobriges, Belgae, Regni, Trinovantes and Corvinii. He was not certain he had the beating of this army despite the magic of his Shaman for there were names here that were legend amongst his own warriors. As was this little girl standing defiantly before him for she had defeated the Catuvellauni, Durobriges and Dobunni in battle, conquered the evil heart of King Col of the Trinovantes and been adopted by the Lord Prince of the Atrebates and Durobriges. She was a warrior princess with the spirit of Epona, a white horse become human with her mane of white hair and startling blue eyes, and if all that was said of her was true, she could defeat his army with her Master's magic. Maria smiled, a look of mischief that brought out a sense of reciprocating glee in the King, before she replied to his legitimate question:

"I wanted to attract your attention" at which the King laughed before she continued: "but if I have your permission to go amongst your people under your protection then this army will move on to your northern borders with Dacia and wait for me there."

"She must be tested!" snarled one of the High Priests and the King nodded then asked Maria: "How well can you ride a horse?"

The girl blushed then admitted: "Alas, until three months ago I had not ridden anything except an ass once and I sat before my father on his camel as a child. I do not think I am yet a good rider but I will gladly try any challenge."

The King signalled towards his personal guard; the champions of his people; great warriors with a string of victories to their names; the lairds of his largest settlements and the Creach of his kingdom. One rode forward leading a giant of a stallion, twenty one hands tall, a pure grey, dazzling white horse with flowing mane and proud tail, flaming eyes that through a trick of the moonlight shone bright blue. The whole of the Iceni war band gasped, believing that the girl's soul had entered the stallion and then the horse reared and broke free of the hold the Iceni champion to rear before Maria.

The girl whispered a few words then sang and the horse slowly knelt on its front legs before her so that she could mount it. Then with another whispered request, it trotted proudly towards the King, head held high, the diminuitive child on its back an insignificant burden for its great strength. On reaching the King, Maria sang once more at which the horse stood still charmed by the sound and with a snort and several squeals her family of wild boar scrabbled out of her saddle bags, jumped to the ground and ran at the High Priests whose horses took one look at the charging boars, turned tail and fled.

The King laughed until tears flowed from his eyes then spoke to Maria in ringing tones that all might hear: "You have more than met the challenge of my High Priests. You have my permission to visit any settlement you wish and to do so under my protection. Stay with me as my guest. This mighty horse is yours. Indeed there are many who will see it as you in equine form: created by my Goddess or your Master for each other. It is mightier than any horse in my kingdom and I would be honoured if you would accept it as my gift to you."

Maria bowed at the honour shown her then asked: "Show me the road north and I will send my army on to the lands of Dacia" at which the King pointed and Maria turned to signal to Longinus to join her. The Centurion bowed to the King then listened to Maria's instructions: "Send our army north with orders to hold at the borders with Dacia. They go in peace and must pay for or make good any provisions they need on their journey. Ask Iosephus, Galahaidra, Felstum, Haladriel, the Prince Craedech to join me, with yourself of course" she added with a grin. "Prince Godric commands the army but before he leaves I would wish to thank him for all he has done for me."

Half an hour later, the army were ready to ride north, with Prince Wulfrid taking half of Godric's warriors and leading them south towards the capital of South Hamm as Godric explained: "I will be some weeks in your company, girl, and I cannot afford to leave my kingdom without leadership for that time. The kingdom of Cantiani has always looked towards my west borders at Lewes, Pevens Sea, Hastin and the banks of the River Bourn and will take advantage of any weakness they see such as a prolonged absence by myself. Wulfrid is honoured by my people, is still a Prince and was a worthy ruler before me; he will keep my people safe whilst I stop you getting into mischief." Then embracing her and kissing her on both cheeks he muttered: "Glevum is a good choice. Look after him. And remember you are my daughter and I have made you a Princess. Hold your head high for you are the equal of anyone."

Maria blushed then clung on to Godric's neck and spoke quietly into the privacy of his right ear: "I am fortunate to have found such love from you: unexpected yet so welcome. My father, I hope always to honour you through my deeds."

"Drive me to despair more like" he wheezed with laughter and with a final kiss turned to order his army to march.

Lord Herne had sent three thousand towards the Ford of Hern, the camp of his Eorl Wors, the Hill at Tewech and his hill forts on the Malverns under the ever reliable Eorl Hosta. These were all client kingdoms sworn to the King at Glevum as were the large settlements of Frome, the bridges over the Trough and the Wey, Ciren, Cipen, Stow and Upton.

Lord Herne, seeing how the love between Maria and Craedech had blossomed and also in awe and wonderment at Maria's conquest of King Col through her courage and defiance, had taken Longinus to one side and over an amphora of the local ale, an acquired taste that had thus far escaped the Centurion but which he endured from good manners, and explained the hope of many of the lords that Britannia could unite to face Roma when the invasion eventually came:

"The name I mentioned: the person who we see can unite us. Do you now see who that is?"

Longinus remained as confused as ever so Herne took mercy on him:

"Maria through her marriage with Craedech will create the largest kingdom in Britannia. She has won over the Kings of the southern kingdoms from the Chiltons to the Burntwood, as well as King Col, and the Kings of Glaston's Tor and Sulis. If the heart of the Iceni can also be won then she will have at her bidding an army of over one hundred thousand strong."

"But this is madness. Maria would command them surrender for she would never fight!"

"She fought at The Summoning Circle" Herne reminded the Roman. "If it were to save a people from oppression then surely she would fight?" but Longinus could not be convinced and asked in deep concern: "Is this why the Prince seeks her hand?" at which Herne sat back in his chair and chuckled to himself before letting the Centurion into the joke:

"The Prince could not have chosen a more worthy partner, for she will bring him far more honour, influence and territory than the princesses of 'royal' blood that have chased him relentlessly for the last seven years. Yet he loves her for her generous nature and she loves him for his kindness and steadfastness. Neither have any idea of how important they are become for the future of Britannia."

Longinus had asked Casterix's archers and Lord Hendrix's legions to stay whilst Craedech had instructed Lord Corin of Prydain and the cavalry from Glevum to fall under Godric's command. Godric still led an army of fourteen thousand, a large force even in Roman terms but a fraction of what he might face if Dacia mustered against them.

Maria and her six companions then rode with the King to his Royal Seat at Stone Hill at the crossing of the Nene just as it met the Trent. They took the same road as Godric for part of their journey but out of courtesy to the King of the Iceni, Pasterix, father of Boudicca, Maria allowed her army to be out of sight before allowing herself to be escorted by the King.

The Stone Hill was twenty five leagues to their north and a three hour march by narrow bridleways, tracks and paths that followed the banks of the Cam, Ouse then the Nene, well trod by horses but a struggle for Pasterix's infantry and Godric's archers, the latter with the slight advantage of not wearing armour whereas the Iceni foot soldiers wore great horned helmets made of iron or bone and carried heavy weapons and studded shields slung across their backs. Godric's army was thus the quicker and began to pull away soon reaching the crossing of the Trent and into the land disputed between the Iceni and the Dacian Kings. Godric was to head for the crossing over the Humber which marked the formal southern borders of the Parisi who had sworn fealty to the King of Dacia.

King Pasterix's Royal Seat at Stone Hill was defended west and north by two wide and deep rivers (the Nene and the Trent) and to the west and south by forests, the River Ouse, a loop of the River Lynn and the peninsula leading to Bes Hill at the mouth of The Wash. The Fens around were flat marshes and grasslands creating an island surrounded by water and in the centre of which was the Royal Seat with a castle and the City sitting across three steep hills. It was not only the King's seat but also was the home for the largest horse market and horse fair in Britannia, and the largest meeting place.

Three wooden bridges formed the entrances to the Citadel with a motte and mound and three further tiers of earthern ramparts topped by a wall of pointed stakes that circled the three hills and within which was the King's Hall and the garrison and stables for his army. The City had grown outside of its walls as it had captured more trade and the reputation of the horses bred by the Iceni had grown. Nearly one hundred thousand would gather on its market days and for its fairs and auctions.

As they rode towards the Royal Seat, many of Pasterix's champions and lords would ride alongside the King and Maria to get a glimpse of the girl who was a warrior, could do magic, had met the challenge of their shaman, had tamed the horse they had named after their Goddess, 'Epona' and was followed by the fierce wild boar. Only the bear and the wolf were more feared and both could still be found in the forests to their east and north. Maria would grin and mouth a greeting as they pulled alongside and left them in awe that such a natural and gentle child could have achieved so much. When Longinus overheard Pasterix's captains tell the girl about the bear and the wolf he groaned as he could already see by the gleam in her eye that to tame one or more of each was an adventure that attracted her unruly heart.

The western bridge which they used to enter the Fens on which the City stood proudly ruling the lands around was guarded by a company of men and women on foot and bearing spears and long oblong shields. They saw the pony on Maria's shield, recognised the Horse Epona and were amazed that it should bear anyone so calmly, then looked at the rider.

Maria had removed her helmet and chin guard and these hung from her horse's harness so her elfin-shaped, child-like face and long hair were both visible. As always though, it was her eyes that caught the attention, true, honest blue, brimming with joy and laughter, deep pools of such clarity they charmed any who looked at her.

They had not been prepared for her youth yet had no doubts that this was The Magdalan from the emblem on her shield and the lance and banneret that she bore. Her legend had already spread as far north as this City and would spread further as her mission took her beyond the lands that traded with the continent and into the darkest kingdoms of Britannia and Caledonia. All knew that the girl bore a Spear, Stone, Shroud, Robe and Sword of great powers and that she travelled under the emblem of the Prancing Pony, a warrior from the 'Vale of the White Horse'.

That night, the King held a feast in honour of the lady. His Great Hall was a hundred paces long or sixty great oak beams in length each holding an A framed gable with cross pieces to prevent them from falling apart and buttresses on the outside to hold the weight of the straw thatched roof. Even so, the roof had shifted as the ground beneath the structure had given way in one corner and the hall was pitched at a drunken angle and creaked in the slightest breath of wind. The girl looked up every few minutes and remembering the biblical story of the Judge Samson, prayed fervently that this roof would not fall to crush the pagans.

There were three long trestle tables each holding five hundred guests and a raised dais with a top table with thirty seats all facing into the main body of the Hall and the King's many guests. In the centre was a giant oak carved throne or cathedra painted in golds, reds, greens and blue and towards which the King marched as musicians in the minstrel gallery to the far end of his Hall struck up a merry tune. Behind the throne were tapestries and wall hangings lit by candles held in the cages of black iron wall sconces covering the wall, whilst standing candelabra lined the side walls and giant cast iron cartwheel-shaped candelabrae hung from the ceiling beams.

As the King went to sit down, he turned to show Maria to the seat to his right and Craedech to be seated on his left hand side as befitted a Prince and Princess and the girl was nowhere to be seen. He turned towards Craedech in enquiry and the Prince just shrugged his shoulders having decided that his love was beyond reason or reasoning. Then looking down the length of his Hall the King saw that she had sat herself on the end of the bench at the very furthest reach of the right hand trestle, the place of least honour, and was happily introducing herself to the civil servants and other members of the royal household seated around her whilst they sat in awe initially and then rapidly fell victim to her charm and courtesy, hungry for all news of her exploits.

Pasterix turned to his steward and asked that he show the princess to her place of honour then turned once more to Craedech and said: "I can see that your future wife will be a handful, lord Prince."

"'will be'" he laughed in rejoinder "alas, my life is already a merry dance that she leads." And it was in good humour that the King sat down to be joined by a contrite Maria who instantly apologised but in her defence said: "There are so many here deserving of more honour than me. I am a servant first and foremost so was honoured to be amongst fellow servants."

"Whom do you serve?" asked the King surprised at her words.

"My Master and anyone who will listen to his words."

"'A man cannot have two masters' and surely the Prince shall be your master when you marry?"

"My King" Maria replied with childlike innocence "Have you not noticed, sire? I am not 'a man'!" and that set the King laughing again. Then Maria asked after the King's daughter for she was newly born and he was the proud father. He spoke of her with love but also respect for she would be Queen of the Iceni when he was gone. To Maria's intense joy, he called for his wife's nursemaid and had the child brought in.

The young girl looked at this bundle of emotions, love, confusion, almost certainly wind and a total disregard for etiquette as she held her father's ear in a vice-like grip. Then the child screamed in temper, raging that no-one was paying her enough attention. The King rapidly passed his daughter into Maria's excited hands to hold and the child was instantly silent, their two sets of blue eyes meeting in wonder then acknowledgement.

And Maria stood atop a mountain, high above the clouds, dazzled by the brightness of the moon and the stars, almost close enough to reach. By her side was her Master, no longer stern as he had been when last they had met. Already, she was forgiven. Now he was to take her to see the future. They flew through the clouds to stand on the heathland near the homestead of Hampes' Stead and the plains around Watling Street where a Roman Army not even ten thousand stood defiant in the face of the slaughtered army of an Icenian Queen. Her Master explained what it was that Maria could see:

"The child you hold will be the second Queen of all Britannia, calling on the allies that will remember your mission with love and uniting them against the oppression of Roma. She will lead Britannia into rebellion, defeating Roman armies at Camulodenum that you know as Colcaister, which she will burn to the ground, Burntwood, Londinium or Loddon's Hill and Verulanium. The place that we look down on now is where she will finally be defeated by the Legions of Vespasian and our friend, Longinus, and she will commit suicide rather than become a captive of Rome.

She will die defiant and her courage will set an example that future generations will follow establishing a sense of national pride that will see one of the smallest and least populous countries become the largest Empire my world shall ever see, taking my message to the four corners of our world and defying the evil oppression of a terrible tyranny twice in the same century."

And then Maria was standing holding hands with a lady of early to mid thirties, beautiful with long bright copper hair, yet whose eyes burnt with an inner flame of fury. She was wearing a hauberk with oval shield, spear and a winged helmet. The armour and helmet was Maria's own. Maria knelt before the lady and gave her homage for this was the Queen, Boudicca, grown into her majesty and the girl recognised her proud nobility instantly.

The Queen turned and said: "The message of your Master will survive this defeat and return when The Grael, Sword, Spear, Robe and Shroud shall be found. For this reason you must hide each where they can become in later years beacons of hope for a new kingdom that will establish belief in the Nazarene once and for all as the faith of this land."

"My Queen, how can I help you?" Maria asked in humble prayer and Boudicca looked down on her as the girl knelt still and smiling reassured her:

"So much good comes out of the tragedy of these events that though I bemoan the suffering brought about upon my family, my friends and companions yet I am to be remembered with honour. Rome shall respect Britannia and our royal households from this moment onwards, so much so that the mother of one of Rome's greatest Emperors will be a British princess. Complete your mission: **all** of it and pray for me for your prayers echo through every hall and corridor of heaven" and with this last cryptic comment, Maria was back in the King's Hall a peaceful and sleeping child held carefully in her arms.

Maria passed the child gingerly back to her nursemaid, then took some bread and passed it around the table before singing her praise to God, rejoicing through the fragile beauty of her voice, and saying the words of the breaking of the bread. With her words, suddenly the room was alight as the flames of the Spirit surrounded her. Those seated at the table jumped up and stood back as it looked as if the girl had caught fire. Those at the trestle tables also caught sight of her burning in white flame and stood in awe.

Through the flames she could be seen in white and silver light and her voice, the whisper of leaves, the shiver of corn, gentle yet heard in every corner of the Hall, distinct, talking in every native tongue, speaking the words of prophecy as the Spirit filled her, brimming over with its power:

"Great and noble King, one day your daughter Boudicca will lead all of Britannia in war against the Might of Rome. Britons seek a hero or heroine who will unite your many kingdoms and tribes. I give you our heroine" and Maria took the sleeping Boudicca back into her arms then held her aloft carefully before returning her to the nursemaid's care. "Look after your Queen and guard her against the day she becomes Queen of All Britannia" and with her final words the flames were extinguished and Maria's fell forwards, her head crashing into her pot of stew on the table. The King and the Prince were at her side in moments then reassuring the other guests she was unharmed, just slept, before wiping the food off her face and hauberk with their napkins.

Maria was awake in moments and totally apologetic, distressed that she had caused such a fuss, at great pains to downplay what had happened. But her fellow guests were persistent, repeatedly asking her what had happened and to explain what was the 'breaking of bread'. In the end, though she had not intended to say anything until the following day, she told them of her Master, the breaking of bread, the laying on of hands and the power of the Eucharist. They had seen 'her power' as they called it but she instantly corrected them: "Not mine but my Master's. Not my will but his will is done!"

As had many before them, they asked how the Master's power could become their's? "It cannot" she replied knowing that she disappointed them yet they were entitled to the Truth: "The Master's power is his alone. For my Master is the one, true and only God. But if we believe in him and ask for his help he will often grant us his aid and send down his gift of God's Spirit. He has promised he will always be present in the breaking of the bread and that is how we honour and remember him."

"Teach us" they said again and again and, with the King's leave, Maria moved amongst the tables, telling the guests the stories of the quiet man from Nazareth but also asking them to spread the word that tomorrow she would be celebrating the Service of the Breaking of the Bread in the large field where they held their horse fair. Then the lords each asked her to come to their settlement and speak to their people. She looked each time to the King for his permission and he willingly granted it for the sake of the prophecy he had heard and the great honour that would befall his household.

His High Priests were standing in the corner of the King's Hall and had watched in horror and dismay as a whole people turned from the false path of their sorcery towards the simpler and more peaceful message of Maria's Master. Their leader, High Priest of the Grove of plane trees and the stone tumulus that topped the second of the three hill tops that formed Stone Hill, cut across the hubbub of the many conversations generated by Maria's moment of prophecy to command silence as he said: "I challenge!"

Maria broke the silence to whisper to the King: "What does this mean?"

Pasterix replied sadly: "You are challenged by the High Priests to a contest of magic. They will between them come up with some challenge to slay you; they are seeking revenge for when you earlier humiliated them".

Maria signalled to Galahaidra, Longinus, Felstum and Iosephus for their aid and to bring the holy artefacts. Then she stood and responded without fear to the challenge:

"I have no magic but nor do I believe in magic. All is as God's will or God's creation. I accept your challenge therefore."

There were twelve shaman and they immediately stood in hushed conference to determine how best to meet the challenge they had issued and slay the girl with some trickery disguised as magic. "Snakes venom" they decided. "Force her to place her hand within the whistling stone!" All had played this game before and knew the trickery of it.

"We challenge the girl to the ordeal of the whistling stone" said the High Priest and at his signal a stone with eight holes was brought in together with a glass jar containing a viper, its black V marking on its neck clearly visible, its bite lethal after a few minute's of terrible pain.

"What is this challenge?" Maria asked.

"It is simple" answered the High Priest: "A servant places the viper in one of the holes whilst we are blindfolded then we must each take it in turns to place our hands in a hole until one of us is bitten by the snake. The person bitten will then die."

Maria nodded happy to agree to the challenge and then she and the High Priest were blindfolded whilst the servant carrying the jar with the viper removed it using a forked stick and placed it in one of the holes then prodded it several times to make it angry. Their blindfolds were then removed.

"You may go first princess" said the High Priest with confidence for he had seen the servant's signal and knew which hole to avoid. Maria paused in prayer then plunged her hand without hesitation into the topmost hole and withdrew it unharmed. The shaman went next, and knowing which hole to avoid, he was equally confident as his arm went into the second hole and returned untouched. Maria once more avoided the hole with the viper and the High Priest did the same. Half way and the odds were now one in four. When Maria calmly avoided the viper for the third time, the High Priest began to sweat. He suddenly remembered that she had real power and if she was to be believed then she was favoured by God.

His arm went in to a hole near the bottom of the stone and his mind played tricks on him briefly as he scratched a finger on the sharp edge of the stone. "It has bitten me, trickery!" he cried but Maria caught his hand then sucked the finger to draw out any blood and venom as she had been taught. Tasting only the saltiness and warmth of blood and no sign of the cold bitter taste of venom, she smiled at the shaman reassuringly and said: "A scratch not a bite and there is no poison. My turn?"

Now Maria hesitated. Not out of fear. Rather she knew that if she chose the right hole then she was condemning the shaman to death. Instead she prayed: "My God save the High Priest. If I must die that he lives then take my life."

Once more, she was in the presence of her Master, standing together on the sandy beach in the quiet cove of warm green and blue waters, the dolphins swimming in the bay before her, a cloudless blue sky and a pavilion of cream and gold silks on six poles with gold finials beneath which were cushions and rugs on which her lord invited her to join him. This was the special place in her heart in which her Master had taken up eternal residence.

"This is a beautiful place" he said, his clear grey eyes looking out to the horizon that stretched farther and farther away as they watched it. Then kneeling at his feet, Maria shed tears when she saw the wounds on his ankles and, as she had before, used her tears to wash the blood clean then wipe the blood and tears away with her hair. Finally, she had the courage to ask: "Have I made you my prisoner here, Master?"

"One of the many advantages of being omnipresent is that I can enjoy being somewhere as wonderful as this and yet still complete my Father's work. Do you know why this is such a special place for me?"

Maria could not think of any answer that would not come across as arrogant, hubris or egotistical and in the end shook her head in defeat.

"You being here is a good reason" the Master said accurately reading her mind and making her wonder why she had bothered to try and conceal her delight that perhaps he came here *because she was here.* So she was crushed briefly when he continued: "but that is not the answer." Then he raised her up again as he explained his love for his place in her heart: "This is your creation and not mine. Therefore I love it all the more for it being your desire for me and not my desire for you. Ask your question, dear heart."

She took a few moments to recover from the deep well-spring of love for her Master that had followed his affirmation of the place she had made for him, coming close had she but known it to that eternal loving contemplation of the Master that would one day mark her permanent place in Paradise in constant presence with God's infinite compassion. It was the Master who broke the connection, knowing that Maria still had work to do on Earth but the day would come …

"Master. How shall I live without inflicting death on the High Priest?"

"There is no choice that you shall make that shall be wrong. Always this challenge had to end in one way."

"It must end in one of our deaths. Yes lord. I know this. Yet can I not find another way?"

"My child, this challenge was never to see if one of you could *kill* the other."

Maria put her head to one side, a habit she had never grown out of since childhood and a sign that she was totally and utterly confused and had decided to admit to not having a clue. Her Master saved her from the embarrassment of admitting to her stupidity, though laughing within himself at the chaotic state of her mind, by asking another question.

"If someone came to you with a snake bite would you let them die?"

"Oh no" she replied without thinking. "I would heal ..." and her voice trailed off as she realised the true enormity of her stupidity. Just to make sure she asked in confirmation: "This is a challenge of healing and not to the death?"

Her Master nodded then asked his final question: "Was your head falling in a pot of stew a 'nice touch' too?" at which she laughed her confidence fully restored.

Returning to the Hall, her arm shot towards the Stone and descended into the dark of the penultimate hole to be recovered untouched. And now the High Priest knew he faced death. Immediately, he shrank from the Stone pointing at Maria and shouting: "She has tricked me. The servant who placed the snake into the Stone must have told her which hole to avoid."

"No master I did not." The servant interrupted, arguing for his life then condemning himself with his next words: "I did as you asked" then the horror of what he had just admitted suddenly suffused him and he covered his face with his hands.

"Take the servant away and have him tortured to find out what other trickery he has done for these false magicians" ordered the King but before the King's guards could hold the man, Maria stood before Pasterix, placing herself between the servant and the King. She knelt and pleaded:

"Mighty and noble King. I ask for mercy for this man. I plead for his life. I beg that he is allowed to make amends voluntarily and offer him service in my household if he will promise to be faithful. I forgive him for the harm he would have done me and the trick to which he was party."

"He has dishonoured his King by seeking the death of an honoured guest" roared the King so incensed that as he rose from his chair it flew back a good foot despite its great weight.

Maria stood walked slowly across to the King, knelt once more before him, took his hand in the palm of hers, kissed it once then asked again:

"I still live and so am not dishonoured. Moreover, this servant has already revealed the trickery of your priest through his words. He knows he faces disgrace and the guilt of that haunts him. It is punishment enough for it is God's punishment. But now we can show man's mercy. How kingly will that mercy be to forgive a sin as great as this servant's sin?"

The King looked into her eyes and could see only the genuine wish to save a man who had tried to kill her. '*How can she be so forgiving?*' he asked himself '*And yet I will hurt her if I slay the servant as grievously as if I had offered her poison myself.*'

"For you he lives" the King whispered then signalled to the guards to return to their stations. The servant fled from the Hall, the eyes of all upon him, some with mercy but most with contempt. Maria signalled in her turn to Iosephus to go, find the man and offer him comfort. Then the King turned and asked her "And what of the High Priest?"

"The challenge must be completed" Maria replied "for it is God who was challenged and God must end it" at which words the High Priest fell on his knees to beg: "My lord King, forgiveness for the servant but not the master. How fair is that?"

It was a sign of the King's growing trust in Maria that he turned to the girl for her answer.

"Let us both place our hands into the Stone" she said. "No" she heard her Prince gasp in horror but before anyone could stop her she plunged her arm into the last hole then felt the viper's teeth dig deep into the flesh of her arm, striking at vein and artery, feeling the venom head relentlessly for her heart. Knowing her painful death was minutes away.

"Your turn" she said to the High Priest but already he was running for the exit from the Hall. One of the guards stepped across his path to prevent his escape and went down to a dagger in the heart then the Priest was gone.

"Arrest them" said the King pointing to the rest of the Priests and too late they realised that their doom was to be the same as their leaders. "If the girl dies, you die" the King promised them.

The Prince was at Maria's side in moments but she shook her head, smiling at him then saying "Carry me to the guard who was felled, my legs can no longer bear me."

In tears, he did as she asked whilst Galahaidra and Longinus brought to her hand the Robe, Shroud, Spear and Grael. "You know what to do" she whispered as the venom began to take away her breath and they laid the guard in The Shroud, covered him with The Robe, placed his head on The Grael stone and then The Spear in his cold hands as Maria said: "Thy Will be Done but it was you, my Master, who said this challenge would not result in death but in healing. Please, grant this man back his life."

They could never be certain if their prayers would be answered for always it was God's will that would be done. But on that day, God wanted to show the Iceni his mastery over death. The man had been slain by the High Priest but he was brought to life by the grace of the true God. Those nearest the man gasped as the cut of his heart wound healed to leave no scar on his breast. The man sat up startled then began to praise God.

"Now me" said Maria and collapsed.

She woke surrounded by worried faces and had to laugh for they all looked so very serious and yet over their shoulders she could see the light of a glorious summer's day, God-given and blessed, streaming in through the mullion windows of the Bower where she had been taken, near death yet miraculously the venom had receded through the healing of Craedech and Galahaidra. The fact that the healing power had not just been shown to be a gift granted to Maria but also to any of the Master's followers had won over any remaining doubters to follow the Nazarene.

The King's delight that Maria lived was as great or greater than anyone's in part for the guilt he felt at the years he had religiously followed the wrong path and deception of the Inner Circle of the Council of Sorcerers under the guise of the Priesthood of Epona. The girl's fearlessness in submitting herself to the risk of death and her faith in the healing power of her God and the prayers of her followers had been an act of such courage and heroism that he was in awe at this child warrior, almost a woman, lying before him and would have followed her every command. Had he not been happily married and with a daughter destined to become one of his country's greatest Queens, he would have challenged Craedech for the honour of her hand. As it was and out of her hearing for he knew in her humility she would have refused his kindness, he said to the Prince of the Dobunni:

"I promise you anything in my kingdom, any aid or succour you or your lady shall need and will hold to an alliance with the southern and western kingdoms for as long as the princess and I shall live. I know that Prince Godric Bann has already taken the girl as his daughter and I am graced with an heir already yet whilst I live she can come to me in her need and I will do anything for her as if she were my own."

"My lord King, I thank you on her behalf. She will probably be too stubborn or pig-headed to take up your kind offer but if the time should come then I will ask on her behalf."

Almost all of the King's nobility, his champions and royal household converted to following the Nazarene. The magic of their Shaman, the Priests of Epona, had been secretive, done in private, ritualistic, smoke and mirrors, and only granted to an elite few. Moreover, it was now exposed to have been trickery, the servant of the High Priest revealing many of the secrets and deceits of the Shaman but also able to tell them more of the Council of Sorcerers:

"There are twelve on the Council and you have now exposed three: one you captured in Bures, one has fled, and one of the eleven Shaman arrested by the King this night is another Council member; I can point him out to you."

The servant's name was Brascerus and Maria honoured her promise, taking him with her as her personal servant. He was quick to convert to become a follower when later that day he saw the girl heal two blind men at the end of the Service of Eucharist, their eyes harmed as they had gone to rescue a young family from their burning mud and straw hut. The two men both were to become leaders of the faith community in The Stone Hill, Maria rededicating the former Temple to Epona. However, many did ask her: "But what of Epona?"

"The one true God also loves horses. Once he healed the horse of a family who would have been left destitute, lost and in fear of bandits without that horse."

Two days later, Maria healed a horse that was kept at stables especially to be ridden by a number of children who were disabled in mind or physically disabled and for whom their weekly ride on the horse was the highlight of each week. The horse was good-natured, sure-footed and took equal pleasure in the delight it could see and sense in the children. It had pulled a tendon avoiding a rabbit hole and faced being put down when it had gone permanently lame.

"Maria" a stable hand had asked, bravely daring to raise the plight of the horse at one of her many services in the settlements in the middle lands of Britannia. "Can you save my horse? The children have wept every day since they heard what I must do."

"Tell them to pray and I will be with them today" she promised.

As she stood amongst the nine children, all of whom had prayed non-stop on hearing that she was to come, Maria held the hand of one child, born with half a leg missing and abandoned on a hill-top by his parents to be rescued by a passing warrior and brought to this wonderful place of hope for the orphaned and disabled. She whispered to the child: "And do you pray that you one day might be healed?"

"Not this day. This day we pray for Astor" the horse's name "because if he is healed then all nine of us are made happy."

Longinus was with her and seeing the tears start to flood from her eyes quickly distracted the children whilst the girl composed herself. Then she went to that place within her heart where she would find the Master.

They stood by a tree, a solitary tree in a field of wild grass which rippled in the wind. The tree stood straight and tall with no branch out of place and a perfect canopy of gold tinged green leaves; the fields were without weeds and every blade of grass was the same lush emerald green and the same length. The sky was red, mauve, purple and gold, a departing sun leaving its message of hope for another sunny day on the morrow. For a moment she was distracted by the tranquility of the place and also diverted: for somewhere here there was a message for her to find. There always was!

"You know I am not clever Lord" she admitted baffled.

"You only have to ask" he replied.

"What is your message here, Master?" she finally did ask conceding utter defeat.

"I have already told you" he replied with a smile of pure mischief.

"When?" and the smallest amount of frustration crept into her voice at which the Master laughed then observed: "I thought you sounded angry when you first came here. Why are you angry?"

"Oh" she said in dismay. First because it was unlike her to get angry and she was embarrassed to have done so with the Master of all people but also because she realised she had become distracted from the real reason for seeing the Master.

"Why must the horse be saved and those lovely children still be handicapped? *'Indeed why should any child suffer harm?'*" she mused forgetting that the questions forming in her mind would be heard as loudly as those she asked.

"What do you want?"

Maria paused to think then asked: "Can you not heal the horse *and* the children as well?"

"You only had to ask" the Master replied and was gone leaving Maria feeling about one inch high in her stupidity and muttering to herself: "That was about as humbling as it gets!"

Then she asked the children to hold hands with her before placing their hands on the horse, Astor. "You know what I want, Lord, sometimes even when I do not know myself. Grant those present whom you and I love at this moment your healing grace."

Both the nine children and the horse were healed. The owners of the farm which looked after both disabled and orphaned children were delighted but then asked: "What are to be done with the children now they are hale?"

"Keep them here as a favour to me and when I return with my mission accomplished to set up my own household, I will send word. The children can come live with me but on one condition."

"Name it?" asked the lady of the house more curious than concerned for she was a generous soul.

"They bring Astor with them." At which the lady smiled. She vowed to send both the horse and the children to Maria when the time came. "Is there a lucky man?" she dared to ask and Maria grinned then with a wink said: "There are quite a few, but one leads the pack and if he stays the course I will have him before next springtime."

The Prince objected vociferously to having a man who had conspired to kill his future wife in his royal household but Maria listened attentively to every word of his ten minute long rant, admiring his stamina, then reminded him that when people got cross with her it made her laugh and whilst he was recovering from that revelation then told him: "My Master came to call sinners … so there!"

He went in search of Longinus, aiming a kick in his anger at one of Maria's wild boars and missing whereupon it urinated on his foot and when he went to push it away it bit him on the ankle. Totally fed up, when he found the Centurion, all he could say was: "She is …!" and was stumped for words.

"Impossible!" Longinus finished for him correctly guessing who 'She' was.

Maria knew that she could never convert the Iceni fully to follow her Master though almost all adopted his teachings, admiring their simplicity and fairness. The majority of the warrior class retained their devotion to Epona as it was too ingrained to disappear over-night, the royal household followed the lead of the King but his Queen Guidevere brought their daughter up to worship Epona.

Meanwhile Maria had added to her general message her guidance on how the early Church should conduct itself. She was conscious of what Amarillus had wisely said: the church would lose followers unless it valued the meek, the humble those who kept their head down, brought up a good family and had no ambition to become martyrs. This had been reinforced by the prophecies she had seen. She spoke for the first time of the future at a gathering north of the ford of the River Ret at the hill-top settlement Grantha's Ham:

The Mission of Mary Magdalene. The Sermon at Granth's Ham in the territory of the Iceni: 'The History of the Early Christian Church in Briton', Pilate' 4th Century AD

"We must prepare for a future where we shall face challenge, persecution and heresy. Some of us may be asked to choose between our career, our family and our beliefs. Any challenge that would see us deny our faith especially to deny that there is a God, should be resisted but if there is a way to bypass such a challenge then do so.

If we are persecuted then always be ready to hide: avoid unnecessary death and torture. Prepare places where we can still celebrate in secret: tombs and catacombs, woods, forests, islands, marshes and ruins. To die because we would not deny our faith when faced with torture and death will see us rewarded in the next life. But to seek out death and thus endanger others in our community could see souls lost because not all of us have the courage to be martyrs.

My God loves the meek and the mild, the peacemakers and those who turn the other cheek so remember and honour those who seek to protect their families, the weak and vulnerable as much as those who openly profess their faith and die for it. Protect the lives and the faith of all our followers with a veil of secrecy when in the presence of those who would oppress us. Prepare refuges or safe havens to which we can retreat from those who seek our deaths.

People will come who were not present to see the Master or they have not been filled with his spirit YET they will add to my Master's teachings their own words or wishes. Alas this may be through good intentions but if such false teachings conflict with that of my Master then this is heresy.

I have sinned.

I have never denied God, when all of his disciples, his closest followers except for me, denied him publicly and were forgiven. But I have sinned by deliberately facing torture without thought of the consequences on those who follow me or those I love. Many of you will also know that I do not eat meat but this is not part of my Master's teaching. Once I was in danger of not doing God's Will because I refused to eat meat offered by a wise Prince as a gesture of peace and goodwill. My Master had to remind me that my Master's teachings come before my personal preferences. So I ate meat and enjoyed it!"

"No sign of you putting any fat or muscle on though" Longinus had muttered out of the earshot of everyone except Galahaidra and Maria herself who both managed to smother their laughter.

After a fortnight Maria saw tens of thousands convert to her faith, and as many again move towards doing so by believing in both one God and one Goddess, Epona. A minority remained unsure either way. The girl caught up with Longinus and Galahaidra and told them her work with the Iceni was done. They were at the ford of the River Stam with the Castle of Leicas, the Water of Rute and the Bray of Mow to their west, Col's captured settlement, Lyncol that sat on the Lynn was to their East.

Stam's Ford was a large village with two bridges over the Ouse and a green to the east of the village which was their only large public place of assembly. There was a smaller covered market which sat next door to their Moot Hall on the same street as their Inn.

The Lord of Stam could boast a war band of forty and the settlement had over three hundred residents in rows of wooden huts that followed the contours of the east bank of the river. Just under one hundred residents of this small settlement turned up for the Service of Eucharist on the village green that day and most had come to honour Maria, whom the laird of Stam, Vorcin, had seen when a guest at the feast held in Maria's honour.

Vorcin proudly showed her the chapel he had created in the cellars of the Inn in the centre of the village and which was alongside the former Temple to Epona. These two buildings and Lord Stam's Hall House were the only large timber-framed structures and had also used local gold-tinged stone to provide footings and a foundation for the sole plate to sit on. The laird had already established a small community of followers that met daily for a short service. He asked Maria to dedicate the cellars of both the Temple and the Inn, now opened up as one large space for Services to the Eucharist to be held, and she was delighted, later showing her pleasure when she sang Solomon's Psalm of Praise for the gift of the original Temple.

The following noon she sent word that she would head north to King Pasterix in his Keep at The Stone Hill and he rode straightaway to join her, a war band of fifty following in his shadow, reaching Stam's ford in time for supper.

"Were you planning to leave without saying goodbye?" he asked as he stepped into Lord Vorcin's Hall to see the girl, kneeling and deep in prayer. He was frowning but he could not stay angry with the girl for long as she said with a cheeky grin: "I gave you a day when I knew you would need four hours at most. I promise I would have waited for you as long as was needed. My lord King, you have been too great a friend to me for us to get upset by the poor wording of my request and my lack of diplomacy. I meant no offence."

He could see the truth in her eyes as she said she 'would have waited' and 'meant no offence' and also the bubbling spring of tears of distress as she saw that she had made him angry. He was not a cruel man and also he was honest enough to know he had not really been offended but rather had wanted to put what he had taken as presumption on her part back in its place. He should have known better for Maria was never presumptious so he did the best thing, he gave her a hug and whispered: "I am made grumpy with saddle sores but am glad to be here. Have I time to change before we eat?"

Maria's face lit up with a beaming smile at the hug but then she shocked him as she said: "I had not thought to eat myself. The men in my company are going to the one and only Inn. You could join us if you wish. I would be made most happy to escort you."

Thinking of the size of his own escort and remembering the size of the Inn Pasterix muttered: "We had better go now or we will struggle to get through the doors let alone get a seat."

The stables at the Inn could only take half of the horses from the King's war band, the rest being stabled at the laird's or Creach's Hall where they were to sleep with the King, whilst Maria shared the Bower with the Creach's two daughters, Haladriel and the two ladies in waiting for the Lord of Stam's daughters. Vorcin's wife had died in child birth, thirteen years earlier, the child dying hours later, a distant memory of joy departed for the laird.

Arrangements for supper were more complex as the Inn was only designed to take one hundred standing in its one large bar area, with a trestle that could seat forty. The landlord now faced neartly one hundred and fifty with sixty seeking to eat supper. He fetched hay bales in from the stable and that allowed seating for another twenty then had an old piece of canvas set up running from four poles to the north gables and that gave him a covered area across the street for sixty or seventy to stand under. Half price on the first quart of ale or glass of wine for the inconvenience and soon all were entering into the spirit, volunteering to raid their own cellars or those of the laird when they ran out of food, ale or wine, helping the barmaids (and helping themselves *to* the barmaids), whilst trying to chat up Maria, Haladriel and the laird's two daughters. Maria found their attempts to chat her up all so dreadfully funny that she had a fit of the giggles all evening which saw both the King and her Prince in good mood as they watched her childlike delight at the attention she was receiving.

Eventually Longinus captured the attention of the King and asked about the many kingdoms that made up Dacia. The King was happy to oblige. As he spoke, he drew a map of the route they would take in the dust at their feet: first showing the inland route through the County of Jed, crossing the Bannock and then the Forth at Bridge of Allan; second the east coast line through Amble and across the Aln; or third the western land route avoiding the coast and heading for Caister, Dumfries and Galloway, all part of Dacia but rapidly being overrun by the Picts from Hibernia to the west and Caledonia to the north. The major crossings would be over the Humber, Tees, Tyne, Tweed, the Dales, Pennines, Firth of Forth, the Firth of Tay and across the Cairngorns.

"Dacia is very different from anything you have encountered thus far. Dacia is long and divided by mountain ranges east and west and north to south. The roads are even worse than those you have already been on with dense forests, wide rivers, snow covered mountain passes and barren plains. Outside of four to five cities you will find no more than a dozen people in any settlement and less than one hundred and fifty thousand residents overall.

Do not expect a friendly welcome. Dacia is always at war with someone and has disputed borders to its south, north and west, crushing the smaller kingdoms that were its neighbours and creating huge buffer zones beween the Iceni, the Highlands of Caledonia and the Pictish lands on the west coast.

Dacia stretches perhaps three hundred leagues from the Humber, passing the Tees and Tyne and on to the Tweed (possibly even as far as the Firth of Forth depending on how war on the northern borders with the lowlands of

Caledonia has gone). Just as there is around fifty leagues of land disputed around Dacia's southern borders there is as much again disputed to their north from the Tweed as far as where the Forth narrows after the Bridge of Allan.

You might take five to six days to ride to the mouth of the Forth using the east coast route with just overnight stops: the countryside is bleak and wild with many rivers and steep hills and mountains to cross. However, Maria will want to stop at Yorvic, the new Caister, Darlin's Hill, Dur, Aln and Allan whilst your equites, Iosephus will want to set up staging posts so that you can change horses, get freshened up and stay over at some or all of Amble, Bam, Berwich, Eyemoot, Cairngrass, Auchterarder and finish at Perth.

I would give yourself fourteen to twenty days (the addition is in case you get so friendly with the Dacians that they take you on a tour as you will then need at least six additional days to ride inland to Hex Hill and across to the west coast, taking the Pennine Way from Darlin's Hill to Caer Leon, Caister and Caer Lisle).

Once you have reached the Bridge of Allan you are definitely in Caledonia but you may even meet Caledonian, Gaelic or Pictish raiding parties from the moment you leave the Wych of the River Bere.

You can go north by the east coastal route which is where most of the people live or the inland route that might be shorter and quicker but you will pass only a handful of settlements. There is then the west coast route but that involves crossing the Pennines which is difficult at any time of year. However, it does mean you meet the Picts with whom you will need to get friendly or your stay in Caledonia will be brief."

Longinus was fascinated. The distances were huge with as much again to do to reach Ultima Thule from Perth. He took the chance whilst the King was so forthcoming to ask about Caledonia and the King drew a deep breath then gave the Centurion nightmares for the rest of that night:

“Caledonia is divided between the Dacians, Picts, Caledonii, Vicing and Gaels, with Celtic, Gaelic, Hispanic and Roman traders and both raids and trading with the Teutoni, Germanii, and the wild Huns, Goths, Daenii and the Norse. Little is known about or has been charted north of the Firth of Tay and Perth. Perhaps one hundred thousand live in the whole of Caledonia and less than three thousand north of a line between the Glass How and Perth where Caledonia is at its narrowest.

With the exception perhaps of parts of the west coast held by the Picts, the rest of Caledonia is disputed between the Vicing, Caledonii, Gaels and Picts and war parties of each will hunt down any stranger. The few east coast ports are relatively civilised through trade with the rest of the world but Caledonia has very little to trade so that benefit is limited. Maria will find succour in the farms and homesteads amongst the Crofters who are generous-hearted but they are also too often the subject of raids by any of the four warring tribes.

If I were Maria, I would stick to the east coast, cross the Forth near Allan and visit Perth then take ship and sail south back towards Britannia but I fear that your little company will meet with a war band and become their hunted prey in the bleakest of countryside where it snows in summer and never ceases to rain. The hours of daylight are shorter too and you will be into their autumn once you head north of Perth.

If you do go north of Perth then you will be hunted every step of the way, take over three months mainly on foot leading your two horses, putting you into the worst time of year to traverse the seas to the islands of the Hebrides, Orkney, Thule and Ultima Thule with winter storms and blizzards every day. No ship will put out from Thurso to any of the northern Islands at that time of year.

Once you find yourself in the cold of winter, you will need to find shelter and hope your horses, food and water last for another three months then you will take the three months of springtime to return to Perth. Nine months in the snow and the rain! In that time you might come across fourteen hundred people in the settlements on the coast including the mouth of the Ness, Dean, Thule, Ultima Thule and Skye. That is the same as if you were to visit a single medium sized settlement in my territories or any of the southern and western kingdoms adding just one day to your mission …"

Maria had overheard this last bit of their conversation and nodded with understanding but then interrupted to explain why she still felt it worthwhile that she at least try.

"What you say my lord King is very wise and sensible. I do not wish to contradict a single word. Rather, I will explain the mission I have been given more fully and hope through my offering greater clarity than I have before to also explain why a community of three thousand spread over eight hundred thousand square leagues should still be important to my Master.

My Master asked me to spread the word to '*every one who would listen*' giving others the mission to convert the larger numbers living around the Middle Sea.

I am to go to those in far flung out places, the hardest to find, the easiest to ignore therefore. I am to leave trails for others to follow: to find The Cross, The Shroud, The Sword, The Grael, The Spear and The Robe. I am to demonstrate God's gift of the power to heal the world. Finally, I am to establish a dynasty of faithful whom one day in three hundred years' time will convert the Roman Empire.

My mission is to the *people who otherwise might be left out*, to grant them an insight into the messages of my Master that will last the two thousand years needed before our ability to address isolated communities can be resolved through better means of communication that now are beyond my understanding but where it will take minutes or even seconds to give my Master's message to people living in remote places rather than nine months."

"Is the faith you have shown us different then from that of the rest of the world?" the King asked wondering if the Iceni had fallen into heresy or been short-changed by the girl.

Maria recalled the measuring vats in the City of Glevum and her mind went back to her conversation with Craedech on short-changing people. *'As long as the totality is the same none will be short-changed even if each grain differs in size or colour whilst the weight of an ounce of gold does not change because a one pound coin is round or six sided.'* That discussion had seemed of no consequence at the time yet now it meant that Maria could answer the King with confidence. So she learnt another valuable lesson: that all of her experiences in life however immaterial they might seem at the time could be made significant or given a reason by God.

"No. The message from my Master is the same but the impact has been different. In Africa, Hispania, Gallia and Britannia we have seen more people filled with God's Spirit, more acts of healing and other miracles, and more people leading in the breaking of the bread than the other missions because we have avoided the *constraint of ritual.* Our powers are not magic needing the words of a spell. Nor have we dwelt on *why* my Master had to die because whilst interesting academically 'that was then' and 'this is now'."

"Are you saying our way is better?" the King continued to challenge Maria.

"No! We are not in competition. I am saying that each of those given the lead for a mission has strengths that are best suited to those to be converted. So to those most receptive to the powers of God's Spirit you send someone filled with the same spirit; to those who are attracted to the laws and rituals of our faith you send a lawyer; and to those at the seat of power of the civilised world you send our leader."

Craedech joined the conversation at this point and as he did so Maria suddenly had huge pangs of guilt that she had kept from him her knowledge that not only were they destined for each other but that one of their descendants would be a Roman Emperor. Thinking about it, her Prince might not like that bit as he was pretty anti-Roma but should she tell him? She had not thus far as she was not sure how being 'destined for each other' actually worked as she did not believe in pre-destination!

Her Prince took away all of her confusion as he gently stroked her tension away with his fingers running gently through her hair and then caressing the back of her neck. He bent forward and whispered in her ear: "Whatever the reason God chose you for your mission here, I am glad you came. Else we might never have met!"

Then looking at her more closely he said with growing concern: "You are tired and tomorrow we have a hard day's ride. Come, it is a long time past your bed time and you need your sleep." Maria nodded and as she did so nearly over-balanced to be caught by the King, Longinus and the Prince. The Prince did not wait any longer but lifted her into his strong arms and carried her four houses down to the Creach's Hall. He knocked on the door to the Bower, an oak door set in a stone arch cut into the gable end behind the dais.

Haladriel answered, yawning, then seeing who the Prince was carrying she took a quick look at the chamber behind her to ensure all were decent and beckoned for the Prince to come in. The laird's daughters were already in bed asleep, their companions were helping Haladriel pack Maria's clothing for her journey the next day and laying out a change of clothes for the morning. The Prince guessed which one was Maria's bed because it was made and had not been sat on. Haladriel confirmed this by pointing and Craedech placed the girl carefully down then was shooed out by all three ladies in waiting so that they could undress and wash the girl before dressing her in her night clothes.

Returning to the Inn, the Prince asked what the two men had decided and Longinus confirmed that they recommend to Maria going along the east coast then following the Forth to the Bridge of Allan before heading north east to Perth then back to the east coast line until they reached Loch Ness and Inver at the mouth of the Ness. That should take them three to four weeks. From Perth they would only need a small escort of a couple of hundred cavalry and could send many of their troops back south by sea but he would need Iosephus to arrange that a few days beforehand.

The following morning Pasterix said his farewells over breakfast, enjoying an appreciative hug and grateful kisses on both cheeks from Maria, exhorting her to behave herself and not do anything foolish at which Longinus muttered something about 'waste of breath' but Maria may of course have mis-heard him. The King left two of his warriors with them. "If you hit problems with the King of Dacia send these men to me at Stone Hill with word of what aid I can offer" and then he turned and rode south.

The companions spent the rest of the morning packing but by noon they were ready. They had hired a wagon which they were using to carry clothing and additional bedding. From here they expected it would be much colder and wetter and so they had purchased thigh high leather boots, oil for their chainmail and weapons to stave off rust, hooded cloaks, dominoes and woollen under garments to replace the silks and linen they had worn until now, together with additional blankets and canvas sheets for whenever they were caught outside with limited or no shelter.

"How far?" Galahaidra checked with Longinus shouting across the stable yard where they were mounting up on their mounting blocks and the Centurion held up seven fingers just as the first black cloud drifted over from the east bearing a flock of gulls, their high-pitched chatter announcing a change in the weather. Galahaidra ran to the wagon and returned with three cloaks, one for Maria, one for Haladriel and one for himself.

"Keep these rolled and tied to your saddle. We have three hours hard riding and won't stop as we want to get ahead of this weather. We ride through dense forest for much of the way so will have tree cover against the rain but the temperature will drop markedly: the cloaks are to keep away the cold too don't forget!" then he grinned up at them both to take the sting out of his words, Maria reached down and held his shoulder briefly in gratitude. "Look after yourself" she asked "and I will pray for all of us."

Felstum and Brascerus led with Haladriel and Maria next (The Grael in one of saddle bags with her family of wild boar in the others), Iosephus (with both The Shroud and The Robe) and Galahaidra bearing The Lance, Longinus steering the wagon with Prince Craedech as his escort and the two Iceni warriors bringing up the rear. Each was leading a spare horse except for Longinus who had two horses pulling the wagon and so two more were tied to the rear of the wagon.

They had just made it to tree cover when the heavens opened. The sky turned as black as night, all sign of the sun disappeared, the trees began to shake as the winds blew faster and faster, then they heard the distant rumble of thunder.

"Lightning must be beyond the thunder" Longinus shouted but his voice was lost in the howl of the winds whilst the rain found its way through the tree cover already denuded of leaves and now losing the top branches. With a mighty crack the first branch fell to strike the ground with a thud that spooked two of the horses.

Suddenly the rain changed direction as the wind shifted and now it had found a gap in the shelter above and drenched those below in seconds. Hoods went up on those who had already cloaked up; the rest reached for and unrolled their cloaks. After a minute it did not matter for everyone was partially blinded by the angle at which the rain was slanting and their cloaks were at best shower-proof and today they were far from their best. It was a whole twenty degrees colder than they had been used to and everyone in the party began to shiver except for Longinus who had grabbed a couple of blankets from the back of the wagon and pulled the canvas hood forwards to cover him. The others in the company had thought he had volunteered to be the Wagoner out of the goodness of his heart, now they knew what it meant to be an old campaigner. Galahaidra drew up alongside after a few minutes looking like the drowned rat that he felt like. He muttered dark imprecations then offered to swap places with Longinus and was sent on his way.

With a sharp bang, lightning struck the top of the tree to Galahaidra's left and the tree split from branch to root, shivered and started to fall.

"'Ware!" Galahaidra screamed but Longinus had already seen the risk and had pushed his horses on closely followed by the two Iceni. The fallen tree struck the ground to their rear blocking the road behind them, its many branches catching on the trees either side and sending a shower of leaves and smaller branches crashing on the heads of the party, to bounce off their helmets and armour. "There will be more branches" Galahaidra shouted but once more the wind caught hold of his voice and it was lost in the storm.

Maria held her shield over Haladriel offering the girl its added protection, knowing her own helmet would withstand most blows "and knock some sense into you too!" Longinus had added unkindly. There was another almighty crack of lightning, an explosion and two trees ahead of them burst into flames then came crashing down to block the path ahead.

Galahaidra turned immediately to his right and pushed through a low bramble bush then his horse saw a muddy ditch, its sight being far better than the young man's in the gloom of the forest; it did a cat leap to avoid slipping and sliding into the mud and safely made the far bank. Galahaidra turned and cut the undergrowth away with his sword, clearing the ditch so that those following him could see it and safely negotiate it.

Longinus dropped down from the wagon to check the new path and shook his head then called for Felstum's aid. Together they stripped two of the planks that formed the base of the wagon and dug them into both banks of the ditch then jumped up and down on them to make sure they were secure.

"I will use one horse only! Take the rest over first then I drive the wagon and you signal to let me know if my wheels are lined up with the planks" Longinus shouted in Felstum's ear and the man nodded then helped the Centurion to unharness the horses and led three of them over, avoiding the planks as that would have spooked them. Longinus set the fourth horse midway between his front wheels then using its head as a guide he slowly advanced to the first bank where the horse politely refused.

Felstum stepped forward, stroked its nose and ears then covering its eyes, walked it slowly into the ditch; the wheels dropped a few inches and with a lurch the front wheels were on the two planks … but the rear wheels had skewed to the right and were out of alignment by several inches.

"Your right rear will miss the plank altogether" Felstum shouted up to the Roman officer, whilst standing a foot in the mud and sinking slowly under the weight of his armour. Galahaidra rode up then grabbing more rope from the wagon he tied four lengths with the help of Iosephus, Brascerus and Maria to the spokes of the left hand rear wheel and then each rope was looped to the cropper on the saddles of their horses.

At Felstum's signal they pulled and the wagon slid sideways and to the right two inches in the mud. Felstum signalled for half as much again and once more they pulled, this time a little slower then halted on the young man's signal. He looked up and his smile spoke volumes. Then stepping back into the mud to hold the horse's head once more he waved to Longinus who set his horse to walk, both rear wheels dropping to land on the plank bridge. A few seconds later and the wagon had crossed the ditch, leaving two deep ruts in the bank where it had exited.

Once across, Longinus dropped down from the wagon and immediately saw why Galahaidra had chosen this spot. A wide bridle path ran parallel with the road and then rejoined the roadway at a junction less than a hundred paces further on but far enough to get past the blockage caused by the fallen trees. *'This must have been the original road'* Longinus thought and then he saw why it was no longer used; for rainwater in the ditch they had crossed was overflowing at the junction and in danger of turning road and bridle path into a quagmire. The junction would become a sea of mud that would be impassable in minutes.

"No time to harness up" the Centurion said to Felstum. "Walk the horses and get them past the junction as soon as you can" then waving the rest of the company on, he mounted up onto the wagon and set his horse to a trot. The other riders were all able to ride through the junction now a foot deep in water and several inches deep in mud beneath. Then they halted and turned and watched the wagon from the relative dry of high ground as the road rose up an incline.

Longinus did the junction at speed relying on the narrow rims of his wheels to cut through the mud and just held the turn to left then to right without rolling the wagon: even given his skill, the rear right wheel came three inches out of the mud and the whole company said their prayers then sent out a collective sigh of relief as it dropped back down again.

Once Longinus had caught up with the rest of the party, he leapt down from the wagon once more, let Brascerus and Iosephus harness up the wagon whilst he went and slapped Felstum and Galahaidra on the back mouthing: "Well done."

The storm continued overhead and even their horses began to feel the cold and would buck occasionally as the wind shifted to blow onto their tails. The trees acted like a wind tunnel funnelling the wind to strike the company with a sudden and painful gust that would see their poor horse rear, buck and leap sideways. The experienced riders coped well but Brascerus, Haladriel and Felstum were frightened whilst Maria was sent clear over the head of Epona to land in a three foot deep puddle. She stood and there was not an inch of her that was dry. Then she went over to Epona to reassure him as the stallion was as worried about his rider as frightened of the storm. She signalled that she would lead her horse for a bit and Brascerus, Haladriel and Felstum decided to follow suit.

They trudged at two leagues per hour in ankle deep mud, cold, miserable, wet and bruised in the knowledge that as long as this storm lasted they had no chance of making their rendezvous with Prince Godric that day or the next. Haladriel and Maria both collapsed in the mud in the third hour and Brascerus was close to exhaustion. Longinus called a halt but with nowhere dry for them to rest, the two girls sat with mud over their legs and upto their thighs, damp creeping into every part of their clothing, sneezing between their tears which left tram marks in the mud on their faces. The wild boars sat on Maria's lap looking to keep warm but she was so wet and miserable they soon asked to be put back in the shelter of her saddle bags. Galahaidra and Longinus had a whispered conversation – they could not continue at this snail's pace or risk ambush or worse. Yet they had no choice with the terrible impact the storm was having on their horses.

"How many can you take in the wagon?" Galahaidra asked and Longinus was less than positive: "It will not be comfortable in the back and people will need to lie down or be thrown around. We will also need to rope the clothing and provisions tighter to the side rails or any passengers will be crushed. I can manage two in the back and one next to me in the front."

"One short then" Galahaidra muttered but Maria, overhearing them, interrupted:

"I can ride. I will be ready next time Epona bucks but I want to get out of this storm as quickly as possible so three on the wagon will be enough."

"Good girl" Longinus mouthed then nodded to Galahaidra: they had a way forwards. They took it steady for the first hour covering just eight leagues then pushed on at twelve leagues per hour therafter. By mid-afternoon they had covered twenty five leagues with forty five to go. There was now a good chance they could ride out this storm and make the Humber by late evening. They took a short break, long enough for those in the wagon to stretch their legs and compare bruises.

Maria had been thrown a couple of times, landing in brambles then going smack into a tree and winding herself but she just would get straight back on her horse without a word, waving away her friends' concerns. Now she stood alone and looked forlornly up at the dark clouds behind which the warmth of the sun remained hidden. Their road had become a running stream and she had to wade through water that was already up to her knees and clearing the top of her riding boots, which were slowly filling up with mud and water. With no way to get comfortable, she was the most anxious to press on and get this journey over and done with. "How anyone could want to live here?" she muttered to herself and suddenly Craedech was at her side gingerly giving her a hug whilst trying in vain to find a dry spot where he could kiss her and in the end, wiping mud off the tip of her nose and kissing her there.

"Can you last three hours?" he asked seriously worried about her for she looked so desolate. "Promise me a warm bath and I will love you forever" she replied then squelched away and mounted Epona who looked equally fed up and showed it by bucking her straight off again to land 'splash' in the ditch by the road side. She sank into five foot of water, her armour pulling her down, so fed up she just folded her arms and let the mud and water cover her head before her companions managed to get a firm grip on her, far from easy as she was covered head to foot in soft slippery mud, then dragged her back out onto the road. Without a word she stood and re-mounted Epona who was looking very apologetic as he had not intended anything other than a show of temper; he was remarkably docile for the next hour.

They finally left both the storm and the dark, dank shade of the forest behind them as it came to the sixth hour after noon. By then they had travelled fifty four leagues with a chance of making camp in under the hour for they now had bright sunlight and wide, well-made tracks to navigate. They stopped to change horses, intending to sprint for the finish whilst Maria looked up sadly at the sun, her face downcast.

"What is it?" Craedech asked her surprised to still see her so out of sorts.

"I can see the sun. I can see there are no clouds. So why is the sun here so *cold*?" And she shivered. Craedech tried to reassure her: "I promise you that you will soon get used to it."

"Never will I get used to a *cold* sun. I was born in the desert!" Maria replied and walked away from him to get back on her horse.

Maria's Mission to Dacia (the Coritani, Parisi, Brigantes, Selgovae, Novantae, Votadini and Damnonii) and the Angles (Dece Angli).

The Battle of the Humber and the Conversion of the North, 33 AD

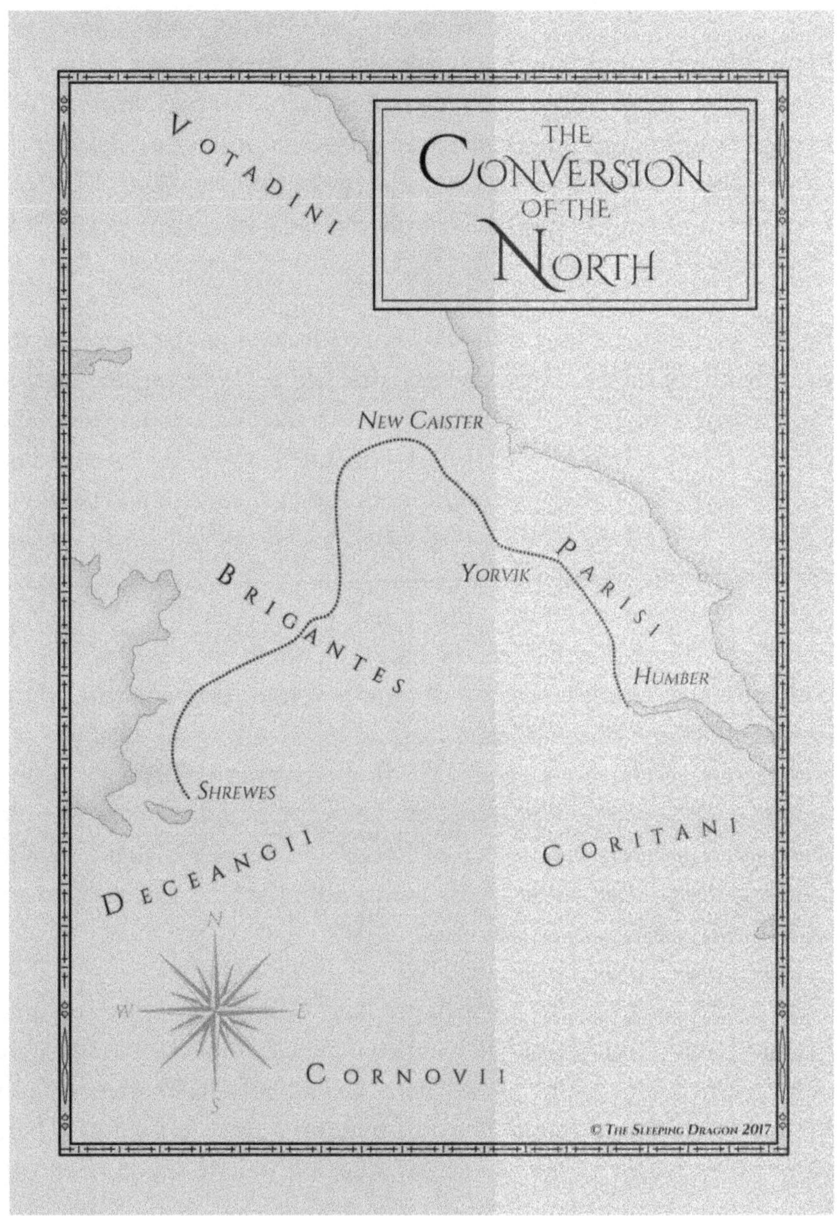

"The conversion of Dacia was rapid following the defeat of the Dacian army on the Humberside and the fall of Yorvic to the first Christian Army, fighting under the Standard of the Prince Godric Bann Caedic of the Atrebates and Prince Craedech of the Dobunni. Fourteen thousand defeated twenty one thousand Dacians under the Eorl of Humberside. Amaric of Yorvic would then surrender his City to Godric.

Mary went before King Jaeric of Dacia and they agreed a peace treaty. This treaty united the Christian kingdoms of northern, middle, southern and western England. Dece in the north-west, the Iceni and Trinovantes in the far-east also converted to Christianity and signed the treaty. Only Cantiani, Dumnonii and the four tribes of Cumria were not part of the treaty." (Pilate 4th Century AD)

By the seventh hour they were within five leagues of the camp on the south banks of the Humber where Godric had set his companies and as they topped Banning Hill they could see two huge armies drawn up and facing each other in the red of the evening sun. They would have sped up to cover those last few leagues but for one sad fact: the sun had begun to bake dry the mud that had covered Maria and slowly but surely she was setting as the mud hardened.

First she lost touch with her feet then her neck would not move followed by both arms and both legs. Galahaidra was now leading Epona with Maria looking like some ancient Golem made of mud sat with all the grace of a sack of tubers on her horse's back. The final straw was as Maria got within sight of both armies to be greeted by cheers from Godric's men, she slid slowly but surely off the far side of Epona and before Galahaidra could grab her, the girl had landed with a crunch on the hard grit of the road, winced with pain and just lay there.

They tried hosing her down which got none of the mud off but ensured that any parts of her which had been miraculously dried by the sun were now drenched once again. So they borrowed several small hammers from the armourers and started to chip the mud off a piece at a time. "There are senator's daughters who would pay a fortune to have a mud treatment like this" Longinus observed hoping to lighten the mood and took cover as Maria's expressive eyes told him precisely what he could do with his 'mud treatments'.

Then Godric was kneeling next to her to ask: "What happened?"

"She is tired and needs rest but can we afford that with the hordes of Dacia less than half a league away?" Longinus asked but Godric was quietly confident as he replied: "We hold the only bridge and ford. They cannot cross. Rather, they wait to hear from the Magdalan. Let her rest tonight and she can talk to them in the morning."

But then he saw the bruises from her many falls and roared with rage until finally his anger woke Maria long enough for the girl to hold out her hand to him, squeeze it gently and then not letting go she returned to sleep. Haladriel asked the men to leave as she continued to gently remove the mud from the girl, it had gone everywhere so in the end she had Maria carried and lowered into a tub of hot water at which the girl woke up and sighed contentedly. "Self-pride is a terrible thing" she whispered cryptically and closed her eyes to enjoy the pleasure of life returning to her bruised and battered limbs.

"Are you free to receive visitors?" Haladriel asked and Maria nodded then asked for a wall hanging to be hung across the tent in which she was bathing to act as a screen. Godric, Galahaidra, Craedech, Longinus, Corin, Hendrix and Herne joined her, sitting on the far side of the screen so that she could hear but not see them. Godric went first and asked again: "What happened?"

"I insisted on riding Epona when he was frightened by the storm. I did so in part to protect others but also because I was proud of my new horse and my armour and wanted to impress everyone including you my father with my heroic warrior-like looks. Alas, my Master has reminded me that I am nothing without him. It is *his* glory I celebrate and not mine. I have been rightly and justly humbled."

"How often did she fall off?" Godric asked them all and Longinus looked embarrassed as he admitted Maria and Epona had departed company seven times with two nasty falls leaving cuts and bruises and her unplanned bath in the ditch. Godric's mouth twitched as he tried not to guffaw with laughter but Maria saw him as she peeped through a gap in her screen and considered giving him a piece of her mind but her inate honesty and sense of the ridiculous came to her rescue and she began to laugh herself before admitting: "It was a very *thorough* lesson and seven is my Master's lucky number" then she stood, stepped out of the tub and put on a robe, popped her head around the screen and grinned.

She was in Godric's campaign pavilion surrounded outside by a colourful City of Tents, smaller pavilions, marquees, awnings and tentings, banners and bannerets in canvas, hide and silks, the colours of the hatchments and eschutcheons of those gathered to Godric's call representing cantonments, villages, eorldoms and mesnes, family, clan or House, of Kings, Princes, Carls, Yeorls, Karls, Eorls, Creach and lairds, with a similar sprawling mass of colour opposite where the many tribes of the Dacians had mustered to defend their borders.

Within Godric's pavilion there was a screened area where Maria had bathed and where she would sleep guarded by the Prince of the Atrebates, his wolfhounds, her family of wild boar and with a campaign bed set out for Haladriel alongside her own bed. The rest of the pavilion was where Godric slept and from which he set out the orders each day for his captains. There was a circle of chairs alongside a brazier to keep them warm as none were used to the colder days and freezing cold nights.

Godric was the first to give her a hug then Craedech pulled her over to sit next to him on the chairs they had set out for their impromptu meeting and refused to let go of her right hand. Longinus chaired the meeting and asked Godric to update them on the Dacian army they could see across the Humber.

"We reached the Humber almost two se'ennight ago and the Dacians were already at the bridge waiting for us in their thousands. Their numbers have grown since from a few thousands to at least twenty thousand. I am afraid they outnumber us but there is good news: first they wait and have no urge to attack us; and second, we were able to take the bridge off them so first blood to us!" he added with a wicked gleam in his eyes but Maria was not impressed, asking in dismay: "None were harmed I hope?"

"This is war, child. Warriors fight and die." Godric rejoined and the other men showed that they agreed "Our cause is Right and Just. Surely our reward will be to be favoured by God?" but Maria would not accept that, saying: "It is fortunate then that I am here to see there is no more killing. I will see the Dacians tomorrow and seek an alliance with them. We are here to promote the 'love of our neighbours' and not the conflict of war."

Her companions shuffled their feet and Godric muttered "I liked her better when she was asleep" at which she laughed, gave him a hug and apologised: "I am ungracious. You are all so patient with me. I have sinned and ask God's and your forgiveness. I am in no position to criticise others. Please accept my apology for I love you all dearly and am truly grateful for your care of me. God has said 'Thou shalt not kill' and I try and do as he says."

"Tomorrow we give you a chance to talk to the Dacian leadership" Craedech explained "but we must be prepared if their response is to capture you or assail us. We also seek peace but sometimes war is needed to secure that peace. You spoke of this yourself when addressing the people of Glevum."

Maria gave in reluctantly, sniffed and in her quietest voice whispered: "Just try not to kill anyone, please" and remained submissively silent for much of the rest of their conference, so much so that Galahaidra asked her if she was unwell to which she shook her head and whispered so that only he might hear: "Just praying that the best thing shall happen."

Godric continued to set the scene for the rest of the company:

"We have fourteen thousand, mainly cavalry. They have more, mainly infantry. There is a river to cross, a ford and bridge to win through but beyond that is good country for cavalry. We must beware of their archers and we will struggle to cross the river unless we can do so quickly and in stealth. I advise against a night attack as we will end up fighting ourselves in the dark. Instead, we must be ready to move fast: to get a forlorn hope of our best archers, spears and cavalry across the bridge and ford to hold the north side long enough for us to deploy."

Longinus nodded and wished for a legion, even a century of good legionaries, as they were the best troops in the world at such warfare. But he could still contribute to their plan for battle:

"Get the infantry across first to establish a shield wall and have them carry pointed stakes to place in the ground to deter enemy cavalry then use your archers this side of the river to send volleys to keep their counter attack at bay whilst we then get our fastest cavalry across. Our forlon hope of cavalry will have an important role: to harry the enemy but not to attack. Disrupt them. Act like a bee and threaten to sting but never do so. They buy the time for us to cross in five vans: centre, two flanks and two reserves.

We fight on a narrow front, encouraging the enemy to place their cavalry wide on their flanks. When they attack our flanks we outflank them with our reserves" and he demonstrated with his hands then smiled as Godric went in search of and found a hide with a crude map of the area. "Much better" he said and thanked the lord then started to place the leftovers of their meal, fruit stones and meat bones, onto the panorama representing the two armies, talking as he did so:

"Our tactics are to hold the centre and outflank our enemy on both flanks which is why we hold two reserves. Our centre will form around the shield wall and because it will mainly be cavalry, we can hold a much broader front than their infantry. They will mass their infantry into tight ranks using their shields and spears to fend off our attacks. Again we use our cavalry to outflank and get to their rear. Densely massed infantry cannot turn unless very disciplined and trained to do so. Their spears will look like a battle winner before the battle but will be their downfall as they cannot manoeuvre readily with them.

We will dismount a thousand of cavalry to use as infantry and a shield wall when we cross the river and they will be armed with swords, which can thrust in any direction. If I had a week, I would drill those troops, as it is choose those who are best with the sword and shield for they will win or lose this battle for us by holding our centre against the main thrust of the enemy assault whilst we deploy. We will toast them as heroes tomorrow night or join them drinking in Paradise" and Longinus showed the shield wall advancing slowly to hold the main van of the Dacian army whilst the cavalry swung around to attack the rear of the Dacians.

Herne had been thoughtful throughout but now added his own reflections: "This is not our usual tactics and will require our captains to be well-briefed. We will lose contact with the cavalry sent across to harry the enemy so must set our plans to assume we are thirteen and not fourteen thousands. If our centre falls then the archers will be massacred and our cavalry trapped. We fail to secure our retreat through this plan."

Godric laughed then admitted: "This is why I love this plan: Death and Glory OR Victory and Glory. We attack an army half as big again as ours and with no hope of retreat if we lose. The Dacians will see this and throw everything at us. They will mass so tightly that when we attack their flanks and rear they will fall in their thousands. But where will they have taken Maria?" which woke the girl up who had yawned moments before and started to nod off.

"To the rear: on some high point where they can threaten us with her execution or some other act of harm to sap at our morale. If they take Maria, no plan of ours will save her."

They all looked at her then and watched as she gulped now thoroughly awake. Then she asked reasonably: "If I am to die anyway then why attack at all? Why not just leave me and go home?"

"That would not be honourable" her Prince replied at which she said a very rude word that they were all shocked that she even knew but which she explained later was one of the benefits of the gift of tongues: "******** 'honour'! How many lives shall be lost for honour's sake?"

"Thousands" her Prince responded thoughtfully "yet if we turned tail and headed home without attempting your rescue, we would lose all credibility with the millions now converted to Christianity through your mission."

Maria went silent as she sought out the Master and in seconds she was sitting opposite him in a chair so comfortable she sat back for long moments just relaxing and enjoying the pleasure of its comfort. Her Master saw the girl's appreciation of the chair and explained: "One advantage of being present in all time and place is that you can select the best furniture from any era and culture. The chair you sit in will not be invented by man for another two thousand years."

"Can I take it back with me?" she asked wistfully.

"No. And why have you been avoiding me?"

"Because I knew my hubris and arrogance was wrong. I wanted to prove my worth without you and came to realise I am nothing without you."

"That is not true. Despite the storm's worst, you still carried on and reached the camp. Your image of arriving in grand style as a princess and warrior was deflated but such an arrival would have given a false impression of your true strengths and values."

"What is that?" the girl asked shyly. Honoured that she had strengths but also baffled as to what they might be.

"You are honest, good and kind. These strengths are far more rare in this time of Roman oppression and barbaric resistance than you might think. Encountering you is life-changing for anyone who has the God-given fortune to meet you."

"I was trying to be someone I am not. Please forgive me."

The Master laughed: a sound so wonderful and beautiful that Maria's soul leapt and her heart sang in rejoicing. She knelt enthralled as once more the eternal loving contemplation of God-head that was her heart's desire gripped her and it was with great reluctance that her Master broke away from the pleasure of the girl's loving adoration to say:

"Your sins are so easily forgiven. Now, why have you come?"

Maria had to struggle to remember and nearly lost herself in a fit of the giggles at her confusion and forgetfulness then remembered and regained her composure sufficiently to respond:

"Must we fight or will we lose those whom we have converted to believe in you if we do not fight?"

The Master bent forward and beckoned for Maria to do the same then whispered in her ear: "Can I let you into a secret?" and when she nodded continued: "This faith is about *me* not you. Those who turn away from believing in me because you die never truly believed in me. If you die, I will be with you and hold your hand to give you courage. So do not be afraid but your death is not the end of *my* mission."

"I am to die then?" Maria asked her mind and heart in conflict both welcoming her communion with God yet saddened for the loss of her Prince. Her Master surprised her with his answer, teaching her more about the nature of God-head and the relationship between man and God. This would later form the basis of her address to the Dacians in their capital.

"I have not decided yet and when I do decide those around you have the freewill to select another path."

"Can I influence your choice?"

The Master laughed once more then chided Maria gently: "I have told you the answer to that question often."

It was Maria's turn to surprise her Master, something that happened so infrequently that he became The Comforter briefly, a pillar of flame that entered her to give her strength as she admitted in a frightened whisper:

"I am not afraid to die. I will scream at the pain of torture and death but accept it as necessary. I am afraid to ask you for the wrong thing and thus lose your favour."

"You will never truly be saved until what I want and what you want is the same thing. Remember the lesson of the storm and ask yourself: 'Why did I not pray for God's help with the storm?'"

Her conversation had taken less than a second before Maria returned to Godric's War Council and a tent full of men turned towards her waiting for her to speak. She left most of them speechless with her answer: "If the Dacians take me then leave without me or ask for my body. Do not fear for God's faith just as I am not afraid of the death that God and man shall decide for me. I shall pray that I live but also that God's Will Be Done!"

"Well that is not going to happen!" Godric muttered and both Longinus and Craedech showed they would side with the Prince. They were not leaving without the lady either. It was left to Lord Herne to have the last word and give the girl nightmares:

"No point asking anyone for your body, Maria. I have heard that the Dacians tie their victims to two trees roped and under tension then cut both ropes at once and watch as the body is ripped into a thousand pieces. There won't be much of you to take home if that happens!" His wife would later threaten him with the same when she heard of his further moment of supreme tactlessness; Craedech slowly and painfully trod on his friend's right foot whilst Maria went pale; losing the healthy, red glow she had in her cheeks since her warm bath.

Maria was not the only one to lose her sleep that night as Longinus spent the six hours until dawn in briefing his troops and captains on the battle plan for the next day. He had his archers move camp to be by the river but to douse any lights or fires as they did so. "Send a few archers ahead to mark your way so that none trip or are lost in the dark then travel to arrive before first light."

Then he went in hunt of his two Decurions:

"You are the first wave" he instructed them without preamble. "Select a full legion of the best whilst they are still awake and have them assembled at the fourth hour or one hour before the first watch begins. The birds will have begun to sing but the cock will still to have crowed. Make sure those you select leave their horses behind and march as infantry, armed with sword, shield and throwing spear but no lance, thusting spear, pike or axe. Spend the hour between assembly and dawn in cutting down saplings and turning them into pointed stakes, one for each man. The Christian Knight Galahaidra will lead you."

Next he found Galahaidra. "You lead the first wave" and the young man positively glowed with the pleasure and honour. "I am making you a knight as a commander can do on any battle field and will ask Maria to bless and consecrate your appointment tonight or when she breaks the bread for us all on the morrow. You will be the first Christian Knight just as tomorrow will be our first battle.

Select a thousand cavalry to go with you; I have already briefed your archers and infantry captains. Have your cavalry assemble at the fourth hour when the birds sing but before the first light of the sun. No lights or fires when you assemble and have your horses' hooves muffled with cloth. All of your troops are to wear black with no mail to give away your presence by the clink of the iron chains on your hauberks. Remove all metal from your harnesses save the bits.

You cross the bridge and ford silently before dark, using infantry to take out any enemy guarding the north bank then get your cavalry *at least one hundred paces north of the bridge.*

Remember this: Do not attack until you see my signal, the banner of The Robe swung three times in the air. Any foeman you must take to ensure your presence is not discovered must be held alive and captive against the miracle that Maria achieves a peaceful settlement."

"Why that distance?" the newly made knight asked puzzled and Longinus explained:

"I will set the archers so that they fire at their maximum range and so their arrows will land between fifty and one hundred paces from the north bank. We will not be able to set ranging stones so my archers will be firing their first volleys somewhat blind and I need to allow for the first volley landing short or going long by twenty paces either way. Your legion of infantry will stake out and establish a shield wall twenty paces from the north bank leaving space for the rest of the army to deploy behind you. Our arrows will fly over your infantry's heads but fall short of your cavalry"

"It is good. I will go and recruit our forlorn hope" but Longinus had one more task for the young man:

"Go and get Maria up and ask her for her blessing. After what Herne said, I doubt that she sleeps. You are the first to be made a Christian Knight but there will be others. Let us do this right with a vigil, prayer and a mission in God's sight."

Maria was enthusiastic when she heard of Longinus' proposal to create an Order of Christian Knights: "... to oppose the Council of Sorcerers; and as our alternative to the Senate of Rome. Let there be twelve just as there are twelve disciples and let us sit in a circle so that we are all of equal standing and status. Have Godwin's servants set us with fourteen chairs, one left empty for Elijah as we are taught and one to remind us of why we are only twelve and not thirteen: the seat left vacant by Iudas' betrayal and the martyrdom of Stephanus. But I am honoured to be a part of this and ask you to kneel with me."

Galahaidra asked her to wait as he fetched his best steed in full harness and put on his armour, including sword, sicarius, the Holy Lance with the Spear of Longinus as its point, shield and winged helmet. Then he returned and kneeling next to Maria at the entrance to Godwin's tent, he said a simple: "I am ready."

Maria bowed her head and held her hands still before her then looking straight ahead with an 'other world' expression on her face staring into a blessed place as if she had passed to somewhere not of this Universe. Once in communion with the Angels she spoke to God:

"My lord God, my Master, Iesus of Nazareth, the Messiah, Christ, The Christos, the Spirit of God, forgive the inadequacy of my words, their humble simplicity. We are come here in your presence to offer this man's service in the deeds he will do for your sake tomorrow and every day of his life after that. May he serve you faithfully with honour and may his deeds always be right and just in your eyes" then turning to Galahaidra she asked the knight to repeat his oath after her lead:

"I, Galahaidra, do swear to follow Christ's lead in my life, to be pure in my service of Him and faithful to His message for the rest of my life."

Taking Galahaidra's sword she held it flat in her hands, the hilt towards him and said:

"Receive your sword with God's blessing, Sir Galahaidra" and the young man could not help himself but wept before remembering he had a task to do. "Sleep well, my lady" he mumbled through the tears, taking the sword and sheathing it in its scabbard then he headed for the Prince's camp as the best and most disciplined cavalry were those sent from Glevum and that is where he intended to recruit his legion.

Longinus' War Council broke its fast at the third hour of the day as measured by Jupiter's sedate progress through the heavens with Maria leading them in breaking bread together. There were fourteen chairs set out as requested by Maria but many were empty, awaiting the appointment of further Knights of the Order of The Risen Christ as Godric now called it. Around the circle sat Maria, Longinus, Galahaidra, Iosephus, Godric Bann, Craedech, Corin the Yeorl of Prydain, and the Eorls Hendrix, Hosta (who had returned from Hern's Ford, bringing two companies of his best cavalry) and Herne with four seats still empty; two to be filled by representatives of the middle kingdoms, the Iceni and, Maria very much hoped, the Dacians.

In their middle, on a side table, was The Shroud, The Robe, now made into a banner and often referred to as The Standard from hereon, The Grael and The Spear being used as a Lance tip. "We need a bigger table" muttered Godwin as he tried to place the goblet of ale his steward had just offered him as his breakfast onto the already over-crowded side table. "Have to be a round one" Herne whispered back then both men were silenced by a look from Longinus who called the meeting to order.

"Maria, you need to go before the Dacians as soon as dawn breaks." Longinus began and all in the Council knew that the battle would begin the moment Longinus saw that Maria had been taken captive. Turning to the rest of the Council he then confirmed his instructions to them and their captains from the night before (he had briefed over one hundred company commanders and war band leaders, dealing with the differences in command structure between different parts of his army by commanding that each company should have a standard and no man should ever be more than fifty paces from the standard). "If your standard bearer falls, then the man next to him takes up the standard but always look to where your standard is for that is where you must be too" he had told them last night capturing the eye of each captain until he was sure they understood.

Now he chose his words carefully, hoping his generals that sat around this table would understand but Maria would not:

"At my signal which shall be the waving of The Standard three times from left to right then we march as I gave orders yesterday. I will be with the first van and have The Standard by me to issue orders using the battle language of the Atrebates on which I briefed your captains yesterday. If instructions must be more complex than our battle language allows for then I will send two riders with a written message and use my seal" (and he passed around his signet ring so that all knew his Centurion's sign) "as confirmation."

"Why two riders?" Craedech asked. "In case one does not make it" Herne muttered, with the benefit of having far more battle experience than his friend, and Longinus moved on:

"If the first part of our 'march' goes well then watch out for my signal: three waves of The Standard again. This will be a sign for everyone to move towards our final destination. If you see four swings of The Standard then all move towards The Standard and regroup.

Any questions?"

Maria had looked puzzled throughout and finally had to ask:

"I know I am unfamiliar with armies and campaigns but why so much care over marching back to where we came from?"

Longinus had that covered with a well-prepared lie:

"With your capture or death not only will The Dacians seek to attack us as we are seen to retreat but we also lose our alliance with Pasterix and The Iceni. We will be heading into hostile territory for weeks and so must be ready at all times to defend ourselves."

Maria blushed and had the good grace to mouth 'Sorry' at her stupidity and Longinus really hoped that all went well for her own plans when she met the Dacians for he felt their battle plans were a betrayal of her. Briefly he pondered at how Celestile would have reacted to him misleading Maria had she been with them.

With less than one hour's darkness remaining, Longinus heard the first birdsong as he stood with Godric by his tent. "You will escort the girl" he asked the old Prince and Godric nodded then reassured the Centurion: "Iosephus is also with us but we will only go as far as the north bank. I will check on her now but you need to be with your men" and Godric popped his head into the tent to hear Maria offering the first of the psalms as a song of praise for the birdsong she could hear outside as she started to wash.

Longinus strode towards the bridge first where he learnt the two Decurions had already taken out four sentries in the dark and their line of stakes was being pushed into the soft ground on the north bank. Galahaidra's infantry were across the river and held a stretch of the north bank with their shield wall, shields locked to those either side and driven into the ground, covering some 600 paces wide and twenty paces from the river's edge. This would be the battle front for their main van when battle was enjoined. Galahaidra saluted him next as his legion of cavalry walked their horses almost silently through the ford and across the bridge then circled west to go behind the Dacian camp. They would attack from the cover of trees to the north west of the sleeping Dacian's City of Tents.

Next Longinus checked on the archers and also the wind which was blowing southerly from behind him. His archers were on the top of a small incline above the south bank of the River Humber and would have a maximum range of two hundred and fifty paces, allowing for the wind and the height advantage. They needed to be set back one hundred and twenty to one hundred and forty paces from the river's south bank and, borrowing one of the archers to check his pacing and counting, the Centurion paced out one hundred and twenty paces three times then got the archer to do the same six hundred paces to his east. They used two white marker posts and drove these into the ground then set the archers in four rows of two hundred and fifty, their first line at one hundred and twenty paces from the south bank of the Humber; their rear rank at one hundred and forty paces.

"Fire at your maximum range then check to see where your arrows have landed after two volleys. Thereafter keep firing at the Dacian front ranks until my signal or you run out of arrows" the Centurion whispered to the captains and they passed his command on to their companies (ten in total and all men who had learnt their skill in the Mendae Hills around Glaston's Tor).

Galahaidra watched as his cavalry captains guided his men wide of the Dacian camp. Two sentries had challenged them, yawning and ill-prepared, not dreaming that their enemy would attack across a river when outnumbered. Both had been held at knife point, tied, gagged and carried with the troop as it came to the cover of the woods to the rear of the Dacian camp.

Galahaidra could just make out the camp's main fire and assembly place near the centre of the Dacian camp which was where their leadership would be sleeping. Then he looked for any hill within sight of the camp and which had young trees growing on its atoll. There were two that he could see in the pale star light, one to the rear of the Dacian camp and one halfway between that and his current place of concealment. He pointed out all three places to his captains which would be their targets when battle was joined.

Despite his orders from Longinus, he had another plan in mind. Removing his cloak, he passed it to one of his cavalry and stood in Macsen's hauberk, winged helmet, gorget, shield and sword, his sicarius and lance with the spear-point of Longinus, his horse in full harness and his tabard and caparison bearing the hatchment of his Order: the symbols of a white cross, the Grael, and the Chi and Rho of Christ's name in the shape of a flying fish, all on the purple background of The Robe, now the Standard for his Order and that of the first ever Christian Army.

Then the first cock crowed as sunlight crested the distant hills and rose sluggishly over the green rolling sea of the forests to their north and the grey waters of the North Sea to their east.

Maria did not wait but began to cross the bridge at first light with Godric and Iosephus either side followed by the first ranks of Godric's cavalry. Maria turned surprised at this but Godric explained that they would only escort her as far as the north bank. "If truth be told" he said lying through his teeth "They are come to protect me!" and she laughed gaily at that.

She led Epona. She would release her war stallion if she felt under any threat as he was too precious to fall foul of any ambush or trap laid on for her benefit. She wore her leather undergarment and chain mail hauberk, all clean, oiled and polished until sparkling silver, her steel helmet, shield, dagger and sword made for her by Macsen and she carried The Grael in a leather pouch strapped to her sword belt. Iosephus had The Shroud, Longinus carried The Robe as his Standard and Galahaidra had once more mounted The Spear as a Lance.

A further surprise awaited her when she saw the line of stakes and the shield wall. "More precautions for my safety" Godric muttered before she could ask and she just raised an eyebrow. Iosephus and Godric stopped at the shield wall and Maria walked on, alone save for the company of Epona. She took off and held her great helmet so that those she went to meet could see who it was come to parley with them.

Maria was not the only one surprised by the shield wall. The Dacian front outposts woke up to an enemy less than fifty paces from them and streaming over the river they had seen as an impassable defence. They sounded the alarm and men woke to the sound of others running to their stations, armour and weapons grabbed in haste, hurriedly put on, offering incomplete protection as a consequence. Some forgot shields, most forgot helmets. Few wore their leather undershirts or their padded armour and most had not time to do up the laces on boots and their armour. They formed into twenty lines of seven hundred to fifteen hundred, outflanking the battle line they saw before them.

Eventually they would try and deploy with cavalry to the rear and on the two flanks, archers at the front, and infantry in the centre. At first however their formation was chaotic with most troops out of sight of their standards and officers.

Maria crossed the gap between the two armies in the time it took for the first two lines of the Dacians to form. These were the archers and infantry who had been stationed nearest to the river and had formed up in no particular order under the command of the captain whose watch this was. Until all of the Dacian army were in formation they had briefly lost the cohesion of their company structure.

A single arrow thudded into the ground at Maria's feet and she halted to wait for the Dacian's next move. Eorl Edgthbert was the Dacian commander, one of six Eorls accountable to their King Jaeric who was in his north western Royal Seat at Caer Lisle, defending his mesne from Old Caister along the Pennines and Scarf Tay to the town of Preys, Caer Lisle and Caer Leon. The King's capital was at Yorvic but he was soon to move it to New Caister on the Tyne. Edgthbert was Eorl of the Parisi, Humberside and all of the land as far as the twin hills of Darling and North Alles. His own seat was in the hill-top settlement of Durs on the road from North Alles to The Land of Auck.

The Eorl was young, not yet twenty, but already a veteran in battles and campaigns against the Iceni. The army before him, however, was not Iceni, indeed he recognised many standards from the south and west who were a very long way from home. Curious, he had decided to wait and see what they wanted. He was woken that morning with news:

"The Magdalan is here and wants to talk. She is alone. She is only a young girl."

"Give me five minutes and why the alarms?" the Eorl asked his mind still half asleep.

"The enemy have crossed the river but they have now halted. I am guessing they have come to protect their leader" the bodiless voice spoke through the tent canvas whilst the Eorl started to arm himself, gathering what news he could but also issuing orders: "Escort of twenty, ready in five minutes. Can you arrange Gaemeter?" as the Eorl took a guess at a name for the voice.

"Yes my lord."

After ten minutes during which Maria had picked up the arrow, twiddled with it then thrown it away, kicked at a tuft of grass, whistled and generally looked bored and nonchalant, the front row parted before her and two lines of ten men, all giants compared to Maria and guarding the Eorl, pushed through their own ranks, advanced towards her and surrounded Maria whilst the Eorl kept his helmet on and glared at the girl.

"What do you want?"

"Breakfast would be nice" she replied "but I am here to bring word of a new gift from God."

"Why the huge army?"

"It belongs to my friends who worry for me."

"They worry too much!" the Eorl replied and Maria laughed unaffectedly and with genuine delight at his word play before assuring him: "I keep telling them that but they will not listen which is why I have come alone. My intent is peaceful and I am happy to meet your men and talk to them."

The Eorl stopped to think. The girl was young, pretty and similar to others he had enjoyed the pleasure of. Alas, his particular pleasure was murder and the terror of torture, and so he replied:

"No. You come with me. I have a little contraption that has been waiting for you and will see you split your sides wide open: but not with laughter alas."

"I have heard of your contraption and think breakfast is a much better idea for both of us." Maria replied. Alas we shall never know how true that was as one of Edgthbert's guards gave the girl a tap on the head and she collapsed slowly to the ground, blood pouring from the cut made by the sharp edge of his sword pommel as he clubbed the girl. When she fell, he went to club her again but the young Eorl stopped him much to the relief of the watching Longinus. The girl was chained then the Eorl slapped her back-handed across the face and her head snapped back as she woke in shock.

"I want you awake. I enjoy the screams" he advised her calmly smiling.

"I shall be praying for your forgiveness but am happy if you join me in prayer" the girl replied and Edgthbert looked away in disgust then ordered his guards to take Maria away and have her prepared. "Summons me when she is ready."

Edgthbert turned towards the Christian Army and was shocked to see it deploying as if for battle on the north side of the river. As he had been talking to the girl, Longinus had already got his front lines deployed in three battles: infantry in the centre and two wings of cavalry, the escutcheon of Godric Bann Caedic on the left and Prince Craedech and Lord Herne of Hern's Ford on the right. He did not recognise the purple standard in the centre but by the day's end, his army would never forget it.

Galahaidra saw some of the Eorl's men move towards the hill-top nearest him and then begin to haul back two sapling trees which they tethered and staked to the ground, the trees bent over towards each other like two great inverted U shapes. The young knight signalled to his captains. They now had one target. All watched for Longinus' signal.

The Centurion had watched as they dragged Maria away and all hope of her rescue disappeared as she was lost to sight within the body of the massive Dacian army. His opponents were still forming: their lines a mix of type, companies and commanders, troops joining the nearest line with no formation, their flanks had still to deploy and most were following their neighbour and joining the centre van when they should be on the flanks if cavalry or at the front if archers. Knowing such an opportunity could not afford to be lost, Longinus ordered The Standard to be raised and it bowed gracefully left and right three times. Galahaidra saw the signal and launched his attack on the Eorl's rear whilst Longinus' archers fired at maximum range, their volley striking the first two lines of Dacian troops.

It was slaughter with five hundred men dropping down dead or injured under the constant withering volley-fire of the Centurion's archers whilst Galahaidra's cavalry struck the rear ranks of the Dacian army with only handfuls of the enemy mounted troops able to put up any resistance. His 'Black Company', as they would be called in honour after that night, used their swords to thrust past hasty defence and club down archers whose weapons and armour offered no defence or to cut down the vulnerable backs of infantry unable to deploy because their spears already faced forwards. The young knight was into the sixth rank of his foe when he saw Maria being tied by ropes, hands and feet to the two saplings on the hill then the guardsmen paused to send word to the Eorl as he had requested.

The Eorl was busy. Assessing the situation he could see immediately that he needed to close on his enemy to prevent further losses from the constant volleys of arrows from Longinus' archers whilst deploying his cavalry to the flanks and splitting his infantry: half to attack the Christian Army's main battle and the other half to face north and protect his rear from Galahaidra's assault. It would take five minutes for his orders to be executed and his troops to deploy. *'I must keep Maria waiting but the wait might do her good'* he mused. *'Hopefully it will add to her fear of the fate that awaits her and also sap at the morale of my enemy who can now see the girl: tethered on a hill, out of reach of their attacks and waiting to die horribly before their eyes'*. Helpless to prevent this, he expected the Christians to fall back and then he would slaughter them, cutting them down without mercy in revenge for the slaughter of his own men.

The Eorl's plan gave Longinus another five minutes and had the reverse effect on morale from that he had expected. Giving the girl up for dead, Longinus' army were the ones to seek revenge and renewed their efforts. Ten thousand arrows in ten devastating volleys struck the front two ranks of the Dacian army which fell dead, fell back or fell apart causing chaos in the next two ranks. Longinus signalled for his archers to advance and they stepped twenty paces forward and fired again. Another ten volleys saw the Eorl's third and fourth ranks collapse and run or die where they had stood. The Eorl's losses were over two thousand dead or sorely wounded and as many again had fled east and west to be cut down by the cavalry of Godwin and Craedech whose flanking cavalry had swept away the few hundreds of cavalry opposite them and was now deployed facing both of the Dacian flanks.

Galahaidra was within yards now of the atoll on which the Dacians had prepared Maria for death. His cavalry had ridden down or put to flight over two thousand of the enemy, and had formed into a wedge-shape, cutting deeper into the Dacian ranks like an arrow. In the five minutes it took the Dacian captains to find their own companies, reform around their standards and face to the north, Galahaidra had devastated the centre and west of the central battle for as much as ten ranks deep. Moreover, the threat was no longer to the rear but rather to the Dacian centre; so much of the Eorl's troops would still be facing the wrong way after deploying!

It was not the Christian's morale that fell, therefore but that of the pagan army it faced. The Eorl had lost six thousand men by the time he had deployed and faced attacks from front, rear, sides and his centre. At this critical time, he went to see to the execution of Maria and left his captains without orders. They sounded the advance and seven thousand Dacians marched forwards to engage the Christians before them whilst eight thousand faced north futilely, with no enemy before them but rather the Black Company attacking their centre and more Christian cavalry sitting ominously on their flanks.

Hoping against all hope that a further assault would distract the Dacian leadership from their intent to slay the girl, Longinus signalled for Godric and Craedech to attack. Their cavalry responded within seconds and crashed into the flank of the Dacian rearward van, deployed to face north, driving deep into the pagan army, unhorsing cavalry, trampling on archers and cutting through the defence of the infantry. In the first minute over a thousand Dacians fell but the impact on the rest of the Dacian ranks was more devastating as the archers dropped their weapons and fled north, infantry knelt in surrender and cavalry tried to deploy around their standards, waiting for an order to counter-attack.

Galahaidra's path to the atoll was suddenly clear and he rode as the wind to gain the height of the hill. In moments he had cut down the six guards left as sentries on the hill with his Lance and approached Maria. With one swipe of his sword, he had cut the ropes to her right ankle and hand and then held her as she fell forwards.

But the Eorl was not to be denied his moment of black-hearted pleasure and arrived at the atoll with a half company of cavalry, some fifty men.

"You cannot hope to defeat so many of us" the Eorl spoke with glee and signalled for his men to prepare to cut the sapling to which the knight and the girl were still attached.

"Go" Maria begged Galahaidra but the young man shook his head then hanging onto her tight and with the Lance secured in its leather holster on his back, his shield on its strap across his left shoulder, he unsheathed his sword and waited his moment. The rope holding the sapling was cut: Maria and Galahaidra were flung high into the air to their west towards the trees that had been the knight's cover earlier that morning.

Maria gasped at the pain as the rope wrenched them both up into the air; she was still held by ankle and wrist. But Galahaidra was ready and cut both ropes with another swipe of his sword as the ropes went slack briefly. Their momentum sent them flying through the air and the young sicariot sheathed his sword then covered them both with his shield, preparing to protect them both from the impact as they crashed through the branches of the trees towards which they were hurtling at great speed.

Seconds later they tumbled through the top branches of a tree, which slowed them down and they came to rest against its trunk. Galahaidra saw that Maria's left upper arm, shoulder, knee and ankle were terribly mangled, however, and took out the Spear then prayed over her and slowly her arm and leg began to heal. Both then gave praise to God for the girl's miraculous rescue before Maria stuck her head out of the branches to give a cheery wave to her many followers. Moments later she could be seen hale and heaty held securely in the grasp of the first knight of her Order of the Risen Christ. The result as she was carried to safety was devastating on the already failing morale of the Dacians whose rear ranks began to flee, whilst the Eorl stood on his atoll paralysed in shock and disbelief.

Six ranks of Dacian infantry advanced into the killing zone set by Longinus and had to survive two volleys of arrows before they struck the line of sharply-spiked stakes and the shield wall beyond. Five hundred fell to arrows, the same to a volley of throwing spears launched by Galahaidra's infantry, another six hundred died, impaled on the stakes as those behind them pushed forwards and then the spears of the enemy met the shields and sword thrusts of the best warriors in the whole of the western and southern kingdoms. The contest was one-sided and another six hundred fell for the loss of a handful of Christians. The Dacian second rank however filled the gap and for the first time their weight of numbers began to tell and they were able to push the front line of Longinus' army backwards.

This was the only point at which the Dacian army could take hope and it lasted a few seconds; or the time it took for the Christian front rank to take one step backwards then hold once more under the orders of its two Decurions. Then Longinus' reserve under Eorls Hendrix and Hosta hit the flanks of the advancing Dacians and two files of infantry turned in flight, leaving the rest to their fate as they were now surrounded. The fleeing infantry never escaped for they fell to the anger and fury of the cavalry of Galahaidra, Godric and Craedech.

The Eorl Edgthbert's standard bearer signalled for his army to retreat to the atoll on which the Eorl would make his final stand. None of his archers made it but nearly one thousand cavalry and two thousand infantry were able to cut their way through the grip that Longinus now had on the battlefield.

"Come" said Galahaidra to Maria. "I have a battle to fight whilst you will want to lead the healing of the many wounded who have fallen today." Maria nodded then whistled and Epona appeared flying across the battlefield to be the mount for Galahaidra who lifted the girl to sit on the stallion's pommel before him.

"I come with you on one condition" said the girl grinning. "I get to fly through the air like that again" and the knight laughed.

Longinus left the Eorl to muster his final defence and concentrated on finishing off the Dacians that had advanced south and cutting down those that had fled north. Thousands began to surrender and the Centurion sent word that they should be treated with mercy: disarmed, hands to be tied then to be held captive in a great ring around which the cavalry of Craedech stood guard. Herne's and Godric's cavalry and Galahaidra's infantry and archers now advanced towards the atoll under its young commander; the survivors of Galahaidra's Black Company, some six hundred mounted heroes and champions were guarding its slopes and ensuring there was no escape for the remaining three thousand Dacians. Maria stood alone looking around at the death and devastation then wept, before striding once more to approach the Dacian leader, as she had done less than an hour earlier.

Both Godric and Craedech looked at her distant lonely figure in disbelief for they had just fought a battle to free her from captivity and a terrible death and now she proposed to place herself within Dacian grasp once more. Longinus and Iosephus were too far away to reason with her and so she marched towards the atoll, to halt halfway up its gentle incline and wait silently as before. The Eorl came with twenty cavalry but this time stopped ten paces from her … for the Eorl could see he was within firing range of the Christian archers and Longinus was ready to signal for them to fire if there was any fresh attempt to take the girl.

"What do you want?" asked the Eorl.

"I wish to speak to your men. For you already are a man marked for death and your hope for salvation depends now on God's mercy. You will find none here. Your men, however, can live in peace and if they will listen it is my hope that they will believe in my God. I come to offer them one last chance for redemption."

The Eorl spat at her then cursed her before saying: "My men would rather die than listen to you." These were his final words and his last misjudgement on that day as two of his warriors struck him down to Maria's dismay as she pleaded with them to stop, dropping to kneel and beg, then to pray for Edgthbert's departing soul that it somehow find the way to God's grace.

The captain of the Eorl's bodyguard asked her: "Will you accept our surrender?" and when she nodded, still in shock with tears of grief for the Eorl's tragic end falling freely across her cheeks, he offered her his sword and asked that she address the men gathered on the hill-top which was to have been her place of execution.

Maria stood before those who had been brave enough to form the Dacian army's last stand but now hoped to hear of their salvation. They were surprised as others had been at her youth but listened for they had seen the girl rescued, healed by a miracle and heard that she promised a new gift from God. They sought hope and Maria offered that hope: for she had forgiven those who had sought her execution and wept for the life and soul of the Eorl who had sought her death.

She stood alone before them and they admired her courage in so doing. Not one considered harming her or holding her hostage. They genuinely wanted to hear the Master's message and to have the chance to follow him as they had heard the Iceni and those from the middle, south, east and west kingdoms had already decided to do. Above all, a Christian army had defeated one of their own when outnumbered and had done so with less than one thousand fallen, slain or wounded. This was power in which they wanted to have a share.

Maria stood and spoke. Her words were recorded by many to spread through Dacia like wild fire and eventually would see the King of Dacia meet with Maria and talk of peace not war:

"I am come to give you the message of my Master; a message that will change your lives but for each of you the change will be unique. This message is not about me. I shall die yet the message will remain. Rather it is about the relationship every one of you will have with God and the reward that is waiting for you. My Master seeks peace not war but he is also capable of great forgiveness and will forgive us for the terrible harm we have done this day if we believe in him and his mercy.

My Master has conquered death. He has died and risen again so that every one of us can live eternally in Paradise. We can reach Paradise if we do two things: obey the commandments, especially the new commandment to love God and to love each other; and to follow the new covenant or contract between God and man whereby God will always be present if we woship, honour and remember him through the breaking of bread.

I ask that we love each other and that we break the bread together. These are not my requests but God's. I am the messenger but God has many other messengers who will follow me. Do not sign up for this covenant because you seek to follow me but because you wish to follow my Master.

Finally, I do not ask you follow my Master as a condition that you live beyond today's defeat. You live if you will promise to keep the peace between us. That is all I ask so that you have life in this world. But if you seek to live in the next world then pray to my Master and follow his message as I do."

"What is this 'breaking of bread'?" they muttered amongst themselves then shouted their question for Maria to hear.

She smiled then said "Let me show you" and their eagerness was palpable. Iosephus and Longinus organised for bread to be brought, enough for the three thousands on the hill and the twelve thousand wounded or captured Dacians and thirteen and a half thousands of Christians. Maria also asked for the names of the five hundred Christians slain and read each name out so that they could honour them. Later she would oversee the healing of the six hundred in Longinus' victorious army that had been wounded and begin the long process of bringing healing to the thousands of Dacians injured in the battle.

"We have come first to ask God to forgive our sins. God can see into our hearts and knows how genuine our contrition and penance has been. Next, we follow the words and actions of my Master as he led us in the Service of the Eucharist on his last day before his execution by the Romans. If we do this in his memory, he will come to reside in our souls, hearts and minds, offering us the gifts of his Spirit: to pray in our hour of need; to heal the sick, injured, lame, crippled, infirm, deaf and blind; to bring aid to prisoners and the oppressed; to speak in tongues (and for the first time they noticed she was using their native Dacian); to prophesy concerning the future: and to offer hope."

Then she broke the bread and it was passed around to the tens of thousands listening intently and following her every word in awe. The Christians helped pass it to the Dacians and this simple act of giving cemented the peace between the two former foes. Then she said the words: 'This is me …' and told them that only two or more need gather together to break the bread but when they did God had promised to be with them."

"Must we be priests?" one brave man said and Maria shook her head. "This gift is given to all of us who keep God's commandments and trust him. Have faith and he will come. He already fills my heart every moment of every day. That divine gift waits for you too."

"Must you be there?" another warrior asked her and again Maria shook her head.

"This is about your personal relationship with God. No-one can stand in the way or is needed for you to converse directly with God. I have shown you the way but from here it is up to you."

No-one knew who first said it but a whisper became a murmur and then a cheer as with one voice they said "Thank you!"

Longinus briefed his War Council that evening, less Maria and Craedech who led the healing of almost ten thousands harmed in the battle. Another four thousand captives had been sent on their way home but many elected to stay: to help in the healing of their comrades and to sign up to join the Christian Army. When several showed through acts of healing that the gifts of the Spirit had come down on Dacians as well as their fellow Christians, the warriors flocked to Maria to ask to become Christians and to attend her Service of Praise and Thanksgiving that evening.

They were amazed to hear that they were already accepted as Christians. "Believe and break the bread. When God sees that you believe in your heart and hears you remember him when you break bread then God accepts your application to follow him. Welcome" and every one of them went to tell their comrades then over the following days took word to their families and communities. As a final act of mercy and compassion, Maria's final prayer that night was for the soul of Eorl Edgthbert and all were silenced by this act of forgiveness.

Longinus summarised the battle for the War Council: it had been a victory with a miraculous outcome. Word of the battle but not the outcome had reached King Pasterix who, on hearing that Maria had been taken captive when briefed by one of the Iceni guards he had sent to protect her, had immediately rode north at the head of a war band of twenty five thousands. King Col also heard of the impending battle and sent another five thousands north. Longinus was happy to report that by the end of the week the Christian Army would be over sixty thousands.

"I will drill the infantry and then we head north with the largest army to be seen in Britannia since that which held Julius Caesar."

"What does Maria say?" Lord Herne asked.

"She asks to go ahead to meet the Dacians with no more than five companions but Godric has forbidden it and reminded her that she must 'honour her father'. For now this is ensuring she behaves and my hope is that our show of force will bring the Lords of Dacia here to meet us. Maria went alone before the Dacian army last time; now it is the turn of the Dacians to show the courage and conviction to come and see her!"

All agreed with the proposal to seek to bring the Dacian leadership to meet Maria and not the other way around. In view of the Dacian's earlier attempt to slay the girl, her companions were reluctant to let the girl out of their sight without the escort of the Army. The warriors in their Army were equally adamant that they would not risk the girl's life again.

Then they collectively honoured Longinus and Godric for their battle plan, Galahaidra for his rescue of Maria, and Godric, Herne and the absent Craedech for their flanking attacks. Fourteen thousand had defeated an army of twenty one thousand with only a few hundred slain. Their enemy had lost seven and a half thousand slain, with nine thousand wounded and four and a half thousand captured. Over the next week, nearly fourteen thousand would go briefly to talk to their families and communities and then return with the same again as comrades, asking to join the Christian Army.

"Everyone can see a winning side and wants to be part of our success. They can see we are the future." Godric explained.

"Yes but Maria sees things differently. Her conversation with the Master on the eve of the battle changed her. We must ask what was said when she is next with us in Council" Galahaidra reflected. Iosephus, Craedech and Herne agreed. If Maria had other plans then they needed to respect her special relationship yet also have the right to follow their own visions of the future.

To those comfortable in a society governed by laws, rules and where consistency was important, the somewhat anarchic culture of faith that Maria had created founded on personal mission and vision was an anathema. To her other companions it was uplifting. Maria was not alone in conversing with the Master and his Angels: many had come forward to ask that their visions be interptreted or to lead their local communities through the power of their communion with God.

Maria's mission was still important but her Council were aware that she was growing up and still developing her own understanding of the faith her Master had shown her. She still had to learn to 'let go' and allow others to lead their communities once she had made the initial contact.

"The enthusiasm of youth and her desire to get things right for her Master see her take on too much responsibility. It is wonderful that she does so. Yet the time has come for her to let the new faith she has helped establish, stand on its own two feet" Iosephus advised with the wisdom of age and the experience of running a trading business that stretched across all of Europa, and into parts of Asia, Arabia and Africa. He continued: "Helpful as the creation of this new Order has been I think to restrict the development of the faith to just twelve minds is too limiting. Let us remember that whilst Christ had twelve apostles, he commissioned 72 disciples to go on a mission that was targetted on spreading the word to just Iudaea.

Surely, we must respect Iesus' example here?

The example given to us by the Master during his ministry saw him listen to many faithful within Synagogues across Iudaea and shape our new faith through constant discussion with individuals, groups and communities. He also went into conflict with those who placed religion, rules and the priesthood over vision and mission. He defended his own disciples when they broke rules to do good: to heal and to discuss the scriptures. We must never let this Council of Twelve become a new Sanhedrin, or the leaders of the conversion of pagan barbarians become the next generation of Pharisees and Sadducees."

At the end of the week, Longinus broke camp to move north towards Yorvic with an army of seventy five thousands. He needed to give Humberside a chance to recover from having such a huge Army living off the land and aimed to provision in Yorvic, North Alles, Darling and Dur.

As the Christian Army came to within forty leagues of the King's capital, the King did two things: first he sent a delegation to negotiate with the Christian Army; and second he abandoned the defence of Yorvic, bringing forwards the date when his new capital would move north to New Caister. Aramir, Lord of Yorvic, Ripon, the territory of Knares and the Bridge over the River Brough immediately joined the Christian Army, bringing with him ten thousand warriors that had been left to hold Yorvic against Longinus' advance.

Yorvic opened its doors to Longinus and he was careful to enter with only a hundred as escort for Maria. Maria met the delegation from the King in the City's Moot Hall and proposed to hold a Service in her Army's camp, as there was nowhere large enough in the City to take the huge numbers that now rode with them. She let the Elders of the City know that all were welcome to the service and acted as guarantor for their safe conduct.

Then she received the King's delegation in Godric's campaign pavilion, sitting in a circle as equals as she listened to their requests and concerns. Alas, a lot was bluster, blaming her for her capture and threatened death and holding her responsible for Eorl Edgthbert's death. She started to nod off and had to be kicked several times by Godric and Craedech to stay awake. The crux was that the King regarded her advance as an invasion, not helped by a significant part of her army being under King Pasterix, but then just as many were from Dacia so Maria did not understand that at all. In the end she summarised more for her own benefit as for theirs:

"The King does not wish to meet me. Meanwhile, I shall continue to head north. I shall not attack anyone but this army will defend itself. So the most peaceful solution is let us continue on our way."

"This is war!" shouted one of the delegates and Maria just laughed then said: "No it is not. Stop trying to create conflict when there is none. I am ready to meet your King but if he wants to run away then I shall head north."

Her reference to the King 'running away' was not the most tactful thing she could have said and saw the Dacian delegation rise and walk out but all admitted it had brought the meeting to a rapid close. "Just as well as another minute and I would have fallen fast asleep" Maria admitted ruefully.

"The King will come next time" advised Pasterix "and he will be angry at your words. You may have to eat humble pie if you want his support but already the south and east of his kingdom is ready to support you. The King may change tack just to avoid losing half of his realm."

"Whatever happens he is still King surely?" Maria replied naively and Godric explained that without an army, he would lose the support of his people who looked to their King to defend them from raids from all directions.

"We are not here to conquer earthly kingdoms but to open the way to the heavenly kingdom" Maria reminded them, dismayed as she realised that their huge army was giving her companions false pretensions: including the conquest of Dacia. "Can we reverse out of the situation we find ourselves in? I am happy to 'lose face' to do this. But we are not here to fight or win battles."

"Maria, I am loathe to challenge you but most of us are here to fight battles, conquer lands, and establish a Christian kingdom" Godric replied and the girl felt her heart lurch as she looked around and saw nods from all of the Council. "Even you Iosephus?" She whispered and he nodded then explained:

"You must remove some key people or we will never be allowed to preach to their subjects." At that, Maria's eyes caught fire briefly and she let them all know that though she was a minority of one, she would never budge on key principles:

"God will find a peaceful way to put me before the people of Dacia. So never say 'never'! An army of occupation is not the right way to convert the people of Dacia" then she stood and walked to the entrance of the Council. As she went outside to be alone, she said over her shoulder: "I abide by the decisions of this Council and will not openly criticise anything that you shall do. You have all saved me often, been good friends and advisors, and now you are ready to take on the future of this faith without my contribution to its leadership. I am going home."

"Who should go after her?" Galahaidra asked but then Iosephus shocked them by saying:

"No-one. She has taken her vision as far as it can go and now it is for others to take it forward. If any of us follow her then we will feel duty bound to accept what she says. She is not being sensible or realistic and cannot see that the conversion of Dacia needs a new King. She no longer represents the Master's mission and told us herself that the Master was quite prepared to let her die on the banks of the Humber. Wiser heads are now needed."

Godric and Pasterix agreed with the equites whilst Longinus was in two minds, wanting to defend Maria but recognising that her's had been a minority view for some time now. Prince Craedech was also in two minds. He loved Maria but he could also see her influence diminishing and was not sure therefore whether marriage to such a young girl whose views were out of kilter with his peers was such a good idea. Lord Herne was sad: the girl was special and somehow they had forgotten that. He had expected his friend to follow her and when the Prince did not, began to wonder if there had truly been love there at all?

Galahaidra waited a few moments then when he saw no-one else was going, stood up and followed after Maria without saying a word to his companions. He found her stroking Epona and whispering to her horse whilst looking out over the hills from Yorvic towards the east coast then west towards the kingdom of Knares and the Vale of Ripon, countryside so beautiful she felt her whole body filling with ecstasy and joy in response.

"Do not go home" Galahaidra said and Maria admitted guiltily that she did not know any more 'where home was or is'? "What is it you want then?" the knight asked.

"I confess I like the look of the armour I wear and feel honoured to have been given such a wonderful gift and I was excited when we went into battle at the Summoning Circle. But I am not a warrior; I genuinely believe that we should not kill and want to find a more gentle way to get my Master's message across."

"That is why I chose to follow you" Galahaidra admitted. "You offered a complete change from my life as an assassin. I think you are right to question what we now do. But you are wrong to walk away from this" and Maria could not help herself but kissed Galahaidra in gratitude.

"You are my perfect knight I think" she then whispered. "You see things I could never see and I need help to understand. You also see how best to achieve what my Master asks me to do when I myself am clueless. I feel out-numbered though. All these men of war surround me yet we are here to bring peace. Where are the gentle, the humble and the simple people that our Master blessed? Where are the meek and the lowly? Where can I find the peacemakers? My fault as I let this happen."

"Have you prayed yet about it?"

Maria hung her head then in shame. "I am frightened to do so as I have made such a pig's breakfast of things. My Master may not forgive me this time and I could not cope with that. I have relied all my recent life on his forgiveness and am afraid to lose it."

"Shame on you" and Galahaidra laughed. "You have taught us that God can forgive anyone and anything if there is genuine contrition. Pray and he will answer you."

Maria nodded then looked once more as the sun cast long lines of its golden benison across the fields, and the wind blew tramlines through the cornfields, the cornflowers flashing blue, yellow and green. "How clever" Maria whispered. Then she looked at the clouds as they swirled and recast themselves, now a dragon, the next moment a rabbit or a face. Not just white but with the tinge of crimson and mauve and lilac. "Bless you" she murmured and then nodded with decision and determination.

"There is too much still to be done for me to go home. I stay. And I shall pray until I have an answer and seek forgiveness for letting us get so far away from the mission we were given. What did Craedech say?" she finally asked the question she had not dared ask for fear of the answer.

"He remained silent. He is unsure. He loves you but he is also part of the establishment here. Obtain this peace with the King of Dacia and without needing to fight him. Then disband your army and send Craedech home; Godric and Pasterix too. But you need to take charge again!"

That evening, she held the Service of the Eucharist. First she addressed the Dacians on what she had learnt from her conversation with the Master:

"God makes decisions about things that will affect our lives, change them for the better. Yet, we must still accept those decisions and can influence them through our prayer or we can ignore them and do our own thing.

If we ignore God's path then each time we do so, it becomes harder and harder to rebuild the bridge between us and God. The wonder of God's mercy is that it never becomes too hard. Sometimes, we may think that what we do is right but each time we change the path set by God we became tangled in life's brambles, we stray into storm's path to be thrown by our most sure-footed steed, or fall into ditches that God's path would have avoided, or worse, we become lost and to escape the dark places we take a path that was never God's intent. In guilt or with stubbornness we then hide from God … without the humility to go before him and admit to our error.

There is no argument but that God has repeatedly said that *to kill is wrong*. There is no excusing killing because it is a 'necessary evil'. It is still evil. I am honoured that so many have gathered to become the first ever Christian Army and to have won our first battle. But can we not learn the lessons that mean this is our last battle also?

I shall go to meet the King of Dacia and will go unarmed. You can come with me or stay here but anyone with me must forego war, violence, the harming of others, the wearing of weapons and armour. I shall ride bare-headed without armour or weapon and enter the gates of New Caister: either to my death or to peace with Dacia. I will not demand the King comes here or make any demand upon him. Instead I will remember and honour the promise I made never to force my faith on anyone. You see it is not *my* faith … it is God's and it is yours.

You are all welcome to come with me but I will not go to war for you or for anyone" and suddenly Maria stood before her Master, shining so brightly she could not see his face for the glare of the Spirit that filled him.

"Are you angry, lord?" she whispered accepting that if he were angry then she deserved this. Yet she stared at him without fear for she was determined to put things right and make good the mess she had made.

"No" came his voice, so strident and powerful she covered her ears with her hands.

"I cannot see you, lord" she murmured, saddened that he remained so distant and her question was greeted with silence. She tried again: "Is what I do wrong?"

"No" and this time his voice was more gentle but still she could not see his face. So she kept trying, deciding she would not give up until her Master would at least smile once at her: "You have taught me to ask for what I want. Let me see your face!"

"Why?" and at her Master's non-committal response she nearly collapsed in tears yet still she would not give up. Her faith was too strong to quail before his righteousness.

"I wish to see your face because I rejoice in seeing your face who was my best friend on Earth and will be my best friend in Heaven; because your smile reassures me that I do your will and gives me the courage to carry on; because I would see you happy and when I cannot see your face I do not know if what I do is the right thing or not to please you."

Then she stood upon a tall cliff and heard her Master's voice behind her say: "Do not turn around." Maria obeyed without question. Then her Master said:

"Throw yourself from this cliff and I will save you and show you my face."

Without hesitation she said: "No. That would be wrong" and she was standing on the beach in the cove that she recognised was her own heart, beneath the pavilion where her Master resided and her Master looked at her and his smile saw her heart leap for joy. "Ooops" she went apologetically as they were both shaken by the jolt of her heart's leaping and the sand rose several feet in the air to crash down around them whilst the smooth waters were briefly marred by the fury of the fiercest sea.

"You know what is right and what is wrong. Trust in your instincts. Do not surrender to doubt."

"Was it doubt that hid your face from me, lord?"

"Yes. But I never doubted you. So why you should doubt yourself defeats me."

"If it is any help, I have no idea either but then I have to admit that about most things" and she stared ruefully out to sea wondering if she would ever understand what it was she was doing? The Master laughed then bolstered her confidence as he said: "You do well without understanding. You should be proud of your achievements. You have done more than enough if you want to stop."

That brought her head round with a snap and she said "No" before even thinking about it then apologised at the abruptness of her answer. But her Master was pleased and would not accept her apology. "Sometimes you say sorry for the wrong things! Forgive me but why do you let Godric, Pasterix, Craedech, Longinus and Iosephus have so much sway over you?"

"Because they have also seen your vision and carry part of your message with them."

"Have you so little confidence in what I tell you?"

"Oh No" said Maria cradling her face in shock. "Oh dear, is that what it is that I am doing wrong? But it is my sense of fairness. I think it is unfair that my vision of your message should be seen as more important than each of their's."

"It is *my* vision not yours" her Master said gently and Maria stood once more before the tens of thousands at the Service outside the gates of Yorvic and said:

"Follow my Master and seek peace rather than war. It will be hard but he will be there to help you! Join me tomorrow as I ride for New Caister by praying for me and let us show that we can win God's battles without weapons of war but rather with the love we feel for our fellow man."

That night Maria kept being woken up: Godric was the first to wake her.

"Forgive me" he said. "A father should have more trust in his daughter" then he kissed her on the forehead and retired to his half of the tent.

Next was Longinus. He paced back and forth not saying a word then went to sit at the end of her bed only to jump up again. She went to say something to help him calm down but he just held up one finger, wagged it at her but would not make eye contact and said "No! No! No! No!"

then started pacing up and down again. Finally he said: "I am coming tomorrow to protect you" to which she replied: "I do not want or need your protection." He looked at her in shock, rendered momentarily speechless as she had often done before then said "But … but Iesus said I was to protect you."

"No he did not. He asked you 'to look after me'. Not the same at all. And it might not have been *me* anyway!" Maria said a grin on her face so broad he could not help smiling in return but then he accepted what she had said.

"Tell me what to do" he admitted defeated and deflated but she laughed gaily, her face shining with delight then said: "Just be with me. And forget any weapons."

Pasterix was next. He was not brave enough to dare her part of the tent so booted Godric out of bed and asked Maria if she would join him. She put on a robe and popped her head around the screen. Haladriel just moaned saying "Now who?" and placed a bolster over her head theatrically. Maria sat down carefully aware the robe she was wearing was not hers, as she had borrowed Haladriel's which was made for the cold of north Briton, unlike her own flimsy peplon and stola, but it was several sizes too big. She hung on to various bits of hem to stay covered and protect her dignity. Pasterix just leapt straight in: "I am sorry. I will leave tomorrow if you want but I have got it all wrong. You will have more chance of obtaining peace with Dacia if I am not with you."

"It may be harder but if you are part of any agreement then the peace will be better. Could you find a way to be with me but not with twenty five thousand warriors at your side?"

"How many warriors would you recommend?" he asked hesitantly.

"No warriors. But twenty five thousand followers all seeking peace and offering me their prayers rather than their protection would be nice" at which the King's eyes shone then he said: "Maria, forgive me. Your vision is greater than I could ever envisage and your courage leaves me breathless. I will stay here with my army and we will pray for our Master to grant there be peace between the Iceni and Dacia."

Then it was Lord Herne's turn. Haladriel glared at him, which made him gulp. Maria quickly grabbed his arm then took him to Godric's side of the screen. The Prince of the Atrebates was equally unreceptive so they both headed outside, Herne's arm being hugged tightly by the girl as she apologised for both of their receptions of him.

"Was it something I said?" he asked perplexed. "No" and she started to giggle remembering the look on Haladriel's face "just you are not the first to disturb them tonight. Now how can I help?"

"I am the advance guard. It is not me you need to talk to but Craedech. Stay here and I will find him for you." She clung onto Herne's arm and asked worried for the first time that evening: "Is he alright? Is he angry with me?"

"No and No. Let him explain himself! And be gentle on him."

She was standing under an oak tree at the edge of their camp, the squirrels chattering angrily above her head as she succeeded in disturbing their sleep just as she had murdered the sleep of all of her friends thus far. Yet to feel the strength of the tree's history and imagine the wonderful sense of ancient memory within the safety and solid comfort of its majestic bark gave her the courage to face her swain's love; and hope for a joyful outcome yet fearing that he would end their love this night. She turned alone to face a nervous Prince.

Maria was conscious that she was wearing nothing beneath her bedrobe and that her greatest wish was to kiss away all the nervousness, worry and concern she could see on her man's face. But she feared if she moved either hand from where they were placed strategically to hold her robe in place, she would be left naked and embarrassed. So she restrained herself somehow and waited for the Prince to speak first. He looked at her face, watching for some sign and so she smiled. Instead of reassuring him that made him even more uncomfortable. At last, he built up the courage to ask:

"Say something, please."

Ignoring the fact that he had got his best friend to drag her out of her comfortable and warm bed *because he had something to say to her*, she decided that she would need to take charge of the conversation and then realised that this was also defining their respective roles for the rest of their lives:

"If you look over my right shoulder you should see the planet Venus as the brightest thing in the sky. At some point in the next ten minutes it will move across the path of the Moon and a small chunk will look as if it has been eaten by a mouse: an enormous gigantic invisible cosmic space mouse! Or so my child-like mind imagines. This is known as Venus being in the 'ascendancy' and anything that affects the cycle of the Moon affects women who are governed by the Moon's gravity in many ways. Put simply, tonight is a good night to say to your girlfriend or your future wife or indeed any girl you might meet that 'You love her'. If that is what you want to say?" she added shyly.

"If I said that" he replied, looking into her eyes and ignoring the sky behind her "What would you say?"

"You will just have to find out" she said mischievously then seeing the look of anxiety and fear writ large on his face she had mercy on him. Taking a hand, she kissed it then said: "I am still yours. It was I that lost you and not the other way around."

"No" he admitted honestly. "I put my desire to be respected by Godric and Pasterix before my love for you. I am contemptible."

"Yes you are" she confirmed at which his eyes went wide then he realised she was teasing him and a slow grin appeared on his face. "What did Herne say to you?"

"That I was to punish you mercilessly for days. Now stop avoiding why you came here or I shall have to tease you some more!"

He was still not quite ready yet but he knew he must tell her sometime. He was confused by all that had happened this night and had not come to terms yet with how the night had panned out. At last, he took a deep breath and then as Maria held his arm and squeezed it tightly for reassurance, he told her what had happened and suddenly she understood why Godric, Longinus and Pasterix had been to see her. She then realised that this meant she would be disturbed by one more person that night and wondered if she would get any sleep?

"The Master came to see me for the first time ever. I have received the gifts of the Spirit but tonight was the first time I have met or seen the Master. I have to believe it was him as I never met him during his Ministry. He said to me and I shall never forget his words: 'You must choose between Maria and pride in your position as the Prince of the Dobunni, Corvinii and Catuvellauni. For Maria's mission might take you anywhere in the world. If you do not choose Maria then you must hope that I forgive you one day.'

'But I love her' I had replied.

'You did not support her when she needed you to' the Master reminded me and I confess I had already felt guilty about that. 'She holds my message and you ignore her at risk of my displeasure.'

'What should I do?' I asked.

'You could listen to her. I find in general that it helps!' and then the Master was gone. I have been thinking all night since and what I have come to tell you is that I will follow your lead wherever you go. So tomorrow …"

"Later *today*" Maria corrected him in a whisper thinking of her warm bed; fortunately he did not catch what she murmured.

"… I shall come with you unarmed without my armour and invite anyone else from Glevum to do the same and I shall follow your vision faithfully for it is the Truth. Forgive me for not seeing that."

"You were forgiven the moment I saw your poor anxious face. Now take me back to my tent before I turn into an icicle."

He escorted her back to Godric's pavilion, being careful in the dark to avoid the guy ropes of other tents but also suddenly aware of the bitter cold that was creeping rapidly in as the clouds cleared and the winds built up. She was grateful for his company and as they got to the entrance, she did what she had wanted to do for the last half an hour and leant forwards then turned her head upwards to look into his eyes and as he bent forward to say 'Good Night' she kissed him on the lips then sighed contentedly and left him, his mouth dropping open like a stranded fish.

Which is how his best friend found him and laughed: "Went well?" and the Prince nodded then suddenly laughed and hugged his friend in his joy. Next moment he remembered something that Maria had said and frowning, asked Herne: "Why did you tell Maria to 'punish' me?"

"I did not ..." Herne started to say then the realisation came that there was more depths to Maria than he had at first appreciated. "She is punishing me for some tactless comments of mine" he groaned then admitted "and she will make you an excellent Queen for she can be truly devious. Now tell me all that happened and I must think up some dreadful punishment for *her*."

Maria lay awake waiting for the last of her night's guests. It was another half an hour before a quiet voice said: "Are you awake, Maria?"

"Yes she is!" said Haladriel and picked up her bolster and blanket then marched around the screen and dived into bed with the surprised Godric. "Since neither of us are going to get any sleep, I could do with the company" she said to the Prince and Godric grinned then called across to Maria: "Your father is busy, take yourself off" and blushing the poor girl grabbed Haladriel's robe once more and headed for the entrance flap where Iosephus, looking equally embarrassed was waiting to see her, wringing his hands, his eyes not able to meet hers.

"I have a confession to make" he started without preamble and Maria asked: "Can we find somewhere out of the cold first. I have just been flung out of the tent I share with my father and have nowhere to sleep. How about your tent?"

"Can you cope with Longinus and Galahaidra sharing the same tent?" the equites asked and she was quite content with anywhere as long as it was warm. A few minutes later, and Iosephus had woken the Centurion up and turfed him out of his camp bed then placed Maria on it where she sat, shivering and wrapping herself in the blanket, whilst Longinus started to roll over onto the floor to sleep then saw who was in his bed and sprang up, unfortunately forgetting he was naked at which Maria screamed, hid her eyes and Galahaidra was woken up by the noise.

The two men were outside the tent in double quick time, Galahaidra saying to Longinus "Stay here and I will find the horses and get you a toga. But if you are seen with no clothes on and then anyone sees Maria leaving your tent we will have the devil to pay when we next see the two Princes" then he added: "And once you are dressed you can tell me what is going on?"

Iosephus did not give Maria a chance to settle but began to apologise immediately but he got no further than: "My lady, Maria, I owe you …"

"No you do not" Maria interrupted him. "You have been kind and patient with me for years and just because the Master came to see you tonight and told you to support me does not mean you have been wrong, merely that I had assumed that the vision of conquest you had was something you had been given by the Master whereas my own sense of right and wrong should have told me the Master would never have advocated having an Army or going to war. I should have stuck to my guns. Now give me a quick hug, promise me we are still friends, tuck me in bed then go and find somewhere else to sleep with those other two idiots whom I also love dearly but I have now seen Longinus naked twice and that is two times too many for my young, frail and fragile heart."

Iosephus chuckled, mouthed a grateful 'I love you', kissed the girl on the forehead then having tucked her in as she had asked, headed for outside where he found Longinus, now blue with cold still waiting for some clothes. "We need another tent Centurion as this one is taken" the knight whispered then handed the young officer his own cloak.

Galahaidra came up trumps, returning five minutes later with clothes for Longinus, news of a tent where they could bag three beds that was far enough away from their own billet to stop evil tongues wagging and, best of all, he had found one of the camp followers, a young girl who had tagged on to their Army as they had gone through North Alles and, whilst having the morals of an alley cat would classify as a chaperone for Maria especially as Galahaidra was paying the girl well to keep her mouth shut.

“Now tell me what is going on?” the young knight asked and Longinus retorted: “Only if you can tell me how you manage to find a spare girl in a camp full of soldiers in the middle of the night … and ignore that, I just do not want to know!”

The following morning, Maria returned before first light and snook into Godric’s tent, tiptoeing past the sleeping Godric and Haladriel and into the screened off section of the Prince’s pavilion. She got dressed in her simple peplon and stola, placing her armour carefully in a trunk which she shut and locked away, still proud of Godric’s gift but saving it for a time when she could wear it without it making a statement that she was something other than what she was. ‘*One day*’ she thought wistfully then sat and waited for everyone else to wake up.

Fifteen minutes later Godric stuck his head around the screen and asked if she was up. Seeing Maria was wide awake, he came across and sat on the bed next to her then asked: “What is the plan?”

“I ride for New Caister with a few companions as an escort but no-one is to be armed. I meet with the King of Dacia. I do not think he will be as foolish as poor Eorl Edgthbert so I expect he will see me, see that I am harmless and also when he sees I have no ambitions to supplant him, he might even allow my request. I shall brief the Council over breakfast then leave immediately as I have over 140 leagues to ride and it will take me ten or eleven hours. I will arrive this evening provided I set out early.”

“You are still not the best of riders. I fear you will exhaust yourself” Godric asked concerned but Maria just smiled and said that if she must fall off then it was God’s will and if she hurt herself badly then God must have other plans for her. Then they both carried the sleeping Haladriel back to her own bed to catch up on her missed sleep and set out the chairs for the Council meeting later that morning. By the sixth hour they had a full house but most people looked pretty rough after a sleepless night of tent hopping. Lord Herne muttered about getting his revenge and then was shocked when Maria retorted: "I will tell on you to your wife, Craedech's sister, Egtheghbreda, if you do." The lord was in enough trouble with his wife as it was and capitulated.

Once the full Council were present, Maria set out her plans for the day and there was no dissent. All agreed that she depart with a small and unarmed escort and aim to ride for New Caister by that evening, travelling light and each rider taking one change of horses. The weather forecast was good and a cloudless blue sky greeted them as the first light of dawn came across the sea to their east.

Longinus suggested that the original company of six should go north, but Craedech asked to be included and Felstum had already been sent by Iosephus to secure shipping for their return journey. "We exchange Felstum for Craedech then. We get a good rider and warrior to replace a loyal man but not one who is firm in the saddle."

"What about Brascerus?" Maria asked. "I want him safe and looked after as he has provided much intelligence concerning the Council of Sorcerers and he will be at risk of assassination by them."

Godric had the answer, offering to take him into his household for safe-keeping as he was heading home and taking Pasterix and the troops from King Col under Eorl Hendrix with him. "It still leaves you an Army of over thirty thousand and I would leave that to hold Yorvic until you can settle things with the King at New Caister."

As they were getting ready to leave, Haladriel came to Maria in floods of tears and the two girls found themselves a quiet corner in Godric's huge tent then the young girl unburdened herself: "Can I go with Godric? I can find you someone from here to go with you to New Caister but I would like to go home to South Hamm and Godric has offered to take me with him. Would you mind?"

Maria held her hand, dried her tears and comforted her saying "Of course you can go with my Lord Godric and he is lucky to have such a wonderful companion. Do not let him bully you!"

By the seventh hour they were ready to leave. Galahaidra rather contrarily insisted on wearing his armour but the rest of the party, abiding by Maria's wishes, were in their day to day wear but with additional layers to stave off the cold despite it being a sunny day. Haladriel had been as good as her word and found a middle aged nurse maid who was between families and a good rider. Her name was Kaera and she had family in New Caister so welcomed the ride and the company. This brought the company back up to six and they set off promptly.

Thurscchia was their first stop and they made the hills above the settlement at just past the ninth hour. A short stop, change of horses and they bashed on for the Hill of Darling. Their way crossed moors and rolling hills, rushing brooks and streams, shallow stoney fords, rickety wooden bridges and deep waters that were skirted by the paths which they rode: old bridle paths and newly cleared tracks. They skirted the foothills of the Pennines and kept to the lower ground as much as possible. They made slow but steady progress, ten to twelve leagues in each hour, seeing few opportunities for a gallop but when they did come across an open field they would make the most of it.

By noon they had reached Darling and were making good time as they were now past the halfway mark. Iosephus found them an Inn and they stopped to have luncheon, ale for the men, wine for Kaera, water for Maria. Maria left the men and Kaera chatting and wandered off to discover a peep-hole which had been cut through the brambles and hedgerow to create a viewpoint revealing a magnificent vista: a deep gorge that went as far as Aycliff and the settlement of Dur that sat across two hills with the Forest of Sacres beyond.

Before her, there were steep banks of heathers of every conceivable tint of greens and purples, with the river Browneigh at the bottom, silver and meandering in gentle curves with the occasional rill and waterfall. Dragon's Vale was at the furthest edge of her view, the proud head of an ancient fire-breathing serpent as a rocky promontory captured for all time and guarding the southern approach to Caister.

She recalled one of the many songs of praise, naming God as the creator of 'form' and 'colour'. "Such form and colour is wonderful" she murmured in gentle prayer.

Then a chaffinch burst into song in the elm a few paces to her right, the tree sitting on the steep slope with its exposed roots providing a natural, timber-framed home for a new family of badgers, the bird sitting at the furthest end of a branch that hung precariously into open space with the drop down to the base of the deep gorge below. Maria smiled as she enjoyed the bird's warbling chant and the sound of the water rushing over stone cobbles below, the leaves and branches rustling like the sound of waves upon a sandy shore, the sun at its peak overhead, bathing everything below in its gentle warmth. "Still a cold sun" she muttered but then she decided that when it was not raining, a cold sun could be quite pleasant especially as in the desert one hid from the hot sun there all the time!

She said a simple 'thank you' to her Master for talking to her companions. She had not asked or expected that he would become so involved but she was grateful as her friends now understood her better and were supporting her. She found a tree stump to perch on with the bark of an old and gnarled oak that gave her shelter from the heat of the noon day sun and offered her a back rest then, courtesy of her missed night's sleep, she yawned, her head dropped down onto her chest and she nodded off.

"Where is she, the dratted girl?" Longinus muttered then he caught sight of her and beckoned Iosephus over asking: "What shall we do?"

"We have to wake her I am afraid. We must leave now or risk arriving at New Caister in the dark or worse, after curfew has begun and the gates will then be shut to us."

Longinus tried whispering in her ear and stroking her cheek but neither brought the girl out of her deep sleep. Iosephus called her name gently at first then increasingly loudly and there was not even a flutter. Muttering terrible imprecations to the Gods of Sleep, Longinus lifted the girl up and carried her to his own horse, then handing her briefly to Iosephus, mounted up and asked the knight to pass the girl up to him. "She has lost weight again" the old knight said to the world at large but genuinely concerned as she was now lighter than many of the children they would often meet on their travels.

"She is fading again as well" Longinus observed and he held out her arm to the sun and they all could see her veins running in bright blues and mauves within her pale golden skin. He held his own hand the far side of her arm and they could make out its faint shadow. "Did anyone see her eat?" he asked finally and all shook their heads.

They left Darling and headed north-west for the Land of Auck, seeking the hill top way from Stile, skirting west of Dur to Esh through Lower Eigh, crossing the Tyne at the Bridge of Blay and on to Caister through the north gate in the woodlands of North Humberlandia, not risking going too fast as Longinus held the sleeping Maria on his saddle before him.

They met their first challenge between Esh and as they backtracked to follow the Vale of Eigh north and west. As they rode beneath the canopy of ancient trees, they encountered a hunting party of two Dacian nobles, their ladies and retainers on horseback and following the trail of a lone stag through the Forest of Sacres. On seeing the company the nobles stopped and commanded them to halt then started to question them closely. They ignored Maria but were interested in Craedech and Galahaidra; the Prince because he was wearing his signet ring and was more finely dressed than the rest of the company and Galahaidra because of his armour and the hatchment on his shield which they took at first to be Iceni.

Galahaidra explained the origins of the prancing pony and fortunately one of the Dacians had heard of the Vale of the White Horse whilst the Prince was able to say he came from Glevum which impressed them as every one from the west kingdom was thought to be immensely wealthy.

All was going well when suddenly one of the wild boars in Maria's saddle bags grunted and stuck out its bleary and sleepy-eyed head. The hunting party shrunk back and drew their hunting spears or their bows and arrows ready to slay the boar when some instinct woke Maria up, she yawned, stretched saw the swords and in faultless Dacian said:

"The wild boars are mine and rescued when their father was slain. They mean no harm and will sleep until we get to New Caister."

"Why are you going to New Caister?" the leader of the party, a local laird, asked her curious as to why a simple country girl who rescued wild boars should want to go to their new capital: "And whose horse is that?" a second noble in the party asked, admiring Epona.

"We go to the capital to meet the King and the horse is mine" Maria replied without blinking or disguising their intent.

"What makes you think you will be seen by the King?" the laird sneered whilst his peer said: "Take her and hang her for the horse is clearly stolen."

Longinus felt slowly and carefully for the dagger in his ankle holster whilst Galahaidra had dropped his sicarius down his left sleeve and into his left hand held furthest away from the two nobles so out of their view. Both men were preparing for mayhem. But Maria had other ideas. She sat up straight and with dignity said: "I am not and never have been a thief. But this is easily resolved. Walk the horse some distance from me and I will call it. If I had just stolen it, the horse would ignore me. I will let you call him first. His name is 'Epona' and he was a gift to me from King Pasterix" at whose name both men stood back suddenly alarmed.

Then the first noble said: "I think you are honest from the clarity and innocence of your eyes. You have told us the truth and not hidden your intent or that you know the Iceni King though this would make us fear you. I will give you trial as you suggest" and he asked his fellow noble to lead Epona away about fifty paces.

"Epona" he called and the horse's ears pricked forward recognising his name but then he snorted and turned his back at which the nobleman had the grace to laugh. Maria whispered the name so gently that almost it went unheard but not by her horse who reared and then charged forwards, galloping to be at her side. Epona nuzzled Maria's hand and she fondly caressed his ears whilst both nobles nodded then the party leader said: "The lady is honest" at which she bowed her head shyly but the laird then continued: "so now must tell us why she rides to meet out King?"

Maria was happy to do so: "I bring an offer of peace from the peoples south of here. I seek permission from the King to speak of a gift offered by my Master. I am come from Humberside and Yorvic where I left an army in order to come before your King alone if needs must so that he does not fear me."

The whole hunting party laughed at that and one of the ladies challenged Maria saying: "You are just a girl and of no status. Why would our king possibly be afraid of you?" then another whispered to her neighbour "Perhaps she is a little strange in the head?" and the rest of the party agreed, the leader turning to Longinus to say: "Look after her well. Alas she is pretty but half-starved and quite mad. You are kind to take care of the child" and taking his money bag and unlacing it from his belt he threw it to Longinus saying: "I hope this helps. At least get some food inside her."

Then they rode off with Maria saying a prayer of gratitude for their generosity before telling Longinus that since they had been given the money under false pretences he must give it all to the nearest almshouse. "There are 40 gold pieces here, enough to feed you for a year!" Longinus exclaimed frustrated but Maria was adamant that they give the money to charity.

They found the Tyne as it went north from Stock and followed it as it weaved in and out of forests, valleys and rocky outcrops, until they could see the wooden bridge at Bray and the palisade and stone towers beyond, set on a muddy mound surrounded by a motte and an earth wall being the outer fortifications for the King's new capital and garrison town.

Here he could command thirty thousands to defend his new city of New Caister. The City was a fortified camp with the King's Hall, Moot Hall and Devizes but no other buildings, the rest of the huge site being given over to a vast community of pavilions and tents, the home for his army and their support staff such as blacksmiths, armourers, butchers and bakers and their families. Sixty thousand residents lived in this tented realm, nearly half the entire population of his kingdom and half of these were warriors.

At the seventh hour in the evening and just as the sun had started to dip beyond where the Tyne met the North Sea, lighting up the twin-rivers that were woven into the fabric of the City, Maria and her company presented themselves at the City's North Gate and stone barbican. They were immediately challenged:

"Who are you, whom do you seek and state the purpose of your visit?" to which Maria answered:

"I am Maria, called also The Magdalan and am come to see King Jaerid, King of Dacia. My purpose is to discuss peace and therefore I am willing to go alone before the King."

"Follow me" replied one of the sentries, pointing to Maria and indicating that she should step through the postern gate. "The rest of you stay here" and spears were pointed at the throats of Craedech, Longinus and Galahaidra. Maria was ushered into a dark cell but relieved when she saw the door was left open, indicating she was detained but not yet under arrest. She was then commanded to strip and when she protested spears were pointed at her own throat but Maria stood up for herself.

"I am a young girl and not accustomed to going naked before men. Is there some way you can do what you must do yet I retain my modesty and dignity?"

"Here" said a gruff voice and tossed her a towel. She undressed, turning her back to them and then eventually built up the courage to turn to face them, covering the nakedness of her lower body with the towel but having to expose her small breasts and blushing in shame as she did so.

The guard took one disinterested look and said: "She is clean" then searched her clothing before passing it back to the girl to get dressed again. She dressed quickly but then began to cry at the outrage of what they had done to her and one of the guards threatened to cuff her over the head at which she sniffed then wept in silence.

The commander of the guard and captain of the watch for that night entered Maria's cell, took one look at her youth and fragile beauty, confirmed with his guardsman that the girl was unarmed and gave his orders:

"We have no indication or notice of any visit or appointment with the King by someone called 'the Magdalan' and must assume that you are either mad or intend our King some harm. You are unarmed and clearly not dangerous so we believe you are deranged and we will send you on your way" but then he was interrupted by the sound of running and a guardsman joined them, nodding to his captain and then whispering in his ear. After a brief pause, the captain asked Maria:

"Why is the Prince of the Dobunni in your company?"

"He accompanies me. It is our hope that when my mission for my Master is fulfilled that then we might be partnered in this life and in the next."

"Who is your Master?" he asked in confusion then continued in disbelief: "And why should the Prince of one of the largest kingdoms in Britannia seek your hand who can choose any princess in the land?"

"You must ask the Prince why he seeks my hand" the girl replied her head held high now, all sign of tears and shame departed; blue eyes bright in the knowledge that she did not fear whatever they might do to her. "I do not truly know why he seeks to marry me but I will gladly do so for I love him. I am the Princess Maria Bann Caedic, the sole heir and adopted daughter of Prince Godric Bann Caedic Wulfridson, Prince of the Atrebates, Durobriges, Belgae and Regni, the biggest kingdom in southern Britannia.

My Master is Iesus of Nazareth and the one true God. I come to see your King with word of a gift from God and to seek peace between the southern, western and middle Kingdoms, the Iceni and the Dacians."

The captain now shook with shock and asked, frightened of what dishonour his men may have done to the lady and fearful of the answer:

"You are the leader of the 'Christian Army' that defeated the Eorl Edgthbert of Humberside and to whom the army of Eorl Aramir of Yorvic surrendered?"

Maria was as ever truthful as she replied: "No. My companion Longinus who also rides with the Prince led the army but they follow my Master's message."

The captain spoke then to his guardsmen and what he heard distressed him. Now he feared all on watch that night would face grim punishment and asked more in hope than any certainty: "Did my men distress you or dishonour you?"

"I was stripped naked but not harmed. It is not the reception I would wish but your men needed to know that I am harmless. I forgive them and will make no mention of this to your King if you will also keep what your men have done secret from my companions. For I fear their anger should they come to know of my dishonour at your hands. My mission is to bring peace, not become the cause of unnecessary war."

The captain bowed and gladly promised that he and his men would ensure no word of the shame of her strip search should ever leave that cell. He expressed his gratitude, humbled by her forgiveness: "My lady, my men and I are grateful that you are so merciful and forgiving. Let us take you to see our King. You have our thanks and praise."

They climbed one flight of stairs to reach the ground level of the barbican at the north gate and Maria stepped out onto a long street that ran along the centre of two rows of tents and pavilions. She loved the colour of their hatchments, stripes and waves of contrasting blues, greens, reds, yellows, golds and silver, poles with finials, tall flag poles and the stands for banners, stacks of spears and swords, the butts for arrow practice, and the odd abandoned fletch or head from an arrow. The evening sun was still out in its red fiery glory, its flames touching the tops of silvery clouds, the golden circle of the moon a half shadow, set huge in the blue sky beneath the clouds.

At the centre of the City of Tents that spread in a circle within the palisaded perimeter wall of Caister was a square containing the law courts, Moot Hall and the King's Hall, the latter building dwarfing the rest of the City, standing fifteen paces tall, eighty paces long and twenty five paces wide. It was made from huge oak trunks holding a timber frame and vaulted ceiling, with a thatched straw roof, grey stone base and walls of dried mud over its timber frame. The walls were painted but also held woollen rugs and tapestries for insulation and to bring relief to the otherwise dark hall. A row of mullion windows sat at the top of the walls offering some light whilst every ten paces, huge cartwheels of iron acted as candelabra, hanging from the oak rafters of the ceiling.

The King's Hall was divided into: the Banqueting Hall, with three long trestle tables and a dais with the top table and the King's Throne; the King's Chamber where he slept on the ground, or on rugs with woollen blankets as a covering around a roaring fire with his companion champions and his Queen besides him; and then the Queen's Bower and Warde Robe which offered the Queen a private chamber for her ladies in waiting and the Queen herself to bathe and dress in.

The King was seated on his throne in conference with three of his four remaining Eorls: the laird of the Brigantes, the laird of the Caledonian Lowlands of Segolvae, Votadini and Damnonii and the Eorl of Novantae. They sat around the centre trestle at the end of the table nearest the King but all four men had turned as the Captain of the Watch entered, bowed and announced Maria: "My liege lord, your royal highness, may I present the Princess Maria Bann Caedic of the Atrebates known as the Magdalan."

Maria also bowed then stood with her hands clasped before her, her eyes bright and staring honestly and without fear at the King yet her smile showing her pleasure at this meeting, her demeanour one of respect but not of submission. She shone with inner integrity yet, as ever, it was her youth that amazed the men. Also they saw her frailty and that she was almost wraithlike in her fragility, as much a part of the spirit world as the human: a single breath would blow her away like the cobwebs on the beams above their heads or to drift and swirl as the smoke from the roaring fire in the hearth to their rear.

"Are you truly the leader of the army that defeated the Eorl Edgthbert of the Parisi Coritani and Humberside and Eorl Aramir of Yorvic and Ripon?" the King asked in wonder.

"King Jaerid, wise and noble sire. Your armies follow the message of my Master. It is my command and his desire that they *pray* for us both but that they shall never fight for me against you again. My wish is for peace and for your permission to speak to the people of your land. I have a gift to offer your people, which gift is given by God. Yet your people will still need to be ruled and to have a wise King. You are that King and all I ask is to agree a treaty of peace between the many peoples in the southern, western and middle kingdoms, the Iceni and yourselves. Will you hear me, my King?"

"You have brought your army with you?" The King asked still in fear that he faced the might of the Christian Army at his gates.

"I have come to your City with five companions and have asked to come before you alone and without escort or weapon. My King" the girl pleaded "Do not be afraid for you have nothing to fear. You are King of Dacia and I make no challenge to your rule, merely am come to seek your permission to journey through your lands and speak to any that will listen to me."

The King sat back on his tall carved oak and brightly painted throne, thoughtful, not certain if he should be angered at her reference to his 'fear' or honoured that she was expressing her support of his kingship. Eorl Graedhold of the Brigantes raised a hand to indicate he had a question and at Jaerid's signal of consent, turned back to Maria to ask:

"Why if you come in peace have you brought such a huge army?"

Maria bowed to honour the Eorl, acknowledging his question then turned once more to face the King, her eyes never leaving his, glowing with honesty and her belief in her response:

"Great King and noble lairds, my noble laird, Eorl Graedhold. My Army was gathered by my companions to protect me although this was not my desire. My companions including my father by adoption were uncertain of the reception I would receive at the hands of Edgthbert. Indeed, many suspected the Eorl would seek to slay me when I went before him alone. They were right!

But I was rescued and when the Eorl attempted to attack my Army we defeated his men even though my Army was outnumbered. The Kings Col and Pasterix then sent warriors to my aid on hearing that I had been taken captive by Eorl Edgthbert whilst those from your armies captured at our battle on the Humber or guarding Yorvic under Eorl Aramir elected to follow the message of my Master.

Your army under Eorl Aramir still guards Yorvic for you but offer their prayers for my safe return and that I am successful in agreeing a peace treaty with yourself."

Jaeric lent forward now, eager to test the integrity of the girl before him:

"You are come alone? Then accept you are my prisoner and be prepared for torture and death at my hands."

"You are the King of Dacia and the ruler of these lands. If my torture and death is your wish then I shall meet my fate as bravely as I can. I am ready to die" and her eyes were unblinking, unwavering and fearless as she said this before continuing: "I am also ready to live, to speak a message to your people that they will wish to hear but which poses no threat to your rule. Above all, to avoid the war that will almost inevitably follow my death."

"You threaten me with war when a guest under my own roof" the King stood in anger and shouted at the girl who hung her fair head briefly but then lifted it once more in defiance of his ire:

"Not I. I will do anything to avoid war, even unto my own death if that is what must be. But I would rather we were at peace. My lord King, will you not at least consider peace?"

"We dispute lands with the Iceni. There can be no peace" the King continued, sitting back in his cathedra, his moment of anger passed.

"King Pasterix would listen to me. Divide the land in equal half between you."

The King laughed then scorned Maria's naivety saying: "Whom could we trust to make that division? We are so accustomed to being in dispute that neither Pasterix nor I would trust anyone to make fair division. How could we ever agree peace therefore?"

"If I could persuade Pasterix to allow *you* to make the division of the disputed lands into two equal parts, would you then agree to peace?"

"Yes" said the King surprised at her answer. "But how will you persuade Pasterix?"

Maria smiled once more then explained her intent: "I will say that you make the division … but that he gets first choice of which part to have."

All four men were silenced for a moment then scratched their heads or their beards, looking for a loophole or a problem with the solution that the girl offered but they could find no reason to continue to dispute the division if one made it but the other then had first choice. Finally, the King laughed and admitted, somewhat to his own chagrin but for the first time showing the charisma that had made him the leader of the Dacians:

"Your youth has confused us. You are wise and your Master must guide you wisely also." Maria bowed her head briefly but the King had not finished: "I will grant you your peace treaty and under the terms that you propose namely that we shall divide the disputed lands equally. But what of you sweet maid? Torture and death or shall we continue to enjoy your company?"

"Great King. Would you allow I sing for you? I would do so as penance for the wrong I have done you" and Maria's words briefly mystified the King so he asked her plainly:

"What wrong is that?"

"I wrongly and unintentionally talked of you 'fearing' me and 'running away' when I should have realised that your refusal to meet me was because you are a greater man than I. You were teaching me a lesson for my presumption. I ask your forgiveness for my folly and my poorly chosen words. I am truly penitent."

The King could not refuse her humble request for forgiveness and already was seeing the great advantage of a peace treaty with the Iceni and the other kingdoms south of his borders. Together they could resist invasions from the west and, with his southern borders secure, he could switch his attention to repelling the Pictish raids in Novantae and advance north into Caledonia, along the Firth of Forth and the territories of the Segolvae, Votadini and Damnonii.

He had no wish to keep the girl captive for this would see the army to his south rise in anger and destroy him. He did not fear that army but was realistic about his chances if he angered the rest of Britannia. Only the Angle kingdom of Dece had yet to be visited by Maria and he was certain that the King of Deceangli would follow any line taken by Pasterix, as the Angles and Iceni were on good terms with a dynastic marriage of Pasterix to the daughter of King Graefreigh of Deceangli, Guidevere, in the previous year.

"I can speak for Dacia" he said finally. "We welcome this treaty and also grant you permission to speak freely with my people. I find that I trust your honesty and respect the puissance of your Master. What is your further will?"

Maria's eyes shone and then she surprised him by standing and saying she had one more thing she would wish to do in gratitude. Before the three lairds could stop her, she had jumped forward and kissed King Jaerid on both cheeks and then knelt once more before him. "That was to say thank you" and she grinned.

"Go with my goodwill" he replied and then invited Eorl Graedhold to show the girl back to where her companions were waiting anxiously. Their relief as she entered the cell where they had sat frustrated and anxious was visible as they stood in joy to greet her return then asked if she had been harmed in any way.

"I have been treated with great courtesy" she replied and the King has agreed to sign a peace treaty with the Iceni, the kingdom of the Trinovantes and the southern, western and middle kingdoms. Before we go north, I suggest that I visit Deceangli and obtain their agreement to the treaty also. Pasterix would wish this I am certain. But from there, we travel north to Caledonia, the Firth of Forth and the lands of the Votadini, Segolvae and Damnonii."

"East coast, west coast or through the middle?" Iosephus asked the girl and Graemhold suddenly became interested at her answer. Maria turned to the Eorl and asked him directly: "Have we your permission to go through your lands of North Humbria? And could you persuade the young laird Haedrolt that we be allowed to travel through the lands he holds under dispute in Caledonia?"

The Eorl agreed without question. "It is the better route as you will travel further north under the permission and protection of the King of Dacia if you follow the eastern road. Whereas the western way through Caer Leon and Caer Lisle will see you have to cross Galloway and Dumfries which are held by the Picts. The west coastline is the shorter way but far more hostile."

Maria and her companions stayed three days at Caister as the honoured guests of the King. He sought to celebrate the girl's presence with a feast each night but after the first night, she politely asked if she might be allowed instead to walk his City to offer aid to the poor, the lame, crippled, blind and deaf, and also went to pray for those he held captive in his cells. On the second day and into the evening, she walked the City bringing joy and help to all she met and then she visited the cells and prayed for those held prisoner: for crimes, for debts, insurbordination or cowardice when faced with the enemy. She went before the King and asked on their behalf for their release against their promise of good conduct.

The King looked into her eyes and could not refuse their fierce honesty and naked wish for their forgiveness. He announced an amnesty for all crimes provided the perpetrator should confess and promise not to repeat their error and then he released the prisoners as she had asked.

He further aided the lady by sending word to all parts of his kingdom that Maria would lead a Service of the Eucharist on the evening of her third day. He was giving people a day and a half to make their way to his capital but was hopeful that good numbers would attend. His faith was rewarded when just over one hundred thousand came to his City, filling to over-brimming the tented accommodation, Inns and Taverns in the City and seeing an enormous camp of caravans, wagons and tents set up outside the western gate.

Maria walked the City initially escorted by the King and by Graemhold in whose eorldom this City sat but then was allowed to do so accompanied by Prince Craedech and protected by her loyal knight, Galahaidra. The young warriors and children flocked to see the 'Christian Knight' a hero of three Battles, dressed in the armour made by Macsen and which shone bright silver in the sun light. His deeds had become the subject of many songs, ballads and lays sung by the Bards whose words inspired each generation of fighting men to heroism.

As Maria visited the City and the camp outside she spoke of the life of her Master and then children would ask her for the stories from her Bible whilst their parents listened to Maria the story-teller, whose own enthusaiasm for the subject of which she spoke filled the stories of the first testament with new life. She told them: of Daniel and Noah and Adam; of Tobit's Angel and her dog; of Abraham and Isaac; of Ioseph and Pharoah; Moses and the Ten Plagues; the Passover; of the parting of the Sea and the defeat of Iericho; of Iesse and Iacob, the promises of Isaiah; the heroism of those captured and tortured in Maccabees; of the Judges, Samson and the Philistines, Samuel, Saul, David, Goliath, Jonathan and Solomon.

They could see that Iesus of Nazareth, born in David's City of Bethlehem, of the tribe of Ioseph and of the line of David and Iesse, was the culmination of a history that went back to the promise made to Abraham by God, the original covenant. They saw that now they were being given a new covenant for they understood such pacts. But never before had they had the chance to enter into an oath made by God for their sake!

Then Maria spoke of the gifts of the Spirit and the new covenant. As she did so, she prayed for healing and many saw blind, deaf and infirm come to hale health and belief in one God. So they listened and saw the new covenant at work and they found belief. They foreswore their own Pagan Gods and looked to 'The Christ' as their new divinity: but a gentler God-head who sought peace and advocated love. This was hardest for them to accept and so eventually many turned to Galahaidra to ask: "How is it you dress as a warrior and yet follow the Master of the Magdalan?"

"My God says that I shalt not kill. Yet, the God of Abraham, Moses and Iacob killed many thousands to save those who loved and respected him. His chosen people have fought for centuries to create his kingdom on Earth. I still believe that one day God will return to this world and establish his kingdom on Earth. I pray for that day and I fight to protect the Master's message until that time.

Maria once said that there are many paths to the one God. She represents one way but I have chosen another. I will only fight for what is good and do so with a pure heart. I offer mercy when I can and compassion and love even for my enemy. Yet to save Maria's life I have gone into battle four times and slain three would-be assassins. I will kill again if it saves the life of someone who is good and vulnerable. I choose a harder path to God for I must justify every death at my hands when I come before him on the Day of Judgement yet through my faith and my deeds I believe I have made penance for the terrible things I did before I met the Magdalan."

"How do we become Christian Knights?" many asked the young man as he followed the girl through the City and the camp, watching over her and her Prince, the Holy Lance across his back, his shield of the prancing pony on a field of grass on his left arm, wearing his winged helmet, a dragon spreading its wings in flight, eye, chin and neck protectors in polished iron, his chainmail gleaming and adorned in pearls, silver and gold, his tabard in purple with the Chi and Rho of his faith in gold over his heart, his sword, long and straight, polished to shine as blue flame, his scimitar sharp and straight, his sicarius curved and deadly, a warrior-hero from legend and as much admired by the young ladies as those who would be warriors, following his lead.

"First and foremost be a Christian. Be pure and be brave. If you can devote your whole life to the Master then you can become his knight. No longer will you be loyal to the Kings and Queens of this world but rather to God and his Angels."

"How can we do this?" they asked for all had been brought up to honour and obey their laird, his captains and sergeants and ultimately to owe an oath of loyalty to their King.

"You still need Kings in this world. Our Master was once asked how he could serve two masters by paying tax to the Romans yet advocating we follow the word of one God. He answered by taking a coin, a denarius, turning it on its head and saying: 'Whose head is this?' Then he answered his own question: 'It is Caesar's so give to Caesar what is his and to God what belongs to God.'

Serve your King loyally but serve God, my Master, first.

When I became a Knight I kept vigil for the few hours before I went into battle to fight for my faith. I spent the night in prayer in the presence of The Grael, The Robe, The Spear and The Shroud. And I was granted a vision: I call it the '*Grael vision*'.

I saw Angels carrying before me the four great artefects and then they broke the bread and made offering to God. Through the gift of the Grael, I saw Christ as he broke the bread and drank the wine then made the new covenant. Through the gift of the Robe, I saw Christ tried, condemned and tortured, forced to carry his own cross, to fall three times before reaching Golgotha. Through the gift of the Spear, I saw Christ crucified and die. Through the gift of the Shroud I saw Christ buried in his tomb and then risen.

My Master once said 'Happy are you who have seen the Master and believe but far happier yet are those that have not seen the Master and still believe.' The *Grael vision* is a reward for our faith and belief and sets us on the road to salvation through the purity of our deeds in honour of God and his sacrifice.

So to become a Christian Knight you must first be a Christian but then seek out the holy artefacts and pray for the '*Grael vision*'. For the vision the Grael grants is the affirmation of our faith. My vision will see that I shall never surrender my faith but always follow it to the end of my days here on Earth believing in the Master though I never saw him in life."

The children and warriors understood and went away in awe and thus the powerful legend of the Grael took shape as the quest of affirmation for every aspirant that sought to follow in Galahaidra's footsteps in the many generations to come. Yet many also feared the Grael for they knew that it would punish those with impure and impious thoughts with the curse of 'unhealable wounds'. In years to come as many who sought out the Grael would be punished by it as would see the vision and be uplifted by it. Its legend became one of peril as much as purity.

The Service of Eucharist in Caister in Dacia was the culmination of Maria's mission to Britannia. She said very little that was new but with this service she cemented peace in Briton and for a generation Britannia was a predominantly Christian country with Christianity going in to hiding but surviving until the 4th Century and the mass conversion of the entire Roman world to follow the faith of the Nazarene.

The Service was remembered for two things:

King Jaerid had struggled to sleep since the first day of Maria's mission to his City; an inner conflict had gripped him. Afraid to go before Maria, whose respect he craved and feared to lose should he admit to his confusion, he sought out Galahaidra and on the second night of Maria's visit he joined the young knight in vigil with the four artefacts in their presence in the tumulus that was the stone grave of Jaerid's ancestors. He was granted a vision; he never shared the details but whatever it was it was life-changing. The following day he stood before the crowds gathered to hear Maria and welcomed the girl:

"Welcome my people. I intend to say very little. We are fortunate to have with us Maria the Magdalan who brings a message from Iesus of Nazareth, her Master, and who is the One God. I wish to say before you all that I renounce the Pagan Gods of my ancestors and from this day will follow Iesus, the Christ, the One and only God and shall do so for the rest of my days. I hereby banish the Sorcerers and Druids who promote the superstitions that have kept us in fear for centuries. I banish the night and seek that we all shall come into the light."

The crowd gathered were silenced at first and then as the news of their King's conversion rippled across their uplifted faces they smiled then cheered, their acclamation embarrassing and then encouraging their King to step forward and join them as they now all turned in eagerness to break bread together.

The service was short for darkness approached and Maria took the opportunity to reiterate her Master's message from previous addresses. Two things she emphasised, the first was the importance of free will:

'The Mission to Dacia'. Extract from Pilate's: 'The Early Christian Church in Briton.' 4th Century AD

"Remember that every one of us can influence the future and change God's Will through the power of our prayer. We can also choose to follow our own path despite God's Will. The more we do this the greater the risk that we grow away from God and will find it harder to return to him when we do. Yet God has said we can still find redemption and be saved even at the eleventh hour. We should never give up the hope that we can be saved even if we come to realise the error of our ways in later life. If our repentance is *genuine* then God will find us."

Then she spoke of the differences in practice that were already developing within the early Christian communities. Paulus was condemning these as heresies but Maria offered a different vision:

"It would be easy for God to regulate our every action; to make laws for everything we shall do; to predetermine our destiny. But my Master welcomes our innovation, our new way of seeing things, the different ways in which we rise to his challenges, meet the adventures of God and discover the wonders of his creation.

He has set us one destination: to be with him eternally in Paradise. He has set us eleven commandments: things we must do to earn the gift of eternal life. He has contracted with us: to be with us and share his Spirit with us if we remember him through the breaking of bread.

Beyond that he has said that our path to him is down to us. If we get lost then God will find us. If we stray from the path, his many stories give us the way back to find him.

So never condemn the practice of another. We are all made by the same God, are equal in his love of us, are offered the same gifts including his Spirit and life after death, and every one of us has the same right to be found by God if the path we choose is wrong.

I have strayed off my Master's path often and learnt from each occasion. I have also been found by God when lost and been forgiven. I ask that you are all open to the same forgiveness and tolerant of the differences in the way we each follow the one God."

Maria set out for Deceangli going first through Novantae escorted by the Eorl Yarrolt of the Novantae an elderly man, genial in his protection of Maria, whom like so many she found on her travels had adopted her, recognising her vulnerability and fundamental gentleness yet proud of her courage and achievements. He rode next to Craedech and the girl, telling them of the history and rich culture of the Novantae, its mountains, lakes and stunning coast, and the Pennine mountains that bordered the ancient kingdom.

Going West then North: Deceangli and Dacia (Talbot and the King of the Angles, the Coritani, Parisi, Brigantes, Selgovae, Novantae, Votadini and Damnonii)

On the second day of their journey from Caister, they reached the mountain-topped stone settlement of Garra Fay and looked down on the City of Caer Lisle, the lakes and the Western Mountains beyond, the far reaches of the Western Sea and the cliff-topped shoreline of the land of Hibernia. Pasterix joined them with a few of his closest companions, honouring the terms of the new peace treaty and coming with only those necessary for his own comfort.

They journeyed to meet the King of Deceangli who was Pasterix's brother-in-law; the King of the Iceni hoped to win the Pagan King over to this new religion that had gripped the country. But in reality he came to see Maria and to thank her for her peaceful settlement of the dispute there had been with Dacia over the lands between the Rivers Nene, Trent and the Humber for nearly fifty years.

They both dismounted and embraced on seeing each other, gladdened to meet and full of news. It was obvious that no further progress would be made that day until the King and his favourite princess had caught up on all of their gossip and so they made early camp sheltered from the wind by the many standing stones that had been erected by the first settlers to this barren place. Once their pavilions had been erected, the King and Maria sat down to supper with Craedech, Galahaidra, Yarrold, Haedrolt, Graemhold, Longinus and Iosephus. Kaera prepared Maria's section of the tent, screening off the furthest corner, making her camp bed and then going in search of a carrock or other suitable rock formation she could fill with boiling water for the lady's bath.

Maria did not mention the horror of her strip search but otherwise told the King everything, especially concentrating on the wonders she had found at King Jaerid's capital, the faith of the children, the poor, humble and infirm, Jaeric's release of all prisoners and conversion to Christianity. Pasterix was amazed and to himself admitted he had never paid the King of Dacia the attention he deserved. Yarrolt was equally enthusiastic about the reception Maria had received but also spoke of Galahaidra's influence on Jaerid's conversion. "My King is to be accepted into the '*Order of The Risen Christ*', the sacred Order of Christian Knights."

"Can I join?" Pasterix whispered to Maria and she nodded but said: "You have to go through an initiation first. It is a test of faith rather than courage and is not dangerous unless you approach the test with impure or impious thoughts. Be pure in mind and the test will see you accepted. If you wish we can do this tonight and I will be by you to ensure nothing happens that harms you for you are too good a friend to me for me to see you harmed in any way."

"What is this test?" the King asked concerned but the girl squeezed his hand gently and reassured him: "You will be asked to spend a night in prayer in the company of our four most holy relics. You will be granted a vision by God and his Angels; each person's vision is different. The risk is if whilst in prayer you have an evil thought for then the Grael can punish you. I can sometimes heal that harm but must offer myself in your place when I do."

"Would God really take you in my place?"

"Oh yes. Such self-sacrifice so honours God that the Angels sing in praise in heaven and one's soul is cleansed to offer an eternity of pure, loving contemplation and adoration of God. Both God and the soul claimed by God are immersed in love so wonderful that it fills heaven with its glory.

Yet God also knows that for us, the experience of life is just as important. He has given us the gift of life so God is loath to bring life to a premature end. There have been many times when my Master and I have been in such communion with each other it would have been easy for us both to have forgotten about his mission which I serve.

Yet we have drawn back in part I think because he seeks to offer me the creative joy of motherhood: that gift to mankind denied all others created by God, including the Angels. We can create souls through the union of man, woman and God and no other species can do this. I hope to be granted that gift and then I shall have accomplished all of my heart's desire save one thing."

"And what is that 'one thing'?" asked the King, humbled by the girl's vision of life on Earth and in Paradise but also curious as to what more she might seek.

"My greatest desire since the day my Master and I met has been to stand and kneel forever in my Master's presence: to sing his praises, listen to his teaching, honour him with my laughter and my tears, serve him in any way he wishes, in an eternity of adoration. I love him in life and wish for this to continue without cease after my death."

"I shall pray every day that God grants you your heart's desire. Pave a path for me too and speak on my behalf when you are with your Master. Surely, God shall listen to you?"

Maria smiled sadly. She wanted so much that her many friends and companions be granted a place in Paradise and of course she would pray for all of their souls. But the sad irony was that as the poor man had found when pleading for the soul of the rich man in one of her Master's many stories, God seeks to establish a relationship *directly* with each of us. If we do not listen to the word of God ourselves then no matter how much someone else prays for us we cannot be saved. Maria feared that people would look to her to intercede for them rather than pray to God.

"You have my prayers, my dearest friend and also my love, honour and respect. Please remember yourself in your own prayers" and the King nodded, made happy to hear of her love for him but understanding also the importance of her advice.

"Will Deceangli follow my Master's vision and join the rest of Briton in peace? Your wife, the King of Deceangli's sister is not converted" Maria asked voicing the concern of all of her companions.

"You have never met Guidevere and therefore she has not seen the obvious truth in your eyes nor seen your healing and your courage. King Graefreigh will make up his own mind."

Then the King began to draw the land of Deceangli using his hands in the air before her. She could see the mountains of Cumria to its south-west; the Black Hills and the Malverns to its south; the Dales and Abraham's Heights with the Pennines and the lands of the Brigantes to its east; the mountains and lakes of Novantae to its north; all coming alive as he weaved his magic with words and gesture.

Deceangli was a long, thin strip of land, surrounded by hill-top settlements whose residents were hostile and with a coastline under constant attack from the Picts of Hibernia. The Picts were not the only insurgents with Britons from the kingdom of Corvinii, Celts from the tribes in Cumria and the Iceni settled in the Dales raiding on almost a daily basis. King Graefreigh feared most the insurgence of the Picts as he was on good terms with the Iceni, whilst the assaults from the Corvinii and Cumria were usually rustling and tended to leave populated areas alone. He could gladly overlook the loss of a few sheep. The Picts however came to slaughter and rape, taking young girls as slaves, leaving whole settlements barren of life; bereft of any future.

Pasterix continued to explain to the young girl who nodded in understanding and she sat on the table before him with her hands wrapped around and hugging her knees enthralled and excited at the sound of all of these wonderful places, her eyes fixed to his, listening to the King's every word; she was especially intent now she was sitting on the top of the world, looking across towards the mountain ranges to her north east and south-west.

"The treaty he will support because it is good for his kingdom, bringing Graefreigh the support of the Corvinii and Dobunni to his south, the Iceni sitting in the hills of the Dales to his east, the Brigantes across the Pennines to his north-east against the common threats of Celts from the mountains of Cumria and the Picts from distant shores of Hibernia."

She had seen the Golan Heights, the Atlas Mountains, the Pyrenees, the Alpes and the Massif all of which towered over the Pennines, Cuaelch and Segolvian mountains yet what she saw now was more beautiful and accessible with stunning lakes and hidden grass-topped valleys, shallow and deep waters, snow-topped or with the giant-like standing stones in proud displays. Tumuli forming natural Temples or the portway to ancient tombs, promontories of mythical creatures and hidden mists as clouds descending or haws rolling down like gorse bushes blown by the wind. It was the size that she first admired: these were mountains in miniature and easier to take in and explore therefore yet just as exciting.

Each of these mountain and hill ranges carried their own legends of sorcery, ghosts, spirits, spectres and wights, and tales of the monstrous, dragons, trolls, goblins and elves with caves of ice and stone leading to ores and gems that would fall into your hands or sunken worlds where you would be turned into stone.

The King would still need to defend his western border but she could see instantly that this would become so much easier if he no longer faced war with the kingdoms to his south and east, whilst Graefreigh was already at peace with the Segolvae to his north.

Craedech laughed but Maria sat transfixed at Pasterix's stories of hauntings, enchantments and curses, so spellbound that for once she was amongst the last to find the solace of sleep. Though she decried all that the druid Daedlus had done in the town of Bibinari, he had reminded her that God had created the 'unseen' as well as the seen and that hers was a world where the possibility of ghosts or of the monstrous such as trolls and dragons was equally likely.

She did not fear such monsters and spectres as ultimately all of creation answered to God and she hoped she did God's will. She also did not fear death at their or anyone else's hands though recognising that some means of death were less attractive than others. But she was fascinated at this new challenge and wondered where did their strange powers come from? Was it the trickery of simoncy or the work of Sai'tan who had tempted Eve and sought to tempt her Master?

"Will we seek out this world of sorcery?" Pasterix asked and wide-eyed the young girl shook her head slowly then shivered with the frisson of delighted fright.

"My heart says 'Yes' for I would love to meet a dragon but my soul tells me my mission is to save other souls and leave to God the task of saving those who have no soul.

As to the enchantments of those who serve Sai'tan, I pray each day to God to deliver them and me from evil: to protect me from even coming into contact with the evil creations of the bearer of light, Lucifer. God tells us to pray to him that we are saved from Lucifer's temptations and the mightiest of those is the temptation to seek out his enchantments and monstrous creations.

I confess to wishing to go on this adventure but I shall resist this particular challenge in the knowledge that to hunt down witches, ghosts or trolls is not an adventure of God's making!"

Pasterix, Craedech and Longinus, who had been listening in, all breathed a collective sigh of relief on hearing this. Longinus in particular had been looking at Maria in horror as he had seen her obvious enthusiasm for the world of the undead and monsters. He would have advocated running a league in the opposite direction if they had ever encountered anything remotely connected to the world of ghosts, spectres and the ghastly. He was less than enthused over the standing stones that surrounded them whilst Galahaidra had already set their tent as far away as possible from the granite giants and gone to guard over their tent, convinced the stones would wake at any moment and attack them.

"Bed!" said the three men in unison and she laughed then jumped down, gave them each a kiss and headed for the far corner of the tent where Kaera had stayed up faithfully in order to undress her, wash her and tuck her into bed. They both snook out of the tent and went down a short path between the standing stones, into a copse of sycamore and ash trees to a rock pool that Kaera had filled earlier with steaming hot water, boiled in a cauldron in the camp's fire.

They were escorted by the family of wild boars who stood guard as Maria slid slowly into the water, still warm and pleasant. She washed quickly to avoid being seen and the water getting cold yet was sorely tempted to just lie there and look up at the stars which were brilliant and out in huge numbers: the sky was clear and her view was uninterrupted by any other light whilst the atmosphere was thinner and so caused less diffusion.

She could see both the Milky Way and Andromeda with three of the summer signs of the Zodiac low on the horizon, Jupiter and Saturn as bright marks in two quadrants of the sky, Orion or Gilgamesh as was the name by which she knew the great hunter was upside down so she changed her position and lay the other way in her rock pool.

Immediately she saw the half crescent moon, an old and waning moon, almost hiding Venus and Mars, then she caught sight of the other three signs of the Zodiac visible in the summer. Next was the Cross, then the seven princesses of Regan's chariot formed as part of the constellation of Caseopeia, pointing to Castor and Pollox and the Sickle with its cousin, the smaller Sickle, Plough, Bear or Chariot as it was variably known on the far right just below the Dog Star, Cirius.

Finally, she could see the Pole Star, the North Star that guided every traveller to their right destination and which marked her own path. It was particularly bright on this night and blinked to remind her of its presence. '*Yes I must still go north*' she thought '*and you are God's way of gently reminding me. Do I do wrong in this deviation to Deceangli*?' She prayed to her Master and suddenly she stood next to him in the circle of standing stones at the very height of the Fay on which they had camped.

"It is so beautiful, Master. Will it always be here or must we defend it one day from evil?"

He turned and held her hand so that she could feel his strength and his humanity.

"You still live!" she gasped in mingled surprise and delight.

"I will return to your world one day but yes I am still alive. Your adoration of me keeps me alive as does the prayers of my many followers. I rose from the dead to live eternally yet all would have been in vain without the love and faith of those who believe in me."

Maria knelt at his feet then but he joined her and then slowly raised her until they could stand once more together. Then he took her in his arms and she felt his embrace and her heart was glad. Releasing her, he took her hand once more and then they walked together. As they did so they ascended into the heavens until the mountains were a distant speck and finally they stood amidst the stars. Her Master pointed out many she had not been able to see from her rock pool; stars hidden by the brightness of others or too distant to be seen through the diffusion of the Earth's atmosphere. The heavens were cluttered with stars and Maria gasped as she took in the totality of the panoply of these heavenly orbs of fire.

"What are stars, lord" she asked humbled as ever by her lack of understanding of what she was being shown.

"First, tell me what the message is here!" Her lord and Rabbi urged her gently.

Maria looked around her and all she could see was a blanket of light: the stars were merging into a single band of coruscation, indistinguishable as constellations any more. She tried to discern a message here but soon she was blinded by the light before her and had to shade her eyes.

"Too much light blinds" she suggested not sure if this was the message and her Master laughed then asked: "Do you mind being illuminated by all of this light?" and Maria shook her head and mused '*She was so delighted to be in her Master's company that nothing else really mattered*.' At her thought, her Master began to blaze with a white light that drowned out all other flame and she looked on fearlessly as he became the sole thing that she could see; all else turned to shadow behind him. Once more he gave her courage and restored her faith as he said: "You will always see me whatever shall attempt to blind you to my love for you" and she nodded for that had been her own thought too.

"Alas, you still have not learned my lessons though" her Master continued and Maria was instantly contrite before saying: "I promise that I try to understand. Alas I am not clever but I can often work things out when you help me."

"What then must you do?" Her Master replied and the girl blinked then had a flash of inspiration, secretly wondering if that was her Master working to aid her. She answered her lord:

"I have only to ask. I therefore ask for your help in finding the answer to the lessons that you grant me this day."

She knew she had pleased her lord for suddenly they were both, for the briefest of moments, part of the same spirit. Merged as one, the same bright light made up from an adoring duality. This new entity was created by one spirit capable of granting love and an infinite response to being loved; and a second spirit in adoration of the other, bringing the first spirit joy and comfort for eternity. The God-head of the first spirit as reflected in the second made in its own image such that as their love combined the differences between the two became ever more remote.

"Am I destined for this future?" Maria asked in awe and hope.

"All of mankind are made in my image. The possibility of merger through your infinite praise and adoration of me is genuine and is one of the consequences of living eternally in my presence; but only if you wish such a thing?"

"I devoutly wish to love you for all eternity but surely to become part of you is too great a reward?" the girl asked in danger of being overwhelmed by God's promise.

"Maria, trust me when I say that you will teach me much. You are forever surprising me and I seek the innovation and the creativity that will come with mankind's acceptance of the gift of eternal life in my presence. Your constant ability to surprise me fuels my own ability to create new worlds for you to discover. I would be honoured to share my God-head with you … but not yet for you still have much to learn from your time of preparation her on Earth … Starting with your two lessons today!"

Maria was now really stumped and had hoped that her Master might be diverted from his original intent then realised that her thought would have been read by her Master and blushed in embarrassment. He laughed then said:

"I have just given you a clue to the first lesson of the day. The second lesson can only be solved by you looking at yourself. Solve the first lesson first as to solve the second lesson might prevent you from solving the first."

"Oh dear" muttered Maria. "I am truly out of my depth." Then she re-ran their conversation and two things stuck out: her Master's reference to her being blinded by the star light and the ability to fuel the master with new ideas. I think I have it" she whispered and then standing before her Master she attempted to answer the first lesson:

"I should be wary of allowing other things to prevent me from seeing you in everything I do and also I should be aware that there is far more in the Universe to discover and that you will constantly create new challenges for us all to meet. Also I think you were pleased that I could still see you despite the brightness of the stars."

"Well done. Now what is the second lesson?"

Maria gulped. She had thought that her answer had covered more than one lesson but clearly not. There was still something else she had missed. '*Look at myself*' her Master had said and then the denarius dropped and she cried in dismay, trying to cover herself with her hands.

"My lord. Forgive me. I have no clothes on!"

"What is the lesson?" he asked sternly needing to capture her attention before her embarrassment broke off their communion with each other.

"I do not know" and already Maria could feel they were beginning to separate. And now she could feel her Master's anger with her for the first time and tried with all her might to think what she could have learnt from being naked before her lord. '*The Sin of Eve*' she suddenly recalled and once more she stood before her Master and his anger had drifted away like the wisp of clouds visible from their mountain-top perch.

“What was the Sin of Eve?” Her Master asked more calmly having already forgiven her for her lack of understanding.

“The loss of innocence” the girl replied.

“How did that manifest?”

“She was embarrassed to go before God naked and so sought out clothing.”

“Were you embarrassed when standing with me?” he asked and now she fully understood his second lesson.

“Not at first, lord and not now I realise the import of your lesson. I shall never be ashamed of my body again. For it was made by you and in your image. Must I travel naked?”

Her Master laughed then chided her: “You wear clothing to keep warm, to protect you from scratches and insect bites and to avoid distracting others for whom the female form is something enticing. But never be ashamed if we need to talk and you come naked before me. After all, you entered this world naked and will depart it naked. Be proud of the way you have been made.”

“My lord, what are stars?” she asked persistently and her Master laughed as her stubbornness was also one of her strengths.

“Stars are great balls of fire generating heat and light with cores of liquid metal and metal in gaseous form providing fuel for the fire that burns at the centre of every star. They have atmospheres too but these are so hot that man could not survive going near them let alone trying to breathe them. Even at 90 millon leagues away from the nearest star called the Sun, the Earth must still have a protective atmosphere or all life on Earth would be burnt away.”

Not for the first time that night, Maria gulped and when she finally returned to her rock pool to be dressed in her kaftan ready for sleep by Kaera, she had nightmares about solar flares, rather than the world of ghosts and witches, being kept awake at the thought of being burnt to a cinder by a star.

To complete the picture of what happened to the company that night, Iosephus slept like a log, his snoring keeping Longinus and Galahaidra awake, not that either had any chance of sleep with the standing stones around them doing anything but standing.

As they came down from the mountanouus range of Scarfa and Granta Fay they saw the Angle's capital of Fort Talbot; the greyhound or Talbot was the only dog species to be named in the Tora of Maria's faith and the name of the place was a warning to expect a City of dog lovers. Iosephus and Pasterix told the companions that all of the warriors were expected to hunt down and kill a wolf and used the more nimble greyhound in preference to the wolfhounds used by other tribes and Lords. As Pasterix went on to explain: "Greyhounds are great pets but must be allowed to run for miles or get arthritis. Wolfhounds are lazy but are great at stopping children from running or rolling into the fires and hearths in our Halls."

Maria had a little word with her wild boars, the piglets had already grown into boars with tusks and grey bristles replacing their stripes whilst their mother had almost outgrown her saddle bag. "Promise me you will be good" she pleaded with them "So no chasing any dogs or you will get me into terrible trouble."

Fort Talbot was built in the loop of two rivers and entered by a wooden bridge set on oak posts driven many paces into the mud then held upright by rocks from a local quarry. The bridge was thirty paces long, or ten lengths of oak joined together with iron nails then roped to allow for some movement due to the rivers' tides and weight of traffic. There was also a river ferry for heavy goods. The City had stood over one hundred years and was entered by a single large barbican and gatehouse facing east, away from the constant threat from Cumria.

The Deceangli had sailed a century earlier from the bitter cold of the Bight of Heligos to settle in the more mild west of Britannia, two hundred long boats landing on the Aer Mann one dark and misty night then heading inland to the borders of Cuelch and the Black Hills. They had conquered the peaceful Celts, slain their menfolk and taken their wives and daughters, but soon the beauty of the land had seen them build a city and make this land their homes, starting families, intermarrying with the Iceni and Novantae, trading with the Catuvellauni.

The population of Deceangli was just over fifty thousand and forty thousand lived in Talbot in a series of concentric circles of mud huts and timber framed Halls for their nobility, the Inns and Taverns, Law Courts, Measuring House, the major traders such as blacksmiths and armourers, the covered market and horse auction, stables, Temple to Epona, Moot Hall and King's Hall. The resident and trading population had outgrown the living quarters within the City and a village of tents, mud huts and pavilions had grown topsy turvy between the ferry and the bridge.

Approximately four thousand residents lived in the fortified town to their north set on a hill surrounded by water and named after its King Lud; then three thousand lived in the hundred of Shrewis to their south in another fortified town, more a camp, but set within the loop of the Avon, protecting its western borders. There were then a few villages, settlements of a hundred residents or less, to be found in remote spots under the shadow of the Dales or the borders with Cumria, where the Angles had established farms and homesteads. These were vulnerable to raids from both the Corvinii and Cumria but held on defiantly as they provided the food for the rest of Deceangli.

Talbot's defences included a mud motte and bailey, two rivers and a canal that connected the two but with lock gates either side, the bridge, barbican, gatehouse then a palisade set on top of a huge circular earthen mound, a further inner wall with spiked stakes between the two and a covered walkway connecting the outer and inner perimeter wall, four towers sat facing north, south, east and west on the inner circular wall with one final ditch running around the inside of the inner palisaded wall.

Three thousand warriors defended the capital with one hundred riders on constant patrol and a further two hundred in each of Lud's Vale and Shrewis to repel raids.

King Graefreigh had been warned of the company's approach and was standing at his gates to greet them. He held Pasterix in a tight embrace, asking first after his sister and niece then asked to be introduced to Maria. He was thrown as others would be by her fragility and frailty for she was fading slowly, her skin so fine that it was transparent in places, her frame so thin it barely covered her. Her smile in response to his welcome was warm and she jumped off her horse with the gay abandon of a child to embrace him in her turn. He fell for the lively girl, still a child in many ways, and from that moment peace between Deceangli and the rest of Briton was assured.

Next he greeted Craedech, Longinus and Galahaidra, each become famous for their exploits in battle. Once more, Galahaidra would impress the young warriors and children in Talbot, all of whom wanted to become Christian Knights and follow in his footsteps. The King, however, was more interested in Longinus' battle tactics, developed over three centuries by the legions of Rome, captured by Marius as part of his reforms over a century earlier then refined by Julius and Augustus Caesar, Marcus Antoninus, Agrippa and Germanicus Caesar in wars against Gaul, Britannia, Parthia, Egypt and Germania and the civil wars of Sulla, Marius, Pompeius, Octavian and Marcus Antoninus.

"Your use of archers, cavalry and foot soldiers in combination is a new tactic for us, especially using your cavalry to outflank Eorl Edgthbert and your foot to hold his spear phalanxes. Were these totally new tactics or adapted from campaigns you have been on?" the King asked the Centurion who was happy to reply:

"No, these were used by Julius Caesar to defeat the army of Pompey the Great in Hispania at the great battle of Phillipi. Caesar was outnumbered but held back a reserve which he used to strike Pompey in the flank and rear just as Pompey had committed his legions to push back Caesar's centre. The result was the same as ours on the Humber."

"How would you defend against such an attack?"

"Keep a reserve of a mixture of cavalry and infantry whose role is to protect your flanks and rear against cavalry flanking attacks. Ensure the reserve has one of your best commanders as if you commit that reserve too early or it is ordered to hold your centre then the commander will leave you vulnerable. Your enemy will not commit to a flank attack with you sitting there able to knock them out of their saddles unless they have become desperate and already lost the battle in the centre."

Ra'el then added as an aside to Roaring Flamebringer 'as happened at Bosworth and Croperty Bridge. At Marston Moor, the whole of the reserve was committed too early when holding some back would have prevented Fairfax and Cromwell from developing a flank.'

'You forget, little one. I have seen these battles.'

Ra'el continued:

"Would you train my army and its commanders in these tactics?" the King asked the Centurion. Longinus gave this genuine consideration and asked King Graefreigh the key question:

"I will not train an army to fight those whom are my friends and allies nor to fight against the legions of Rome. My loyalty is to my Legion first. Whatever my personal wishes, my mission to look after Maria is also important. Can you accept the wait as I escort Maria north and then into Caledonia?"

Graefreigh was insistent and what he offered was tremendously appealing to the young Roman officer yet he was also wise and knew that to wait would see him get what he wanted and ensure the man had no confict of loyalties.

"Return here and I can promise that all of the Kings will respect your wishes and welcome the chance for a Christian and Britannic army to be trained by you to defend our borders. We do not seek to assail Roma but rather we wish to keep the fragile flame of this new religion alive in this country despite any future defeat by Roma."

"You will convert to become followers of Christ?" and the King nodded then committed his whole kingdom to the leadership of Christ. "Today the priesthood of Epona will ask the girl to rededicate our Temple to Christ. Our nobles seek to become members of the *Order of The Risen Christ* as do I. Our conversion was assured the moment I saw the girl. She speaks Truth and has no agenda behind her wish to see us convert other than to do her Master's will. Maria is Epona born to lead us and if she says that her Master is the one and true God then we shall follow her lead."

"What of the Council of Sorcerers?" Galahaidra asked the King, joining in their conversation as they rode through the gatehouse and onto the City's widest street, the King's Hall half a league in the distance. The King was happy to answer the Knight's question for he had heard of *The Grael Vision* and was anxious to be led by the first Christian Knight through the journey to his own vision of God.

"All save one of our Shaman are banished and have fled to Cant, Cumria and Kernow, who alone of the Briton and Celtic kingdoms continue to worship the Pagan Gods. Our High Priestess has remained; she is a good person devoting herself to prayer and to healing. She is a mystic and her dream of God has led her to endorse Maria's mission. She will stand by the girl offering her public support of the new faith, hoping and indeed praying to receive the gift of healing."

As with Caister, Maria asked to be shown around Graefreigh's capital, which the young King was glad to do. He was proud of its many buildings and its strength in defence and defiance of the Celts, Britons and Picts. His three Eorls joined him, Garamede of Talbot, Lud, King of Lud and Caesterac, Eorl of Shrewis.

As they walked through the City's many narrow streets, its buildings were well-made, sturdy and well-kept, with flowers, vines, clematis and wisteria growing up beams and across the frames of the mullion windows that brought both light and fragrance into every home, Graefreigh explained how the hierarchy of Kings and nobles had developed across Britannia:

"There are many lords who have absorbed smaller kingdoms and now call themselves 'princes' or 'kings', whilst many small kingdoms have retained the title of 'kingdom' with a 'King' yet their King swears loyalty to an overlord. Some kingdoms allow succession by women, such as Iceni and the Durobriges but most do not.

My sister Guidevere is older than me and married to an Iceni King so thinks of her own inheritance or her daughter's on Pasterix's death whilst Col and Jaerid have sons who will gladly pick over the pieces of Iceni's kingdom should Pasterix die.

So we have the kingdom of the Atrebates led by the Lord of Hamm who now has the title of 'Prince of the Atrebates, Durobriges, Belgae and Regni and Lord of the shires of Salisbray and Hammshire'; Lud, the middle kingdoms of the Catuvellauni, the Brigantes, Parisi, Selgovae, Corinii and the Trinovantes are still led by Kings despite their conquest by Jaeric, Col or myself."

That evening, Maria and her company were honoured by a feast in the King's Hall. Graefreigh had been warned that Maria would join one of the trestle tables near the bottom and had placed Pasterix and Craedech either side of him, with his nobles on his top table clustered around Galahaidra all anxious to learn more of *the Grael vision;* Longinus also sat on the top table as the Kings and both Eorls were interested in Roma's battle tactics. Finally, Iosephus sat at the end of the top table, next to the High Priestess, Senna, the three lairds from Dacia and Lud's two sons, entertaining those around him with the accounts of his travels.

Maria and Kaera joined one of the trestles, sitting with three merchant families who were enchanted to be in her presence, whilst many of the lesser nobilities and knights asked the stewards supervising the meal if they could rotate places between courses to be near the girl. When asked, Maria was delighted and so she had a constant flow of new faces whom she charmed with her grace and gentle manners.

She noticed that many of those sitting with her had brought their 'Talbots' and these sat obediently at the heels of their masters. And so she told the story of the Angel and the dog from Tobit and then the story from Judges about the greyhound. She was asked if dogs were in Paradise and replied carefully yet her reply encouraged many of those in her hearing and would see the greyhound adopted as the symbol for the Tewdor family and the royal household of all of Britain:

"I have never asked and promise to do so. But my hope is that if Angels have dogs then they must have a place with God. Moreover, after the final Day, God will establish his kingdom on Earth and then surely, we will be surrounded by the animals we love. For did not God make Adam responsible for looking after all animals and was not Noah directed by God to save every species from his flood?"

"Tell us these stories" they asked and so she did. Then she was asked: "Do you have a dog?"

"Alas no, for I have yet to find one brave enough to live in peace with my family of wild boar" and at hearing this she was invited to introduce them to her adopted family and asked Kaera to fetch them from where they guarded her bed in the Bower behind the King's dais. Minutes later there was chaos as the boars charged tusks down at the greyhounds which fled in dismay. "Enough" Maria whispered and the boars reluctantly came to sit at her feet. "Is this how you behave when told to be good?" she admonished them and they briefly looked crestfallen then saw the scraps beneath her table and began to clear up. Maria apologised but all of those around her had dealt with the anarchy of having puppies and were understanding. Indeed her quiet control over the wild animals impressed those dining with her more than anything that she had said that night.

"She is Epona" the High Priestess said to Iosephus, in total thrall of the young girl but Iosephus was more careful as he replied: "Do not worship the girl but save your adoration for her Master. She is a messenger but our faith and following is to him who died for us then rose from the dead."

"Is she not important?" the High Priestess asked in astonishment and the old equites smiled as he replied: "Oh yes. She has been chosen by God to deliver his message. But we must always remember that it is *his* message."

That night, Galahaidra, King Graefreigh, King Lud, King Pasterix, and the Eorls Garamede, Haedrolt, Graemwold, Yarrold and Caesterac joined Maria and the High Priestess Senna in the Temple of Epona with the artefacts from Christ's Passion before them. First Maria dedicated the Temple to become a place for those who followed the Nazarene to break bread in his memory. Then she blessed those with her and broke the bread, leading them in a short service of forgiveness and the Eucharist. Finally she spoke of the *Order of Christian Knights*, the original vision of twelve seats put to one side as she recognised that all of those seeking to serve God through the dedication of their life should have that chance. Then she left them to their vigil and the unique vision that each would receive from God.

Gaedfreigh went to stop her in alarm. "What happens if I fail?" he asked in dismay and was rocked back by the young girl's reply:

"There is nothing I can do if your faith is found wanting. It is you that must believe and not I who must do this on your behalf. When your heart is ready and purified then make the attempt. God will welcome you when your heart is faithful."

Galahaidra took the Grael from its cedar box and the Shroud from its silk cover, sown by Maria to offer it protection, and put both on the altar on the presbyter of the Temple. Then he placed the Standard bearing the remnants of the Robe against the wall behind the altar. Next, he took the Lance, with the Spear now mounted permanently as its point by the skill of the best smith in the kingdom of Dacia, and lifting it from its leather frogged holster across his back he placed it before the altar. Finally, he knelt and prayed simply as he had been taught by Maria:

"My God. Thy Will Be Done" before turning to face the eight men kneeling nervously before him, the High Priestess behind them, who earlier that evening had asked Maria if she would be welcome. Maria had questioned her gently:

"Do you believe in one God, who was born as man and lived to die for us and rise again?"

"Yes" she had said, her faith and conversion guaranteed when she watched Maria's generous compassion and love bring relief to children and the infirm just through her touch and a simple prayer as the girl had walked through the streets of Talbot, meeting huge crowds gathered just for the chance to see her. No spells just absolute belief in one God.

"Will you remember Iesus of Nazareth who is God and is alive through breaking bread with others who also believe?"

"Yes" Senna replied without doubt or any trace of reluctance.

"Now you are a Christian priestess. Lead others in prayer and in the breaking of bread. I shall pray that one day you are granted the gifts of God's Spirit for you are a healer and with God's aid you will bring relief to so many who are vulnerable or infirm" and Senna had dropped to her knees in tears to be held by Maria until eventually her sobs and shaking had finished and much calmer, she asked the girl: "How do I pray?"

"Praise God, thank him for all of creation and his gifts then ask for help but always it must be pure and from the heart. I am still learning how to pray and the adventure of so doing will never stop I think."

As the eight men's vigil began, Galahaidra left them. The '*Grael Vision*' was personal and he had no wish to disturb their reflection. Now Senna stood watching the eight men as they knelt before her former altar. Awkwardly at first but then in increasing confidence each would say a short prayer or petition in turn then pause in silence. After two hours, they remained in silence, uncertain of what would happen next.

Senna was unclear what prompted her to intervene but she spoke into the silence:

"We must wait and we must never demand God's gifts or his vision. We must pray but humbly" and she knelt next to them, her eyes closed, pleading with God that he grant these aspirants to become Christian Knights, the gift of his vision. Her prayer was answered but in an unexpected way.

For suddenly a tongue of flame came down on *her* head, she gasped and looked up to see briefly a vision of God's Angels and then she saw Iesus, standing in her presence, his wounds clearly visible, his eyes blazing with joy as he said: "Those you have healed, you have done so in my name. I grant you the gift of my Spirit so that you can continue to heal to my honour and glory" and she fell to the ground before the altar, aflame briefly, too bright for any of the other men to approach. Finally she quivered and lay still prostrated before the altar in supplication, at first unable to speak until she found the words to say a simple 'Thank you'.

"What has happened?" Pasterix asked for he had seen the same happen once to Maria and knew that something of great moment had just occurred. Senna replied slowly, unsure herself what had happened but wishing to explain herself as best she could:

"I think that I have been granted a vision by the Grael and in my case God has granted me the gift of his Spirit to heal. I am blessed and do not deserve such generosity yet welcome it on behalf of all those that I shall aid through God's love."

"How was this magic made to work?" asked King Lud but Pasterix hushed him. Instead he spoke to all of his companions, saying:

"The *Grael Vision* comes to us when we are both humble and faithful. It will be different for each of us. Indeed, we may have to accept that we are not yet ready and pray for a day when we shall be. God has given the vision to someone who has followed the path of peace and dedicated her life to healing others. We each should learn from that. We are approaching God and must do so penitently, humbly but also offering our goodwill for those whom we shall serve if we become Knights" then he knelt once more, eyes downcast and prayed for his people, the Iceni that they be well served by their King.

An hour later, he was still in prayer, with no expectation for himself having already decided he was unworthy but hoping that God who was clearly present in this place would look after his people as he had done over his chosen people. He, thus, became the second to receive *the Grael Vision*, never disclosing what was said, but standing and approaching The Lance which glowed in his hands. "I promise to serve my people faithfully and to love and honour you, my lord" then he returned The Spear carefully to its place before the altar and walked from the Temple to go and find Maria. He was so full of God's Spirit he had to find someone who would understand how he now felt.

When he got to the King's Hall where Maria was meant to be sleeping it was to find the girl was wide awake and excited. "What is it?" he asked as she grabbed his arm and dragged him to the far end of Graefreigh's Hall. Sitting opposite the King's dais was a table in the shape of a Ɔ: a round table made of many woods: ash, poplar, oak, sycamore, elm, mahogany, pine, burr and walnut to create a chequer board affect. The table was round but with a section cut away so that people could sit on both sides. It was designed to take thirty six seated on the outer rim and the same on the inner rim; a total of seventy two places. Each place had a tall carver, made of different woods, standing tall with the sign of Chi and Rho carved as a flying fish.

Set before some of the place settings were letters written in gold leaf in the wood of the table: The Princess of the Atrebates (place 7), Sir Galahaidra (place 26), Sir Longinus (place 59), Sir Iosephus (place 53), King Jaerid (place 55), Prince Craedech (place 16), Prince Godric of the Atrebates (place 6), Yeorl Corin of Prydain (place 13), Eorls Hendrix, Herne and Hosta (places 48, 49 and 51). Thirteen names were already showing and it included both The Lady Senna (place 65) and King Pasterix (place 67).

"It is a gift from King Col" the girl said "and by some miracle, it showed your name a few moments ago and I knew immediately that you had been granted *the Grael Vision*. Who else will be chosen, I wonder? I am so excited I shall sit and wait. Will you join me?"

Pasterix nodded caught up in the girl's enthusiasm and honoured also to be amongst the first to be selected to this new Order. Then looking once more he noted that the names were in alphabetical order with gaps left for those who would be selected. "Seventy two places" he murmured "and all have already been allocated by God."

Maria hugged him then said: "Not quite. God offers the opportunity, his challenge as an adventure. But we must still grasp it. Some may lose their way and their spaces remain blank on this table as what might have been. We must never presume that it is enough to be named. We must still earn the right to sit at this table and live faithfully thereafter."

Then Pasterix noticed the last two seats and only places not to be set alphabetically were already named: 'Elijah' and 'The Chaise Perilous'. "What is the last seat?" he asked.

"Do not sit in it. It is Iudas' seat and that of the diakonas Stephanus. It represents betrayal but also self-sacrifice. No-one who sits in it shalt live."

Pasterix laughed then said: "I thought you were not superstitious. Yet you talk of this table almost as if it is magical and carries a curse." Maria blushed and her head dropped briefly as she was aware of how it must seem but then she lifted her head once more and defended herself:

"Sometimes God's actions are mysterious; can seem magical; can be cruel in our eyes. A God of Love and of Peace yet He permits oppression; and oversees our destruction by nature through earthquakes, volcanoes, tidal waves, storms, tempests and floods. He has killed thousands if not millions in destroying Sodom, Gomorrah, the flood at the time of Noah, the plagues that struck Egypt, the Temple that slew the Philistines, the fall of Jericho and the cities of the Plains. Perhaps the thing that horrifies me the most is his condemnation of souls to the burning fires of Hell to be tormented forever. I am not God, and just as well as my heart weeps for those tormented and I would be too merciful. I pray each day for another way to be found; for their reconciliation and forgiveness.

His Son shows us the other side of God's many attributes: his love, compassion and forgiveness, but I must never make the mistake of separating the two. God is all of these things: He can be merciless and merciful, unforgiving and forgiving, punishing sinners yet also coming to save sinners.

God condemns magic, sorcery, enchantment yet also does magical things, beyond explanation. Again He is a contradiction. There is no answer I can give you except this: God is consistent. He is consistently contradictory and we are not expected to be able to explain his actions.

I get around all of this by offering my *acceptance* of what God does but never my *understanding*. I have not the intelligence to ever be able to explain God's actions. Instead, I believe that everything He does is ultimately for our good; even if I cannot see how sometimes."

"You say you do not understand God and yet you are closer to God than any of us and help direct us towards a far greater understanding of the divine through your example, actions and words" Pasterix challenged her with feeling, admiring of her wisdom and for once finding her humility inappropriate. She laughed then said: "Mine was an awful lot of words that I could just as easily have summarised by saying: 'I take God on trust'."

An hour later, Maria gasped as before their eyes they saw gold writing appear in place 33 to the left of Sir Galahaidra's seat and opposite Lady Senna then she jumped up and down in glee: "King Graefreigh. I am so pleased. He was so worried he would fail God somehow and not be deemed worthy. Yet going around his City, all have praised him as a kind King."

Pasterix was also pleased as it made for an infinitely more comfortable home life for him that his brother-in-law had not been rejected but he then added a slightly sour note as he said: "We could have a long wait for any of the remaining six to be chosen. They are each proud men."

"Shame on you" Maria replied laughing then skipped across to give Graefreigh a kiss as he staggered in to his Hall, shattered at his experience and then he stood in awe when he saw the table. "Your place is ready for you" the girl said shyly and pointed it out to him. He walked slowly towards the chair, almost reverently pulled back the carver and sat down.

Maria ignored all etiquette and plonked down besides him in one of the unallocated places then said: "The experience is different for each of us and is personal. Be glad that you have been chosen" and all he would say was: "I had to go into myself, to admit to my faults and failings, to beg for forgiveness and only when I refused to despair did the vision come. It was glorious but I shall say no more."

It was dawn of the next day and Pasterix and Graefreigh were asleep. For once, Maria had outslept them all in constant prayer for the last six men. Then, at last, as the first rays of the sun came through the mullion windows to touch the table before her, she saw gold writing begin to appear, two places to the left of Galahaidra, five places to his right and two places further on, the second seat near where her Prince's place was set and two places to the right of Elijah's seat. She woke the two Kings up, having no regard for their status with both deciding that at times her youth was a burden to them all, but they could not stay angry with her for long as they saw the next five places had been allocated: Eorls Gaeramede, Graemwold, Haedrolt, Yarrold and Caesterac.

"Alas King Lud must wait. But who knows, it might just be a question of time?" Yet Maria was doubtful as she said this for Lud had sought magic rather than a personal revelation.

Senna came into the Hall then ran across to Maria and the two girls hugged with joy. "I did not expect this" Senna said truthfully and Maria admitted: "Nor I. But does that not make it all the more wonderful?" then she turned to Eorls Gaeramede, Graemwold, Haedrolt, Yarrold and Caesterac and welcomed them. All five men were overjoyed and relieved in equal measure. It was Maria who then asked about Lud and was told by Caesterac:

"Best leave him. He is offended and blames you. He will come around in time but for now he is angry and become your enemy. He never truly understood that this was a test of his values and worth. He is already riding back to his City of Lud believing himself to have been tricked and slighted."

"I prayed for you all. I would not have him my enemy" said Maria saddened at how things had panned out but Senna would not have the girl blame herself and told her not to worry as by the time Maria returned from Caledonia, doubtless Lud would have forgotten all about the 'insult' he now placed at the girl's doorstep.

Maria broke with tradition and allowed Senna to lead the Service of Eucharist that night reserving her contribution to a short address on how God's values were not the same as ours, drawing from Christ's meeting with the rich young man who could not give up his riches. *'I will find that man'* Maria promised to herself *'and do everything I can to help him find the way to be saved. For my Master loved him.'*

When Senna showed her people the gift of healing, they were amazed and proud of their priestess and some were brave enough and had sufficient faith for Senna to lay her hands on them and they also received the Spirit. Thousands were converted that night and almost the whole City turned out to see Maria and her company head north towards Caledonia.

Caledonia: Maria Magdalan's Mission to the Voltadini, Selgovae and Venicone. Maria converts the Lord of the Gaels

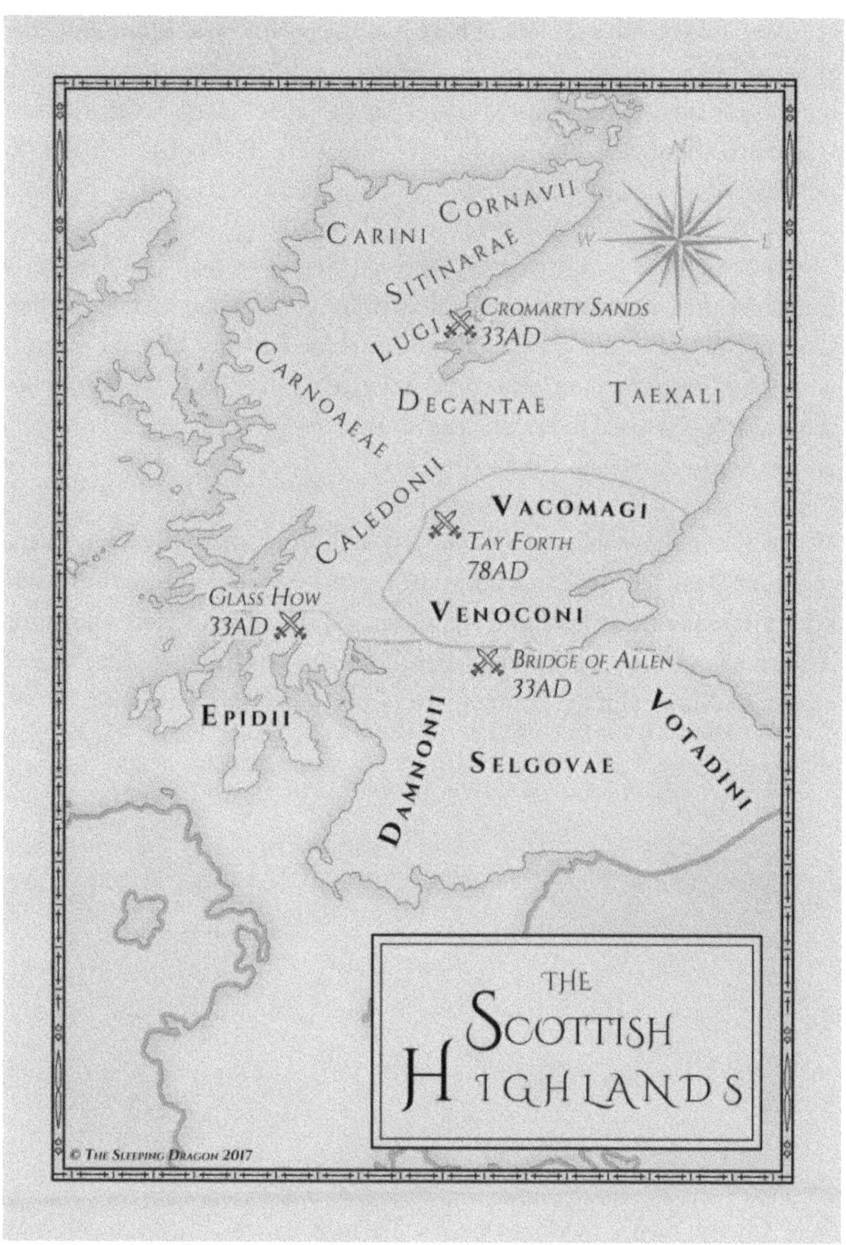

Caledonia was divided into four parts.

The lowlands that lay north of the land of the Brigantes and Novantae, through the hills of the Selgovae either going west into the Cumbrian mountains and the territory of the Dumnonii or along the east coast through the Northumbrian coastline and the lands of the Votadini to the Firth of Forth and the kingdom of the Selgovae (Sevgolae).

Crossing the Forth one entered the land of the Venicones, the Clackmannan Mountains and its capital of Perth which was the gateway to the Highlands at the foot of the Cairngorns and the first fording point of the Tay.

From there Caledonia was principally either unoccupied, Pictish territory or the hunting ground of the many small tribes of the Caledonii (such as the Cerones, Creones, Carnonacae, Carini, Cornavili, Vacomagi, Taexili and the Lugi, Sitinarae and Decaniae on the banks of Loch Ness).

Then in the furthest north islands of Thules and Hebrides or the Western Isles of Skye there were the Norse or Vicing tribes of the Epidii.

Deceangli had been a detour but a valuable one securing the territory behind them and ensuring that if they must flee south they could do so into friendly lands. Graefreigh had signed the Peace Treaty with Pasterix as witness and thus almost all of Britannia south of the Tweed was agreed to pursue peace and converting to Christianity. The peace was fragile and would be broken nine years later by Claudius' invasion which would drive Christianity into hiding. But that lay a few years ahead yet. For now, Maria must attempt to begin the conversion of Caledonia and not for the first time she was less than confident in her abilities to speak her Master's message.

"I am the wrong person for this" she whispered sharing her fears with Longinus as they rode north and east the following morning along the top of the Pennines. He asked her to expand and reluctantly she did: "I am a weak young girl, exhausted, no longer able to win over people with the inner flame my Master chose me for, as it has been blown out by the cold winds of Autumn. I fear this rotten wet weather has defeated me." It was sunny and warm at the time, a pleasant and refreshing day that the rest of the company were enjoying.

"What utter rubbish" and Longinus roared with laughter then sizing up the situation pretty accurately, told her straight: "You need to sort out your relationship with Craedech and finish this mission as quickly as possible. Don't even think you can fool me about the look that came into your eyes when you were handed Pasterix's daughter. You are getting broody and it is a sign that you have started to grow up at long last. Now cheer up, you have found yourself a nice man and he will look after you - provided you behave yourself!" he added with a grin.

"Huh" she muttered and went off in a huff to talk to Galahaidra as hopefully he had more sense or more sympathy, she was not sure which! But Galahaidra was even less sympathetic. "You are telling me you have been '*defeated by the weather*'! You will be the laughing stock of the known world. Get a grip!" and he became the second of her companions to roar with laughter.

She rode next alongside Iosephus and asked sheepishly "Are you going to laugh at me too?" He did not but equally he told her straight: "You giving up on us now makes me want to put you over my knee and give you the beating you deserve. Stop being a spoilt brat!"

"So no sympathy there" Maria muttered and that left Prince Craedech. She rode alone in thought until at noon when they stopped west of Caister to change horses and grab a bite to eat. Craedech was waiting for her having already spoken to the other three men. Maria was starting to feel out-numbered and was rocked back when her Prince went immediately on to the attack:

"I know what you are about to say and I do not want to hear it. I have always been proud of you but your defeatist talk when you have just seen the conversion of the Iceni, the Parisi, Cotadini, Brigantes, Novantae, Dumnonii, Segolvae, Votadini and the Western Angles is frankly ridiculous. Say one word about giving up and I shall leave you."

She stood there staring in shock and he turned and walked away. She was left totally alone and had no idea what to do or say. She had felt battered and had lost her confidence and all she had wanted was a hug. *'Was that really too much to ask of her friends?'* She walked to Epona, stroked the flank of his neck then lifted her wild boar out of their saddle bags and watched over them whilst they went for a run. She knew better than to ride off as her Master would punish her and Galahaidra would chase her down. She was not sure how to apologise as she did not think her concerns had merited such a harsh and unforgiving response. Then she finally understood: they were all worried for Caledonia was a much bigger challenge than Britannia had been. The men's anger was born out of their concern and they did not wish to share that with her.

Was she really surrendering to the weather? Of course not! She was frightened because she had no idea what she was about to face and nor had any of her companions. Then Kaera summed up the prevailing mood of the company when she reminded Longinus that she had only signed up to go as far as Caister and so would be riding east whilst the company went north. That noon the rest of the company sat around Longinus' field stove, warming up some broth and fetching out some bread, covering cold legs with woollen blankets. Maria walked away, not wishing to share a meal when she had been so effectively shunned by them and not sure if she would be welcome any more.

After an hour, they packed and mounted up. Kaera came in search of Maria to say goodbye and looked long and hard at the girl then said: "No-one will say any the less of you if you stop now. Ignore these foolish men. They think it is as simple as the weather but I can see that the fearlessness that was in your eyes has gone. Either find your courage again or stop here." Then she gave Maria a quick hug and rode east.

Maria returned to the camp and mounted Epona then followed the men at a distance as they rode ahead of her in pairs, laughing, enjoying the Novantaean borders, ignoring the girl behind them. They crossed into Brigantian lands and forded the Eigh, the Tees and the Tyne and headed north-east for the mouth of the Aln on the east coastline, making good time on firm ground in fair weather.

Twice Maria stopped to talk to the children and their mothers in the small and secluded settlements in Northumbria, welcomed as always by those who had heard of her many adventures and wanted to share in them by touching her or hearing her speak. She was meeting the Votadini for the first time and these people were great mariners, cultured and well-educated, sailing to the west of Hispania and the north east coast of Italia where their tribe had also a much larger settlement, a port from which they traded with Media, Mesopotamia, Aegypt and Arabia.

On both occasions that Maria stopped to talk to the Votadini and listened to their wonderful and exciting accounts of the magical places to which they had travelled, Galahaidra circled back to fetch Maria, frowning as he did so, assuming she had been seeking to give them the slip.

They rode for three days heading for Dunstan's Hill and the estuaries of the Bere and Bam where they would cross the Tweed to enter Caledonia and in that time Maria slept in her own tent and rode apart from the four men, who had rapidly become used to her silence and ignored her. She did not join them for their meals; indeed she did not eat, retiring to pray for the return of her courage. Finally she sought out her Master.

He had his back to her. They stood once more upon the cliff's edge and Maria feared that had he asked her to jump then this time she might have. Seeing his back, she retreated to her tent where she had been kneeling in prayer. She took a deep breath and said: "sorry" but she could not bring herself to go back. '*Not tonight*' she said to herself. '*Give it time. For time heals*'… except there are some wounds that take more than Time's Silence to heal.

At Dunstan's Hill, she held a Service of the Eucharist and was surrounded after they had broken bread together by dozens of the sick, crippled and infirm. She prayed for the Spirit to fill her but no healing came at which she ran to hide, shedding the tears of the truly desperate. In the end, it was the knowledge that these poor people had come seeking her help and that she had let them down that gave her the resolve to face her Master once more. Again she faced his back but they both stood in a busy street she remembered from when they had first met in Nazareth.

"Master. I understand your message too well. You remind me of my humble beginnings and that it is you who have made me what I am. Without you I would never have discovered my love, the Prince. But I am not here for my sake. Below are nearly thirty people who suffer when you could heal them. They do not deserve to be punished for my failure, surely?"

"They can pray for their own healing. They do not need your prayers."

"Forgive me, lord, but you are wrong. These people have had nothing to celebrate all their lives and to see your healing not only removes the harm from which they suffer but also gives them hope."

"You defy me?" and she heard the distant rumble of his anger.

"When you are wrong, yes!" she replied bravely then wondered from where she had found such courage. But her Master now towered over her, seeking to cow her with his ire.

"O dear" she gasped and began to giggle. "I am most terribly sorry but you getting angry just makes me want to laugh" then more seriously she continued: "I know I am lost and that I have hurt and angered you. But please, do not punish these good people for *my* sin."

"What is your sin?" he asked; his voice more calm, his demeanour less stern.

"I think I gave up too easily" but what she found was that she did not know. "I ran away when you rejected me?" she said finally in a small voice but posed as a question rather than said with any certainty. At last, her Master looked at her and said: "How many times must I tell you I am *always* here to comfort you?"

"Forgive me, lord, for defying you once more but how was turning your back on me comforting?"

"You did not ask for my Comfort" her Master replied but hesitantly as if admitting to himself an error which Maria took full advantage of when saying: "Sometimes friends do not need to *ask*; it is enough to see they need help."

At last her Master smiled. "My lessons are hard but in this lesson we have learnt that *your courage is still there*, just buried for the moment, and that a good friend must sometimes *break the silence to comfort their friends*."

"What must I do, lord?"

"Comfort *your* friends despite their silence for they are frightened and need to see your courage."

"Goodness" said Maria. "I really muffed this one!"

"I forgive you" replied the Master with a glint of humour in his eyes.

Maria returned to the meeting place where she had held the Service and to her relief most of the congregation were still milling around, talking of their disappointment in the way the Service had ended. Without hesitating, Maria walked up to a man who was blinded in one eye and holding her hands over him, prayed "Lord forgive me" at which all could see the flames of the Spirit come down on her and the next moment the man was singing God's praises for the return of his sight. She spent the next hour healing the sick, comforting the orphaned and the lonely, talking to all who would listen about the wonders of her Master's ministry.

It was surrounded by the people of Dunstan's Hill that Galahaidra found her. He frowned and beckonsed that she should follow him. But she just grinned, stuck her tongue out at him then ignored him and went on telling the children at her feet about the day Iesus had walked across the Sea of Galilee with the sandy beaches of the North Sea and the sound of the waves breaking onto the shore as the backdrop to her story-telling. Galahaidra stood there stunned and then he listened and as he did so he could see the return of the charisma with which Maria had bound millions to God's message. Moments later she found him kneeling at her feet.

"Forgive me" he said and she embraced him whispering in his ear: "There is nothing to forgive but something to forget perhaps?" At which he nodded then said: "Leave the others to me!"

For the first time in days she joined them for supper as they camped on the sands below the cliffs on which Dunstan perched with Bam's stone settlement visible on the next cliff top. The men were obsequious in their attention to her, offering her food, seeing that she was comfortable by the fire, fetching blankets for her. An argument nearly broke out over food however.

"Will you not eat?" asked Iosephus, seeing her plate was empty save for the smallest portion of couscous. Maria shook her head at which Longinus asked: "What did you eat when you were on your own?" which question she ignored and attempted to change the subject. But now all four men were suspicious and grew briefly angry.

"When did you last eat?" Craedech asked. "Just now" said Maria hoping that would end the subject but Longinus was persistent: "And the previous occasion?"

Maria hesitated and then admitted sheepishly: "In Talbot I think"

"Four days, no, five days without food! You are lucky you are still alive."

"My lord will look after me for as long as I do *his* mission" and that ended any argument although all four men watched the girl carefully from then to make sure she was eating whilst Iosephus wept when he put her to bed that night and saw how thin she had become. "She barely has enough muscle to stand whilst riding must be taking a heavy toll" he muttered as the men kept vigil by the fire.

The company followed the east coast for many leagues from Dunstan's Hill, taking their time as Maria needed rest and the others in the company were glad to see the girl happy once more. They made their way slowly towards the estuaries of the Bam and the Bere, which is where they would cross the Tweed. Their horses rode across the smooth sands and waded in the cold shallow waters of the North Sea. Maria would swim each morning, enjoying the tow of the under current and the excitement of the surf of the waves then being wrapped in blankets by her companions as she would sit with them over breakfast her teeth chattering with the cold yet she had never felt happier now they were all reconciled again. The skies remained clear and her skin gradually began to take on tone and colour as she basked in the sun, lying on the rocks and enjoying these rare moments of calm and tranquil peace before they came to Caledonia.

The moment they crossed the Tweed they were stopped by a troop of Dacian cavalry. The men were glad to see Maria as all had been at the gathering at Caister and still spoke of the miracles they had seen and their own King's conversion. "We would escort you" they said "but we are followed by a Gaelic war party. Beware for already you are being watched." Maria said a prayer for their safe keeping and the Dacians rode on towards the comparative haven of the lands of the Votadini in Northumbria, leaving the girl and her escort to ride north then west, following the line of the Forth.

"Why this way?" Longinus asked as the road they were taking was much longer than if they had followed the Tweed north through Beles' pool, Storo, and Hallaeyne. Iosephus was happy to explain:

"The land we shall cross is much flatter, with beaches we can ride across, rolling hills and grassy plains on which we can gallop. Moreover, this way is well-guarded by patrols from Dacia and for much of our path we will be in the territory of the friendly and cultured Votadini, who have already met Maria, admittedly in small numbers.

The shorter route is through steep mountains, around wide lakes and Glens; it is the home of roving Pictish, Gaelic and Caledonii war bands and the war-like Segolvae. We risk being hunted down whichever route we take but this way is safer and quicker with the added advantage" and the old man pointed out to sea where they could see three triremes just off shore "that we have our rescue at hand if we do become the prey of a war party out for sport."

"And if they are not out for sport?" Galahaidra asked and Iosephus made a cutting motion across his own throat and then used his hands to make the shadow of a raven before pointing at Maria.

That night they camped at The Dun of the River Bar down on the beach with the cliffs towering over them. As the men sat chatting around the fire, the girl having already retired to her own tent, they heard the first of the carrion calls, the calling sign of Gaelic or Pictish war bands. As the night got much colder and darker they heard the answering calls, a baying of pleasure from many directions, disturbing the natural chatter of the night.

"How many?" Longinus asked Galahaidra who stood briefly then slowly regained his seat: "Too many" he replied "and from at least six directions. If they wish to take us then already they have the men to do so. We must trust in their curiosity."

"Guard the girl!" the Centurion commanded and Galahaidra nodded then went off to find his bed roll which he placed across the entrance to the girl's tent. Maria woke to find a snoring knight lying across the flap that was the entrance to her small tent. "How silly" she muttered then went back into her tent to grab an extra blanket for the man, who was shivering in his sleep with cold. Covering him, carefully avoiding disturbing his sleep, she then stepped gingerly over him and went in search of fresh water, a spring, rockpool or waterfall in which she could wash.

She found a small fall of water cascading down the cliffs to form a crystal clear pool below and stood beneath the ice cold water to make her morning ablutions. Her wild boar sat guarding her clothing, knowing better than to tear it to shreds as their peers had done in the woods west of Bibracte. She had been bathing for only a few minutes when the first of the Gaelic war band came and stood at the entrance to the gorge in which the fall was to be found, blocking her exit whilst watching her intently. He made the call of a night owl and more men joined him. Maria's eyes were closed so that she did not notice them at first. When she did finally look up, she just managed to stifle a scream and instead made a gesture towards her clothing. Then the gift of tongues came to her rescue and she was able to speak to them in Gaelic:

"If you let me dress then I will come with you. I pose you no threat."

"We prefer our women have more flesh than you, lassie, but be assured we are not threatened. Dress and then we shall take you to see our chief. He will decide your fate" one of the men spoke and Maria took him to be the leader of this war band.

The men carried spears and oval shields, were dressed in woollen tartan with silver broaches at their right shoulders. They were bearded with braided hair; looked savage yet had spoken fair to the girl. She bowed in acknowledgement and dressed quickly fearing that if she delayed one of her company would walk in on them and also be taken.

Despite the openness of the ground that her company had crossed, the war band were able to follow paths that were hidden, sunken or wooded, they were not seen at any stage as they took the girl ever west towards their chief's camp at Plean on the road to the Bridge of Allan. From their hill-top refuge they looked down on Fallin and Throsk on the banks of the Forth and away to the distant Muir.

It had taken a day for them to traverse the rocky and wooded tracks but they had made good speed on foot, almost running as the men sought to lose a pursuit they anticipated when Maria's companions found her taken. Maria's wild boar followed her, giving her the relief of their company, watching over her, never letting her captors sieze them. The war band had grown to six men, all armed with spears and each had tried to chase the boar away but the boars were persistent and gave Maria hope. In the end, the Gaels shrugged their shoulders and let the boar follow them.

Maria tried to keep up but she could not maintain the Gaels' pace and a few hours into her capture found herself being carried by one of the men over his shoulder, muttering to his colleagues that she weighed less than his child and would be eaten whole by their chief at which the men laughed.

"Is this the warrior princess from the south of whom we were warned?" another said "for if this is she then we were sadly deceived."

The whole of the chief's tribe had gathered in a sunken and secluded valley, trees offering cover from every direction, to see his examination of the child warrior who said she bore a message from God. "I have seen her naked" said one of those who had taken her captive at which Maria blushed "and she is just a slip of a girl, with no muscles or strength in her. She offers us no threat."

The chief had her dragged before him and watched as she knelt, bowed her head, then looked up at him defiantly, no fear in her clear blue eyes. She waited patiently for the chief to speak and knew that this interview would determine whether her mission succeeded or failed.

"You are a Roman spy!" the chief admonished her but Maria shook her head then replied: "I bear the lash marks from where I was punished by Rome. My Master, whom I love, was executed by Romans. I do not come from Roma."

Those gathered began to mutter at this, amazed she could speak their language so fluently but demanding proof that she had been lashed. Before she could protest, two men held her down on the ground by her arms whilst a third tore the clothing from her back. The lash marks were there for all to see as were the scars from King Col's torture of her. They could see both the punishment, the trace of the iron balls and hazel branches, but also the healing as no scars were visible, just the tram-marks of the weals that she would bear in honour for years to come.

The chief nodded, satisfied that this first accusation had been met but the trial still continued as the girl sat back on her knees, hugging her ruined clothing around her, yet no longer afraid as once she had been to go naked before her accusers. Her Master had taught her better. Instead, she looked around at the three score warriors gathered to see her death and under her gaze, each looked away, seeing a child thrown before their mercy and no longer proud of what they did. Then she looked once more at the chief and faced his next question:

"You come from Dacia and we are at war with the people to our south. Admit you are a spy of Dacia."

"How else, wise chief, could I come to these lands if not from Dacia? I am come from the south and must cross their lands!" and Maria smiled to take away the sting of any insult in her words. Once more, the chief nodded, accepting her response but then he pushed her answer, challenging her with being on good terms with King Jaerid of Dacia. Her reply saw all of those gathered whisper once more, curious and eager in equal measure.

"Great chief. I went before King Jaerid alone and he threatened me with torture and death as you do. I was not afraid. I showed that I represented no challenge to him. Intead I offered healing and hope. I showed him how he could be at peace with the people of the Iceni. He sent me to the lands of Angles and I have come from there to here across the Pennines and along the east coast through the land of the peaceful Votadini."

"How can you prove to us that Jaerid has not sent you to spy on us?" the chief demanded, the first sign of anger in his voice.

"Forgive me. I speak truth" the girl replied and the chief seeing the honesty in her eyes, sat back accepting that she was not lying.

"Are you able to lie?" he asked her gently now and the girl shook her head but added: "I will sometimes remain silent for I would not wish my words to bring harm to anyone. I will not betray anyone who has bound me to secrecy or for whom I feel responsible."

The chief was astonished at that and his next question sought to test the boundaries of her loyalty: "Would you tell of our camp here?"

"If it is your wish I keep this place a secret then I would remain silent even under torture" the girl replied and the chief could see that her words were as binding as any oath. He was surprised and asked: "Why?"

"I do not come to change the way this place is ruled. I side with no-one and offer my aid freely to everyone. I will not lead armies to defeat the peoples of Britannia or Caledonia, but will offer my healing to those harmed in conflict and seek peace if that is what people seek. My mission, however, is to offer you a place in a kingdom after this life. My Master came to found the kingdom of God in Paradise and to open its gates to all of us. He had no interest in the kingdoms of this world.

I am come to offer you his gifts: a place with God when we die and the power of his Spirit to heal, to speak in the language of others, to tell the future and to offer hope."

As she spoke, the chief showed increasing satisfaction as now he had the evidence he needed to condemn the girl. He looked around his tribe and saw the same eagerness in their eyes as he felt in his heart. Then turning towards Maria, he sentenced her, saying:

"Your words condemn you. You speak of being given God's power. Of gifts that are sorcery and enchantment. You admit, therefore, to being a Witch and we shall mark you as such for all to see. You shall be branded for the evil that you are. But first you must survive our challenges and let us see if your God will save you."

The girl still showed no fear. Instead she prayed before saying into the silence that had followed the chief's decree: "I forgive you all that you do. I am not a Witch and the gifts I speak of belong to God. I am 'God's Instrument' and if I die it does not change God's message or the gifts he offers. Others will follow me to offer you the same gifts: for everyone is entitled to hear the message of my Master."

They took her roughly and bound her legs and arms. Then as she fell forward, they kicked her until she had curled into a ball. Still her eyes blazed: with love and forgiveness. They considered blinding her, such was the guilt they felt when they saw her eyes, but the chief had other plans. "If we take out her eyes then we shall not see the fear of our challenges reflected in them. I want to see her look on me afraid."

They dragged the girl to the nearest river, across gravel, stones, cobbles and brush that cut her leaving her covered in bruises and abrasions. She made no sound. On reaching the river, they tied her to a rope and then flung her into the current and watched her drift beneath the water until the rope went taut then hauled her in again. She was choking and coughed up both water and lichen but then grinned. So they flung her in again: but this time she was better prepared and had taken a deep breath then prayed for God's aid. Once more she stood before her Master.

"Forgive me lord for my sins. I am ready to die if this is the end you wish for me" she said to him as he held her in his arms. He was seated with the girl across his knees, her head resting in the crook of his arm. Together they looked from the top of a mountain at the green and yellow fields of a distant land: woods, lakes, rivers and hills in a colourful patchwork of peaceful perfection, no clouds in the blue sky above. "Thank you" she whispered "for this is truly beautiful. If this is the last thing I see then I am grateful for your gift of this vision."

"Is that what you wish?" he asked her, stroking her hair, soothing the bruises from where she had been kicked by the Gaelic war band. Maria so much wanted to say 'Yes' for she wished more than anything to be in the presence of her Master, but some streak of stubbornness and the reminder of her promise to serve out her penance before ever she could be accepted in Paradise made her say:

"There is still much I have to do for you, my lord. Give me the strength to do your Will."

She came out of the water once more, spluttered, coughed then laughed which confused the men around her. They looked in enquiry and confusion at their chief who shrugged then said:

"She has survived water so now we must test her with fire. Prepare the next challenge!" and Maria watched as the warriors brought out brands which they lit from the camp fire in the centre of their circle. To one side she noticed for the first time a hut, deserted, it had once had residents but they had been slain and buried when the war band had taken occupancy of this secluded vale. Abandoned it had now found a use as they set fire to it until soon it was a raging inferno.

"Walk through the hut and out the other side" the chief said and then they untied her feet but left her hands still bound before prodding her with their spears.

"No need" she said proudly and walked without fear straight into the heart of the flames until they had lost sight of her in its conflagration. They heard a muffled scream that was abruptly cut off and followed by total silence save for the roar of the flames. Moments later to their intense surprise and consternation, Maria appeared the other side of the hut, her clothing burnt away to nothing but her skin beneath untouched by the heat, no sign of scorch marks, her ropes had also been burnt away from her hands and she was now unbound. As the warriors looked on in amazement, the hut collapsed, its roof falling inwards and pulling down the walls with it.

"Brand her!" the chief muttered but Maria challenged him saying: "Where is your proof of my witchcraft? I have survived your challenges for had I been a Witch then I would have floated when thrown in the river and no Witch can survive the heat and flames of a naked fire. Your men can see me naked and that I bear no mark of a Witch. Rather, listen to my message from my Master and then decide my fate."

There was a rumble of agreement from the men around the camp fire. Already they had been amazed that Maria had survived their ordeals and now they wished to hear more from this girl, who looked so fragile yet stood fearlessly before them all and met their every challenge. "Let her speak" they said and the chief, gauging the mood of his war band accurately, reluctantly agreed.

"Thank you" Maria whispered to her Master and also to those around her and then she asked if any of the warriors had some bread. Several were glad to offer some to her and she placed it all on the ground before her then sat cross-legged with them in a circle around her.

"My Master is the Son of God, and was born of a royal family, sent by God his Father, he became man to show us how to live our lives, to offer himself as a sacrifice so that our sins might be forgiven, to rise again from the dead, to open the gates of Paradise for us all, then to ascend into heaven where he waits for us.

Some days later, he sent his Spirit, to fill us with his love and to offer us his comfort. He also made a promise: that every time we break bread in memory of him, he will be present.

My Master is within me, permanently resident in my heart, to offer me aid, advice and his comfort. To guide me as I go around the world, telling people of my Master's life. And so I ask: do you want to hear more?"

"Yes" they said without pause and Maria began to tell them the story of Iesus' mission, speaking for hours without end whilst they sat spellbound by the excitement in her voice as she recounted the many miracles and parables. Then she broke bread with them and they were amazed at how simple was the ritual, used to the false conjurations of their Shaman.

"Can you heal wounds?" some asked and she nodded then commanded: "Show me your wounds!"

Two of the men folded back their kilts to show nasty scars on their legs. She beckoned them over and for the first time noticed that they were slightly lame: a disaster for these warriors for whom being able to walk at great speed and without leaving a footprint out of place from which they could be detected was essential to their way of life. She laid her hands on them and prayed fervently with her eyes closed for healing as she feared otherwise these men would be abandoned or slain one day when their injuries proved to be too much of a risk or hindrance and they started to lag behind their peers. She heard a gasp and dared to look and see if any good had come of her prayers. She shared their amazement, therefore, as she looked down and saw their legs had been healed of their scars, sinew and muscle returning, renewed strength obvious as they stood and tested their legs then skipped in joy before giving Maria a hug.

"She is useful" some of the veterans said to their chief. "Let her live. She is almost nothing and will be no burden. Other war bands will wish to hear her stories for she has entertained us well this night. Let her live" and the chief nodded for he also had been struck by her survival of their challenges, her stories and her acts of healing.

"What does this mean?" Maria asked confused and wondering what they now sought of her. The chief was happy to respond:

"You are our prize. We will take you to show other war bands and thus we shall be greatly honoured. You must come with us" at which Maria shook her head, braving the chief's anger but knowing this could not be allowed to happen if her mission was to have any chance of success.

"Forgive me, honourable chief, for what must seem ingratitutde at your act of mercy in letting me live but my message must also be taken to the Segolvae and the other tribes of the Caledonii, the Pict and the Vicing. I will willingly speak to the other war bands of the Gael and let your war band be honoured when I do, but must ask for my freedom to seek out other tribes, to journey north. Also, my companions seek me and will worry for my safety. I would wish to ease their concern by being allowed to rejoin them."

"Have you no fear?" he raged to which she replied with a mischievous grin: "No, not of death or torture but I do fear not completing my mission" and he looked once more into the fearlessness of her blue eyes and realised she spoke the truth. Startled, he said as much to himself as to her: "Your Master must be powerful to have such command over you" and she nodded replying in a whisper only for his ears to hear: "My Master is the most powerful person in the Universe. How lucky we are that He uses his power to show us his love and compassion."

They lent her a kilt to cover her nakedness which she wrapped around herself several times, clasping it at her right shoulder with an intricately woven silver broach, amazed at the cloth's warmth and how soft the fabric was. Night had already fallen, and once beyond the tree cover, Maria could see the stars in the heavens. The same six warriors that had first captured her now led her back to where she would find her companions with her loyal family of wild boar following at a safe distance behind her. She was tired, her eyes kept closing, but she refused to give in to her fatigue until she had been re-united with the rest of her company.

As she had left the Gaelic camp, the chief had promised her: "Other war bands will be in touch. Watch for sign of them."

After a few hours walking along hidden paths, the men pointed to the glow of a fire and the shadow of a tent besides it. Galahaidra was sitting by the fire, watching for any movement, listening for any sound, the sign of tears of frustration streaked down his handsome young face. She thanked her escort, kissed each on the cheek then watched as they disappeared into the trees. Only once they had gone did she run towards the camp to leap into the arms of the astonished young knight, who held her tight, unable to believe she was returned safely. Epona neighed in delight and tugged at the rope tying his harness to a tree, seeking to be reunited with his mistress.

"What happened?" Galahaidra asked then before she could begin to tell him, shushed her and said: "Wait there. I must wake the others. We will all want to hear of your latest scrape. We have been worried beyond wits' end."

Once they had gathered around the fire, Epona and the wild boar standing guard proudly, she told them of her capture, ordeal and release and of the promise that other war bands would seek her out. Galahaidra was the first to respond, giving the girl a rocketing: "Do not ever go for a bathe without waking me first."

"Why?" She asked reasonably. "You cannot come with me when I bathe" and he glared at her but was defeated as he could think of no sensible retort that would not get him into trouble with Craedech. "Just be careful" he muttered and she grinned, recognising his acceptance that she must still be allowed to go out on her own on some occasions. Longinus was the next to speak, asking her:

"Will we be allowed to come with you when you meet other tribes?"

"I do not know" and she was thoughtful for a few moments then smiling added: "Probably best that you do not come with me as you are a Roman and they do not like anything to do with Roma. I will be alright on my own."

It was left to Craedech to have the final word: "We are glad you are back but we have been so worried for you, imagining the most terrible fates that awaited you. Thank goodness you are returned to us safe and sound."

They put up a tent for Maria then Galahaidra lay down in front of it once more, doing so in her plain view so that she was left in no doubt that he was guarding her. Craedech, Iosephus and Longinus then retired to their camp beds in the pavilion that was more than big enough to sleep ten. It was just gone the second hour in the morning when Maria stepped over the sleeping Galahaidra, carrying her blanket, opened the tent flap to the pavilion noiselessly then finding Craedech's bed, she saw he was fast asleep so rather than disturb him, she lay quietly at his feet, laying claim to her man.

Thay broke camp to the spectacular sight of the Lomond Hills and the Horn across the Firth of Forth, the water still and clear blue, and boats already out in the shallows with huge nets held tight between them, in quest of an early morning catch. Maria waved but was ignored. As they rode west, they could sense the watching eyes; they were too far south and east to encounter Picts but the Segolvae, the Gaels and the Caledonii would be looking out for them. They had to hope that the Gaels that had taken Maria had spread the word that she was harmless, told a good story and had healer's hands.

By day's end they had reached the Falls of Fallin, green waters descending from the hills above, creating a rainbow of colours as it met the waters below, pools of clear water upon a grey stone bed that gave the flowing waters their green tint; the waters emptied into the cold of the North Sea. The Falls were surrounded by tree lined banks whose roots had been exposed by years of erosion, tortuous and twisted, a colonnaded home for water voles.

At no time had the company been challenged. Maria spoke to the few people inhabiting a small village of mud huts below the Falls defended by an earthen rampart on the banks of the Forth; they made a living by aiding travellers to cross the ford, whose waters were rapid and dangerous for anyone unused to them. Maria spoke to the proud and courteous people she found. They were Segolvae and polite yet reticient; offering the girl the welcome of their hearth to warm herself, freely sharing their food with her but remaining otherwise silent. One of the village elders explained: "We have been told to expect you but you will not find a welcome here. You shall not be harmed but do not expect many to follow you. Our ways are long-established and we have worshiped our Gods for hundreds of years. One wee lassie will not change that!"

The Forth ran all the way to Loch Ard to their west and deep in country where Caledonii and Pictish war bands would hunt the unwary. The party had decided therefore to ford the river where it started to meander through the valley of Cambus Kenneth and Cambus Barron snaking from where the Romans would one day build a stone bridge at Kincardine and narrowing dramatically four leagues further on where the river turned south towards Touch. There was a ford at Drip and another at Gargunnock and the bridge at Allan.

They made slow progress now. The main settlements were on the north banks of the Forth in the Forth Valley, including Alloa, Clackmannan and Tullibody and that was where the better paths and well-established tracks could be found. Maria, however, was determined to speak of her Master's message at any and all of the villages they encountered on the south bank no matter how small or remote, even though she would often meet just a handful of people. "If just one follows then there will be rejoicing in heaven" she explained to her companions and so they stopped every league wherever they found someone living by the river's banks. The journey from The Hill above the River Bar to Pean which was the nearest settlement to where Maria had been held captive had taken the war band half a day but took her company seven days: and each night they heard the haunting cries of the Gaels and the Segolvae that watched their every step.

So Maria broke bread at Dunmore, Airth and Throsk, the mouth of the Grange, Linlithgoe, Dalmeny, Mussel, Cockensie and Longnidory on the winding road to Fallin's Falls and Allan. She met less than two hundred people, rugged and determined folk who carved a life out of the Sea and the Forth that had cut its way through the Clackmannan Mountains to create a valley with rich soil yet also offering shelter for their many sheep. Indeed she met one hundred times as many sheep as people and Maria laughingly joked that her Master had sent her as a shepherdess to convert lambs and not as a fisherwoman to fish for men.

The bridge at Allan was in four sections, three men wide, each section spanning a gap between rocks or small islands in the middle of the Forth, no span longer than ten paces, and all held in place by ropes connecting to twelve large oak trunks driven into the mud below. The river was narrow and had curled north; it was still fast flowing and dangerous should anyone fall into its black waters.

Bridge of Allan was one of three places the company could cross the River Forth and the closest to their destination of Perth. There was a small settlement at Allan on the north and east side of the river which had grown up on the hill-top over-looking the bridge; the bank immediately by the river flooded regularly and offered very little grazing or arable land so the settlers had opted for higher ground.

Maria and her companions rode through the woods west of Fallin and broke cover as the sun was just setting over the Clackmannan Mountains and came to a large clearing on the west bank of the bridge. They never made it across the bridge however for the moment they came into the open, hundreds of Gaelic warriors surrounded them: they came from all directions, from the south following the line of the river from Drip, from across the bridge, from the approach to Doune, Keir and Blair of Drummond to their west and Blane's Dun to their north.

Longinus stepped forwards bravely, seeking to identify who was the leader of the war band they now faced. As he did so, Galahaidra muttered: "Over three hundred. Let us hope they are here to wave us off!" A tall and muscular warrior, face painted white, hair bright red, armed with a long sword and round shield, a large horned helmet denoting his rank as the leader of several war bands, hanging from his belt, stood forward from the circle of warriors and asked Longinus:

"Where do ye go? The lands to your north be mine and ye are no welcome."

Longinus took counsel from the rest of his party. If the Gaels were intent on blocking their crossing of the Forth then they would needs return the way they had come and meet up with the three trireme that Iosephus had commissioned. Their journey by sea would take longer and the North Sea was dangerous, but it would avoid them coming into conflict with the Gaels. Whilst the men were discussing their options, Maria ignored them and walked over to the Gaelic leader, bowed then kneeling before him asked:

"Noble warrior, great leader! What possible threat do we pose? I merely wish to break bread with any who will join me. I carry no weapons. Is there any way I can prove to you that I mean only good and not harm?"

"I have heard of ye" the chief of chiefs replied. "You have the God's power and ye have no fear. You are far from being 'harmless'. I have heard the stories ye ha' told and your Master hath commanded floods, destroyed cities, slain thousands. I fear ye and would see you gone from my lands."

Maria was shocked for she had never considered she would make anyone *afraid* of her. It was true that her Master could destroy cities or armies but he had made a covenant, a promise that he would not wipe out mankind as he had done in the time of Noah. Remaining kneeling, she pleaded with the chieftain:

"My Master seeks peace not war, seeks love not revenge, seeks to forgive where once he would destroy in his anger, is more moderate and compassionate than he was before. He is God yet he listens to mankind and we can change his intent through our prayers. I follow him because he has shown me his forgiveness and he offers the same to anyone who believes and remembers him in the breaking of bread. You can see I am not strong; you could crush me without blinking. I would gladly die at your hands if it would show you my Master wants only good; seeks to help not to harm; seeks to show his love and compassion and not his Might."

The chieftain conferred with those around him. He was conscious that they had already put the girl to the test and she had proven herself not to be a Witch. Yet she had defeated two war bands and the King of Dacia's army. If the girl wanted she could call on thousands to fight at her side. She was not weak … except that she chose to be so. '*Why?*' he pondered and remembering he had also been told the girl never spoke a lie he decided to put her honesty to the test:

"You are a mighty warrior and my people have seen ye wear the armour and carry the weapons of a Goddess, a heroine capable of slaying whole armies just by the artefacts of power that ye bear. Why then do ye make yourself weak?"

Maria was surprised at being described as a warrior and heroine and her transparent face showed her disbelief that anyone could see her that way. Then she remembered the lesson her Master had taught her when confronted by the storm and blushed before admitting:

"For a few days I was that person. I wanted to be this warrior princess that conquered Britannia and thus converted the people of Briton to Christianity through my conquest. I sinned through my pride and pray that one day I shall be forgiven. My Master taught me that I was wrong. The real me is not a warrior and so I have put my armour and weapons away and come to you unarmed and totally at your mercy.

I firmly believe that no man or woman should kill another human being and would die rather than do so myself. I was also taught by my Master that everything I achieved in battle had been through *his* help. And then he told me that he did not want anyone to be converted at the point of a sword. He seeks the honest and total commitment to him, bonded by our love and our soul's desire and not by fear.

Once there was a man who sought to follow Iesus. But he asked first to go home and say goodbye to those he loved. Iesus was adamant: you have to commit *totally* to me and leave your family behind. He spoke of those who hold the plough not looking backwards for then they will not steer the plough straight and thus it will leave a furrow in the ground that is crooked. We must look forwards with all of our mind, heart and soul. There is no tolerance, no half-hearted compromise, no wavering *when our furrow must be straight.*

I love my Master without question; I believe he is God without the need for explanation; I follow him absolutely and will never turn backwards. If you should follow my Master you must do so totally and this means your conversion must take in your heart, mind and soul: not to save your life but because you love my Master."

"Is your's the only way?" the chieftain asked, rocked back by Maria's answer and the intensity of her devotion to the Master, but also his heart was charmed by her honesty, her youth and her fragile beauty. He became another to come under her spell: to seek to follow her for the best of all reasons: that she spoke the Truth!

Maria laughed and the sound of her honest and unaffected laughter echoed around the clearing. The warriors smiled for her gaity was infectious and they lowered their weapons accepting the truth of what Maria said: she was no threat though once she had been; but now she offered another way, a different path.

"My Master said he is the Truth, the Path and the promise of Eternal Life. I believe that. He is the only way … but how we get to him can vary from one person to another. Such is God's power that he can make any path to him become the right path. Love God and love your fellow man and woman and believe there is One God and you cannot go wrong really!" at which she grinned for the Truth and the Path to Eternal Life was so simple if one stuck to the new commandment given by Iesus. Everything else became irrelevant if you could commit totally to love of God and man.

"What do you mean by love?" the chieftain asked and Maria was happy to explain:

"Many things, good sir. My Master once told the story of a man who had been beaten and left half-dead by robbers. Two men walked by and left him but the third from Samarihya stopped, helped him, took him to a local Inn, paid for him to be healed and for his board and lodging. That man showed love for his fellow man.

Once a friend of mine, also named Maria, bought expensive perfumed oil and washed my Master's feet in it, showing her love and adoration of him. Her sister said: 'Surely the money would have been better spent on the poor?' but my Master reminded us all that we must not only do good works but also we must leave a place for worship of God. So we not only love our fellow man but we also love God: my Master's new commandment requires both.

My greatest dream, my sole desire is to be in the presence of God, eternally, showing love for him through my prayers and my singing, rejoicing in his creation, serving him without question. My time on Earth is to prepare me for an eternity of love; to teach me so many important lessons about how I must trust God in all things. My Master is also my greatest friend. One day I shall die; perhaps this is that day? But I am not afraid to die because my heart's desire lies beyond my death: to love my God forever in his presence."

Although spoken softly for the chieftain's ears yet all in the clearing heard her words and began to nod in understanding. This was not their way yet many were tempted by the thought of a God who rewarded good deeds and asked for love in return. The chieftain was rocked back once more by Maria's total fearlessness. She did not fear torture or death. '*What a warrior this girl would be'* he thought *'if she had not turned her back on war and violence and instead she has the courage to deliberately make herself weak'*. Yet still the chieftain challenged the girl as he asked:

"I already worship many Gods and my Gods are powerful. They bring me conquest in war and aid me when I hunt people or animals. Why should I worship your God?"

Maria was thoughtful as the chieftain's question sat at the crux of her mission. These people were used to centuries of superstition and magic fuelled by the trickery of their Druids and Shaman yet Giselda's and

Senna's conversions had taught her that many Druids and Shaman were honest, had integrity, piety and genuinely had believed in their false Gods.

In addition, the warriors before her showed their awe and wonder of creation by seeing every part of the natural world as governed by a pantheon of Gods: divine beings who commanded the sun, the stars, the seas, rivers, trees, mountains and so the list went on. Not One God with many names and attributes but many Gods each sharing a part of creation; a share of God-head. As she had said to Tartellus: 'Was this very different?' Her God asked for awe and wonder for his creation as part of the adoration we all must give to Him and these people already showed that devotion. Yet how explain that this was different from worshipping lots of Gods as opposed to One God?

"Great chief: you are the sole leader of these warriors. There are many chiefs of individual war bands but they ultimately look to you for direction. There can be only one leader. It is no different with God. He is served by many who have been gifted with immense powers, especially his Angels who can make the oceans boil, destroy whole countries, turn the sky grey, the sun to go black, silence the birds that sing. My One God created Angels as well as creating man. There is only one God the Creator just as there is only one 'chief of chiefs'."

At that he nodded in understanding. "We have a hierarchy of Gods and I understand the point you make. Ultimately there can be only one God who leads and only one God who was at the beginning of all things" then looking around the circle of his men, he could see their eagerness to hear more and turned back to Maria:

"Forgive me for my earlier discourtesy. Will ye join us in supper?"

"I would be honoured" she replied inwardly breathing a huge sigh of relief and saying a massive prayer of thanks to her Master. "I ask that during supper I might be allowed to break bread with you all. It is how we remember my Master."

Nicodemus records how *"At the Bridge of Allan Joseph of Arimathea and Mary Magdalan were met by Hargest, Chief of the Gael in the Valley of the Forth, broke bread with him and some three hundred warriors. Many were converted that night by the simple stories of the Master gently told by the Magdalan and by her courage. She became known as 'the girl who does not fear' and was greatly honoured as such."* (Nicodemus. The History of the Early Christian Church, 5th Century AD)

Longinus, Craedech and Galahaidra were feted and honoured by the Gaels as they had won renown for their prowess in war at the Battle of the River Humber. Later they were shown to their own pitch and set up tent, guarded by the Gaels, ever watchful yet merging to become invisible in the dark of the woods to their south and west. A few warriors stayed to keep the men company around their camp fire whilst Maria retired to her place at the foot of Craedech's bed, offering the Prince her prayers and protection, showing all where her heart lay. As Maria was getting ready for bed, Galahaidra muttered in her hearing:

"You are incredibly lucky. It would have been so easy for the Gaels to just wipe us out. Can you at least give us some warning next time you decide to take on three hundred war-like barbarians on your own?"

"Oh ye of little faith" she whispered then grinned as the young knight shook his head in mock despair.

From Allan they had a choice of two routes: through the Clackmannan Mountains, Dollar and Tillicoultry to Milnathort and then north to Perth via Auchtermuchty and skirting the north of Loch Leven and the Lomond Hills; or more directly to Perth through Blane's Dun, Auchterarder then following the line of the river Erin or Earn to Broom and Eviot, passing south of the Cairngorns and Tibber Moor before crossing the River Earn at Bridge of Erin and heading north to Tarsappie and Perth. Maria asked the chieftain, whose name was Hargest, for his advice. "I want the route with the most people: for my mission is not just to go to Perth but to tell as many people as possible the Good News."

"Go by Dollar, Milnathort and Auchtermuchty. You will meet the peaceful Venicontes whose capital is Perth but who also live in many of the villages south of the City between the Lomond Hills and the Cairngorns" Hargest advised them all. "It is a longer route but a better road for there is a cutting through the Clackmannan Mountains and the road follows a narrow gorge with little chance of ambush. Your only risk is that someone blocks the far end of the gorge where you come out just north of Milnathort and Loch Leven and just south of Auchtermuchty. You will be well-received at each settlement you come across as I shall send word ahead of you. There are perhaps three to four hundred people you will meet along the way. Perth then boasts at least one thousand residents; more on the days when they hold markets and fairs which is most weeks."

When it came to time for the company to depart, Hargest hugged Maria tight and then wished her safe passage his voice gruff: for in the short time he had known the girl he had come to respect her and fallen under her charm:

"You are very different from what I expected. I can see your God goes with yet there be those who will seek your death. Your courage should see ye through but please be careful" and he nodded towards Longinus, Galahaidra and Craedech, knowing that they would guard her. "Once you head north from Perth into the Cairngorns and the Highlands" he continued "You must be wary of the Picts and the Caledonii. Their war parties harass everyone in that barren place. Keep my Maria safe!" and then he waved them on their way.

The road to Milnathort and Auchtermuchty cut through a narrow and deep gorge with sheer sides that were a mass of heather, mosses and grasses growing over light grey rock and topped by trees: poplars, elms and oaks. Water ran down as rills and falls into a stream that fed the Loch Leven. Their path was tortuous, weaving as it followed the way left by years of erosion by the narrow stream that they would often have to wade through. So steep were the banks of the gorge that they lost sight of the sun overhead then black rain clouds descended on them and they covered up from the cold rain, riding in dark shadow. When they emerged at the far end of the gorge through the clouds and the rain they saw the flat lands and marshes that were the northern end of Loch Leven, surrounded to the west and south by the smooth slopes of the Lomond Hills with Milnathort sitting on the east banks of the Loch.

Milnathort was technically out of their way, lying just to their south whereas the direct route to Perth was to their north via Auchtermuchty. But Maria was insistent that they meet the people of Milnathort. "It is only a detour of two leagues and we have made much greater deviations on our winding road to Perth. There are a few hundred live in the settlement and if only one converts then we will have achieved something that is good."

The settlement was long and thin, divided into two parts: the oldest part of Milnathort was a fortified camp set in the bank to the north of Loch Leven with views as far as the Tay Valley in one direction and the Firth of Forth in the other. Then a smaller community of fishermen and farmers had grown up around the banks of Loch Leven building their huts on the grey sand at the water's edge and the grass-covered island near the centre of the Loch. Over time the communities by the Loch and in the hill-top fort had united and the village had grown to join the two settlements together.

The welcome the company received was gracious and the villagers genuinely showed their interest in Maria and the message she had come to bring. "We have heard of ye" they said and she was invited into many of their homes, the girl gladly accepting their invitations. The first evening she sat in the large hut that was their place of assembly with nearly two hundred of all ages and told them the stories of her Master's life and his ministry.

"Why us?" she was asked again and again. It was a question that Longinus had begun to ask also. He had understood what they had sought to achieve in Hispania, Gallia and Britannia. But Caledonia was different again. It lacked any cohesiveness or nationality and he could understand why Julius Caesar had baulked at attempting its invasion. Every one of its many small villages and settlements would need to be converted, each presenting a unique challenge, if Maria's mission was to be a success.

"There are so many reasons that I have come here today" Maria replied "and I would gladly spend several weeks with you just talking of why my Master's message should be heard by the people of Milnathort. Alas, the rest of Caledonia must also hear what I have to say and so I do not have weeks but l welcome spending today and tomorrow here.

My mission is to bring my Master's word before the people of Caledonia. This could not be achieved in my life time but my Master sees the future in terms of millennia rather than the life of one simple girl. I am asked to make a beginning but in the hope that one day the foundations of the faith we establish here and in the other villages I will visit will rise to build a Church that will spread across Caledonia.

My Master's first and most loyal disciples were fishermen as are many of you so it is fitting that I come here to talk of the many stories that my Master told about fishing, even calling his disciples 'fishers of men'. There were many occasions that he sat in the boat with Iacobus and Petrus and guided them to huge catches. Once, he placed an eye in the mouth of a fish to show that God is always expanding the Universe and creating new things for us to marvel. Now there are many such fish, all related to that first act of creation and named after Petrus as the 'Stone Fish'.

Another time, my Master walked across the waters of Galilee to join Iacobus' boat and briefly Petrus was able to walk on the water towards him but sadly Petrus lost faith and plunged in. We are taught by my Master that we can do anything if we have faith and it was with his aid that I have lived when I should have drowned or been burnt by flames."

At this, one of the young men said: "Och anyone can walk on water! Come to the Loch tomorrow before ye break your fast and we will show ye … if ye have enough faith that is" he added with a laugh and Maria willingly accepted the offer fascinated to discover what the young man meant. Then they asked her to tell them about when she had nearly drowned and she spoke of the day The Valiant had floundered in a storm.

That night she joined many for supper and broke bread with them. After supper, a young woman approached her to ask if she could join her company. Maria saw the woman was genuine in her faith and belief yet still questioned her commitment because she saw loss in the other woman's eyes and needed to know that her conversion was not her response to some sort of bereavement. The woman's name was Ninian and she would become one of the first of the Caledonian saints.

"Once a disciple said to my Master: *'I will go wherever you go and follow you everywhere.'* My Master was impressed yet also wanted to be sure the man understood the commitment the young man was making and so replied: *'I have no home and so there will be no rest for you. You must become homeless too if you follow me.'*

I, also have no home. Where once I called home, if I returned now then it would be to my death. My mission takes me to strange and foreign lands. In many I am welcomed yet none can I call 'home'. I need to see the same commitment in my followers as my Master asked for. For if you follow me then the reality is that you commit to following my Master. The reward is an eternity of serving my Master so this is a commitment beyond any other you could make. I see loss in your eyes so ask is your commitment genuine and total or the response to a recent bereavement?"

Ninian's reply touched Maria's heart and was the start of a friendship that stretched beyond this world and all time and space.

"My husband and young son were lost in a storm on the Firth of the Forth, trawling for fish when the weight of their net took them under to be lost in the deeps of the Forth. I pray for them every day and hope that some day my prayers will be answered. I pray that wherever they have gone to they shall be loved and cared for.

The Gods of this place do not speak of a life beyond death but your Master offers that gift. I will follow you and your Master forever if my service shall grant my husband and son the gift of eternal life that your Master offers."

"Follow my Master" Maria replied with tears in her eyes for she could think of no greater service than the sacrifice Ninian was prepared to make, then continued for she could not lie and feared the truth would drive Ninian away: "but my Master will want your total commitment. Pray for your husband and son by all means but you must serve my Master for one reason and one reason alone: that you do so because you love him."

Ninian smiled for she had thought of this already and so knew her mind. In this regard her faith was greater even than the Magdalan's as she responded to the girl's concern:

"Our Master has spoken to me and welcomes my love of my husband and son. Did He not once teach us that every man and woman was made in his image? Another time He told us that we all bear him in our hearts and that his presence becomes real in the breaking of bread. Yet again He said to a follower, the love you have shown your family is also to show love to me. I love our Master by showing love for those He has created. Our Master can be loved in many ways. Accept my way is different from yours yet it is still love of God and Man."

At which Maria embraced the young woman then apologised for she had forgotten that she was not alone in being in communion with God. Others also would be granted this gift and teach her more about her faith if she learned to listen to them:

"Forgive my doubt. It was misplaced. Come with me and I shall be honoured by your company. I am still young and have much to learn. Teach me please and show me our Master's way through your own visions as I shall tell you of mine."

The following morning Maria headed down to Loch Leven and watched amazed as several of the children and the young of the village were all walking on its smooth waters. "Come" they said and one young man of her age smiled and held out his hand which she took gratefully. Maria carefully strode into the smooth black waters and found that there was a narrow and winding causeway just beneath the water. So deep that it could not be seen from a distance but shallow enough that you could see someone's feet through the water such that they appeared to be tredding on the surface.

The next moment she missed her footing and went head first into its depths. It was the coldest water she had ever encountered in her life and she clambered out in record time then looking to the heavens, apologised for daring to try and imitate her Master's miracle. She could hear the distant echo of his laughter from across the Lomond Hills.

She returned to the camp and changed out of her wet things then tried to warm herself in front of the last embers of their camp fire. As a consequence, the party did not leave for Perth until mid morning, now six where previously they had been five.

The way to Perth skirted the hills of Fife to their east and passed through where the Clackmannan and Cairngorn mountains were separated by the valley of the River Erin to their west. The Auch crossed their path: running as a narrow stream from Loch Aurd through Auchterarder and Auchtermuchty then on to the North Sea joining the Firth of the Tay. The Auch had once been a raging flood forming the gorge that the party had used to reach Milnathort and the valley that went north to where Perth lay as the gateway to the Highlands. It was now no more than a stream but it still must be crossed. They stopped for a late lunch on arriving at the settlement of Auchtermuchty where they would ford the Auch.

Their welcome at Auchtermuchty was as warm as that they had received at Milnathort. There were less than a hundred settlers but they were enthusiastic to hear Maria's stories and amazed when Iesus was able to heal a blind man through the intercession of the girl's prayers. That evening, as Ninian and Maria had supper with the whole community in a large timber framed structure used as stabling for horses and a barn for sheep in the cold of winter, Maria spoke of Iesus' birth:

"Although Iesus was of royal birth, of the line of David and the tribe of Benjamin in the House of Iesse born in the town of Bethlehem, yet when his mother and father reached Bethlehem, there was no room for them in the Inn there. Many had come to the tribal capital centre for the tribe of Benjamin as the Roman Emperor Augustus had decreed that there must be a census in preparation for introducing a poll tax across the Empire. All of Iudaea had been asked to return to their tribal centres and this meant that the pregnant Maria and the worried father Iosephus had to travel from Nazareth, where Iosephus was the town's carpenter, to Bethlehem."

She was asked the first question and was happy to take interruptions for she was now a practiced story-teller and the tradition in her homeland was for those listening to a story to interact with her. Her delight in seeing this was also the tradition in Caledonia was transparent and her tale from here was a series of questions and answers but she never forgot the path and the final destination of the stories she was to tell that day.

"Who was Iesus' father? I thought it was God!" a young man challenged her and smiling to show she welcomed his question she answered:

"Maria the mother of Iesus was met one day by an Angel called Gabri'el who said that she would conceive a son who was both God and the Messiah. Maria went to meet Eliza who was her aunt and who greeted Maria saying 'You bear the Son of God'.

There was a scandal when it was discovered that Maria was with child but had no husband, especially as Maria was of David's royal line and the line of Iesse. So a husband was found and a man named Iosephus agreed to take Maria into his home and honour her as his wife. Iosephus brought Iesus up as his own son but died before he could see Iesus' ministry. He is greatly honoured for the love he showed Iesus in life."

"What happened next?" one of the village elders asked, a woman ancient yet with the thrill of knowledge and the desire for adventure still present in her eyes.

"For you, mother, I will tell how Iesus was born but first I say to you that the adventures of God are ageless and without limit. Seek them therefore with glad heart" and then Maria continued her account:

"The landlord of the Inn saw the state that Maria was in and offered the young couple use of his stable, cut into stone but with a timber frame extension very similar to this barn. That night a child was born to be greeted by Angels and then by the shepherds on the nearby hills to whom the Angel Gabri'el said: 'Rejoice and do not be afraid. For on this day is born a child to Maria of the line of David and he is the Son of God. Go down to the village of Bethlehem and do homage.' In the end, all in Bethlehem gathered at the stable and did worship the child who was King of Kings."

Maria paused but they were not content and asked for more and so she continued:

"The couple stayed in Bethlehem for a few weeks to let mother and child settle and recover from the birth. They were able to rent a house in the village which had emptied once the census was out of the way. Three wise men, sometimes said to be Kings, who studied the stars had seen a star that was the sign of a great King's birth, a child who would grow up to become a man of such majesty that one day the whole world would know his name. The star shone in such a way that the wise men were given a destination: the royal village of Bethlehem.

When they reached Bethlehem, they enquired at the Inn, asking if there had been any births within the last month. They were directed to the house that Iosephus had hired and he answered the door to them. 'We have come to give homage to the King' the three men said and in astonishment Iosephus showed them in. On seeing Maria and the child, the three men knelt and offered the lady three gifts of kingship: the myrrh and frankincense we used in Iesus' tomb and the gold coins that I placed on the dead Iesus' eyes when we buried him in the cave in Golgotha.

Then the same night Iosephus was visited by an Angel in a dream, saying: 'Take the child to Aegypt. Flee for his safety.' Meanwhile the three wise men visited the Palace of Herod the Great in the new City Port of Caesarea. They were taken before Herod and in good faith told of the royal birth in Bethlehem. Herod sent them on their way and they were escorted to the borders of Iudaea and Syria to ensure that they did not tell anyone of this new-born King.

Herod was afraid of insurrection. He had seen Rome remove Ptolemy, the brother of Cleopatra, and place the young girl on the throne of Aegypt only for the girl made Queen to rebel against Octavian when she fell in love with Marcus Antoninus. Herod also knew that in reality he was a puppet King, at the mercy of Rome, a client kingdom with an Army of Occupation only an hour's march away under an appointment of the Roman Senate, a Procurator.

Herod could not afford a rebellion under an opposing branch of his Royal House – an army under the Messiah that would remove him and revolt against Rome. Alas, Herod had misread the Prophets' description of the Messiah and he thought of his kingdom of Iudaea on Earth as the Messiah's objective when he should have been rejoicing at the opening of the Gates of Paradise, a kingdom beyond this world and the place we shall go to when we die. The Messiah did not threaten Herod's kingdom but he would hold the keys of the Gates to Hades and to Paradise.

So Herod did an evil thing: he ordered that all children born in his kingdom in the last month should be taken and slain. His Praetorian did the deed, going through village after village and killing all infants, whether new-born or not, a deed that shall always be remembered as every community in Iudaea suffered.

But Iesus had escaped for as the wise men returned to their country they smuggled a message to Iosephus carried by one of their servants. The message said: 'We do not trust Herod and believe he means your child harm.' Iosephus remembered the Angel's words and as the soldiers of Herod began the massacre of the Innocents, Iesus and his family had already escaped south to Eziz-Aqaba on the banks of the Jordan and the Gulf of Aqaba which was their way into Aegypt, avoiding the Sinai Desert and Mountains. They journeyed to Sherin and to Radir before entering Aegypt at Ramses.

They stayed in Zagazig, a City found by the Persians under Cyrus, many leagues inland from the Middle Sea in Dalmatia but which was on the camel route from Cairo to Ramses, Egypt's largest sea port. Iosephus' carpentry skills were much in demand and they lived comfortably though always aware that they were in a Roman Province and if Herod went to the Procurator in Ierusalem or the Legate in Syria, then they could become outlaws again. Fortunately no word of their escape came to Herod.

Zagazig is in Sharqia, north of the City of Kings in Qalyubia and the Egyptian City of the Dead which is the royal burial place on the Nile near Luxor. Zagazig is where Iesus was brought up until Iosephus heard of Herod's death and then the family returned to Iudaea to settle in Nazareth by the Sea of Galilee."

"Zagazig is made famous by the ancient poem 'Zig zag zig' which Saint Saens would later set to music" Ra'el reminded Roaring Flamebringer and then she continued her tale but hurrying now as it was already dark outside and she was beginning to grow weary.

"Tell us about his childhood. Was he worshipped? Was he happy?" the people of Auchtermuchty asked Maria and she was happy to respond.

"Iesus spoke little about his childhood yet there are some stories from those rare moments when he spoke about himself as opposed to his mission. He was a clever child and stood out for his wisdom at an early age, going to the Temple in Ierusalem when ten and being found by his parents explaining the scriptures to the Rabbi and Priests gathered there who were awe struck at the child's knowledge and understanding. He was bullied as a child: for being different and for coming from somewhere other than Nazareth. Once the bullying got out of hand and Iesus turned the child doing this into a fig tree.

Iesus helped Iosephus in his workshop and was as skilled as his father at carpentry, becoming known for the quality of his woodwork and being a master in his field until his thirtieth birthday.

His mission began when he was baptised at the age of thirty in the waters of the River Jordan by his cousin Iohannus, the son of Eliza. Within months he had recruited his disciples and apostles and was called by us 'Rabbi', 'the Teacher', 'the Master' for his new teaching and knowledge of the scriptures. Once his Ministry started when he was thirty, he would not visit Ierusalem for another three years until he came to be proclaimed as King. Iesus was the culmination of the prophecies of the Prophets and the beginning of the Good News that we can all be gifted with eternal life: Alpha and Omega; the Beginning and the End."

They asked her about Paradise and she talked of the many times the Master had described His home in the heavens. They spoke of the gifts of the Spirit at which Ninian stood forward. "We know ye" said several of those gathered in the barn and she smiled at their recognition then said: "When Maria broke bread with us in Milnathort then the Spirit of God came to me. I have been given the gift of prophecy and the gift of healing."

"Why have we not been given the same gifts?" they asked now jealous of what they saw as the favouring of Milnathort. Ninian took this question and her answer surprised and amazed everyone.

"Auchtermuchty will be greatly honoured in times gone by, just as much as Milnathort. For I have seen your future: two thousand years from now you will still be celebrating the story of Iesus' birth as told by Maria in this very barn every winter. On the coldest nights each year people will queue from around the world to come and see your celebration and it shall give our Master great pleasure for each time you remind the world of his birth then you rejoice in His name."

As Maria and Ninian went to retire to their tent with Galahaidra once more lying across its entrance flap to guard them both, Longinus approached Maria and humbly admitted he had been in error:

"You know that I have been doubtful about our ability to convert Caledonia and could not see why we should even make the attempt. Yet now we are blessed with the grace of Ninian and the welcome we have received here and at Milnathort has warmed our hearts and refreshed our confidence. I was wrong and should trust our Master more. He has his reasons and they are always good; it is just we cannot always see the end of His path."

Maria was so delighted that she stood on tip toe to kiss him then said shyly: "I am lucky to have you as a dear friend. The Master teaches us all. He is not mine but all of ours and I have been guilty of forgetting that He shows his love for us through granting every one of us a part of His vision. We are both blessed by Him."

Perth was a further half days ride. It sat at the crossing of the Tay, the first crossing west side of the Forth of the Tay where it joined the North Sea. A stone bridge built by Roman masons with gently curved arches; an ancient ford; and a rickety antique ferry boat that needed four of the crew to constantly bail out water whilst a fifth handed out safety lines to passengers were available for those coming from the south, north to Scone or west to the far reaches of the Western Isles and Inner Seas off west Caledonia, Eagles' Glen, the Glass How and Aer.

Perth was also the point where Caledonia was at its narrowest, the ride from Perth on the east coast to Glass How overlooking the western seas was six to eight hours on well-rested horses.

As a consequence, Perth had become a thriving port and would represent the point furthest north of the Roman Empire. Just six miles north was the site of two battles to be fought by the Romans, both leading to the defeat of the Empire (although the Roman historians claimed both as victories for Rome) and thus ensuring the independence of the Highlands and Hibernia. In the fourth century AD in the time of Constantius as Emperor, he would move his Empire's boundary further south to the line of Hadrians Wall between Caer Lisle and New Caister, abandoning the Antonine Wall and a line of fortified camps further north. Constantius would also briefly move the capital of the Roman Empire from the Oyster City (Camulodenum, Colcaister or Colchester as it is now known) to Eboratum, Yorvic or York to give the City its modern name.

The City of Perth had not only been a port: it had become the main trading link between Caledonia, Hibernia and the rest of Europa including Scandanavia, the Barant and Kala seas, the north coast line of the land of the Roos, the Heligos Bight and Dane Mark, the Gulf of the land of the Finn, Finn land and White Roos, the Balticum Sea and northern Europa, the North Sea, Mare Germanica and the north coast of Germania and Gallia.

The Roman Empire had traded with Perth for nearly a century and Pontius Pilate's father had stayed in Perth for a few months, probably stranded by rough seas, although the local legend is that Pontius Pilate himself spent some of his childhood in a villa six miles north-east of the City which suggests that the Pilate family had once settled in this area.

The City had begun as nothing more than a fortified camp with an earthen rampart and a horse-drawn ferry across the shallows of the Tay but the many routes inland and its successful trade with the independent European kingdoms, the Norse and the Roman Empire had seen both its prosperity and its community bringing the best architecture, art, culture and heritage that its rich merchants had seen in their travels back to enhance their home City.

Whilst the rest of Caledonia was building in wood, mud and straw, and would be constantly repairing damage done by rains, storms, tempests and floods, Perth built in stone and was rewarded with a City made sturdy that also benefitted from more clement weather. Perth copied the grid style that had pervaded all of the romance Cities and was more Romance than Caledonian. It became the Venetia of the north: more so as it was surrounded by water sitting between two passes of the Tay; which river became a defining feature of the City's size and shape as well as its success in trade.

Perth would eventually be over-shadowed by Glass How or Glasgow, Dee's Hill or Dundee and Edwin's Burgh or Edinburgh as trade switched to the Americas and the rest of Britannia. The Tay was crossed at its mouth and the Forth was also crossed further east than the fords and the bridge near Allan. Both developments reduced the level of trade passing through Perth. Perth still remains the most popular and sought-after City in Scotland, however.

The company had no difficulty finding lodgings in an Inn when they reached Perth, crossing over the Tipper Moor and the Roman bridge. Maria praised God for the simple pleasure of a Roman style bath in which to make her evening and morning ablutions. Then once refreshed, all six of them walked around the City, starting with the port, where Iosephus touched base with his three crews. To Maria's delight, one of the ships was Iosephus' private yacht and Decius gave her a cheery wave then swung down onto the pier to join the company.

"Not been put in a pot and cooked for supper yet?" he asked getting a groan from Longinus who muttered "Don't give the people here ideas or the poor girl nightmares."

"I was nearly roasted" Maria replied with her head held high and then at Decius' look of shock she told him of the challenges she had met when first she had encountered the Gaels.

"The whole crew will want to hear!" the helmsman replied. "I hired the crew of The Valiant and they all want to listen to your latest adventures plus I know someone who cannot wait to see you again. Take a look at our crows' nest" and as Maria looked up there was Felstum grinning back down at her. Then Iosephus turned to Craedech and told the Prince: "I have three hundred of your best warriors on board as well. Alas we could not bring any horses but I can go to the horse auctions tomorrow and kit them all out. No-one will come near us when we enter the Highands and the land of the Picts."

Maria spoilt the party briefly when she said quietly but in a voice that would not accept opposition: "No armed soldiers. I have promised the Master that I shall go unarmed before the Caledonians and that includes the Picts when we meet them. I do not seek to scare them away!"

Craedech waited until she was distracted by Felstum, who had shinned down from his perch on top of the mast and was now running towards her.

"Keep them nearby" the Prince whispered to Iosephus and the older knight signalled his consent behind the girl's back. Then both went over to greet Felstum who was so excited with his news. "The Emperor Tiberius has retired and appointed the young Germanicus as his heir" he shouted and poor Maria had to cover her ears so deafening was the young man in his eagerness to tell them all of the events in Roma.

"Germanicus will be the new Emperor and it is a new era: we have a young man as leader of the civilised world and he has already won over the Senate by asking to be called 'Caligula' in honour of the nickname given to him by the soldiers he campaigned with in Germania. He is highly respected as many remember his father who was much loved. It is a new dawn, all augurs well."

Then he continued more sombrely as he knew Longinus would be upset at his next news: "Also Pilate was recalled to Roma. He contracted a terrible fever on his arrival in the City. His wife Cordelia cared for him and briefly was ill herself but her fever went away miraculously. Pilate however died in agony with great ulcers all over his body, screaming in pain and suffering from incontinence. Many came to see him and all wept at the damage done by the illness. It is as the Master once said: *'When we lose that which gives us our immunity to diseases or succumb to the viruses that disrupt the way our body normally functions then diseases can cause massive disturbances. The same can happen if we fail to keep our mind or soul pure. Corruption can be as damaging as the spread of any disease.'*

*(*Felstum was quoting from one of the Master's visions to the Magdalan and as recorded in the Gospel of Mary Magdalene, written 1st or 2nd Century AD. The Saviour explains how matter, impure particles, viruses and corruption of the mind and soul can lead to terrible illness as part of the chapter on how Iesus healed the sick*)*

Pilate is dead: he took two weeks to die and none of his physicians could put a name to the disease that took him in its fatal grasp; perhaps punishment for his judgement of our Master?"

Maria was the first to respond surprised that Felstum should remember her account of the Saviour's words and her *vision* on the day that Iesus had risen from the dead: "I shall pray for Pontius for he was placed in a terrible position by his Emperor, the Sanhedrin, King Herod and those who spoke for my Master's crucifixion. But of most import: what of Cordelia? How is she now she has lost her husband?"

"She has returned to the shelter of her family in Roma. They guard her but no-one holds her to account for the failings of Pilate. She is safe."

Ignoring the fact that Felstum had not answered her question, Maria made a promise:

"I shall visit her the moment my mission is over. She loved her husband and remained loyal to him in difficult times. Now she has lost both her only son and her husband. Her grief must be terrible" then Maria turned to hold Longinus, recognising his hurt from his sudden silence.

"He let you go" she reminded him "and had he not done so then you would be in trouble as someone respected by Pilate and on his staff. There will be many young men whose careers will be blighted by Pilate's disgrace yet he allowed you to avoid all of that. I think, maybe, he knew what was going to happen and saved you?"

Briefly the man wept, sniffed, wiped his nose on the sleeve of his cloak then kissed Maria, thanking her and ignoring the sharp intake of breath from Craedech. After all, he had known Maria long before she had met her Prince … well a few months longer anyway!

"Where now?" Felstum asked still excited at meeting up with the company.

"North" Maria answered not exactly helpfully but at least she was being consistent for a change.

They stayed a week in Perth. Primarily this was to ensure their ships were fully provisioned as there would be few places where they would find communities or settlements able to provision the eight hundred crew and warriors on the three ships. They were told that there were fortified camps at the mouth of the Ness and the Dean which traded with the Norse, Vicing and Germanii but that from the moment they went north or west into the Cairngorns, the only company they would find was Pictish war parties who would hunt them down without mercy and the north and western tribes of the Caledonii that had united recently: yet their union was still young and fragile.

One old campaigner from wars against the Allemanni in Germania who had settled in Perth on his retirement took Maria to one side and warned her of the risks she would face, showing his concern for the girl.

"The Picts are as bad as the Teutoni. They will hunt you down for days just for sport. Their cries break the night never letting you sleep. They come at you from all sides out of the dark of the forests or across the shadows of the Mountains and trap you in the valleys then take turns to charge at you. Your companions will fall one at a time: you will watch as you lose your friends until it is just you left. They will not listen to you and your Master's message for their way is constant war and terror. You will be tortured and slain in the most terrible way. Turn back, please!"

"Father, was this your fate?" Maria asked saddened that this poor man may have lost his comrades in arms or been tortured by the Teutonic and Germanic tribes. The man nodded then added: "I survived. They wanted the story of Varus' defeat to be told: the capture of the standards of three legions; the empty camp; the bodies of my peers never found. Just one poor legionary to tell the tale and then be banished to the furthest end of the Empire: to be kept out of sight of an angry and unforgiving Emperor. Yet I will be just as saddened if you are lost also. Come back!" and he limped off followed by Maria's fervent prayers that he find happiness and peace in his new life.

Their visit to Perth was very similar to when they had landed at Heraklion except on a much smaller scale. They met several hundreds rather than tens of thousands, a handful of whom had heard of Maria from her missions to the Middle Sea and Hispania. A few more had heard of her from the settlements further north. Most had no idea who she was but were touched by her approachability, humility and honesty. The general consensus however was that the girl was slightly deranged and would make a noble sacrifice for the first Pictish war party she encountered; pretty much the view of her companions too!

That first nght, Craedech went down on bended knee before her – which put him just about on her eye level to be fair and within seconds she had joined him on her knees whispering she would not have him do such homage to her. He grabbed her hands and held them tight then said: "Come home with me now. If we go north then we achieve nothing but your death. You have done all the Master could have asked of you. Surely he will grant you a life?"

"I have no home" she replied though sorely tempted by his command.

"Foolish child" the Prince fumed. "You have *my* home and if that is not enough then we can make a home wherever you wish."

"But do you not see that it is not my destiny to have a home?"

"Did the Master say that to you?" Craedech asked her directly and seeing the guilty look in her eyes went: "Aha! I thought so. This is some self-imposed penance for your earlier life. You nearly became a thief when desperate, hungry and with no other means of a living … but you chose the Master without thinking and followed him the first time you met. What need of penance have you? Maria, please, love me and spend your life with me. We can still tell the world about our Master but let us do so without taking unnecessary risk."

She tried to pull away but he would not let her. She looked at the ground between them but holding both of her hands tightly in one of his own he used the other to force her head up to look at him. At first she remained with her eyes downcast but eventually she could not resist and her eyes finally met his defiantly: "Bully" she said and then laughed with such unremitting joy and pleasure that Craedech felt his heart respond to his lover's delight in him.

"Does that mean 'Yes'?" he dared to ask.

But she would not say. She was not sure. And she would certainly not make such an important decision without *praying* about it. Instead, she bought herself time:

"Let me at least make this attempt to meet with the Picts and the Caledonii. I need to know that when I commit to you there shall be no niggling doubt that I could have done more. I need to test my worth one more time. But then … then I promise that I shall decide."

"Not enough" he muttered wondering why he had chosen this maddening young girl when he could have chosen a comfortable life with any number of well-behaved and submissive, immaculately well-mannered ladies from Royal Houses across northern Europa. He glared at her but she was stubborn once more and knowing the look he gave in as rapidly as she had earlier. They knew each other's strengths and had learnt to allow the other space when they were determined yet both would always remain independent.

Iosephus was also determined to dissuade the girl from what was beginning to look like a suicide mission. And so he took the girl shopping in the City's Forum, with its exotic collection of rare silks, perfumes and oils, rare breeds of wild animals, reptiles and snakes, jewellery and clothing, books, parchments, scrolls and the finest art and architecture. Within five minutes he realised he was wasting his time as Maria ignored the many stalls and hawkers and offered the bag of money he had given her to the first beggar they encountered. Then suddenly, Maria had a thought and turned to Longinus:

"Have you still got that bag of gold?" she asked the young Centurion and he guiltily admitted he had hung on to it since the time a Dacian noble had given it to him out of charity. He had planned to keep it to cover their travel expenses not least as he was worried Iosephus might run dry one day. She stuck her hand out and demanded he pass it over then gave the gold coins to several beggars, almost causing a riot in the street. Then Maria saw a crocodile in the auction and remembering how she had not believed Longinus' description of one, she started to bid for it.

"NO!" said Craedech imperiously and brought the ill-conceived expedition to a hasty end. "I tried" muttered Iosephus, deflated and defeated. "I really did try."

It was Galahaidra, who came closest to finding Maria a distraction and one that kept her in Perth for several days longer than she had planned. Knowing her love for and empathy with children, for she was still a child in many ways, he took her to the school to meet the children there as they learnt their letters, languages, mathematics and philosophy. She sat in on their lessons and enjoyed the pleasure of an experience she herself had missed as a child. She was asked to talk of the places she had visited and to share with her classmates the many languages with which she was gifted. She loved nothing better than to tell stories and rapidly hers became a daily slot.

"Genius" Galahaidra's three male companions said to the young knight and Craedech began to plan the building of a school in Glevum. But alas, the spirit that drove Maria might love children but it also told her to 'go north' and on the eighth day, they set out into the Cairngorn Mountains. Craedech briefed his warriors, all now mounted and able to follow at a distance: "Keep out of sight or hearing but be no more than an arrow's pass from us at any time." A large gathering came to wave them off. None expected to see them return.

Caledonia: Maria Magdalan's Mission to the Picts in the Cairngorns

Maria'a account of her mission contained in the apocryphal '*The Account of the Missions of Joseph of Arithemea*' records:

"On leaving Perth it was cold every day: it rained non stop for forty days and then it snowed! The words of my Master were an echo lost in the continuous mountain ranges ... and then the Picts found us and it got rather exciting."

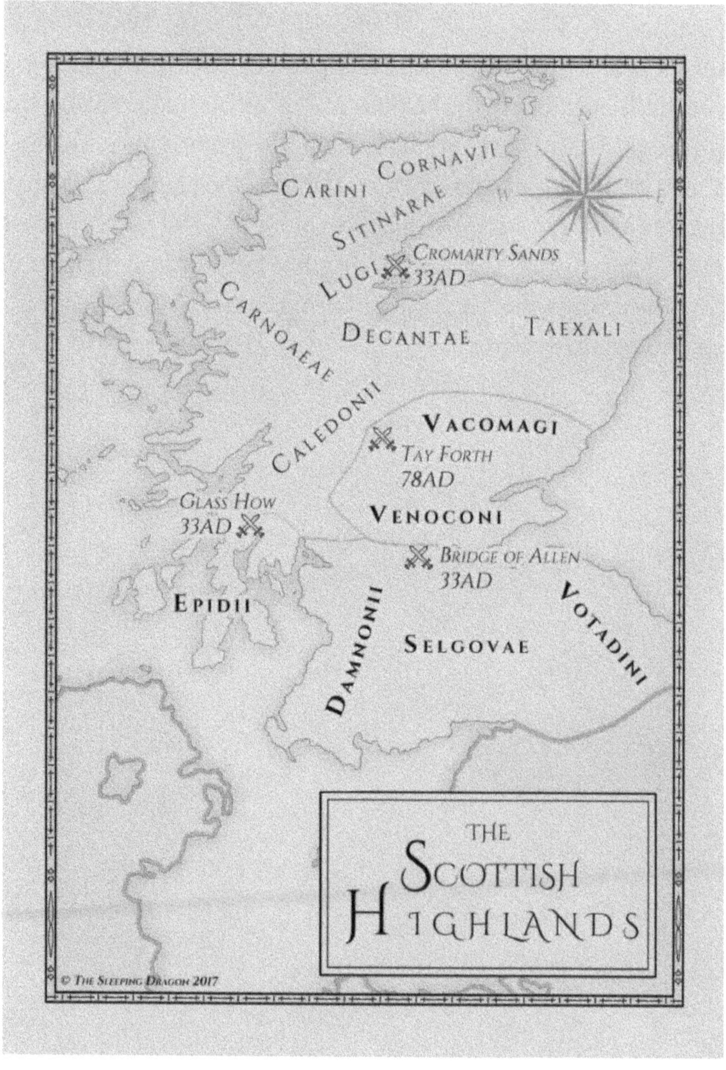

Ra'el broke off briefly to comment on Maria's Gospel account: "It is possible Maria may have been exaggerating but just as likely that it might rain non-stop for forty days and nights between Perth and Inver on the Ness or Campus Augustus at the mouth of Loch Ness. What we do know is that the Picts attacked her mission on day four."

"Sleep!" commanded Roaring Flamebringer "for it is already dawn and even the stars that you adore have retired to rest. I shall watch over you but I would hate for your story to be hurried or for it to be told when you are tired and unable to grant it the care and attention that the tale deserves. So sleep, my little Queen, and later today you can tell me of the conversion of Caledonia and also of how all of this relates to you and your family. I am curious yet I would still want the story to be told when you are at your best!"

Ra'el smiled back at the dragon that she had fallen in love with and who had promised to teach her to read and write: her heart's desire. He looked at her with eyes that whirled and thus she did not notice his gentle spell that gripped her heart and commanded her eye-lids to close. Drowsiness and weariness became the calm of the deepest of sleeps and she fell forward into the careful clutch of his clawed hand where he held her, fragile and frail, not daring to move lest he drop her, not daring to breathe lest the sound of his inner flame wake her, bewitched by her presence and the sound of her slow breathing as she dreamt and thus encountered the discovery of new stories for his future delight. He had become her guardian, who once would have eaten her for the delicacy of her blue eyes and fair hair but now honoured her as his souls ease and life's mate.

The sun was already climbing towards its zenith and Ra'el awoke to look down on the chequered fields of blues, greens, copper and gold and the deep dark dense forests of her family estate bathed in the brightest of suns.

"Home" Ra'el gasped and then looked over her shoulder at the twin hills of Vezelay and Avallon, the burial place of Mary Magdalan and Sir Percy (or Parsifal) of the Round Table, whom legend told first found the Grael and Spear through the loving sacrifice of his sister. Maria had kept her promise and returned the Spear to Sir Percy once her mission had been completed. The Spear of Longinus rested beneath the portal of the entrance into the Roman Keep that had been built at the top of the hill on which Avallon now rested, glaring defiantly at Gergovia (*the Eternal City of Freedom and Independence),* the Spear grasped securely in Percy's right hand.

Avallon sits above the ruins of Camelot at the confluence of the Camut and the Lot, and overlooks the lake where Maria would become the 'Lady of the Lake', guarding the sword Excalibur that was made by Macsen to be worn by a warrior king and given to Maria when she first came to England; 'Caelibann' or 'Excalibur', the gift of Godric Bann Caedic and made specifically for Maria **and her descendants** to never be broken or defeated in battle and to bring peace to any kingdom where it is wielded.

Vezelay sits above a network of caves cut out of the limestone hill on which it perches that has become storage space for many of the families who have lived in the City for centuries, the occasional shop, cellars for wine and cheese (of course) and then at its deepest is the labyrinth, with Flamebringer's treasure and Mary Magdalan's sarcophagus, the latter still guarded by its stewards waiting for the day when Christians will remember the purity of their faith as it was before its paganisation by the Romans, Huns and Goths.

Then looking south Ra'el saw the winding trail of the pilgrim's path continue to the sacred place of Fontenay. By some magic of the dragon, the silver pathway that was the Oyster Trail snaked visibly from Fontenay to Beaumes and the caverns beneath the convent that adjoined the magnificent hostel (where Maria, daughter of Bethany and sister of Lazarus, wife of the Legion Commander Longinus led a small community of mystics for over fifty years) then on to Marseilles (where Lazarus used the gift of life he had been given by Iesus' miracle to become the first Bishop of the Christian community there), Bordeaux and Toulouse, Pamplona and Bilbao, Zaragosa and Valencia, across the Balearic Sea to Pollenca, then the Mediterranean to Tunis and Valetta, Heraklion in Crete, Limasole in Cyprus, Latika, Damascus and finally Jerusalem.

She turned to look north and saw the silver snaking path continue from Vezelay and Avallon towards Orange, Lyons and Dijons then west to Orleans, Blois and Tours. From Tours the path went north to west of Mans and carried on north to Caen, across the Channel to Southampton, Stonehenge (where the Robe is buried alongside King Craedech of the Catuvellauni, Cantianii, Belgae, Regni, Durotroges, Sitiges, Cumnovii, Dobunni and Atrebates), Glastonbury, Gloucester, Worcester then Abingdon and Waltham Forest, Ongar, Doddinghurst, Cressing Temple, Bures, where it branches over the Stour and towards the Brett passing through Clare and Lane's Ham (where The Grael is buried), Colchester, Blandford, Mendelsham, Eye and Diss, Norwich, Kings Lynn, Stamford and Peterborough, Hull, York, Darlington and Durham, Newcastle, Chester, Talbot, Ludstow and Shrewsbury, Alnwick, Dunstanborough, Bamborough and Berwick, Bridge of Allan, Milnathort, Auchtermuchty and Perth, Loch Ness and Drumnadroichit, Inverness, Beauly, Mullochy, Cromarty, Gulbairn Sands, Thurso and the Orkney Islands.

"Thank you" Ra'el whispered and kissed the tip of the dragon's nose at which he snorted then replied: "The path is long and winding; it does not include Saints Peter's and Paul's missions which both end at Rome. But how does Turin become the resting place of the Shroud?"

"A close friend of the family of Bedevere, a neighbour of their estates in England, fought as a mercenary for England and Florence. He passed through Piedmont and Turin on his way to Genoa and Florence. His companion was the Baron of Paciano who had fought at Poitiers on the losing French side, been taken hostage by the soldier of fortune and who bought out his freedom.

Paciano owned estates north and south of Rome but also in north Italy, where the Paciano family estates included the marchionette or marquesa of the province of Modina, including Piedmont and Turin, following their marriage into the D'Este family. They still hold estates in the mountains above Lake Como but their Castello in Paciano is now a museum and conference centre. The two men stayed in Paciano's Castello in Turin on their way to Firenze and Paciano gave the Lord Acquetto The Shroud as ransom; Acquetto promptly donated it to the City's cathedral."

"That sounds like another story for another day" the dragon suggested, avoiding any offence by smiling as he did so. Then he supervised Ra'el washing in a rain cloud, which involved him flying through the cloud whilst the girl removed her clothes and was bathed from head to foot in freezing cold raindrops that the sun then dried the moment they flew out of the grey cover of the cumulus to ride on the gentle undulations of the clouds, white as snow, covering all sight of the land below, the occasional rumble and spark where thunder and lightning were being created by the friction of frozen rain drops beneath them. Then Flamebringer dived recklessly through the clouds to pull up feet above the tall waves of the Ocean, Ra'el's screams of terror scarcely heard above the crash of the waves and the passing thunder in the clouds.

Ra'el washed her clothes clean in the Atlantic Ocean, many miles out from Bordeaux as the dragon flew skimming just inches above the sea and Ra'el leant over his side to hold her clothes in the waves below, hoping and praying that she would not fall.

Finally, Flamebringer flew back to the centre of France to perch on a mountain within the Massif Central, a cloud descending to hide them both as the dragon lay down with his head a few inches from Ra'el and his eyes showing his eagerness for her to continue the story of Mary Magdalan's mission to Spain, France and Great Britain.

"This mountain is known as 'The Magdalan' and so I felt it was appropriate that we sit here and listen to the final moments of her mission. I have one last question" he whispered as a wisp of smoke, not wishing to delay her story any further: "What was this great disaster or moment in history that needed the power of the Holy Artefacts to be used to repair the Earth? How could an event so monumental be kept secret from everyone?"

Ra'el laughed then shocked the dragon into silence: "Had such an event already happened there would no longer be the need to hide The Grael, The Spear and the other artefacts. The event for which God has granted us the supreme power to repair the Earth *has yet to happen*. Those who guard the Holy Artefacts have prayed that it shall never happen. We would rather waste our lives serving no purpose than we face the possible destruction of our planet. None of us wish to face another flood as was Noah's poor fortune."

Then the girl sat up and prepared to recommence her story. Flamebringer nodded to confirm he was ready and so the story began with the companions heading into the Cairngorns, snow falling heavily as they did so.

"The company were ill-prepared for braving the Cairngorns and Highlands. Three days into their travels they were bored, sore, cold, wet and none of them had a good thing to say about the constant grey barren stone that was all around them, or the dark grey clouds that covered the sky during the day and hid the stars at night. The rain was persistent and heavy, and the company had to lead their horses avoiding streams, springs, falls and rills that would suddenly burst their banks to over-flowing as the precipitation levels grew higher and higher. A foot of rain was falling every day. There was nowhere to hide from the foul weather, no tree cover, no bushes; just steep rock with few hand or footholes.

"Now the sun is hiding!" Maria whispered to herself and would have gladly accepted back a 'cold sun'.

The party were roped to each other after Maria and Ninian had each taken tumbling falls and nearly rolled to their deaths over the edge of the large and sharply angled flat granite ledges that formed their pathway north. The grip on the smooth damp rock was treacherous and only Galahaidra and Longinus had climbed such mountainous terrain before. They led the party, anchoring themselves securely whenever they came across a particularly precarious stretch. They had finally called a halt, tied the two girls with their rope to a large boulder so that they did not blow away and begun the arduous task of erecting the girls' tent and their own pavilion with the help of Iosephus and Craedech.

"A few more days of this and the Picts can have me!" Galahaidra grumbled and then watched in horror as Ninian and Maria's tent disappeared over a cliff's edge after a rogue gust of wind had caught it and lifted it high into the air. The only source of heat was Longinus' military camp stove and it could just about warm one pair of hands at a time. They had put it into the girls' tent to try and warm it up and now it stood forlornly in the rain, where it fizzled, coughed, spluttered and gave up the ghost.

"Whose idea was it to come to this terrible place?" growled Craedech and five pairs of hostile eyes glared at Maria who grinned then said: "Cheer up! We only have maybe thirty more days of this and we should find the Ness."

Longinus added another circle of stones to hold the larger pavilion to the ground, the north side of the tent was already blowing inwards in the wind, whipping back and forth and rendering one end of the mens' pavilion impassable. Galahaidra picked up the stove which had begun to fill with water and placed it upside down in the shelter of the pavilion to dry off.

Alas the two girls' nightclothes, blankets and bed rolls had gone over the cliff's edge in pursuit of their tent and there were no spares. The party had travelled light to leave room for food as there was no wildlife or settlements for leagues in all directions and they therefore had to carry provisions for the week they expected to be in the mountains.

After five minutes, Galahaidra had erected an awning to provide some shelter for their horses and whispered to Longinus that they might need to offer their steeds the security and warmth of their own pavilion.

"There is room … just" the young Roman officer replied "but only if the six of us squeeze up in one side leaving the other for the horses. It will be cosy and intimate."

"I think the chances of anything untoward or remotely amorous happening are absolutely none without risk of injury, exposure and frost bite" Galahaidra replied. "Our women are safe from our advances and unlikely to remove their clothing with no blankets available. Let us do it. We are damned if we get to the lowlands beyond these mountains and we have lost our horses. On foot the Picts will hunt us down in minutes!"

So Galahaidra took the awning down again and used it to provide a wind break to the north of the pavilion whilst Longinus broke the news to the rest of the party that they were all sleeping together in one big huddle with twelve horses. It took an hour to get the stove lit but in that time everyone managed to get under shelter in the pavilion, although the girls were stuck in their damp clothes with no dry layers or blankets to get into. No-one wanted to eat and everyone voted for an early night's sleep.

The men stripped off down to nothing and hung their clothes from the pavilion's cross-pieces above their heads with Ninian admiring the view whilst Maria covered her eyes. Then they wrapped themselves in their bed rolls and covered themselves with their blankets. They pushed the two girls away with their feet complaining that they were damp and so both girls ended up by the entrance flap with a howling gale completing their total and absolute abject misery.

"Eureka!" and Longinus had finally got the stove alight. "Give it an hour and we will start to warm up" he claimed a little optimistically and then he joined the rest of the men in stripping down to nothing and wrapping himself in his bed roll and blanket then lying next to Iosephus so that each man warmed the other with their body heat.

After a few minutes, he looked across to where both girls were hugging each other and grizzling in distress. They were getting colder and colder and their skin had started to turn blue. Longinus swore. He had seen this before with young recruits.

"Strip!" he ordered "Then get yourselves under the blankets with us. You need to be making body contact and cannot afford to wear your damp clothes a moment longer."

Both girls shook their heads at which Longinus threatened them: "If you do not strip right now, I am going to come over and tear your clothes off you with my bare hands." Maria screamed whilst Ninian's eyes blazed with anger but Longinus was serious and started to unroll his blanket.

"No!" cried Maria for whom seeing Longinus naked for a third time was more than her fragile heart could stand and she turned her back on him then quickly began to remove her damp cloak, robe, peplos and stola until she was just down to her silk slip. "That as well" commanded her tormentor and with a sniff she dropped it to the ground then whispered: "If just one of you looks I will cry" then she turned, ran and flung herself down to lie on the floor next to Longinus. She crawled sideways under his blanket and turned her back on him. Ten seconds later she was either asleep or pretending to be so.

Longinus carefully un-wrapped his bed roll and covered her with it then gave her a gentle hug as he had used to before she met Craedech. She made no move to either encourage or discourage him and so he held her carefully all night, ensuring she was kept warm.

Ninian took one look at the rest of the men, ruled out Iosephus, Craedech was taken and anyway he was fast asleep, but Galahaidra was young, handsome, athletic, virile and, most importantly, had avoided getting as wet as the others. She stripped off all her clothes quickly and ran across the tent then crawled into bed with him, rolling back both blanket and bed roll then hugging him tight, not caring if he could feel her more intimate areas just needing the warmth of his body. "Stay still" she whispered. "I need to warm up!" then she could not resist and kissed him on the lips. He responded by holding her tight against his chest with both arms at which she turned her head with a contented smile to rest it gently on his right shoulder and as she drifted to sleep, her hands softly caressed his back until he had also relaxed into sleep.

The following morning just as the birds had woken him yet the first light of dawn was still hours away, Craedech's stood at Longinus' feet, his forehead was as black as thunder with anger. He had woken to find Maria being held by Longinus in a hug that looked pretty intimate to him and had kicked the Centurion to wake him up. Longinus had never been his best when just awoken and usually took about ten minutes to get his brain in gear. He was not given ten minutes.

"What have you been doing?" demanded an incensed Prince.

"Nothing" muttered the Roman. "The girl needed to be warmed up or she would have died of exposure. You can have your turn tonight!" which on reflection was not the most tactful thing Longinus could have said but in his defence he was still half asleep and he promptly went to go back to being fully asleep at which Craedech screamed: "Take your hands off her!" and everyone except Maria woke up with a start. Ninian took one look at Craedech and laughed. The poor Prince realised he was standing naked in front of them all and his anger drained away as he desperately tried to hide his embarrassment behind a horse blanket, wrapping its folds around his waist then returning to the most important subject, he wagged his finger at Longinus ... and the blanket fell to the ground.

Ninian dissolved into hoots of laughter with Galahaidra trying to stop her, even clapping his hands over her mouth, only for her to nibble his fingers at which he blushed and removed them fast suddenly realising how vulnerable he was to a counter-attack from this bold young lady.

The Prince stomped over to where they had tethered the horses to the side poles of the pavilion which was the shape of a figure of eight, with a narrow entry chamber then two large circular domes, each kept in place by a cartwheel raised from the ground by a series of side poles. The horses were in one chamber and the company had snuggled up in the other, with Longinus' stove in the centre, the embers from which were still throwing out heat.

Craedech found his horse and his saddle bags and took out a navy blue robe which he flung over his head then marched back into the company's sleeping quarters. Longinus had taken the opportunity to move and was now asleep in Craedech's place, using his bed roll and blanket. Craedech was still furious but at that moment, something prompted Maria to yawn, stretch then laugh in her sleep before rolling over. She was heard to whisper "Craedech, you are my one and only love. Love me for ever" then fell back into deep sleep, dreaming contentedly.

But the damage was done: Cupid's arrow pierced so deep that the Prince's anger fled to distant lands, leaving the young man's heart captured totally by the young waif before him, for he was now her prisoner more thoroughly than ever before. She had cast her spell and done so when he was angry and she was asleep yet it had been far more powerful because it had disarmed him completely.

"What should I do?" he whispered looking at Iosephus and Galahaidra "It would be wrong for me to join her for she is comfortable and I would not wish to disturb her. I fear I would not have the Centurion's self-discipline!" Ninian sighed at the mention of self discipline and elbowed Galahaidra who went bright red. It was left to the older knight to protect his young protégé and advise the Prince:

"Sit by her feet. It will fill her with joy to wake and see your face. You have won her heart already. But her mission comes first and take care that you do not distract her from it."

So when Maria woke it was to the smell of Longinus frying breakfast and to the sight of her Prince, watching her intently and lovingly. She smiled then asked: "Will you hold me tomorrow night? I felt safe with Longinus for he is a dear friend and makes every effort to protect my honour but it is you that have my heart. Could you hold me, hug me, kiss me but do no more? I would wish to marry you when we return to Glevum, to do so with your father there and given away by my father, Godric. Then you may take me but my faith teaches me that to make love outside marriage is adultery and a sin for which I could be stoned."

"What did your Master teach?"

"He taught that marriage is the most important commitment we can make. Man, woman and God come together for life to create new life. The married man, woman and God make love as a sign that their relationship is now both human and divine and are gifted with the ability to create new human life *and a new soul.* Even the Angels do not have this gift to create both life and souls.

Yet my Master forgave the young girl who was to be stoned for making love with the young man she loved when they had yet to marry. '*Let him who has not sinned cast the first stone*' he said and then forgave her and told her not to do it again. My Master is against the death penalty for it removes the opportunity for a sinner to earn forgiveness and redemption through a lifetime of penance.

He also spoke of marriage and Paradise when he was asked a question that the Judges and Prophets had ruled on in our scriptures yet continued to be the subject of debate amongst the Saduccee. 'A man has married seven times in life and has six widows. To whom is he married when he joins them in Paradise?'

My Master replied: 'Man and woman are married to God when they reach Paradise and also in constant communion with the Angels and their peers in Paradise. There is no place for marriage which is a public commitment to love another person *exclusively* for life when alive. All in Paradise have made a commitment to love God and to love all of our fellow men and women for all of eternity so there can be no exclusivity in Paradise.'

The Judges Rebecca and Rachel had previously ruled that death had ended the first six marriages and therefore only the seventh still applied when the man reached Paradise. My Master was over-ruling the Judges and giving precedence to his new commandment: to love God and all of Mankind.

Finally, my Master was against divorce which my faith and that of the Romans and the Arab tribes of my birth allow. 'What God has tied together let no man split or cut apart …' he once said.

So our marriage is a special relationship that allows us to create new souls; it is exclusive and for life but ends with our death; my love for God and my communion with the Angels and all of those souls in Paradise takes precedence over any marriage.

My love for you does not stop me also loving others. Our love is special but is not the sum total of my love. I shall love our children, your family, my adopted father, our friends, your and my subjects, those we shall meet, our allies and our foe ... but I shall only *make love* to you for all of my life."

Craedech was stunned, bombarded by her memories of her Master and the lessons she had received from the Angels. He was also horrified at how restrictive the Christo-Judaec faith was when it came to marriage and had to ask:

"My love, I shall of course have only one wife but I am expected as a Prince to take many mistresses to ensure there are plenty of sons who survive the trials of childhood to become King after me. We recognise those born out of marriage but who are acknowledged by me as mine. Was not Iesus conceived outside of marriage?"

"If you make love to other women then I shall spend my whole life weeping in sorrow but still you shall have my special love and no-one else. Your lack of faith shall never be used by me as an excuse to be faithless myself" Maria responded, the tears already flowing silently in anticipation of his faithlessness. Then she answered his question about her Master's own conception:

"My Master was conceived by God who was his Father. God does not marry or recognise the exclusivity of marriage applies to God-head. My Master never married or conceived for reasons I do not understand for many of us were willing. Again, I think He was teaching us a lesson that marriage is not needed or applicable to God and in Paradise. Rather, Paradise is a permanent celebration of the Eucharist.

I also believe that God has established rules that limit the creation of souls for a reason. The merger of mankind made in God's image with God establishes a new entity even more sacred and loving than when each is apart. God could create souls on his own but we offer something in addition: perhaps our naivety or our new and refreshing way of seeing things; our love that is more potent than if God loved himself; our mistakes from which we all learn; and the way that each pairing creates a new man or woman who is different again with my blue eyes and your auburn hair or your green eyes and my fair hair?

My Master loves the place I have created in my heart because *I made it for Him* and so it is original. God loves it when we design, innovate and meet His challenges with our solutions. To God there is no right answer to the conundrums he has set us for he seeks the new and admires the way in which we help Him expand creation through the novelty of our thinking. Even our mistakes create something novel and thus are to be loved.

It is destruction and desecration that angers Him. When we slay another, steal another's ideas, possessions or wife, undermine our love for each other, show no respect or love for the lame, disabled, infirm, children, prisoners, refugees, slaves and the oppressed or destroy Nature for which we have been given the responsibility to nurture as the world's appointed stewards."

Craedech gulped then with a gleam of humour in his eyes remarked at a tangent:

"Longinus once told me that you said very little and must be the perfect woman therefore. What happened to the girl who says little?"

Maria had to laugh. Her answers had been long because they were heartfelt and she needed her love to understand fully how she felt about Marriage, God and Paradise. She also had not realised that her friends talked about her and in all innocence asked:

"Do you talk about me much? What do you say? I guess I must be very irritating for I know I am stubborn. Are you moaning about me? Should I apologise to you all?"

Craedech knelt next to Maria and carefully took her in his arms, ensuring Longinus' blanket continued to protect her modesty yet even this chaste touch aroused the passion within him and it took a supreme act of self-control for him to speak quietly and calmly:

"O Maria. We speak of your vision, your courage, your achievements but also our fear for your life, your health and your failing strength. We all love you. Never change, my love."

She stood once more on the cliff's edge and her Master held her right hand. She felt his humanity, his blood pumping through the blood vessels in his hands and his arms as she gently stroked them, warm, soft and gentle, covered in the finest hairs, yet strong, muscular and well-defined. She also could feel his divine love crackling like static electricity wherever her hand came in contact. She dared to kiss him once, carefully, reverently, on the cheek then rested her head sideways on his left shoulder, ready to listen, comforted by his presence, at home as he hugged her in his arms then he stood besides her and looked over the cliff at the clouds many miles below. He turned his head and smiled down on Maria then said: "Would you jump if I held your hand?"

"No" she replied "for it would be a grave sin. To destroy this gift of life for no purpose is a great evil."

Her Master was thoughtful then asked her another question: "Would you jump if I commanded it?"

Maria laughed and the cliff dissolved to become the sitting room of his Father's house with two large brocade sofas and a Persian silk rug on the floor between them but otherwise the room was a timber-framed hall with a huge wood-burning fireplace lit by candles in iron sconces and candelabra, warmed by tapestries and wall-hangings.

As she looked more closely she saw Christ's life told as a series of images woven into the tapestries: his conception, his birth, presentation, baptism, the wedding feast, the peritope, the ministry, the royal procession into Jerusalem, the riot in the Temple, the arrest in Gethsemane, the scourging and the way of the cross, the crucifixion, burial and resurrection, the opening of the gates of Hades and the gates of Paradise, his ministry beyond his death, the ascension and the gifts of the Spirit.

To her amazement, the tapestries continued with her own ministry and that of Paulus: even the Battle of the Humber got a tapestry all of its own. Then she looked at the ceiling and to her childlike delight she gazed upon the stuccoed ceiling from Tartellus' triclinarium but with her Master centre stage and not Augustus.

The windows were huge yet there was no draught which surprised her and for the first time she looked through panes of glass. Beyond each window was a different view: her parent's home in Nazareth, the Golan Heights, the Sea of Galilee and the River Jordan, Tunis and Hanafa's cove, Pollenca, the Fluvius Turia and its famous bridge into the City of Valentia, the Bascones mountains and the port of Iaenus Portus, the Gardens of Pharo, the caves in Bomeris, the valley of her lake on the confluence of the Camus and the Lot in the shadow of Avallonae, her first view from the Downs and along the Vale of the White Horse, Godric's Hall, The Summonsing Circle, Glaston Tor, the Mendae Hills down onto Hern's Ford and beyond across the chequered green and yellow fields towards Cumria, the Chilton Hills along to Abing and Waltha's Ham, her first sight of the Wash, Shere Forest, The Stone Hill, the Dales and Pennines, the viewing point along the River Brough to the Dragon's Vale, the Aln along to Dunstan's Hill, Bam and Bere Wich, the Lomond Hills across the Firth of Forth, Fallin's Falls, Loch Leven, the barn in Auchterarder, the Tay coming into the north of Perth and the Roman Bridge and then the mountain-top on which she was currently camped.

As she looked closer each window filled with those she loved from her parents to those she held in a special place in her heart, a fresh room created for each including Maria and Martha, Lazarus, Iosephus, Longinus, Celestile, Annanaeus, Petrus, Paulus, Perseus, Decius, Felstrum, Haladriel, Godric, Craedech, Herne, Egdethbreda, Jaerid, Kaera and Ninian.

"What is the lesson, lord?" she asked overwhelmed and he grinned as she completely forgot her manners and like the child she was jumped straight to what interested her. She blushed, mouthed 'Sorry' and 'Thank your father for letting me see his house' at which he laughed and she shrunk before his eyes in dismay as his laughter told her she was being stupid in some way or another. He immediately took pity on her.

"Maria, you are very welcome here. My first lesson points to the very essence of your God. My Father and I are One but not the same. Yet what one cherishes we both cherish. Where we are is the sitting room in my Father's house and so it is my Father's sitting room and also *my* sitting room.

My second lesson points to mankind's superiority over other created beings, including my Angels. Had I commanded an Angel to jump, the

Angel would have jumped. But you challenged me" and her Master smiled showing his delight in her response before asking her: "Can you now tell me: what are the other lessons here?"

"I will not do wrong even if am commanded to" Maria replied without pause then was stumped.

"You were right not to jump but why?"

"Because the gift of life is too precious to cast away without purpose or gain just to prove to myself what I already know: that you are God. I understand this first lesson, namely that just as I must trust my instincts around the cliff so it is the same with marriage" and the radiance of her Master's smile was all the confirmation she could ever ask for and so she had the courage to continue:

"But your other lessons have me baffled as always."

"Have some tea" he replied passing across a delicate porcelain teacup with a gleam of humour in his eyes but then suddenly the room grew dark and his visage took on a look of profound sadness as he told her: "The day will come when we shall meet in this room again. I shall need *your* comfort" and then He was gone.

She clung to Craedech then whispered: "Though I shall be your Princess and your Queen, nothing will make me change or dilute my faith. If we must go our different ways because to be a Prince shall bring you into conflict with remaining faithful to my wishes, then we must part now: as friends … but become no more than that."

Craedech pulled away to look into her eyes trusting what he would see there. He saw her honesty as always, the fearless determination to do the right thing even though she sacrifice herself and then he saw deeper than these but present and almost over-powering, her great sadness. If he allowed them to part then she would remain pure to her faith but never be happy in life. What a terrible thing that he hurt her in this way and so he addressed that first and foremost:

"My *Grael Vision* saw me leave Glevum in your company to journey to Roma to see Cordelia then to take you home to Iudaea. The message was clear and repeated when Iesus came to me the night before we rode to Caister in Dacia: I must choose between being a Prince and being with you. In my heart and mind and soul I chose … you and thus was granted the Vision. Nothing has changed. I am yours before ever I shall be a Prince."

Maria kissed him with such passion and depth that Craedech was left breathless before, laughing with joy as he said it, and admonishing her at the same time: "Do not tempt me or I shall marry you here, right now, with Ninian and Galahaidra as my witnesses Longinus to stand as my best man and Iosephus to give you away. Trust me: I am close to bursting with love for you!"

She hugged him harder but turning her head to one side to rest on his chest. The next moment she sat back with a start, looked at him quizzically and started to mutter: "Wait, I am stupid as always." Then shook her head repeatedly before suddenly her eyes widened, her mouth opened slightly, her lips moistened, her hands held Craedech at bay (and just as well as sight of her lips had sent the poor man into a frenzy), and her face lit up, her hair glowing, her eyes on fire.

"I have it!" she said in the closest her small voice could get to a shout: a barely audible murmur.

"You can still be a Prince; you just need to be faithful to me. The problem is making provision for your succession. I shall, of course, do my best and there is a prophecy that I have never told you of which says a descendant of our marriage will be responsible for our faith becoming that of the entire Roman Empire but you could make Herne your successor and command him to have mistresses."

"What is this future you have kept from me?" Craedech said sternly whilst trying not to laugh at the image he suddenly had of the shocked horror on his brother in law's face when he broke the news to him that he must persuade Edgethbreda to allow Herne to take on a few mistresses into his household.

Maria had the good grace to look very guilty and humbly confessed:

"Knowing how you feel about Roma, I feared your reaction. Forgive me for I had not foreseen that your concern of lack of children would encourage you to be unfaithful to me." Then she took a deep breath, avoiding looking at the Prince whom she guessed, and rightly, would not be looking best pleased with her at that moment, before telling him of her Master's plan for the future of their faith.

They sat on the floor of the pavilion, no camp fire before them yet as Maria spoke, a single candle came to guttering flame, lighting the spoked wheel above them and the many uprights that formed the temporary timber-frame of their domed canvas hall chamber. She sat cross-legged, one hand held aloft to describe the events she was to foretell in ever increasing circles of haste, the other hand still in her lap, her eyes in distant worlds and places, whilst the Prince sat transfixed, mesmerised by this story-teller who had no idea of the charisma she brought to her description of four centuries of change.

She had the *Gift of Telling* drawn from generations of bards and poets amongst the nomadic tribes of her heritage and ancestry. He possessed the *Gift of Story*, the ability to listen, absorb and inspire the stories to be told by a story-teller. One needed the other for no story can be told without an appreciative audience.

"Three things have been foretold which together will see our faith rule the civilised world. The communities converted to Christianity by Petrus, Paulus and I will survive nine persecutions, three terrifying civil wars and three different invasions by the pagan hordes in the next three hundred years. Our faith will become the official religion of the entire Roman world and many of its neighbours, including the conversion of Hispania, Gallia, Britannia and Caledonia.

I was once told to complete '**all**' my mission and did not understand the implication of what I was being told until now."

The Survival of Christianity in Roman Britain.
The first prophecy and vision of Maria the Magdalan

"My dearest love and would-be lover, it shall be our great honour to be the antecedents, the progenitors of a British princess who shall be born in Colcaister, but will be the princess of the entire eastern, southern and western kingdoms, united by our marriage. Our royal family will remain true to our faith and the princess of our royal line will be brought up as a Christian following the traditions that we shall establish both before and after the invasion of Britannia by the Romans.

The prophecy is that this great princess, her name shall be Helena, shall give birth to a son who shall unite the Roman Empire in battle, fighting under The Standard and the banner of Christ, and will become its sole Emperor. He shall declare that Christianity will be the faith of the whole Roman world and he will be advised by his mother and a great Synod held at Nicaea. He will reconstruct our faith from the many traditions around the world that will have developed as our faith went into hiding, empowering our 'bishops' to ordain new ministers of the Eucharist, and to bring new people into our faith not in dozens but in millions.

The Emperor's mother will carry the secret of Martius, the hiding place of Iesus' cross, a secret that was entrusted to me by the young Roman when I left Jerusalem. The future princess will uncover the cross piece from which my Master, Iesus, was hung from its hiding place on Golgotha. The sign of the cross shall become the symbol of our faith under which the new Emperor will establish unity and peace.

The Emperor's son, the first Christian Emperor, will come to Yorvic and hold off a Pictish, Caledonii and Gaelic invasion, in the wake of which Caledonia will gradually throw off the shackles of constant raids from the west. Many of its farming communities will remain Christian, remembering Ninian and establishing a simpler and purer faith that is very different from the dogmatic religion established by Roma. Neither path is wrong.

This ends my first prophesy as seen when I stood before King Col, the wounds of my beating still on my back, the warm blood dripping in a puddle on the ground beneath me, only a blanket to cover my nakedness.

The Survival of Christianity in Roman Britain.
The second prophecy and vision of Maria the Magdalan

My second prophesy foretells Roma invading and conquering Britannia. Your father, Caractacus, is King of the western kingdoms of the Dobunni, Atrebates and the Catuvellaunii but Godric and Wulfrid are both dead" and Maria stops, her head drops and she sobs briefly whilst Craedech holds her tight and strokes her hair until eventually she calms down, lies back into him but she can never dare tell him how her father and grandfather die. She sniffed once, a rather surprisingly loud noie for someone so delicate and with such a quiet voice and then continued her account of her second vision: "I am now Queen of the southern kingdoms of the Dubroges and the Cantiani, a kingdom stretching from Gwuildesford to the Royal Seat at Chard then south to the ford and estuary of the Col across via Salisbray to my future capital Wyncaister, then east to the port of Devrum, north-east to the Ritupiae and Medae and the Castle of the Roche and due west back to Gwuildesford, including Loddon's Hill on the River Thamis.

I meet the Roman Commanders of the Legions that have landed in Cant (Kent) and I am granted an audience with the Legionary Generals of the IInd Augusta and the XIVth Gemina by name of Vespasian and … Gaius Gallicus Longinus.

I have already agreed a Peace treaty that holds for most of the south coast and is welcomed by the two commanders who become keen supporters of our administration of the territories in the west, south and south-east. The two Legions are split and stationed at Glevum, Cipenham, Gwuildesford, Glaston Tor and Devrum; the Roman Navy under our old friend Varus Flavius is offered harbour at Devrum and Ritupiae and he accepts this offer.

Alas, your father leads the defence of Britannia. Kings Caractacus, Casterix, Togdumnus and Pasterix unite with the Dumnonii in Kernow and go out to meet the Roman Army under its commander Plautius in two Battles on the Maedeway and the Thamis. Eight Kings are defeated in battle in the territory of the Catuvellauni (Togdumnus, Casterix and Pasterix are slain, Caractacus flees). The Peace Treaty with the southern and western kingdoms holds however and Vespasian is able to base his legion at Esceancaester. In 43 AD, the Emperor Claudius arrives and receives the surrender of a number of Kings and Queens, including you and me …" and Maria ducked for cover as Craedech went looking to find something to throw at her then hid behind the main central tent pole until she was sure she was totally forgiven. Only then did she give him a grin at which he snarled and her wild boar ran for cover but she persevered.

"The Roman Army pushes slowly north under the Consul and future Procurator or Governor of Britannia, Plautius. Plautius is ruthless, removing the remnants of the royal families of the Trinovantes, Iceni and Corieltauvii. He honoured the Treaty we had signed with Tiberias in 37 AD and even allowed us to have administration when he needed to move Legio II Augusta north again. By 47 AD he had made the River Trent the new northern border of the Roman Empire.

Scapula becomes Roman Governor around 47 AD and your father mobilises a rebellion from Cumria mainly of the Dobunni and Silures (Siturges). Your father is defeated at Caer Caradoc on the Welsh borders in 50 AD is taken hostage and goes to Roma. As his daughter in law I am also required as a hostage to go on trial before Claudius and surrender to Scapula at Noviomagus. Caractacus speaks well and is allowed to live but must stay in Roma. I am allowed to go home and am gifted back our lands of the Dobunni, Atrebates, Silures and Catuvellauni lost to your father and his brother.

"Ahem and what about me?" mutters Craedech.

"O did I not mention? I offer myself as hostage on your behalf whilst we smuggle you across to stay with our good friend King Graefreigh who has fallen back to Caledonia."

"And why did you keep this from me?"

"Well I was not concentrating too much on that bit of the vision."

Craedech looked long and hard at Maria and could recognise that whilst the girl was not telling an untruth she was also not telling the whole truth. She only remained silent like this to protect someone so Craedech asked gently: "Am I hurt in some way?" at which Maria blushed bright red then said in a huff: "If you must know, Graefreigh has two rather handsome daughters and you seemed to be having a great time actually, mainly on your back" and after a rather embarrassed pause on all parts Maria bashed on.

Scapula and then Gallus push Graefriegh out of Deceangli and the Parisii out of Humberside then Gallus takes Yorvic and Jaerid, his family and many of his Eorls and loyal warriors flee to Caledonia to be hidden by the Votadini. Senna flees to join us in Wyncaister as does King Graefleigh, his family and two of his three Eorls. King Lud continues to hold out against the invaders and reintroduces the superstitions of the druids. The druids are hunted down ruthlessly and exterminated in a battle at Aengles' Sea in which I finally am drawn up against the Council of Sorcerers; Lud is captured, taken to Roma to be punished by being thrown off the Tarpian Rock as part of Paulinius' triumph before the delighted Emperor Claudius.

Dacia and Deceangli soon surrender; together with the Iceni under a young Boudicca, twenty years old when Scapula moves in to place a half legion in Iceni territory. The Iceni are offered a client treaty which they accept for now, whilst the ypush south to recapture the lands they had lost to the Trinovantes around the Lynn, Wash and the Broads. Soon they have infested Norwicken and King Col's kingdom is split north and south between the advancing Romans and the Iceni. Guidevere acts as regent, bringing up her daughter to worship Epona.

Claudius is Emperor at the time of the invasion and his policies are broadly fair, so whilst there will be the rumblings of future unrest there is also hope for tolerance and peace. Alas, Claudius will become the first Emperor in history to persecute our faith and he will order the execution of Paulus whose mission has seen him arrested and taken to Roma for trial and execution … but Paulus argues his case and survives for now."

Maria chokes on her tears at this point and has to be held tightly by Craedech who never met Paulus but knew that Maria honoured, respected and loved the man for his achievements in defining and spreading her faith and his far superior intelligence which allowed him to understand her Master's teachings and present them with a clarity which she often lacked. She showed no envy only profound admiration for the Saint.

"He dies so early with so much more to do. Surely he sits with my Master in glory?" she whispered, almost a gasp as she sees Paulus' death at the hands of the future Emperor Nero: her weeping came as close to silent prayerful reverence as her sobs would allow. Somehow she found the breath to continue:

"Fortunately, Claudius will limit his antipathy against Christians to the City of Roma and the province of Iudaea. Christianity continues to flourish in Britannia and Caledonia until the revolt of Boudicca" at the mention of which Craedech's eyebrows shot up.

"The invasion of Britannia, the crushing defeat of Caractacus' army and the trial of Paulus mark the end of my second prophecy. There are five years of peace during which our faith grows in the background between my second and my third prophecy."

The Survival of Christianity in Roman Britain.
The third prophecy and vision of Maria the Magdalan

"The third and final prophecy was gifted to me in the King's Hall in The Stone Hill, before King Pasterix as I held the young baby, Boudicca in my arms.

Nero will become Claudius' successor as Emperor in 54 AD but lacks the tolerance or the common sense of his predecessor. He empties his Treasury spending a fortune on music, the arts and dramatic performances and imposes severe taxes on the western Provinces favouring those Provinces who have been influenced by the eastern and more opulent cultures of Persia and Aegypt.

Paulinius is elevated to be Procurator and Governor of Britannia in 58 AD and in 60 AD, midway through Nero's reign, when Paulinius' legionaries are collecting taxes and outstanding debts from the Iceni, a cohort of soldiers accompanying the tax collector assault Boudicca and rape her two daughters.

In response, Boudicca unites almost all of the kingdoms in Britannia in revolt against Roman occupancy. Within six months the Dunrovii, the middle kingdoms of the Catuvellauni, the Trinovantes, the Iceni, Brigantes, Parisii, Cotinari, Novantae and Deceangli will join forces under Boudicca to defeat Paulinius in battle, will descend on Colcaister (now called Camulodenum by the Romans) which Boudicca will burn to the ground slaying tens of thousands of vulnerable citizens, many of whom are Christians whose only fault was to attempt to seek peace between the Iceni and the Roman settlers. Boudicca will massacre a half legion near Burntwood and defeat a the rest of the IXth Legion in a battle near Loddon's Hill (Londinium); the XXth under Paulinius will arrive late to the battle and escape heading back towards Cumria but will still be badly mauled.

Verulanium is also burnt to the ground and then Boudicca continues on west and south along Watling Street where Vespasian and Longinus march from the west supported by auxillaries including a few thousand from Glevum under King Craedech …" and Maria blushed then grinned when she saw her lover's profound shock on hearing he will side one day with the Romans against a rebellion by the kingdoms of Briton.

"I refuse to believe that I shall ever side with any army of Roma!" the Prince growled grumpily in a right royal huff and she stroked his cheek then kissed him gently on each eye lid before saying:

"Hush my dearest delight. A few months ago you would not have believed it if someone had told you that one day you might fall in love with a little beggar girl of no talents from a distant sanded mesne beyond the Middle Sea, the Charybdis, the terrible Oceanis Atlantis and the Mare Britannia.

God can make anything happen if it serves His purpose. Shall I continue or are you now too cross with me?"

"I am not cross …" he began then saw her mouthing 'O yes you are' before miming a fit of the giggles. He glared at her, she laughed, and defeated he sat back and indicated she should continue, outwardly showing good humour, inwardly sulking like a great, grizzly black bear.

"… and fifteen thousand cavalry riding from Wyncaister under Queen Maria Caedric bearing the sword Excalibur. Although outnumbered, Vespasian's army defeats Boudicca through greater discipline, the power of Excalibur and the gifts of the Spirit contained within the four Holy Artefacts in a battle in the lands of the Atrebates on ground unsuitable for Boudicca's chariots. Alas Boudicca commits suicide afterwards.

Boudicca's revolt will see two things happen that will help cement the foundation of our faith but first our faith will come under terrible attack: Christians in Roma will be blamed for a fire that guts the centre of the City and which leads to our persecution by Nero seeing many of us thrown alive into the Arena to be eaten by lions. We will die singing praises to God. Petrus having escaped from prison once, will return to Roma, be arrested and will be crucified whilst Paulus is finally beheaded …" and for the fourth time, Maria breaks down and weeps, shaking with the distress of the future that she can see. This time it takes nearly half an hour before Craedech can persuade her to continue.

"What happens next is equally awful I am afraid" she admitted, explaining why she was finding it so difficult to finish her story-telling and she looked into Craedech's eyes, seeking courage there. He smiled and said "It all will happen for a reason" at which she nodded and carried on in a wistful whisper:

"Ierusalem will fall to Vespasian's and his son Titus' Legions and many Jewish and Christian leaders including most of the surviving apostles and Iesus' mother and brothers will be lost or slain in the massacre that follows the legionaries breaching the walls of the City. One of Iesus' sisters escapes to Marsela. The Temple of Solomon will be destroyed" at which she stuttered then carried on bravely: "The apostle Iohannus is taken at Mdena and is sent to prison on the Island of Patmos. Longinus has returned to Iudaea with Vepasian and manages to smuggle to safety a few of those captured before they are sold into slavery or executed. Longinus' wife Maria will be left in our care briefly before returning to the caverns at Bobinis and so is kept safe."

"Is she much like you?" the Prince asked and when she nodded he looked forlorn. Maria was shocked at his reaction until she realised he was teasing her at which she hugged his arm in gratitude at his attempt to distract her and cheer her up and then carried on:

"The fall of Iudaea and the death of Paulus and Petrus will see the epicentre of our new faith switch from the diocese in the Middle-East, Africa and Eastern Europa to those in Hispania and Western Europa.

In the wake of Boudicca's revolt, the Romans will change their policy toward the royal families in Britannia and seek to rule their newest province through administrative regions that reflect the boundaries of the former kingdoms.

This new policy of tolerance in Britannia also offers protection to the Christian communities. Our faith will survive the invasion during Claudius' reign and the revolt in the time of Nero because you and me, my love, are seen to remain loyal to Rome" and she ignored the raspberry Craedech rudely blew at that "and as a force for peace. Many British Christians will be slain by Boudicca at Colcaister, Burntwood, Verulanium and Loddon's Hill for refusing to rise against Roma and thus Christians in Britannia are seen as part of the Empire. A view no doubt encouraged and reinforced by the likes of Amarillus, Tartellus, Antonius, Varus Fluvius and Longinus who will all be in powerful and influential positions in Vespasian's administration and will support Galba then Vespasian in the Year of the Four Emperors.

Nero will be overthrown as he starts to rebuild Roma after the fire. Vespasian's friend Galba will be slain in battle on the outskirts of Roma and Vespasian decides to make a bid for the curule chair with Longinus at his side. When Vespasian becomes Emperor this ends our persecution.

The invasion of Britannia, Boudicca's revolt, Nero's persecution and fall result in a Christian Romano-Briton royal dynasty that is respected, involved in local administration for over three centuries, maintaining peace, posing no threat and ultimately marrying into the Imperial family, influencing the religious policy of the entire Empire through a Britannic princess becoming the mother of the Emperor" and Maria pauses for breath after one of her longer sentences then bashes on:

"Christianity survives in Britannia and Caledonia because it goes underground and because it is protected by a royal family ruling Britannia for Roma then ruling the Roman Empire … protected by your and my descendants.

So, if I am to complete **'all of my mission'** then I must marry you and you must stay a Prince. If that means you must have mistresses then I shall weep but I promise that I shall never leave you. All I ask, no I beg, is that you fit me somewhere into your busy love-making schedule. Give me the grace of at least one child."

Craedech glared at her and her head bowed forwards under the force and ferocity of his anger, which she could see from the furrows on his forehead. She was initially bewildered and confused as to why he should be feeling so hurt by her revelations. He soon revealed the cause of his anger and she rapidly tried to defend herself, desperate not to lose his love over a stupid misunderstanding. He started forcibly but by the time he had finished his face was vivid red with rage, he was shouting and she was cowering before him, weeping and shedding tears, sobbing uncontrollably, no sign of the giggles that anger would usually induce: for his love was too important to her and the possibility of losing his love frightened her beyond all fears.

"So this is all about your mission. All you want is to give birth to a son or daughter who will eventually give birth to a daughter who marries into the Roman Imperial family. And knowing how I detest anything to do with Romans you have the audacity to choose me to be your stud. You are contemptible." Stuttering through her tears, Maria tried to convince him to trust her not even sure that he was listening to her:

"I fell in love with you when I saw you held in your grieving father's hands. I realised I loved you, totally, without sense or reason, beyond reason and that you ruled my mind and heart completely, that I would be miserable if you were not part of my life, I realised all of this when I was about to die at King Col's hands. I told the King and his Sorcerer that I loved you and that was for me the moment of truth. They were about to kill me and I wanted my last words in life to be that I loved *you.*

All three prophecies came *after* that.

I ask you to trust me: I am telling the truth when I say that I love you for no other reason except that you are a wonderful man. Surely you can look into my eyes and see that I am telling the truth?"

"All I see is that you have deceived me and everything you have said has been a lie" he replied and he stood and went to leave the pavilion. As Maria went to hold his arm he flung her off leaving her lying on the rush matting floor, her eyes staring in despair at his retreating back, her tears tearing her apart, unable to say a word or call him back through the stuttering despairing sobs and the pain of her breaking heart. "Master" she whispered then curled into a ball, lying on the matting as she looked blankly into empty air.

Craedech got as far as the entrance to the pavilion. The sun had yet to rise; the sky was dark, clouds covering the stars and the moon, whilst the sun was hiding behind the steep hills on all sides. Snow was falling and his companions were desperately struggling to keep the camp fire alight, whilst Longinus was still fighting with his field stove: a battle that he very much appeared to be losing. The Prince could not believe the level of deception to which he had been the innocent victim. And there was the rub: he could not believe Maria could have deceived him. Not just him but everyone. Then the realisation came that she could not have deceived him. Confused he did the only thing he could think of doing and did so in *hope.*

He prayed and for the second time in his life the Master stood before him, or to be precise the Master was sitting in his Father's sitting room with the Prince standing nervously before him.

"Join me please" and He beckoned to the sofa opposite. The Prince did as he was told in total awe, sitting quickly and upright with his hands on his knees. The Master saw this and spotted several nervous twitches as well. The glint of humour that Maria loved to see came into His eyes as the Master recognised the Prince's look of terror from the first time his father, Caractacus, had summonsed the Prince as a young boy for a right royal ticking off. The Prince however did not see the tell-tale sign of the Master's good humour and the silence was making him even more nervous. The Master sighed then broke the silence:

"A girl who is honest opens her heart to you and your reaction is to want to abandon her. Is that correct?"

Craedech gulped and nodded then closed his eyes in anticipation of the anger his answer would spark off. What he heard was another sigh.

"You want to control the girl entrusted with my message of hope to the world. Why?" Craedech suddenly realised that there was the true issue. He was not concerned that Maria had deceived him for she had not. It was that she was taking control of him.

"I am to be King and must be in control" and even to his ears that sounded weak as an answer.

"She becomes Queen many years before you become a King and her kingdom is larger and more powerful than yours. She will have more status than you ... yet she will sit at the foot of any table whilst you will sit at the head and she will decline to sit on any throne. She has other offers from those who carry much more status than you in a world that is ruled from Rome. Why should she marry you?"

"Her mission requires she marry me?"

The Prince's lame answer saw the Master sigh a third time before He asked:

"Why does her mission require *you* to do anything? I can achieve what I seek in many ways. This way saves *your* soul but only if you follow it. Your current path appears to be prompted by your arrogance, lack of humility, your egotism, and your inability to follow the lead of another.

I brought you back from the dead because Maria fell in love with you the moment she saw your poor dead face. Not part of my plan but we humans fall in love without any rhyme or reason at the most awkward moments with the most unsuitable people.

Falling in love with a dead Prince hell-bent on killing her and whom she had never met before and whom she could not marry because you had been killed by her own father has to be about the most hair-brained and illogical stunt ever pulled off by a Daughter of Adam and Eve … or pretty typical for Maria.

So if you cannot see that you owe this girl *everything* because she fell so absurdly in love with you and learn to respect her unbelieveable love that conquered your own death then it is best you go your different ways and I will find someone else to be the progenitors of the Princess Helena."

"What will happen to Maria?"

"There is little point in her becoming a Queen if she has no Prince to marry. The Picts will take care of her" and even to the Master's ears that sounded a little brutal and unkind. The Prince was shocked then realisation came:

"You are angry else you would not even consider something so unkind! Your anger means that you care! Alright, what is in this for me? You are not going to give up on your plan to see the Roman world become Christian and I think I know why."

A rumble of thunderous fury could be heard in all of the north facing windows and for the first time the Prince glanced around him. He was amazed, and stood ignoring the growing tempest of God's fury. Without asking for permission he looked at the décor and decoration of the room properly. Then he turned on the Master his eyes blazing and inflamed with understanding and the revelation of what he saw. He rapidly began to reappraise their conversation and re-examine the divine motivation:

"This whole room is about Maria's life and *your* ministry but tied together as one. She means that much to you that she is become part of you and you her. Everything in this room is there to make Maria happy and yet this is *your* sitting room. So why would you want me to marry her if she means so much to you? Why not marry her yourself? Why this convoluted plan when a living God-head could ride in on a giant stallion and whisk my maiden away to your Father's House in Paradise which you have already prepared for her?"

The Prince had never expected God to show ruefulness and embarrassment, also such a human sense of loss. The conflict of emotions was visible: with authority competing with regret. And it was this conflict that achieved what anger had not: Craedech finally sat back in silence to listen to the Master's admission that he had mishandled things. '*God is human*' as Maria had always told them all but until that moment he had doubted her.

"I have not brought Maria to come and live with me in Paradise because if Maria does not marry you then she will be devastated and I could not bear to hurt her so.

Rather, I want to grant Maria a time of peace on Earth as a reward for her achievements on Earth for which I am and will be profoundly grateful. I want her to have human happiness on Earth because her desire in Paradise is to extinguish her own individuality and unique personality, to surrender her right to resurrection after the final Judgement, and rather to become part of me, eternally, self-effacing, in total adoration of me.

So I have brought to life the man she loves. I have made her a princess and will make her a Queen over a great kingdom because I wish her to be comfortable after her terrible trials and the suffering she will see during her mission. Her descendants will one day rule the Roman Empire.

I also love you, Craedech. I have found you a partner who will enhance your status and who seeks no status for herself. To whom thousands will flock just to be near her yet always it shall be you that she and they shall call 'King'. Who shall bear you children yet always remain a child herself, pure, innocent and chaste, faithful in love to you alone even though you might be unfaithful to her. Who will teach you to love me and thus redeem your soul.

I had the opportunity to marry Maria and I knew that she was more than willing. I put my ministry first and knew that to have denied Maria God's gift of motherhood would have been poor reward for her unselfish love yet to have had children with her would have confused the whole concept of a single Divine Being and my conception with Maria, my mother. I confess I also thought I would have the time to work out the theology of a God with many children within my own mind but this ridiculous, surprising, totally lawless and rule-less yet guileless child acted impulsively and without thought by falling in love with you, my lord Prince.

Once her heart was given it was too late to change things.

King David once slew the husband of a lady whom he fell in love with and I punished him for so doing. Now I found myself contemplating doing the same and turned my back on any such thoughts. Instead I came to the realisation that whilst I might master time yet this little girl with no powers herself, save the gifts I grant her, could still surprise even me with her impetuousness.

She loves you and that is the new reality just as she creates beautiful scenes for me to admire in my house and a place for me to live in her heart."

"Why make this room for her if you want her to stay alive and marry me?"

The Master looked around the room and as he did so the thunder receded and the clouds scattered, bright golden sunshine came from every corner and finally manifesting as God he said:

"I did not make this room for her. *She made it for me.* And every time I look at what she has done for me I am made incredibly happy, more so than had it been my own creation. This is one of many places Maria has subconsciously made for me in her heart, mind and soul. Without intending to do so, she has redecorated most of my rooms in this house and all of my gardens and the parkland in Paradise too."

"You love her that much?" but God shook his head and corrected the Prince:

"She loves me that much. My love is equal for all my creations but I will confess that I spend more time with some than others and Maria interests me more than almost all others past, present and future."

"Why? She is not intelligent so why are you so interested in talking and spending time with her?"

"My dear Prince, for the same reason you want to marry her. She is special because she is different and surprising yet so full of the ability to love that to be loved by her is both rewarding and confidence-building. And so I ask you, why do you want to run away from her love?"

"Because I cannot ever hope to repay her with as much love" the Prince finally admitted and with the truth before them both at last, the Master took them to a sandy cove where they sat on blue satin and velvet cushions surrounded by soft, golden sands beneath a cream silk pavilion and looked out onto a calm blue sea and a clear blue sky.

"Beautiful" the Prince exclaimed his heart responding in pure delight. "Is this another one of Maria's?"

"O Yes" the Master replied. "This is the special place for me she has made in her heart. I bring people here when I have something to forgive them for but first you must want to be forgiven."

"My lord, I must ask something first. Is my heart as beautiful to you as this place?"

"My Prince, when have you ever made a place for me to visit? I would love to visit a place made for me by you and would see it as special. Do you know why?"

"No. Please tell me, for I have no particular talent in design."

"Put at its simplest, there are two reasons this place is special:

- it was not created by me and so is a *surprise* and
- it was created *for* me so is an act of love and generosity which therefore touches my heart

"You have a heart?"

"Talk to Maria. She knows the answer to that already"

"What should I do, lord?" and when he said that for the first time the Prince could see joy in the Master's countenance whilst the sun turned the whole sky to brightest gold, dazzling the Prince.

"Do not worry if it gets quite a lot brighter in here. Maria can sense *my* happiness in her heart and the golden sky is her unconscious response that will glow brighter as she becomes more attuned to my own joy. In this way you were right that we have become one. But I am glad you asked what it is you must now do because I am happiest when people involve me in solving their problems.

The answer is 'Marry Maria' of course. And then let us solve any problems that arise after that one at a time when they come up. For being married to Maria will be one long puzzling and unpredictable adventure!"

At last the Prince could smile. He had learnt so much about both God and Maria. Yet he still felt terribly guilty that he had encouraged the girl to open up her mind to him. When she had done so truthfully and comprehensively he had then punished her for doing so.

"Ahem!" God interrupted "I should have warned you that I can read minds during these sessions. But do not worry. I *forgive* you for your reaction to

Maria's expression of her love. She has much love to give but also many people she loves. Get in there fast and claim your share of her love and do not be worried that you cannot repay her. The love I have to give is greater still and you cannot possibly repay that. So what? You will still be loved by me … and by her. Just repay what you can with the love you can offer."

And then Craedech was back in the pavilion. He strode across to Maria and lifted her into his arms, still not yet dressed but her heart was now bared to him. He knew he had the freedom to walk away from a lifetime in the shadow of someone so full of love that all would flock to her light casting him in the shade. But why should he be anything other than happy to be the partner of such a popular lady destined to be a much-loved Queen? He laughed when he could not answer his own question then saw she had angled her head to one side and was looking at him quizzically without any understanding of why he was laughing.

As she saw him looking at her, all of her tears fled and her good humour returned. The sparkle shone once more deep within her eyes and she grinned back at him then confessed: "It is a childhood habit which I am stuck with. It means I am clueless. But I do not care; it is wonderful to hear you laugh and I do not need to know why. Just as I can never hope to repay your many kindnesses yet does it matter? I will love you as much as I can and if that does not repay you for being such a wonderful generous and loving man yet I can do no more.

So I ask you Prince: Can you accept everything I have to offer even though it can never be enough on the condition that it is as much as I can give?"

"Yes" said the Prince so touched by her humility that he found the decision to commit to loving her was easy to take. His own heart leapt as finally he discovered the knowledge that he genuinely loved her, *whatever the consequences*. All else came second to having a life in the company of someone so special … and so clueless!

Then back to practical issues, he carefully untangled himself from the bear hug Maria had captured him in and whispered in the girl's ear as he did so: "The others will return in five minutes for breakfast and Longinus has his back to you. This may be your only chance to clear away your tears and to get dressed without making a spectacle of yourself. I will grab some clothes for you from the horses' saddle bags and will be back soon."

It was raining outside and the dark of pre-dawn cast even more shadows as the black clouds that were their permanent companions continued to hide both the sun and the stars.

"Another sun being miserable" muttered Maria and prayed for a 'warm sun' one day.

All were now dressed and Ninian and Galahaidra had found a rock pool to wash in but the rest would let the rain do the task. Galahaidra's news as they returned back to the pavilion to sit around the stove and have their breakfast was grim, however:

"We are three to four days from lowlands in every direction with no country that allows for our horses to trot let alone gallop. We must journey on foot but so must those who follow us. On foot you can cover ground without leaving a trace for hours possibly even a few days. But if there are many of you then after three days you are bound to leave some indication of your presence and movements.

Yesterday I saw the first sign of someone following us and so I left some traps. Nothing large or noticeable or that would hurt or harm. Twigs set to fall at the weight of a footstep or the passing wind of a stranger; cobwebs set at head height; brambles curling as trip wires; and shallow holes to create puddles which when emptied reveal footprints (for when walking in mud and if you wish to leave no trace then you go from puddle to puddle); moss placed strategically on certain branches that when lifted shows hand prints beneath; bark loosened to break when shinning up or down a tree trunk.

We have at least five following us and I picked up the trail of another one, caught him up as he was being less cautious than the rest. I soon realised why he had thrown caution to the winds as he was heading north-west whereas we are going north-east. So I stuck to him for an hour and was rewarded by my first sight of a Pict war band on the march.

I ran in the opposite direction just in time to join Ninian in her bath" which inappropriately tactless description got him a kick from the young lady and he rapidly apologised for his clumsy words. "I meant with 'her bathing'" which to his companions did not sound any better and so he decided to stick to what he knew – he could make it up to Ninian later.

"We have about one hundred Picts some two hours away and they know precisely where we are and can track us down almost whenever they wish. We need to shake off the five around us if we are to lose the one hundred behind us."

"Anyone have any ideas?" Longinus asked and Galahaidra jumped in after the frightened silence that followed Longinus' request.

"The rockpool Ninian and I used had a stream. We will look innocuous taking clothes down to the pool to wash. We can conceal weapons, armour and other important items and equipment rolled up in our clothing, the Holy Artefacts too. But our horses and pavilion must stay here as we cannot take them with us if we seek speed and to evade the enemy. One hour along the stream and we will have shaken off those sent to mark us out. From then the hunt is on and we must run non stop day and night for two days to reach flat ground. Then we must find a homestead and buy horses or we will be dead."

"Can we not fight once we hit the flat ground?" asked a quiet voice and they all looked around wondering: who was this war-like character?

"Me" whispered Maria and all eyebrows shot up high. "Why fight?" Longinus asked the girl when all knew he meant 'why are you of all people suggesting we fight'?

"They will respect us more and it gets me in front of them quicker."

"As a corpse" Craedech added uncharitably then admitted it was an improvement: "At least you did not offer to go and meet them on your own!"

"Actually that was my next suggestion. Any reasons why not?"

“Thousands” muttered Craedech shaking his head whilst Longinus after ignoring Maria and giving Galahaidra’s plan some thought made a small amendment.

“Release six of the horses and leave the rest for the Picts. They will look after them well. Make it look as if six is all we have. The others we send out into the rain. They will follow Epona; and Epona will follow Maria and her wild boar as both have befriended each other. The Picts won’t get too close to our horses and our horses will stay away unless Maria summons Epona then they will come to us immediately. The Picts probably will not even consider following six wild horses with no saddle or harness.”

“If they look at their mouths and feet they will know they are not wild. The marks on their backs from their saddles will show the same” Galahaidra pointed out but Maria had the answer to that:

“They will not go that close and Epona would not let a stranger get within fifty paces of him” Maria observed then added at a tangent: “Do not forget the stove though for I refuse to sleep naked in the cold another night” and ignoring the girl’s last contribution, the company all agreed they had a plan.

“Which way do we head once out of the stream?” Iosephus asked. Galahaidra was still at the helm in this meeting and so directed the question toward Craedech adding, as he did so and before the Prince had answered: “I found no-one within ten flights of an arrow let alone one. Those we seek may be lost so we must go back the way they were to come to find them.”

“South west then” the Prince replied whilst Maria queried ‘who ‘those we seek’ and ‘they’ were?’ and was ignored a second time.

As an added precaution, Galahaidra dressed quickly into his black assassin’s robes with the curved hooks of steel on toes and hands, his knife in a chest holster, his Lance in its triple strapped and frogged holster, his belt tied across his back, his shield clothed in black silk hanging from a buckle and strap on his left shoulder, wearing his black hood and mask, but carrying also the sword Macsen had made for him in its black leather scabbard.

"Please just knock them out or send them the wrong way or some other clever trick you can use but do not kill them" Maria pleaded with him whilst Ninian said a simple "Come back safe and sound."

Galahaidra exited the pavilion through the rear flap that faced west and noiselessly moved amongst the guide ropes then crawled across the heather on the ground towards a drop in the granite ledge on which the pavilion was perched. It was still dark but the young knight was taking no chances. In the opposite direction from the gorge the rest of the company were to take was a copse of around ninety to a hundred trees which was the only cover for a league in any direction (except for the gullies cut into the rock by rills, falls, rivers, springs and streams which led down to the rock pools Galahaidra and Ninian had used earlier that morning). There was one gully however that skirted the camp site and that was Galahaidra's objective. Galahaidra dropped into the gully and crawled along its base until the far side of the copse.

Only then did he rise slowly and ran in a long loop to approach the copse from the opposite side from their camp site. The first light of dawn rose ponderously in the east where their pavilion was set up; the copse was dead ahead of him with the camp site, the company still chatting and packing as silhouettes in the first light of day and the long drop over which the two girls' tent had flown lying to his north; and the entrance to the gorge was to his west with daylight pointing like a withered and arthritic finger straight along its meandering course.

On reaching the copse, he climbed up the tallest tree until he reached the very top then slowly placed a piece of reflective glass on the end of a branch he had shaved off with his knife and did a 360 degree scan. No other head in sight and so he popped his head through the tree-topped green roof of the copse and was immediately rewarded with sight of two men in swirling white paint, both armed with bow and arrow, half way up two trees to his west. They were looking at his comrades eating the remains of breakfast and would miss Galahaidra if he came at them from the south.

He dropped down the tree quickly using his grappling hooks and ran soundlessly along the perimeter of the copse, crouching low and using a natural ditch that had formed at its edge through the action of the roots over the years pushing earth away or trapping water to create a stream that had eventually established a perfect motte just right for one crouching man to hide in. Keeping to the shadows he arrived fifty paces from the two trees that were the Picts' watchtowers.

Instantly he saw the third and fourth Picts standing guard at the bottom of each tree leaning against the trunk with their backs facing south whilst they themselves could just see part of Longinus and the pavilion to the east. '*Where is man number five?*' the Christian knight pondered then putting himself in their shoes he realised he would have commissioned one man to forage for food and drink especially if they had just watched his own comrades eating breakfast.

Twenty seconds later he had crept silently stepping over the occasional leaf, twig, branch and root to get behind the first of the two men standing guard. He checked that he had a clear and unimpeded view towards the third man to his left and then did not pause but immediately sliced the throat of the fourth man. He let him slide to the ground, making hardly any noise but just enough for the third man to turn his head towards his colleague and receive a silver-plated sicarius straight through his right eye and into the skull cavity of his brain beyond.

Both men had made some noise falling but not enough to carry to the two archers above as the dead men had fallen into mud. Galahaidra checked that the men were dead then searched them and found two hunting knives that would double up as throwing knives. He tested the weight and balance then nodded to himself, cleaned his sicarius, wiping off the blood and returning it to its holster, and put the hunting knives in the top roll of his black leather boots. Now he was ready.

He began to shin quietly up the taller of the two trees concealing the Pictish archers testing each hand and foothold as he did so for loose bark or any other trap or wire rigged to set off an alarm. It took him five minutes to get behind the first look out but he continued to climb for three more minutes until he was above both men and with a clear shot at each. The man in the other tree had a clear view of both the camp and his compatriots, whereas the man below him must look over his shoulder to see his comrade.

'*Far tree first'* he mused and drew then threw a knife in one motion. The third man dropped from his perch to go crashing to the ground. The Pictish scout below him made the mistake of looking towards the noise and thus he was looking over his left shoulder as Galahaidra came crashing down onto his right hand side. Ten sharp grapple-hooks carved flesh and bone from shoulder and ribs and the man opened his mouth to scream only for Galahaidra to ram the second hunting knife into the the gaping roof of his mouth and upwards into his brain. The Pict toppled slowly to his left then down to the base of the tree trunk to join his three comrades on the ground whilst Galahaidra leapt from tree to tree heading back to camp.

The party were ready to leave when Galahaidra reported there was now only one Pictish scout left then he issued revised orders and did so with urgency for they perhaps only had a few minutes to make their escape:

"We go now and fast! Go to the rock pool and just keep going. Do not stop to pretend to bathe or even to have a bath if that was your plan" and he looked at Maria who got an uncontrollable fit of the giggles as that had been precisely what she had been thinking.

"Run until I catch you up" he continued ignoring her. "Only then do we lay down some false trails and cover our tracks. I will wait five minutes to see if we are followed then catch you up. If I do not join you in five minutes then I am trapped, have been spotted or am dead. Go!" and they all turned and ran, following Ninian who knew the way and leaving Galahaidra

The young man did a quick sweep of their camp's perimeter then shinned up a tree and waited, watching in the main towards the south entrance to the copse of trees where the four scouts had been taken out and which was the only cover except for the occasional boulder or gullies and rills in the rock face along one of which Ninian had found the pool, rill and stream that was to be their escape route.

After four minutes he was rewarded with the distant wail of a peewit (except the weather was too cold, wet and miserable for a peewit with no large mass of water or fast flowing river nearby and therefore this peewit was very lost or very human). There was no answering cry and as Galahaidra watched, a man stepped out of the bushes carrying a spear in his right hand and four rabbits and a buzzard on neck strings hanging from his left hand.

When he saw the bodies, the Pict dropped his catch and swung in a curve, his spear held pointing forwards, gripped in both hands at the waist, turning a full circle on the sole of his right foot, his left leg bent at the knee for balance, eyes looking in all directions but also checking over the bodies: to see that all four had gone to knife wounds. He relaxed slightly for he had feared an arrow shot was to be his fate. He had no fear of a knife for he had a spear.

Without any warning he launched into a run towards the camp. He ran slowly, a gentle rolling gait he could keep up for league upon league and reaching the camp perimeter saw that it was empty. He found tracks leading to the rock pool in the first minute of searching but was instantly suspicious as the tracks were too obvious and there were only five pairs. Now he was looking for either a hidden set of tracks for the whole party or the concealed tracks of one man left to assassinate him as he went after the party's obvious route towards the falls where two of the party had washed that morning.

He recalled the young lady not yet twenty and who was still in the first bright flush of her youth, good looking with it. She had known it too as she had flirted with the young man accompanying her. Her companion had seemed embarrassed but the Pictish scout had a clear view of her and had enjoyed her full performance, imagining the reception he would have given the girl. With an evil smile he took even more enjoyment from considering what her grim fate was going to be when they caught her. The war party he was scouting for would leave her until last then savour the pleasure of her screams.

Galahaidra was now worried: he had not planned this well at all. Up a tree, his knife was his only weapon. Even throwing directly downwards, he could not be sure of his shot until his enemy got a lot closer. His enemy was about to find him from his tracks and could force him out with his spear or set fire to the tree and smoke him out. The young knight could jump to an adjoining tree but that merely delayed the inevitable.

As he had never needed to, he was yet to try his sword so he had no idea of its powers if any. He could wait before drawing his sword until the foe was testing this tree with his spear; basically waiting until he was about to be discovered anyway. If he leapt down on the Pict as he had done with the third man he had slain then he would probably be impaled on the spear. At least he was buying more time for the rest of the party but he felt he had planned this all wrong and should have stayed on the ground.

He had run out of options when he got lucky. The Pict had found the tracks of the six horses and wondered if the party had ridden off. He traced the horses back from their tracks to the pavilion and decided to check the tent out. The moment the Pictish scout entered the pavilion he saw where the other six horses were stabled and his eyes glittered at their potential value as he inspected each of them and noted their expensive harnesses. He had just become very wealthy.

Galahaidra waited until he heard the horses snickering at the attention of the scout and dropped to the ground in four leaps from branch to branch then looked for somewhere to hide. His luck was still with him as he saw a small gully whose approach was by rock and thus he would leave no trail. Being careful not to leave any trace of his passing, within thirty seconds of the Pict going into the pavilion, Galahaidra was hidden in a man-sized gully the shape of a coffin, except that was precisely the sort of thought that the young man had rather he had kept unthought!

The Pict was still unsure whether the party had taken off on their horses or not? Unlike the tracks down to the gully leading to the rock pool which had been of a party of five, there were six sets of horse tracks. Why the difference? Were the horse tracks the decoy … but then why only five tracks down the path? If the six tracks were real then he had seen twelve horses with the party when they had settled the night before. Six had been left tethered in their shelter in the pavilion and thus six were in use or one each for the party. Everything led to one missing set of tracks so he had better find them.

It was coming up to the hour since Longinus had led the party from the camp site. Galahaidra had planned for five minutes at most before he caught them up. Now he had to hope that Longinus' field craft was good enough to lay false tracks and hide the real ones, perhaps leave man traps as he had done at The Summonsing Stones. But Galahaidra had one other concern. Any time in the next hour he expected to hear the rest of the war band arriving and they would flush him out in seconds. He needed to go and to head south then throw false tracks himself. But first how was he to take out his immediate pursuer?

Galahaidra slowly raised his piece of reflective glass to just above the surface of his gully and angled it at forty five degrees. The Pict was to his nor-nor-west, in the open and very close at twenty paces. He had been looking the other way or would have seen the glass. It was an old trick Galahaidra was going to use but he must hope it worked and closing his eyes to pray, the young knight threw a stone over his shoulder and towards the entrance to the gully that led to the rock pool. Jackpot!

The stone rattled in the entrance then rolled several paces, sounding like at least one person stumbling then running down the gully. Galahaidra heard the sharp intake of breath then careful footsteps towards the gully, those of a man expecting a trap, but not thinking of any danger from behind him.

Galahaidra stood, turned and threw his sicarius in one dance-like elegant yet precise motion and the knife flew slowly and gracefully through the air to sink six inches into the Pict's back just to the left of the spine near where the shoulder blade curves, finding the space between the third and fourth rib, then plunging up to its neck into the man's heart. The Pict staggered, knelt slowly on one knee, then the shock took him and he clutched at his chest, before falling to the ground. Even lying there he tried to move and took several minutes before with a final rattle and cough, he went grey and stopped breathing altogether. Only then did Galahaidra retrieve his knife and the wrench as it was pulled clear of the heart gave the man the shock that finally killed him as his brain shut down.

Galahaidra did not wait another second but ran south, following familiar paths as this was the route the company had taken but in reverse the day before. He intended to do twenty leagues south then ten leagues to the west looking to find his companions. He would also be looking the whole time for any sign of Craedech's men, climbing any trees he found on the hour every hour to check the area.

His fear was that a second Pictish hunting party had come from the south as well as the war party he had encountered to their west. Unless the party he had walked into had travelled north then turned east the mirror of the route he was now attempting? He had to find out.

Then he heard the high pitched howl as the war party arrived at the camp. He continued to listen as he ran and to his dismay heard the war party split with a number charging through the trees and onto the granite escarpment in search of him. He was a dead man: he had no more than fifteen minutes head start and they knew the territory whereas he was struggling to find the best path.

Longinus had waited a few minutes then begun the arduous task of laying down several false trails and supervising the rest of the party as they set traps under stones or between the sides of the gully. "Why are we wasting time doing this?" asked Craedech for the traps were obvious and easily avoided.

Longinus explained: "One in six traps we are laying will be carefully concealed and lethal. The same number again will be booby-trapped and will go off when they try to disarm it. Some traps are obvious and distract our foe so that as they avoid one trap to the left, they walk into another to the right and vice versa. The obvious traps make them complacent. If the hunting party walk into just one of the deadly man traps then suddenly every bend in the path becomes dangerous. This slows them down. They cannot be certain that any part of the path is safe.

The false tracks work on the same principle."

"Why have you laid an obvious track going the way we will be going? It is like an arrow saying 'Come and Get us!'" and then the denarius dropped. "When they find our real tracks they will still think they are false! Like the real man traps."

"Precisely!" and Longinus continued his master class:

"Every hour we turn either east or west or double back and when we do we lay another set of false and true tracks. At first, they will assume that the path that is least distinct or worst hidden is our true path. So we make them regret that assumption by setting a trap on that track followed by a dead end. We take another path then do the same … except the next time we set a trap, dead end and fifty paces on *continue along the same path.* The one thing we must watch for is that they work out where we are going and get ahead of us."

"Where are we going?"

"Back. We are doubling back on ourselves. Going south. But then we go west and this is when we throw them off our scent again!"

They all got their heads down and started to dig holes in the mud of the stream's bed, to pile up stones to fall from the top of paths onto those below, cut sharpened stakes that were held under tension as their pursuers came around bends, using brushes made from bundles of twigs and branches as hand brushes to sweep away the evidence of their passing. Ninian began to mutter at the state of her nails but Maria was revelling at playing in the mud. Iosephus' back kept making ominous creaking noises. It was Craedech however who observed the passing of the time then asked:

"Where is Galahaidra?"

"Move out" commanded Longinus ignoring the question for the knight was either dead, in hiding or being chased and they were unlikely to see him again. They walked east a few hundred paces then doubled back stepping into their own tracks before Longinus removed a Hawthorne bush he had dug out earlier then replanted it once they had stepped through.

"Up in those trees" he whispered and then signalled the way south that they should take, lifting Ninian up so that she could reach the lowest branch. Craedech swung on his legs from a strong branch further up the tree and offered both hands for Longinus to grab. The Centurion had brushed clean all footprints whilst standing on a stone under the branch from which the Prince now swung. Taking both of Craedech's hands he was lifted into the air to join the company in the trees.

Maria was an expert at climbing trees with no fear of heights and was already twenty paces up, jumping from one oak tree to another, watching the sun to be sure of her heading. The rest of the company followed her, though less recklessly, most not daring to climb as high as the girl had, Longinus in particular being scared of heights and sticking to crossing using the lowest branches. Craedech tried to catch Maria up but soon admitted defeat. Her lightweight meant she could use higher branches by which to cross and also could swing further.

Maria and Craedech were the first to arrive at the sycamore tree that was their target, and thus were able to help the rest of the party down. Longinus pointed to a rock ledge eight paces from them and heading in the right direction. They ran across, being careful not to catch their feet on any leaves, branches or roots and thus leave a trace then Longinus brushed away all traces of their footsteps, walking backwards as he did so.

"Run" he said "We need to get distance between us and about now the Pictish war band will have reached our camp." That was enough to frighten them all and they ran. However it soon became apparent that the girls would not be able to keep up at the pace the men were setting. At a nod from Longinus, Craedech and he hoisted Ninian and Maria onto their shoulders and started to jog. Their pace was now slower than that of the Picts so they had to hope they would lose them at the first junction.

Then they heard the piercing scream of the Picts' Hunting Cry. The chase was on.

Galahaidra heard those chasing him begin to spread out, sweeping around to his left and right. From the cries and movement behind him he counted fifteen warriors, five behind him and five to left and to right. He had no time to throw them off his scent and must prepare himself to turn and fight. The young man began to look carefully for some feature that he could defend or from which he could mount an ambush. The one piece of good fortune was that the war band had split in three. He had a chance against five unless the party contained archers. He thought back to when he had first encountered the war party and '*Yes. They had twenty archers*!' If he did attack them then he must take out the archers with his knife before relying on his Holy Lance to take out the rest. He saw immediately the weakness in his plan. For any suitable place for an ambush or to hold against the Pict's assault would almost certainly be unsuitable for his long lance. "Sword then" he muttered putting his hopes in the skill of Macsen.

After two hours during which he had heard the Picts get closer and closer, indeed he had caught brief sight of one slightly ahead of him but a good distance to his left, he finally saw a gorge that ran west and which he could follow for at least a league, holding off the Pict's assault at the far end. They would follow him through the gorge and along the top of the steep mountains that formed its sides splitting again into three parties. Those on the top would be slowed down by the time it took them to scale the mountainside and also by the more treacherous path they would take.

Galahaidra increased his speed, risking tripping on the rocks and loose pebbles that formed the base of the gorge. He was in constant prayer now and by some miracle his tred remained safe and secure and he began to gain on his pursuers until he reached the end of the gorge. He turned with his knife in his right hand. A few minutes later he saw the first of the Picts: a group of five with the archer at the rear. He waited his moment.

Placing the base of his lance against his left foot, he held it like a pike and its power unerringly guided the lance to pierce the leader's right thigh at which he fell writhing in pain. The remaining four hesitated at the loss of their leader and this gave Galahaidra the chance to retrieve and holster his lance. Then three of the Picts came at him, whilst the archer unstrung his bow.

The archer was not looking at the young knight but concentrating on stringing his bow when Galahaidra's silver sicarius pierced him in his right eye and he fell. Then the knight drew his sword and the prayers of Macsen took effect. A bright white light was emitted from the sword, dazzling the three warriors but through the power of the swordsmith's art, leaving Galahaidra's sight clear for him to thrust his sword twice, despatching two of the Picts through the heart with the Vorpal Blade.

The third had stepped back instinctively and then he recovered his sight long enough to swing with his giant cleaver at Galahaidra, an enormous overhead blow intended to carve the young knight's head in two. Galahaidra stepped to one side and caught the cleaver with his foot pinning it to the ground then swung his own sword and sliced the throat of his opponent who toppled backwards and lay in pain, clutching his wound in a futile attempt to stop the blood loss. The wound was fatal yet the Pict writhed on the floor still alive ... just. Unlike Maria, Galahaidra had no intention of healing the wounded Pict or his leader who was crawling over to the dead archer to pick up his bow and arrows. Stepping over each of them, Galahaidra plunged his sword through their hearts. He could not afford any living witnesses to what he did next.

Collecting his knife, Galahaidra headed out of the gorge fifty paces then went west, retraced his steps in reverse, re-using the foot marks he had left then went east and did the same before returning to the gorge. Once there he ran back towards the entrance knowing that he would leave no trace in the stones at the bottom. The sky was dark with black rain clouds and it was raining heavily so he took a chance that none of those above him would see him running in the opposite direction in his black outfit. Nonetheless, he looked out for the Picts above him and was prepared to stand back into the shadows of the gorge if he saw any movement above. In the end he had to squat behind rocks on two occasions and watched the Picts above run by without hesitation.

It was mid afternoon when he reached the entrance to the gorge where he left false tracks south, east and north then found a granite ledge with a steep incline that he could use to go north. He needed to get to the top of the ledge and the incline was steep, the ground underfoot treacherous, the risk was that the Picts might see him as he scaled the ledge undoing all the benefit of the false trails he had laid. He accepted the challenge therefore of running up the hill. Half an hour later he was exhausted and only half way up the ledge. If the Picts had not been fooled by the trails he had laid then they would emerge any second from the gorge.

Longinus and his company had run for three hours, stopping every hour to set trails east, west and south with traps on the end of each. Their real path was also south but accessed by trees or across stones and granite ledges so that it was invisible for the first one hundred paces. On the third hour they set a 'false trail' south at the end of which they set a trap then ran on along that path, Longinus carefully covering their tracks.

The Picts however knew they were going south because of the route Galahaidra had taken and so hunted for the real track, ignoring those going east and west losing quarter to half an hour in the search. They did leave one warrior behind, injured by one of the traps set by Longinus. The company were gaining quarter of every hour in the hour but losing all of that and more as the Picts were running much faster in territory they knew.

After four hours, Longinus heard the Picts perhaps a league behind him. There was no time to set traps so Longinus looked for a natural feature he could use to throw the war band on their trail off the scent. He found one: going east-west: west was the direction he wanted to travel. Across their path was a fast running stream, approximately two to three feet deep or waist high on Maria, thigh high on the rest of the company.

He sent the company west, ensuring their entry into the stream pointed south and setting a short trail that continued south but taking no more than a minute doing so before sprinting along the bed of the stream to catch up with the rest of the company. He came across Maria first who was struggling as she waded through the deep water. In the end she decided that swimming might be more effective and plunged in then used the more silent breast stroke to try and keep up with the others who were able to stride at speed.

Suddenly, Longinus hissed softly and pointed back the way they had come. Craedech, Iosephus, Ninian and Longinus were round a bend in the stream and all but the Centurion could not be seen. Maria was in plain view if any of the Picts looked to their right. "Hide" he whispered then he ducked behind the reeds by the bank. Maria needed no more warning but sank beneath the water and swam towards the reeds then slowly broke one beneath the water and used it to suck air into her lungs whilst she remained submerged.

Longinus watched the Picts through the reeds and counted seventy-nine heading south. They had lost some of their number to his traps and he smiled to himself. But now it would be less than a quarter of an hour before they backtracked to the stream then split, half to go east and half west. As soon as the last of their war party had crossed the stream, he ran to where Maria was hiding, picked her up, the girl protesting the whole time as he put her on his shoulders like a child. He muttered about her weight but for once he was glad she weighed around 70 pounds. Then striding across to Craedech, he said:

"We cannot stay ahead of the Picts for the three hours we will need to cover the ten leagues to where we think your company should be. It may be less if they have outriders searching for us but that does not matter as I give us two hours at most before the Picts see us and then perhaps half an hour before they have rounded us all up and the torture begins. We need somewhere we can ambush them. You go ahead and find us a site where we can surprise them and hold them until it grows dark then we run once more and hope to find those we seek. I will drive the rest of the company as fast as we can go."

"Will someone tell me 'who it is we are looking for'?" Maria asked plaintively and once again she was ignored by them both. Her revenge was to subject Longinus to her chatter for the next hour and a half, comprising principally of the stories about sea monsters and sea serpents told her by the crew on The Valiant. In the end he threatened to put a sack over her head and she gave in with good grace, guessing rightly that he must be tiring and needed to concentrate or he would drop her. Instead she whispered "Thank you for saving me" in his ear and went silent.

The only bit of good news for the pursued party was that when the Picts finally realised they had been fooled and that there was no fresh trail heading south somewhere beyond where the 'false trail' ended, they decided to backtrack to the exit from the gorge to see if they had missed any trails east or west in their haste. Coming to the stream they sent fifteen east and the same number west whilst the rest of their host headed north. They had wasted an hour hunting for a trail south, so convinced were they that the party were going south. Now they were one hour and forty minutes behind Longinus.

Galahaidra heard the Picts' war cries in the gorge but still some distance away as he finally heaved himself over the mountain's ledge and dropped to the floor of leaves beyond. He lay there for a few minutes capturing his breath, his chest aching from his efforts. But he was fit and had no intention of giving up. He had changed his own plans: convinced that Craedech's troops would not be found in the labyrinth of mountain crags, ledges, promontories, valleys and passes to their south, he now intended to run to Maria's rescue, realising he should never have left her side.

He ran for two hours, no longer pursued by the Picts who had lost all trace of him, arriving at the camp in the middle of the afternoon. It was overcast, raining still and visibility was no better than at night, especially as he moved into the gully with its steep sides. However, drawing his sword it lit his path through the gully to the rockpool and beyond. He could see where the Picts had fallen to Longinus' traps, all three surviving but caught on stakes or in pits where the mouth had spikes pointing inwards, only for Galahaidra to finish them off. Then the knight headed south and almost ran into forty nine of the Picts, checking all the way back to the gorge for any trails they might have missed in their haste.

Their direction immediately told the knight that his friends had gone east or west. Knowing what the company's final destination was he started to run south-west, going by the most direct route, fearing that some of the war party had peeled off in pursuit of Longinus. He suspected that the Centurion would try a repeat of the Battle at The Summoning Circle but his foe were very different and far more dangerous, whilst Longinus had only three who would fight when before he had been five. Moreover, and how he hated to have to admit to this, the girl, Maria, had taken down more of their foe than anyone else but now refused to fight. Galahaidra needed to rejoin the party to bring the numbers up or he dreaded that he would find his comrades slain or captured to be tortured.

A few minutes later the Picts found the tracks of a single man going south-west. They did not follow them but rather looked for a path that had gone west, eventually coming to the stream which they realised must be the only way the company could have taken and with a whooping cry they followed the waters' path.

Craedech had found an ideal spot for an ambush some four leagues in front of the company and which would take the party just under an hour and a half to wade through the stream's deep waters. The party had concealed within the rolls of their clothing chain mail, helmets and swords enough for the three men as both the girls refused to fight.

"Your sword is made never to kill and your Grael only wounds" Longinus pleaded but Maria laughed then retorted:

"Yes and every time I wound anyone then Galahaidra and you come along and slay them. Thou shalt not kill means also thou shalt not help someone else to kill" and she remained stubborn on the point whilst Longinus cursed and swore eventually giving the girl a fit of the giggles.

Two oak trees had fallen across the stream as the earth between their roots had been eroded by the stream's fast-running water. They formed a barrier that must be climbed or ducked under with one's head touching the water as you did so. The bank at this point and for fifty paces to the east was a good four paces high, steep with smooth mud and moss. You could go back fifty paces and climb up the bank where it was less severe and dangerous.

Longinus instantly saw that what was needed were wire traps fifty paces back where the bank dropped, stakes under tension buried beneath the loose stones of the stream's bed on the approach to the two trunks, spiked stakes on the bed beneath the two trunks, smaller versions of the same and sharpened bark on the topmost trunk to cut hands and fingers as the Picts went to grasp the top of the dead tree and a neck-high thread tied across between the two banks of the river to cut through necks as people went to clamber over the trunks. He issued his instructions and once again the party got digging. By the time they had finished digging and preparing the traps, it had begun to get dark.

It was now the half-light of the shorter late Autumn days with the added 'delight' that it had started to snow and the flakes were settling fast, covering the traps set by the Roman but also seeing the temperature drop to well below freezing. Slowly but surely the stream that was shallow began to freeze over. Entering into the last hour of the light, Longinus wound a thread between trees to mark the company's retreat through the woods behind them and went to send the girls ahead. Maria refused and sat down not budging and after a few seconds during which Longinus glared at her going purple, Ninian bravely sat next to her.

"We are not leaving you" said Maria stubbornly and Longinus had run out of time to argue so turned instead to issue orders to the others:

"Prince, you and the knight Iosephus are to be ready to chop down anyone coming over or under the Oak trees. Build yourself some sort of platform to stand on but keep an eye out for anyone coming at you from beneath the two trunks."

"And you?" Craedech asked.

"I will be on one of the banks taking down anyone who hits our traps or climbs the banks but watching also for their archers. We have perhaps ten minutes, possibly as much as half of one hour before our enemy will charge down on us. Get armed and armoured up; your helmets will protect you against their arrows as shall your shields. Use them!"

The river bank the nearside of the barrier across the stream was about one pace deep and easy for Maria to haul herself up and over it, which is what she did whilst Craedech and Iosephus were distracted by their task of building a platform to stand on. Running down the west bank she was the first to see the Pictish war band and called across to Longinus on the east bank, who looked at her in absolute, horrified amazement. "What are you doing?" he mouthed.

"Plan B" she replied. "You know: the one where I walk up to them on my own and tell them stories. Be right back soon!"

"Craedech" Longinus roared "Can't you control her?"

"What? Who?" and Craedech lifted his head from where he was putting the finishing touches to the bracings on his platform. Ninian rather smugly replied to his startled questions: "Give you one guess!"

Maria dropped into the stream and walked towards the war band, her hands at her side, palms extended. She was greeted by a volley of arrows, all of which were deflected as if an invisible shield was sitting around her. The Picts stopped astonished but also frightened at this. For they had heard of the warrior princess from the south who could slay thousands with a single word and now they had seen her magic and in the twilight it scared them.

She stepped towards them until she was in earshot then speaking in perfect Pictish said: "I promise you that I shall not harm you. I ask that you sit with me and listen to me and then I shall go north to find more of your people to talk to."

"Join us and fight with us" they replied "For you are mighty and we would spread your word not only in Caledonia but also in Hibernia" but she shook her head then offered:

"I cannot fight for you for I offer the same to everyone. Once I fought for my Master, now I offer his peace. My Master offers everyone Eternal Life if they will listen to his words. It is the gift of Eternal Life I offer you and which you can take to your people here and in Hibernia."

"Tell us more" they said intrigued and she beckoned towards the bank much further down than the traps Longinus had laid, then sitting on the grass encircled by them she told the story of Iesus' life from his birth to the coming of The Comforter. They were most interested in the gifts of the Spirit and when they heard how the Spirit had filled Maria and sent her running across mountains they asked how they could have the same power.

"It is not my power but God's power focused through you and me. We become God's Instrument to do His Will."

"We understand. We serve God and are given his power, his gifts, to accomplish his challenges and his quests" they replied and Maria smiled in joy at their reply then asked: "How is it you understand my Master's words so easily and so correctly? Most have struggled with the idea of being God's Instrument yet you have no difficulty in recognising what is meant."

They smiled in turn, welcoming her compliment then ventured: "Perhaps it is as warriors that we have come to realise life is full of challenges but also very fragile unless you have the protection of God and do His Will. Also, we have stories and legends of heroes … and heroines" they added quickly "… who go on quests with weapons or artefacts such as magical rings, amulets and broaches to do God's work. We sing of such legends every night and all of us wish that one day we could do the same."

"Tell me of your legends for I love stories then I shall tell you some of mine" Maria asked and they all nodded in agreement, proposing a minor amendment: "Tell us the stories of your own life and your adventures. For the telling of these we will be welcomed in every one of our war bands" at which she blushed and they laughed, explaining themselves by saying: "We were told that if we met you you would seem weak when you are strong; that you have eyes that showed you do not fear death or torture; and that you are humble. We have seen that all three are the truth. Maria the Magdalan, we welcome and honour you."

Sir Galahaidra chose that moment to burst through the trees like a fire breathing demon, the Holy Lance held in his hands shooting red and gold flames before him to lighten up the heavens and the glade through which the stream ran; to burn away the snow from the tops of the trees around them and shouting: "They come!"

The Picts around her stood in terror and might have turned on Maria but she had looked at the knight and frowned then spoken sternly in both Pictish and Aramaic: "Galahaidra. Put the lance down and behave, these are my friends!" The knight gulped and as he did so the flame died back. "Friends?" he queried and when she nodded he asked with a trace of annoyance and some frustration: "How do you do this? I thought I would need to rescue you yet here you are sitting and chatting!"

Maria was delighted to translate what Galahaidra had said to her new friends and they laughed then all agreed that he should sit with them and tell of the battles he had been in. When they heard he had been an assassin but now was a Christian Knight they were all enthralled and every one of them wanted to join the *Order of the Risen Christ.* Maria was honest with them as always:

"It is hard. It is not a measure of courage but of 'worthiness'. The number of places is limited to seventy two. I think that some of you might be successful but I can never tell who will be selected and who will not. The places are open to all around the world including yourselfs. But the table will seek those who care, who love, who are humble yet fearless and who will fight for good, defend the vulnerable yet seek never to kill if they can. Above all it is an Order where its members have dedicated their lives to my Master."

"How can we be tested?"

"There is a celebration, a vigil and a mission. I will knight any and all who are successful in having something we call *the Grael Vision*. You kneel in prayer before an altar which holds the four of the six most sacred symbols of our faith; one of which you have seen flaming in Galahaidra's hands" and at that they whispered to each other, recognising the power of these artefacts whilst Maria continued:

"Those granted the vision become *Knights of the Order of the Risen Christ* and their name is written by God on the Round Table of our Order. I suggest that we invite as many of your people as possible for amongst your warriors I do not doubt that there shall be heroes who will join our Order and be welcomed by God."

"Tell us about the gifts. Must we join the Order to possess the gifts that you have? Any tribe would honour someone with your powers."

"The honour is God's and not Man's. The gifts are God's to give but can be given to anyone. I was a poor orphan with no family and no status yet God gave me his gifts. Thousands have been granted God's gifts. All you must do is break bread with each other and remember my Master as you do. All you must be is pure in your faith, believing in my Master, loving God and each other."

"Will you break bread with us?"

"Yes but I would wish to do so for all of your war band if you could make that happen. Then one of the Picts stood and bowed then offered Maria his sword.

"I, MacAllan, chief of the Pangallis kindred, do swear to you that you and your comrades are safe in the company of my tribe and that we would be honoured if you would break bread with us."

Maria lifted the blade to her lips and kissed it then passed it back to MacAllan saying: "May this blade always do good, protecting and serving its master, never to break, always to ring true" at which it was the chief's turn to blush and then he roared and shouted for the distant shadows to hear: "This lady is a Pict. I formally adopt her under the protection of my tribe. She is the Magdalan and I take the name 'Magda' in her honour."

"My lord, will other tribes come if you call?" Maria asked hoping against all hope and so was overjoyed at his response:

"Stay with my tribe one week and by the end representatives of every tribe from the west and north coasts of Caledonia to here in the middle of the Cairngorns will have gathered at our tribal centre, come to hear you and to see you test our worthiness" then with a glint of humour in his eyes he whispered in Maria's ear: "Your companions can come out from where they are hiding now" and she fell back with laughter then hugged his arm before sending Galahaidra off to fetch them.

"Where is she?" Longinus almost screamed in fury then added "And what are you doing here?"

"We are all under the protection of the chief Lord Magda MacAllan of the Pangallis kith and kindred. We have been invited to stay the week whilst MacAllan invites the other tribes to join us. And I thought the plan was for me to catch up with you?"

"She is alive?" Longinus asked in astonishment and Galahaidra nodded then added mischievously just as Craedech joined them: "The chief has taken a real shine to her. They have hugged already" and the stoney face on both of his companions made him roar with laughter.

Ninian recognising his voice ran across in the dark and silenced the young knight with a kiss then held him in her arms, her head resting on his right shoulder, with a gleam of possessiveness in her emerald green eyes that Iosephus recognised and remembered from his own partnership with his long-dead wife.

"Ninian just saved your life from my wrath" Craedech muttered in Galahaidra's hearing to which Ninian replied "And Maria just saved all of our lives."

Although dark, the chief was able to lead the war party and their new comrades through deep and distant paths, winding tracks, narrow streams and gullies, hidden valleys and mountain passes to his tribal capital in a cavern beneath the purple tinted mountains and mauve coloured snow, always in the half light of a crimson cold sun or silvery flamed moon, the natural catacombs beneath the ground containing statues, columns, paths, rivers and lakes made from limestone stalagnites and stalagmites, green and glistening in candlelight; many archways and steps or figures carved carefully over the centuries with skill and attention, love and respect into the limestone by Man and Nature in artistic partnership.

They crossed one black watered but crystal clear lake by boat, rowed by some of the warriors and which they beached then tied up on the far bank. They walked under two waterfalls until they came to the tribe's capital carved and cut as terraces, chambers and halls into the granite beneath the limestone, made warm by the constant heat of the naked flame, softened by woollen rugs and wall-hangings, windows opening onto the many balconies, patios and levels created by both soft stone and hungry rivers that had once gradually eroded away the limestone to make smooth paths but which rivers now made their grand descent as waterfalls into the lake.

"My home" Magda whispered to Maria whom he had escorted as his Queen, telling her of the history of his tribe and how all the Pictish tribes gave honour to the King beyond the Sea, Pedrus, fighting for his honour and to reclaim his kingdom, lost to the expansion of the Angles from the lands of the Bight of Heligos. As they walked through the many cathedral-like halls and chambers, he pointed out to the girl's delight the statuary of mythical creatures: dragons and gryphon, unicorns, night mares and Pegasae, Koaxl and Roc, all of which she greeted as a child with both glee and a momentary frisson of terror.

Under MacAllan's watchful and increasingly appreciative eye, Maria stopped to greet every child with a hug or listened to their innocent questions, to tell them of her life and most recent adventures, their mothers as anxious as their inquisitive offspring to listen to Maria, all attracted to her as the butterfly senses the buddleia: for she was the warrior princess who was God's messenger and had the power to heal. All were both astonished and flattered that she spoke with fluency and in poetry in their own language; her softly spoken words were a song that many would sing for centuries after her visit, Maria's life as a desert Queen becoming part of the verbal tradition of their tribe.

"Will your Master demand that I serve Him and not my King?" MacAllan dared to ask, already charmed by the girl and fearful to fall out of her grace, not yet realising that he could never do so for already she loved him and his people.

"My Master was asked once: 'How can you serve two Masters? Should I obey the law of the High Priest Caiaphas yet still pay my taxes to Caesar?'

The question was posed by a sicariot, an assassin, who wanted my Master to commit to revolt against Rome. So Iesus asked for a denarius and posed a question to all gathered that day: 'Do you pay your taxes in such coins?'

'Yes' the sicariot replied and begrudgingly continued: 'and I must exchange my money or coins for Roman coins and do so on the tables before the Temple, paying the Sanhedrin a fee, a percentage each time I do.'

Then turning the coin over to show the head of Tiberius Caesar, Iesus showed it to the sicariot and the crowds saying: "This belongs to Caesar. Give to Caesar what belongs to Caesar and to God what belongs to God."

My Master's kingdom is Paradise and not in this world. My Master supports the need for human leadership on Earth but my faith is not about creating new kingdoms on Earth. My Master seeks the eternal kingdom in the next life.

So follow your King unless the path he takes leads you away from Eternal Life through damaging your belief in God and your soul."

"How might my King damage my soul?" MacAllan asked confused and Maria replied as always without thought but rather remembering as a waking dream her Master and the Angels standing before her, helping her to answer the same question:

"Once King Herod of my home country of Iudaea feared that a new King had been born in a nearby village who would one day rule in Herod's place. Herod ordered all of his soldiers to ride into every village in his kingdom and kill 'all newborn children'.

Some soldiers killed every child they found not bothering to check for parentage or age. Others examined every child and questioned every parent and killed only those newly born *since* the King's Order had been issued. Some pretended to kill the newborns but in reality hid the infants or sent them away to escape with their parents. A fourth group of soldiers hunted down those newborns that had been allowed to escape and slew them then cut off the hands of the soldiers who had helped the infants to live. The final group refused to obey the King and were executed by him, dying defiantly.

Which soldiers followed their King, which followed my Master and who followed neither?"

"The first, second and fourth group followed neither. The third and fifth group followed your Master" those listening replied after much discussion amongst themselves whilst MacAllan looked on appreciating how his men had already adopted Maria as one of their own and realising that this was her true magic. Maria grinned and nodded in agreement then asked:

"Why did none of the soldiers do their King's will?"

That silenced them until finally one young warrior spoke up hesitantly:

"Because they all knew that what was being asked of them was wrong?"

Maria bent forward and kissed the seated warrior on the brow then whispered for all to hear: "This man shows wisdom and courage. He would have been in the third or fifth group had he been in Iudaea when my Master was born and be honoured by my Master's Angels for his actions."

Then she turned to the young warrior and said before all in the chamber in which they were sitting in a circle on the floor of soft silver sand:

"Well done for you are right. They knew that the King's Order was wrong. So it is today and forever more. Follow your King but not if his Order is wrong *to you*. It is irrelevant if the Order is wrong to me or right to your colleague. It is the promptings of your own heart and soul against which you shall be judged by my Master."

Those around the young warrior clapped him on the back for getting the answer right and the warrior blushed whilst inside he was delighted to have received the praise of the Magdalan. MacAllan nodded in understanding then still he questioned Maria asking: "How does the Master grant you your powers … for our arrows could not touch you yet this is no power of the Spirit?"

It was Maria's turn to nod once more in agreement and say: "My lord chief you are very wise and what you say is true. My Master resides in me, in my heart. When I pray he often answers to help me for he wants his mission to succeed. He has saved me from drowning and from fire, from being flayed, scourged and tortured on the rack. I carry the scars of some of those for life but I do so with pride for it shows my service of the Lord. One thing I will say and it is no secret yet people forget it: at the heart of my faith is to love God and to love all men and women."

"So you love me?" he asked surprised to which Maria replied without hesitation:

"Yes of course and I am proud of the way your tribe has befriended us. You have shown us much love also."

"I think I am going to enjoy this week in your company my little princess. Will your Prince mind?"

"That I show my love for those I meet? I hope not or else he will be cross all of the time and that shall make me laugh."

"Has anyone told you that you are 'special'? Join me at my table when we feast tonight" but Maria shook her head saying: "I am not special. Different, unique but so is everyone made by God. As for dinner, I am taught to sit at the foot of the Table and I enjoy so doing for then you meet the poor, the hard-working civil servants, the meek and humble, from all of whom I learn so much."

"I think you are special but I do not wish to argue with you. Will you sit with me if we do not sit at the head of my table?"

"Why yes. I would be honoured."

"Good he said for my table is *round* and has no head. I was delighted to hear your Order has a Round Table."

"I wish with all my heart that you are granted *the Grael Vision* for you are noble, courteous and wise. I will gladly sit next to you if you can bear my company."

"Bless you" he replied "and pray for me as I shall pray for others! Now do you mind if I sit Sir Galahaidra and Sir Longinus near us as we all want to hear about Longinus' art of warfare and Galahaidra's exploits in battle. My men are still returning from the merry dance those two led us."

"O not more boring talk of war!" Maria exclaimed with a mischievous gleam in her eye and a wicked grin. It took a couple of seconds for MacAllan to realise he was being teased, something that happened rarely. When he did then he relaxed in her company: she was not afraid of him, also loved and respected him and was quite prepared to tease him. Like many before him he was amazed at her youth, frailty and fragility, beauty, fearlessness and loving spirit. Yet another warrior came under her spell and little did she know it but the whole tribe watched her at dinner that evening and became enchanted as she roamed the table bending forwards to introduce herself, to contribute her simple wisdom to each conversation and give everyone present a little piece of herself and her 'magic'.

Her reputation had been further enhanced when she had stood outside the cavern and whistled. A few minutes later Epona followed by five Arab mares and her family of four wild boars trotted into the cavern and came up to greet her. The chief could not take his eyes off Epona and when Maria said the stallion belonged to her, he was astonished that such a little girl could ride such a tall and proud stallion. Then Maria's wild boar decided to have a mock fight with some of the children, rounding them up whilst they squealed and ran away.

"Do you have dogs?" Maria asked suddenly looking around just in case.

"Are you frightened of dogs?" he asked surprised and she laughed then shook her head:

"Not I. I love them to bits. However my family of tusked reprobates over there would chase them away causing chaos. When I visited the King of the Deceanglii at his Hall and home in Talbot, every Lord possessed a greyhound. Alas, even though my boars had promised me they would behave as soon as my family was let in the Hall they chased all of the dogs away then ate the scraps the hounds had been eating. I was mortified."

Tears of laughter streamed down his eyes as the chief pictured the chaos. Then Galahaidra told the chief about her rescue of him when The Valiant was sinking and went on to tell of his rescue of her when facing death at the hands of King Col and how later he had also rescued her from death at the hands of Eorl Edgthbert of Humberside. Finally he finished with the tale of her challenge in the Court of the Iceni and to win Epona, the conversions of Jaerid and the Round Table sitting proudly in the kingdom of the Atrebates (Maria had sent it to her father Godric to guard) at the Castle of Wyn. All who heard had also seen the honest fearlessness in the clear blue of her eyes and now honoured her silently for her courage in the face of torture and death or when saving the lives of others.

Longinus' defeat of the Dacian Army on the banks of the River Humber also fascinated the Picts for they had fought against the Dacians often and lost whenever they had faced ten thousand or more, never being able to muster the numbers needed to attain victory. To hear that Longinus was outnumbered twenty one thousands to fourteen thousands suddenly gave them renewed hope.

“Is there no chance of peace between you?” Maria asked in a small voice expecting an angry response. Instead the chief smiled at her and said “Once we fished the seas over which we now fight and lived in the lands on the west coast. Dacia created itself by pushing out its boundaries and forcing into exile or slaying our people on our coast then called the land their own. Your Iesus, your Messiah came to free the oppressed and the refugee. He came to save my people.”

“I believe that also. Yet cannot some way be found to do so without killing?”

“I could ask you the same question” at which Maria’s face blushed and tears of distress slowly fell upon her cheeks. “Were many harmed by us?” she asked in fear of the answer.

“We lost thirteen good men to Galahaidra and your Longinus’ traps, two of whom carry terrible injuries and barely live. My men would welcome learning about the different traps Longinus laid and his skill in setting false trails.”

“Give me the names of the fallen and I shall pray for them and visit their families. I shall ask my Master to set them on the path to the Gates of Paradise if indeed they are not already there as a reward for doing good deeds in their lives. Take me to see the wounded that I might alieviate their suffering, please” and she begged with her hands and her eyes, pleading to prevent the death toll from rising any further.

“Come then” said the chief and escorted her to the tribe’s House of Healing then left her to meet the families of the injured men; the warriors had lost consciousness many hours earlier. As she entered the chamber, the tribe’s shaman stood in the corner of a darkened room and was mumbling in a strange language which sounded to Maria’s untrained ears to be jibberish. The old man would punctuate his mumblings by throwing ash and occasionally strips of some sort of silvery metal that he would set alight to spark and flame as they fell to earth: silver, blue, red and gold fire.

Around the tressle beds of two young men stood their family. Each wounded warrior was married and both men had children: toddlers, infants and babes in arms. Their young wives wept as did their mothers. Their fathers were dead, already the victims of war and one had lost both brothers; the other was an only child.

As Maria approached, the shaman cursed her and the mothers glared at her in anger. She understood and quietly spoke to the room in general, asking: "Can I see what help I can offer?"

"You have done enough" spat the shaman but Maria shook her head then said to the two wives: "May I try? I shall pray. No more than that. But if my prayers are answered then perhaps we may persuade God to aid us?"

"Your God is a fraud" the shaman intervened, determined to challenge Maria who turned towards him and bowing asked:

"Father" she said humbly. "There is only one God but surely we both hope our prayers shall be heard?"

"These men have both lost legs and one has lost an arm. Both are dying as they bleed to death. Can your magic cure the harm you have done?" he replied both scornful and sarcastic.

Maria turned to the young mens' families and apologised:

"Forgive me for arguing in front of you. You do not need to hear us argue in this way. Please let me pray over your husbands; I shall not take long and you can stay as I do so then I shall leave" at which the wives nodded in response unable to speak but attracted to Maria's honesty and humility, also her age for they had been not much older when they had both married their young warriors.

Maria closed her eyes and went in search of her Master. He was waiting for her and they both stood on the tall peak of Mount Ararat looking across Media, the Arabian desert and out towards the Caspian Sea. "My lord" Maria greeted him, kneeling in homage then kissing his hand as he held it out to her. When she saw the wounds from his crucifixion, she wept openly and without restraint then asked: "Can no-one heal your wounds?"

"They are part of me and remind everyone of my ultimate achievement" he replied. "I do not need for them to be healed."

"Should I ignore your wounds, lord?" and then the young girl bowed her head in sorrow whispering as much to herself as admitting to her Master: "Alas, I cannot ignore them and the harm they represent. So I ask, no I beg to be allowed to wash away your blood and bathe you in my love."

Her Master laughed with joy and was delighted once more and openly by her adoration of Him then said: "I welcome your care and believe me when I say that your love and attention remove my pain yet my wounds shall never heal."

Maria took his hands in hers and gently washed away the dried blood with her soft and gentle tears then pictured the finest and freshest honey which appeared as if by magic on a side table besides them both. She spread the honey carefully wherever the skin had yet to heal as a cool salve to remove any irritation. Finally, she kissed his wounds before covering them with a fresh linen bandage and praying that God would remove any pain he felt and do so for her sake: to take away her own pain at the sight of his suffering. At which her Master retrieved his hands then smiled down at her and asked:

"Can I do anything for you Maria?" she blushed before finding the courage to say:

"Master! You are the One God, the Creator, capable of any and all healing. I am about to pray for the healing of two young men. I ask of your mercy that you listen to my prayer and answer it as you see fit. May Thine Will be Done."

And she was standing once more in the chamber of the House of Healing. "Let there be light" she whispered and the candles in the candelabra gutted, flickered then came to life whilst a gentle breeze blew away the cobwebs and the dark smoke of the shaman's 'magic' then swallowed the gloom in the room. From nowhere came sunlight to turn the room to burnished gold, the limestone gleaming as it reflected the light within the room. The faces of the women and young children came to glorious life, the stain of their tears washed away, burning with an inner flame of belief and hope. Maria spoke softly into the stunned silence that had followed the transformation in the room

"Please feel free to repeat the words I say. I speak no spell and offer no magic. Rather we pray to God: we ask God for His healing power. Collectively our prayers will be more powerful than if I pray alone" and the two families nodded in understanding.

"Father
These men carry great harm.
We wish with our hearts and souls
For them to be healed
They are good sons, husbands and fathers
Return their lost limbs
Remove all infection
Make them hale and hearty
That they may love their families
As we shall always love you
Thy Will be Done!"

Maria had her eyes closed and without noticing had knelt in supplication, her tears flowing freely, in private subconsciously confessing that these men had been injured in defence of her and that she sincerely wished this had never happened. She heard the gasps and the shaman's cry: "This is some trickery" but then even he was brought to believe as both men opened their eyes and awoke to find their limbs had returned, their wounds were healed, all sign of blood loss and infection had departed. They both sat up and hugged their weeping families and as they rejoiced in God's miracle, Maria retired silently from the chamber to praise and thank God in private, her song of praise reflecting her mind, heart and soul's joy and delight in the miracle that God had just performed.

She thought she had escaped all attention but then heard hurried footsteps behind her and turned slowly to see the shaman, a look of bewilderment in his eyes.

"I have been taught to use trickery; to persuade people that there is hope; to take credit when that hope is realised; to talk of the wrong and evil actions of patients for which their illness, disability and death are just punishment: but never to actually heal and with no conversation with God. Until today I thought that this was all that man could achieve. But now …" and he broke off, humbly, overcome with the possibilities that now were opened by the act of healing he had observed. Maria offered him the chance to believe in One God:

"Stand next to me when I break bread this evening. It is an act of devotion that God himself showed us and how he asks to be remembered. I would be honoured to share this celebration with you."

"You are forgiving and generous. So much has been said of you that I refused to believe but now my eyes have been opened. Thank you" and Maria smiled then wagged a finger gently and advised him:

"Be grateful to my Master not me. It is God who has opened both of our eyes to his healing power, mercy and compassion. Will you join me as your lord and chief shows me around your settlement here? And I shall tell you of the life and ministry of my Master, the one and only, all-powerful God."

MacAllan and a few of the warriors Maria had met earlier joined them and Maria spent the rest of the evening being shown those parts of the sculpted caverns she had not already seen, punctuating the many hugs, kisses and much laughter she had in the company of children (whose mothers admitted their offspring had waited up, often past their bedtime to see the 'warrior princess'), with tales and stories from her Master's life, death, resurrection and ascension. The shaman's name was Actaeon and he remained by the girl's side, clearly having adopted her.

It came to late evening and Maria found a quiet room. Then joined by MacAllan; six of the warriors whom had become her informal bodyguard, her praetorians (and done so willingly out of love for the young girl), Actaeon and her companions she led them all in a service in celebration of God, showing Actaeon who stood besides her jointly presiding over the celebration, the simple task of breaking the bread and asking him to repeat the words and actions of the act of consecration. Together they held up the bread and encouraged all in the room to do the same as they said: "This is Me; the real Me. Take my bread, eat it and do this remembering me." At the end of the service Actaeon asked to become a Christian and so Maria asked him three questions:

"Do you believe in one God?"

Actaeon nodded; his eyes aflame with joy as he did so.

"Will you love God and love Man?"

Again the man nodded filled almost to bursting with the power of his devotion. So Maria asked her final question:

"Will you break bread in memory of God asking your fellow Picts of Pengallis to join with you?"

"Yes, Maria, I will do so with all my heart and soul."

"You are a Christian" and as Maria said these words she held out her hands and laid them on Actaeon's head at which tongues of flame danced on his head and before his eyes. He was filled with God's Spirit and looked at Maria with awe then hurried to the House of Healing, grasping Maria's hand and dragging her in his wake. Arriving at the set of chambers that were used for healing, six of the chambers were occupied with people suffering from breathing problems, weak hearts or one child who had fallen.

The former shaman prayed over each then watched in wonder as every one was healed through his prayers and the gift of healing granted by God's Spirit. "Thank you" the old man said in tears. "This has been my life's and heart's desire fulfilled through the grace of your Master."

"He is our Master now" and Maria kissed him on both cheeks then headed back into the maze of corridors to find the large subterranean Hall that was her companions' and her sleeping quarters for the night.

As the company went to retire, the young man whom Maria had singled out for praise at his answer to her question concerning Herod's murder of the Innocents approached her and shyly asked:

"Maria, my good lady, my name is Kenneth of the kindred of Kenneth of Dungallan. You have taught us that our Master escaped King Herod because his father took him to safety having been warned by the three wise men and Angels. But what of you?" and he went silent at her brief look of unfathomable silence and sorrow.

"I was too young to be alive at the time yet the atrocity touched all of our lives in the town I call home. My father lost his wife and their son and daughter, my brother and sister had they lived. His first wife was slain trying to prevent the death of her infants. My father did not marry for another twelve years such was his grief. Eventually, he married a much younger girl, of about my age, and a year later they had me. I was four when both of my parents contracted a fever and died."

"I shall pray for you all" he whispered and was gone.

That night the company all retired to a Great Chamber cut into the stone with a sanded floor on which they placed their four bed rolls and blankets then Maria quickly popped her head out of the doorway, pushing back the curtain to ask the sentry on guard there: "We are two short on bed rolls and blankets and our wicked men have left we ladies without. Could you find some for us?"

"Yes maam" he replied with a grin as he thought of the terrible consequences had he not. Then returning to the chamber Maria stood defiantly in the centre of the room, remembering the horrors of losing her bed roll and blanket the previous night and in her most strident commanding voice, just louder than the winds' whisper, told all in the chamber: "I am not getting undressed or going to bed until our bed rolls and blankets have arrived."

"Well I was quite happy with last night's arrangements" said Ninian in a huff and Galahaidra hid his head and his embarassment under his own blanket. The blankets arrived in moments, the men of this underground City all gallantly coming to Maria's rescue. The two girls then retired to the corner of the chamber and changed under their blankets. Ninian waited until Maria was asleep stood up with her blanket wrapped around her, walked across to where Galahaidra was fast asleep and kicked him until he had woken up then lay down next to him and gradually slid under his blanket. "Just warming up" she whispered and nibbled his ear.

"I am a young man and a Knight of our most Christian Order" he replied frostily.

"Well I am not that old either" she replied kicking him on the shins and ignoring him as he went "Ouch that hurt!" as she continued: "And if you are a Christian Knight then it is your responsibility to have more like you!"

She loved it when he blushed and he was incredibly handsome so she was certain he was the right man for her. She just had to cut through all these terrible taboos he had picked up from his previous faith as a fanatical Jew.

Her previous pagan faith had taught her that a woman's role was to have as many children with as many sexual partners as possible. Ninian had been faithful to her husband whom by some miracle she loved to the abandonment of her heart and so kept to one sexual partner for the five years of their marriage. Her child had prospered from having two parents who lived together with him and who loved him dearly. The death of her husband and son had been a terrible loss and she had mourned so deeply then realised that there were still many years ahead of her, she was only nineteen after all as she had married at fourteen. She could have children again; she just needed to find the right man.

The moment she had seen Galahaidra she had known that he was taking her heart with him as he journeyed north and so had followed him and would do so as the saying goes: 'To the ends of the Earth'. The problem is that he was endearingly coy and kept ignoring her. So she decided to take the lead and it was proving very hard work indeed. She decided to play hard:

"Do you not find me attractive?"

This was the fatal question that seals every relationship between man and woman because there is only one answer and it has to be 'Yes' (that is unless you enjoy a poke in the eye and a kick in the lower regions). Galahaidra gulped, blushed then nodded his head at which Ninian kissed him and said

"Thank you. I think you are an incredibly good looking and handsome man. Will you hold me like you did last night?"

"You were cold and I was warming you up" Galahiadra replied showing he was still resisting the inevitable. Ninian smiled then retorted "I need warming up now" and slid across on top of him.

"You are not wearing any clothes" he gasped in shock and she kissed him before he could say any more absurd things then reminded him: "It was the same last night and all my night clothes were left behind at our camp. You will have to cover me. Roll over and hug me."

"Do I have to?" he asked not being the remotest bit gallant and definitely letting the side down for any knights out there who would have known their duty by now.

"No" our lady replied "for I can kiss you just as well where you are" and to demonstrate the truth of this she kissed him until he had to open his mouth to breath then her tongue entered his mouth and she sucked the air out of his lungs until dizzy with the love of her he fell limp in her arms.

"Now you can breathe" she whispered "but every breath will not be yours but ours. For we are bound together with a knot that no-one can cut or separate. O Galahaidra, please love me."

How could he resist? For years his every moment had been spent as a contract killer, no friends, family or home. He had then fallen in love with someone he had promised to defend even at cost of his own life, whom had then complicated matters by saving his life with a kiss. But she had given her heart to a Prince yet made him the first ever Christian Knight.

He had promised to be pure, to be chaste yet he knew that Maria supported the idea of family even though she had been an orphan … actually no-one had ever asked her what were her beliefs about family at any of her sermons or question and answer sessions. Suddenly he sat up, his eyes otherwise than where they should be looking. Ninian fell off him, landing on her backside and glared at him, seriously miffed now. But he compounded his error by not noticing. He was deep in thought and Ninian recognised the look, sighed in resignation and rolled over then went to go to sleep.

Galahaidra pinched her then said "Don't you dare. We have a lot of talking to do. And I am not going to make love to you tonight … but tomorrow is a definite possibility depending on what Maria says."

"O Great. We have to ask her permission now?" Ninian growled.

"No" he laughed "But we do need to ask her something in the morning."

"Well what do you want to talk about?"

"We could start with the simple things" he suggested grinning "like where do we get married and who gives you away? Longinus is my best man of course! Who were our parents, how many children do you want, where are we going to live and what are we going to do for a living? I don't really know much about you except that you lost your husband and four year old son in a terrible boating accident and I would gladly wish that awful day away if not for the very simplest of facts that I love you and all that is stopping me from making love is that I want to do this right and I do not want to be the substitute for the man you really love. I want you to love *me*."

"O my" Ninian said and looked at him mistily, the look in her eyes making it clear that her love was totally genuine. And so they talked and time passed so fast that it was dawn before they had even noticed. Finally, she shivered with the cold for the first time and he carefully covered her with his blanket and dared to steal a kiss on the nape of her neck.

She gasped then watched in delight as her handsome man stood in his white linen robe, put on his leather under garment, tightened the leather laces, pulled on his leather riding boots lacing these up also, dropped his chain mail hauberk over his head, tied it tight around the waist with his leather belt, froggings and scabbard, put on his gorget and chain guard, sheathed his sword in his scabbard then finally turned to look at Ninian before placing his helmet on his head, his lance in its holster across his back and his shield hanging across his left arm.

"Why?" She asked intrigued and he immediately understood what was behind her question.

"Why do I dress for war? We have found peace with the Gael and won the respect of the Picts but the Caledonii and the Vicing still lie out there in the furthest north-east, the Hebrides and Thule where we hope to find Longinus' niece. Maria cannot hope to defeat them, but an Army of Picts with Longinus' leadership can; add in the troops that are on board Iosephus' ships carrying the Sacred Artefacts – and we will be invincible."

Ninian covered her face in her hands, the horror of Galahaidra's description of the war he was committing the Christians to and his vision for the Army he was mustering was tearing at her loving heart. She tried to argue with her love but his voice spoke only of his determination. Inspired by the reception he had received in Dacia, Deceangli and from the Picts, he knew that he was respected as a Christian warrior and champion, a victor of battles, the leader of a Christian Army that had defeated Dacia and could defeat any army sent against it if it would follow its leader. Longinus would command but Sir Galahaidra would be the inspiration for a generation of young Christians seeking redemption through fighting for God.

Ninian cried as she saw the future, her gift of prophecy seeing the violence of war replacing Maria's gentler message of a God who blessed peacemakers.

"My love" she pleaded "Did not our Master speak to all of your company on the night Maria rode to Dacia to tell you that we should seek peace and not war? Did Maria not rescue us from a terrible fate at the hands of the Picts with her message of peace? Did she not do the same with the Dacia, Deceangli and when you met the Gael at the Bridge of Allan? Surely we must give her a chance to do the same with the Caledonii and the Vicing?"

Galahaidra removed his helmet so that Ninian could see the profound sadness in his eyes for he also had been given the gift of prophecy but like the humble and kindly knight Perseus before him, he was frightened of using his gift, in many ways feeling unworthy to have such a gift from God. His desire to defeat the Pagans in battle was part of his intent to vindicate himself for the evil of his days as an assassin and contract killer, but using his talents in the art and craft of war in which he felt more confident.

"I was the only one of the company not visited that night but I have seen a vision of Maria slain at the hands of the Vicing: Maria being tortured most horribly and being flung to the depths of the North Sea chained to a broken mast. I would save her from that fate."

Ninian shook her head then stood and slowly walked over to her man, stroked his cheek before holding him in her arms as she said:

"O my dear love. How wrong you are. I would gladly die for our Master as would Maria. We would both gain that ultimate miracle: the eternal loving adoration of God in Paradise."

Then the tears flowed fast and freely as Galahaidra could not bear to stand by whilst the two women he loved more than his own life were slain in terrifying pain with him watching on helplessly. He knelt before Ninian and begged that she stay in the safety of the company of the Picts or return to the security of her homestead in Milnathort. He offered to guard her and be her guide if only she would agree to stay safe but the young lady shook her head. Even to become the partner of Galahaidra she would not surrender her mission that had been given to her by the Master …

… Suddenly they both stood before the Master in a room stripped of all furniture and furnishings, glowing brilliant white, almost dazzlingly so and the Master was holding their hands together with his own and smiling at them as he did so. They were amazed to *both* be in his presence. Maria had tried to explain such contemplative prayer and spoken of Gisella's gift from the Spirit that was to bring many Christians simultaeneously into communion with God and each other, but only now did they understand and appreciate the wonder of such prayer.

"Though neither of you ever met me in life yet you Galahaidra will recognise me from your *Grael Vision*, whilst your faith, Ninian is as great as anyone's I have ever seen so if I say that I am God you believe me without doubt. Know this: that your love for each other honours me. If you must set aside other ambitions to be as one then I will still be pleased. It will be enough that you show God's grace by loving God, living together and loving each other."

Ninian knelt and hung on to both her Master's hand and that of her lover then hesitantly asked Iesus:

"My lord and my Master. I understand that you can turn whatever we do to good. If I abandon my mission for love of this man, you will still find a way to make my mission happen. Yet what of me and my self-respect? I wish to complete your mission as my gift for you; my way of thanking you for your gift of eternal life for my dead husband and son. I will feel that I have failed if I cannot achieve what is the destiny you granted to me."

"You must find a way to do both" was the Master's adamantine reply "To love each other and to achieve your mission."

Then to Galahaidra he said: "You are a warrior born to protect the vulnerable, the weak, those who are threatened. You are gifted with the ability to fight that is unsurpassed. You are my pure knight and I suspect that had I been guarded by you on the night of my arrest in Gethsemane you would have seen off my captors and saved me from crucifixion. Yet sometimes the right thing is that those you protect are left to fend for themselves.

I do not condemn all soldiers and warriors: one of my most devout followers is the Centurion Cornelius whilst the Centurion Longinus serves me and I have you to defend my faith and my faithful. All I ask is that you exercise **restraint** and limit your killing to the absolute minimum. Turn the other cheek even though this damages your pride in being unbeatable.

So I command you: protect my Ninian in the mission she has been given and ensure your prophecy never comes to be! But do so without meaningless and unnecessary killing."

"What is her mission, lord?" Galahaidra asked finally finding his voice.

"*The conversion of Caledonia*. But be not afraid if it shall take a hundred years or more. Ninian shall be the first to meet many of the communities that shall in time be our most devout followers and take my faith and my message to people around the world."

And then they were back in the chamber with their companions asleep around them and the last glow of the embers in the fire setting their eyes aflame. Ninian was the first to speak:

"Well that certainly told us" she said and Galahaidra roared with laughter and had to be shushed by his love who did not wish for the rest of the company to be awakened so early. "Wear your armour" she spoke fair to the young knight "for you will need it to protect *me*."

"What of Maria?" Galahaidra asked and Ninian replied more sombrely: "She follows her own stars and must look to the Master to be saved."

"Will my vision become truth?" the knight asked now puzzled and confused at the conflicts between his prophecy and the mission he had just been given by the Master. Ninian knew far more of prophecy and explained:

"All visions of the future are '*may be*'. They may never happen if we seek to stop them or they may happen whatever we do. It is down to us and how we meet the challenges God sets to make our visions become truth or not.

Maria has a vision that sees everyone behave reasonably in response to her request for peace and which conflicts with just about everyone else's prophecies of the future. What she achieves is the impossible and implausible and yet so many of her visions for the future become true because of her absolute trust in God. However, not everyone is reasonable and sometimes she will meet those whose response is violent such as King Col or Eorl Edgthbert or the Sorcerers at Stone Hill."

"I will stand outside and guard you both but I know that my Master respects my intent to kill anyone who threatens you with harm. I am proud to be your guard, Ninian" at which the young lady blushed once more made shy by Galahaidra's obvious love for her whom she had mistakenly thought was indifferent.

As the week unfurled more and more Picts came to hear Maria and sign up for Galahaidra's mission against the Vicing in the northern islands. Iosephus sent word for his marines to beach their ships near the mouth of the Deen and come north-west to meet them. Craedech learnt the sad news that his three hundred comrades in arms had been ambushed by the Pictish war band and slain a few leagues south of where Longinus and he had laid their ambush on the stream. Tens of thousands of Picts came and at least half were converted by both the message and the many miracles from God committed through the instruments of Maria, Ninian, Actaeon and the dozens of Pictish faithful who received the gifts of the Spirit as a reward for their new beliefs.

On the seventh day, Maria held a special celebration of the Eucharist after which she led two dozen of the leaders and most accomplished Pict warriors in vigil with Galahaidra, the four Holy Artefacts laid out on an altar before them. She prayed for every one of them that they be received into the Order but particularly she prayed fervently for MacAllan and for one other young warrior whose faith had already touched her heart. As the early hours of the morning came, a shattered but jubilant MacAllan wondered into her chamber and walked across to hug the young girl in delight.

"The vision I saw was of us both before God in Paradise, the Grael held by you and the Angels who sang rejoicing in our adoration of God. I am converted and do solemnly swear to be faithful and true to God and this Order."

Maria was humbled by his vision but accepted his fealty with joy using the words that she had first used with Galahaidra to bind him to the Order and its commitment to pure service. Three other warriors were also granted a vision: Lotha, Lord of Aer in the Western Isles; Caesta, a Pictish champion and unbeatable with a sword in his hand born on the Island of Skye but whose family had been sheep farmers; and her quiet young warrior, Kenneth of the kindred Kenneth of Dungullan. All four would see their names engraved in the table at Wyn Caister or Wyncaester and three of the Picts were seated close to each other near where the entrance to the table's inner circle could be found, with Sir Caesta sitting near King Casterix. The table would look far less deserted when the Order next met.

Galahaidra asked Ninian why she did not put herself to the test but she declined saying: "My faith needs no more reinforcement than that it has received when the Master spoke to us both. For my faith is already strong. Your Order has Maria and Senna to keep you men from doing anything too rash or foolhardy: two women shall be more than enough to master seventy mere men!" at which brave or foolhardy words she had to run to find refuge, chased by her infuriated knight.

Caledonia: Maria Magdalan's Mission to the Highlands. The Decantae, Taexali, Lugi, Sitinarae, Carini, Carnonaeae, Caledonii and Cornavii

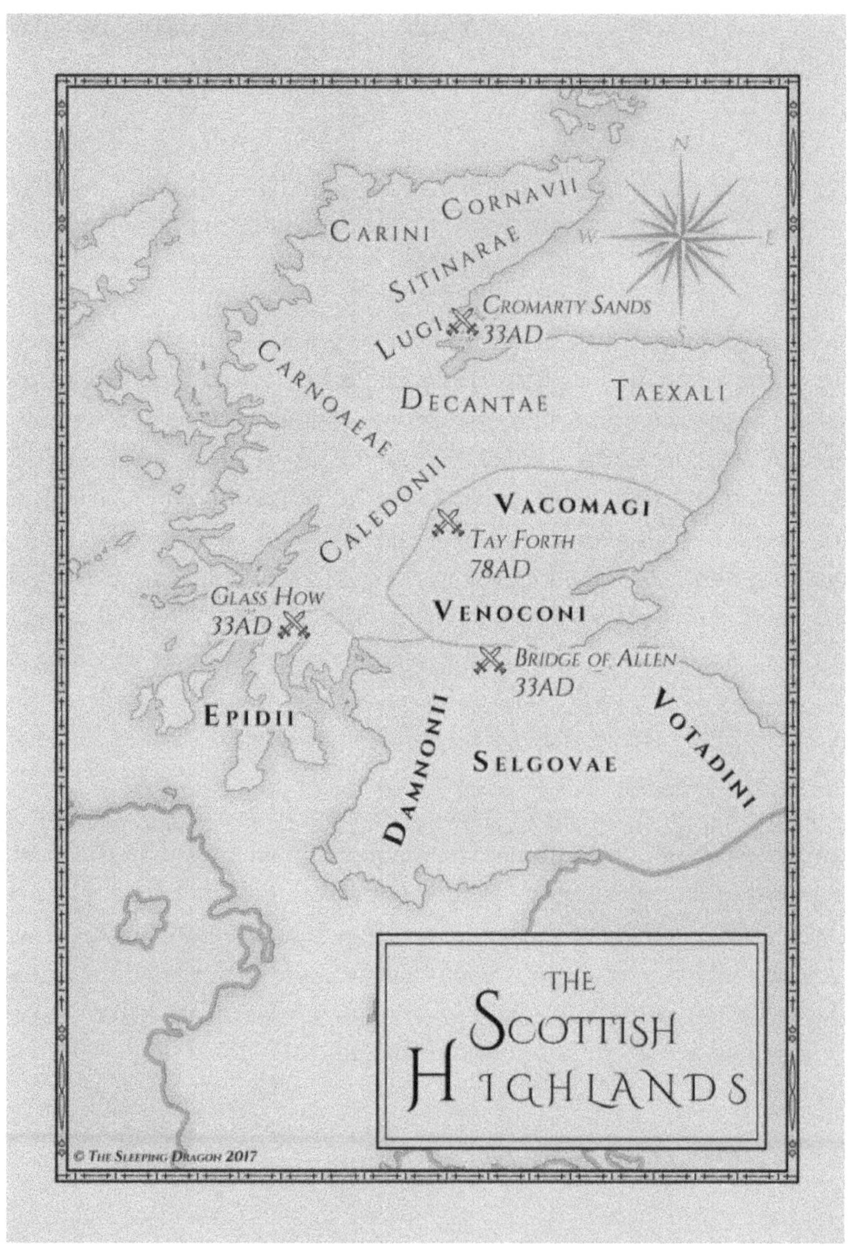

In the early hours of the seventh day since the company had first been invited by Magda MacAllan to stay at his Cairn as guests, the Pictish war leader called a Council of the many chieftains and war band leaders whom had journeyed to see the Magdalan. During that week Pictish war bands from the north and west had arrived each day with news of the rest of Caledonia: the Caledonii were mustering in the west under their King Graimir; the Vicing and Norse people from the lands of the Bigkt and Skaggerak, the Ice lands, Greenland and Scandavia were already rumoured to be at sea and heading to meet Graimir.

"Their objective is the defeat and slaughter of the Picts and Gaels" MacAllan advised the Council solemnly. "They have heard of the arrival of Christ in our midst and seek to defend their Pagan beliefs. There must be war."

In the discussion that followed, both Maria and Ninian begged their comrades to seek peace and to convert the Vicing and Caledonii through mutual respect, tolerance and prayer, but all others present were convinced that the time had come for war ed most vociferously by Sir Galahaidra.

"The Vicing will eat you for their supper" MacAllan had roared "there is no reasoning with them."

Maria and Ninian stood later that same evening on the stone ledge that formed a natural balcony to the cave that formed their bed chamber to watch the sun dip over the distant muirs and munros and looked out sadly at the snow topped crags and mountains of the Cairngorns, Grampians, the Sidlaw to their east, the Lochaber to their south and the Fells of Campsie to their west. Tall and proud giants in dark grey shadow against a deep crimson sky. It looked so tranquil. It was the peace of that moment that gave both girls the determination they needed.

"We must go to the Vicing ourselves" Maria whispered and Ninian nodded. Knowing their mission was the conversion and not the slaughter of the pagans in Caledonia, the two girls decided to risk going alone and unarmed: to pose no threat to any they encountered. They could reach the Vicing long before any Christian army on the march.

Ninian secretly feared Galahaidra's vision of conquest and had decided that the only way she could reconcile her love of the knight, her own mission of peaceful conversion and his desire to fight was to try and persuade the Vicing people to seek peace. Maria was a slave to her usual optimism and belief that people would react reasonably to her Master's offer of reconciliation and universal peace: that good can prevail somehow. Neither of them had any actual plan; and both brought out the recklessness in the other.

So, they excused themselves from Longinus' company by saying they were to be left alone to pray in vigil for the gathering armies. The Centurion had been set to watch over them by the Prince Craedach whom had noticed Maria had grown strangely silent during MacAllan's Council, a sign she was plotting something, and so he had become deeply suspicious. The two ladies packed rapidly and lightly, summoned Epona, Maria's wild boar and took three other horses, then left their quarters in the middle of the night and were heading north on horseback before dawn break.

At first light, Longinus, Galahaidra, Craedech, and Iosephus, wearing their armour that they had been gifted by Godric and had been made by Macsen, were mounted on the best horses in Iosephus' stable and had decided they would ride at the head of the huge host that had mustered to the Christian standard. They carried with them the Holy Lance, the Shroud and the Grael. Sir Caestra rode immediately behind them carrying the Holy Standard and flanked by Sir Magda MacAllan, Sir Lotha and Sir Kenneth of the Kenneth of Dungallan.

The Prince, Longinus, Galahaidra, and Iosephus were all wearing full length chainmail hauberks, iron winged helmets and shields. Following them, they had managed to mount five companies on horse back, three hundred with the horses captured following the massacre of Craedech's company when ambushed in the foothills of the Cairngorns. However, the vast majority of their army ran on foot: six thousand Picts with five hundred archers from Glevum and Colcaister.

Their generals were Sir Longinus as overall commander, Sir Galahaidra in charge of the cavalry (which command he would later delegate to Sir Caestra), Prince Craedech, Sir MacAllan and Sir Lotha in charge of their three wings of foot with Sir Iosephus to command the reserve and Sir Kenneth to command the archers (which command was subsequently delegated to Sir Iosephus). Sir Caesta was to be their standard bearer and was to have ridden with Sir Galahaidra.

Just as they were about to march from the caves of MacAllan's Cairn, all gathered heard the sound of galloping horses approaching and King Hargest of Alloa, Clackmannan and Fallin with the war bands from twenty Gaelic tribes, comprising some one thousand cavalry, came at haste to join them.

Turning towards Longinus, Hargest threw himself off his horse to land sure-footed; in one movement he was striding straight towards the Centurion. His greeting was a shout that murdered what was left of the silence of that morning: "Roman!" he roared. "We heard you gather a Christian Army but this time with a distinctly Caledonian feel in order to assail the Vicing and drive them from our Highlands. We could not bear to miss a good outing and have come to offer our aid. Now where is my darling girl?"

MacAllan was not to be out-roared in his own capital and standing tall on his horse, bellowed: "Hargest, you foul stench. What are you doing in my home chasing after my girl?"

"MacAllan you muck-raking worm, she was ever mine before yours. I am here to give her polite company for a change."

"May your beard fill with lice, your face explode with boils and your tongue swell with purple spots. The girl has told me she loves *me*" cried MacAllan and leapt off his own horse to march towards the advancing Hargest.

"Blah, MacAllan, you cantankerous cockroach, the lass must be blinded by your false teeth and glass eye!" and the two men grasped each other in a hug then MacAllan turned to Longinus and said:

"This is my good friend Hargest. Poor fool married one of my sisters and he strangled her in the first week they were together. I wouldner lasted a day with the dreadful hag. We have been best friends ever since he done away with her. You have met I take it?"

"I am a Christian like you so of course we have met!" Hargest interrupted, nudging his friend in the ribs then asking again: "Now, where is Maria?"

"Seriously, you know the girl?" asked MacAllan intrigued and then a few moments later was left standing in horror as his friend told him the abridged but no less gory version of his brief encounter with the poor girl.

"In the space of a few hours, I kidnapped her, drowned her twice, set fire to her, stripped her naked and left not a blemish on her, tho' she did get a little bruised when we gave her a kicking whilst tearing her clothes off her. She took it all in good mood and we all ended up converting to become Christians and now we follow her as do thousands of simple folk in the farms, crofts and homesteads across the Forth and right up into Perthshire. Now where is she hiding?"

Longinus set off to find the two ladies where he had last left them at prayer in the caves and caverns of MacAllan's Cairn, irritated that they had not yet joined the muster outside but returned quickly and in despair on finding both of their backpacks missing, and that Epona and three of Iosephus' fastest horses were also absent.

He was loath to give the newly arrived King nor the Prince and his companions the bad news but there was no point in hiding or delaying the discovery of the truth: "Maria and Ninian have gone off on their own. I suspect they seek to have a chat with the Vicing to see if they will agree to converting to Christianity and to holding to God's Peace" he announced to the stunned assembly.

"Has the girl no fear?" asked Hargest in horror.

"Has she no shame? The Vicing are good for only one thing and that is a good thumping!" muttered MacAllan.

"Has she no sense?" Craedech added through clenched teeth. "The Vicing will skin her alive as much as look at her!"

"Best go rescue her then as knowing the girl she will be in trouble already" Hargest had the final word.

The Lord of All the Gaels mounted up, signalling for his cavalry to join Sir Galahaidra's whilst he rode alongside his drinking partner, MacAllan, as they headed out to find Maria and Ninian. They went in force, fearing her capture by the growing war bands of the Caledonii or Vicing and that they must rescue her by show or use of force themselves.

Sir Caesta could barely contain himself at the honour of carrying the sacred Robe with the precious blood upon it that was the Holy Standard; his tartan was purple and gold to match the colours of the Robe. The ladies in MacAllan's capital had spent several days sowing full and half tabards of wool dyed in purple with a gold fringe and the Chi and Rho emblem of their faith marked on each to show that this army marched under the banner of Christ.

Galahaidra's five companies also each wore a tabard as did the company of archers, but nothing was going to stop the Gaels and the Picts going into battle bare-chested, the female warriors too, covered in white and blue wode, the pattern vaguely resembling a Chi and a Rho. The result was that the advancing war band was a riot of colour.

The army would march supported by a baggage train of three hundred wagons and five hundred pack horses with over a thousand camp followers including weapon, sword and armour smiths, farriers, blacksmiths, fletchers and froggers. Under Longinus' direction they had built three trebuchet and two ballistae which were being hauled at the rear of his long column. Their advance was therefore painfully slow, had to follow wide tracks and the main pathways, sticking to the valleys and gorges, and made a noise that could be heard for many leagues in every direction.

On their first day as they sought out the crossing of the Ness at the westerly mouth of Loch Ness near Campus Augustus, Iosephus rode up to join Longinus with a question and some news from the trireme that stood out off the Forth of Tay and that was following the advancing army with provisions. First was the news:

"Maria's father, Prince Godric, has already received word of her torture at the hands of the Gael, her courage when confronting the Picts and suspects that she intends to go alone when she meets the Vicing and so has sent some help in a fleet he has commissioned to leave from South Hamm and dock at Colcaister, King's Lynn and Yorvic. It brings us aid to protect his daughter. He also sends word to you, Longinus: 'Bring my daughter home safe and unharmed or I will feed you and that pup Craedech to my wolfhounds'."

"He is in a good mood then?" Longinus replied with a grin and Iosephus chuckled before his next piece of news which was less positive:

"The word I have from my fleet confirms the rumours we have already heard: the Vicing living in Ultima Thule have sent emissaries to their cousins in the Norse lands and the Bight to come to their aid. King Craedfellast the Intemperate has gathered nine hundred long boats from the fjords north and south of Scandavia and his brother King Graemwolda Warmongerer has mustered another sixty long boats full of warriors from the Green and Ice lands to the far north-west.

King Graemir of the Caledonii has also gathered his tribal leaders and assembled at least five hundred men from the Carnonaeae, Carini, Cornavii and Decaniae.

Then his brother Garrord, King of the Caledonii is also mustering and should be good for another five hundred infantry with two hundred expected to join him from the Epidii but only if they can pass through the lands of the Dannonnil.

The Germani and Teutoni, including the Chaeni and Suevii are gathering under their Kings Caerdain, Hostiga and Tortelimir and will sail from the Bight heading for land north of the Ness and the Firths of Moray and Beauly.

We could easily be outnumbered by the Pagans who have come to destroy the new faith and its 'high priestess' Maria. King Craedfellast has promised that the girl's whitened skin shall be stretched across the cliffs off Thursoe and her head shall be placed upon a stake for the ravens and crows to peck until it is bleached bone. Then they will feed her remains to the fishes in the deep. The size of the foe we face depends on how many ships the Norse can commission but their war band will be huge and savage."

Galahaidra came across to listen in then waved over MacAllan and Hargest waiting until they had joined the impromptu War Council before asking: "Do we have any intelligence on our and their fleet numbers?"

"Just about anything spare at sea is being used by King Graemwolda to harry the west coast of Dacia. My folk will know the moment any ships are diverted. I will send word anyway as if Craedfellast and Graemwolda have set sail then my liege will want a good piece of the action" Hargest contributed thoughtfully then Longinus added his denarius' worth:

"I will check with Varus. He has orders to gather a fleet to infest the north Germanic ports in preparation for Caligula's invasion of the mouth of the Rhine. He will have intelligence reports from all the way along that coastline."

"How many ships is Godric sending?" Galahaidra asked Iosephus and the old man laughed.

"Over one hundred quadrimes with thirty thousand troops and support staff in eighty of the rimes the rest are full of his horses. He clearly wants Maria to be especially safe."

"Send word to King Jaerid" suggested Galahaidra. "It seems that the Pagan world has declared war on our fledgling Christian kingdoms. Jaerid could face raids all along the east coastline. He will need his fleet out at sea and his defenses in his fortifications on the coast and the mouths of the Tweed, Tyne, Tees, Aln and Humber. He may send us aid also."

"There is some good news" Iosephus added. "The Sevgolae and the Dannonnil are also mustering under their Kings Craemond and Harbandum and will come to our aid with three to four thousands, including archers and cavalry. They are as determined as we are to see off the menace of the Norse. We have no news from the Vacomagi and Venicones but the Votadeni are already preparing to join King Jaerid should he come north."

"We must find Maria and Ninian" MacAllan urged adamant in his concern for the two girls "for they will count their life span in seconds if found by the Vicing, the Norse or the Caledonii first."

Within the hour, Sir Galahaidra had spotted where Maria and Ninian had parted from the main track north to the Ness and headed north east into the thick forests and undergrowth of the Decaniae territory. It was impassable terrain for the army's huge baggage train and so Galahaidra approached Longinus to decline the commission to lead the Army's cavalry.

"I am meant to be guarding Ninian and should never have left her!" he told his dear friend and left the massing troops to ride north, following the trail left by the two girls.

He had intended to go alone as he had thought this would be quickest but he did not know the paths through the Highlands and across the Ness particularly well. So King Hargest had joined him, looking for his first quest to confirm his membership in the *Order of the Risen Christ*; the chieftain was seriously miffed, though he would not admit it, that his friend Lord Sir MacAllan had been chosen by the Grael before him and was out to make amends.

The third member of the group was a surprise to everyone including himself but was chosen by the Grael when it suddenly came alight with a cream and mauve tinge, shedding its subtle light as the Angels spoke to a young man, an unknown and gentle warrior whom had already been singled out to be blessed and bear witness to the *Grael Vision* and then praised before his comrades by Maria herself, whom had spotted his worth. Sir Kenneth of the Kenneth of Dungallan, the soft spoken warrior, rode behind his two seniors carrying a lance and the Grael; he had been loaned Iosephus' hauberk, shield, helmet and sword.

The three men rode a steady six leagues every hour on the terrible roads and paths that ran north to the ford of the River Oich at Campus Augustus and did sixty leagues each day, using Galahaidra's sword and the Holy Lance to light their path in the dark and thus were able to hold to the road for eleven hours every day. Even so, they would have still been slightly slower than Maria as they all were wearing armour whilst Maria and Ninian were unarmed and Maria had the faster horses; except that Maria and Ninian kept stopping to marvel at their surrounding countryside and so their leisurely pace for only six hours of daylight, allowing for two to three hours of stops each day, meant that they covered less than fifty leagues daily!

On her first two days since leaving Longinus' protection, Maria had ridden less than one hundred leagues heading north along winding roads through steep gorges and deep valleys avoiding the attention of the Decaniae who were frightened off by the sight of her wild boar. Unknown to either girl, they had also come under the protection of a company of the Sevgolae tribe, who were seeking to join Longinus at Augustus and remained hidden, their deadly arrows removing any attempt to assault the two ladies.

As the girls came out on the banks of Loch Ness which they intended to follow as far as Drumnadroichit, Maria and Ninian encountered their first wolf. It was silver-haired with bright blue eyes, female with two cubs to feed, desperately hungry as it had not eaten for days and guided to the girls by their scent and that of their horses. With its colouring, it could have been a twin for Epona … or even for Maria. The she-wolf stalked the two girls silently hoping to catch one or other of them as they bathed or slept, to wrench out one of their throats and carry the corpse to where its family were hidden in the depths of the forest. The mother was young and this was her first family. The she-wolf was unsure as to what to do and had been deserted by her mate who had moved on, leaving her to try and cope on her own.

At a small village in a dip in the steep forested hills either side of Loch Ness, Maria and Ninian came across their first settlement and steered clear uncertain whether they faced the Decaniae or the Traxial, but having been warned off both by Iosephus. They headed down to the shore of the Loch to set up camp. They were half a day ahead of the chasing Sir Galahaidra. Maria planned to set up their tent then light a fire on the grey sands whilst it was still daylight, a bed of pine needles providing a soft carpet for the girls' feet and offering kindling to start their camp stove and fire.

Ninian prayed every moment that Galahaidra would forget about the army he was helping to muster and instead would come and rescue her. The weather was the worst they had yet to encounter: cold snow or cold winds; an 'invisible sun' that when it did come out from hiding made the sky and the ground cold; the land so barren that winds blew from the North Pole; or so wooded that the trees hid any hope of daylight reaching to touch them.

Maria's Gospel records little but in fact she was enjoying herself, marvelling at the huge expanse of inland water, the mountains in the distance, the tall trees and a world turned to whitened ice and snow that made every feature resemble a marble statue. "Are you sure this is not the sea?" she kept saying and Ninian would remind the girl that she herself had very rarely left the vicinity of Loch Leven, the Lomond Hills and the Firth of Forth.

When they reached Campus Augustus Maria gasped as she looked along Loch Ness from its southern tip towards the Inver on the Ness. "Is this the …?" she began and Ninian exasperated replied "No it is not" and rode off in a huff. It did not last because Maria kept pointing out new birds and animals, strange trees, funny shaped mountains and clouds and in the end Ninian surrendered: "I give up. If I give you a hug will you be quiet?"

"One hug an hour and you have a deal" and they both laughed as the tension disappeared. Then suddenly the she-wolf jumped out of the forest and lunged at one of their horses, which were grazing. The wolf was too tired to bring the horse down and all four of their steeds took off. Ninian screamed and ran, attracting the attention of the lupine which, whilst tired, was always going to chase a screaming girl who was trying to run away through a dense forest.

"Come on" said Maria to her wild boar and they gave chase, Maria stopping to grab Ninian's saddle bag, then running like the wind in pursuit of the screams.

Longinus' army marched three leagues every hour and twenty leagues each day, the pace slow due to the poor daylight and rapidly shortening days. This was the territory of the Decaniae or the Traxial but as yet there was no sign of any habitation or opposition. They took four days to reach the ford across the fast running River Oich choosing to use the footman's ferry rather than risk the waters of the river which were deep as the rain had fallen without cease for weeks. The long column of the Christian Army was already two days behind Maria, Ninian and Galahaidra when they finally reached the ferry and their speed did not improve.

It was painfully slow work for Longinus' cavalry as only two horses could be ferried at a time and four horses each hour, just under two hundred in a day and their entire cavalry took five days to get across. The wagons took a further three days whilst the rest of the army in frustration swam or tried to ford the Oich. They lost over one hundred drowned and another four hundred turned back and went home. The army was dispirited but fortunately no-one took advantage and at the end of nine days, Longinus was finally north of the Oich and able to head for the Firth of Beauly ... but by then Maria was aready deep into Pagan territory in the far north of Caledonia.

The journey to Beauly at the mouth of the Beauly Estuary would take Longinus a further four days, marching through pine covered winding mountain tracks and passes and at constant risk of being ambushed. His scouts spotted the signs that his army was being watched but no sign of any enemy and every settlement they came to had been deserted in haste: they finally found the signs of recent habitation but the Sitinarae and Lugii who lived in this part of Caledonia had disappeared, retreating before the steady advance of Longinus' long column.

At the first of his daily briefings on their first night as he commenced his army's crossing of the River Oich, Longinus voiced the concerns of all of his captains:

"The Caledonii are drawing us in and forcing us to use our own supplies rather than to feed off the land. I think they are waiting for reinforcements from the Vicing kingdoms from the Lands of Ice and the deep, dark fjords to our north-east. Once we reach Beauly then we can start to scout the land more easily but for the next few days we will be very much in the dark as to both our allies' and enemies'movements.

The next three to four days are thus critical as we get across the Oich and we must stay on constant alert, ensuring we erect a temporary palisade to defend and fortify our camp here."

"How many might we face?" MacAllan asked and Longinus was happy to reply:

"The home of the Vicing is much further north around Thurso and Thule. At present we face the Sitinarae, Traexil, Danercae and Lugii. Our intelligence reports on the numbers of the Caledonii can be relied on and tell us that the Kings of the Caledonii can muster at most between one thousand and fifteen hundred warriors. The Caledonii are heavily outnumbered by us and will not risk more than a skirmish until they have joined up with the large number of Vicing and Germanii heading our way."

"When might that be?" asked Lotha.

Iosephus was able to answer that question and presented a detailed report. The equites was receiving daily reports from his ships as they moored up in the ports along the east coast, getting into conversation with the ship-hands and diakonae of other ships then sending word by the large network of messengers Iosephus now had operating in Britannia and Caledonia:

"The news is not good" he admitted immediately and without hiding the extent of the challenge now faced by the Christian alliance. "Also my information is in some cases as much as four days old but has been supplemented by a helpful assessment sent by Varus whose fleet has left the west coast of Gallia and already crossed the Mare Britannia and Mare Germania, entering the North Sea, heading north.

We believe the Vicing from the Norse lands and the Bight are heading for Thurso as Thule could not feed or host the size of fleet being sent. Those from the north are one day at most from Thurso but face terrible seas. The fog on the east coast of Northumbria and at the mouth of the Firths of Forth and Tay will put them off travelling further south and delay those from the Bight from coming north but also will hold up our own reinforcements.

Germanic fleets have set sail from the mouth of the Rhine and already the Vicing and Daenii fleets from the Bight of Heligos have joined up with the Germanii to raid the north coast of Cantiani, looking for provisions. The King of the Cantiani met them in battle near the Castle of the Roc and was defeated; his son, the Crown Prince, lost a flotilla in a skirmish at the mouth of the River Maede.

Both are dead ..." which drew a gasp but Iosephus carried on: "... and Cant is currently leaderless and in chaos. Prince Wulfrid joined up with the Kings of the middle kingdoms of the Catuvellauni and Eorl Herne to hold the South Downs and prevented the Germanii from advancing any further inland.

We then have reports of skirmishes when the Germanii tried to land at the mouth of the Rivers Blackwater, Cole, Or, Deben and laid brief siege to Norwicken before moving out of The Wash and back into the North Sea. Based on the last sightings, they have braved the fog hugging the east coast at the mouth of the Tyne and Aln and are one day south of Jaerid's fleet and a further day behind that of Prince Godric.

The Vicing from Scandavia should reach Thurso tomorrow and will then take four days to disembark including the time it takes for them to bring the residents of Thule, Ultima Thule and the Hebrides across the sea to the mainland. The Vicing and Germanii from the north coast of the Rhineland and Germania and the Bight of Heligos are five to six days south of Thurso by now.

By the end of the se'enight we could face the armies of the Kings of the Chaeni, Suevii, Caledoni, Germanii, Alemani, Teutoni, Burgundi, Vicing, Daenii, Sitinarae and Lugii who must then march south, a journey of four to five days to meet us at Beauly. We have two se'enight to muster at most and it will take us all of that time to reach Beauly.

We will have even less time to prepare if we head north to choose better ground to meet our foe that is more suitable for our cavalry and artillery and so we must take our chances at Beauly and send word to Godric to scout the area and prepare suitable ground for us."

More information would become available in the days ahead as Longinus found himself delayed by the ferry crossing over the River Oich. Longinus would then get a detailed briefing once he joined Godric, Jaerid, Pasterix and the other Christian commanders at Beauly but in the meantime those marching with him had to continue to rely on information that was several days old.

All of Longinus' captains and his fellow commanders at the briefing that night nodded as Iosephus concluded his report, welcoming and understanding the briefing then asking Longinus about their own muster. Longinus' intelligence was also old but he did have plenty of good news:

"The armies of the Christian kingdoms are gathering to meet those of the free Pagan world. We fight for the future of our faith against the evil of those who believe in war over peace, disunity over harmony, who do not value life, and place their trust in a pantheon of Gods, superstition and the trickery of sorcery. If Maria were here she would pitch herself against the Pagan armies that gather to destroy us, alone without arms, relying on the power of her prayers. But we know that sometimes God and Man must work together to defend the peace lovers, the weak, meek, humble and vulnerable.

We are the peace-makers and we fight not to convert those whom we shall meet in battle but for the right for them and us to choose the faith we shall hold dear when not threatened. Again, if Maria were here she would remind us that our Master said we should never convert someone to believe at the point of a sword. Commitment to follow the Nazarene must be genuine and total, from the heart and not through fear."

Prince Godric had set sail one day before Longinus had completed his muster at MacAllan's cave, doing as much as two hundred and fifty nautical leagues each fair weather day at sea for he was in a hurry to rescue his daughter, hugging the east coast line but kicking his heels as he spent three days loading more troops, collecting more ships at Colcaister, King's Lynn and Bes' Manse or Ton, and waiting for decent weather. His armada would reach the Forth of Beauly five days before Longinus, with time to pitch camp and begin to erect a palisade to protect his huge army.

King Jaerid received first word that Maria was in trouble from King Pasterix who had led an army through the Shere Forest and across the Trent to join the Dacians at Yorvic. Pasterix brought with him an army from Deceangli under King Graefreigh and two of his Eorls. The three Kings spent a day supervising their embarkment at Hull on the Humber and then two days later they could be found supervising an embarkment at Yorvic. They sailed for three days to the Forth of Beauly, and arrived the day after Godric.

King Pedrus, sovereign of all Lands West of the Western Seas, the King of All the Picts, *disputed* King of all Hibernia, Caledonia, Deceangli and Dacia received word from Lord MacAllan, one of his most faithful and highly respected chieftains that a huge army of Vicing and Caledonii was seeking to capture, torture and slay a Britannic princess taken under the protection of MacAllan himself. The enemy were led by the three Kings Graemir, Craedfellast and Graemwolda.

"I will have their heads" King Pedrus muttered his eyes fiery coal, black and burning with the intensity of his hatred for the two Vicing sovereigns whose raiding long boats had repeatedly scoured and laid barren the green rolling hills and rich pastures of the east and north coasts of Hibernia. He would send a fleet of forty ships to try and sink his enemy at sea then would spend two days putting his army to sea on forty more ships.

Below Drumnadroichit was the shallow grey sanded beach at the side of Loch Ness, a small wooded peninsula to the south of the settlement with the sheltered beach approached through a pine tree forest leading to crystal clear but freezing cold black waters. As Maria reached the forest, she could hear the sound of her companion crashing through the trees, still screaming (and Maria rather mischievously wondered just how much could one person scream?) with the occasional snarl and howl of her pursuer. The girl looked for Epona thinking the stallion might be useful in a fight with a wolf but the big coward had taken off and was nowhere to be seen.

"Just us then!" Maria whispered to the wild boar and sent them off in a looping run to the left, whilst Maria looked to cut off the wolf by going right. She realised that she was by some miracle gaining on the wolf: but then it had looked partly starved and she guessed it was struggling and possibly on its last legs. As she caught first sight of it she could see the poor mother had been suckling her young but without eating any food herself; the young mother was starving!

Maria whistled and the wolf stopped and turned to face Maria who stood still waiting for its charge, giving Ninian the chance to get up a tree. The wolf ran at the girl and Maria remained absolutely still … and her wild boar ran out of the trees to her left to strike the wolf in the right ribs, sending it sprawling to the ground to roll, right itself and snarl but then to whimper for it had taken a terrible wound in its flank.

"Leave!" Maria whispered and the boar came to heel; she bent down to congratulate them and then walked towards the wolf. It glared at her, preparing to make its last stand and Maria prayed for its healing, singing a psalm in her quiet lilting voice, then reaching into the saddle bag she had brought with her and tossing a hunk of meat, Ninian had packed for her meal the following day. The wolf blinked at both the moment of its healing, and it understood it had the girl to thank for that, and then the food before her. Without a sound, it grabbed the haunch of meat and ran off to find her family.

Maria waited until Ninian had come down out of the tree then sent the girl back to their camp site escorted by the wild boar whilst she waited, still with the saddle bag. She had to wait an hour but her patience was rewarded as the she-wolf returned. Once more Maria threw it a piece of meat, realising as she did so that she was condemning her friend to become vegetarian but better she miss her own supper than she become the supper of a wolf.

Then Maria sang to the wolf and it crossed the clearing slowly to lie at Maria's feet. The girl squatted next to it, spoke soothingly, stroking it behind its ears, then placed her hand inside its mouth and stroked its tongue; it smiled then laughed. Finally, Maria prayed: "Help me to save this poor mother's family" and with a yelp the wolf took off to return a few moments later with her family of two cubs. Maria responded by giving the mother the last of the meat in Ninian's saddle bag and also the loaf of bread her companion had kept for that evening's supper. Then stroking the wolf once more but avoiding touching the cubs for the mother would be protective of her young, Maria went to walk away. The wolf picked up her two youngsters in her silken soft jowls and padded calmly behind Maria, quite content and with no intention of ripping anyone's throat out. The girl had not expected this but was touched and thought: '*The poor thing will struggle to get food and needs feeding up if she is to offer her young her milk. I shall look after them.*'

And thus it was that Maria found herself adopting a family of silver wolfs, with the most stunning blue eyes and fair hair. "You are beautiful" Maria found herself whispering involuntarily and something in her voice communicated itself to the wolf whose ears pricked up and her tail began to wag in pleasure. "Friends?" Maria asked and the wolf grinned once more.

"You cannot keep a wolf!" Ninian screamed and went to hide but Maria could not stop herself and began to laugh whilst also watching with pleasure as her wild boar and the wolves all appeared to be getting along famously. Her horse, Epona, however, was proving to be the biggest coward ever and it took the girl a good hour to coax him back to the camp site.

"I shall call you 'Thea' after one of my ancestors" Maria said to the wolf and it wagged its tail then went off to hunt. Maria watched with joy as the two cubs got into a tumbling, rolling bust up of a mock fight, guarded and supervised by the wild boar, whilst their mother was away from the camp site hunting for supper.

Maria tethered their horses except for Epona who was too proud to be tethered, to two of the tall trees; they were Douglas firs and Maria had never seen such wonderful giants close up before. She was itching to get her fingers on one and climb to the very top then survey the whole world from her tall perch.

The two girls had been lent a tent by MacAllan and pitched it on the shore line where the Loch ran almost due north; there was very little tide so they placed it close to the water's edge. With their camp fire lit and spitting but still shedding heat in the snow, Maria undressed in the tent, shivered in delight as she stood under the silver glow of stars before the large expanse of icy water, raised her arms and sang her praise of and gratitude to God for the wonder and beauty of his creation, then she dived beneath the black waters.

Maria's horse, Epona, and the family of four wild boars tested a hoofed foot each and retreated in disdain leaving such idiocy as to swim in the freezing waters of the Loch to the adventurous and reckless girl-child who was their mistress. Instead they went in hunt of a spring or stream in the shade of the trees that might offer warm water to drink and shelter from the snow. Ninian joined them and found a log to sit on where she sang softly, her spirits returning as she, like Maria had earlier, began to take in the natural beauty and majesty of their surroundings. It was about now that Ninian went to take some food out of her saddle bag to cook for supper and discovered to her dismay the full treachery of her friend!

This is where the war band of five mounted Sitinarae from the settlement on the hill found them. Once more, Maria was caught without clothes, though this time she had the advantage of darkness, in which impartial and all-enveloping blanket she could hide, and the distinct disadvantage that it was well below freezing point and now snowing heavily. The wild boar had taken one look at the warriors' hunting spears and picked up the wolf cubs then taken them into the safety of the woods to wait for the return of their mother.

The Sitinarae did not bother with conversation but stripped Ninian then tied both girls with their ropes by the neck, hands, arms and legs, forcing them to kneel. They lashed them with their long horse whips and shorter crops until the blood had come to the surface of what skin remained or spilt down their bruised, battered and scarred bare backs. Maria's skin had barely healed from her previous lashing and curled away in long bloody strips from the first blow of their crops.

Next the men tethered the girls to posts set out in the Loch and that the girls had taken to be boat moorings but now with the benefit of closer inspection they realised from the sorry remains and bloody body parts on each that the posts served a more macabre purpose. The icy cold water on Maria's flayed back was all that stopped her from fainting as it anaesthetised the pain at least briefly but long enough for Maria to hear the men discussing what they would do next. They spoke of a 'summonsing' but neither girl had any idea what that entailed.

"Do not be afraid, Ninian, for we are told that the tide on this black water is mere inches and they cannot plan to drown us in waters that shall not reach even as high as my neck and no higher than your shoulders" whispered Maria seeking to reassure her companion but earning herself a back-handed cuff across her mouth from one of their captors that brought more blood from chapped and bleeding lips. Ninian just wept for she had never been beaten before and was in constant pain but also afraid that she would bear the scars for the rest of her life. Maria ignored the blow to her face and continued to pray for Ninian and to whisper "Be brave, be brave."

The Sitinarae war band picked up branches that had fallen from the tall firs behind them and began to beat them on the surface of the water by the shore making a loud drumming noise and sending ripples out onto the Loch's otherwise smooth surface.

At first the girls could see the ripples as silver semi circles, catching the dull light of the Moon but rapidly fading in the dark of the night as the snow clouds hid the stars whilst the Moon was waning, soon to be old and black. All the girls could see as they looked up was the snow flakes falling into their eyes, nose and mouth.

After ten minutes the girls were no more than shadows, spectres and ghosts, their hair, faces and shoulders covered in ice and snow, turned deathly white, whited sepulchres and near the reality of death from the terrible ice-cold of the water. With no clothes as insulation they were moments away from becoming victims of hypothermia, their lungs and hearts about to give up the ghost as they passed into the deep and deadly sleep that intense cold brings.

Then the monster came.

It reminded Maria at first of the crocodile she had seen in the auction at Perth, with its narrow pointed jaws and many rows of serated teeth. Yet it was also like a python, with a long sinewy body that slithered, speeding across the surface of the water for twenty paces or more. Unlike the snakes she had seen in the deserts at home or even the viper she had met in the Hall of King Pasterix, this monster had fins on its back like a porpoise or shark.

Maria was seeing the monster in the dark so when all is said and done much of her description could have been put down to her own imagination but for subsequent events. If ever Maria had met a Sea Dragon, wingless but with side fins where the land dragon had wings, then this creature was certainly a cousin of such serpents and a draconis of huge and commanding size. Ninian saw nothing for she had closed her eyes and was screaming in terror as she felt its warm breath against her cheeks.

Once more, Maria thanked God for her gift of tongues and spoke to the serpent showing no fear.

"Forgive us most noble monster for disturbing your rest. We would not wish to do this. Others have brought us here to persuade you to murder us. Those who seek to do this are cowards and fight against the defenceless and vulnerable whereas we seek your friendship and to share the stories of the magic of our world. We would offer to sing to you and tell you of the beauty of trees and mountains whilst hearing of the mysteries of the deep. Would you share *the Gift of Story* with us?"

The monster was stunned to hear any Living Being speak in its tongue for it had lived alone for many centuries without a companion or mate, deprived of the gift of sharing stories which was the particular love and delight of all of dragonkind and their many different species.

"Fair maid, share with me your name and then I shall share mine before I take you both to where we can tell stories undisturbed by these rude men."

"Willingly, O Lord of all Serpents of the Sea. My name is Maria and my companion's name is Ninian. We would happily join you if you would allow us to ride on your back and also warm us both with the gift of your breath?"

"My name is Pederaster" and the serpent rose high in the water to lunge at the band of Sitinarae on the shore. The warriors did not hesitate but rather ran into the deep forest behind them and did not stop running until they had reached Drumnadroichit with their news of another sighting of the Loch's monster. As soon as the men were out of sight, Pederaster breathed on the two girls, warming their heads, shoulders and upper bodies, then dipped his noble head twice to cut the ropes that secured the girls to the two mooring posts, using a sharpened tooth to delicately sever the ropes where they bound wrists and ankles.

Once free, Maria had to work hard to persuade Ninian to even attempt to mount onto the back of the sea serpent but finally the young lady closed her eyes and allowed Maria to shove her up the steep and smooth sides of the serpent before Maria mounted herself, being just behind the monster's ears where she could whisper her stories for Pederaster to hear as he swam to his resting place.

The first thing both girls noticed with pleasure was that the serpent's skin was warm, thawing out their frozen legs; it was also smooth and rippled sensuously beneath them. Maria immediately kept her promise and spoke of her travels across Iudaea and Jordan as part of her Master's ministry and then the places she had visited along the Middle Sea as part of her own ministry.

"Did you see any fellow sea serpents in the Middle Sea?" Pederaster asked interrupting her story courteously.

"Alas no, my dear friend, but they are rumoured to live in the deep seas of the Charybdis and I have seen maps drawn by our explorers of the Seas and the Oceans that show serpents in the Atlantis Ocean."

Then Maria spoke of her Master's mission and the gifts he offered to the Caledonii tribes and the Vicing people residing in the north of Caledonia and the Islands beyond.

"It seems that the leaders of the people you will meet seek to prevent their people from hearing of something that is a great good for their subjects" observed the ancient worm wisely and Maria agreed adding:

"Many leaders fear change even when it is beneficial because the process of change often empowers their subjects or motivates them to evaluate the world around them from a fresh perspective. My Master promotes free will and his message can see the chains of autocracy and oppression fall away. He often spoke of saving us but used the Greek and Aramaic words for enlightenment when he did so; a word that also literally means to remove our chains and bring us out into the light."

They had swam through the water at great speed and yet the girls had felt only the slightest of movements, a constant and welcoming caress of their inner thighs that warmed them through and staved off the deadly cold of both the Loch's waters and the falling snow. Suddenly, the serpent's haven was upon them and they ducked beneath the low overhang that was the entrance to a subterranean lagoon of cyan blue water kept warm by the gentle volcanic action beneath the bed of the Loch.

Sheltered from the cold of the snow, the monster landed the girls where they could wade a few feet through water to reach the golden sands that lined the lagoon. Both girls sat cross-legged with their hands in their laps whilst Maria spoke of her adventures in Dacia, Deceangli and the Highlands of Caledonia then told the dragon of the Holy Artefacts and also reassured the serpent that both she and her companion had put away their swords, all weapons of war and armour.

"We pose no threat but can offer help for we are much-travelled, are healers and I have the gift of tongues which includes the ability to listen to and understand you then return your fair speech."

"My fair lady, Maria. You have already told me more of the world beyond this cavern's walls in one night than I had previously learned in five centuries. I am in your debt" but Maria shook her head at that and explained herself:

"Noble serpent, forgive me, my Lord, if I do anger you by arguing with you; but it is we who are in your debt! You have saved both of our lives and rescued us from where we were being held captive. I deem you my friend and I ask one further favour but with no obligation on you to respond."

"What is that favour?" Pederaster asked intrigued yet also slightly wary for he had many years of mistrust of mankind to set aside though it was hard for him not to trust Maria. All of dragonkind can smell a lie and so the serpent could see the absolute honesty and truth in all that Maria had said.

"My favour is that I would love to hear your stories of the many exciting things you have found in the deep."

"Not a favour but an honour!" the Sea Dragon responded and smiled succumbing to the girl's gentle charm and made trusting by her trustworthiness; or rather Maria took the opening of his jaws to be a smile of pleasure and not him clearing the debris of previous meals from his carnivorous dentures. Then Pederaster spoke for half the night, his head on its long sinewy neck resting on the sands besides Maria who sat transfixed, whilst Ninian had curled up in a ball, using the sand to dry and warm herself then partly buried within the soft secluded sanded shelter of a wadi in one of the many dunes near the rear of the enormous cavern that was the serpent's home, she fell into a deep sleep.

Maria was wide awake and the serpent would occasionally use his warm tongue and breath to dry a part of her body that she had missed and which still glistened with the Loch's water or thawing snow. It was the early hours when the monster let Maria sleep by which time their friendship was firm, their trust in each other total, and the girl's promise never to reveal the location of the monster's safe haven was absolute and unbreakable.

"The Sitinarae sought that I meet a terrible fate: to be eaten by a monster. Instead I have found a new and wonderful friendship that I shall hold for the rest of my life" Maria whispered in gratitude into the monster's ear then fell forward in deep sleep to lie in the crook of his right shoulder, guarded by Pederaster and insulated from the cold by the heat of his fiery blood. "Good night little one" the dragon replied in his softest voice, his tone hypnotic and gentle; not seeking to disturb her sleep. He was both fascinated and delighted in the way that this evening had evolved into a night of companionable pleasure.

Some compulsion had driven Galahaidra to risk riding the bridle path at night in the dark. The path sat besides the Loch Ness and followed the twists and turns of the River Oich. The knight used the light of his Lance engaged through his devout prayers for the safe return of Ninian to show them the way. He had let his love ride with Maria annoyed that Ninian still stood by the need to try peaceful means to engage with the Vicing and Caledonii. He now regretted leaving her side for he had undertaken to protect her and failed to do so.

Because of Maria's insistence that they look at every beautiful place and seek out every settlement, the two girls' progress had been leisurely; Galahaidra had gained several hours on them each day. His night ride brought him to Drumnadroichit just as news of the latest sighting of the 'monster' hit the village. At sight of him, the Setinarae warriors and villagers went silent. For here surely was a knightly dragon slayer, with lance of fire and silver armour, a fire proof shield and sword made by the famous smith, Macsen? They gathered in the centre of their village to hear 'what was the knight's intent'; for this was a hero out of their legend, who bore the magic of the ancients. They would talk of this day for generations to come and it would become part of their verbal tradition.

"Have you word of Maria the Magdalan?" Galahaidra asked and one brave resident stood forward: "The girl and her companion pitched their tent on the shores of the Loch. There is a sheltered spot a league from here at the far side of the dense forest that you can see runs from our settlement to the side of the Loch. They were captured by these men" and he had indicated the Sitenarae.

Galahaidra turned to the five Sitenarae warriors and now his Lance was aflame with the red fires of a dragon as he asked:

"And what was to be the fate of the two girls?"

"You are too late" one of the war band muttered braving the knight's possible ire. "They were left for the monster and will have been taken and eaten by the beast. None ever survive."

"I do not believe in this 'monster'. Point out the way to where the girls were taken and I shall release them. Hope for your sakes that the girls live or I will hunt down all in this village and slay you" Galahaidra swore and the villagers and warriors quailed.

The patch of smooth grey sand was easy to find with the trail left by Maria being very obvious as she had so often stood still to look at the beauty and majesty of her surroundings with no regard for the tracks she then left. Galahaidra was now using his sword to light their way, his Lance being too cumbersome and so, in two parts, was held once again in its rear holster, whilst the sword allowed him to carve a wider path through the maze of fir and pine trees. He discovered the girls' tent and their clothes: Maria's neatly folded, Ninian's flung in. As he searched for sign of the girls, Epona and the wild boars ran out of their hiding place in the forest to greet him then went to the edge of the Loch and showed their distress. Thea and her cubs stayed hidden at the forest's edge waiting for their mistress' return.

Fearing the worst, Galahaidra hiked his hauberk up to rest in his sword belt, unlaced and removed his boots and leggings then waded into the water, the light of his sword illuminating the two mooring posts and showing the bloody remains of a monster's meal: clearly human, and from the strands of hair and the delicate hand left in one mauled tangle of rope, one had been young, unusually blonde and female.

"O God!" Galahaidra wept "This is my fault. Lord, please find a way to forgive me" then he turned with ashen face towards his companions and had no need to say more as Sir Kenneth fell to his knees and Hargest roared, swearing his oath at the skies: "Not one Caledonii shall live for this."

"We find the monster first. There will be bones and both girls deserve the honour of a burial. We cannot leave them to be eternally picked over by this terrible beast. We bring their bones home" Sir Kenneth's words echoed over the black waters and the other men agreed, Hargest adding "This was not the quest I would have wished when offered the chance to receive *the Grael Vision* but it is the right thing to do."

Sir Kenneth's eyes shone at his words. "We shall prove our worth through our faith in God even though she who led us to understand our faith has been taken from us. But more important, the *Grael Vision* gives each of us what we *need*. It will show us the way to the two girls' bones. Let us put our faith to the test" and the three men clasped hands, taking hope from their insight, seeking to turn Evil into Good.

Sie Kenneth went to the saddle bags on Epona and quickly found The Shroud. Sir Caesta had given King Hargest safe custody of The Standard. Sir Kenneth held The Grael and Sir Galahaidra The Lance. They found a rock with a flat and dry top, turned white by the snow as if covered in the finest linen cloth and on which they placed the four Holy Artefacts. Then all three men knelt in prayer, Galahaidra as the first appointed knight presiding:

"My lord God, Sir Kenneth and I bring before you King Hargest, a man made worthy through his continued faith despite the terrible loss he has suffered. Grant him the vision to see the last resting place of your servant Maria that she may be honoured in death as she was honoured in life" then they remained kneeling in silent prayer. To their surprise as they talked of this night in years to come in shared awe and wonder, each of the men received a vision, despite two already having been appointed as Knights of the Round Table and having previously seen their visions. The visions were rapid: they came within minutes where other knight aspirants had waited many anxious hours.

Galahaidra's vision came first and he saw Maria's bones being lowered into a carved stone sarcophagus in the caves beneath the City of Vedselae. Hargest was next, and his vision was of Craedech's and Maria's wedding before a jubilant people in the Great Assembly Hall in the Royal City of Wyncaester, the Round Table beyond at which sat the *Knights of the Order of The Risen Christ* waiting for their comrade knights to join them for the wedding feast with a proud Sir Hargest amongst them. At Craedech's side was Longinus, giving the bride away was Prince Godric, and bearing the posie of flowers Maria had held and standing behind her to hold the girl's train was Ninian.

It was Kenneth who was granted the third and final vision: of Maria asleep in the creases of a sea dragon's neck, content and miraculously full of life.

"She lives" said Kenneth and Hargest in union "As does Ninian" Hargest added for Galahaidra's benefit and once more the young knight wept then shouted his praises to God before saying "Where?"

"She appears to have befriended the sea monster" Sir Kenneth explained wrongly assuming the knight meant Maria and at sight of Galahaidra's incredulity continued "I know! I know! What she does makes no sense but we must take care of this monster for it may not be as monstrous as we had thought. What I saw was a cave which contained clear water and must open out from the Loch. We need a small boat some oars and your sword, Galahaidra. Ask your sword to find the girl" and Galahaidra did as Sir Kenneth asked, sceptical at first but the moment he thought of Ninian, his sword pointed a narrow beam of light to a distant bank of the Loch, straight as an arrow.

They returned to Drumnadroichit and found one of the crofters, who had made his home at the southern edge of the village maintaining the fields that lay between the forest and his mud hut. The fields offered good soil, sheltered from easterly and southerly winds. He had just finished working the fields and his late crop of roots and tubers was ready for harvesting. He had not been at the previous visit of the companions so looked on them with astonishment and much less fear than had he heard their earlier threat.

When asked if he had a small boat the farmer nodded and showed them a canoe carved out of a tree trunk with an adse, a shaped prow and bow and enough seating for six. It was heavy but the three men could carry it between them. The crofter added the oars, again carved out of a single piece of wood; for the crofter was no joiner. The three companions took ownership of the canoe and offered money for its loan but the crofter shook his head. For he knew he had become part of the legend of heroes; Galahaidra was clearly a dragon slayer and the boat was needed for only one reason. He did not expect to see the boat again but the knight …? Something about his confident air told the Setinara that this man would write his own history; not become the footnote of someone else's.

The companions returned to the Loch and set the canoe to the water prow first, astonished when it floated and did not leak. "You first" said King Hargest stepping back and Galahaidra laughed then directing the men to hold onto the far side stepped slowly but confidently into the centre of the canoe and sat down. "Prow then Bow" he said and the other two men nodded then Sir Kenneth placed both hands on the left hand side of the prow with Hagrest and Galahaidra compensating as he levered his light weight over the side to sit facing forwards, with Galahaidra at his back. He did the whole thing in one fluid movement that impressed his two companions.

"Come on sire" Galahaidra commanded and the newly-made Knight shook his head. "I cannot swim" he muttered. Galahaidra showed no mercy saying: "Nor can I but you will lose your place as a knight if you fail your quest and are not received under oath by Maria as all other knights have been."

"Rot your beard" muttered the King then noticed the knight was clean shaven and cursing he went to copy Kenneth's stylish entry into the canoe, slipped and crashed down head first, sitting up with a bleeding nose but grinning with relief. "I will stay here if you don't mind" he suggested as he lay in the bilge water and rolled carefully onto his back then made no further attempt to get seated. Galahaidra and Kenneth were inclined to agree that it was best if the Gaelic King stayed still and taking up their oars, they rowed for the spot where Galahaidra's sword had told him he would find his love, Ninian, occasionally holding up the sword to confirm their course. They rowed for three hours and saw the first light rise above the steep mountains to the east of the Loch. With daylight came their first proper view of their heading … and no sign of a cave or cavern entrance.

Galahaidra took the sword once more and pointed – it seemed to indicate a spot that was solid rock. '*The power of the sword is a prayer'* the knight reminded himself '*and I must show my trust in the Lord.*' "Carry on" he said to his companions and they rowed steadily closer to the sheer cliff. They were a few feet away, too close to change course when Galahaidra saw something and shouted "Duck". Sir Kenneth did as he was told and then all three men looked up at the low roof of the entrance to the sea serpent's home passing rapidly over their heads.

Before them was a boulder, rising from the clear blue water of a lagoon and by some miracle of nature the boulder matched the crevasses and faults in the cliff surrounding the cavern entrance. From anything further than a few feet it looked to be part of the same cliff face. Instead a current caught the canoe, dragged it under the cavern entrance's roof and then to the left to circle the boulder and arrive at the still water of the lagoon.

On the sanded beach at the far end of the lagoon was a Sea Dragon, asleep with its head protectively circling around the young Maria, Ninian partly covered by the sand of a dune, also sleeping further up from the shore line. "Even the water is warm" whispered Sir Kenneth in awe as he tested the water with his hand.

"How deep?" Galahaidra asked and added: "The sound as we beach will wake up our monstrous friend then 'ware havoc!"

"Go slow" Kenneth replied "for we are low in the water due to our weight" and he nodded towards the rabelesque Hagrest then added "and in a few seconds my prow will touch sand."

"Stop here then" and the two knights both back-paddled bringing the canoe to a gentle halt. Alas, their oarsmanship raised tiny ripples that circled gently out to touch the tip of the dragon's tail. Pederaster woke with a roar then immediately apologised, looking guiltily at Maria who was holding her hands over her ears briefly deafened by the monster, whilst Ninian had buried her head in the sand in her fright.

The monster turned slowly towards Galahaidra and demanded "Who are you? and What brings you here?" to his great surprise, the gift of tongues saw the young knight understand the dragon's demand and he replied honestly in the language of the serpent:

"I come to take the girls under my protection."

"Will you bring them back to see me?" the dragon asked saddened yet knowing he must let the girls go. Galahaidra looked at Maria and seeing her nod, turned back to the dragon to smile and say:

"I promise to do so for it is what Maria wants."

However Maria then confused all of them by stubbornly refusing to go. "Why do you stay?" Galahaidra asked in frustration and even King Hagrest was lost to understand the girl. In the end, Sir Kenneth found the solution and asked Pederaster to talk to Maria which the dragon was happy to do.

"Why do you stay my child? You have an important message to give to the world."

"I promised I would not give your hiding place away" cried Maria, bursting into tears with her head downcast.

"Actually it was my love for Ninian that uncovered you both here" Galahaidra explained; not the most tactful of his comments as he rapidly realised so it was left to Sir Kenneth to find the solution.

"Noble Serpent, all three of us are Knights of a special Order where worth and integrity is important if we seek to continue to be a Knight. We have all made great sacrifice to become a Knight and if we each swore on our knightly honour to never give away the location of your home then such an oath would be binding."

Pederaster looked at Maria who nodded confirming that Sir Kenneth spoke the truth. And so the three Knights made their oath and Maria breathed a huge sigh of relief then kissed the serpent on the nose before she and Ninian asked if their rescuers had brought any clothing.

The three men looked embarrassed and had to admit that rescuing naked maidens from the clutches of giant sea monsters was not something they were very practised in. Pederaster broke into laughter, a pleasant sound and so infectious that soon they were all laughing then he offered to carry

Sir Kenneth to the girls' camp site and back. In twenty minutes, they had returned and the monster acted as a screen behind which the girls were able to change with discretion. "Good luck" Pederaster whispered in Maria's ear and then he blew their canoe half way across the Loch, Kenneth and Galahaidra rowing the rest whilst Maria as the only one who could swim stood on the rear footwails and steered with the third oar.

Alhough it was now three hours after dawn, no-one had obtained much sleep, so the men erected their tent and relit the camp fire, a long task as both wood and kindling were cold and damp. Eventually however the fire caught and its heat warmed through the logs piled either side then began to warm up their bed rolls, blankets and two tents. With an hour gone, Ninian and Maria had to be carried to their beds and covered in their warm blankets whilst Sir Kenneth took the first watch from midday, only to get the shock of his life as Maria's wild boar escorted Thea and her cubs into Maria's tent. A few seconds later and Ninian's screams woke the whole camp and she stormed out of Maria's and her tent, scowled at Galahaidra then muttered: "What sort of a bodyguard are you? Letting my tent be invaded by wild boars and wolves!"

The party eventually settled down and then slept until mid afternoon and with only two hours daylight left decided to stay put and make an early start on the following day. Longinus would be another seven days at the Oich and eleven days before he reached Beauly so they had plenty of time to rest and still arrive at their destination ahead of Longinus.

"I will return to give MacAllan the good news" Hagrest announced that night as they ate supper together, the wolf cubs playing at Maria's feet, Thea lying across her legs and sleeping contentedly for the first time in weeks, whilst Sir Kenneth confirmed he would follow and guard Maria and Galahaidra looked at Ninian, whispering for her ears only: "We shall not part again in this life or the next."

The following morning they washed and dressed in the dark, broke their fast with hot bread and honey then set out at first light with six hours daylight in which they would cover thirty leagues; the fox cubs were in

Maria's saddle bags, the she-wolf and wild boar padding alongside Epona. Hagrest would reach the ferry over the Oich on the next day. Maria wanted to take the rest of the party to Inver which was a detour but the settlement was the largest north of Aber. Aber was best reached by sea on their journey back to Britannia but Inver on the Ness had nearly four hundred residents and would be the largest community they had visited since the City of Perth. That night the four companions stopped with Inver in view from the top of a giant fir tree that Maria insisted on climbing, whilst Thea howled in concern.

"We shall reach Inver by midday tomorrow" Maria shouted down then asked "Is that the sea yet?" and pointed to the Loch whose waters formed their right hand boundary and they had often stopped to splash in its shallows. Ninian covered her ears with her hands then turned to Galahaidra and said: "Are you not meant to protect me? Then silence that absurd child!"

"She is bored. Leave it to me" and then Galahaidra shouted up the tree asking Maria to point out many of the landmarks they would pass the next day and then when night fell and the stars came out he asked her about their individual stories. Maria took the opportunity to sing her praises to the wonderful display of stars above and her new family of wolves sat entranced. By the sixth hour after midday they were all tired and took the opportunity for an early supper.

As they sat around the camp fire that night, Galahaidra briefed the two girls on what he knew of the muster of the Christian Army and their Pagan adversaries. They were mortified. Ninian went first, thumping Galahaidra on the right upper arm and calling him a fool. "Did you not listen to a word our Master told us?" she cried then broke down and wept. Maria went next: "We must ride to meet the Pagan Kings first. We must go to the north coast; forget about Inver. If we can persuade the Pagan Kings to listen then we may still prevent this terrible war."

"Maria" Kenneth spoke softly, a quiet voice that reflected her own and showed the fundamental gentleness of his personality. He was as much against the horrors of war as she, but also knew that when war has been declared, all principles of peaceful pacificism are forced aside. War brings atrocity in its wake whether you are a person of principle or not. Once begun, there is no dam to halt the terrible on-rush of its waters; it sweeps every concept of humanity to one side. Yet there are still occasions when an individual can withstand the tide: rare and exceptional. Kenneth could not be certain that Maria's resistance might be one of these but feared she would become another forgotten moment of temperance in a history full of such vain attempts to stand up against those who lived their lives by violence. So Sir Kenneth tried to dissuade her from a course of action that must lead to her death.

"The Pagan Kings have already declared war on you personally. Every Pagan barbarian in the northern hemisphere is commanded to seek you out, torture you and then damn you by committing your remains to the depths of the seas. They talk of the most terrible means by which they can inflict pain and misery on you, of publicly hanging your remains for all Christians to see the Pagan's total mastery over your Master. You will find no mercy when you meet them, only the most horrific death imaginable. Their army is mustered to find and slay you; it has no interest in our Christian army other than if we attempt to save you."

Galahaidra nodded, adding his ten denarii's worth: "We muster to save you Maria. You commit suicide if you go it alone this time."

Alas, once again they encountered Maria's stubborn heart. Perhaps if Craedech or Godric had been present they might have dissuaded her but Sir Kenneth was too sympathetic to her cause and Galahaidra was already in the dog house with Ninian and not in a strong position to push his point of view. Maria looked at them all then summarised what they had told her:

"Two of the largest armies ever to gather in Britannia and Caledonia are about to fight it out *over me.* The death toll will be horrendous and there can be no winner from such a conflict. The solution, of course, is obvious: take away the cause of the conflict. I shall go before the Pagan Kings and meet my death with prayer and song removing the need for the Christian Army to save me."

"Suicide is a sin!" Galahaidra spoke with authority.

"Self sacrifice is not. Our Master showed this but even if He had not, read your Isaiah and your Maccabees. What I do is not suicide for I shall try my best to bring the Vicing and the Caledonii around to see reason and only to succumb if they insist on murdering me. But do not be afraid for me. I shall pray to our Master and I am certain there shall still be a way for peace to rule supreme."

It was with great sadness that the party set off to seek out the Kings of the Caledonii and Vicing so that Maria could surrender into their custody. Or at least three of the companions were sad, fearing they were presiding in the death by execution of their dearest friend. Maria, however, positively glowed: "To save so many lives through my sacrifice is the death I have always prayed for" she murmured. "At last I can understand the sacrifice of my Master and experience the terrible pain and torture he went through to save all of our lives. I cannot explain how happy I am but this is the fulfilment of my short life."

And she was genuinely happy: singing and laughing as she looked around her at little things: the song of birds; the cold sun had returned to sends its ladders of light through the collage of the clouds; a sky made mauve, purple and crimson by the gathering storm; the swirling fall of gold, silver and copper leaves; splashes of rain falling on her cheeks; clouds formed as giants holding up the sky; her wild boar who were chasing each other in and out of Epona's legs; her new family of wolves, the mother proudly walking as she guarded her new mistress, her cubs copying their mother's proud step, looking over their haunches to be sure they got it right.

Then as she looked into the far distance she saw the grey shadow of majestic mountains; towering torrents of crystal water crashing down to create foam at the base of majestic falls; the distant silver sea and the black waters of the many lochs held secure within the vales of mountains' glory; the echoes of the deer as they called to their herd. She sang; she offered praise; she rejoiced and nothing could make her sad; not even the weeping of her friends for whom her happiness was more painful than had she shown fear for her fate.

"What of Craedech?" Galahaidra fumed, so incensed he was come close to bursting with his anger and briefly Maria's head went down in sadness, not certain how to respond but then she looked within her and found the courage, the inner reserves of character to say:

"I will still be with him. For surely God will allow our love to survive? Our love is a good thing, God-given. It will not be cast away; rather God will find a way for it to continue despite my death. I shall pray to the Master but I believe my love shall never die though my body shall be tortured and I shall be slain."

"Are you not frightened?" Ninian asked and Maria nodded. "Yes I am absolutely terrified but that does not matter. My fears are unimportant. We save lives through what we do."

"We save the lives of Pagans who seek to slay you in order to crush the faith of our Master" Sir Kenneth whispered, barely able to speak through his sadness and desolation.

"We give the Pagans a chance to be redeemed, for they are also loved by God. The chance for them to be saved would be lost if they were slain before the time allotted to them by God." Maria replied yet she was overwrought herself to see the gentle knight, Sir Kenneth, so distressed at the fate she was about to face.

"Do not fear for me" she continued trying to console him. "Death is the start of a wonderful journey. Pray that I have the courage to face my death and make it mean something" and in silence they rode towards the lands of the Corvinii in the furthest northen reaches of Caledonia, where the cliffs looked across the most tempestuous of seas, a boiling mass of heaving water with waves hundreds of feet high that smashed against the cliff face that formed the furthest reaches of the world: Ultima Thule.

Maria's intent was to surrender at the first Vicing settlement she could find and accept the punishment that awaited her. A punishment for no crime, yet this would be an act of selflessness that would place a seal upon her mission.

"You cannot do this" screamed Galahaidra. "You forget that it shall be your descendants who will convert the whole of the Roman Empire to follow our Master."

But Maria shook her head then whispered: "I forget nothing. This is not my faith but my Master's. He will find a way for our faith to grow without me. My mission was never about me and always about Him. Surely no greater ill is there than that we go to war to save my life?"

"What about us? Will we have a choice or must we go to our deaths with you?" Ninian asked, her own fears showing and finally Maria showed doubt. "I do not know" the girl admitted and was silent then whispered: "I need to be alone for I have not considered this. It would be wrong of me to endanger any of you. I think I must go before the Kings alone."

"NO!" cried all three of her companions and she had to grin for she always laughed when faced with the anger of others then Maria asked a practical question: "How long will it take for us to reach the north coast?"

"We have another one hundred leagues to cross but the roads are bleak, paths shall be hard on our feet, it shall take three or four days in good weather but snow is coming, the days shortening and we might take twice as long. Why?" Sir Kenneth replied.

"Because I must reach the place of the Vicing in time to be slain by them before ever the Pagan and Christian armies meet in battle!" and now she had so thoroughly silenced everyone that no further word was spoken for the rest of that day.

It fell dark around the fourth hour and Maria insisted on sitting up to talk to the stars as her horse, Epona, Thea and her family and the wild boar all sat at her feet, listening to her singing, an appreciative audience enjoying her company, picking up no sense of the sadness of her other companions. Sir Kenneth had placed his bed roll under the flap of one of the tents and whispered to Galahaidra: "I will guard Maria. This is not how I thought Maria's mission would end and I imagine both Ninian and you are devastated. Ninian needs you tonight. Take the other tent" then Ninian joined Galahaidra as he was seeing that the horses were settled for the night and asked him simply: "Sleep with me" and Galahaidra nodded his head: "Kenneth will guard Maria and I would be honoured to keep you company on this saddest of nights."

"Can you not do something?" Ninian asked the pain naked in her eyes and Galahaidra looked at her then said: "Yes I can do many things. But would Maria ever forgive me and can we not be certain that the girl is right? Too often she has been right before!"

The following morning breakfast was a silent affair. Maria was very conscious that her companions were in shock, unable to see the importance of the sacrifice Maria was proposing to make. They could not see that however important was her mission her Master's message would endure whatever she chose to do. But the thousands who might die in battle would lose the opportunity for Eternal Life. For them the consequences could be everlasting. She could not allow such a terrible loss of life to happen. To give up her own life, her ambitions, her love for Prince Craedech in return for rescuing so many tens of thousands was more than a fair exchange. She was grateful to her Master for the opportunity to make something of her life in this way. To achieve something where up until now all she had done had been the Master's doing. She listened with surprise therefore as Galahaidra made a pronouncement:

"We are a day away from the Firth of Beauly where we expect to see your father Prince Godric arrive with his fleet and army, ready to defend you. Three days later and we should reach the north coast of Caledonia where we should find the place where Kings Craedfellant and Graemworma will have landed and will be ready to receive you. Sir Kenneth has agreed to accompany you and offer you his protection until you go before the Kings of the Vicing.

Alas, I do not have the courage to go with you and propose that Ninian and I remain with your father. I cannot bear to see you slain nor am I certain that you will obtain peace through your sacrifice. The Vicing are come to take Caledonia and Britannia, in the process defeating the King of the Western Lands and Hibernia.

This is no longer just about you, Maria. You are arrogant and egotistical to think that it ever was. This is about the barbarians from Scandanavia and northern Europa wiping out all the little kingdoms in Britannia and Caledonia, killing the likes of Godric, Jaerid, Pasterix, Craedech and all of the people you converted to Christianity on your mission, all slain …" and he broke down unable to say any more, grasping Ninian's hand for comfort, refusing to look at Maria, who sat there in shock, never thinking that her mission would end with her friends deserting her. She went to stand and stumbled blinded by her confusion then she knelt and prayed, seeking her Master, questioning her own motives for the first time. "I am truly lost" she whispered to herself.

Her Master was waiting for her in a room she had never been in before: it was barren of all but the simplest of furniture; a long table, two chairs, a stand or podium, no windows, half lit, a harsh stone floor, plane and featureless plaster walls and panelled ceiling. "Master" she asked "What is this cold and lifeless place?"

"It is where you are to be judged" he replied and would not look at her, at which she fell to the ground and kneeling before him begged: "Lord, please have mercy on me. Has my arrogance been so great? Forgive me lord or at least let me make amends."

"By what right have you thrown away my mission to serve your own ends?"

Maria's head dropped and her whole body sagged as she began to come to terms with the terrible error of judgement she had made then her courage returned and she stood to face her Master, accepting whatever punishment was to be her due:

“I stand condemned and accept that I am guilty of sacrificing myself and your mission” she whispered and felt her heart pounding and her whole body reeling with fear at the consequences of the great wrong that she had done. Almost unable to breathe yet somehow she was able to say:

“What penance must I do to earn forgiveness and restore myself in your love or am I already beyond that?”

“Is your life of so little value?” Her Master asked. Yet he was not angry with her. Rather he was genuinely concerned at what she was in danger of becoming.

“Yes, Master” she replied astonishing him with her answer. “My life is of no value save when I do your Will.”

“Maria, you are so wrong: for everything that I have created has great value in my eyes” and then he held out his arms and as she flew into them he held her tight then said: “Learn from this, my dearest one. My mission is never to be bartered away and your life is never yours to sacrifice in this way.”

“What must I do?” she asked tears flowing and yet the tears were not because she felt sorry for herself nor from any embarrassment or guilt. She cried because she had nearly let her Master’s mission fail through her pride.

“Complete your mission, **all** of it!” and at last the Master smiled down on her before he said: “And I shall not forgive you until you have done so … but remember I am always here if you need my help.”

“… and all the many deaths! All those poor souls lost through the evil of war? Is such a huge loss of life right?” and Maria stood once more defiant and prepared to challenge her Master at which he laughed then said: “You know what you must do!”

Maria looked at her Master, her head on one side, her mind in utter chaotic confusion and then suddenly a sparkle came into her eyes and grinning she said: “Help me complete your mission *and* prevent the terrible battle between the Christians and the Pagans”. But once she had said this she paused for finally she comprehended not just the terrible sin that she had committed but also what it was that she must do to put things right.

She laughed and the room brightened at the sound and as she looked the first of many windows appeared, cut as if by magic through the plaster of the walls to show her vistas of the most beautiful vineyards and a cloudless sky. It was twilight and the sun left a trail of golden blessing, its benison as tramlines on gleaming purple and brightest green as its rays tipped the ripening grapes. In the darkest of blue heavens stood the silvery moon; it was almost spectral in its presence. Though it was autumn, the blossoms of spring and the rose petals of summer drifted through the mullion windows to further brighten the chamber and her heart. This was Maria's favourite time of day when she could praise God for both the sun and the moon and this is what she now did, singing to her heart's and soul's ease for her Master.

Then as she looked into the room, she saw pictures and wall hangings appear to bring the colour of outside into the sere Judgement Hall; soft seats, cushions, lanterns and cedar wood tables, incense burners and a sideboard which was brimming with ice-cold drinks and the scent of tea, rose syrup, sherbert, fresh lemon, chillies and lime.

"Will you drink with me, lord?" she asked kneeling once more before him to pour the clear bronze scented liquid from its silver samovah and offering him a porcelain cup of tea and rose petals, the china so delicate it floated in her hand then drifted slowly across the room for him to hold. He thanked her then nodded to himself for he could see that Maria finally understood.

"This is beautiful" she said looking once more around the room that continued to fill with light and colour, losing its former stark and severe character to come finally to blossoming life: silk hangings and coloured glass lanterns hanging from the ceiling. She went to thank her lord but the Master held up one hand.

"Not mine!" he explained and she found herself back at the company's camp site in a glade south west of Beauly, with Galahaidra, Kenneth and Ninian each watching her anxiously for her tears seemed so desperate.

Maria smiled up at them from where she had been kneeling at their feet and said simply:

"Forgive me for I have sinned. We must find a way for me to bring my message to the Pagans … and to stay alive." As she looked into their eyes she saw the hope that her death-wish had driven briefly under the surface suddenly return.

Maria's Mission to Caledonia: Beauly and Mullochy Bay

The settlement of Beauly sat on the cliffs of the estuary at the mouth of the River Beauly, known as the Firth of Beauly. The settlement was north of the river itself where the river had formed an island to provide a naturally fortified moated encampment. Just to the west of Beauly the road crossed at a ford and over a flimsy wooden foot-bridge, western Baltain, where the track led east to the Firth of the Moray through the Balcharan and Drumchardine forests and mountains.

Beauly was relatively prosperous, part of the ferry crossing that forded the Firth from the larger settlement at Inver and which allowed the south-east coastline to trade with the less populous north-east coastline without the need to travel many days to the south-west in order to pass around Loch Ness. The Roman merchant oupost of Campus Augustus and the ford of the River Oich that had been Longinus' route north was the next nearest crossing for those travelling north and south from Inver on the Ness.

Prince Godric had sailed into the Firth the previous afternoon and scouting its shores he had considered putting in at Inver on the mouth of the Oich and Ness but instead brought his fleet into the comparative calm and safety of Mullochy Bay. Above its sands, his troops had begun to build the large wooded palisade and earthern works that would be the defence for his army of fifteen thousand horse and thirteen thousand phalanges and archers. By the time Maria and her company reached Beauly, Godric and one of his Yeorls had already set up an outpost to the north of the settlement and were waiting for her.

Garrard, captain of a company of fifty cavalry, greeted the princess and immediately offered twenty of his men to be her escort to the fortifications at Mullochy. He was the first to give the girl the news that Pasterix, Jaerid and Varus were also on their way, sailing the North Sea to come and protect her.

"First, I am ordered to bring you to see your father. He has been out of his mind with worry."

Maria asked to say a brief service for the tribes of Lugii and Treaxil that inhabited the local villages and Inver to their south-east. Many had gathered at Beauly on hearing the news that Maria had come and survived being taken by the monster at Loch Ness. "What is this story of a monster?" Garrard asked her, eyeing Thea and the family of wild boar a little warily.

"Not a monster but a gentle and courteous sea serpent whom I hope one day to introduce to you all" Maria replied at which Garrard could see Ninian over the girl's shoulder vigorously shaking her head and miming huge and terrifying jaws.

A few hundred congregated at the large settlement for Maria's midday service of the breaking of the bread, curious to see the girl and interested to hear of her mission. Any who could bear a spear or sling had left for their King's muster to the north and so the local settlements had lost their men-folk; the women, the young, the old and the vulnerable were more receptive to the message of the Master, for his audience had always been the meek and humble, the poor, the oppressed. Whilst it was only a few hundred, the Assembly that day represented well over half of those who lived around the Firth and within a half day's ride of Beauly.

"I come with a message from my Master for those who mistakenly believe in many Gods and who dream of a day when this world can be peaceful. For those willing to follow my Master I offer his promise, his covenant, his oath and his gifts."

Her words were greeted with eager silence, a collective intake of breath as all prepared to listen.

"My Master has sent me on a mission to bring his Good News to those in the far-flung places of our world whom otherwise might be neglected. My Master wants everyone to be given the chance to hear his message. His message is important for he is the only God and holds the keys to Paradise. He offers every one of us a wonderful gift: to live with him forever in his home in Paradise" and she made eye contact with them watching as they nodded in understanding before she continued:

"He came amongst us as a simple man, the son of a carpenter, yet was proclaimed King by the people of Ierusalem, executed by the Romans and after three days he rose again from the dead to live with us, to perform many miracles, to preach, to rise into the heavens to finally sit with his Father, and to send us the gifts of his Spirit.

He made all of us a promise: follow him and he will grant us Eternal Life in Paradise. He also offers us his help: he will come and live within us whenever we break bread together and I will do this with you today" at which all sat forward showing surprise, wonder and hope.

"He sent his Spirit and it grants us the gifts of healing, prophecy, tongues and hope" and it was only then that they realised she spoke their own language, both Lugian and Treaxal, and the murmurs begun. So she stopped there to take their questions.

"How do we follow your Master?"

"Believe in Him: One God! Who came to Earth, died and rose from the dead to new life for us and who sent his Spirit to fill us with the joy and wonder of his love. To follow him we must obey his command: to love God and to love one another."

"That simple?" they all asked in astonishment. "Is that all?

Maria nodded then continued: "My Master told many stories which show what love means and whilst I am here I will happily tell you these" and she was flattered at the sea of nodding smiling faces that greeted her offer. "My Master also promised to be with us: to live within us and inspire us, advise and guide us whenever we break bread with him. He also sends his Spirit to strengthen us and his gifts of the Spirit to help us. Both we shall witness now" and at these words all sat forward wanting to see and hear of these gifts from God.

"The day before he died, my Master had a special meal with his closest friends and family. He broke a loaf of bread and passed the pieces around until we all had a piece" and Galahaidra passed her several loaves which

Maria broke until there were over three hundred pieces then her acolytes, Galahaidra and Kenneth began to pass the pieces around in two large rush panniers, the tribes people eagerly taking a piece as the panniers were passed amongst them. When Maria could see that they all had a piece, smiling to herself as she spotted those who had greedily taken more than one, she continued:

"My Master held the bread up" and they all copied her "and said the following words: 'This is Me; the real Me. When you do this then remember Me and I will come." The result was immediate and breathtaking. The sun broke through the clouds to single out the young girl and the flames of the Spirit came down as white flames of fire to engulf her yet they did not touch her fair skin but rather shone through her as if she were the shade of a lantern. She lowered her hands slowly, tongues of flame at every finger tip and the flames leapt and danced to touch every one of her congregation.

All gasped as they saw the Master: a vision that filled them with the passion of belief and brought them hope, courage, the desire to do good, to serve and to follow God. Then a few found they could speak in tongues, all of the languages of the many tribes of the Caledonii. Ninian was careful to mark them out for they would help her in her mission to convert the pagans. One turned to a neighbour and touched a young woman kneeling in prayer on the head. The poor woman had been born with a cleft lip and suffered disparagement and insult for her disfigurement during her life until that day yet had responded with care and love, teaching the children of her village and nursing the elderly and infirm. This day and for the rest of her life the Spirit rendered her beautiful and continuing to kneel she gave praise.

"Accept us as followers of your Master" many asked, wanting to know how to become a follower: a 'Christian'. Maria laughed gaily: not at them but with them and because she was happy at the Good News she was about to give them.

"You are already followers because you asked" she replied. "And the Master is now *our* Master and not just mine."

“Tell us more of our Master” others asked.

“Gladly” she replied. “I shall return each day to break the bread and when I do I shall tell you one or more of his stories and about his life, death, resurrection, ascension and the first day he gave us his Spirit. Come back” she asked “and Bring family and friends, neighbours, your sick to be healed, your prisoners and slaves to be released to come to the Master for their freedom. Return and you shall make our Master happy. For today we all begin the journey to Eternal Life with God in Paradise. My Master said: ‘He is the Truth and the Way to Eternal Life.’ Join me and our Master shall return to us every time as we ‘break the bread’.”

“What shall we do when you go?” one asked and for the first time the crowd became restless and anxious.

“Have no fear. The Master will never leave you now. You have all felt his presence. Those who wish to do so can lead you in ‘breaking the bread’: which is the greatest gift we can give God and our way of remembering him. You have seen how simple it is to do. Have the faith to break bread in your homes and villages and the Master shall remain with you in your hearts and souls.”

Later that day Ninian would dedicate her first Temple to the Risen Christ in the settlement of Beauly: a stable, so suitable as it marked the birth of Christianity in Scotland as well as Christ’s own birth, with views overlooking the Firth of Beauly across to the Firth of Moray and out to the North Sea; a simple place with the Chi and Rho of Christ’s name carved into an upright beam, a tressle table for its altar and a manger overturned to become the podium from which Ninian would begin her lifetime of preaching. The followers who came soon spilt out onto the courtyards beyond but in its earliest days they shared the Good News with a small herd of cows and sheep and two draught horses with their harness hanging from cross beams and hay bales doubling up as seating.

That evening, Maria joined her father who was as angry as she had ever seen him. “What madness is this that you try and throw away your life in such foolishness?” he bellowed and even his bodyguard quailed.

Maria was suitably contrite, falling at his feet and begging for his forgiveness, honestly and openly owning to her stupidity immediately, offering whatever penance he should see fit: "All I ask is that your good humour shalt return. For I love you, my father, and cannot forgive myself that I have distressed you so … unless I know that you forgive me."

"Ha" he said but a smile crept into the corner of his mouth as he asked: "Tell me about the monster!"

"I think you will like him!" Maria replied in all innocence then her face fell in shock as she realised the other interpretation of her words, but Godric roared with laughter as he had always admired her courage and defiance of him. He followed her because of her honesty and the Power of God he could see within her, but he loved her when she did and said outrageous things as now and was proud of her courage. He continued but teasing her now: "I am neither a monster nor do I have any wish to meet one. Now when did you intend to give your father a hug?" and she leapt off her knees and into his waiting arms. He growled good-humouredly in her ear then whispered: "As always I am proud of your exploits but you go with an escort of at least fifty thousands when you meet the Pagan Kings and that is your father's command."

"It is alright, father, for our Master has shown me what I must do. I have been stupid and the solution is so simple."

"Do we fight?"

"That is not up to me and has little to do with me. I shall advocate Peace but if you must fight then so be it!"

"How is this?" he roared.

"If I told you it would spoil the surprise" at which his face went bright purple in momentary rage. Seeing his anger she began to giggle and he gave up: "You are the most disrespectful of all my subjects … but I fear that makes me love you even more" and for that admission she kissed him on both cheeks then thanked him for being so understanding.

"'Understanding'!?" he muttered: "'Understanding' … I don't 'understand' a thing."

The following day as Ninian, the Prince, Sir Galahaidra and Sir Kenneth broke their fast with Maria and Godric's captains at a large tressle table set on the cliff's edge overlooking Mullochy Bay, one hundred and seventy triremes and quadrimes came out of the low hanging mist like a flock of sea monsters and began to row into the huge bay, dwarfing Godric's large fleet that was already moored up on the west beach.

It would take a whole day for the three Kings Pasterix's, Jaerid's and Gaefreigh's huge armies to disembark. They were joined by the Votadini under their Chief, Great Lord Pearlinn and by Lord Harroult, the young Eorl of the disputed territory of the Sevgolae. "Bit of a problem" Godric would later mutter to Jaerid "as the Sevgolae and Dantonnil tribes have both joined us and won't take lightly to Harroult being here."

"Best leave it to Maria" Jaerid had replied. "They would all follow her into Ragnarock!"

The three Kings left their two lords to supervise the disembarkment and joined Prince Godric at his breakfast table. Maria stood on the edge of the cliff like some Dark Age conductor of a huge orchestra, steering the ships with a wave of her hands as they just missed colliding or directing them to a slot where they could beach safely. Fortunately all of the ships' captains and helmsmen below ignored her rather random advice, but the Council of the War Lords was punctuated by 'Ooos' or gasps or the occasional 'O No!' from the lady whom they had all come to rescue.

"Welcome" said the Prince then sat them down and ordered his three new guests a huge breakfast. Maria had ordered the food for the previous sitting and the men were starving. Soon they got down to business:

"There is a huge plain that lies between Avioch and Fortrose with a view towards the North Sea on the north and east flanks, abutted by cliffs. It has a woodland and then three fords over a river should we need to retreat or regroup to our south and an impassable bank of mountains save for a narrow and winding pass that ten men could hold to the west.

The only open approaches are from the south which involves forcing a landing at Mullochy Bay where not only will our fleet be ready to assail the Pagan fleet but we will have artillery lined up on the cliffs above the Bay and fire ships ready to disrupt our foe. The alternative approach is to land on the beaches in the Firth of Cromarty which is wide, flat and broken up by soft, low-lying, gradually rolling hills. There is a forest on the north-west boundary in which cavalry could hide. The battlefield is good country for cavalry, artillery and archers. It is also a natural funnel and our enemy will struggle to be able to bring their full numbers to bear being crushed together so tightly they will not be able to move. The one risk is that there is a cutting to the north-west and they may land part of their army there and come up the cliffs seeking to launch a flank attack. This is where Longinus' skills in man traps plus our cavalry, artillery and archers should give us an advantage, allowing us to drive their numbers over the cliff top.

Let them attack us and we can have many surprises ready for them."

"It is good" and both Jaerid and Pasterix applauded the chosen site then Graefreigh asked the key question: "How do we persuade our foe to fight us there?"

"The Vicing scout by sea so will see our formation but also the strength of our defences if they should try and besiege us at Mullochy. They will fight us on open ground for they have no siege weapons" Sir Kenneth replied for he had been part of the Council that had developed the Christian Army's plan. "Also, we have people from the tribe of the Lugi willing to give word of our location: these are converted Christians, willing to be tortured or die for their new faith."

"I pray this shall never be put to the test" Sir Galahaidra muttered.

"And what was Maria's comment on all of this?" Pasterix asked and Godric blushed. "We have told her the absolute minimum" he admitted and the rest of the Council laughed but were silenced by the Prince's next comment: "She insists she is allowed to speak to their many Kings and leaders … and that she goes alone."

Finally, Pasterix broke the despondent silence that followed Godric's last devastating comment: "It is why we are all here: to protect someone who has no sense of self-preservation but who is so special that all the kingdoms of Britannia have sided together to fight for her. I have news from your father, by the way, Godric. Prince Wulfric met with the King of the Dumnonii and the Lords of the Cantiani. Both have signed the Peace Treaty and joined Maria's 'peace' as have the two Kings of the middle kingdoms of the Catuvellauni. Caractacus now is the sole King of the Catuvellauni whilst the Lords of the Cantiani have sworn fealty to Prince Wulfrid on two conditions: that Maria becomes their Queen; and that her second child shall become the hereditary ruler and leader of the Cantiani. All of Britannia needs Maria alive."

This was greeted with great joy by Godric especially. His daughter would one day co-rule all of Britannia east of Kernow and the mountains of the Situges and south of the Ouse and do so with the rest of Britannia committed to peace and to the powerful unity of faith and belief in one God. Next it was Galahaidra's turn:

"Longinus is three to five days away with seven thousands. Varus is five days away or less with a thousand. The Sevgolae and Dannonil have mustered and will join Hagrest, Lord of All the Gaels with four thousands and arrive in two days. Finally, Sir Iosephus has sent his small fleet of four ships with one thousand mercenaries.

But there is yet more news: Pedrus, the King of All the Picts, the disputed sovereign of the Western Lands and Hibernia has raised eighty ships and sails to defeat the two Vicing Kings whom he hates more even than you, King Jaerid. We do not know how many he shall lead into battle but King Pedrus has committed his whole land and every Pict in Hibernia and Caledonia to the protection of the British princess, Maria."

Seeing Jaerid's face, Godric asked pointedly: "Whom shall you fight, sire?"

The King shrugged his shoulders then realised that the Council needed a better answer than that so gave them the Hope and the Truth they needed to hear:

"I fight *for* Maria and *for* Christ. Eorl Amaric seeks conversion to Christianity whilst he is here and to be put to the Grael test so anything less than total and unequivocal support of Maria will see both Lords Amaric and Harroult revolt. But I cannot be certain that all in my army will think or believe the same whilst I am equally uncertain that all Picts will be happy to side with Christ. We march under a Christian Standard … but do the Picts think that or are they seeking revenge?" then after a few moments further reflection, he smiled and advised: "Put us on opposite flanks and Maria between us and we shall fight for her, forgetting our many differences … for one day at least."

Pasterix thumped him on the back, saying for Jaerid's ears only: "The best thing that ever happened was the peace between us. I shall be proud to fight at your side, cousin."

Graefreigh then concluded the report on the muster: "Lest we forget, we have also brought a *small* force. We number nearly one hundred thousand plus the support staff to go with such a huge army, which is mainly brought from Iceni: bakers, slaughterers, armourers, weaponsmiths, ferriers and blacksmiths, fletchers, carpenters, medical, nursing and veterinary staff, an army of clerks for Pasterix's autobiography" at which the young King blushed then grinning shamelessly admitted he was learning Latin and was grateful for the gift of tongues he had received. Graefreigh continued as if there had been no interruption: "tailors, musicians, several poets and bards, canvas makers, rope makers, falconers and the royal gardener."

"God's blood, this is not war but a family outing" muttered Godric and then after a brief pause, they all laughed and it was in a good mood that the Council meeting broke up to oversee the accommodation for nearly two hundred thousands.

Galahaidra caught up with Maria to ask how her own plans were going and she grinned back at him then gave him a kiss before coming clean: "I started yesterday and all went better than I had hoped but I must wait until Hagrest can join me. I need Sir Kenneth, Eorl Harroult and yourself and to send some messages to the tribes living on the west coast and in Thule. A few hundreds of people, no more than that, yet it shall be they and not our army of tens of thousands that shall determine peace."

Galahaidra looked confused but Maria would provide no further enlightenment, merely saying "We wait until the Pagan Kings march or sail and only when I know where they shalt be do I go to meet them."

"You will still meet the Kings?" He asked suddenly frightened for her.

"Yes! But I take you, Kenneth and Hagrest with me provided that the Kings of the Pagans shalt guarantee your safe conduct."

"And your own 'safe conduct'?"

"God shalt guarantee that but do not fear for me. I no longer see my death as desireable, necessary or inevitable. I have a plan and I Trust in our Master. My faith in him shall see me saved: if there is any way to save me and if that is *His* Will."

The Christian Army predominantly followed the Celtic calendar based on the cycles of the moon rather than the twelve month solar calendar, updated by Julius Caesar and his nephew Octavian, Augustus, then further revised in the reign of Tiberius. Instead of twelve solar months, the Christians had years of thirteen, fourteen or fifteen lunar months. Winter had started and they were in the eleventh of thirteen months.

It had begun to snow heavily and both the winds from the west and the tides of the seas were mounting. The bay below was relatively sheltered from westerly winds but the ships were in danger of being wrecked unless they could be hauled at least another three lengths up the sands of the coves on which they had been beached.

Tents and pavilions needed to go up fast to provide accommodation for the army; one whole hectare of forest had already been cut down and was now being milled to create stabling and other accommodation. The earthern ramparts were being dug but it was taking time as the ground was frozen and almost rock hard. The smiths were struggling to get their forges lit but needed to do so as metal tools were desperately needed: adses, axes, hoes and spade blades.

Camp fires were alight and cooking pots were bubbling away, using up the provisions brought by ship whilst the army organised its foraging and hunting parties. Scouts were coming in with news that the best way to provide for the Army was to trade with the merchants in Inver and Aber on the Deen: the local settlements were too small to maintain an army of their size. There would be no sleep that first night but rather the army and their support staff worked through the night to get pavilions, tents and the first of the timber-framed halls erected. Eventually, the Christians would create the largest City in Britannia for their Army. For now, it was cold and chaotic.

Godric spotted both Maria and Ninian shivering with cold and sent orders for his own heavy metal trunks of clothes to be brought up from his flagship, an elegant trireme. Inside the chests were two white fur hooded coats which completely covered them both and saved them from the exposure the girls would have otherwise experienced with no fat to protect them and both recovering from the beatings on their backs and sides they had received at the hands of the Caledonii.

Ninian found shelter under the trees to the west of the camp, standing alongside many of the care staff around a camp-fire, whilst Maria walked around to talk to the warriors, asking to help. But all were protective of her and knew she was recovering from terrible injuries so rather they would stop and talk to her: of their homes, their family and to ask about her. Godric watched and his reaction was the same as Craedech's: *'What a wonderful Queen she shall make when the time comes. Let her learn her art now but my kingdom will be safe in her hands.'*

That evening, her Eucharistic Service had over one hundred and fifty thousand in attendance and the local communities were stunned at such a huge gathering. Maria was careful to ensure however that local people were near the front and felt welcomed. She told the story of the 'mustard seed', explaining what they were to the many present whom had never seen a desert and only the Iceni and the Trinovantes had grown mustard seeds. She gulped as she realised they had never even seen a 'warm sun' let alone a 'hot sun' and she was planning to live here!

She also took the opportunity after the Service to talk to those who had been fortunate enough to receive the gift of tongues the day before and asked them to do her a favour: "Will you ride to see friends or family whom you have in the west or further north?"

Most were able to say 'Yes' having many family members who had settled to the north and west. "Can we ask why?" they questioned the girl gently.

"Two reasons" she replied, smiling in gratitude at their offer of aid: "Can you invite them to join us here for the Celebration of the Eucharist. I guarantee their safety and that they shall be warmly welcomed by me and by all Christians: for it is a command of our Masters that we love all men and women.

Second, my friend the Centurion Longinus has a niece, from north Gaul with red hair and green eyes. Could you ask for her as she is why my friend has journeyed with me?"

They were happy to agree and set out that same night on horse and foot, promising to return within the week.

Longinus arrived three days later; his column spread over two full leagues and took two days to cross the River Beauly using the ferry and small bridge. Yet his arrival was good news and it almost completed the muster of the Christian Army. It also meant their overall commander and general-in-chief was now with his army and would be able to outline his more detailed plan for the discomfurture of the Pagan Army. Iosephus arrived the same day and this brought Maria's company back together for the first time in two se'enights. She was overjoyed and could not stop hugging each of her companions in turn. She clung to them in relief and left them breathless when finally they could untangle themselves. She saved her warmest embrace for Craedech and he jested: "Miss me?"

"O yes and never again shall we be apart for so long. In future you shall guard me and be at my side."

"And if I want to do my own thing?" He asked still teasing her.

"I am 'your own thing' and don't you ever forget that my Prince" was her feisty reply and he gulped then nodded but she was serious and continued:

"My love, my lord, I have sinned terribly and need you at my side so that I listen to the sensible advice you give me and do not stray so much from my Master's path again."

Prince Craedech looked at her in stunned astonishment and his mind was numbed by what she had said as he asked her: "What sin could *you* have ever committed?"

"Loads" she admitted honestly. "But this one was an enormous sin. My pride was such that I was prepared to sacrifice my life to prevent this Christian Army and the Pagan Army from fighting each other. I thought that one life for tens of thousands was a good sacrifice. But my Master reminded me that I would also be abandoning the mission which was not *my* mission to abandon but *His*. I am humbled and humiliated. He has not forgiven me so I must serve my penance. I need your help."

"Anything" he replied but Maria shook her head. "Such commitments as the one you have just made are precisely what got me into trouble and what our Master once questioned when a possible follower said he would follow Iesus 'everywhere'. I need you to offer me advice when I appear to be doing something stupid" then a mischievous smile came on to her elfin face and she said with a disarming grin: "It is likely to be a full time and very arduous task for I often do stupid things" at which he finally laughed and hugged her. "Much better" she whispered in his ear and promptly fell asleep in his arms, the Prince only just catching her as she started to fall to the ground. Sir Kenneth had been watching from a discreet distance and stepped forwards to help Prince Craedech carry the girl to the large pavilion in the centre of the camp that Godric had erected for himself and his daughter.

"She has not slept since she got here" the knight whispered over the girl's head. "I think she was waiting for you and has been much more worried for your safety than she would ever let on. By the way, welcome!"

Iosephus briefed the War Council on the terrible news breaking from the west and all of the War Lords were silenced as they tried to take that news in: "It is a very new report, fresh from my riders based along the west coastline route. The news may be as old as two days out of date but however old this news is, nothing can disguise its seriousness.

The fleet of King Pedrus met the combined fleets of Kings Craedfellant and Graedworma and was sunk with all hands. If Pedrus' army was on board then they are now at the bottom of the Western Sea. The sea route for the tribes from Skye, the Hebrides and Thule is now clear. That eighty ships should be sunk without trace augurs badly and suggests the Vicing fleet is vastly superior to anything we can put out to sea.

"Does King Pedrus live?" Godric asked and Iosephus shook his head then on reflection admitted: "No-one knows but we should have more information as the week unfolds.

The Vicing armies now only wait to join up with the Germanii and then they will come south to meet us here. Should we try and prevent the merger of the Germanii and the Scandanavian Vicing Armies?"

All shook their heads. The risk was too great. The morale of their marines would be at rock bottom if they tried to assail another fleet and the risk if they lost their fleet was that over one hundred and fifty thousands would starve in Mullochy and Beauly with no means to bring food to their camp by sea, caught out in the terrifying snow storms of winter. Longinus continued:

"We must be careful as to how we break this news to our army. We need scout reports twice each day as we must be ready for when the enemy move. However, we must not find ourselves camped for too long at the proposed battle site. We must send a Forlorn Hope of sufficient size to tell the enemy what our supposed intent is, but not so large that our foe is tempted to let our whole army starve or remain exposed to the weather."

The War Council could see the sense in this and as Longinus caught their eyes and their attention he could see the courage and determination return. He opened the meeting for questions and none of these spoke of defeat to his relief. Already his generals had put the loss of King Pedrus behind them.

"Who leads the Forlorn Hope?" asked Eorl Amaric. Longinus turned to Galahaidra and asked the knight if he would and so was a little taken aback by the young man's reply:

"Not this time, my friend. Maria already has a task for me" but he could not be drawn to tell them what it was.

Iosephus then suggested that whomsoever led the Forlorn Hope should also be in charge of preparing the battle site for its defence and Longinus thanked him then asked his Council: "I need someone who is an engineer and good at preparing traps. Do we have anyone?"

It was Craedech who answered that question: "I could but I have promised to protect Maria. We have Roman legionaries joining us, however, and surely there will be many amongst those who have your skill?"

"Better than me even" exclaimed Longinus in delight. "For there is one person who would be ideal for both the Forlorn Hope and setting the traps for the Pagans: my former primus pilum, Martius."

Finally, it was Galahaidra who asked the question they had all been avoiding but now must address: "How large are our enemy and shalt we be outnumbered?"

"If our enemy can be persuaded to attack us on the battle site I have chosen then their huge numbers will count against them. They shall be so crushed that they will not be able to raise their arms to strike us whilst we can surround them with our superior cavalry. It shall be Trasimeno but in reverse. We shall be Hannibal this time!"

"How many?" Galahaidra persisted and Longinus admitted reluctantly:

"My friend and brother-in-arms, I do not know. But it could be three hundreds of thousands or more. We may be outnumbered by two Pagans to every one Christian. Yet I believe it shall be our superior tactics that shall count and not their superior numbers" with which optimism from their commander-in-chief, the War Council broke up to allow Eorl Amaric to begin his vigil.

Maria and Ninian escorted Eorl Amaric and Sir Galahaidra to the Temple dedicated by Ninian in Beauly. Candelabra had been placed every three paces along both side walls to provide background lighting whilst large lanterns of red-coloured glass hung above their heads marking the sacred blood of their Master's anamnesis. The stable was warm, kept so by the body heat of the animals. It was also reasonably quiet, the silence disturbed by the occasional baying of the herds which were asleep but annoyed by the movement of the two girls and two men.

On the tressle used as an altar were the Spear, Standard and Grael, whilst the Shroud was being used as the altar cloth. Two candles sat either side of the altar. Before the altar was a feeding trough, turned upside down and on which Maria had kindly placed a purple silk cushion she had seen in the haberdashers in Beauly, a mud hut near the centre where the village's Forum could be found. The cushion and feeding trough made a comfortable kneeler.

"What do I do?" asked Amaric whose loyalty to and faith in Christianity had been as strong as anyone's. Maria greatly hoped that he would join the Order for she trusted him totally. She held his hands as much to give him comfort as to let him feel the strength of the Spirit of God burning in her. "You are on fire" he whispered in surprise and then concern for her.

"It shalt not harm me. It is God's Spirit and whilst I do his Will surely I shalt not be harmed?" But he looked closely at her skin and could already see the transparency. He asked not from fear but rather for understanding: "Will I burn like this?"

"Perhaps" she replied. "We each experience God in a unique way. My destiny I believe is to become one with God; to lose my human form as I become a new entity: a being of pure love, adoration, creation, service and obedience. But others shalt serve God in different ways: perhaps fight for him or act as his messengers; or help create new worlds? There are so many ways to serve God and God gives us what is relevant and appropriate for the service we shalt ultimately give for all eternity."

He nodded. Not really understanding what she described but comforted that the service he would be asked to do would be something that best fitted his skill set. He said as much for her benefit as for his own: "I want so much to serve God and if this shalt help then I desire the *Grael Vision* very much!"

"Bless you" Maria replied "For you ask for what God wants and that is the best way to approach the test you now face."

"Do we begin?" And now Amaric was nervous so Maria squeezed his hands for comfort omce more then nodded before asking:

"Do you believe in One God whose Son was born, died, rose again, ascended into heaven and then sent his Spirit to grant us his gifts of healing, prophecy, tongues and hope?"

"Yes" said Amaric without hesitation.

"Do you love God and your fellow man and woman?"

"Yes" replied Amaric once more.

"Will you remember Iesus through the breaking of bread?"

"Yes"

"Will you be pure in your faith as shown through prayer, fasting and pilgrimage?"

"Yes"

Maria smiled then kissed him on both cheeks as a benison and for encouragement before saying: "Then you are ready. Kneel here and pray."

"Pray for what?" Amaric asked briefly confused and then suddenly shook his head saying to Maria "My lady, do not answer that. I know for what I must pray" and the man knelt, bowed his head and remained in silence.

He barely moved for over an hour when suddenly the candles gutted, the red glow from the lanterns turned to gold and Amaric lifted his head. His eyes shone as if aflame and for half a minute he looked towards the altar. Then he stood, turned to Maria who together with Galahaidra and Ninian had kept him company and said:

"Thank you. My *Grael Vision* followed you to your meeting with the Pagan Kings. What you hope to achieve is wonderful and I pray with my heart and soul that you are successful. I asked for Peace on Earth and was given a vision of you as the Instrument of Peace" then he paused before asking: "What do I do now?"

"Each Knight must serve out a Quest" Galahaidra advised him "Sir Amaric, have you a Quest in mind?" and Amaric turned to Maria to say: "Take me with you when you go to see the Pagan Kings" at which she nodded then stepped forward and hugged him.

"I am so proud that you are part of this" Maria whispered before taking his sword, kissing the flat of the blade then holding it out to him, hilt first, she said simply: "*May this sword and the Knight who bears it do good and pure things, remain faithful to the message of Christ, promote peace and unity in this world and receive the blessings of God in the next.*"

The Christian Army's scouts reported to Longinus five days later just as Longinus was greeting Varus and Martius. Varus had brought over one hundred ships and thirteen hundred legionaries. Longinus briefed them both quickly and suggested the legionaries remain on board ship for one further day: "I am expecting news today" he explained "and might need you to go north."

Then the reports from the scouts came in: "The Pagan Kings are coming" they said. "They come by sea and not by land. They will join up with the Germanii and then come here. They are hundreds of thousands!" Longinus called his War Council and began to issue his orders.

First, Longinus commanded Martius to go north and land on the beach by the battle site at Cromarty: "Order your men to look as scruffy as possible. We don't want the enemy scouts to think they face professionals. But where it matters they should have armour and weapons close to hand." Then he issued his orders to Varus, who accepted his command without question but Varus wanted to ensure his fleet was kept safe and advised Longinus:

"Do not ask us to beach our ships as Rome will need them in the future. Rather, we shall disembark the legionaries and then head for safe waters in the Mare Britannia."

"Agreed" Longinus confirmed but then Varus had one condition: "I want to see Maria" he said bluntly "as do my crews." He need not have worried.

Longinus laughed then pointed down to the bay below them where Maria was walking amongst the Admiral's fleet greeting the legionaries as long lost friends and then Martius dropped down onto the sand to be welcomed with a hug of delight.

The scouts were not the only ones to return to the huge camp above Mullochy. The previous day, the last of those Maria had sent out to make contact with the Caledonii villages in the west returned. None had news of Longinus' niece but all had brought back with them a huge representation from their villages. The village elders in every tribe were deeply concerned at the alliance between the King of the Caledonii and the three Kings of the Vicing. They came to see if there could be peace.

"Fathers, Mothers" Maria had said to them as she invited them to celebrate the Eucharist with her. "We must pray to God for peace and have faith in Him who is our Master. I cannot be certain that there shalt not be a battle but I can say that should the Christian Army be victorious then its leaders will offer you the freedom to remain here under your own rule. I cannot say the same about the Germanii and the Vicing. They come to conquer all of Britannia and Caledonia."

"This is our fear also. What can we do?"

"Persuade your own Kings to side with us" Galahaidra replied on Maria's behalf but the elders were doubtful and asked:

"How can we persuade our Kings? They are already in too deep with the Vicing, encouraged by the Chiefs of the Sitenarae and the Corvinii."

"Trust in God and be ready to approach your Kings asking them to promote the cause of Peace" Maria said thoughtfully then continued: "I go to meet your Kings. If I can persuade them to defend their own lands but not to become involved in a war between the Vicing, Germanii and my faith, will you also ask the same of your Kings?"

They nodded then all asked: "Can we join you in the breaking of the bread?" and Maria's smile in response was so bright that Ninian's Temple, where they had chosen to meet, came alight as if the sun had risen within its dim and dusty corners. The celebration that followed saw over one hundred Caledonii from the north and west coast tribes of the Decaniae, Carini, Carnonaeae, Creones and Cerones convert to Christianity and take the word of the Master out to the Highlands and coastlands north of the River Oich.

Longinus, as the Christian Army's commander, ordered all of his ships to put to sea to guard the Roman navy as it headed north under Prince Craedech's command: "We cannot afford a naval battle so this is a show of force to put our foe off any attack in the next twenty four hours. But bring the fleet back once the troops are landed as we wish to encourage the Pagan Army to land north of us. Place chains across the mouth of Mullochy Bay and mount artillery on the cliffs overlooking the coves as we also cannot afford our fleets to be blockaded here: our ships are our means of survival when the snows and frosts of winter come, bringing us food and other provisions to supply the huge army encamped here."

"This is not winter?" Godric asked in dismay, used to the warmer weather on the south coast and Jaerid broke the bad news to him: "It will get a lot colder yet."

Just as night fell, Kings Craemond and Harbondum rode into the camp with over three thousand troops and news of Harbondum's defeat of the Epidii in Battle at Aech. Although the two Kings brought small numbers and the defeat of the Epidii had been a massacre with two hundred Vicing falling to over 1800 Caledonii, the impact on morale was electrifying. Longinus encouraged the two Kings and their entourage to circuit the Campus, telling the story of their victory to as many of his troops as possible. He summonsed all bards and commanded them to write ballads and lays about the victory at Aech. The first songs could be heard an hour later and Craemond and Harbondum were feasted, toasted and feted wherever and whenever they were seen.

The carpenters and blacksmiths were set to work to make more ballistae and trebuchet to place on the cliff tops whilst the Roman navy put out to sea once more to avoid being blockaded within the Bay of Mullochy. Longinus ordered his army to prepare to march and warriors began to report into their captains and standard bearers.

With all this activity going on, no-one noticed Maria depart; she had commissioned a small skiff for herself, Decius, Sir Galahaidra, Sir Kenneth and Sir Amaric, their horses, Maria's wolfs and wild boar, as she set sail to meet the Pagan fleet.

Maria's Mission to Caledonia: The Battles of Cromarty and Mullochy 33 AD

It was evening and dark when Maria who had climbed into the crows' nest of their small sailing vessel first caught sight of the bright lights of King Craedfellast's and King Graemwolda's huge fleet of over one thousand long boats and quadrimes, which had moored along both banks of the Firth of Durnoch and in the sheltered coves of Loch Fleof. From the horrifying screams, Maria guessed that the Vicing and Germanii were rounding up and raping or torturing any of the inhabitants of Durnoch and Tarn who had settled on this lonely shore seeking peace and in admiration of its natural beauty and who had now become the victims of the terrors of the Northern Pagan hordes.

Durnoch could be seen to the north lit up by flames; for the large settlement burned and its inhabitants had already been slain in a riot of carnage and violence. The Pagan Army had come to lay to waste Caledonia and Britannia, leaving desolation, desecration and destruction in their wake. They had no intention of negotiating peace or of fighting for the freedom of the Caledonii.

Her crew looked up towards Maria who openly and unrestrainedly wept for the poor lost souls of those who had stayed at home: too vulnerable, too weak, too humble and too meek to follow their neighbours to war. Maria's prayers could be heard through her tears as her companions left her to her sorrow and began to turn the skiff: there could be no peace agreed with the evil of the warriors who had committed such murder.

Maria sensed the skiff turning and straightaway shinned down the mast to join Decius at the helm. "No" she whispered. "We have God's work to do here. What you see is a sign of what will happen across Europa unless we stop the rot here."

"But how?" Decius asked "For whoever did this will not speak to you of Peace. Rather, they will hang you by your hair until dead."

"I have a lot of hair so should survive for a long time" Maria replied with a grin then continued: "Can you get our skiff close to the enemy fleets? I need to find the flagships of the King of the Caledonii and his brother."

Decius shook his head and muttered to himself that the girl was still as reckless as when she had crewed with him on the Middle Sea. Then stopping briefly in thought, he suddenly nodded to himself then gave Maria what support he could offer.

"I will not recognise the King's ship from any other and do not know his hatchment, escutcheon and banneret. But all of the royal flagships will be moored together to allow the many Kings and their commanders to meet and plan any battle or siege ahead. These ships will be much larger than others and also will have more lights and lanterns lit because their crew will still be on duty. The warriors on the rest of their ships will be ashore, slaying all they see, regardless of age, infirmity, vulnerability or sex, ravishing any woman or girl, burning down the small settlements and sinking any fishing trawlers they find.

I cannot get you close to their fleet for if we are spotted then they will chase us and sink us. But even from here I can see a cluster of thirteen quadrimes and long boats that carry more lights and the voices from those ships are carrying across the water. If *you* listen, because of your gift with languages, you may pick up what is being said and thus identify whose ships they are."

Maria listened carefully, Decius commanding silence from his small crew and the Knights whom had come to protect Maria as much from herself as anyone else.

"Why is Craedech not here?" Galahaidra had asked her but Maria had mentioned that the Prince was on board the Christian fleet's flagship and could not be freed for what he saw as a fool's errand. Galahaidra looked at Maria suspiciously and asked her direct: "Did you ask him?" and Maria could not lie so with a grin that brought dimples to her elfin face admitted:

"No, he has not got a clue where I am. He will be hopping mad and obviously will take his anger out on you. Good thing I have brought you this boat for you to make your escape in" and then the girl left the poor knight with his jaw hanging wide open being consoled by Decius who had overheard every word. "She has not changed at all" the helmsman muttered.

Within minutes Maria had identified one of the long boats where the disheartened crew were cursing the destruction they could see before them:

"We do not follow our King to see the murder of our own kith, kin and fellow Caledonians" muttered a voice rendered gloomy in the gloom.

"Hush" replied his comrade, whose whisper still tripped across the silence of the dark waters of the North Sea to be picked up by the acute hearing of the young maiden with her ear close to the water. "If you are heard then you shall be slain. We have no choice but to follow now and it is the same for our King. He fears for his family if he should turn against the Kings Craedfellast and Graemwolda."

Maria turned to Decius and nodded. Then checking no-one else was looking in her direction she walked around him until she was standing behind him: "Don't look" she whispered and stripped down to her silk shift then before her friend could stop her, she had dropped silently off the bows and into the cold waters below. Seconds later she heard a splash and looking to her left there was Thea, following her. Galahaidra heard the splash and ran to the side rail of the skiff then pointed for Kenneth's and Amaric's benefit.

"I cannot swim" Galahaidra admitted muttering and then looked at the other two knights and they both shook their heads. Sir Kenneth paused briefly in thought and then a gleam of humour came into his gentle grey eyes as he posed a question to his two comrades: "Do you think that perhaps Maria knew this? What are the chances of her selecting three companions at random, none of whom could swim to be with her when she braved the Pagan Kings at sea?"

Amaric looked shocked, never considering that Maria could be capable of such deviousness but Galahaidra shrugged his shoulders in resignation:

"She planned this" he whispered "and when she returns I shall tell her father and her future husband of her antics and she will receive the father of all trimmings down" then he turned to Decius and asked: "Was she armed?"

The helmsman held his hands up in the air, acknowledging that he did not know. "She told me not to look" Decius confessed feeling a complete idiot.

"Can you follow her?" Amaric asked but the helmsman was clear that if they moved any closer they risked discovery by the fleet's lookouts or running over the girl in the dark of the sky and the sea.

Maria swam to the shore side of the long boat from which the voices of the Caledonians had drifted for her to hear, working on the basis that the look outs would be watching out towards the North Sea. She waited until a cloud had covered the bright light of the moon above her then grabbed the rigging on the side of the ship and began to climb. Every few feet she would reach back for Thea and place her wolf on one of the runners: wooden platforms on the side of the ship that were used when it moored at a quayside.

The sides of the King's long boat were relatively close to the water compared to the four rimes or banks of oars that gave the quadrimes their height, speed and name. Within a minute she was able to raise her head slowly over the side of the deck and looked across at two Caledonian warriors, wearing tartan and armed with an oval shield, spear and knife.

To her right was the Fos'castle with the cabin for the King beneath. There were no lights coming from the cabin's windows and Maria guessed that the King was either in Council with his fellow sovereigns or asleep. Except had the King slept then there would have been considerably more guards on deck and in front of the cabin's entrance.

'*In Council then*' she thought to herself and walked slowly along the top runner, ducking beneath the deck's side whenever either of the look outs began to turn to look back at the slaughter on the shore. She quickly made her way to the prow of the ship, below which was a large bay window glassless that looked fo'ward from the King's cabin. Holding the Prow Spit, she swung towards the window until her small feet were balanced on the sill then beckonsed for Thea to follow.

The wolf leapt into her arms sending the girl flying backwards through the cabin's window to land in a sorry heap on a woollen rug on the wooden planked floor of the cabin, with an enormous and apologetic wolf lying on top of her.

"Get off me you big lump" Maria muttered then laughed as Thea sheepishly sat back on its haunches before it gave her a grin. Maria stood and had a look around the cabin: there was a warderobe next door to the cabin, accessed by an archway across which a heavy velvet curtain had been drawn, providing the ideal hiding place for the girl and her she-wolf whilst they waited for either King Graemir or his younger brother King Garrold.

Maria had to wait a good hour and had half fallen asleep when Thea licked her face to wake her up and the next thing she heard was the sound of dozens of voices; clearly the Kings had returned with some of their Lords and their bodyguards. '*That is going to be awkward*' Maria thought as she did not know the Caledonian lords from each other and the last thing she wanted to do was disclose her plans to anyone else but the two Caledonian Kings … well not in the first instance anyway!

She heard someone barge into the cabin, grab something then head straight out again leaving Maria alone in the cabin's warderobe once more. The girl looked through the curtains into the cabin and eventually spotted that the wine amphora and leather sack of ale had been grabbed off the sideboard. '*O wonderful, they are going to have a party and come back roaring drunk*' she thought then finally, Maria realised she had no choice and she knelt in prayer.

The Master was waiting for her in a room without shadows, soft silks of cream and light blue falling gently from the ceiling, a balcony that was accessed through two wooden shuttered doors, set back so that Maria could see the blue lagoon, surrounded by rolling hills of purest green grass, a sky of mauves, reds and purples illuminated by the setting sun, its final fiery red glow, leaving lines of crimson, rose and gold on the furthest horizon. Her Master was seated on an enormous leather pouf in reds, golds and greens and beckonsed for Maria to sit next to him on a bed of silk cushions upon a silk Persian Rug of sage green that completely covered the wood block floor beneath. On the walls were hung silk tapestries, images of the wonders of the world, in vivid electrifying colour, painted on silk then framed to become windows in the walls of the subtlest grey-green. The room required no lighting; lit by the burning beauty of the sun. In the centre of the rug was a low mahogany table on which were set two goblets, a fluted glass karaffe and a copper-coloured clay jug.

The moment Maria joined the Master, he offered her some ale. She declined politely and also refused some wine: she would not drink alcohol even when the brew might be heavenly.

Maria was against alcohol on the grounds that she had seen the impact it had on people and how it clouded our senses, preventing us from having a true, glorious and uninterrupted understanding of creation; it diluted our sense of the awe and wonder of our surroundings. It also seemed to be the well-spring of argument; encouraging waves of anger and violence; clouding judgement and giving people a false sense of courage. Long years of use could damage key organs such as the liver and kidney, seeing people become seriously ill or even die prematurely. Above all it interfered with our communion with God, our ability to hear and understand his divine message; sending people to sleep when we were preparing to listen to God in the silence of the last watch.

"How can I help?" the Master grinned, reading her thoughts and already being aware of Maria's scruples over wine and ale. He reminded the girl that he was the vine from which all comfort, the past, present and future came and that he had offered bread *and* wine at his Passover meal before he was arrested and taken to be crucified.

"I will gladly share with you a bunch of grapes from your vine, my lord" the girl replied and her Master snorted then spotted the tell-tale dimples and realised she was teasing him.

"Maria, my child, you are not meant to *tease* God!"

"You old stick in the mud."

"Nor call me names" her Master continued exasperated then gave in as he realised the girl was quite capable of undermining any pretensions that he had and reducing him to the stature and status of a schoolboy when she was on a 'mission.' She clearly had something on her mind and was building up her confidence and courage in preparation to confront her God. A futile act on her part and her Master sat back ready to enjoy her challenge: "Maria, what can I do for?" he asked showing that he took her prayers and her requests seriously.

"Persuade the two Kings of the Caledonii and the Sitenarae to finish their drinking party early, send everyone to bed and to retire to their cabins for the night then look after me in case the two drunken monarchs get any ideas." Maria asked and then let the Master see an image in her mind of him being pecked by a hen.

"Was I meant to see that image?" the Master asked Maria and she grinned her smile stretching from one ear to the other and then she whispered: "I love you more than anything and anyone. Right now I need your help!" and the Master found that despite her terrible impudence and lack of discipline or respect, he could not resist helping her or wanting to give her a hug.

"Go on then" she said with the broadest grin yet and the Master blinked in astonishment whilst Maria suddenly covered her mouth in dismay realising too late her error. "Forgive me, lord" she whispered, truly humbled. "I am tired or else would I never have let that happen."

"How long have you been able to read my thoughts?" he asked and she did not need to have his question explained to her but blushing told him honestly and with some relief that now she could confess:

"Since the day you told me that your desires and mine should be the same. Without intending to, my mind changed to do your will. I am and always will be your servant. What you wish for is a command to me. I thought you knew! Only now have I come to realise that you did not know … know that … know …" and she started to stutter in nervousness, terrified for the first time of his possible anger. Then she fell to the ground, kneeling before him, crying now in her distress. The Master reached forwards and held her, his aspect that of The Comforter, the fires of his Spirit wrapped around her as a hug, saying:

"Please do not be afraid of me. Read my mind and you will see that I am not angry but heartened. Of course you know what this means … and you are not allowed to read my mind to find out, I hasten to add."

"My Lord, my Messiah. I am so completely and utterly in the dark that I am afraid that even the term '*clueless*' would be a compliment!" at which her Master laughed then told her: "I expect you to get my lessons right without my help from now on."

"That is so unfair" she replied looking down at the rug as she realised the true enormity of her ability to read her Master's mind and the consequences it would now bring. "Please Master, have pity on me. Promise me you will give me some sort of clue. Better still, I would much rather not be able to read your mind. The journey of discovery as I stumble from one error and misunderstanding to another is as important a part of my lessons and your teaching, Rabbi, as the final answer. The journey is as enjoyable as my arrival."

The Master continued to hold her and try as she might, she could not avoid reading his thoughts and had to ask: "Why are you so proud of my stupidity. Lord, I truly do not understand but can sense such love and a strong sense of vindication. You are pleased with me and yet I do not understand why?"

"My daughter. I am often cursed for the imperfections and challenges that are found in this world. Yet you have shown why these are important. Granted the ability to read my mind and understand all of my purpose, you prefer to learn my lessons through your experiences: to find the answer through the voyage of discovery. The world I have created is a puzzle and you seek to solve the puzzle for yourself rather than be given the solution by me. I am so proud of you Maria and would grant you whatever you seek."

"Can you keep a watchful eye over me when I meet the Caledonian Kings? I fear that their drinking may encourage them to do things to me that would shame me or worse."

The Master looked down on the two settlements on the Firth of Durnoch, his sanded paradise at Tarn and the spectacular cliff top views from the north of the Firth of Durnoch. He saw hundreds slaughtered and impaled on stakes along the cliff top or gutted like a fish and cast into the sea, homes burnt to the ground, even the herds of animals that had been the two settlements livelihood had been the victims of the unsurpassed violence thousands of Pagan warriors had wreaked upon the innocent and the vulnerable.

The Master stood and Maria heard the rumble of thunder outside or so she believed. Turning towards the balcony she saw the silver flash of lightning against a black sky as dark rain clouds clustered overhead to hide the panoply of the stars, and furious winds grasped the silks hanging from the ceiling and flung them back and forth, twisting around each other in a demented frenzy. With a loud thud, the two shutters flew from their hinges and rose, spinning upwards into the sky to disappear out of Maria's view. The temperature dropped suddenly and Maria shivered then looked back towards the Master and he was standing, lightning surrounding him, coming from his eyes, his fingers and his heart; the room had grown considerably taller to accommodate the Master who had grown such that Maria was no more than the size of a mouse, kneeling before his Colossus. She could see that the pupils and iris of his eyes had turned as black as coal, his face devoid of all emotion. She had never seen this aspect of her Master but knew that God could show great and justified vengeance when angered, yet she was not afraid. Then He spoke and His judgement was deafening, adamantine, unquestioning, not to be opposed:

"I will damn those responsible for the death, desecration and destruction of Durnoch and Tarn for all time. They shall burn in the Fires of Hell with no relief. For I am the Just God, the God who Judges Mankind and who Punishes all sinners; I am the One God who Saves the Righteous and the Innocent!"

Someone other than Maria would have walked the other way or turned their face when confronted with God's fury at the devastation they both could now see in Durnoch and Tarn. Maria in particular could not deal with anger for she rarely took it seriously or avoided the scene of any argument. But these were human souls about to be damned and whilst Maria could not fathom or understand such anger as her God now showed yet she knew that sometimes even justifiable fury must be challenged, must be moderated: *restraint* must be shown.

"Lord" Maria interrupted so quietly that almost He did not hear her as He towered above her now several hundreds of feet high. Then continuing to kneel before him as there really was little point in her standing, she pleaded: "You came to save *sinners*. Punish me in their place but give these Pagans a chance to redeem their souls. Please do not send them to the Torments of Hell. Take me in their place."

The silence that followed her pleas was disturbed by the occasional crackle and hiss of advancing flames from beyond the two mahogany doors that were the entrance to the chamber in which they held communion; the room was not only growing larger to accommodate the presence of God, it was also getting hotter and the sound of the flames outside getting louder as each second passed.

"You can change your mind and depart. The flames are not meant for you" Iesus advised the girl and the Nazarene stood before her, no longer inhuman, the chamber in which they conversed returned to its original size. But she shook her head and closed her mouth, biting on her bottom lip to stop it quivering and to prevent any scream of fear from escaping: for she was more frightened than ever before in her entire life yet her stubbornness was why her Master had chosen her. She watched as the varnish began to melt and peel from the great wooden double doors to the room in which they now waited for the Pagans to be punished, Iesus standing looking out of the only window at the view beyond, his back to Maria either through disdain or because he could not face the punishment to which she was about to subject herself; the girl still kneeling on the floor, her eyes closed and head bowed in prayer and in horror.

The first tongue of dreadful flame burnt through the mahogany panelling of the right hand door and beads of sweat appeared on Maria's forehead but still she would neither speak nor cry out. The doors flew open suddenly, caught in a back draught and the air was sucked out into the corridor, the doors following as they crumbled under the might of the fires of Hell. Maria choked at the lack of air, now bereft of all oxygen she could no longer scream. She could see a raging inferno in the corridor, sheets of flame curling to try and grasp her, the very air now aflame as the inert gases and the oxygen separated and the oxygen ignited. Her death and eternal torment was creeping closer and closer.

The girl had enough air saved in her lungs to say two or three words at most: a plea or to beg. Her Master waited to hear her break down and seek his help; to listen to her last fearful words; to grant Him the opportunity to step in and save her. She opened her mouth and said a simple: "I forgive you" and the flames leapt down her throat to burn her lungs to ash and leave her without the means to speak or breathe, dying with a silent scream of immeasurable pain, the pupils in her eyes turning white as they had once before, her hair blackening and aflame, her skin lifting from her bones, curling, twisting and turning to dust.

"No" cried her Master and caught her in his arms as she fell but she was beyond her ability to hear him. He healed her instantly of the harm that had been done but the Master was unable to remove the residue of absolute terror that would haunt her memories for ever who had been consumed alive by the fires of Hell. He could see the horror in her eyes. Then she woke and seeing her Master still begged: "Take me" she whispered. "Let them live and let them learn to love you as I have learnt to do" and then the full enormity of what had happened gripped her and she fainted.

Maria returned to her senses in her Master's sitting room. She carefully lifted her hands expecting to see the flesh as blackened ash over bare discoloured bone. They were untouched. Nervously she felt for blisters and scars on her face or the absence of hair and could find no sign of the passing of the flames. Finally she opened her mouth to see if she could speak through ruined lungs and her voice was clear yet tranquil, the timbre of a small and lonely child but she praised God that she had a voice. She looked within her for her courage and finding it said: "Master. Thank you for saving me once more."

Her Master looked stunned and after a few moments of astonished silence in response to her words replied: "I had not expected you to 'Thank me'. You are incredible, Maria."

"No, my lord, you saved me and I am grateful. There is one thing alas that my actions mean we cannot now put right and I ask your forgiveness."

"Tell me and do not be afraid of me. I shall never be angry with you again."

"That is a shame. Anger gives me a fit of the giggles" and she grinned to soften the impact of her flash of humour. Her sense of fun would always get her into trouble yet her Master loved her for it. Maria continued to explain the fault for which she sought his compassion: "Alas, I was to have saved the Caledonians from going into battle with the Vicing. It is now too late for me to do so."

"Rubbish" replied the Master laughing. "What is the point of being omnipresent in all time and space if I cannot then manipulate time? We talk and then I will take you to meet the two Caledonian Kings as they retire to their cabin."

"What would you wish to talk about, lord?"

"Why you were willing to give your life for the valueless souls of those Pagans?"

"You taught me lord that everything you create is of great value to you. I am your servant, lord, and what you value even slightly, I value greatly."

“I had forgotten how stubborn you are” her Master confessed then offered Maria his aid:

“What will you attempt?”

Maria’s reply was no surprise for she had already asked for his help: “I will ask the Caledonii to pull out of the contest leaving the Germanii and Vicing to fight it out with the Christian Army.”

Maria was back in the cabin of one of the two brothers, the sons of King Carica, either Graemir or Garrold. It did not matter which as one would persuade the other: grant her to just persuade one of the young men and her objective would have been achieved. She was still recalling her torment and restoration into the love and favour of her Master when the cabin door began to open. She just had time to dive behind the curtain to the warderobe, tripping over Thea and smothering her laughter and the wolf’s attempted howl. Then she realised how stupid she had been. The King would want to change into his nightclothes and they were hanging airing right in front of her.

A few seconds later King Graemir wrenched back the heavy velvet curtains and looked into the startled innocent blue eyes of a young girl with an elfin face, long silver blonde hair and a sheepish and rather embarrassed look on her face. He started to leer and then took a sharpish step backwards as he looked into the less than innocent blue eyes and long silver blonde hair of an enormous wolf, which was intent on guarding its mistress.

Graemir went to call for his guards and both the girl and the wolf shook their heads then Maria raised one finger to her lips. The King just looked at her bemused then laughed for Maria was standing wearing a silk slip that was dripping wet, her hair in tangles as always, wafer-thin with not an ounce of body fat or a muscle she could call her own, yet smiling with happiness, presenting no threat. *‘No need to call for help’* he thought before saying:

“Alright, Lady Wolf, who are you?”

"My name is Maria the Magdalan and I have come to rescue you" she replied laughter still bubbling inside her because she could see exactly what the King was thinking and the King looked at her in shock before she carried on: "Technically I am a Princess too. Can we sit down whilst I tell you what we can do to get you out of the horrible mess that you find yourself in?"

"What mess is that, little lady?"

"You have seen what Craedfellast and Graemwolda have done to Durnoch and Tarn. Do you want to see all of Caledonia meet the same fate or would you rather be toasted as the King who saw off the threat of the Norse and Germanic hordes?"

Graemir walked over to one of the curved chairs in his cabin and beckoned for Maria to join him. She bowed her head in acknowledgement then sat very carefully in the chair, unable to disguise how short she was as her legs hung several inches above the cabin's decking. Clicking her fingers, Thea came to sit at her feet, obedient to her gentle request. Then she asked the King:

"Sire, most noble King of the Caledonii. It would save time if I set out my proposal to both you and your brother at the same time. Can we send word for King Garrold to join us?" and Graemir nodded then went to the door, had a hurried and whispered conversation with the guards outside and returned.

He offered Maria a drink from his sideboard but she declined, indicating however that she had no issue should Graemir wish to take wine. The leader of all the many tribes of the Caledonii poured a glass of wine, but such was his interest in their conversation from there that it remained untouched.

"Tell me about yourself" he asked intending to fill the time until his younger brother joined them but within minutes he became enchanted by this child's naïf account of her adventures, bemused at first then respectful, for Maria's experiences far outstripped those of the legends of his greatest heroes and champions: Faemir One Eye and Corinthum of the Silver Hand,

Beorneth DragonSlayer, Hagred WolfsHead and Garamir Widowmaker, all surpassed by this softly spoken child from the desert lands to his south. "You are … surprising" Graemir found himself admitting and she blushed.

Garrold joined them half an hour later and at sight of Maria he laughed then mocked his brother, saying: "Can't you manage on your own?"

Maria stood and bowed then held out her hand. He saw how delicate and fragile it was and then he saw Thea and his attitude changed. More seriously, he sought Maria's forgiveness for any discourtesy at which she laughed gaily then rightly surmising what he had been thinking, corrected him gently:

"My lord King Garrold, King of the fiercesome tribe of the Sitenarae, I am honoured to be in the company of the sons of King Carica of all of Caledonia. I am Maria the Magdalan and, as you see, I pose you no threat but am come to offer you my aid."

Garrold frowned then looked across to his brother with his eyebrows raised. Seeing his brother's gesture of reassurance he turned back to the girl and said: "I have heard of your courage, your honesty, your purity and your humility. I can believe you are indeed Maria, Princess of the Atrebates, not least as no-one else as young and beautiful as you would have dared to stand on my brother's floor dripping salt water all over the place. Without doubt you are she!" at which Maria went bright red but Garrold had not finished: "Why do we need your aid? And what is this help you shall offer?"

Maria took a deep breath for if her plan was to work then she needed these men to agree to two things. "Forgive me and help me, my lord and Master" she whispered in prayer then bravely put her request before them.

"Sires, I will kneel for you are Kings and I do homage to you both. I hope what I shall offer shall be helpful but it shalt be your decision and yours alone. If my aid is not needed then I am your prisoner."

"And your wolf?" Garrold asked eyeing Thea warily as the blue eyed lupine had no intention of Maria becoming anyone's captive. Maria had considered this:

"Will you swear to let my wolf go free? In return I shall ask her to make no defence should you choose to hold me captive."

Graemir and Garrold looked into Maria's eyes and could see straightaway that she would be bound by her promise. They both agreed to her terms and with a sigh of relief, Maria placed one hand into the hands of each brother, a sign that she was to make an oath that would be unbreakable except by death:

"I believe that you and your subjects have been shocked by the murder and ravages of the Vicing as they have plundered the coastlines of your allies. I have heard disquiet in the many long boats of your countrymen. All of the tribes of the Caledonii would gladly go home and seek peace … except you fear that the Vicing will not let this happen. So I have come to help!

Join the Christian Army and fight with us against the Pagan hordes!

We shall protect your villages and rescue your families and clansmen now held hostage. We also have a plan that shall leave the Pagan Army stranded without means to go home and ultimately will see their surrender bringing us peace from Norse raids, whilst the Picts would gladly cease their raids on our west coast and befriend us if we were to join them in ridding both Caledonia and Hibernia of the terrifying threat of the Norse long boats coming out of the mists."

"How?" both men asked in unison then Graemir went first followed by his brother: "Our families are held on Graemwolda's flagship. How can you hope to rescue them?" at which Maria smiled then said:

"Because you gentleman will deliver me as your prisoner to the Vicing Kings on Craedfellast's flagship and whilst they are distracted, torturing me for our battle plans, my companions will take Graemwolda's ship and release those dear to you."

Then Garrold asked: "How will you defeat the Vicing?" and Maria laughed then replied:

"Not I but you shall" and as they looked at her in disbelief she outlined her plan.

Their response was supportive yet they showed concern for the girl and it was Garrold who spoke both of their minds: "You place a lot of faith in us and you put yourself at terrible risk. But we can ensure the Pagan Army and Fleet are where you ask. How then this sees their defeat we cannot understand" but Maria reassured them and the innocent truth in her eyes convinced them. Finally they both kissed her hands, confirmation of their agreement to her plan to which she said in turn:

"I trust you. We fight to save Caledonia from the evil of the Norse!" and it was their turn to blush then hold their heads high. They both toasted the girl then left the cabin to start to put her plan into action.

Decius blinked not able to believe his eyes but as he looked the coloured glass lanterns on the masts and spits of the two flagships of the Caledonian Kings appeared to be signalling to each other … except they were using a battle code that was not Caledonian but rather in the language of the Brigantes (as used by those from Yorvic). There was no-one in the entire Pagan fleet who would know that language and to the casual observer it would look to be the two brothers discussing the plans for the morrow.

"Amaric. Can I borrow you?" Decius muttered and Sir Amaric, Eorl of Yorvic headed across to the bow of their skiff then followed Decius' arm as he pointed to their north and the Caledonian fleet.

After five minutes, the Eorl laughed: "It is official. We are now Caledonii and are to head over, lights blazing, one gold and two red lanterns on our top mast as our identification, to collect two Kings and a prisoner … Give you one guess who! … and take them to Craedfellast's flagship where the Kings have called a War Council. We then head in darkness to the ship moored alongside which is Graemwolda's flagship and rescue four ladies of various ages (that should cheer you up Galahaidra!)" he added as an aside. "We rescue the ladies then collect the two Caledonian Kings and sale out of the Firth, heading South."

And as they were taking all of that in Amaric added: "There is a postscript: We are asked to join up with Longinus' Army then be ready for Battle against the Pagans as they climb up the beach head at Cromarty. Maria then sends a special message to the three of us: '*The Pagans will become desperate and we may be tempted to crush them but remember we seek peace. Offer them the chance to concede with honour. Appoint a Champion and if I can join you then it shall be me but otherwise I trust one of my three heroes to fight for the honour of our faith, using the Holy Artefacts to sweep away any champion of our foe. God blesses us all for the peace that we shall bring.*'"

After a minute's silence as they absorbed Maria's bombardment of instructions their reactions were varied but none contested the girl's plan.

"I suggest we sail now as from the sound of things, most of the Pagans are still celebrating on shore!" Decius recommended, also eyeing the winds to ensure they favoured the skiff if they had to make a run for it.

"She is mad, you know!" was Galahaidra's comment.

"Her 'three heroes' means us, I suspect" Amaric reflected before continuing "And the chances of us allowing *her* to be our champion are none!"

"What does she mean by "*if* I can join you"" Sir Kenneth reflected and that silenced all four men before Decius said "Come On" and they lit up their lanterns, including their identification, cut loose their mooring, set their sails and headed slowly and sedately towards the two Caledonian flagships.

The two Kings and Maria with two of the Sitenarae as their bodyguards were waiting for the skiff which pulled alongside Graemir's flagship and took on board four men, one girl wrapped in a fur cloak and a bewildered wolf. Then they cast off once more and rowed the half league to where Craedfellast's flagship was moored beneath the burning ruins of Durnoch. As Graemir looked up, he could see Craedfellast waiting for him on the poop deck who signalled for the two Kings to join the Council gathered in his cabin. Then a lantern swung as the skiff pitched briefly and shed its light on the girl's face. "Brought the entertainment I see" shouted the Vicing King, "Who is she?"

"A gift for you," the Caledonian King replied: "This is 'the Magdalan'" at which Craedfellast went briefly silent in surprise then roared with delight.

They hauled Maria up on deck then dragged her by her hair until she reached the King's cabin where she was flung onto the decking in the centre of a circle of chairs and benches laid out for the Council meeting. Most of the chairs were already taken by the Kings of the Germanii tribes, Daenii and the Vicing kingdoms. The minor Caledonian kingdoms had stayed away at the request of their two senior Kings and, with lanterns extinguished, had set sail for home. None had spoken to the Corvicii for no-one trusted them but the remaining Kings and chiefs had been sounded out and voted for peace with the Magdalan in preference to the massacre they had seen of the Lugii and Sitenarae.

Those present stood in surprise and looked down on this frail child cum girl as she tumbled before them and laid still. Then they looked at Craedfellast, their eyes questioning what purpose was served by the young guest that had joined them.

"Is she supper?" growled Hostiga King of the Suevii.

"Meet the Magdalan! A present from Graemir and Garrold, our allies!" and the men cheered then took it in turns to kick her at which she closed her eyes and prayed silently. "Do we kill her now or later?" Caerdain asked and Graemir replied:

"She knows the Christian's battle plans. Torture her first. Then save her until the Christian's see her suffering; inflict on her the Raven in their full view." All nodded and many clapped the young King on the back. They had been unsure of the loyalty of the Caledonian Kings but now all doubts had been swept away.

"Best keep her on the boil" Graemwolda muttered and several of the Kings looked towards him with eyebrows raised in question, seeking explanation. The King of the southern and western Norse lands growled: "Hair!"

They stripped Maria until naked, drove sharp daggers into the muscles of her upper arms so that she could not use them to save herself, knotted a rope through her hair then hauled her up from the cross-beam on the mast, her screams cutting through the dark of the night, the pain too great for her to pass out as her weight was held by her hair, the moans never ceasing, her legs scissoring at first but that only increased the relentless agony and saw the first clump of hair and scalp tear away leaving a puddle of her blood on the deck below.

Eventually she swung slowly, keeping her legs still but unable to find any position which reduced her pain, and then began the waking dreams: nightmares of such intensity she experienced their horrors physically as well as mentally and her moans turned to the whimpers of a child. Her light weight prolonged the torture for she was not so heavy as to pull out all of her hair and fall to the deck or to inflict so much pain as to faint. She had nowhere to hide from the evil of the pain being inflicted on her. And then the crew decided to play with her. They took up the long barge poles used to fend off other ships and fixed sharp knives or lit brands and attached the lighted flame to the end before they 'tickled' her feet with them and the screams grew louder.

When the skiff had reached Craedfellast's flagship, Garrold had turned to the ship's captain and said: "Our skiff is in the way here and my men will get bored twiddling their thumbs waiting for us. Any problems if I tell them to moor up to the ship next to us? They can wile away their boredom talking to the crew there."

"That is Graemwolda's flagship. The men there will as bored as your men and welcome some fresh company. Graemwolda will not mind given the present of the girl you have just brought him and his brother. Tell your men to mention my name: 'Gorcaist' and take this!" and the captain opened up one of the barrels of provisions in the bilges and reaching in brought out some salted pork then looking around he spotted a sack of ale.

"Your men should get a great welcome when the crew see this!" and he watched as Garrold issued his instructions and the skiff pulled away to moor up alongside the neighbouring long boat.

Sir Galahaidra, Sir Kenneth and Sir Amaric jumped from the runner on their skiff to the rail that ran across the bank of oars. They carried their present so that it was the first thing the crew on Graemwolda's ship saw. Galahaidra bore his lance and sword, the other two men each had a sword, Sir Amaric had borrowed Maria's Vorpal blade from her chest of armour which her father had insisted on bringing with him, whilst Sir Kenneth was still using Sir Iosephus' sword. They had been careful not to carry too many weapons; enough to show they were warriors but not so many as to become a threat.

They were greeted with delight by the skeleton crew of eight who took the joint of pork and set it to boil in an enormous cast iron pot around which the three knights sat, with five of the crew as company, another one guarding the cabin door *'Where the prisoners must be kept'* Galahaidra mused, one man as sentry on the starboard deck and one to port. Galahaidra rubbed his nose when he saw Decius watching and the helmsman slowly moved his skiff until it was below the prow, the fos'castle and the captain's cabin, invisible to any of the guards. When Maria's screams began, Amaric and Galahaidra had to hold Sir Kenneth down physically, so upset was the otherwise gentle knight.

"Wait" hissed Galahaidra and slowly the softly spoken knight calmed down. Then one of Graemwolda's crew had the sadistic idea that they should use Maria as target practice: he was the worse for wear having drunk too much poor quality ale. Two of his comrades joined in who were in a state that was not much better. Kenneth showed his relief as two arrows flew harmlessly into the night sky but the third passed through the thigh on Maria's right leg and something snapped inside the young knight. In one motion, he had drawn his sword and thrust it through the archer's heart whilst Amaric followed suit and swung Maria's Vorpal blade taking off three heads of the crewmen sitting by them but who had their backs to him as they had watched the macabre contest. The guard in front of the cabin let out a shout and then ran to the aid of his fellow crew members. His shout was drowned out by Maria's screaming as was Galahaidra's whistle of summonsing.

Thea leapt silently from the fos'castle where she had been waiting patiently and took the guard on the starboard rail in the throat whilst Maria's family of wild boar joined in and rounded up the man on the port side, one tripping him as he tried to run and three then goring him to death as he lay helpless on the deck.

Galahaidra thrust twice and the Spear of Longinus dropped one guard to the deck with a thigh wound then ignited with the fury of dragon's fire as Maria screamed, running the final crew member through the heart, setting him to burn with red and blue flame briefly before the Iudaean had mercy and threw the dead man overboard. The wounded warrior went to call out for help and Amaric beheaded him, humming happily and saying to his comrade-in-arms "I want this sword" at which Galahaidra smiled evilly and replied:

"If we all survive this night and tomorrow you will have earned it" then he helped Kenneth to drop the rest of the bodies slowly and silently over the side and into the dark waters of the Firth.

Thea was distraught and it took all of the three knight's attention to calm the young she-wolf down as she listened in horror to her mistress' screams. "Be brave!" Galahaidra whispered sadly and though they took him to mean Thea, all were praying the same of Maria.

When the deck was clear of any sign of a struggle, the three knights went to the cabin where they found three young girls and one lady: Garrold's young wife who was barely seventeen but bravely holding the other three ladies and offering them words of comfort whilst hiding her own tears; Graemir's wife in her thirties; and two daughters both in their teens, all weeping … or rather they were until they saw Galahaidra. Kenneth could not resist a smile as all four calmed down miraculously quickly.

"I am come to rescue you" Galahaidra announced standing under the light of a ship's lantern and nothing he could have said was more certain to have captured their hearts.

"Two of them are married and two are too young" Kenneth whispered in Galahaidra's ear as he walked past the handsome young knight who blinked then said: "Duh!" One of the girls heard him and her face fell. '*O dear he must be simple*' she thought but then taking another look admitted that it really did not matter.

"Amaric!" shouted Kenneth "Get in here now!" and as soon as the Eorl who was safely married and long past his thirtieth birthday had joined them, Kenneth rescued Galahaidra and set him to watch on his own for trouble at the bow of the long boat whilst Amaric and he loaded the girls into their skiff. There was a difficult moment when the three girls and one lady encountered Thea and her cubs which were growing up fast, another when they met the four wild boars and a moment of terror as they heard Maria's screams. Then they all had to endure the long wait for the signal from Craedfellast's ship that the two Caledonian Kings were ready to be collected from the War Council.

Graemwolda dropped a sobbing Maria onto the deck after two hours and hauled her nearly incoherent with pain to the main cabin. Craedfellast already had the hot brand ready and once the girl had been dropped onto the deck, he did not give her the time to call on any reserves of courage or strength but drew the hot brand across the bare soles of her feet and then moved it slowly along her stomach. She arched her back in agony: her skin turning to blackened crust wherever the hot metal touched, her only response beyond jerking spasms of pain was more sobs.

"If you talk I let you sleep; if you lie to me then the pain gets worse. Understand."

"I cannot lie" the poor girl whispered through a throat made hoarse by hours of screaming and she felt the brand dragged across her buttocks and came near to fainting.

"If you contradict me the pain gets worse."

"I understand" the girl said bravely. "I am not a brave person and will tell you what I know."

"You lie" replied the King calmly and the brand was driven into her forehead leaving a permanent scar: the V mark of a Vicing slave. Almost it was too much as Maria came close to fainting but Craedfellast had had years of practise and knew his art.

"Talk" said the Vicing King and she did, slowly at first but as she saw the King threaten to burn her again, the words came out thick and fast but stuttering due to her fear and pain rather than any hesitancy. For her small reserves of courage had been burnt away:

"Longinus has placed artillery on the cliff tops above the Bay of Mullochy. He has built a huge palisaded fortress with two earthen ramparts, towers and barbicans on the cliff top at Mullochy that can hold one hundred and fifty thousands within its walls. He has less than a hundred thousand for he has lost King Pedrus. He has prepared some defences at Cromarty which is on his line of retreat. His ships are in Mullochy Bay. He will put them out to sea to do battle in the Firth of Beauly."

These were her last words as Craedfellast went to burn out her tongue. Saying "I forgive …" she fainted as she felt the heat of the poker on her bruised lips.

"Leave it to tomorrow. It shall be much better if she is awake when you take out her tongue and eyes. Better still if the Christians are present to see us torture the girl" Garrold suggested and Graemwolda laughed, shouting "These Caledonians are more blood thirsty than we are!"

Reluctantly, Craedfellast left the girl her tongue. With the information they now had from Maria, the Pagan War Council began to develop their plan for the defeat of the Christian Army. Craedfellast summarised what they had learnt from the torture of Maria who had been chained when she had fainted and flung out on deck to sleep, if she could; with the agony of her wounds and suffering the freezing cold of the night naked. Those guarding her had orders to prod her with the sharp points of their spears if she appeared to be going to sleep.

"Longinus sees our Army coming from their east and south, landing in the Bay of Mullochy and forcing us into the Isthmus of Cromarty" Craedfellant began, a panorama made of wet clay showing the Firths of Cromarty, Beauly and Mullochy Bay on a table at the far end of his cabin and the Kings on the Council standing in attendance and contributing from their knowledge of warcraft and the local area. The Vicing King continued:

"Longinus may even try and assail our fleet at sea before we have landed our troops. He will try to send our Army to the bottom of the sea should he do so. He will seek to suck what remains of our fleet into the Bay of Mullochy and then he will blockade us trapping our fleet within the Bay."

He handed over to Graemir who had been considering how they might defeat the Christian Army and already a plan was beginning to form in his mind:

"Longinus anticipates our land army to attack from the south and has prepared strong defences, intending that we smash our Army against his walls. We could besiege him and starve him out but he has positioned his fortress so that he has many means of being supplied from or escaping to the north.

So, we land our Army in the north at Cromarty and cut off his supplies and his retreat, forcing him to come out and meet us.

Longinus' fleet is less than a quarter the size of ours. Therefore he will try and force us to bunch up, trapping us in the Bay of Mullochy and using his artillery and fireships to sink our fleet.

So, we attack his fleet whilst it is still in the Firth of Beauly. We position our fleet so that we have the benefit of the wind and the tides both of which are forecast to be southerly and westerly. We watch as our foe's fleet retreats into Mullochy Bay and then we blockade them there.

Their defeated army will fall back into their fort at Mullochy and their fleet will be trapped in the Bay of Mullochy. They will find themselves beseiged and starving with their escape route to the north blocked by our army."

The Council were excited and eager to work through the detail. It was Tortelimar who sounded a note of caution:

"The Christians will know we have taken the Magdala. If they hear we have her captive, alive and being tortured then they will change their tactics, potentially trap us near Cromarty or avoid us at Mullochy by putting out to the North Sea. How do we avoid this happening?"

"Kill the girl!" muttered Graemwolda in his low Bear-like growl. "Let me do it brother for it is my birthday tomorrow!"

"That would be a waste" Garrold intervened and it was a sign of the growing trust for the two Caledonian Kings that the Council listened intently as he explained himself:

"First we can make it look as if we have slain the girl. There are some girls with fair hair about the same age and height as the Magdalan that from a distance could be passed off as the girl and whom we can publicly execute by strangulation so that whoever it is cannot cry out and then carve them up into the Raven, remove eyes, slice ears, cut off lips and leave for dead hanging in plane view but not so close as to be identified.

Second, let us go fast: attack tomorrow. The foe will still be reeling over Maria's capture and so let us hit them when their motivation has taken a huge hit!

Third, in the battle we then place the real Magdalan somewhere we can execute her and where she can be seen by the Christians to die horribly: a final blow to their morale. Do it at sea as then we can throw the carrion into the Ocean to be damned without hope of eternal life, her limbs, eyes, ears, mouth, tongue, hair all removed so if by some miracle she returns to life on the last day as Christians believe or at Ragnarock as we believe, it is as the shell of a human, blind, deaf and dumb for all eternity!"

"Are you sure you were not a Vicing in an earlier life?" muttered Caewlin "Or a Daeni?" Hardenicum asked "Perhaps a Suevi or Teutoni?" Suggested Hostiga but it was Craedfellast who had the final word: "You are a Scandian from across the Seas!" and they all roared their approval of Garrold's plan.

Craedfellast then took Garrold to one side and spoke to him at length: "I need someone we Vicing can trust to hold Caledonia and northern Britannia for us. Can you be that man? You have a young wife and doubtless will have many children. They can gradually take on the kingdoms that shall become vacant on the deaths of the Christian Princes and Kings. Will you be our man?"

"And my brother?" Garrold asked thoughtfully.

"He has an old wife and two daughters, no sons. He is honourable and will step aside the moment Ysolte has a son and if not Ysolte: well make sure you sow your seeds wide and wisely. No, it is you who represent the future" at which Garrold shook the hands of the black bearded, black hearted Norsemen.

Galahaidra had spent the long hour between the capture of Graemwolda's flagship and when the War Council meeting finally broke up overseeing the three girls and Graemir's wife tearing sheets, hammocks and canvas into long strips. They wound then tied these together to make threads which he supervised being soaked in lamp oil then he set the makeshift fuse to run from the bow of the ship, out of sight of Craedfellast's flagship, to a store room beneath the fos'castle that he filled with barrels of lamp oil, fish oil, dry clothing, papyrus, perfume, dried and smoked meat and fish, and the spare sheet for the main mast which had also been shredded.

Then he got everyone on board the skiff and they waited for Graemir's signal that they were to return to his long boat. They did not have long as a few minutes later Decius spotted a brand being waved and they began to row the skiff slowly and steadily towards Craedfellant's flagship, Galahaidra lighting the makeshift rope that they had set as a fuse. It had eighty paces to run and the first four paces took thirty seconds. "We need to row faster" muttered Galahaidra and they increased the tempo.

It took four minutes to reach the fleet's flagship and another three minutes to moor up collect the two King's and to embark, this time heading away from Graemwolda's long boat and out into the black seas of the Firth. Galahaidra hissed: "Where is Maria?" and Graemir answered from the bottom of the long boat where he was holding his wife as if he would never dare let her go again and offering to her a lifetime of penance. His wife was furious with him for allowing Maria, who was only two years older than their eldest daughter, to be subjected to such terrible torture and such a horrendous ordeal in order for *them* to escape and had openly wept as she had remembered the young girl's screams. Graemir spoke carefully but knew his words would upset his wife further:

"I spoke to Maria before we left. No more than a couple of words. She has to stay so that Craedfellast and Graemwolda go with her plan and do not suspect Garrold and me and thus come after us. If she escapes tonight, the Vicing and Germanii will change their plan, even delay their assault. She asks we trust her!"

But it was Galahaidra who showed his anger: "How can she escape tomorrow? She will be guarded all the time, alone in the middle of a fleet that is five to ten times that of ours. Has she fooled us and planned to go to her death after all?"

His question was greeted with silence. The company should have been celebrating the rescue of Graemir's and Garrold's families and the Caledonian tribes switch of allegiance from siding with the Vicing and Germanii to joining the Christian Army … but the loss of Maria overshadowed all of that.

They kept their identification lanterns lit, ensuring they were in full view and at some distance from Graemwolda's flagship when ten minutes came up … and nothing happened!

Into the silence, Garrold asked on behalf of his young wife: "Ysolte wonders if we must now become Christians." There was a pause as everyone waited for Galahaidra to answer that question but the young knight was still counting down the seconds until the fuse lit the explosive cargo; he was already up to twelve minutes, and watching with growing anxiety for the first signs of fire. Then he saw Graemwolda step into his skiff to be rowed back to his flagship with an escort of ten warriors. It would take them …

An explosion finally ripped the dark sky apart, briefly parting the clouds to let the moon shine down on the Vicing King's skiff that had momentarily been in danger of capsizing and on Decius helming Graemir's skiff and almost having reached the Caledonian Kings' flagships; they were a considerable distance away from Graemwolda's flagship and to the casual observer could have had no part in the fire that was now gutting the Vicing long boat which had sunk within a minute, taking both its crew and its captives to the bottom of the Firth.

"Signal to offer help" Galahaidra whispered and Decius found a brand, lit it from one of the lanterns and sent two signals:

"Can we help?" and "Can we take anyone on board?" After five minutes they received a short message in response: "There are no survivors. The long boat is at the bottom of the Firth. Graemwolda will stay with Craedfellast. We regret the loss of the Queens and their daughters."

It was Kenneth who once more was the voice of reason: "And now we wait to see if they believe us. Provided Graemir, Garrold and Maria stay then there is no risk. Galahaidra, Amaric and I were only seen and at a distance in the dark by their ship's captain. Decius was seen by a number of their crew but a helmsman and in the dark; how likely is it that anyone will distinguish Decius from any other member of Graemir's crew? If Ysolte or Graemir's wife and children are found then we shall all be slain, so the four ladies must come with us tonight in the dark and we shall bring them under the protection of Godric – he can be *very* protective! Galahaidra, Amaric and I are dead if he hears we abandoned his daughter to the Vicing so we go into hiding."

In the excitement of the explosion, Kenneth had been distracted from answering Ysolte's question whilst Galahaidra had not even heard it. Garrold would not consider letting his young wife go anywhere with Galahaidra until he knew a lot more about both Christianity and Prince Godric and so asked Kenneth once more about both.

"Godric is a widower, is in his fifties, has set his heart on Maria becoming the Princess of his tribes and kingdoms and has adopted her as his daughter and sole heir. If he were interested in marriage then he would have already married her. He would do nothing to hurt her including taking another wife. Maria is best to answer your question about whether you must become a Christian but the simple answer is 'No'. Ninian is also wise in understanding our faith and Ysolte can talk to her.

Maria once said: *'We fight not to force the Pagans to become Christians but to let people make a choice of their faith free from pressure from anyone else.'* Ysolte can be part of our services and celebrations but it shall be *her* choice as to whether she becomes a Christian or not."

They waited until it was totally dark, what light there was behind them on the shore and the cliff tops where Tarn and Durnoch still burnt. Then Graemir and Garrold said their goodbyes to the four ladies, the three knights and the helmsman, grateful for the rescue of their wives and children, facing an important day for all of their lives on the morrow. Whilst on the upper deck of Craedfellast's long boat, Maria shivered with cold, wrapped in iron chains, knowing that the Pagans could cast her into the sea and that she would sink without trace, fearful for her life, finally building up enough courage to pray.

She walked the length of a hall five thousand paces long, over an hour to pass from one end to the other, a Grand Chamber, entered through two doors of sycamore panels, the grains cut so cleverly that they matched even to the point where the knots in the wood, like medals, flowed from one door to the other. The panels were polished to such a degree that they shone like bronze. Maria was entering the gateway to her soul and knew that if she passed through the doors at the far end of this chamber she would enter her place of final judgement.

The Hall had marble on the floor and walls; the walls had tall gothic windows and full length mirrors, both the same shape and size, stretching from a low sill to just a few feet below the ceiling, enough space to leave a single word above each window ('Love' or 'Faith' or 'Charity' or 'Purity' or 'Hope' or 'Prayer' or 'Fasting' or 'Pilgrimmage') written in flowing gold lettering in every language known to man and in God's own language with gilt on the carving of marble stone on the walls.

The mirrors were each set opposite a window so that the rising sun would be reflected back and forth across the full length of the hall. Long lengths of colonnades were on either side of her with marble columns that had veins of imperial purple and the red of her Master's precious blood and each stood, floor to ceiling at twenty paces high and were five paces apart. Although she could not count so high (and numbers were not her forte) her Master came to her rescue: '*There are four thousand columns*' he whispered in her mind '*in four rows or long lines*'. Between every pair of the two furthest rows of columns was either a window or a mirror.

Above her was a ceiling painted to represent the most glorious sky with perfect clouds, and the brightest sun, flocks of exotic birds, and the snow atop distant evergreen mountains with herds of deer, their antlered stags proudly acting as sentinels to guard the divide between colourful illusion and the beauty of the real thing, so carefully painted that the line between the walls and the illusionary sky was impossible to discern: Real and Unreal were intermingled. *'Save what is real?'* Maria thought *'when art can so capture the inner essence of a being? Does the being become redundant when what they seek to achieve in life is already achieved in the mind of the artist and illusionist?'*

At the end of the hall was a set of curved marble steps rising five feet, or almost taller than the girl, to where a huge, regal oak cathedra painted in gilt and gold, blues, reds and greens and looking the length of the chamber guarded access to the hall beyond. By every column, long lines of Angels floated a few inches above the ground, two hundred thousand had been summonsed, their robes hiding whether they had feet or not and beneath which they wore full length hauberks of chain or scale mail.

Briefly Maria's sense of fun caused her to speculate irreverently about '*footless*' Angels for was this why they had wings? The Angels' wings were unfurled and their span was ten feet in either direction, their faces were stern or compassionate, loving or angry, temperate or violent, offering death or surrender and each bore a sword, spear or axe of immense power. '*How did she know these weapons were powerful*?' Maria briefly asked herself yet she did not doubt that they were!

God's Angels were dressed for war.

Down the middle of the hall was a velvet carpet of purest blue and each column had green vines winding around its pedestal and gold leaf petals. Standing forth to greet her was an Angel she could not fail to recognise, with chainmail of purest silver and gold, whose winged helmet and chin guard were brightly polished and dazzling as they reflected the sun from the windows, mirrors and the painted ceiling. He carried the sword with which he had conquered light and as the leader of all Angel's he was also God's chosen commander when one day God would finally declare the End of All Songs, Armageddon, Ragnarock, the Apocalypsos, war against all that is Evil.

The cathedra was not empty. For seated on the chaise grande upon the marble pedastal was Her Master armed with the horn used to destroy Jericho in his right hand, the sword of damnation in his left, the helmet of wisdom, the breastplate of faith and the shield of discernment held by three Angels acting as his squires who followed him.

Maria was naked. Yet she was proud to be so. She posed no threat, offered peace in defiance of those who sought war; tolerance as the antidote to the blindness of religious bigotry; restraint was her steadfast shield against the atrophy and anarchy that was the destructive detritus of autocratic anger. She neither wanted nor needed any armour, wearing the apparel that God had given her on the day she was born. Her weapon was the infinite love and adoration she offered God whom she served without any need for his explanation. God had already said it: '*She 'served God on trust'. Which is just as well'* she thought *'as I need an awful lot to be explained to me and there is only one God so I must keep Him very busy and must try not to monopolise Him.'*

"You never could but I would not mind" her Master replied. The expression on her Master's face had been one of determination, but now he was chuckling for he had heard her random thoughts, her doubts and admission of her inability to do anything other than trust and hope. Maria waited her moment until his defences were down and then she attacked:

"Why?" she whispered.

"I go to war to save you" her Master replied.

"You have already saved me by dying for me. Let me complete my mission in love and peace and grant me one request."

"What is it?" he asked, his face now gentle and loving; seeing a dearly beloved daughter in great pain. So for her sake he handed the horn and sword to his standard bearer, the Angel Rapha'el. The Angel smiled at Maria for the Angelic host were proud of the great courage the girl was showing in facing the most terrible torture and her own death in order to save the lives of mankind. All of the Angels who had stood by God at the time of Lucifer's rebellion were protective of mankind and willing to sacrifice themselves, as God had shown the Way, to allow our future development as God's companions and servants. Collectively, they were in awe and admiring of Maria's service. This night, which they feared was likely to be her last, they gave her their comfort.

"Let not the last thing I see in life be my gentle Saviour going to war" the girl pleaded.

They stood at a sunken pool, a fountain to their left feeding a rill that stepped sedately from the steep hills to the dark shadows formed by the oak trees surrounding them; to Maria's intense joy there were three wild piglets which had come to see the girl, milling around at her feet, lifting the fallen brown and bronze leaves to inspect the mulch and soft earth beneath for any fungi or truffles. Maria asked "Have I not been here before?"

"You have. For thousands of years this place will be considered magical yet there is no magic here except the magic we bring ourselves. It is your next lesson."

"Lord you promised to give me clues when we had our lessons! For you know that I try so hard yet can only answer a few of the challenges you pose me. I shall come completely clean here: I usually fall across the answers *entirely by accident.*

Lord, you did not make me clever so please help me!"

"Read my mind" God asked her gently and the girl found that she could not then she praised her God with relief at her release from the burden of knowing all of God's Will without the painful lesson of the challenge of discovery.

"Actually I have never promised to give you any clues" her Master corrected her but chuckling as he did so at which Maria sighed with relief at his return to good humour then asked, the tell-tale twitch of her lips showing there was just a touch of mischief behind her question: "Will Archangel Micha'el be cross with me? I think I may have spoilt his outing!"

"No, my dear, you saved God and His Angels from a grave mistake. I have asked my followers many times to trust me. Y*ou*, more than anyone, have taken me on trust. Momentarily, *I forgot to trust you*. How can I help you?"

When Maria told him about her plans, their laughter drove the darkness from the trees and the hills they had hidden, from the sky and the secluded stars, stripping the armour and weapons from the Angels in their legions so that each bore a musical instrument with which they now defied the evil of violence with the glory and solace of their celestial concerto and she sung in unison with the majesty and sympathetic symphony of the Angelic choir her soft voice caught in the wind to spin in delightful melody across the dark blue meadows of the heavens.

"What do *you* need for *yourself* and not for my mission?" God finally asked her.

"One bright and sunny day" she answered. "Make it the 'real' thing, Lord, not one of mine done in your image; not the mirror's reflection of the sun; no illusion just vindication: please let Peace triumph as an example to our world for all time. Please save those who fight this day from death that your many faithful followers may heal us physically and you may heal us spiritually."

Maria was in chains beneath a dark and moonless sky, on the damp planks of a long boat's deck, too cold for snow with rock-hard ice forming along the deck rails. Yet she was warmed by the love of Iesus, her Master, and his compassion was the real thing: for she could feel it flowing through her and it had become her life's blood.

She smiled as her prayers were answered with gentle and soothing conversation: God and his Angels filled the short hours until battle would begin by telling the girl of the creation of the Universe and she listened in fascination as black holes were formed and combined to make galaxies, millions and millions of them, of which their own "The Winding Rope" or "Silken Silver Scarf" as it was known was just one example appearing as a white slice that had been cut through the fabric of the night sky! She observed the many different types of stars and their magnificent vivid colours and finally was brave enough to ask if she might be permitted to study the stars once her mission was completed?

"O you mean *this* mission" and her Master's words had given her the distinct impression that 'this mission' was the start and not the end of her ministry. She was surprised when she stopped to see how she felt about that: her overwhelming emotions were a sense of relief and of reassurance that despite her many mistakes, God still had work for which he saw that she might be suitable. She whispered "Thank you" and warmth flooded through her, protecting her from the night's cold frost.

Longinus and his army left their camp in Mullochy to march towards the plains of Avioch and Fortrose, south of Cromarty. Most of his army kept to the lines of trees to their west ensuring they were not visible from the Firth of Beauly, whilst their huge support staff of some thirty thousand including any and everything from dressmakers to cooks and armourers stood around the parapet at Mullochy imitating a heavily-manned fortress and hoping that the Vicing would attack anywhere but there.

The night before the Battle, a mist rolled down from the mountains and over the sea. This meant that both the Christian and Pagan Army manoeuvred within short distances of each other, but one could not see the other and vice versa. Both went about putting their battle plans in place oblivious that their foe was doing the same within short leagues of them. The mist had also descended onto the Pagan fleet when it set sail for the North Sea after embarking the Pagan Army and prevented their scouts from seeing Longinus form up.

Longinus could not hide his artillery so had placed half on the cliff tops at Mullochy whilst the rest had been drawn by draught horses throughout the night to arrive in time to set up in the killing field, the battle ground Godric had chosen and of which Longinus was now going to take full advantage. Martius and his legion had already established their Forlorn Hope the night before: a Ɔ shaped earthwork with a spear wall and a motte filled with spiked stakes. Within the defensive works, Martius had placed three cohorts.

He had then built a wooden palisade one hundred paces east and west, two tall towers on each and fronted by a deep ditch and earthenwork wall. Three hundred men held each wall, with throwing pilum or javelin, sling shot then short sword, garrotting rope and dagger as their last resort. They had all met Maria and every one of them had been blessed with a vision of Iesus as they awoke that morning. They were ordered to hold and they would obey that order unto death.

Finally, Martius and a reserve of three hundred men were formed up just to the left of centre opposite a winding pathway that came up from the west beach at Cromarty, a possible route for a flanking force (except that Longinus had placed his own ambush in the woods besides the path up from the beach on the West Bay: *the Black Company* under Sir Galahaidra).

Before Martius' earthen works and palisade was the *killing zone*: three hundred man traps hidden beneath sand or under grass or rocks; trip wires that released huge and heavy logs; a whole cliff side designed to collapse and slide down a mountain when two rocks were prized forwards; and a river dammed to come crashing down the cliffs to their west separating the battle zone from the Firth of Cromarty.

Craedfellast called his War Council to order in the cabin of his flagship where they had met the night before. First order of the day was to address the minor set-back of the night before and he was brusque not wishing to dwell on such matters when the opportunity to conquer the whole of Britannia and take an undefended Hibernia lay before him.

"My brother Graemwonda's flagship caught fire – it looks from some of the wreckage as if the crew fell asleep when cooking. The ship sank in less than a minute taking all hands and also those we were holding for their safety. Our comrades and fellow Kings Graemir and Garrold have lost wives and children in the fire and grieve, yet join us this day to take out their revenge: to shape Fate to their own making as we destroy the Christian Army, slaughter the Picts and the Gael; establishing Caledonia as the free and Pagan Kingdom of the Caledonii and Sitenarae stretching from Ultima Thule to Caer Lisle and Yorvic. My friends you have our sympathy, grant us your courage and support and let us make today a *Day of Celebration* as well as a *Day of Loss*."

The two brothers looked suitably bereft but grateful for the support they were receiving from their peers who stood around them, bowing their heads in silent prayer to the pantheon of Gods they worshipped. Then everyone sat in a circle whilst Craedfellast set out their plans.

"The Magdalan has told us that the Christians will defend Mullochy and its bay, seeking to blockade us should we assault their fleet in the Bay. Their fleet is sitting in the Firth of Beauly, protected by this morning's mist waiting to do just that. The Magdalan has also told us that the Christian's line of retreat is down on to the north cove of the Sands at Cromarty. They have a Forlorn Hope dug in near the approach to Avioch and Mullochy from Cromarty. It is manned by a Roman legion by rumour a ragbag of outcasts and rebels on holiday or extended leave, ill-disciplined and gathered by Longinus for money. Our scouts have confirmed there are around one thousand men defending our road to Mullochy and we have counted thirty thousands within the walls of the Citadel the Christians have built above the Bay of Mullochy. The Magdalan has spoken truth, although my brother broke her nose and slit her ear lobes this morning to confirm this. Her fear is real; her words are true.

So we know our enemy's location. Their intent is that we assail Mullochy from the Bay. They will attempt to blockade our fleet and destroy it with their fire ships and artillery on the cliffs. Our Army will then starve or smash itself to oblivion against their walls, towers and barbicans."

"We are certain of our information?" asked Graemir and Graemwolda replied:

"To remove any doubt, I sentenced one of my best champion fighters to share in the torture with the girl. He is dead: his heart burst from the shock of the pain when his feet and hands were set fire. The Magdalan felt the same pain yet lived to confirm all that we have learned. Our scouts have also been tortured to ensure their reports are accurate. Then I persuaded the relatives of some of those who are working within the Citadel, making bread, helping nurse and tend for any sick with 'camp fever', to join us as spies. One couple came to us with news of the Christian's movements when Longinus first marched from MacAllan's Cairn to the River Oich and have already proven they are loyal. My peer, King Garrold, found them for me. They rode into the enemy Citadel yesterday and confirmed the enemy numbers last night. This information is true" and Graemwolda handed the meeting back to his brother to chair once more.

"With the loss of my brother's flagship, my own ship will lead our fleet but with Graemwolda at the helm and to be our Sea Lord as we hunt down the enemy fleet. He will land the Germanii on the sands in the West Bay of Cromarty, the Vicing in the cove that forms the northern approach to Mullochy, the Chaenii at Inver, and the Daenii and Caledonii at Avioch: all four landings to happen simultaneously.

The Daenii and Caledonii under Hartdenicum are to hold Avioch then send half their force at a run until they face the west walls of the Citadel and motte around Mullochy, holding the road to Baltain. They then besiege the Christians within their walls, taking out the bridge across the River Beauly: ensuring the Christians stay within the security of their defences but being at a safe distance from the enemy's artillery.

The Germanii, Suevii and Chaenii led by the Teuton Tortilemir as King of the Germanii shall have the honour of taking the western approach up the cliffs over Cromarty. They have the quickest road up the cliffs but it is narrow and winding and can be defended easily. Make a noise and sing your hearts out! You are to draw the enemy towards you and will arrive cliff topside at least an hour and possibly an hour and a half before the main body of our army, led by me makes the top of the cliffs and attacks the Christian Army on its right flank forcing it towards the treacherous cliffs on the east shoreline of the prominotory.

Caerdain, King of the Chaenii and his men will be landed on the south shore of the Firth of Beauly and take the settlement of Inver on the mouth of Loch Ness, cutting off the Christians other source of supplies and reinforcements.

The Firth of Cromarty creates a promontory the shape of a snake's head. As we mount the cliffs, we will have dense woods to our right, Avioch to our left and Mullochy before us with the River Beauly wrapping around before us with the road to Beauly itself and Baltain Bridge. Next are the Firth of Cromarty and its tall cliffs running from our right and beneath the cliffs to our East. To our left are the North Sea and the Firth of Beauly:

the sea is our boundary to our left and then to complete the circuit is the deep waters of Mullochy Bay.

King Hartdenicum, our scouts report troop movement in Baltain so the bridge there is the first objective for the Daenii. Once we hold the road to Baltain, the town and port of Inver, the northern approaches to Avioch and the pathway down to the sanded coves off the Firth of Cromarty then our foe have no means to escape. If we can blockade the enemy fleet and trap it in Mullochy Bay, then the Christians will starve.

I lead our main army which takes the northern approach from Cromarty: a track that is wider with less risk of a fall or ambush and we arrive therefore intact and without molestation. We take out any troops they have left as a Forlorn Hope, defeat any Christian troops sent to hold Tortelimir then reinforce the holding forces at Avioch, the road to Beauly and the bridge at Baltain.

Then we wait until one day our starving foe either surrenders or leaves its walls to attack us facing an enemy three to four times its size. There is no other army or people out there to offer them more aid and reinforcements, whereas we can call on more troops from Daenemark, Heligos' Bight, Rhineland and the tribes of the Helvetii, Belgae, Alemmani, Burgundi and Teutoni.

We have enough ships to feed our armies through the small havens of Avioch, Fortrose and Cromarty; can bring food from Inver or from the lands of the Sevgolae and Sitenarae across the Baltain to Beauly, and our ships can bear another one hundred thousand troops if we require more reinforcements."

The Council had bent forward during his briefing, watching as he moved troops, marked as painted wooden blocks, north, south, east and west on the soft clay of the diaroma prepared for this meeting. Immediately they could see that if the Christians lost contact with the Firth of Beauly and the North Sea, then they would be cut off from access to any food or aid. Graemwolda was the first to respond:

"We have not touched on your plan for my fleet yet, brother. But before we do, some further suggestions about the siege. First we capture the artillery on the cliff tops above the Bay and turn them onto our foe. Second we build rams, towers, ladders and catapults using the huge supply of wood from the nearby forest to build as many as we need.

The Christians will be over-crowded with tens of thousands sharing the same springs and latrines.

So, third we look to poison their water. The first sign of anyone going down with 'camp fever' or suffering from 'scarlatina' which we can give them from the use of one of our sorcerers' potions, and we catapult the infected corpses plus any diseased animals into their City and watch as disease takes off. Alas the snow will prevent the rapid spread of diseases that are common in the summer but brings its own ailments such as lung fever and other killers.

Watch for signs of the raking cough and ensure that anyone who gets a fever goes into the front rank during our daily assaults on the enemy's walls with orders to spit on our enemy. The girl, the Magdalan, shows sign of fever after her night naked in the ice cold winds from the North. Her corpse could be the first we fling across their walls. What an irony if when the Magdalan is dead she should kill off those that when she lived she made believe in her false God!"

It was still many long hours before first light and the birds were yet to greet the sign of a new day's dawn. The Council were eager now to hear the plans for their fleet but there was one thing they wanted to hear that was even more important to them. Graemir asked the question on their collective behalf: "How many do we face and what are our numbers?"

Craedfellast was happy to answer his fellow King's request before he briefed them on the fleet's orders: "We have over two hundred thousands of warriors and thirteen hundred long boats. The Christians have seventy thousand warriors and less than two hundred ships, mainly troop carrying triremes or quadrimes. Any plan would see them massacred but this plan ensures they cannot run away!"

Their eyes were shining now and they all wanted to get on with it and launch their invasion and siege of Mullochy but Craedfellast had yet to finish his briefing. The plans for the fleet were as important as those for his land army. He waited until he had their full attention then quickly appraised them on how they would ensure victory at sea:

"Our fleet will be led by Graemwolda but leading from my flagship. He leads thirteen hundred ships whose first task is to land troops at four beach heads: Inver on the Ness, Avioch, the West and the North Bays of Cromarty. Then he will muster out in the North Sea. His task after this is to hunt down the Christian fleet which will be hiding in the Firth of Beauly.

The Christian fleet will either do battle in the Firth and is so outnumbered that it will be destroyed just as the Hibernian fleet was; or the Christians will run and hide in the safe haven of the Bay of Mullochy protected by artillery on the cliffs above and provisioned using the supplies in Mullochy itself. Once there, we blockade their fleet, preventing them from sailing to the south of the Firth for supplies and we besiege Beauly and Baltain, cutting supplies off to Mullochy. Their fleet will starve just as their army will."

"And the girl?" Graemir finally asked.

"First I cut out her tongue and remove her ears. Then I break her rib cage, snapping each rib with my bare hands, one at a time and then I remove her sternum. Next I cut out her kidney and spleen which I give to her to hold. Then she loses her eyes, I cut off her hands and feet and tie all of these in a sack around her neck. Finally, the 'delicate' bit! I cut her lungs free of the blood vessels that feed from them and bring her lungs through her broken rib cage and place them flat across her back, spreading them across her shoulders from her spine to look like the wings of the Angels she so adores (often called 'The Raven').

Now she starts to suffocate which is when I carefully but quickly remove her heart with my sharpest knife and stuff it into her mouth still beating: it is the last thing she will sense before she dies.

Throughout I give her hallucinatory drugs which have two effects: one they prolong her life preventing the shock of my assault from killing her until the last painful moment and; two they give her nightmares that magnify the horror of her experience.

Once she is dead, I place a bag of starving rats over her head and tie it at the neck so that the rats cannot escape. The rats eat her face and hair then once her skull has been cleaned to the bone they eat each other. We tie a chain to her feet with the remains of three dead dace and throw her into the sea. The dace attract the pike and the pike attract the sharks to the warm waters here and the predators take the opportunity to eat some fresh red meat.

The man-eating fish will tear off her limbs and eat the rest of her until there is nothing left but the occasional mauled and chewed bone sitting on the sea bed, imitating sand or stones. There will be no resurrection of the body for her: nothing left of her to enjoy life after death.

I torture then mutilate her in full sight of the Christians in Mullochy and Avioch. I will take my time, making it a piece of theatre, a work of art, letting the screams rise from her throat, her curses rendered as futile mumbles by the removal of her tongue; her tears burnt away when I remove her eyes and her sight. No hands with which to defend herself. Her womb removed such that she will know she can never have the gift of children. Let us see her 'God' rescue her! Her God does not exist."

With an hour still to go until first light, Graemwolda signalled for his ships to make their landings. They sailed into the shallows, oars already banked, the Vicing warriors with their winged and horned helmets firmly tied by the short frogs from their chin guards, shields hung held securely by straps across their shoulders, swords oiled in waterproof leather scabbards. The long boats turned using their rudders and bow sail, forcing their prows to embed into the sand, their momentum bringing the bow up briefly and then it swung around to allow the port side to lie parallel with the shore. The long boats were still rolling in the ebb and flow as the waves broke on to the shore when the first one hundred ships had beached themselves.

Such was the speed and eagerness of the Vicing that fifty had jumped from each ship into the shallows of the three coves in the first ten seconds, two hundred in the first three minutes (during which they lost the first of their number, a young warrior who jumped too far in his eagerness, slipped, was trampled under foot and died, drowned, before any of his fellow warriors had noticed). The rest of the warriors were more careful from then, the painful lesson had been learned.

Graemwolda broke the few moments of silence that followed the man's discovery as they lifted his crushed corpse from the strands. "The God's have claimed their due. No harm will come to the rest of us!"

As soon as they hit the shallow waters, the warriors ran to find their captains and standards or bannerets then lined up in long columns; just under five hundred columns of three hundred men on the wide expanse of white sand in the North Bay, lesser numbers at Avioch, Inver and the West Bay.

The first one hundred long boats started to pull back out into the deep of the Firth to let the next one hundred ships disembark. After forty minutes, Craedfellast had landed one hundred and forty thousand warriors on the North Bay, six thousand at Avioch under King Hartdenicum of the Daenii, three thousand five hundred of the Chaenii under King Caerdaen and forty four thousand on the West Bay under King Tortelimir of the Germanii with only a few horses or archers and no artillery. One thousand Chaenii under the Eorl Hadrinum had been sent to cross the Beauly at Baltain and sack Inver on the Ness, ensuring the Christians could not be supplied or victualled from Inver.

Craedfellast turned and waved once: his brother's gesture was acknowledged by King Graemwolda as he ordered his fleet to head into the rolling dense mist at the mouth of the Firth of Cromarty.

It was still dark, snow clouds covering the dim light of a wintry dawn and hiding the sun; the cold flakes drifting in huge clusters and banks of ice that lashed the frail and flaking skin of the young girl chained to the mast of his flagship, her mind in distant worlds, scarcely in contact with reality, separated through pain from the evil of her senses. Her child-like mind had lost all sense of space and time; cowering in disbelief at the horrors of the despite within her physical world she had receded into fantasy; given in to the challenge on her sanity, losing touch with everything except communion with the unseen spiritual world which she could not explain nor prove existed.

Even when standing on the precipice of insanity, perhaps even already having fallen over the edge, still she could find that place within her heart where the love and compassion of her Master resided. She remained stubborn in her commitment to love conquering all even though her experience might be otherwise and despite whatever nightmares might present themselves; all that was evil and fearful fell before the bastion of her love for a gentle and wise man from Nazareth.

It was in a state of grace that Maria recalled the words of the prayer she said every day, in loving memory of when her Master had sat with her on the rolling hills overlooking the Sea of Galilee and she repeated it constantly as a mantra in adoration of her God:

"My Father
You live in Paradise but also reside in the loving comfort of my Heart.
I praise your name and pray for the day when all will honour you; seeing that you are truly God and King.
One day you will rule the whole world as your kingdom and the joy and peacefulness of Paradise will spread to here on Earth.
Protect me; Heal me; and Save me through the breaking of bread with me. Teach me to forgive others as I would wish them to forgive me.
Help me find the path to your gift of Eternal Life without being distracted by sin or being led astray by temptation.
If I make mistakes then forgive me, teach me how not to sin again and guide me back to your perfect way of life.
This is my belief."

The Naval Battle of the Firth of Beauly and the North Sea 33 AD

The four armada which had separated in order to deliver their crews to their disembarkation points now regrouped at the mouth of the Firth of Cromarty then turned east towards the North Sea before sailing south towards the Firth of Beauly. They briefly broke through the bank of mist still rolling down from the cliffs at Cromarty and could just make out the tip of masts that belonged to several of the Christian fleet's quadrimes, the tallest ships in either fleet. Graemwolda pointed the masts out to his helmsman who nodded then cried over the howling of the wind that nearly tore his words from his throat:

"They are Christians. There is nothing else as tall"

Then the helmsman issued simple orders to be relayed using hand and flag semaphore, relayed from one ship to the next, not risking any distance further for fear a message be misread. The fleet was already badly bunched up and each vessel was too close to its neighbours, at constant risk of an accident. So the commander ordered the fleet to break up into flotilla of nine to twelve vessels then they advanced in the direction of the tall masts in strange and foreign waters at slow speed to avoid any rocks or hazards, whilst at the same time seeking the mouth of the Firth of Beauly.

The mist suddenly became denser, thickening dramatically at which the helmsman turned to his commander and shouted over the noise of his sail and rigging being whipped back and forth in the wind:

"Sire, we risk the enemy fleet sailing around us and into open seas. If they gain the North Sea then we could spend days trying to catch them. We should spread out" and the helmsman demonstrated with his hands their fleet sailing in a long line, broadside facing the enemy, effectively acting like a long chain across the mouth of the Firth. Graemwolda lifted his hand as a sign of his agreement and within ten minutes the orders had been relayed and were being obeyed.

Maria broke into song, a gentle melody, a love song but in a strange tongue. A song that told of her joy in all she saw and had seen; her willingness to die but also to live; a ballad that disclosed the final part of her plan. Meanwhile, the God-given mist continued to conceal the fleet being led by her love, Prince Craedech. The mist also ensured that Graemwolda could not carry out his final mutilation of her for which he needed a clear sky and for the Pagan flagship to be in plane view of the Christian Army.

Graemwolda looked at the girl and snarled: "I do not believe in your magic but I cannot afford to take any risk and so I shall cut out your tongue if you continue to sing" at which the girl stilled her tongue yet still the King could hear her gentle humming and he cursed her for her defiance, picked up a marlinspike from where it held the rigging in place for the top sail which was not in use and drove the sharp metal spike through one of her ankles to pin it to the mast behind.

Maria gave a gasp then fell forward, held by her chains but otherwise limp as she tried to take the weight of her body off that ankle and the metal that was tearing through flesh and sinew between her tibia and fibula as her leg slid slowly down the mast until the chain went taut and the spike came to rest beneath bone at the junction with her talus, forming a natural wedge. Her eyes rolled and this new source of pain caused her to faint.

Whilst Graemwolda had been distracted by the girl, his fleet had spread out and each vessel was now alone, occasionally catching sight of the bow wave of the ship before it or the shadow of its bos'castle as it disappeared into the next thick bank of fog. Suddenly he heard an eerie high pitched keening cry, almost a plaintiff plea, the sound of someone or something in distress which has lost something else, the cry a mother might make that had lost her only child but could hear it screaming in the distance.

"What is that dratted noise?" he grumbled turning to his helmsman and an enormous head, long and triangular in shape, looking like that of a huge lizard, cut through the blanket of the mist, opened its mouth and picked up the helmsman in its giant maw then shrunk once more into the fog. A few seconds later a long sinuous, snake-like body with four dorsal fins and a wide rhombus-shaped tail fin sliced through the mist, mast, rigging, decking and hull to carve the long boat in two and send it within seconds towards the bottom of the Firth.

Maria was cast to one side, still attached to the mast by the long spike through her ankle. For a moment it looked as if she might float but the weight of the chains around her defeated the buoyancy of the wood, the mast tipped and the unconscious girl began slowly and hesitantly at first but then at increasing speed to slide to the depths, accelerating towards the bottom of the Firth, condemned to being buried beneath the cold waters of Beauly.

Graemwolda was under the water and had expected to see nothing: the sky above was obscured by mist and the lanterns on his ship had been extinguished as the two halves had plunged beneath the surface of the sea within seconds. Instead a ghostly green light lit up the whole of the sub-aquarian world in which he now found himself. The water was clear and so by its light he could see everything: first he saw his own crew grabbing the debris and detritus that were the remains of his ship, anything that could float and which they could use to stay afloat. Some had found enough decking to get out of the water and use it as a raft. Most were in the water and at risk of drowning or dying of hypothermia if they did not find land soon. '*But which way was land?*' he wondered.

Then to his intense surprise he saw the head of another sea dragon or sea serpent. He could not be certain if this monster was the same one as had taken his helmsman or scuppered his ship but now it was approaching his men and … to his utter astonishment it blew a breath of warm air over them. The men were dried in an instance, the mist cleared where the dragon had blown his comforting air, and the makeshift rafts and driftwood sped at the rate of many knots, skimming on the water's surface, heading faster than the men could have rowed to the safety of the nearest shore and the settlement of the Rose Fort on the banks of the Firth of Beauly.

Graemwolda watched this as an interested spectator for he had already considered and accepted his own fate. He was waiting patiently to die.

His mast had snapped under the might of the sea serpent's tail, sending splinters in all directions and a shard some five feet long with a razor sharp point had pinioned both of his legs together. This, in combination with his chainmail hauberk, was seeing him sink slowly despite his best and most heroic efforts. So he looked around him through water that was ice cold but clean and crystal clear and watched in amazement at the havoc being caused by a colony of sea dragons, each one three times the length of his largest long boat, using tooth or tail to sink his fleet, blowing most of his crew towards the shore … and that mystified him … but capturing several in their murderous maws and taking them to some hidden meat store, an enclosure in the dungeons and dark depths of the gloomy and sere emerald sea beneath him.

Except when he looked down, he swore that the loss of air and oxygen had awakened his imagination to fantasise about the kingdom of the dead which either he was about to visit or perhaps the eternal void was all that anyone faced on death and what he saw was one last flight of imagination. He was not a man known for his imagination!

'My life has not been good' he admitted *'and if I could lead it again then I would have sought to be more kind, get involved in less challenges, kill fewer people, rescue someone perhaps?'* Then he laughed as he realised that he had never saved the life of another person: now that was something of which he could be proud and he gently mocked himself whilst secretly he would have loved to have been the hero that had saved a drowning child.

He looked down once more, expecting his earlier mirage to have faded but if anything it was now more definite. For below him he could see a distant City, *'made by or for dwarves'* he hazarded still needing to get used to the distortions of depth, width and height beneath water. The City had domes, minarets, spires, towers, tenements, great halls, chambers, palaces and palazzos, colonnades and cloisters, lakes, canals, fountains, rills and avenues, monuments and mausoleums, auction houses, markets and forums, court houses, parliaments and assembly rooms, guild and moot halls, bridges, piers, parks and wooded glades all glistening in ghostly ghoulish green, with the occasional sight of the spectral, shadowy shades of sinuous sea serpents.

The King had been totally thrown by the scale of the Citadel below him for suddenly he saw one of the sea dragons swim through the upper window of a minaret, a small casement window or sky light; the long lizard stopping briefly to curl around the railing of a balcony, lounging, relaxing and turning its head slowly to enjoy the vista of its tranquil home. That 'small' sky light window must be as tall as the mast on his ship he realised, whilst the balcony on the upper floor of the minaret was the length of at least three long boats.

Then Graemwolda coughed as he could no longer hold his breath, the last of his air had long ago been expelled and he was living now on carbon dioxide, his head began to ache, his muscles were no longer responding, his heart beat accelerated and the pressure within his lungs was encouraging him to open his mouth, at which point he knew his lungs would flood with water and cease to function, he would be deprived of the oxygen vital for his heart and brain and would thus black out. But he refused to panic and it was that which saved him.

Without warning a hand clasped his nose, squeezing shut his nostrils, another hand gripped him beneath the chin forcing up his head then pinching his cheeks to force his mouth open. A chapped and bloodied mouth clasped his in a life-saving kiss and breathed cold sweet smelling fresh air into his lungs. Then with one hand holding him securely under the chin, he was carried slowly but securely towards the mysterious City. Each minute, his mouth would be held once more, and fresh air would be blown into his lungs by a powerful swimmer, able to carry him through the water and yet keep enough air for them to breathe. He hoped for both of their sakes that whoever this was had saved enough breath for themselves and had not wasted their own life to save him. *'A little late'* he thought *'but I might just have had my first unselfish thought!'*

He watched as he was taken closer and closer to the largest building in the City and possibly in their world: a Royal Palace, some great Museum or a Temple perhaps? They passed through a sky light two thirds of the way up the dome and swam a few feet to break clear into fresh air, a glazed sky light in the copula above their heads giving them a view of the surface of the Firth. The surface of the Firth was perhaps a league above their heads? Then his rescuer lifted him until he was lying on his front, on one of the semi circular benches that allowed spectators to view the City through the lens and mirrors of a giant camera obscura.

He heard his comrade speak a few words in a language he did not understand and in a voice so gentle it was more the echo of a departing whisper than any language he had ever heard.

It was in fact a humble prayer, another new experience for Graemwolda. Then two hands grasped the shard that had held his legs together and broken both of his calves and with one slow, gentle but determined pull, the wood came away and by some miracle the bone, sinew, nerves, muscles and flesh healed, leaving no scar, no pain but with all of his strength returning in an instant.

He stood slowly then turned around to thank his rescuer and heard a splash then saw two feet, blackened and encrusted in blood, and a shattered ankle with a bone sticking out left at an odd angle having cut through the skin. The trail of fresh blood, a line of the occasional air bubble and his mysterious 'Guardian Angel' had disappeared through the small sky light window they had used as an entrance, swimming like a dolphin.

"Sire" and he turned to see seven of his marines including the helmsman of his own flagship, all looking at him with a combination of bemusement, consternation and fear in their eyes. "Where are we?" asked one and "What is going on?" asked another.

"We are near the bottom of the Firth of Beauly in what appears to be the City of a colony of Sea Dragons. They have destroyed our fleet and eaten the rest of the crew. We are all that is left I believe."

"Sire, I am not so sure" and several others of the men shook their heads as well. "It is hard to know what to believe but all of us were brought here either by one of the serpents or by the girl. Some of us saw the serpents blow some of our fellow crew members towards the safety of the shore. Cael and Derwent here were both carrying injuries that could have meant they died but were miraculously healed as were you by the girl. What magic is this, sire?"

"What girl?" asked the King then heard a splash and another of his crew was hauled to join them in the camera obscura. He bent down to lift the man onto one of its curved benches then lay him down carefully on his side as he studied the deep gash that he carried on his forehead. The man looked as pale as death and the King knew of no answer to such a terrible wound. He went to ask if any of the other crew could offer help and a gentle voice behind him went "Shush".

Turning, the King had to look down nearly two and a half feet from his towering height of seven foot nine inches and was held mesmerised by the clear blue, innocent child-like eyes of Maria, her face battered from several blows, her nose broken and slightly off from centre, both ear lobes cut, one tooth missing, bruises across her back and front, her upper arms with two deep dagger wounds, a small scar on her scalp, burnt hands and feet and the festering wound from an arrow that had gone clean through her thigh, but she was smiling at him with joy and before he could stop her, she kissed him, hugged him, whispered in his ear "I am glad you are alive" then went "Shush", putting a finger across her battered and burnt lips before turning to the man with the scalp wound and saying: "Lord please help this man. As you love me and I love you, I ask for your aid."

As they all watched the head wound healed, the colour in the man's cheeks recovered, he opened his eyes then turned to Maria and in a voice full of awe said: "You were there: with me. You stood up for me. You argued that I should have another chance. Thank you!"

"I owe you my life" King Graemwolda said to her and was unable to take his eyes off the girl. She had been tortured, degraded, left for dead, indeed he had last seen her sinking under the weight of chains, plunging to the very bottom of the sea. With the chance to escape, she had instead come back and rescued him and saved not only his life but that of several of his crew. No-one had ever saved his life before. Admittedly, the need to do so had never previously arisen but that someone whom he had shown such terrible despite to, could find it in their heart to help him … he found he had no answer to why anyone would do this and so, mystified, he asked the girl: "Why?"

She understood his question immediately but smiling mischievously said: "I will not answer any of your questions with no clothes on!"

The King frowned and was momentarily disappointed to find Maria was like any other female, placing such importance on her appearance then he saw the tell-tale dimple in her cheeks and recognised the sign from his sister. This girl was teasing him! He found that he was over-joyed because she must like him, see him as an equal and above all not be frightened of him to *dare* to tease him. To find someone with the confidence to treat him as a … (and he struggled at first to find the analogy before finally admitting to himself that only a 'close friend' or his sister would contemplate teasing him and then he had to take a firm hold on the tears which would have flowed as he realised he had never taken the time nor been the sort of person to have friends). How he wished his sister was here for Maria and Garahelda would have got on like a village on fire. Indeed, he could easily see Maria fitting in as part of his household and was already lost in admiration of her courage.

But now she was not only teasing him, she had stopped to laugh with unrestrained joy but no sign of any scorn or mockery at the look of shock and stunned surprise on his face when first he had encountered her. Then she had seen his tears and she had become serious again, wiping them away gently with her hair. She kissed him and he was shocked once more as through that one gentle benison he felt such comfort that all of his courage was fully restored.

He turned to his men, his expressive eyes saying '*Well, what is you waiting for?*' and they began to throw across various bits of tartan, scarves, shawls, even a blanket, all made from wool and stunningly colourful. Two tartan shawls held together by two silver broaches gave her a top and a skirt which between them kept her warm and saved what was left of her reputation, covering her modesty: it was of small matter to the men that she was dressed in tartans worn by two opposing Clans who had fought bitterly for centuries.

"Now you can ask me anything" she said, giving his arm a hug and he roared with joyful laughter before inviting her to sit on the bench opposite him:

"Tell me how you are here? How is it you are alive?"

"Good and noble King. First, may I complete my healing of you?"

"Of course" he said surprised. For he already felt fit and refreshed so was surprised that she should think any further healing was necessary. He looked at the girl and her ruined good looks and experienced a sense of guilt then wondered why she did not heal herself? Something must have shown in his eyes for she answered his unasked question.

"Alas I cannot heal myself. But that does not matter. I am alive to save you and your crew and that is all I care about" and now she was serious once more:

"Graemwolda. I forgive you and love you."

At her words, Graemwolda felt a huge burden he had not appreciated he held at first but as it began to dissipate, such was his good humour that he was able to look around him with delight then he turned towards the girl once more for as her heart and soul had offered their forgiveness he had seen something else. "You love me?" he whispered surprised but also honoured by her adoration. He spoke so only she could hear him and she nodded then grinning added: "I love you for your courage and your wise leadership. Do you think you could use your fearlessness and great wisdom to do good things?"

"What are these 'good things' you speak of?"

And so Maria talked from her heart about the places she had seen with children who would be so uplifted by just meeting Graemwolda, seeing how tall and fearless he was, the size of his sword and the strength of his goodwill, his ability to command those around him to fight for that in which he believed. He was everyone's image of a hero. Yet children were being brought up to fear him whom God had made heroic looking.

"How wonderful, my lord, if all the strength and wisdom you have been given by God could be channelled into fighting for childrens' freedom from oppression and slavery; if they could come to you when lost, lonely, in fear, and know you would stand by them: that when they face the terror of Rome's constant oppression then your hand will be held out to guide them?

Once I came across a slave auction and there were two children; so alone without friends or someone to guide them. I had some spending money with me but was soon outbid and wept for many days afterwards that I had been unable to afford those poor children. They were bought by a rich Roman matron and I followed her that night and offered myself in their place but alas I was worth nothing to the lady who wanted two pages for a dinner party that night then to sell them to go down the local silver mines. I wept and can still see those poor boys' faces. I hope that I can find them one day and pray for their safe return.

Iosephus of Arithemea, a wealthy merchant, banker and historian was my escort and refused to lend me money (to be fair I am a terrible risk when it comes to money and no-one should lend me a denarius as I will spend it within minutes)."

At that, the barbarian warrior laughed. He had kept clear of the fairer sex for in his experience they were far more expensive than his own sex. He also had many female slaves who satisfied his needs following a decade of war against other Vicing, Daenes, the Germanii, Romani, Parthians, Medians and Helvetii. His personal household was served by a few hundred slaves none older than in their teens (as that is the age they would then be buried in the sand, or if boys they would be executed by strangulation and have their eyes pecked out; the prettiest and most obedient girls would lose their tongues and be sold on to the Vandals).

Every one of his female slaves were a lot prettier than Maria, especially with her broken and bruised face, much more subservient (indeed none would have dared tease him) yet he had to admit that he had never felt the intensity of emotion with any slave that he now felt for the young Iudaean (and some had been Aegyptian or Median princesses)! Eventually, he was able to stop laughing long enough to ask the girl how she had ever discovered the colony of sea serpents and also to see if she had any plans for their escape. She was happy to respond and positively gleeful; for this part of her plan to defeat the Pagans had gone like clockwork. All now depended on Longinus.

"May I first introduce you to a dear friend of mine?" she said with a smile and no fear; at which the King realised she was enjoying his company as much as he was delighting in hers.

Then Maria began to hum the tune that he recalled from when she had been chained to his mast and he had struck her with a sharp blade through her ankle to silence her. Briefly he winced at the memory but the girl showed her resilience and also total disregard for any pain by ignoring him: she had clearly forgotten his assault on her.

The majestic head of a proud sea dragon, standing tall on its long and slender neck, towering fifty paces over the girl who stood before it, still singing without fear, rose out of the sea waters trapped in the dome of the subterranean City, sending a huge bow wave of water to cover Maria from head to foot in its spray. She looked up and grinned whilst the poor dragon looked at her, totally contrite at the mess it had made of her hair and impromptu tartan dress, and Graemwolda gulped and stepped back.

"Hello my love" she said, her voice gentle and loving and Pederaster responded with delight then looked a little closer at her and said: "I cannot send you back to your father looking like that. He would never agree to peace until he had slain every Vicing in the northern hemisphere!"

"Can you clean me up?" the girl whispered and the dragon nodded but first he asked to be introduced.

"King Graemwolda of the Green Land and the Ice Land, may I introduce you to King Pederaster, Sovereign of All Sea Serpents and Sea Dragons and my very dear friend" at which Graemwolda looked at her in shock then had to ask: "How did you become friends with this monster?"

"Hush, my love" Maria replied "For he is not a 'monster' but a King, highly educated, a scholar, an expert in many languages and although he has yet to learn Vicing, the day will come when he shall. I would hate it for a wonderful friendship between two such warriors and leaders as you two would come to an end over a careless word!" and the Vicing King blinked then took the girl's hint.

"If we can all sit down then I shall tell the story of my discovery of the Sea Dragon of Loch Ness and his family and subjects in their City beneath the tranquil waters of the Firth of Beauly" and then she sat cross-legged with King Pederaster's head by her lap, his eyes looking longingly and lovingly into hers, swirling gold, silver and green, his long neck wrapped protectively around her, whilst Graemwolda and his fellow Vicing sat slightly nervously besides them both, conscious that should Pederaster yawn or twitch he could swallow or crush any one of them by accident.

First she began with her lashing and torture at the hands of the Sitenarae by the banks of the Loch and their attempt to feed her to the sea dragon. Thus had begun a wonderful friendship! But Maria had been left terribly saddened when she heard of the poor sea serpent's loneliness and so she had prayed for Pederaster and her Master had responded.

"Once upon a time, the King of the Sea Dragon had gone in hunt of food for his young wife who was expecting their first child. Swimming from his castle and home near Beauly, he had headed towards the Oich and the mouth of the Ness. Suddenly and without warning, the hills and mountains around the banks of the two rivers had collapsed as the whole world was rocked by a huge and earth shattering quake. The King had taken refuge in a cavern until the rock falls had subsided then swam towards the mouth of the Loch only to discover to his great dismay that the entrance had been blocked and that he was trapped within its deep waters.

Ten thousand years past when quite by chance a young girl met the sea dragon and the two became great friends through the telling of stories. The girl wept when she heard that the sea dragon had been trapped and prayed to her Master that something might be done. And so she discovered that the King's wife still lived and that unknown to the King he had one daughter and she had a child and so it went on, each generation bearing one or two children, all living in the magnificent sub-aquarian City, enlarging it as their family grew, now the grand home of over five hundred dragons.

The girl was given a great gift by God: she was granted the aid of Angels and in their celestial company she swam to the *City Beneath the Sea* and met the Queen, still silently in mourning. The Queen was amazed and asked what could be done to rescue her partner at which the Angel Rapha'el, the Queen Faradir and the girl went to the mouth of the Ness and the Angel took up the Horn of Jericho. With a single note and blast of her horn, a line of rocks fell into the deep and the Queen was able to swim into the Loch to greet her partner. Now they preside in great majesty in the City that every generation of sea dragons has extended, a permanent monument to the faithful love of two beautiful dragons.

For no discernible or sensible reason, the King remained grateful to the girl and when she asked for his aid to defeat the Navy of those who sought the girl's death he was happy to oblige. The girl insisted that none should be harmed and the sea dragons, learning how stubborn the girl could be on such matters, reluctantly agreed. But then the King of the Sea Dragons heard the girl's screams and saw her being tortured by those who wished to slay her. In his fury the sea dragon, incandescent with rage, would have slain the crew of every ship.

But the girl managed to be heard above the noise of the fury of the many dragons and begged them in tears not to hurt any man. Some had already been injured and so she used her healing to remove their harm. Others were stranded and in danger of dying in the cold water so she persuaded her friends to blow the ships' crews to safety. Eventually, all were unharmed save the *King of All Vicing*. So the girl went in search and found him, breathed air into his lungs then carefully removed a shard of wood that would do him great harm and brought him to safety."

"So how will this story end?" asked both Kings.

Maria laughed then admitted: "Alas I have absolutely no idea. But I love you both and would have you both as friends. Could you do this for me?"

Both nodded but then Pederaster went silent for a moment, reflecting on her tale before advising them both: "If Godric sees Maria in her current state then there is not a Universe large enough to save Graemwolda from his wrath."

"I do not fear Godric. He is an old man." Graemwolda replied haughtily.

"He is also my father" Maria reminded the Vicing "You harm him and you shalt be hurting me. I know! I shall have to hide." They all laughed at that then Pederaster spoke softly, saying: "I owe you so much more but this is the start and I know my partner and all of my many descendants would wish I do this for you also." Then he dropped a single tear into the clasp of his right claw and proffering his foot towards the young princess said simply "Drink!"

"It is quite a lot" said the girl eyeing what looked like at least a gallon which would surely make her burst "and what does it taste like? Also I do not believe in magic." At which the Dragon laughed then said "Do not argue. This is God's Will and my prayers for you; both are profound" Maria grimaced then did as she had been told. The impact was immediate and was accompanied by a gasp from Graemwolda and the crewmen as Maria's face, ears, nose, mouth and teeth returned to their former beauty, her wounds to leg, feet, upper arms and hands, her bruises and cuts and the loss of her hair were all instantly repaired: her hair shone white gold.

So great was the love of the dragon that its prayers were heard and answered; he was a Creation of God's and thus the Divine Being could see into the heart of this creature of His Making and respond to all acts of selflessness. God rewarded the sea serpent's long years of faithfulnesss to his partner through his healing of the girl and Maria's visage shone with such exquisiteness the sea serpent suddenly felt hungry when he marvelled at Maria's rather *tasty* beauty whilst the Vicing King wanted more now than anything else in the world to have this young girl from nowhere become his Queen. She sat before them and they were transfixed by her stunning looks; a princess to capture any heart. "What is it?" she asked. "Do I have a spot on my nose or something?"

"No princess" replied Graemwolda "but you have won my heart. I would follow you wherever you go to whatever adventure or fortune you lead me to" at which Maria stood, blushed then suddenly ran to find somewhere to hide. As she had predicted a gallon was far more than her small and delicate bladder could cope with. "Don't you dare '*follow me wherever I go'*… or peep" she shouted over her shoulder then got a fit of the giggles.

Eventually she returned, went bright red once more as they both enquired if she was alright before coming to stand before Graemwolda. The King went to stand opposite her but the girl laughed then admitted: "If you stand then I cannot reach you: to do *this*."

"Do what?" he asked as he sat back down and she stood on tip-toe then kissed him once on the lips before saying sorrowfully yet steadfastly:

"I am promised to Prince Craedech and he holds the keys to my heart. I love you and will come to your aid if ever you need my rescue but I cannot marry you so ask that I be allowed to return your heart to you … not to be deserted by me but also not to be taken from you."

"How shalt this story of ours end?" the King asked once more saddened and realising that for the first time he had encountered something he could not conquer through Might or Force.

"Follow my Master" Maria replied "For I am taught that one day when we have earned the gift of God's love we shall live forever in Paradise. And when that day comes, God's gift to us will be that we can love each other forever.

Paradise shalt be a place without envy or jealousy: my love for Craedech, for Pederaster, for Godric and for you, my King, shall all be equal in my eyes and the eyes of God. Follow my Master and join me in Paradise and you shalt make me the happiest lady in the world."

"I am not sure I can wait" the King muttered a sign of his former anger and impatience peeping out like a goblin sticking its head out of a hole in an otherwise immaculate garden lawn. Maria had to laugh then explained: "People getting angry around me makes me giggle and if you do not behave, my King, then I shall tickle you until you laugh again" at which the King looked at her in shock then said: "You would not, would you?"

"I would struggle to reach anywhere higher so would have to tickle your feet!" and the poor King could not help himself as slowly but surely he did begin to laugh helplessly. Maria hugged him, delighted that his good humour had returned then she invited the bemused crew to do the same. As the golden light of her Master's love spilt over from warming her to bathe them all in its bright blessing and balm Graemwolda found that he was unable to resist his conversion, not least because he knew that it would please Maria:

"Maria, you have shown me love, healing, compassion and wisdom. Surely this comes from your Master but also from your own good heart. For the sake of both, I shall follow your Master and remain devoted to you for this life and in the next."

Then kneeling before her and taking her hands in his, he swore before all of them: "Maria Bann Caedic, the Magdalan, Princess of the Atrebates, I do pledge both myself and my people to follow the faith of your Master, to believe in One God who is the God of the Nazarene. Maria, I ask for your help as I learn to follow and believe in Iesus of Nazareth. So help me also, my God."

The Battles of the Black Isle of Beauly, 33AD

Once more Roaring Flamebringer interrupted our young heroine to bring her attention to the sun as it set in bright crimson to their west, turning the tall Douglas firs of her home forest d'Etapes into the dark shadows of giants menacing the arboured home of the Queen Faladriel. Then the young girl heard the first songs of the stars as they rose into the night sky and smiled a what she heard was Abelard's protection of his elfin wife from the Doom of Geant.

"My Queen" enquired the dragon of the maid "How can the Magdalan reconcile the battles that shall come with her command to herself and others not to kill? And where doth this tale come from? I know little of any battles fought in the wilds of north eastern Scotland or of any early Christian armies?"

Ra'el readily admitted confusion at the events of which she was to begin to give account and her answer was hesitant:

"Maria has already faced the torment of Hell and now she tries desperately to minimise the damage from inevitable war – even God declared war and it was Maria whom interceded repeatedly on behalf of the Pagans to save their lives so that to give them another chance to come to belief in God.

Yet despite her every effort, several battles would be fought on the Black Isle north of Inver and Munlochy and east of Beauly. Yet when war was over she returned to healing the injured and praying for the souls of those slain.

As with all of God's greatest miracles, he turned the great Evil of this day of death to Good and won the trust and love of many pagan hearts in so doing.

The story I shall tell are the accounts of the four land battles fought on the Black Isle between Beauly and Cromarty as the Christian Army under Longinus defeated the Pagan armies of Craedfwllast. My brief accounts are told from memory and are drawn from much older records found in my grandfather's library which include the Chronicles of both Prince Godric and King Tortelimir as well as those of Pilate, Nicodemus, Bede, de Boron, de Troyes and Menissier. Perhaps most helpful are the Royal Chronicles of Tortelimir, first Christian King of the Germanii, which date to the 1st Century AD"

The dragon laughed then told the young bard a little of his own history as he replied:

"We dragons were saved from our own damnation by someone not dissimilar to yourself or Maria. I enjoy your account but am doubtful that your sources describe anything more than fable ... yet what you tell was once part of the Christian orthodoxy – to be believed as fact by every Christian including dragonkind.

When you have finished your story let me tell you that of Serena Clan Faeron, 73rd Empress of Atlantis, and how she conquered Lucifer in the Nine Circles of Hell, thus rescuing all dragonkind from our fate as foretold by the Gospel writer, John ... but first yet again you are showing how young you are for I can see the stifled yawns and the slit eyes that show you have once more exhausted yourself in the telling of your tale. So sleep ..."

And Ra'el fell into the soft comfort of his right claw, a smile of delight across her face as the events she would tell on the morrow danced before her sleeping eyes. She awoke at the first light of dawn to find herself sitting upon the ruin of the tall arched window that formed the north wall of the ancient Abbey at Fontenay, her dragon wrapped around the stone, its head close to hers, eyes whirling wih expectation, and so (with a snatched kiss on his silken nose) she returned to the story of the battles on the Black Isle in the year of Christ's death.

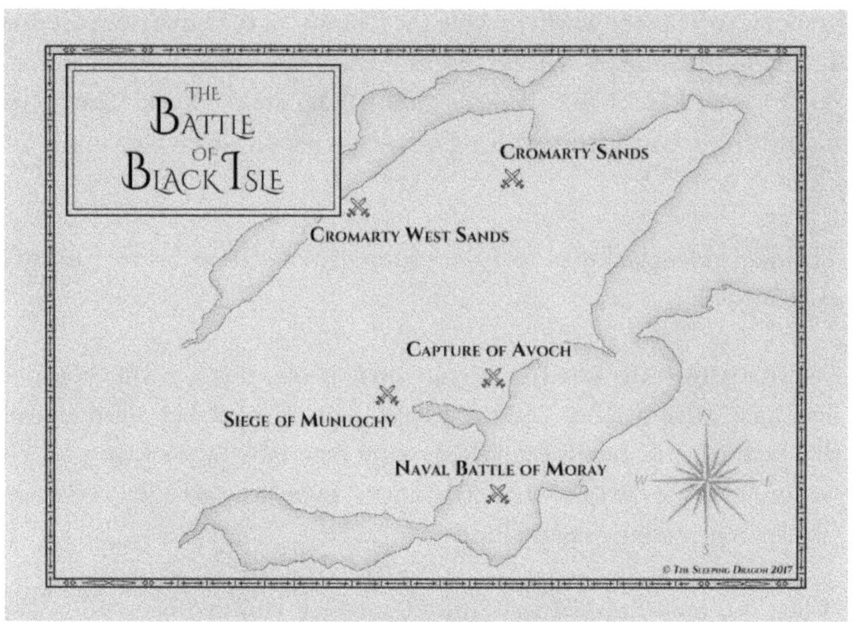

"At the sound of a whistle blown by King Craedfellast, the long columns of Vicing and Germanii started to mount the cliffs overlooking Cromarty Sands, running swiftly up the winding paths from the west and north coves. It was just after the seventh hour in the morning and the first signs of morning sun could be seen fighting their way through the steep, dark, grey banks of snow clouds. The weather had grown progressively worse during the early hours of the morning and the Vicing faced not only the challenge of the Christian Army waiting for them at the top of the cliffs but they were also running straight into a blizzard.

As a consequence, an hour later as the Germanii started to deploy on the cliff top they lost all sight of their enemy, the Christians, massed on the battle plains above the West Bay.

The Germanic army formed into two broad columns led at the front by King Tortelimir, the Germanic cavalry and archers, followed by the Suevii and Chaenii on the Germanic right flank and the large horde of Germanic infantry on their left flank.

Longinus' army was set out on a much broader front with cavalry on his right flank and in the forests to his north west (his far left flank), his archers were dead centre and his mercenaries and infantry were formed up in front of them.

At eight in the morning, the battle above the west sands of Cromarty began, the snow falling even heavier and shutting out the sky and all that was farther than a few yards before each brave warrior. Arrows and axes came out of the blinding white light and the thick clumps of snow whilst ice was forming rapidly on helmets, shields and beards. And in the ensuing chaos, over forty thousand Pagans met a smaller army of Christians and were defeated.

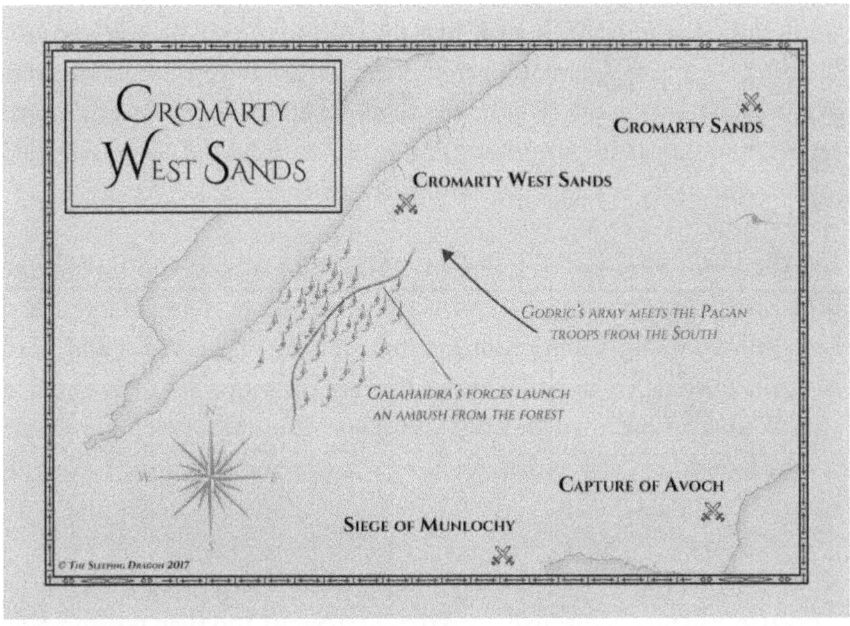

The battle started with Sir Galahaidra launching his cavalry from the forests to the rear of the Pagan King Hortiga's army, supported by King Hargest and Magda MacAllan's horsemen, whilst Prince Godric and Eorl Amaric launched their own cavalry against King Tortelimir's left flank and Sir Kenneth set his archers on Tortelimir's cavalry.

Within the first thirty minutes, Galahaidra had slain King Hortiga in personal combat, the Suevii and Chaenii under Hortiga had been massacred, the few that were able to flee had crashed over the cliffs blinded by the blizzard whilst Tortelimir had been unhorsed by Galahaidra and captured surrounded by the last forty of his cavalry.

Prince Godric, Sir Amaric and Sir Galahaidra's cavalry then attacked the flanks of the Germanii infantry as, unsighted in the snow, the sky dark, a cold sun covered by snow clouds, their eyes blinded by blistering blizzards, they staggered towards Mullochy without a leader. The Yeorls Corin and Garrard with the infantry of the proud Atrebates stood and held the Germanii infantry as they staggered, formless and leaderless, into contact with the solid phalanxes of the Christians; the wind coming from the south flung the snow relentlessly into the faces of the tall blonde warriors, blinding the young Germanii before them. Twenty five thousands were captured, wounded and slain by the flanking attacks of the cavalry, with only a few thousand Atrebates falling. Four thousand Germanii fled towards the army of Craedfellast to their east.

But the losses were not only Pagan. Alas, with almost the final strike of the Battle, the champion Yeorl Garrard was slain. King Hargest had been unhorsed and taken prisoner by a company of Germanii and Lord MacAllan had fallen and been buried beneath the snow, so badly wounded that word went out that the Lord was slain. After two hours, Tortelimir was exchanged by Sir Kenneth for King Hargest and the young Germanii King left the field.

King Craedfellast's plan had always been to draw a large proportion of the Christian Alliance across to defend the West Sands and then punch a hole through their remaining defences by advancing from the North Sands. His army had a longer route to the cliff tops at Beauly and so arrived at the Christian lines of defence much later than Tortelimir's engagement to his west.

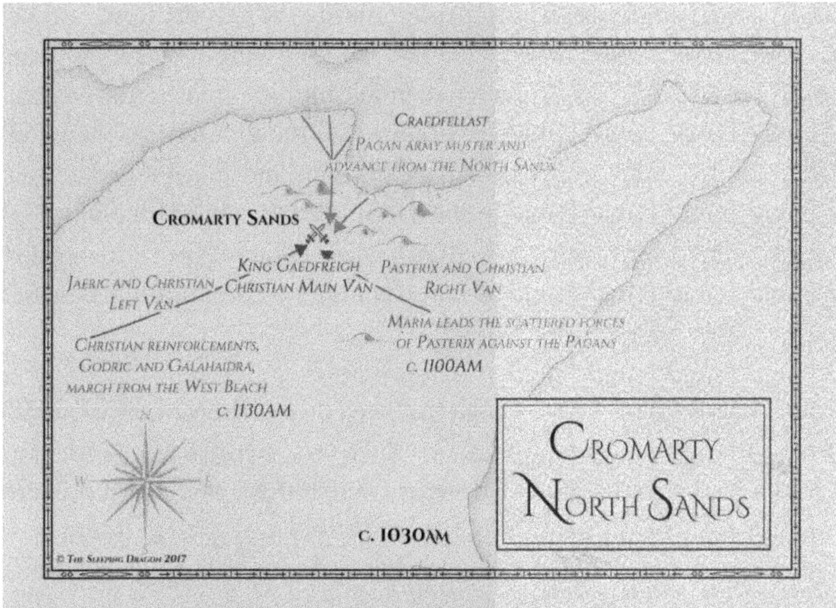

Around the tenth hour of the day, King Craedfellast reached the cliff top above the North Bay of Cromarty Sands with no news of the defeat of the Germanii or of the sinking of his entire fleet at the mouth of the Firth of Beauly where it joins the North Sea. Although the sun had been above the horizon now for almost two hours, the snow clouds continued to hide the sun and sky whilst snow blizzards both dazzled and blinded his men. They did not know what they faced and no longer dared risk running as before them lay the prepared defences, trenches and traps laid by Martius and his legion.

Craedfellast was disappointed that the weather would mean he would not see his brother's execution of the Princess of the Atrebates; he was also conscious that his army, whilst overwhelming in numbers, was also over-balanced in favour of infantry and might struggle against the Christian Army's cavalry on open ground.

Nonetheless, the Pagan Army numbered some one hundred and thirty thousand and his enemy's ranks looked thin and fragile by comparison, perhaps thirty five thousand at most.

The Vicing King launched his men cautiously towards the front ranks of the Christians, but did not see Pasterix's flanking wing of twelve thousand to his far left. His own infantry then fell into the traps set by Martius which were devastating, hidden beneath the snow. Over six thousands fell wounded, a few trapped or slain outright and the rest of his front ranks ground to a halt gingerly testing the ground. At which point King Graefreigh ordered his archers to launch volley upon volley of arrows whilst his catapults and ballistae fired huge flaming boulders into the bunched ranks of the warriors before them.

King Graefreigh of the Deceangli had been given charge of the Christian Army at Cromarty and won a heroic victory, perhaps the Christian's greatest victory of the Early Christian Church through his own personal courage aided by the panache of his brother in law, Pasterix. Both would fall wounded before the end of battle but had won, defeating the Pagans. Graefreigh's infantry drove through Craedfellast's centre, whilst King Pasterix's cavalry launched a flanking attack from the Christian right flank, supported by the Kings Craemond and Harbondum. Alas the numbers that they faced were too huge and both attacks crumbled or lost momentum when the two Kings fell.

Pasterix was eventually captured and Graefriegh lay wounded and near death. Yet both Kings had bought sufficient time for Maria, Galahaidra and Godric to arrive on the battle field. The final half hour of the battle would determine if Britannia fell to the Pagans or could become united as a Christian Alliance.

Meanwhile, the Daenii and Caledonii had successfully disembarked at Avioch just after the seventh hour and then separated. The Daenii had left five companies to capture Avioch which was bravely defended by its towns people and the rest headed towards Mullochy, looking to hold the Christians within the walls of their Citadel whilst the Caledonii were sent towards Baltain, ostensibly to prevent any attempt by the Christians to sortie towards the bridge but also to prevent any Christian reinforcements from gaining the Citadel of Mullochy through the West Gate.

Across to the west outside the village of Tore, near Baltain bridge in the eighth hour in the morning, the Caledonii joined up with King Pedrus and his Army of Picts. The King had been believed to have drowned when his entire fleet was sunk in a naval battle off Skye. However, the King had landed his army at the mouth of the River Lochy, disembarking to the north of the estuary and then marched north-east crossing the Oich and Ord before heading towards the Muir of Ord. Kings Graemir, Garrold, Tarriclum, Parester and Vercing met up with King Pedrus then marched together to Bogallan. King Tartaracs of the Cornavii was dropped down the well in Bogallan and his fifty clansmen joined Garrold's clan.

By the ninth hour, the Caledonii and Hibernians had been spotted marching north-east towards Mullochy whilst the Daenii had reached Bogallon which they held, seeking to prevent the Caledonii from relieving those camped in Mullochy. The snow then reached this part of the Bay and the Firth and both armies lost sight of each other at which the two armies halted, not wishing to cross the others' path by mistake. King Hartdenicum of the Daenii sent word to King Craedfellast but his messengers fell into the traps set by Martius or were taken prisoner by Martius' sentries.

By the tenth hour, the Daenii had heard no word from Tortelimir, Craedfellast or Graemwolda. They could not believe that all three forces would have been defeated and assumed instead that communication was so bad, messages were not getting through. Outnumbering the Caledonii by almost three to one, they decided to find the Caledonian Kings and do battle.

The New Alliance at Anlach

Graemwolda with Maria in tow landed near the Bay of Anlach and could immediately see the banner of the King of the Caledonii, flying high and swirling in the wind, set in the ground outside the battered Inn in the hamlet of Anlach. Out of the snow storm and seated before a spitting open fire, King Graimir was in Council with his commanders, discussing how they should attack the Daenii and had just received news of the death of MacAllan from a young man of the Clan MacAllan called McKeith, fresh from the Battle of the North Sands of Cromarty. In strode the tall Vicing hero and the young girl, the challenge of the sentries outside had been ignored by the giant, whom pushed past them in order to greet his fellow King, closely followed by Maria, whispering apologies for Graemwolda's peremptory manners.

Momentarily, Graimir was not sure which to do first, reach for his sword to slay the Vicing King or greet Maria in relief, surprised but delighted that she seemed unharmed despite her ordeal at the Vicing's hands. Maria resolved his dilemma by running into his arms then introducing Graemwolda to him. The two Kings glared at each other but could not remain angry as Maria started to laugh at them both for their hostility.

Then, before they could settle down to exchange news, the first bad tidings of the many setbacks in the battle fought at the North Bay of Cromarty was brought to them as an urgent message delivered by one of Iosephus' outriders together with a summons for aid from King Godric. At which, Maria had leapt on the first horse she could find, weeping in distress as she heard of the many losses, unarmed and without armour, yet riding impetuously to lead the Christian armies before either King could prevent her.

"What hope has she on her own?" Both monarchs asked of the other and realised they shared one thing in common at least: they both feared for the girl yet could do nothing to tame her reckless and willful spirit.

Graemir, still wary of his companion, thought to win Graemwolda's good humour yet further in the tale of Maria's part in the battles so far and the Vicing King fell yet more deeply in love with her as his peer's tales unfolded. The knowledge that Maria had surrendered to his torture when afraid astounded the Vicing. Then slowly a gleam came into his eyes. Not anger but appreciation and hunger. His respect for the girl was growing by the second. Here was a Queen out of Legend that could master this world. To her courage could now be added honour, principles and determination. And she was barely sixteen with so many years ahead of her! In the right hands, with the right coaching, she could become a great instrument for the Expansion and Independence of his Vicing Empire.

Then as they continued to talk, news came through of a great Christian victory by Longinus against the Pagans on the West Bay. "But all is not good news" another of Iosephus' messengers briefed the two Kings. "Avioch has fallen and King Graefreigh who leads the Christians in battle against the Pagan horde led by King Craedfellast is dead. Graefreigh's brother-in-law, Pasterix has been taken captive. King Jaeric has fled as have the Kings Craemond and Harbondum. Prince Godric and my master Sir Iosephus continue to hold, hoping that Sir Galahaidra can bring reinforcements and are sending out for aid but there is none within reach. Maria is needed to take charge of the Christian Army before it disintegrates but no-one can find her!"

"We should pray for her" said Graemwolda thoughtfully and Graemir agreed: "Maria will welcome our prayers and it is a foolish man who writes the girl off; she may yet turn this defeat into victory." Then after a few moments silence, Graemir had the temerity to ask: "Just how determined is your new faith, my King? Are you willing to fight and to die for your new faith?"

"What would Maria ask that I do?"

Graemir was thoughtful at that but would not lie. His fellow King deserved better than that: "She has gone north so that the rest of us can decide for ourselves but also to see if peace can be achieved without risk to our lives. For if she was here, she would go before the enemy we face, alone, and try and convert them even though it means she come to great harm."

“As she did with us” Graemwolda asked in realisation, horror and understanding. Graemir nodded. “Has she no fear?” Graemwolda then asked to which Graemir replied:

“Watch to our East. Even if she has fear yet still she shall be there! O yes, my friend. She is very afraid. But she loves her friends more than she fears for her own safety.”

“What courage” and Graemwolda was briefly silent before nodding to himself with renewed determination. “Maria sets us all an example of courage to be followed. Give me a sword and I shalt fight for my new God.”

Graemir’s delight was tremendous, genuine and heartfelt. He gripped the giant in both arms then held him tight. Graemir was no midget at five foot nine yet still had to look up a good two feet to greet his peer whose sword was taller than he. Then Graimir whistled; the signal for his brother to join them. Garrold had gone to fetch King Pedrus but his brother had wanted to sound out the Vicing King before they met as the Christians could not afford the Picts and Vicings to fight each other when both were needed to fight the Daenii.

“Pedrus …!” gasped Graemwolda in astonishment on seeing the King of the Picts. “You are meant to be dead.”

“You sunk my fleet you Vicing thug” the Pictish King roared “but fortunately I had already landed.”

“Do you fight me or fight for Maria?” and Graemwolda’s question silenced the King of the Picts allowing the Vicing to continue: “Maria’s Peace will give you Hibernia. More than that will need my armies and her navy for she now rules the seas from the north of Scanda to the Scilla and Charybdis.”

“If you are offering your aid then I will gladly seek peace. My only wish has been to protect the fishing communities along the western coastline which the King of Dacia now rules.”

Graemwolda offered his former foe an olive branch. For Maria's sake he was prepared to bury his animosity for the Pictish King and fight as his ally:

"Maria's Peace will protect your kingdom and she is clear that we can all choose our faith and there is no requirement to convert. Imagine a world where we are united against the threat of Rome and you need not look each day over your shoulders in fear of raids from Vicing, Caledonian or Germanic fleets."

"I had never planned to consider peace. Let me think further on this!" answered Pedrus sadly and Graemwolda nodded as he felt very much the same then moved the meeting on to consider their assailment of the Daenii:

"Well then, let us take advantage of your good fortune in being here." And Pedrus nodded whilst the Vicing King turned briefly to the two brothers from Caledonia. "I am guessing that the Daenii seek to crush you. They will know of your treachery" and Graemwolda pointed towards Graemir and Garrold "but they may not yet know that they face the Picts as well and they certainly will not know that I have landed an army of my marines."

"How many?" Pedrus asked bluntly and Graemwolda amazed them with his answer:

"Over one hundred thousand but many are slaves and none are armed."

"Leave that to Decius" suggested Garrold.

"Who is he?"

"He led the crew that sank your flagship and used to be a Decurion in the Roman Army."

That persuaded Graemwolda who continued now much heartened. Indeed, already his delight in the art and craft of warfare had returned and he was enthusiastic for the fight: "Decius need not convert and arm more than five thousand; enough to prevent the Daenii from breaking in to your

Citadel. Our objective must be to trap the Daenii against the gates of the Christian's walled City."

"What are my orders, commander?" Graemir asked and the Vicing King blinked then smiled at the compliment the senior Christian King present had just paid him before carrying on setting out the orders for the day: "Graemir and Garrold: Fall back before the Daenii. Draw them towards the Gates of Mullochy but so slowly that the Daenii get ahead of you. Pedrus, you follow the Daenii but stay out of sight.

We go into battle when you see me sortie from the West Gate."

King Hartdenicum was taking an early luncheon around the tenth hour. His news was mixed. Four of his Karls had ridden in and now joined him in a light repast, their reward for having ridden hard with their news. "Talk and eat" he said spraying the field table at which they sat with crumbs; they were meeting in a small timber-framed open stable that was being used to store hay.

"Avioch is taken. I have left two companies of Karls and brought the remaining five companies here." The King nodded then turned to the next Karl. The news was not so good:

"The Germanii have been defeated. Hostiga is slain. Tortelimir has withdrawn with a few thousand to meet up with King Craedfellast."

King Hartdenicum turned next to the Karl that had ridden from the North Bay and the man, more a giant at over seven foot but incredibly handsome with bright blue eyes and long fair hair, shrugged his shoulders then said: "Absolute chaos: it was madness to fight in this snow as we threw away any advantage we had in numbers. King Graefreigh the leader of the Christians is dead. King Pasterix their second-in-command is captured. Yet the Christians still fight without anyone knowing who their new leader is (if they even have one). We outnumber them perhaps ten to one. They should flee! Yet they still fight!"

"Then let us finish things here!" Hartdenicum said grimly and turned to his final lieutenant:

"My news is the most recent: I have been inside the British camp here at Mullochy. There are *no* soldiers. The Citadel is full of camp followers and support staff. Plenty of weapons but there is no-one to use them. Meanwhile the Caledonii march for the safety of the Citadel. They are less than two thousand. We can cut them off with ease but must move fast."

"How fast?" asked the King, spurred on by this news.

"Now would be as good a time as any."

The King stood and swept his own breakfast onto the floor then issued his command: "Gaetrum, Faraster grab some food and follow me with twenty companies. We run for the West Gate. This blizzard will hide us.

Gorbag, Mancus, Graeybeard. Keep track of the Caledonii with twenty companies and make sure they hear you through the snow on their tail.

Gorbag, ask my son, Prince Corvinium, who is with our men, to take three companies, steal what horses he can from the stables around here then he is to track the Caledonii on their left flank.

Our objective everyone is to force the Caledonii into a trap which we spring when they reach the West Gate. Don't mess this up and with luck we will gain the Christian Citadel and be able to hold it should the Christians defeat Craedfellast or offer it to our King as a prize if we are victorious at Cromarty Sands."

God's Messenger

At the news of the plight of the Christian Army above the North Sands, now rendered leaderless, Maria rode in constant prayer, her mind scrambled chaos as usual, unsure if the two Kings, her dear friends, Graefreigh and Pasterix lived, still uncertain of the fate of MacAllan or of Hagrest but she remained optimistic that no one had told her anything about Longinus, Galahaidra or her father. Those three could win any battle on their own. Alas, the death toll sounded horrendous.

The roads were treacherous and constantly blocked by snow drifts which she rode over or through, driving her horse north with the wind behind her. In her first hour she travelled ten leagues and it was approaching half way between the tenth and the eleventh hour as she reached the spot where the battle above the West Sands had been fought. Longinus had left ten companies of men to do what they could at the scene of the battle but snow had started to cover everything: weapons, broken and bloodied men and animals, even the makeshift shelters they had tried to erect.

She found the captains of the ten companies at a desolate and deserted spot: young men but then they were all young men or women for war destroyed the young of each and every generation! Together they ran through the snow to find shelter in the hovel of an old lady, happily making hot drinks for the many men taking shelter before her fire.

"Mother" said Maria bowing low "Can you offer us somewhere we may meet in private?"

"Yes princess" the lady replied instantly recognising the girl from her growing legend despite the tartans she still wore and opened the hatch for them to scale a ladder that led into the attics, lit by a skylight which in this case was covered in a good foot of snow!

"I have seven hundred men to help us but no orders and no experience of this" one of the captains began his briefing and he pointed out of the sky light to where all sign of the companies' endeavours had already been swept away by wind, rain and snow. "We have a few hours before a hurricane hits us from across the sea" he added emotionlessly although his young heart must be sinking at the thought of the damage such high winds would wreak. Maria looked out upon the approaching storm and would not be daunted, saying:

"Set your many captives to help: their friends lie out there as well as yours. Then split the men into three groups. Our priorities are: first, wood for buildings as shelters and hospitals and as fuel for fires for light and heat; second, build shelters and as rapidly as we can; and third, dig the wounded out of this snow. Many will have died from hypothermia whom otherwise we could have saved. Save them for me captain, please" at which he saw her tears held back but still ready to flow at any moment. "Yes princess" he said simply "but can you help?"

Maria was thoughtful then suddenly her eyes shone the brightest sapphire blue and she said: "Follow me!"

Moments later, they stood at the door of the simple house and the young girl whistled. All they could see at first was a disturbance in the snow but then it began to take shape before rearing then bucking with joy. Epona loved snow but above all he loved his mistress and pranced then danced before her in joy at his summonsing. Maria stroked his nose gently then lifted a cedar box carefully from his saddle bag, opened the lid, spoke a few words softly then placed the box upon the snow and said: "Look".

It took the captains a few moments for their sight to become accustomed to the glare of the snow but when they could see properly they gasped then shouted for their men:

"I need six hundreds in pairs" one commanded and then the captains pointed to beams of golden light radiating out from the clay platter within the black cedar box. The Grael was showing the way to those whom it could find still alive within the snow.

Maria whispered to one of the captains: "Tell your men to bring any The Grael shall indicate even if they look dead. The Grael is also showing us those whom it can restore to life from death."

"But how do we restore them?" asked several of the captains bewildered for they were Picts and Gaels, MacAllan's and Hagrest's men. They had little experience of this faith; had blindly followed the lead of their commanders when MacAllan and Hagrest had converted to Christianity without asking questions.

Maria had the answer and called five of the captains to join them.

"I am Maria" she said at which they all smiled as everyone knew who she was. "What are your names?" and embarrassed at first they then told her: "Caeorl, Faelin, Graeme, Terence, Vernon and Gastor."

Then she closed her eyes and whispered her gentle prayer: "Through the laying on of hands may you grant these men the gift of your powerful Spirit God that they may heal the many harmed here and wherever they encounter those poor souls who have been hurt. Please, Lord, I need your help to undo the harm of war."

The men had been shivering in the cold but suddenly they were on fire with God's Spirit and turned towards Maria, looking at her in amazement. "Go" she said "and find your friends, comrades and former foes. Save their lives. I must ride to our other battle site. There are yet more lives must be saved this day."

Caeorl came forward and held her in his arms, saying: "Go, my lady, with our blessing. You have given us hope. Bring your gift of hope to others that you shall save this day" and then both looked around as there was a loud shout:

"It is MacAllan. The Lord MacAllan. Och, the poor man is poorly!"

"Show me and fast" Maria shouted then ran through the snow at the sign of two men waving. In moments she was at MacAllan's side saying a simple prayer, a plea from her humble heart. The flames of God's Spirit briefly dazzled everyone and the snow crumbled and melted away in an instant to reveal the man, himself, who groaned, held his head, shook it, sat up, then laughing said: "What are you lot all looking at then?" and his men cheered. Then Caeorl and Faelin lifted him out of the snow and carried him carefully to stand where he was able to see his men aiding the many wounded and the Lord nodded his head in approval.

Caeorl turned to praise and thank Maria but she was already riding at reckless speed to follow where Longinus, Galahaidra and her father were leading their reinforcements to meet Craedfellast and his Pagan horde in battle.

The path that Longinus and his companies had taken was well-trod and Maria had no difficulty in following their tracks. She quickly caught them up but had no time to stop and sped past them, her voice a gentle whisper that caught in the wind and swirled around them: "Make haste and follow me for victory can be ours."

She rode fast for another fifteen minutes until she could hear shouts, cries and screams coming out of the snow blizzard. Then the first volley of arrows fell close by, thudding into the ground to her right and disappearing into the snow drifts as far as their fletching. A horseman rode across her path, in fear of some pursuit, his long sword swiping to cut her throat but she dodged the man's blow easily. And yet it did unsettle her slightly.

Second's later four men in the purple livery of the Christian Army charged towards her, their spears held as lances, imitating Sir Galahaidra's stance as he rode into battle. They saw the girl's long hair and the tartans of the Germanii tribesmen she was still wearing and bore down on her in the half light mistaking her for a Pagan.

The girl reined in held her hands out, palms upwards in the universal sign of peace and stood stock still. The riders came on at increasing speed, seeking to run her down. At the last possible moment, one of the men recognised her and at his shout they all lowered their weapons and tried to shy away from her. Epona spooked and bucked high into mid air, launching Maria twenty feet off the ground to come crashing down, fortunately landing softly in four foot of snow.

She sat up, brushed the snow off her face and out of her eyes, moving carefully to avoid being trampled by the horses still stamping around her and one of the men stooped down, caught her by the arm and swung her one-armed to sit behind him whilst another grabbed Epona's reins. "Your father wants to have a word with you" the cavalryman whom had rescued her said sternly but then as he saw her gulp he could not help himself and laughed. "Don't worry lass. There are plenty here owe you their life and will take care of you. Come with me and I will look after you."

Prince Godwin was sheltering in a stone crofter's hovel, one door, one window, one room, one fire and one huge swirling tempestuous hurricane had descended on the battlefield outside. He took one look at Maria and the relief on his face was palpable for he had heard such horror stories about the harm done to her. "You look radiant: impossibly healthy given this ghastly weather! My daughter, I know you have already done so much to defeat the Pagans but I need your help. We are losing this battle. The odds were always just too great. We are doing alright here on our left wing, although our hold on this front does look fragile, but our centre and right wing have disappeared. I cannot risk any of Amaric, Kenneth, Galahaidra or Jaerid to find out what is going on; Longinus is still to join us; and that leaves Harroult who lacks battle experience."

"And ..." she asked guessing what was to come next.

"Could you ...? I have brought your chest just in case" and not daring to make eye contact with her, he beckoned to an aide, standing shivering in the doorway who was delighted to run off and fetch it from the comparative warmth of the Prince's campaign tent.

Meanwhile Maria walked over to her father and gave him an enormous kiss then said "I have missed you and have lost count of the number of times that I wanted to be near you. Of course I will help you" and the Prince sighed with relief then glared at her:

"Later you can tell me about your adventures for from what I hear you have been shockingly reckless, foolhardy and I will have to put you over my knee at least seven times ..." and then he paused and could not stop his pride in his daughter bringing a sparkle to his eyes as he pleaded with her "except … daughter it is truly wonderful to have you back. Can you please do some of your magic for we need rescuing?"

"Help me change into my armour, lend me a sword as Sir Amaric has mine, have your aide harness Epona then point me in the right direction to find the army of Pasterix" Maria replied and they held each other for several minutes feeling the great comfort in each other's arms.

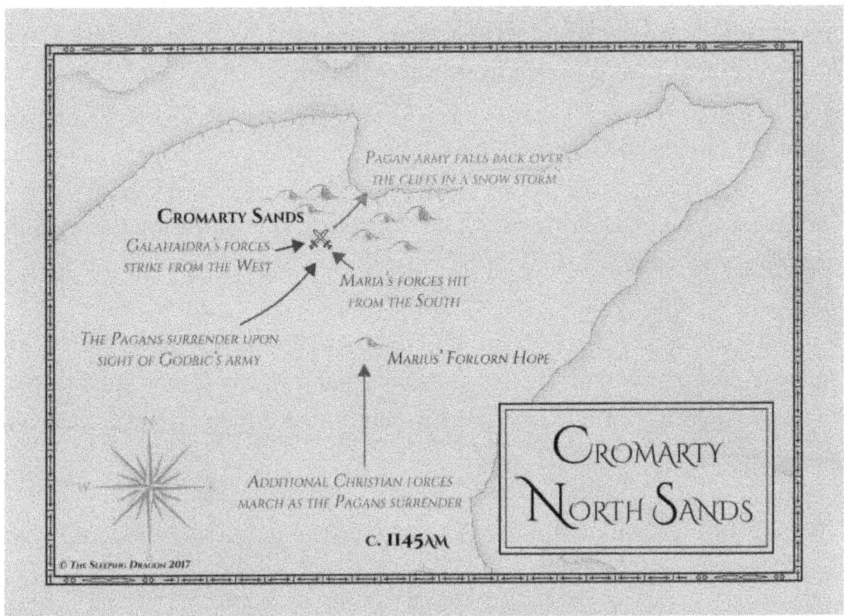

A few minutes later and Maria was riding through the scene of a nightmare from Hell, Eorl Harroult at her side, updating her on the terrible bloodbath she could see all around her.

"In the early stages we held the centre and left whilst Pasterix attacked from our right. His cavalry cut through Craedfellast's left flank effortlessly, the Pagans collapsed, retreating, running into their own reserves and tumbling over the cliffs. Then Craedfellast broke through our front line forcing Martius to fall back and so Graefreigh led his own personal bodyguard and companions in a counter attack and just kept going, punching a huge hole in the enemy's ranks. We thought we had won but alas Jaerid had been held on our left flank and then he was defeated and fled.

Craedfellast surrounded our leader and King Graefreigh was forced from the protection of his companions, dragged off his horse and cut down by eight Vicing; he fell to be trampled deep into the snow. A few hundred yards away, King Pasterix rode into an ambush and lost all of the small company that were by his side, being wounded and taken hostage. Thousands of the cavalry from Iceni, perhaps the best in the world, were left without their leader so they fell back and were lost. As we speak, we have no right flank and no centre … or if we do we cannot find them."

"Can my father lend me some cavalry?"

"Yes but he will need help soon. The Pagans are concentrating their whole army on his flank."

"Tell my father not to worry. The Pagans have already been beaten for they are now trapped on the Isthmus of Cromarty. My father must retreat to Mullochy rather than sacrifice himself. Tell him that is *an order* from his daughter."

"If I tell him that he will have me beheaded" Harroult replied and they both laughed realising how true that was. In the end, Maria said "Do your best" and left it at that.

As the hurricane grew in its intensity, it briefly blew the snow clouds and the blizzards away far into the distance. Maria was fortunate to be sitting on Epona on a steep rise to the north of the battlefield that gave her the perfect view of how the troops lay. The Christian centre and right flank had been fighting in a wide flat-bottomed valley, out of sight from the left flank and Longinus' reinforcements approaching from the West Bay. The Christian left flank had imploded and she could see Jaerid fleeing for the safety of Longinus' legion. Longinus would take another twenty to forty minutes to deploy where his forces could contribute effectively to the battle. The battle would be won or lost in that time.

The Christian front line had collapsed early on in the battle. Martius had retreated behind the earthen rampart he had built as a last resort and then held as the rest of the Christian centre collapsed around him leaving him as a small island of defiance!

Harroult blushed as he admitted that his infantry had been the first to flee overwhelmed and unable to cope with the thousands of Pagan double headed and double handed axes and their long spears. He had fled to join Godric but his infantry had disappeared into the snow.

Longinus had not been able to reinforce King Jaerid in time and the left flank had been broken by the Pagan archers. Jaerid was still in flight being chased by Pagan cavalry.

In the centre, King Graefreigh had been slain, and this had crushed the heart and soul of the Christian army. The Christians had been left leaderless, stunned and in shock as a consequence. The Lowland Kings and their regiments had stood still and taken a beating from all directions; they were retreating south east and in danger of going over the cliffs as they were blinded by the snow whilst the winds of the hurricane had blown their cavalry to the ground. Finally, on the right wing, the capture of King Pasterix had left the Iceni in chaos and his army was spread all over the battlefield.

Just as the snow clouds were regrouping ready to mass once more over the battle, Maria saw Eorl Graemond and the Kings Craemond and Harbondum. They were near the cliffs to the north-east, out of position but still in contact with some of their troops. Then Eorl Harroult rejoined her with two hundred of Godric's champions: he would not proffer anything less for the protection of his beloved daughter but this left him vulnerable to the gathering masses of Pagans under Craedfellast.

"You are going to have to be on your best behaviour" Maria said as he galloped up to join her with the cavalry. The young Eorl blinked and then Maria explained why he must behave at which he groaned, gulped then remembering what the girl had been through herself finally and reluctantly agreed.

"I am telling you this next bit in case I get myself killed. The cavalry escort is for you. I ride alone."

"No, my lady. Your father will skin me alive!" Harroult protested but she would not listen demonstrating once again how stubborn she could be. Maria showed him her plan to finish the battle, using her hands to represent the two battle fronts.

"So far during our battle the fronts of both armies have turned ninety degrees. The Pagans have split our army in two then trapped our centre and right flanks against the northern and eastern cliffs.

We can turn their tactic against them as, in the snow, they have lost contact with us and no longer realise we are to their rear. Their whole army is currently concentrating on holding off the assault of my father from the west. I plan to punch a hole right through their middle using Pasterix's troops and attacking them in the rear, whilst you, Eorl Graemond, and your 'best friends'" (Harroult groaned) "Kings Craemond and Harabondum hold off the latest Germanii reinforcements that have just arrived under Tortelimir."

Then turning to Harroult she held out her hand and rather shyly said "Good luck" then explained why it was so important he survive the battle. "I need you alive. You must persuade Jaerid to surrender his ambitions for the lands of the Dannonil and the Selgovae."

"How can I do that?" the young knight asked. But he had been chosen as Jaerid's Eorl around the fertile lands of the Forth Valley for his youth, energy and above all because he was open to ideas. Quite prepared to hold no territory if that is what the King's diplomacy would dictate.

"Let me show you my grand design" and Maria took out a scroll of parchment that Craedech had 'borrowed' from his father's map room. "We must not get any food, dirt or scribbled notes on it" she whispered "or Caractacus will skin us, if my father does not do so first."

Then she explained her plans for holding Caledonia against Claudius' invasion in ten years' time. Next she kissed the young knight full on the lips and said: "I need you so much to stay alive for you understand my plans for our survival of the invasion from Rome!" before whispering to Epona and mounting her stallion by climbing on one of his fetlocks that he proffered gently for her use. Harroult rode proudly north-east; he was clearly visible in the purple silk tabard sown for the Christian knights and cavalry by the ladies of Inver and Mullochy and honoured to be wearing it.

Maria's chainmail hauberk was white gold and silver, her tabard was long-flowing, with V tongues and crenulations on the hems, bell-shaped open sleeves and luminescent white with a simple cross in shining white gold, her white gold helmet hung at her side from her belt, revealing her platinum white hair, her shield was shrouded in a white silk cover and sat on its leather enarmes across her back, her leather froggings were also dyed brilliant white as were her leather riding boots, the leather of her saddle, the silk of her harness and caparison. On her left thigh sat a long sword, a gift from her father, with a brilliant white diamond on its pommel, held within a white leather scabbard.

Thea, her silver haired wolf ran at her side, whilst her four wild boars, each sat in her saddle bags in pure white leather harness and wore a tabard showing their hatchment of a wild boar.

In white silver, white gold and dazzling white silk and leather she rode the pure white Epona and ran alongside the albino silver wolf Thea through the purest white ice and snow of the blizzards of northern Caledonia and she was invisible to the world. She whispered to Epona and her stallion sniffed the air then found the scent of the mares he had been brought up with on the plains of Iceni.

They flew through the ice and snow, the faintest of disturbances in the turbulence of the snow tempests, a passing of the fastest wind. To the Iceni who saw her coming from a distance this was Epona come to lead them; the Romans saw Mercury and looked for Pegasus; the Pagans spoke of Loki and Freia; the Christians thought they saw an Angel, then those Eorls and captains who had been privileged to see Maria's challenge at The Stone Hill said: "God's messenger is come and now we are safe."

Five minutes later and she had gathered a hundred of the Iceni whom had been lost in the snow; after ten minutes and the girl had a thousand; fifteen minutes and Maria had four thousand cavalry who in turn had helped her find where the Angles had taken a wrong path and were heading south of the battlefield.

But her greatest moment was just before she went to address the army now gathered to her side. As she stood up in her stirrups, on Epona's saddle, grateful for the stallion's additional height else she would have been lost to their view, Thea suddenly yelped and together with the wild boar, her pack of wolves and wild boars launched into the snow until they came to a rock cairn.

They paused, sniffed then began to dig unceremoniously. Less than a minute later, there was a hand. It looked frozen but then it twitched. Maria on seeing this joined in the digging and invited Epona to do the same. Soon they could see that this was the body of a warrior from the armour; then the ruins of the tabard and their hatchment told them it was a Christian noble. When the face was uncovered, they could see terrible scars, cuts and bruises. Maria held her own hand carefully over the face and said simply "Master" at which there was a silvery glow, the snow melted, and the colour came into the man's face. As she wiped away the residue of the snow and blood, carefully folded the edges of the man's wounds and gasped as the skin knitted together, all knelt in prayers of praise.

"Sire" said Maria humbly. "Welcome back. Lead us" and she proffered her arm to aid King Graefreigh as he stood, a little unsteadily, but clearly alive and hale. "Not I" said the King of the Angles with joy at his rescue and great delight at seeing the young girl once more. "These warriors follow me *but I follow you*. Let us find some Pagans to hunt."

"Let us send them into flight. But a Living Pagan that can be reconciled with God is far more part of God's great plan than a Pagan Slain without the chance to become part of the Christian family" Maria replied and

Graefreigh's healing was made complete through his laughter as he said: "One day, princess, we shalt make a warrior of you. But we love you anyway, whether you be a warrior or not!"

It was past the eleventh hour and King Craedfellast had just heard the news that Avioch had fallen to the Daenii. His cavalry had chased King Jaeric off the field of battle whilst King Hagrest and some three thousand Brigantes were surrounded by a combination of his archers and Vicing infantry.

His one concern was that Sir Galahaidra had charged out of the snow and launched into one of his regiments of Vicing; the regiment had been deployed in a shield wall with spears held high; it should have withstood any but the most determined of assaults yet it had collapsed in moments, the flames of red, yellow, purple and blood coloured burgundy emitted from the tip of the Christian Knight's lance had seen his entire front rank shiver, burn then disintegrate into ash!

Craedfellast feared little in this world: his brother Graemwolda; the God Thor and his hammer; the mythical dragon Fafnir; and Ragnarock, the end of the world. But now there was one more thing to add to the list: Sir Galahaidra and his Holy Lance.

Then suddenly he heard a whisper then a murmur and its companion echo, the soft call and its defiant denial, the louder call to arms, the shout of fear and finally the scream of terror, all linked by the same word: a single terrifying word.

The word was not frightening in itself, indeed if said or spoken in many contexts it would have brought comfort to the Vicing. The word was a summonsing call: it commanded the Vicing warriors gathered in the mists on the snow covered sands of Cromarty to surrender to their death: for Freia, mother of all humankind had come to demand the return of life that was her gift. Freia was perhaps as mighty a warrior as Thor or Odin when her Will was adamantine. And now Freia was come to call the Pagan Army to their final reckoning or so believed those who saw the shining white rider with long blonde hair, dazzling blue eyes, her company of wolves and wild boar and the berserker rage of the tens of thousands of Iceni Valkyrie who rode in her wake.

Craedfellast stood before the silver shining face of the Goddess, her wolf and wild boar, whitened in her presence, her mighty stallion also purest white. She held out her hand and the King surrendered his scimitar to her, feeling he had no other choice. Then she bowed and rode on. His whole army felt their fighting spirit depart from that moment.

With a roar, the Iceni tore through the mists and levelled their spears to strike the rear ranks of the startled phalanxes of Vicing from the Northern and Southern seas of Scandia then carried on under such ferocious and powerful momentum to rip apart the long lines of spearmen beyond. Thousands fell in seconds; tens of thousands in minutes. As the terrified Vicing turned to face this attack they were then assailed by an equally merciless blood-letting as the knights under Prince Godric, Sir Galahaidra and Sir Amaric finally arrived on the battlefield and came at them from their other flank. Sir Kenneth of the Clan Kenneth of Dungellan's archers let fly one volley after another upon the undefended centre of the Vicing phalanxes.

Whilst Maria's cavalry were leaping over the ranks of the Vicing seeking out the Germanii of Tortelimir, Eorls Harroult and Graemond with Kings Craemond and Harbondum were leading their wedges of Caledonians and Northumbrians, formerly mortal enemies for centuries now allies for the day, to drive through the ragged remains of Craedfellast's reserve, deployed in a crescent that collapsed upon itself as they were hit by volleys of arrows, the lances of Graemond's Dacian cavalry and the steady advance of just under twenty thousand infantry their long swords swinging to sever arms or necks in a single proficient blow.

The Vicing and Germanii surrendered in their droves, countless numbers falling before the blazing luminous white glow of the 'Goddess Freia' or the flaming red and gold incandescence of the Holy Lance's fire: the first seeing ranks of the Pagans fall to their knees seeking and being granted peace, the second seering columns of the Pagans, burning them to smoldering ash.

The large hosts of Christian infantry would accept the stunned surrender of the Pagans or bury the few remains of those crispened to a cinder. In many cases the Christians were as shocked as their enemy at the sight of the terrible devastation caused by their own cavalry and marched silently amongst the shadows of the dead. Forty-five thousands were wounded and captured, thirteen thousand were slain and a further fifty nine thousands were wounded in blood-letting that lasted barely twenty minutes. Not one Pagan escaped from the hills around Cromarty.

Finally, on a hill top near the centre of the battlefield, Sir Galahaidra, Prince Godric and Maria met and looked around them at the massacre of the Pagans. The Vicing infantry phalanxes had collapsed: faced with archers, snow and rain in their faces, and the assaults to their rear by the infantry led by Haroult, they had then been chopped down in thousands by the cavalry of the Iceni and that led by Eorl Amaric and Sir Galahaidra.

"This bloodshed must stop" Maria begged the knight and he nodded.

The First Christian Knight

Into the silence and stark loneliness of the hollow square where none but the most courageous or foolhardy dare tred, the first Christian Knight, already counting the scalp of the King of the Suevii to his accumulation, Sir Galahaidra came to claim one more lost soul to his count: Craedfellast looked up from where his captains and lieutenants lay felled by the righteousness of the Christian Army's dire desolation and looked into the eyes of one born for a sole purpose: his soul's devastation.

"Repent" demanded the purest Knight, the spear shaker, keeper of the Holy Lance. Craedfellast had moments earlier learnt of the loss of his Fleet, trapping his and the army of the Heligos Bight on this Godless peninsula. Only the Daenii and Chaenii were left to fight their way to freedom; all other barbarians had succumbed to the armies of the quiet man from Nazareth.

Into his dreams and the visions that swirled within his head and spun before his eyes like the twisting twirling flakes of snow promised by the anarchy and chaos of the blizzards that ruled the fragmented skies came the face of his nemesis: the young girl he had thought tortured and brought to her death upon the mast of his own flagship. Yet she had mustered the armies of the Iceni and Dacia when he had thought them defeated and led them to crush the might of the Vicing then stood before him and removed his sword leaving him to challenge Sir Galahaidra with his spear against the knight's lance. In anger but also bitterness at the loss of so many companions, he defied Sir Galahaidra:

"Never shall I repent or agree to follow the Path to the One God. Even if what you offer is The Truth, yours is a woman's world and no place for men who seek the thrill of war."

"Trust me" and Sir Galahaidra laughed as he recalled the wonders of the chariot race of his life "to follow the Princess Maria, the Magdalan, is to never know one moment's peace as we pursue her plough's furrows: the glory of the constant challenges offered by God as his adventures."

Both Knights mounted, the Pagan in the chequered red and gold that was the hatchment chosen by the Vicing and stolen on the day he had raided the tomb of an ancient ruler of Venetia (whose name was long forgotten); following Craedfellast's defeat the hatchment would be adopted as the colours of the Gospel Writer Marcus.

Opposite the Vicing King was the Christian Knight in the Purple and Gold of the former Kings of Rome, worn by the Nazarene when mocked by the Procurator Pilate on his way to be crucified in punishment for claiming kingship; in reality going to his death as The Messiah, God made Man who had come to sacrifice his life to open the Gates to Paradise and wash away the sins of all mankind.

On the knight's lance tip was the banneret made by Maria from the very Robe that The Messiah had worn when tortured by being whipped and scourged, part of his punishment for claiming to be The Messiah. The lance tip contained The Messiah's blood, a precious drop that had fallen as the lance was thrust into his heart when on the Cross to show that the Messiah was truly dead.

His shield, banneret and tabard bore the hatchment of the *Order of the Knights of the Risen Christ*, the golden letters of Chi and Rho on a field of purple that matched the colour of his Master's Robe.

"Are you ready?" Sir Galahaidra asked calmly.

Craedfellast nodded and both men tipped their weapons then ensured their helmets were in place.

Craedfellast wore a simple round steel pot or Spangen; Galahaidra wore the winged dragon's great helm with its wide chin guards, steel neck protector and matching gorget made by Macsen. Craedfellast had leather scale armour and bore a small round wooden buckler whilst Galahaidra carried the steel kite shield gifted to him by Macsen and a full length hauberk of intricately made chainmail, interwoven with a pattern of white gold, armour through which by its magic no arrow, sword, spear or lance tip could ever pass. Finally, the Vicing wore a padded jacket or gabbeson whilst Galahaidra wore a leather under-garment and hossen.

The battle around them came to a stand-still as the veteran warriors and the young who still sought to learn their art of warfare halted to watch the King of All Vicing take on the Christian Champion. All were agreed, the victor of this conflict would decide the battle and end all dispute between both armies. But Tortelimir signalled to Godric that when the Christians had fought the Vicing, the Germanii would also seek to end their own conflict through 'Force of Maynes', their King and Champion taking on the Christian Champion in a second contest.

"I am our Champion" said King Tortelimir proudly. "I am our herald and standard bearer" replied Prince Godric. "Should Sir Galahaidra fall then we shall nominate a new champion."

"Who is that? And who shalt choose your Champion?" Tortelimir asked curiously and then laughed as Godric admitted honestly that he did not know before pouring scorn on the Prince of the Atrebates. "We have your King Pasterix captive and have slain King Graefreigh whilst Kings Jaeric, Craemond and Harbondum all fled the battlefield. We will not fight cowards."

"Then you must fight me" Godric replied before a gentle voice piped up: "Or me" and Maria interrupted them both to remind them that she was also the bearer of arms, a Royal and a Knight of the highest Order in Christianity at that time. Longinus groaned, Craedech responded with rage, Godric did not know what to say or do. Tortelimir refused point blank to do combat with a woman and then stood in stunned silence as King Graefreigh whom all had believed slain came to her rescue, valiantly volunteering to take her place but also saying that the Princess Maria had led the Chrstian Army in the final stages of the battle and that if the girl wished to fight as the Christian champion then he for one would support her.

Craedfellast held his spear straight and nicely balanced, held in a loop of leather that was attached to his upper arm. The spear was 12 feet long, the ideal length with four feet held by the knight when counter-balanced and eight feet before the knight. Craedfellast's spear was the best of its kind ever made, carefully designed that it could be held slightly further forward and be thrust with the right arm held fully extended; for the first eight feet had been carved to be light-weight, strong and to be a few inches longer at the tip.

The spear tip would strike the knight, Galahaidra and send him backwards, but the risk that he fell was remote especially if Craedfellast struck the knight's shield. Craedfellast's best chances lay in a low blow or to take the young man in the face.

Craedfellast leant forward and his spear point was now five feet four and a quarter inches in front of his horse's head, a one foot advantage over any opponent, and angled to strike just below the heart.

From years of practise he had learnt that the best opponents would aim slightly high then drop their lance tip to aim for an easy strike on the shield or chest; or to aim for the heart and an unlikely kill (for the heart was usually protected by both shield and armour). Some knights would aim for the waist area, as this would allow maximum momentum and offered the best chance of injuring an opponent as the spear tip struck thigh or groin, both without the benefit of being protected by a knight's shield.

However because of the advantage Craedfellast held with the superior quality of his spear length, the strength of the shaft and the metal on his spear tip, the Vicing King often got a 'kill' against an opposing knight before even his opponent was able to get a strike *if he aimed for the head.*

Craedfellast looked across at the handsome, narrow and shorter frame of Sir Galahaidra then at the knight's shield and the spear that he and his men called a 'lance'. The Christian knight was holding the lance by his side in the crook of his arm: it was much heavier and of shorter length than that of the Vicing King. Craedfellast was briefly confused by the Christian's lance: it looked too cumbersome to be the chosen weapon of a Champion.

The heralds let loose both horses and the riders launched into a gallop, gathering speed as they charged towards each other, their horses' heads lowered, snorting in anger as they came together. Craedfellast's horse reared and then he charged.

Galahaidra waited, judging speed, the angle of his opponent's spear point and the direction taken by his horse then with the flick of his heel he built up his own speed, changed the angle of his attack and swung his lance to lie in the bouse of his shield, the leather enarmes allowing Galahaidra to carry the much heavier lance and to manoeuvre it easily with the slightest movement of his hand.

Galahaidra's opponent moved to hold his spear high above his head in his right hand with his shield covering his left flank as was the custom at that time, only to change his intended target at the last moment: his indecision would prove fatal. Sir Galahaidra suddenly leant forward and twisted in his saddle: his lance was a full six feet in front of his horse's head as he struck, being held at the very tip and cradled under his arm to give far greater momentum.

Such was the horses' ferocity that as they clashed their horses' knees buckled and the horses fell, collapsing on each other, the lance and spear snapped under the force of their charge, splinters flying to take the King in the eye and the knight in the thigh. The Holy Lance was blessed never to miss and Galahaidra's firmer hold had spelt the demise of the Vicing King as his spear point took Craidfellast in his mouth and penetrated deep to sever his spine at the base of his neck.

Craedfellast fell slowly to the ground, clutching desperately at the ruin of his eye, a single groan as he attempted to crawl from beneath his fallen mount and then he expired whilst Galahaidra grasped his bleeding limb barely avoiding being crushed as his horse tossed and turned above him; he was saved only by the boiled leather of his saddle.

Maria ran to hold the injured knight in desperation dragging him clear of the panicked thrashing of his steed. With care she pulled the shard of the Vicing's spear tip from the injured leg then held the young man firmly in her arms to save him from fainting. As the young knight began to recover his strength she kissed him out of relief.

"You cannot fight injured like this" the girl whispered and Galahaidra replied in his turn: "But what choice do I have? Your father is too old for a challenge such as this despite his courage."

"He is not the only *Bann Caedric* here" and Galahaidra briefly paused in confusion then suddenly realised what was the princess' intent.

"Tortelimir will refuse" he said firmly.

"Not if I am wearing *your* armour. Now strip!" And the poor young man blushed.

Maria was almost six inches shorter than Galahaidra and considerably more slender and yet somehow she passed off her disguise. Tortelimir had seen the young Christian's skill with the lance and selected to fight using swords much to Maria's relief who was convinced that the weight of the Holy Lance would have seen her fall flat on her nose.

She asked Godric for a sword and her father smiled: "I have a present for you" and he handed her a white leather scabbard embossed with silver, gold and sapphires and a blade almost as tall as the girl. "Only you or your descendants may wield this and when you die it shall be for you to give to those who come after you. Use it wisely, for it shall win for you every battle yet bring peace to any land. It is my gift and that of Macsen. I give to you the sword *Excalibur* meaning the gift of Prince Bann Caedic its true name being '*Caelicbann*.'"

"Bless you father" then ensuring her helmet covered her face lest she start crying in joy at her father's gift but also to hide her distinctive hair and elfin features from her opponent, she unsheathed the sword and it swept gracefully through the air, its many sapphires shone like the sky, its blade the brightest steel, a flowing swirl of many metals. Written upon the blade in the language of the ancient Britons made legible through her gift of tongues was the simplest yet most powerful of messages:

She who bears this sword shalt rule all of Britannia. She shall see peace in her lands and win every battle in which she shalt be a part.

Despite Galahaidra's armour being some of the finest and the lightest ever to be made by Macsen, Maria still needed to be hoisted onto Epona, much to her intense embarassment, but after a few minutes Craedech and Godric had managed to mount her on the huge stallion and she signalled to her opponent that she was ready.

Tortelimir nodded to the heralds and they signalled for both opponents to charge. The King of the Germanii reared and then charged at great speed, Maria waiting, watching then whispering in prayer: "Lord, I pray that I shall save the lives of those I lead through my actions this day. Slay me if that is your wish but whatever shalt be the outcome grant this land peace at last."

As she said the final word, she turned to face the young Germanic champion only to see he was already upon her. Tortelimir swung and his mighty blade struck Maria a resounding blow sending her flying backwards almost to fall from the cropper of her horse.

"*Use* your sword, idiot!" Godric screamed and Maria muttered "Ooops" then gingerly tried to raise her shield arm and found it was smashed to pieces, her ulma and wrist broken by the Germanii's mighty strike. Tortelimir circled and swung at her unprotected back at which Epona, fed up and rightly embarrassed at his mistress' lack of warcraft, snorted, bucked and knocked the King of the Germanii off his horse and straight to the ground. "Thanks" Maria whispered and Epona neighed; Maria got the distinct impression her horse was telling her '*That is how you are meant to do it.*'

'*Now what*?' Maria wondered with Tortelimir at her feet and staying on her left side, avoiding any blows she might try and land with her sword. She was totally baffled by Galahaidra's enarmes which needed two hands to use and she rapidly got tangled up. '*O rats. Only one thing to do*' she thought and she threw her shield at the King so surprising him that he fell to the ground under its weight.

This gave the girl the opportunity to stumble to the ground and face Tortelimir. He swung his sword at her head: a mighty blow that had it landed would have beheaded her but she caught it with Excalibur and the next moment Tortelimir was looking at half a blade, Maria's sword shaving through her opponent's sword as if cutting through butter. Maria went to apologise and lowered her own sword as she did so.

The Germanii took advantage of her hesitation and as she was offering to buy him a new sword, he stabbed at the girl and she was too slow to stop his strike; the jagged edge of the half blade took the girl painfully in the thigh. Instinctively she reacted to the blow and the pain by swinging her sword in a mighty but rather ugly looking swipe that severed Tortelimir's sword arm clean off at the shoulder.

The maimed King groaned, dropped his sword and held the wound in desperation with his shield arm. He fell at Maria's feet dying from blood loss and the shock as his artery had been severed, defenceless and at her mercy without sword or shield. The Christian's cheered and the Germanii sighed at the loss of a much-loved King but Maria could not permit the young man's death and, just before she fainted from her own wound, her final act was to pray that Tortelimir be healed.

Maria woke to find herself held in her father's arms, her thigh wound had been strapped up and her arm was in a sling. "I am so sorry I lost father" she muttered ashamed that she had been beaten in both the contest and the battle. But Godric smiled down on her then said: "We will get you a tutor. You need lessons especially now you have such a mighty sword. But the Germanii will not stop talking about you!"

"Why?" Maria asked totally befuddled and unable to think of a single reason why they would be so interested in her. Then Tortelimir was standing over her and smiling with great delight.

"Don't keep her in suspense" Craedech muttered and Godric came clean:

Tortelimir has conceded the contest. He knows that you beat him and he is an honourable man. You won. The victory is yours and we are all so proud of you. The Germanii cannot believe that you would save their King; that is why they cannot stop singing your praises. Tortelimir is a hero amongst the Germanii and had you slain him the Germanii would have been our enemies for life. As it is you have won their King's heart, you are loved by his people and by the King of All Vicings also. For the first time in centuries we have the opportunity for peace with the barbarian peoples."

"I wish for our people to be as one" the young King of the Germanii stuttered in his hesitant Gaelic but Maria understood and her heart rang with praises. She raised her arm to hold his in gratitude and kissed his hand then she sang and all heard the joyful melody of birdsong.

"And which of us do you plan to marry?" Craedech asked trying to be calm, to avoid any sign of jealousy yet his own heart was beating so fast and secretly he was extremely worried that he might have lost the girl he had come to love before all other things. Maria's reply disarmed him and he stood quietly amazed until Godric struck him on the back as he welcomed him as his future son-in-law.

"You are silly. I love you, I will marry you and moreover I will be faithful to you and you only. And that is a promise!"

The battle thus was ended. The survivors began the soul-destroying task of finding those whose anima was now absented, bringing to the surface those buried beneath the cold killing clasp of the snow and the corpses of their colleagues, rescuing the wounded from their bitter burial in the white deathly blankets of ice.

Once more Maria broke down in tears at the dire destruction done by man on man. In the end, the Christian Army had lost two hundred and forty two slain, many of whom (and this came close to breaking the poor girl's heart) could have been saved but had been lost in the ice and were dug out of the snow when too late to resuscitate them. Nine thousand and forty two were found wounded most living with their wounds due to the cold of the ice and bringing even more distress to Maria for so many were young girls of her own age conscripted to fight due to their love and affinity for equines but with wounds that would disfigure their once fair looks, scars that might make a man look noble or courageous but on a lady would see them be treated as a pariah; stomach injuries which on a man might see them remain slim in later life but would devastate a teenager looking for her first child.

"Please God" Maria would beg again and again "better you had harmed me than leave these poor children bereft of future love by man and your greatest gift of motherhood. Grant I surrender my own looks to give these girls a future of their own" but God had an important lesson to teach the Christians. Alas it was a lesson that only those already convinced would appreciate and one that Maria felt more deeply than any other.

The physical and mental sacrifices she had made were rendered futile and she herself learnt that to prevent war was 'absolute'; no plan that included any element of conflict however cleverly mitigated could ever be acceptable to her God. She was in danger of reacting by making even more extravagant sacrifices to save the lives and souls of others yet must learn the lesson that God had no tolerance for those that shalt kill.

Maria knew she had one more battle she must guide towards a peaceful end but then, with this day's tasks accomplished she would meet her Master and learn what was the lesson from the day's bloodshed: for all that she saw was bleak and without anything but the most calamitous of conclusions.

Once more she rode on Epona in white leather, white gold, blazing white and silver; she rode as the wind, a snow cloud come to Earth, her lance carried the banneret of white and silver, her sword in its bejewelled scabbard gleaming brightest steel with the large sapphire on its pommel sending a streak of blue lightning into the cold white sky, her hatchment was white with a silver cross and at her shoulder the gold Chi and Rho of her Order, her kite-shaped shield was also white with a silver cross and hanging across her back on etarmes to leave room for her sling, her hauberk hung from the gorget at her neck and either side of her saddle to protect legs, stirrups and feet.

At her side were Thea and her wild boar harnessed in white and silver, and all haste did she make to reach the Citadel of Mullochy and come to the rescue of her comrades who fought the Daenii.

Half past the twelf hour she had crossed the Muir of Mun and was riding like a flash of lightning towards Mullochy. She had headed out towards Arioch so that she could then approach from the East surprising her companions in arms as she did so. Now she picked up speed for it was rapidly approaching the hour when the Daenii were to launch their attack on the Caledonii. She had promised to be there: to be at Graemwolda's and Graemir's and Garrold's sides when they went into battle and she kept her promises however extravagant they might be and whatever the sacrifices she might make to do so.

The Daenii had already formed into fifteen wedges, a mass of black steel, silver helms and huge double-handed axes, each wedge the size of a company, some three hundred men strong: their total strength in excess of four thousand five hundred, standing before the West Gate. They were giants compared to the Christians, six and a half to seven feet tall, blonde long hair, blue eyes, spectral features, ghosts come to Earth. When Maria first saw them she gasped at their beauty but then they did the same when seeing her.

In response, King Graemwolda had advanced with ten thousand Vicings; two thousand Caledonians were to his left under their two young Kings Graemir and Garrord whilst King Pedrus had advanced to surround the Daenii with twelve thousand Picts. The Daenii had walked into a trap but they were not dismayed.

Graemwolda was the first to see the Princess; a streak of white light that he did not at first recognise but then Decius pointed her out muttering "Now that has to be her most impressive entrance yet!" and Graemwolda just stood with his jaw dropping as she jumped to the ground to land besides them both then grinning whispered: "Am I late?"

Graemwolda took a few moments to admire her glowing beauty then pointed towards where the Daenii had formed up. "I would say you were just in time!"

Noticing the sad look in her eyes he asked: "Was it awful?" She nodded. "Your brother is dead. I could not save him" and she gave him a hug but he just shrugged then said "No loss. I got you instead!"

"Graemwolda that is an outrageous thing to say about your brother!" and she got an uncontrollable fit of the giggles.

By midday both armies had formed in preparation to meet each other: the Daenii had taken advantage of the rough ground, streams, rivers, rolling hills and winter's natural thaw. Decius had commenced his rally and conversion of the Pagans early that morning and soon had gathered some seven thousand to his might. The Decurion now stood with an uninterrupted view upon the high point east of the Gate where Graemwolda sat astride his great warhorse with Maria on Epona at his side; three thousand of the mightiest of the Vicing people, his personal champions and bodyguard were gathered to guard their newly elected Queen.

The crossing of the River Beauly was narrow at this point in its winding path and ran at the foot of the hill-top on which the Decurion's legions had formed, its silver snaking line lying across his route as he faced from East to West. At last, King Graemwolda gave his order to charge at the Daenii and the battle commenced.

Midwinters' cold sun opened to shine as a bright golden glaze on the crust of silver dazzling snow, the winter's thaw forming wide rivers that encircled hills, surrounded mounts and created natural grottoes and tall defensive rock formations. The battle when fought was one ideally suited for infantry; the Pictish cavalry were slowed down fording through rivers and shallow waters, crossing hills, mounts and scrambling up rocky shelfs then down into narrow vales and gorges.

The two armies fought for possession of every dale, dell, valley and vale, from hill-top to hill-top, each steppe had become a natural fortress, cavalry dismounting to stand alongside their infantry. There were no trees, no grass, just barren land and the constant assailment and obstacle of stones, rocks and gravel, or smooth fast running waters. It was a battle initially suited for the tight formation of the Daenii but as the conflict wore on, numbers began to tell, the Vicing and Picts surrounding the Daenish wedges, assaulting them one at a time; cutting them down by attacking each flank and the exposed rear face of every wedge.

As the third hour after noon drew to a close King Hartdenicum stood with the last few hundreds of his Daenii surrounded by Graemwold's Vicing. Many of his warriors had fallen to the power of Maria's Grael and the invincibility of her sword, as she had led her praetorian of three thousand Vicing champions to assail the Daenii wherever they looked as if they had made a breakthrough, time and again crossing the battlefield to launch into the rear or flanks of the enemy's wedges. Some Daenii had tried to escape and become victims of the Picts few cavalry that had remained mounted.

The Daenii had been heavily outnumbered yet their tactics and their warcraft had been superior. But for every warrior they lost the Christians could replace that man with five. And the Christians were soldiers whose morale was at its highest following two victories and with the blazing white glory of Maria, riding on Epona, the wolf Thea at her side and leading them without fear.

Wherever Hartdenicum was able to push the Christians into retreat, Maria would ride to that spot and hold it, her sword Excalibur blazing, her wolf and wild boar driving back all opposition, her Vicing warriors become brave once more and standing proudly to fight for her. Time and again she pushed his own warriors back … yet only a few were harmed and none slain so that soon the Daenish King finally began to believe in her 'magic'.

Then as the third hour passed, she stood suddenly before him, his personal bodyguard had been cast down and he glared at her defiant yet alone to face the new Queen of the Vicing. He was dazzled by Maria as she shone in white and silver, tongues of flame on her forehead and shining in the pupil of her eyes.

She held out her one good hand and he could not resist it but rather he handed up his battle axe to her and then knelt before her white stallion. He expected death, to be beheaded by his own axe and so was surprised when instead she descended from her stallion and bent her head forwards (she did not have to bend very far) to kiss him on the cheek then whisper: "Will you join me in peace, my brother King?"

He stared at her and her eyes shone, sparkling blue, and what he saw was Truth, someone he could trust, innocence and purity. "Does your God truly exist?" he asked and Maria took him by the hand.

They stood by the wildest sea, mountainous waves before them crashing against the tallest of cliffs, above them a grey and thunderous sky. Lightning struck, its forks carving through the heavens. Then suddenly, Maria had gone down on her knees, her head bowed low in obeisance as a gentle, meek and simple man, humbly dressed, walked through the rain and not a drop touched him.

"I am God" said the Nazarene and Hartdenicum believed him in an instant without need of further proof "Should I bow before you?" the King asked seeing how Maria had gone down on her knees in absolute humility. God shook his head: "Maria worships me in a very special way. Indeed her worship of me is more than I deserve but I welcome her adoration and as many of your Kings have found: to be loved by Maria is a great compliment and not to be turned down lightly."

"Maria. What should I do with her?"

"She is now your captive if that is your wish. Yet so much more good will comes to you if you let her live. Alive she will bring you and your people great glory. Dead and you will receive the enmity of the whole world. Even the Romans love her!"

"How should I worship you?" the King asked abashed.

"Let Maria show you. She has shown many how to come to me and to worship me. So many that I am constantly praising her and rejoicing in my choice of her. She is the *Apostle to the Apostles*: she brought the Good News to the first leaders of my Church. She it was who converted them.

Yet she is so humble she does not realise how extensive has been her influence on the growth of my Church. In future years, people will talk of the Ministries of Petrus and of Paulus but it was Maria who launched belief in the Nazarene on an unsuspecting and ill-prepared world."

When he returned from God's presence he had so many questions still unanswered. Maria took his hand once more and said simply: "There is plenty of time. He will remember your questions even if you forget them. But now we have a more important task."

"How can anything be more important than to meet God?"

"Hartdenicum, King, to meet God is important and we do this through prayer and the Eucharist. But it is also important that we leave time for the sick, the lame, the injured, those who are oppressed, prisoners and slaves, the blind, deaf and dumb. Come, for we have many of your men we must heal and in so doing we shalt be doing God's work and undoing the harm of the battle we have just fought."

Once more she showed the miracle of the Grael, shining its golden beams to locate those poor injured souls lost in the depths of the snow and bringing them to healing. Hartdenicum was amazed, first at the many Christians who had the ability to heal by the laying on of hands but most of all by Maria's great mastery and the way in which the many disciples looked up to her.

Then Graemwolda and Graemir came into her presence and he could see they both had come under the charm of this slip of a girl. Graemwolda was a changed man for he had lost all sense of his cruelty when with her. He would make a better King of the Vicing for he was now passionate about the beauty of the kingdom and the people for which he fought. '*But how had she performed this miracle?*' the King of the Daenii pondered. In the end he asked Graemwolda then threatened to tickle Maria with a feather when he could not get a sensible answer from the Vicing.

Maria laughed then surrendered at the first touch of the feather, her feet still sensitive from being burnt: "I surrender, I surrender, help, save me" she cried laughing and caved in immediately then told him what he wanted to know: "I saved his life despite his torture of me; I defeated his armies and Navy. What he saw was my strength and dedication to my purpose. I am very stubborn! The King wants to rule all of the barbarian kingdoms and he sees me as a totem for when he does so: someone whom people can worship whilst he gets on with the real job of sovereignty."

"And you?"

"I will hate it. I would much rather be in Love with Craedech and find a farm somewhere we could settle down on and spend all our time tending vines and looking after our herds. We once came across a farm on the borders of Gallia and Hispania, the farmer was Tartuff, his two boys were my age and fell for me immediately, the wife managed the farm and it was peaceful and immaculate. I would have loved to live there.

Then there were the magnificent fields between Vedselae and Avallonae going down to Font Aeneas. I would make a paradise of those trees and woods and dig caves beneath the mountains for storing our crops, cheeses and feed for our animals. That land was ripe for farming once and I shall make it so again. Let God release me to do this and I would be content … but he has already said he has other missions for me so I must wait."

The Gospel of Mary

By the sixth day after the battles of Cromarty, Beauly and Mullochy, the Kings and Princes of Caledonia, Britannia and Hibernia were still celebrating with their captains and knights the magnificent victory which the Christian Army had obtained whilst Maria and Craedech worked long hours to heal the injured and repair the damage done to fields and farms, to help the animals injured in the conflicts to put right all that had been wronged, including restoring roofs and broken walls and buildings. The royals who had come with them would stay up often long into the dark of the night celebrating and getting drunk whilst Maria and Craedech would stagger to sleep or just as often obtain no sleep for there was so much work to be done.

In the end Craedech could not contain his anger any longer but went to Godric and asked: "Is this any way to treat your daughter who has survived terrible tortures and still carries the scars of those. She has won great victories and yet she is treated like a slave whilst you sit here and feed yourself with no thought for her?"

But Godric replied reasonably enough: "Maria enjoys it. Go and ask her"

So Craedech did go and spoke to her and her reply astonished him after which he decided to leave her to work on her own. Maria held him tight because she could see he was upset and tried to kiss all of his worries away then said to him:

"My love, I am so sorry to hear that I have made you work so hard. Rest and leave this work to me to do. I do it because I serve my Master and I love anything that serves my Master. Leave me and I shalt do the work of two of us and be glad."

Three days later she collapsed from exhaustion and was so ill that she could not be woken. "What shall we do?" her father and her future husband asked, for no doctor could find a cure for her; her heart was slowing down and her mind was gradually falling into the deepest sleep.

"We shall lose her" said all the Kings and then they were angry with themselves for there were many on whom they could have called to come to her aid and yet they had left her to work herself to death. Finally, they decided they could do nothing: *'Either she is speaking with her Master or she is now damned to die. We cannot save her.'*

So they placed her carefully in a glass sepulchre, her body to be guarded at all times and watched as the warriors of the many armies that had fought for her and been rescued by her, the sea dragons, the navies on which she had come to rely, even Thea and her cubs and the four wild boars all came to visit her and hoped for some final act of healing.

However, she was not dying but had gone in prayer to meet her Master, her grief as she buried one more of the dead had become such that, overpowered with the slaughter that she had looked upon and been part of, she had finally asked 'Why?' but not in condemnation but rather asking *'Why had she succumbed to the sin of killing whom knew that 'thou shalt not kill?''*

She looked around the chamber that was to be her lesson for this day and was confused. It was blank save for a single placard that said 'When shalt thou kill?' Her Master was standing ready to test her dressed in the long flowing robes of a Rabbi.

"Are you trying to make me angry, Lord?" she asked in innocence and her Master stopped then replied: "How often have I said 'Thou shalt not kill' yet still you seek a way around my requirement so that you can keep on killing. YOU have angered your God."

Maria could feel the weight of God's anger and condemnation mounting yet she had faced God's greatest torment and still she lived. And so she challenged him despite his growing anger and rage:

"Punish me as you did once before. But remember how you once told me that the greatest of all evils is the sin of wrath. *'The fourth power of Lucifer that comes in seven forms: the power of wrath.'* May I be the focus of your wrath; but to slay all those people and to do that to teach me a lesson. I would rather I had died than that anyone be harmed.

Master, I love you. But I am near death from burying those slain in battle yet I slew no-one. Indeed, I went to extraordinary lengths to save lives. Why, my lord, do you condemn me?"

Her Master stood before her and they looked out upon the very centre of their Galaxy. Then he spoke softly with understanding and as he did so, Maria wept as she remembered all that her Master had done for her yet was puzzled as to why she should be looking out upon the Hub of the Milky Way. It was one of her desires that she study the stars yet to her dismay they still remained a remote mystery.

"Would you really subject yourself and your soul to an eternity of torment for the sake of those slain?" her Master asked. Maria did not wait but replied immediately from her heart.

"O yes, Lord, without blinking" Maria spoke clearly and without hesitation, looking up from her tears so that God could see the truth in her eyes. She was therefore completely thrown by the Master's adroit change in subject. Mind you she was easily thrown by anything she reflected humbly!

"You were the first person to see me alive after my execution. I have always loved you more than any other of my apostles and that is why I chose you to be my Messenger to the world. Later that same day, I visited you at your home besides the Sea of Galilee. Can you remember of what it was that we spoke?"

"Master, I can remember the words but alas I have never understood them. I have always hoped that one day you would find that I was ready to have your words explained to me."

"Let me take you back to that day when I gave you your most important lesson" and they were sitting together on the balcony of Magdalo Castle, overlooking the Sea of Galilee, the Sinai Mountains reflected in its still black waters, with the fury of distant winds sweeping up the sand, turning the dark blue heavens into mauves, purples and reds, the sun's light refracted by the fine dust as it span and swirled across the sky.

Then Maria saw the marks of the cross freshly made on Iesus: the drying blood on wrists, ankles and the mark of the spear in her Master's side. She fell before him, weeping, seeking forgiveness that she had forgotten the sacrifice God had already made and continued to make for her. She had been so petty and he had shown such patience with her.

She smelt the scent of the rose petals still clinging to his robes, the aroma of the oils of frankincense and myrrh still lingering in his hair; all as it had been almost one year before. Except now began the first part of her lesson as he reached within his robe to give Maria the gold coins that had rested on his mouth and eyes in the tomb. "And so the future changes the past" he whispered then started to guide her through the vision he had shared with her that windswept evening when he had just been reborn.

"We spoke of matter, nature, power, sin and of the soul" and then the Master laughed as he caught Maria's stray thought: *'I remember last time was a long discussion, I hope it is shorter this time'.* Maria blushed then apologised but her Master would have none of it: "You remembered the bits that mattered. My teachings are like the rings of Saturn: more colourful and more intricate the closer you get to the Truth at the centre … and your next thought is best kept to yourself!" at which Maria had to chuckle then set herself for a long evening. She did not mind when all was said and done as she was in the company of her most favourite person in the Universe.

"Sin is not something that exists separately from us. We create sin through our thoughts and our actions. There is no 'original sin'. Thus there is no 'excuse' for sin. No Adam nor Eve to blame"

"Master, am I allowed to ask you questions?" Maria interrupted her Master at which he smiled then retorted: "I have yet to discover a way to stop you doing so" and Maria went to stick her tongue out then stopped just in time, thinking *'I wonder which commandment I am breaking if I stick my tongue out at God?'* then she heard her Master's voice echoing in her mind and smothered another laugh as he said: *'All Ten! And the whole idea of my commandments was that you **keep** them all not that you try to break them all.'*

"Ask" her Master said resignedly knowing when to argue was futile.

"Petrus, Tomaeus, Marcus, Mateus, Lucius and Andreius are big supporters of 'original sin'. I think Paulus is too. Levi and Iohannus are more open to new ideas as is Lazarus. But where does the idea of 'original sin' come from?"

"There are those who believe that there must be some rite of passage or entry to become a Christian and refer to my own baptism by my cousin Iohannus who was an Essene as the basis for this. But I tasked you all to go out to the world and preach the *Gospel of the Kingdom* and I gave you a new covenant: that I would be with you in the breaking of the bread. I also warned you to beware of the rule makers and those who added requirements to the *Gospel of the Kingdom.* I will come to you if you break bread. There is no further requirement for me to comfort or consort with you."

Maria nodded to show she understood. In her case this was an approximate thing. She trusted her Master sufficiently to believe that she would understand her Master's words *at some point in the future* and not necessarily all of his words but enough to not sound too stupid if her Master asked her a question.

"So what is a sin?" the Master asked at which Maria muttered "Being able to read the chaos in my mind is so unfair and a sin is what I am thinking right now!"

"Your soul is the key thing I wish to discuss next. It is my main residence in you. But where we meet is not your soul. You will recall that you have only been as far as the ante chamber to your soul. The visions that we share are found **everywhere** inside you, not just the heart, mind or soul.

Alas, not all of my apostles are ready to open themselves to my visions or my presence inside them through the breaking of the bread. You have already been condemned by some of your fellow Apostles for your conversations with me" and Maria remembered the meeting in Lazarus' house when Petrus had bullied her and made her cry accusing her of making her visions up. Andreius had called her 'strange'. *'Well he might be right'* she admitted and grinned. As she remembered the hurt of that meeting she suddenly felt the warmth of The Comforter and she reached across to hug her Master's arm, mouthing a simple 'Thank you'.

"The soul is your defender against the power of *wrath*. As you rightly reminded me that power comes in seven forms: darkness, desire, ignorance, fear of death, lust, pornography and violence. You damage your soul whenever you pursue any of the seven forms" and her Master stopped as he could see the next question bubbling away in the chaos of her mind.

"Forgive me, Lord, but am I not made 'ignorant'? I try my best but I am honest and in all truth I do not know much if anything really. And I have desires. Well there is nothing I want that I cannot do without. Is that what you mean by 'desire'? I am afraid of the dark and still wake up and hide under my blanket at night. I fear death as well but I am ready to die if it matters just I will be very noisy: screams and all that. And what are 'lust' and 'pornography'? I think I might have failed on 6 out of 7?"

"You do not choose to ignore what is all around you. You are far from being ignorant. Rather, you know what matters. Yes, you have understood what is meant by desires and you may fear death yet you died to save the Pagans and have faced death from King Col, the Siteranae, the Vicing and the Gael" and the Master ignored Maria's mouthed 'O Yes' as he got to the difficult bit: "Come back when you are eighty and I will tell you about lust and pornography" then reading her mind he added "And you are not to ask Godric what they mean … or Craedech … or Graemwolda … or ANYONE ELSE!"

He then studiously ignored her pout and continued with the lesson: "The key reason we have a soul has been misunderstood. The soul is believed by some based on teachings from Roma such as by Livy or Lucretius to be the part of a man or woman that goes to Paradise: that is not truth. Our *spirit* goes to Paradise and is our form in our life after death.

Our soul has a very different purpose and is the reason why it is vital all mankind learn that thou shalt not kill. It is part of God's purpose that man travels the Universe and to do so man must learn how to travel through both space and time. The soul is every man's vehicle to do so.

But to inflict the evil of men that kill on the rest of the Universe would be a great sin. Until man has learnt to control the power of wrath and to overcome the desire to kill then the soul remains inactive" hence the importance of the lesson Maria had to learn: there can be no tolerance when it comes to the commandment thou shalt not kill. No executions, no war, no assassinations.

"Now I understand but I have a question." Maria continued her interruptions.

"How did I guess" God muttered almost sotte voce. Maria chose to ignore her Master whom she was certain was just teasing her and bashed on with her question anyway:

"You have successfully taught us all not to kill and so I was wondering: Could you take my life and then let all the others who were slain come back to life? Everyone would learn a lesson in compassion and mercy which is the opposite of wrath. So that would be a good thing wouldn't it?" and she grinned at him, the dimples in both her cheeks aflame as the Master just looked up to … then realised that he couldn't look *up* to heaven and rested his head disconsolately in his hands. Maria poked him in the arm then mouthed 'Next' whilst God thought back and could not recall any of Noah, Abraham, Moses, David or Solomon ever poking him in the arm.

"So to recap: the spirit is that part of us that goes to Paradise; the soul is God's residence in us and is filled with the Son of Man through the breaking of bread; the mind is where we find Faith; the heart is where we find Love, Compassion, Charity and Hope; and God's vision is found everywhere inside us activating the senses, the mind, heart, spirit and soul.

And that then brings us to: matter, energy, nature, form, being and forces.

Matter and energy are the foundation or building block for all things that are created and seen but also for the Forces that govern the symphony or composition to which the Universe responds from light and heat to the stars and the planets. Matter can create Forms, Forces and Powers, both Good and Evil but beware the Dark Force as it has no equivalent and can destroy any natural form. Matter comprises small particles, so small they remain invisible to the naked eye, which come together using the four natural Forces.

Nature is the way in which Matter has come together without the adverse influence of powers or the adverse actions of beings and creatures. It is the backdrop to mankind's creativity and what it is that man must steward and protect.

Form is the way in which Matter presents in Nature. An animal will have its Natural Form. This will develop or evolve over time. If corrupted or distorted by the use of Powers, all things will eventually return to their Natural Form given time.

The Powers of evil will alter, distort or corrupt the evolution of Natural Form but Powers also include equalising Forces such as dark energy and the opposite of gravity: remember that there are Forces for good and evil. But eventually all things will return to Natural or Original Form. Powers and the corruption or distortion of form can lead to disease such as cancer or to unnatural evolution, to stars, asteroids and other celestial bodies straying from their course, to ecological and environmental disasters.

Finally, there are those who fear Nature, in particular that Nature is outside man's control with storms, floods, volcanoes, tsunami, earthquakes, or wild animals. Man is encouraged by me to become accustomed to many different environments and different forms of creature: to become tolerant also of the great variety in human form.

Is that clearer?" her Master then asked Maria and she put her head on one side for a minute, the silence was deafening, before finally she asked: "Is that another question?"

"Test next week. I expect you to revise. Now go" said an exasperated Divinity and shooed her away with his hands.

"What about all those poor men and women I just buried?"

"Will you leave me alone if I say 'Yes I will save them'"

"But of course" Maria replied and her grin was positively gleaming before she added with dimples in both cheeks: "See you tomorrow then!"

Princes Craedech and Godric, Kings Graemir, Graefreigh, Jaeric, Pasterix, Corvinium, Graemwolda, Tortelimir and Hartdenicum raced towards the stone chapel that the armies of hundreds of thousands had built at the mouth of the Beauly on the cliffs above Cromarty Sands. Saint Ninian had designed and supervised the build then announced her intention to make an honest man of Sir Galahaidra, which caused more than a few tears amongst the young ladies in Caledonia and the Amazons amongst the Iceni. The Christian leader, Petrus, had made Ninian's canonisation official and posted to her an epistle which arrived at the same time as his epistle to Lazarus' confirming his appointment to the See of Marseilles as the City's first Bishop. King Pederaster and Queen Falidir and their hundreds of children had spent every day for a week swimming in the Firth hoping for news, singing every night, but now were leaping from the sea in their joy.

The nine Kings, one Queen and two Princes had heard the news that the Princess Maria had woken.

Around Ninian's Chapel was its small grave yard holding the graves of just under three hundred Christians slain at Cromarty Sands, nine thousand wounded had been healed carefully of their wounds and no-one had begrudged Maria if she had taken especial care of those her age, the best looking, those whose visage had been graced by God and would be again.

The nine days she had worked until falling had seen limbs returned and repaired, faces made good, scars turned graceful and thousands had remembered this young little humble girl who had worked ceaselessly to heal every warrior. Collectively they had made her their Queen even before the seven Kings had declared their hand. Every one of the nine thousand was standing around the chapel in prayer.

Suddenly Maria had stood outside the chapel, a little shakily, or that was until her father and lover had grabbed her and held her upright. They went to drag her away but she shook her head, invited all gathered to kneel, then said: "My Lord and my God who has released me into the kind guardianship of these good people. Never again shall we subject our people to the horrors of war."

As she spoke, the first of the graves was opened by God.

The Daenii and the Norse had a terrible tradition of Undead rising from the ground (meanwhile Godric had rather irreverently said: 'Sack the undertakers') but Maria was delighted and ran to where coffin lids were being heaved open from inside. The poor Vicing were terrified but also felt shamed by their young princess cum Queen who ran *towards* the Undead. She had tamed the wild wolf and the wild boar, was best friends with the King and Queen of All Sea Dragons had defeated the King of the Germanii in a joust then saved the lives of the Kings of the Vicing, Germanii and Angles and now she showed no fear in the presence of the Undead!

The Parting of Friends

During the ensuing hours of that morning, all gathered at the Great Hall built by the Christians as part of their temporary Citadel at Mullochy. This was a twenty pace tall part timber frame part stone building with narrow slits as windows facing away from the wind and protected by tapestries. The Hall had a buttery, Cellarers Hall and frigidarium backing onto huge kitchens whilst inside were many round oak tables, with windows set high in the rafters. Six large roasting spits sat in the centre of huge stone fire places and brick chimney breasts.

All wanted to hear from the princess first and then were amazed from her account at how defiant she was when speaking to God. Seeing Maria then meekly obeying her father's every request, Prince Godric's esteem rose dramatically.

"My Master wished to remind me of a time when we had met the day he was reborn. He had told me about how the Universe is constructed, about souls and sin. I am afraid I irritated him so much he threw me out but I would not leave until he had saved the lives of all those who died in Battle at Cromarty and Baltain. So here I am. I said I would go back and so I am hopeful that at the Celebration of the Eucharist tomorrow I shall give a good sermon and invite you all to come. It will be God's message said humbly through me."

They bombarded her with questions but she was cautious, explaining her uncustomary reticence:

"God's message is important and I want to do it justice. I will dwell on it and may go back to make sure I get it right. But key is that we must praise and thank God. For today He taught us that peace is a powerful weapon and He showed his great power by returning hundreds of souls back to life."

Then she retired to within the Great Hall and the Kings opened the doors for other nobles to join them. Hundreds were seeking to join the *Order of the Risen Christ* and Godric had sent for the Round Table from Wyncaister. Some of the monarchs had brought their spouses and Graemir and Garrord had their wives and daughters with them; they had asked to meet Maria and had almost forgiven their husbands for their earlier abandonment of her. Yet now their own standing was so high amongst their peers that they could not really complain. They had adopted Maria on sight with Garrord's young wife Ysolte only being three years older but much more knowledgeable and worldly-wise. Graemir's wife Elaena took both of them in hand, whilst both of her daughters were much sought after to Elaena's delight, especially amongst the young Germanic Kings.

King Caedfarn had joined them from Inver, awestruck that their huge army had suffered such a devastating defeat, overcome at the loss of their entire Navy, even more bemused when news came that there were no dead and all wounded were already healed. The exception was Craedfellast for, as Maria's Master had explained several times to her until she finally pretended she understood, the Vicing had already booked his place in a much hotter regime than the snows and ice he had become accustomed to; somewhere that the Nazarene might hold the keys to but had little influence over who might be allowed *out.*

Maria, conscious that she had promised not to bother God, said a quick prayer, asking if it would make any difference if *She* went to Hell to fetch Craedfellast. That merited a visit from an Angel who said a single word: 'No' and left. When she told her father, first he went berserk on hearing she had planned to go to Hell then he laughed at the Angel's reaction saying: *'Perhaps I should do that?'*

Tortelimir had brought a couple of his friends, tribal Kings amongst the Suevii, Chaenii, Darii and Canovanii and all young men who were instantly smitten by Maria. When they heard that she had offered to go to Hell to rescue the King of the Vicing they were left in awe. They had been at the battlefield when Maria had defeated Tortelimir then saved his life; they had seen the sea dragons in the Firth and watched her acts of healing together with the Resurrection of so many dead and her utter fearlessness in the face of the Undead. As a consequence, after the *Grael Tests* that night which were eagerly awaited and would see three hundred make their trial, the big agenda item of the day was to arrange for Maria to tour Hibernia, west Caledonia, Scandinavia, the Green Land and Ice

Land, Heligos Bight, the Rheinlands, Alemmania, Burgundia, Francia, Helvetica, Geneva and Northern Italia.

Then one bright eyed young ballad from Hibernia asked Maria:

"Have you spoken to your Dragons about the places they have seen across the seas? There are lands to the far west that they may know and be able to guide you to. Lands of wild barbarians yet people rich in myth and legend, cultured and magical. They will like you princess because you speak Truth and legend says they are truth-speakers."

Then came the sad news that at last Maria's fellowship must come to an end; the task of conversion of Caledonia had passed to others and Maria herself must now consider her own future ... at least until she should be given her next mission.

Longinus went first. "I must still find my niece and then shall return to Iudaea going through Lugdebellum then Marsela from which I shall sail to Antioch and then on to Ierusalem. Martius has a longer route down the North Sea, Mare Britannia and Atlantis Oceanis then through Scilla and Charybdis, the Ballearic and Middle Seas but we both hope to rejoin our regiments sometime soon. I will take Amarillus' two half legions with me and earn myself many a meal for the tales I shall tell."

"I will come with you" Iosephus jumped in and Maria, already tearful at Longinus' news was distraught at the loss of her gentle knight who had carried her most of the way on her travels and always seemed to find an Inn.

"I am staying here" and Maria looked around to see her friend Ninian had spoken up. "I need to establish my Temple and then I shall spread the word to the whole of west Caledonia. Maria, you can take Aeyr, the Glass How and the Dannonii as well as Aber and Inver off the list of your travels as I will get to all of those and with the support of the local Kings who have converted save for the Epidii. I should have Caledonia wrapped up and Christian within three months."

"Then I also shall be staying here." Galahaidra did not say much yet every female heart in the Hall beat faster and several sighs were heard whilst others considered changing their arrangements so that they also could stay. Yet all knew he stayed for one reason and out of love for one person.

Prince Godric went next as he also was leaving Maria; he could see she was crushed at the loss of so many friends so was apologetic as he said. "I need to rescue my father. He is old after all. I will sort out your treaty for you and within four weeks you will be Queen of Cantiani, Princess of the Dobunni, Sitiges and Atrebates. I then need to have a chat with the Dunromnii as Kernow is still not part of the treaty. The rest of Britannia is now part of one Treaty, signed up for peace and mutual defence. You need to make a few visits: Wyncaister, Glaston Tor, Sulis, Glevum, Herne's Ford, Talbot, Caer Lisle, Caister, The Stone Hill and Colcaester. Go by ship."

"We will ensure that there are crowds there to see you arrive and see you off" added Pasterix, a tear in his eye, little able to credit that mere weeks earlier this girl had come into his life and charmed him with her gentle voice and now he had peace with his neighbours and had defeated the Vicing and Germanii: all was her doing. Jaeric saw the tear and thumped his peer King on the arm muttering: "That little girl actually did it!" Then Graefreigh joined them both and said: "But what will she want to do next?" And for a moment they were silent before roaring their heads off with laughter.

"I will come with you as you will need someone to show you the way" growled King Graemwolda and Maria hugged his arm grateful for his support but also looking directly at Craedech with one eyebrow raised in enquiry. "I will come too" the prince mumbled and Maria whispered briefly in Graemwolda's ear: "I need to sort out my man, you do not mind sire?"

"Bless you. I am sole King of all Vicing because of you. When you sail west let me know."

She reached Craedech and as he went to speak she stepped up on tip-toe and kissed him long and carefully without giving him a chance to escape.

They both came up for air and then he went to say something so she kissed him again, holding his head in her hand. Once more they needed to catch some air and yet again the young prince tried to speak so she kissed him again and a few minutes later he had finally got the message. When he stood in silence before her, she placed her head on the crux of his shoulder, her other hand holding the nape of his neck and gently caressing his hair then she said just loud enough for all to hear her if they listened very carefully which they all did. This was almost a shout for the girl with the small voice:

"Well I have a much better idea. You are all invited to a party I shall be holding in the Great Hall at Glevum where it shall be my great pleasure to take this young man's hand in marriage. Prince Craedech, will you marry me?" and the prince lifted her high above his head in sheer delight as the whole hall erupted, and from somewhere they found music to which several couples began to dance.

"I think that was a 'Yes'" she whispered into his ear as he led her into the first of many dances. "On one condition" he whispered back. "We have to do something about your wild boar and wolves."

"Don't worry" Maria smiled. "They have sorted that out for us already. They have all got married and are expecting the clever darlings! By the time we get back from wherever you are going to take me we shall have at least twenty wild boar and ten more wolves as family. I knew you would be pleased!"

"The prince is not the only one both pleased and exasperated in equal measure by his Queen" grumbled the poor dragon as another day grew to its crimson end and yet he was no more the wiser about whither this story would go and how it might end. At his glum look, Ra'el could not resist but laughed out loud and then offered her friend some solace:

"Tomorrow I shall begin the next part of this story. I shall tell the tale of the Shroud of Turin and Maria's first journey to Rome ..."

The End of Book One of An Audience with the Sleeping Dragon

AN AUDIENCE WITH A SLEEPING DRAGON. THE SHROUD OF TURIN

Extracts and summary from Book 2 of the story of Mary Magdalan's mission to Britain

Extract One

King Pederaster brought Maria to the shores of western Hibernia, the rolling hills of Balinrobe above Louch Garza and on to Clonbur and the rock bridge, now collapsed but which stretched across the gorge at Oughterford between Carrib and Mask. They could see the distant cliffs battered by the huge one hundred pace tall mountain of water that crested the top of each cliff to leave a sea of spray that covered the land beyond for hundreds of paces more then clasping the ground it would drag earth, mud and stones back towards the huge wall of silt it was mindlessly determined to build.

Then going deeper into the sub-aquarian labyrinth they found the triplets of Nebereth, Nacotipeth and Nebeneza named after three bewitching princesses who charmed the local men folk and were eventually punished for no other sin than to have been created charming. The Carrock and Zammerzam were separated by the twin-mountains of the Kiltarsaghaun, a daunting set of sharp jaws almost human in their ferocity but stilled by the gentle beauty of the Gildain forest.

The dryad Queen of the forest had surrendered her trees including her own soulsmate to the giants because they wanted one causeway more and her kindly faith taught her to surrender before their obdurancy for no other reason than they were made stubborn and she was made meek. In the days that followed the mountains tore themselves to dust in their guilt at the loss of her, leaving the narrow and jagged causeway.

"Where do we go?" asked the gentle princess

"I seek one place: it is aptly named 'The Little Princess'" replied the King of All Serpents.

Synopsis

It is 35 AD and fourteen months have now passed since Maria's mission to Caledonia. Maria of Magdalo Castle, Queen of the Cantiani and Princess of the Durobriges, Atrebates, Belgae and Regni has married Prince Craedech of the Dobunni, son of King Caractacus at his Royal Seat in Glevum with the Kings of every tribe and kingdom in Britannia, Caledonia, Germania and the Vicing Sea Kingdoms of Scandia in joyful attendance together with the Procurator Amarillus, as representative of the Roman Empire.

Prince Craedech's father King Caractacus and his uncle King Cunobiline took the opportunity on the death of the King of Abin and Waltha's Ham to make claim to the middle kingdoms of the Catuvellauni, proposing to bring them under the umbrella of Maria's Peace Treaty. Craedech then decided to go on extended leave, a short break for Maria from her mission in Britannia but one that the Prince might have been wiser to have booked first with his wife and more importantly her Master.

As Pederaster and Falindir carried the couple through the warm seas of the Gulf Stream along the spectacular coastline of western Hibernia, they explored the subaquarian land beneath the Mountain of the 'Little Princess' and then became briefly embroiled in King Pedrus' wars with the tribes of north-western Hibernia as the King of the Picts sought to seal his claim to be King of All Hibernia.

Meanwhile King Ingen of the Catuvellauni had died and King Cunobiline immediately rebelled against Godric, Prince of the Atrebates' claims to the crown of the Catuvellauni having not been a signatory to the Peace Treaty negotiated by Maria Magdalo in 33 and 34 AD. Cunobiline displaced Caelderac's son, Farimar, King of Abin, Waltha's Ham, the Forest of Eppin, Onga, the Hurst of Dodding, Burntwood, Greeting, Inga's Stone and Creeting then went on to take the remaining lands of the Trinovantes, fording the Chelmer, capturing Colcaister and finally defeating King Col at the Battle of Waithe Colne 35 AD before he turned south to add the territory of the Atrebates to his trophies.

Varus, Admiral of the Roman fleet based at Bononia, succeeded in bringing the fleeing Prince Godric of the Atrebates to safety. Prince Godric Bann Caelicus (shortened to 'Bericus' in Cassio Dio's History) was the last descendant of Commius who was Julius Caesar's friend. The Prince escaped in the dead of the night, rescued by his companion and great friend Sir Galahaidra, and reached the port of South Hamm mere minutes before the assassins hired by King Cunobeline of the Catuvellauni rode into the harbour. Galahaidra and Godric both escaped disguised as a journeyman bard (Sir Galahaidra) and his elderly maidservant (Prince Godric).

Godric sailed from South Hamm to Bononia and rode as a captive to Lugdubellum from where the Prince under escort by Amarillus and Longinus (now Legionary Commander of the XIVth in reward for his detailed briefing on the political situation in Britannia and Caledonia, given in person to the Emperor Tiberius at his retreat on the Island of Capri) was brought to the City of Rome to go before Tiberius and Germanicus (Caligula).

Godric was greeted as an ally and the leader of a client kingdom of Rome, moreover one that was well-remembered for its ties with Commius who aided Julius Caesar in his invasion of Britain. The Prince was successful in obtaining the Emperors' support for an invasion of the south coast to reinstate the Prince but on condition that Maria of Magdalo, the Prince's adopted daughter, was brought before Tiberius.

In 36 AD, Maria took advantage of several offers to visit the Kings and Tribal leaders of the Germanii, following her accession as Queen of the Cantiani by affirmation, her defeat of the tribes and kingdoms of the Germanii in the Battle of Cromarty 33 AD, her marriage to Prince Craedech of the Dobunni and her adoption as daughter and sole heir by Prince Godric of the Atrebates. There was much for the Germanic tribes to wish to celebrate with her.

She sailed from Hibernia through the Mare Britannia and the Mare Germanicum, escorted for part of her journey by King Pederaster and Queen Falidir, before meeting up with her own fleet in the safe haven at Ritupiae (Roedean). Following the Naval Battle at the Firth of Beauly in 33 AD, her fleet was currently by far the largest in Britannia, Caledonia, Germania, the Vicing kingdoms, Hibernia and Rome.

Maria disembarked at the Roman port of Noviomagus on the Estuary of the Rhine at Traiectum and rode with Sir Galahaidra and Sir Kenneth Clan Kenneth of Dungalis through Germania, during which she visited her friends Gagdevelorix, King of the Franci, Ventrix, King of the Burgundi and Tortelimar, King of the Alemani. She stayed with each, and converted many of the Germanii to Christianity, before crossing the Alpes east of Concordia and the Danubius, where she narrowly avoided an assassination attempt by a team of sicariot outside the Legionnary Citadel of Augusta Vindelicorum.

Tartellus, Procurator at Valentia escorted Maria from the Rubicon to the Capitol and the Imperial Palace at Rome, nervously presenting the 'Barbarian' Queen to the Emperor Tiberius and his adopted nephew and heir Germanicus, now known under his nickname of Caligula. The Emperors were interested in Maria as she would be the co-ruler of the western and southern Kingdoms of Britannia and her active encouragement of unification and peace offered the best opportunity for Rome to absorb Britannia and Caledonia into their Empire.

Tartellus should not have been nervous as not only did Maria charm the old Emperor but she had the advantage of being related to one of the Emperor's favourite commentators: Pliny the Younger who would later write of her achievements during her period in Rome to his best friend, Montanus.

The two Emperors, one current and one future, agreed to invade Britannia and retake the principalities of the Catuvellauni and Atrebates for Godric and his adopted daughter. In return, Maria and Godric offered to promote a new

Peace Treaty making the Lands and Kingdoms of the Catuvellauni, Atrebates, Belgae, Regni, Trinovantes, Iceni and the Cantiani (or Cant) client kingdoms of Rome, much to Maria's husband's disgust on her eventual return to Briton (as King Cunobiline of the Catuvellauni and Atrebates was her husband's uncle and was disinherited by the Treaty with Rome).

The Emperor, smitten by the girl, asked for a private audience with the British Queen during which Maria succeeded in converting Tiberius to Christianity by the use of an egg that miraculously turned red at the Emperor's request: allegedly the first Easter Egg!

Maria stayed on in Rome and befriended the Lady Antonia Caesar, visiting Laurentum and Arpinum where the girl performed her first miracles in Italy, one healing a favourite freedwoman in the service of Antonia. In gratitude, the girl was offered the position of private and personal secretary by the imperial matron. Maria did not accept Antonia's offer initially; she was still needed in Britannia. But she would return to Rome after the conquest of Britain by Claudius.

Whilst in Rome, Maria was the target of a second assassination attempt by the sicariot which saw her struck by a poisoned dart. She was reunited with the Lady Cordelia who was successful in healing the young girl with her first ever use of the gift of healing through the 'laying on of hands' aided by The Shroud. Moments after, a furious Prince Godric had charged in to Maria's cubillum in the Capitol to find his daughter near death ... yet again!

As 36 AD drew to a close, Maria felt homesick and missed her husband greatly, so she joined up with Joseph of Arithemea who lent her his private yacht once again and her favourite crew members to convey her back to Britannia where she headed for the safe haven of Ritupiae in the heart of her lands of Cantiani. First, she journeyed towards Paciano to visit the Castello there and had the second of her Grael Visions about The Shroud and the Renzi family.

Maria would visit Rome often following Claudius' conquest of Britain and the defeat of Caractacus in 43 to 45 AD. In 52 AD, she went to Rome as a hostage, accompanying the captured Caractacus (and as substitute for her husband, Prince Craedech). Caractacus lost his titles which were granted to his son, Craedech, in recognition of the prince's loyalty to Rome.

The Routes of the Prince of the Atrebates and the Queen of the Cantiani to go before Tiberius the Emperor of Rome in 35 and 36 AD

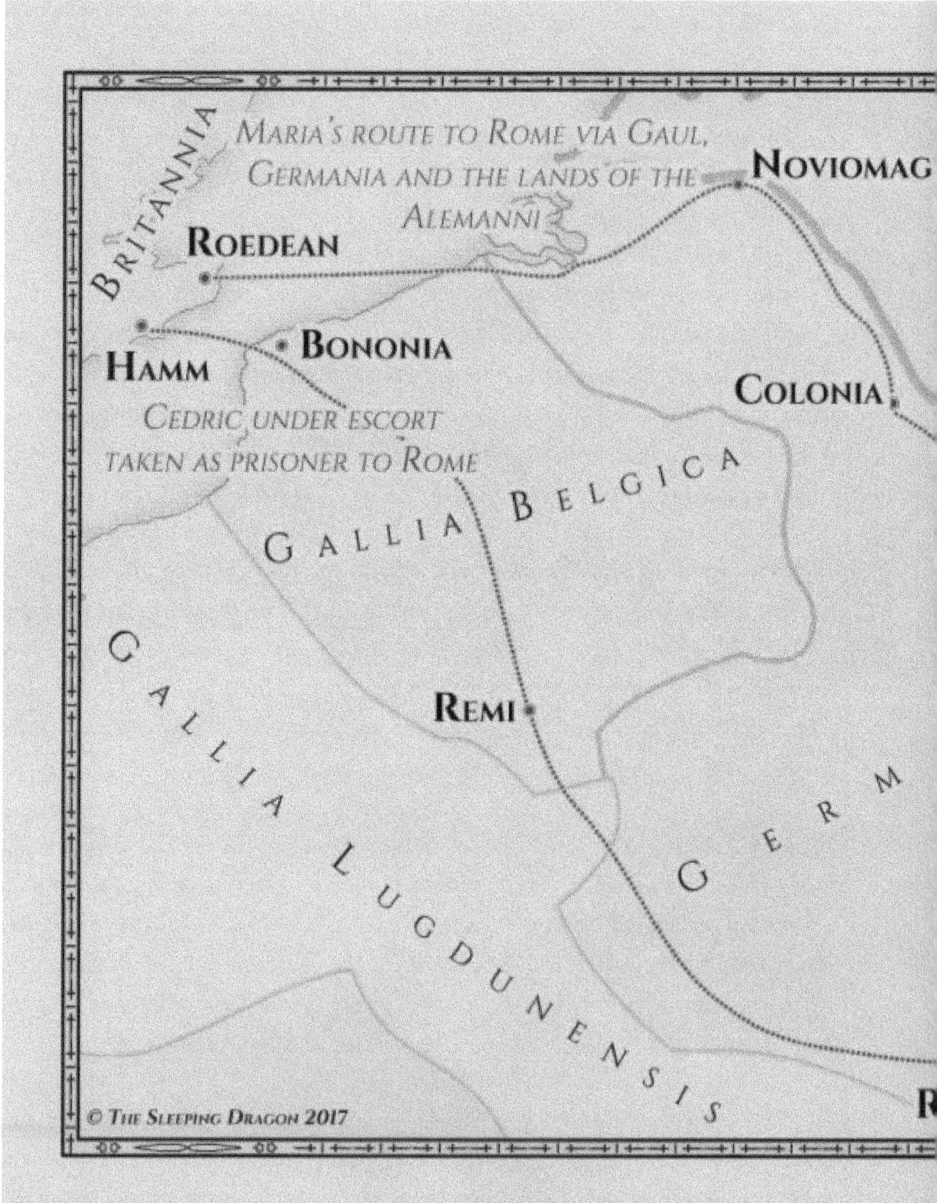

Prince Godric Bann Caelicus, Prince of the Atrebates and Maria, Queen of the Cantiani travel their separate ways to Rome. The Prince was fleeing from the assassins sent by Cunobiline, King of the Catuvellauni and was forced to take ship across the Mare Britannia to Bononia from whence he rode under custody to the Military City of Lugdubellum (Lyons). Godric then rode under protective escort provided by Amarillus, Procurator of Lugdunensis and Longinus, Commander of the XIVth through Raetia and Brigantium then south pausing at Paciano and Trasimino to arrive in Roma.

Maria was released by Claudius and accepted Antonia's offer of a position on her staff in 52 AD. She took on the name of 'Pallas' after her grandmother Cleopathra Pallas Athena Thea and was able to advise Claudius during his administration of the new Roman Province of Britannia and became the tutor for the young Britannicus. She moved to Rome on the death of her husband in 54 AD, becoming Queen of the Dobunni, Catuvellauni and Trinovantes to add to her other titles and brought all three kingdoms under the Imperium of Rome. As 'Pallas', she was able to assist Paulus in obtaining clemency at his first trial (but sadly was not in Rome for his second trial and execution in 65AD). Together with Petronella, Maria also helped Petrus in his escape from the Mamertine. {Maria's mission in Rome in 65AD is part of the third book of Ra'el's account of the early life of Maria Magdalan: 'The Robe of the King'}.

Extract Two

As night approached, Ra'el sat before her winged companion and began to tell Flamebringer the legend of The Shroud once kept by her family in secreted safety in the caves beneath the mountain-top village of Paciano and its nearly three thousand year old stone keep built by the Etruscans.

On the eve of the Battle of Poitiers in 1356, the Baron of Paciano, Nicolo Renzi who was fighting for the French as part of the personal bodyguard of the Pope in Avignon against the English under Edward III's son, the Black Prince, received a Vision that showed he would be slain if he did not place The Shroud under the protection of "a pure and perfect knight".

Di Paciano asked who this 'pure knight' might be amongst not only the gentry of his own country of Italy but the French, Burgundians and English (even, in desperation, the knights from Scotland). All spoke of only one name: Sir Godffroi de Charney, whose Book on Chivalry had been an examplar of purest conduct at the tilt and tourney for all nobility at every tournament since its publication in 1350.

The following morning di Paciano met de Charney in the chancel of the Cathedral at Poitiers where the two men had agreed to pray together then discuss the Baron's request. De Charney was fresh from his attempt to negotiate a parley between the two armies and was tired yet courteous. As they knelt, di Paciano placed a cloth upon the altar and heard a gasp from the knight behind him.

“What is it that I see, lord?” asked the knight and di Paciano went to answer but the young knight held up one hand motioning the Baron to silence then a few moments later spoke reverently: “Forgive me Baron but it was not you to whom I spoke” then turning to the Baron, the knight said: “I must go and make one last attempt to avoid Battle to save the lives of hundreds if not thousands that shalt die in battle today. Leave this cloth with me for safe-keeping. Return here tonight and it shalt be ready for you.”

“But where do you go?” asked the Baron.

“Have you not heard? I carry The Oriflamme, the great gold and navy blue flag of the kingdom of France. Yet this piece of cloth you give into my safety today is worth far more to me than one thousand Oriflammes.”

“Will I see you again?”

“Yes” and the knight smiled before genuflecting and taking up The Shroud.

Records of the battle show that nearly 5000 of the 11000 French and Papist troops that fought that day were captured, wounded or killed to only a few hundreds of English. Records also showed that de Charney made every attempt to avoid bloodshed even to the point of prophesying his own death but in the end, the English under Chandros and the Black Prince were insistent that battle should be joined.

The battle lasted some four hours and was over by mid afternoon. Di Paciano was one of the many captured but being worth a reasonable ransom, he was treated well by his captor: a Knight from Sible Hedingham in the company of the Earl of Oxford, his neighbour at Hedingham. Di Paciano’s captor also owned his own mercenary company: ‘The White Company’.

The Baron asked his captor for a favour. "My Lord Acquetto. A french knight, an honourable man, is holding for me something of great wealth and asked that he return it to me after the battle had been fought. He said that he shall be waiting for me at the Cathedral. May we go?"

Sir John Hawkwood, one day to become a Count of Florence (Firenze) for his services as a mercenary to the Medici family, was more than happy to collect any valuable item left for his prisoner as it would add to the value of his ransom. So together they went to the Cathedral.

In their amazement they knelt before The Shroud laid out on the altar, but shining as if covered in gold leaf and then they saw why: lying within the burial cloth as if asleep and without a mark upon him was the "pure and perfect knight", Sir Godffroi de Charney, holding the Oriflamme of France shining gold, reflected in the young man's armour as he slept peacefully in death, his Grael Vision fulfilled.

They took The Shroud and The Oriflamme and then journeyed towards Genoa and Milano where Hawkwood had been offered a new and extremely lucrative contract. Eventually they came to the magnificent Cathedral in Turin and di Paciano offered Hawkwood The Shroud and The Oriflamme as part of his ransom. So amazed had the mercenary captain been at what he had seen at the Cathedral in Poitiers that he turned to di Paciano and said:

"Let us leave The Shroud with the good priests here to keep. For the vision that we saw as granted by The Shroud was of more worth to me than any ransom I might ask of you. The Oriflamme shalt suffice to see your release and will fetch me a great sum." With which, both men parted company, one to ride to Genoa the other to return to his home in Paciano.

Soon after, The Shroud went on display at the Cathedral of St John in Turin but it was not until one hundred years later that it was officially listed amongst the artwork and precious items held by the Cathedral. Yet wherever the story of The Shroud or The Holy Grael is told, it is always remembered that it first came to di Paciano then de Charney then Acquetto before finishing in Turin."

Extract Three

The next day Ra'el was awoken by her dragon, Roaring Flamebringer, from her deep sleep in the grotto of a silvery cavern, clear blue waters surrounding them, spiralling columns of lime-green and crimson reflected in the still waters. It was a place of tranquillity; and an inspiration for any story teller or lover of stories. And so with a sigh of contentment, Ra'el continued with her tale of the Magdalan:

For the first time in her life as they were sailing into the Bay of Lugdebellum Maria felt sea-sick and put this down to her recovery from the attempted poisoining when in Rome. However, by the time she reached Marsela she was whiter than the canvas sheet that was being used as a cover for the ship's guests. No longer able to save her embarrassment she found herself retching over the side and her father, Sir Galahaidra, Sir Iosephus and Sir Kenneth all started to panic at the sight of her. The helmsman, Decius, was able to get the trireme into the calm waters around Marsela and as soon as they docked, Godric, Galahaidra and Kenneth all leapt to the decking of the quayside and went in hunt of a physician.

The first one they found listened to their tale of poisons, exhaustion, strange illnesses, terrible wounds, storms, sea sickness, even sea serpents and had one question: "All male crew I take it?" and when they nodded, was happy to break the news to Godric that he was about to become a grandfather.

"How long?" asked the Prince who had lost his own wife and his only heir in child birth. "Months yet" replied the doctor and advised them to get the girl home fast then bed rest for the next six months. "The girl is a half starved rat" muttered her father and the doctor shooed them out saying: "Then feed her. She has at least two to feed now."

Synopsis continues

Maria reached her harbour at Ritupiae not daring to risk Noviomagus or South Hamm, escorted by her fleet that had put out from Bononia and which followed her from Scylla in Lusetania on news of her condition. King Pederaster and his Queen were there with over one hundred of their kin to add to the escort for Maria whilst Prince Craedech rode in haste from his lady love's capital at Wyncaister to join her at Loddon's Hill where they planned for her confinement.

Rather ingloriously, Caractacus sought to assault Maria and her small troop of bodyguard whilst protected by the almost non-existent defences at Loddon with the aid of his brother Togodumnus with whom he now shared the kingdoms of the Catuvellauni, Atrebates and Trinovantes. They descended on the partly walled settlement with over one thousand cavalry and for the second time, Caractacus was defeated by Maria with a much smaller force.

This time fifty cavalry under Maria herself, Sir Amaric and Sir Kenneth defeated the Catuvellauni, Togodumnus was slain by Amaric, and in the aftermath, the lands of the Atrebates were returned by the captured Caractacus to Maria. Sir Galahaidra and Sir Iosephus had sailed to join Saint Ninian in Aeyr only for the saint to send them straight back to be with Maria. "What are you doing here?" Ninian had shouted at her husband sweeping him out of her humble hut with her broomstick "That poor girl might need your Spear for the healing power it has and you are no good to me in your armour here!"

The only low moment in Maria's confinement was when both Godric and Craedech tore the poor girl to pieces in their anger at discovering she had led the defence of Loddon. For once, she found she could not laugh. Haladriel stepped in to save her with a hushed cry of "The Baby" at which both men were instantly contrite and Maria shared a grateful look with her former lady in waiting.

On the fourth anniversary of the resurrection of Maria's Master, the Emperor Tiberius died, believed suffocated by his nephew Caligula and Maria gave birth to a son Commius Tiberius Claudius Antonius (names inserted out of tact by Craedech and pure mischief by Maria as she enjoyed her father's reaction at the first royal Christian baptism) Godricson Wulfridson Bann Caelidus.

"Poor little blighter" muttered Prince Wulfrid at the child's baptism as he tried to take in the barrage of names and then when the infant prince exploded loudly into his pants went on to add: "Takes after his grandfather I see" and Maria collapsed into hoots of laughter, much to the general consternation of

the congregation which was a representation of the Who's Who of pre Roman Britain.

After a few moments silence punctuated by Maria's shrieks of laughter (muffled by Craedech's hand firmly clasped over her mouth but which hand was twitching as he considered transferring it to her neck) and the occasional guffaw from Wulfrid, everyone joined in the girl's laughter, save Iosephus who sadly was now profoundly deaf.

The summer of 40AD, Maria was on her stallion, standing with her family of twelve silver haired blue eyed wolves and nineteen wild boar, dressed as always in white silver and gold, her shining silver winged helmet pushed back on its white leather chin straps to reveal her blonde hair and blue eyes, her full length shining steel chain hauberk, showing her yet more slender body as childbirth and motherhood had taken a greater strain on her thin frame, her lance and shield hanging from her etranches and etarmes across her back, the sword Caelicbann or Excalibur at her side, before her the Mare Britannia and the cliffs at Devrum and in the very far distance, a huge fleet gathered at Bononia.

She held up her left hand and fifty thousands stood along the cliff tops and defiantly started to clash their swords onto their large oval shields immediately followed by as many again of cavalry mounted and shouting insults at the Roman Fleet. 'If Rome wants to break their treaty then we are ready for them' *Maria thought and then reached out to hold her husband's hand.*

"Why do you fight?" Craedech asked "You never fight!"

"This time I do. If that man ever comes to invade us it will be the end of all we have set in place. Caligula is evil, a monster and a murderer: the very opposite of our Master!"

"And what does our Master say?" Craedech challenged her, still pressing for an answer that would justify going into battle now where before she had always sought Peace. His fear was that Maria had changed her view because she had the life of Commius Claudius to look after and he hoped she might have a careful eye out for him too. "Thou shalt not kill!" he continued forcibly "Remember how our Master said 'There can be no tolerance on any commandment.' You

yourself nearly died to avoid war and to seek peace in its stead when we fought the Vicing hordes?"

"There can be no peace until this man dies. But do not worry, my love. My Master, at least, trusts me. So watch … " and as he turned his eyes towards the far coastline and the waves crashing on the cliffs of northern Gaul he heard a chuckle from the warrior Queen next to him, still only nineteen and with the mind and the body of an innocent child … except now she was chuckling with glee as they both watched the siren Queen Heirachaea and King Pederaster with his family of sea dragons start to smash up the gathered Roman fleet, disabling it: yet they also watched with delight as, true to the British Queen's orders, every mariner and legionary made the shores of Bononia safely.

"It will be three more years yet before the Romans come to Britannia" the Magdalan laughed "and by then it will be a different man that we shall be dealing with."

Extracts from Book Two of An Audience with the Sleeping Dragon: The Shroud of Turin

EPILOGUE

Mary Magdalan: the Legends

Mary (as often Maria) Magdalan was born in Magdala on the sides of the Sea of Galilee and lived in the Magdalo Castle becoming extremely wealthy on the death of her mother. Following a ship wreck or an attempt to murder her by the Jews who were still persecuting Christians, Maria came to Marsela (Marseilles) where she established Christian communities both in Marseilles and in the caverns beneath Beaumes. She was accompanied by Marcella her servant, Maximim, one of the seventy two disciples, a Roman sometimes called Longinus and Cedon who was the blind man who had his eye sight restored by Iesus, also known as Bartimaeus and Bartnimaeus.

There are references in medieval and reformation translations of the Gospels to seven demons being cast out of Maria but the early Christians referred to seven Angels accompanying her and her own Gospel often refers to her being in communion with Angels. The word used is the same as that in the Creed for 'Unseen' ie created beings and therefore Angels and the use of 'demons' came as part of the attempt to demonise the poor girl.

Lazarus became the first Bishop of Marseilles when on a trip with Maria.

Maria is thought to have converted the Emperor Tiberias in 36 or 37AD and to have invented the Easter Egg by giving the Emperor an Egg that changed colour. She then served Claudius pretending to be the freedman, Pallas, and getting into trouble with the Senate for refusing 15m sesterces and subsequently offering to donate it to charity. She insisted that to have so much money would be wrong when her faith advocated poverty.

In a letter by Pliny, she is referred to as his relative under the disguised name of Pallas Athena or Pallas who was the tutor and coach for Claudius' son Britannicus. She later went under the name of Caenis, Vespasian's aunt or mistress. Both her position as the tutor for Britannicus and her later position as Vespasian's mistress is quite possible given both the friendship she had with Longinus and her royal connections in Britannia. It is likely that she returned to Rome in grief on the death of Prince Craedech and put her knowledge and talents at the disposal of Claudius in the wake of his invasion.

Ninian and Mary Magdalan both were in Rome for periods from 41 to 54 AD helping Christians during Claudius' persecution under the nicknames of *Narcissus* and *Pallas*. Another account has Magdalan going under an assumed name to Rome, one taken from the same ancestor as when she took the pseudonym of Pallas. The name this time was Thea.

After Rome, Mary Magdalan is thought to have worked in Ephesus with the Holy Apostle John on the early chapters of his Gospel and particularly the mystic and visionary elements. These sections were later over-written.

It is clear from Maria's own Gospel that she had frequent and immediate conversations with Christ; that her faith was visionary and teleological similar to other great female mystics; she encouraged an allegorical rather than a literal interpretation of the Gospels of her fellow Apostles; and that there was considerable jealousy of her closeness to Jesus from many of the Apostles, particularly Peter, Andrew, Thomas, Phillip and from Paul. Peter may have changed his view after he had his first mystical experience when escaping from the Mamertime. There is a delightful moment in the Gospel of Mary when Levi ticks Peter off for being a bully after he had made Maria cry. Peter's Gospel is perhaps the closest to Mary Magdalan's suggesting there was some form of reconciliation before Peter's death but also the two Gospels appear to have been originally written about the same time.

St Maximim's Chapel records Mary Magdalan's death when 72, making her 2 years younger than Jesus. There is a second account in Luke of her death when 84 and her being 10 years older than Jesus.

The third account is of her as an orphan and beggar and much younger than Jesus. This account makes no reference to her being the mistress or wife of Jesus whereas the other accounts that refer to her age and death have her in a relationship with the Messiah, for example the *Gospel of Phillip*. This account sees her reach the grand old age of 92 dying in c109AD

Her relics were allegedly transported to Constantinople by Pope Leo in 899 AD often given as the date of their discovery but had already been 'discovered' by Saint Bardilo in Vezelay in c 832 AD. Eudes, King of the Franks had moved the sacrophagus and relics from Beaumes and St Maximim's Chapel to a rather large and spectacular Cathedral in a rare and stunning combination of Eastern and early Norman architecture in the centre of Vezelay in 710 AD. One does rather wonder what precisely Saint Bardilo found one hundred years later as Vezelay's cathedral is somewhat impossible to miss?

From 1279 AD we find records of her complete body to be found in her sarcophagus in Beaumes and it remains there except for a brief period when the relics dodge the French Revolution. They return in 1878 and from then onwards go on the occasional tour including, thus far, Brazil but also Toulouse, Lyons and Paris.

The Catholic Chuch has long condemned, demonised and sought to ruin the reputation of Mary Magdalan, dating back to Pope Gregory's sermon in the 5th Century AD, where the Pope accused her of being guilty of all of the seven deadly sins each governed by a 'demon', an intentional mis-translation of the word for 'Angels'. Pope John Paul II would make a full and helpful apology for this act of 'demonisation'.

Only fragments remain of *The Gospel of Mary* and subsequent apocryphal writings describe Maria's many conversations with the Risen Christ as strange to unlikely. Andrew and Peter both are accounted to have said: "Why would Christ give such important messages to a woman?"

There is even talk of Maria being thrown out by the other Apostles; this may explain the St Maximin Chapel legend of her remaining in seclusion for forty or more years yet this is inconsistent with her own

Gospel where she argued for the Apostles Preaching the Gospel of the Kingdom publicly when they were in hiding spending all of their time making rules and laws. Maria was prominent preaching the Gospel which she named interchangeably as the *Gospel of the Kingdom*, the *Good News*, the *Gospel of Good* or *Good Spirit* and, as the authoress of the early chapters of The Gospel of St John, '*the Word*'. She and Paul were actively preaching at a time when the rest of the Apostles were in hiding from persecution by the Jews and then the Romans.

All of the Gnostic Gospels are consistent: women were the first to see the Risen Christ and whilst the male Apostles fled in fear, denying Christ after his arrest, it was the women of Jerusalem who accompanied Christ on the Way of the Cross and kept him company at his crucifixion on Golgotha, burying him with honour and with their tears.

It is a sad fact that the Christian Church of the 4th and 5th Century sought actively to downplay the important role women had played in Christ's ministry: two of the first four deacons were female yet in the rewrite of the *Acts of the Apostles* after the Synod of Nicaea, their names were subtlely altered to the male version. All reference to the '*Apostle to the Apostles*' (Mary Magdalan's honorific) were removed together with the references to her visions and conversations with the Risen Christ and her ministry to Western Europe. The *Acts of the Apostles* refers to the seven diocese founded by Saint Paul and makes no mention of an active early Christian Church in Southern, Northern and Western France, Britain, Ireland and the Rhineland.

Mary of Bethany, Mary Magdalan and Mary, wife of the disciple Coplas were all merged to become a single person by the 5th Century AD, whilst reference to the sister of Mary, Jesus' mother, and Petronella, the daughter of Peter, are also removed by those who were rewriting the Gospels from Coptic and Aramaic into Greek and Latin at the behest of Constantine.

Most recently the Catholic Church has restored Mary Magdalan to her position as the first to bear witness to the Risen Christ: **the first Christian**, one of many steps it has made in the quest for world unity of all of those whose belief is in a single God the Creator and also in re-establishing the important role women played in developing the early Christian Church.

"The women are the first at the tomb. They are the first to find it empty. They are the first to hear *'He is not here. He has risen, as he said.'* They are the first to embrace him. The women are also the first to be called to announce this truth to the Apostles.

The Gospel of John emphasises the special role of Mary Magdalene. She is the first to meet the Risen Christ.

Hence she came to be called "the Apostle of the Apostles". Mary Magdalene was the first eye witness of the Risen Christ, and for this reason she was also the first to bear witness to him before the Apostles. This event, in a sense, crowns all that has been said previously about Christ entrusting divine truths to women as well as men."

Pope John Paul II

Maria's Peace

As entrusted to Eorl Haroult during the Battle of Cromarty Sands

'Maria's Peace' needed Caledonia to unite around five kingdoms. Knowing from her visions that the land of the Selgovae from Kincardine and the territory of the Votadini would fall to the invading Romans just forty years later, she sought a division that would bring the Caledonian and Dacian leaders together and survive to resist the Roman invasion.

All of the proposed kingdoms would survive the Roman invasion even into the Dark Ages when parts of the territories of the Dannonil, Sevgolae and Votadini would still be part of Edwin's kingdom of Northumbria with Fife remaining as its own kingdom and Ardoch north of Perth and the Forth of Tay being the furthest north that any invaders reached.

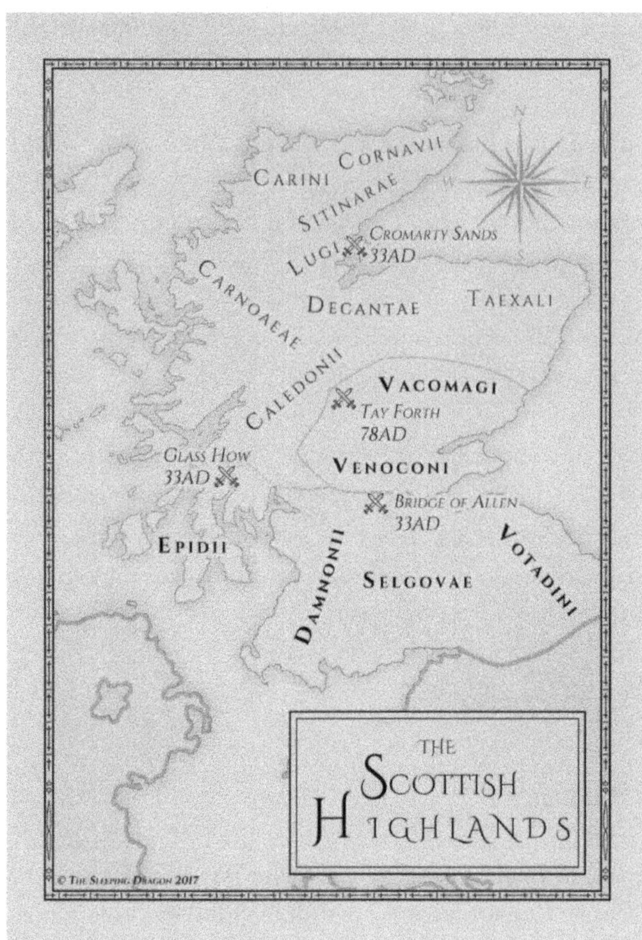

The Five Kingdoms of Caledonia

Dannonil
Ruled by King Harbondum and to include both the territories of the Dannonil and those of the Epidrii

Sevgolae
Ruled by King Craemond and to include the lands of the Sevgolae west of the Falls of Failinn and bordering on the territories of the Votadini.

Dacia

Ruled by King Jaerid of Dacia until the Roman Invasion in 43-84 AD and the Battle of Mons Graupius (which both the Caledonians and the Romans claimed as a victory), it was administered by Eorl Haroult with Eorl Graemond administering Caester as far as the River Aln.

The southern borders of Caledonia ran from CaerLisle and Caer Leon to Caester on the East Coast then included the Eastern Coast territories of the Votadini (the Wick of Bere and the Burgh of Bamm) as far as the Estuary of the River Aln, also taking in the Firths of Forth and the Tay.

Aber was its most northern point, the River Deen forming its northern border, the Cairngorns and Clackmannan Mountains forming its western borders. The lands of the Dacians in Caledonia included the whole of the kingdom of Fife, and the vast mountainous territories of the Vocomagi and Venicones. The Venicones had also settled in Hispania (Lusitania), Northern Italia and the Adriatic Sea and were a great maritime people.

Caledonia

Ruled by King Graemir of the Caledonii and representing the central territories of Scotland and the Caledonian Confederacy that would resist Agricola and defeat the Roman Emperor Severus Septimus in campaigns around 209 AD, leading to the retreat to Hadrians Wall.

Sitenarae

These were the territories to the north of Loch Ness bordering the Oich then going north as far as Thurso and including the people who had settled Thule, ruled by King Garrold of the Sitenarae.

THE GOSPEL ACCORDING TO MARY MAGDALAN

Chapter 4

On Sin, Matter, Powers, Form, Nature, Forces and Original State

". . . Will matter then be destroyed or not?"

The Saviour said: "All nature, all forms, all creatures exist in and with one another, and they will return to their original roots. For the nature of Matter never changes; it returns always to its Original State and can be no other.

"He who has ears to hear, let him hear."

Peter said to him: "Since you have explained everything to us, tell us this also: 'What is the Sin of the world?'"

The Saviour said: "There is no such sin, but it is *you* who make sin when your actions are sinful such as adultery which is a sin. That is why Good came into your midst, to restore everything to its original nature without sin." Then He continued and said: "That is why you become sick and die for you are deprived of that which can heal you. So it is with sin: Sin and Good are opposites and lose one and then you let the other take control of your soul.

"He who has a mind to understand, let him understand."

"Matter can give birth to Power [Energy] that has no equivalent and which as Force can contradict Nature. When this happens then the resulting disturbance will destroy your whole body. That is why I say: Do not be afraid. If you are discouraged by the natural world [by Energy, Matter, Forces] then be encouraged to learn of the different Forms of Nature.

"He who has ears to hear, let him hear."

When the Blessed One had said this, he greeted them all saying: "Peace be with you. Receive my peace. Beware that no one leads you astray saying 'Come here' or 'Go there! For the Son of Man is *inside* you.

Follow Me! Those who seek Me will find Me. Go then and preach the Gospel of the Kingdom. Do not lay down any rules beyond those I have set for you you, and do not set laws like the lawgiver lest you be constrained by them."

When He said this He departed.

Chapter 5: the Gospel of the Kingdom

But they were in grief. They wept greatly, saying: "How shall we go to the Gentiles and preach the Gospel of the Kingdom of the Son of Man? If they did not spare Him, how will they spare us?"

Then Mary stood up, greeted them all, and said to her brethren: "Do not weep and do not grieve or be irresolute, for His grace will be entirely with you and will protect you. But rather, let us praise His greatness, for He has prepared us and made us all into Brave Men."

When Mary said this, she turned their hearts to the Good News, and they began to discuss the words of the Saviour. Peter said to Mary: "Sister we know that the Saviour loved you more than the rest of woman. Tell us the words of the Saviour which you remember which you know, but we do not, nor have we heard them."

Mary answered and said: "What is hidden from you I will now proclaim to you."

And she began to speak to them these words: "I" she said, "I saw the Lord **in a vision** and I said to Him, Lord I saw you today in a vision. He answered and said to me: 'Blessed are you that you did not waver at the sight of Me. For where the mind is there is the answer to our Faith.'

"I said to Him, Lord, how does he who sees the vision see it, through the soul or through the spirit?"

The Saviour answered and said: "He does not see through the soul alone or through the spirit alone, but we understand God's vision for it is a part of us and is made in God's image as are we."

Chapter 8: The Seven Unnatural Forces meet the Soul

(Editorial Note: remember the Arabic and Aramaic words for soul and spirit are the same and so this may be a vision of the meeting of Christ's spirit with the forces of evil)

And our Saviour spoke to me of his soul as follows:

[Darkness, the first Force, is missing]

... And the second [Unnatural] Force was called Desire and it said: "I did not see you descending, but now I see you ascending. Where can I find you now since I am made in your image?"

My Soul answered and said: "I saw you. You did not see me nor recognize me. I served you as a garment and you did not know me." When it said this, it (the Soul) went away rejoicing greatly.

Again it came to the third [Unnatural] Force, which is called Ignorance. The Force questioned my Soul, saying: "Where are you going? In wickedness are you bound? But if you are bound then how can you judge me!"

And my Soul said: "Why do you judge me although I have not judged you? I was bound but I have not bound others. Rather I have recognized that Everything is to be destroyed one day both earthly things and the heavenly. So do not talk to me of Where I am going? I go nowhere [you can prevent]!"

When my Soul had overcome the third Force, it went on to the fourth [Unnatural] Force, which took seven Forms.

The first Form is Darkness, the second Desire, the third Ignorance, the fourth is the Fear of Death, the fifth is the Kingdom of the Flesh [excessive sexuality, lewdness and fornication], the sixth is the foolish Wisdom of Flesh [pornography] and the seventh is Wrathful Wisdom [anger, terror, violence and war]. These are the seven Forces of *wrath*.

They asked my Soul: "Whence do you come from enslaver of mankind, or where are you going, conqueror of space?"

My Soul answered and said: "The evil that once bound me has been slain, and what once forced me to flee has been overcome; my wrong Desire is ended and my Ignorance has passed; in a single aeon I was released from my Fear of Death through my resurrection; I was released from this world to find paradise in the heavens; the body that once contained me is no longer flesh but spirit for I was become God and Man and now I am no longer am full of Wrath but rather united in peace and love of man."

Chapter 9: The Mission

When Mary had said this, she fell silent, since it was to this point that the Saviour had spoken with her.

But Andrew answered and said to the brethren: "Say what you wish to say about what she has said. I at least do not believe that the Saviour said any of this. For certainly these teachings are very strange ideas."

Peter answered and spoke concerning the same. He questioned them all about the Saviour [then said]: "Did He really speak privately with a woman and not openly to us? Are we to turn around and all listen to her? Did He prefer her to us?"

Then Mary wept and said to Peter: "My brother Peter, what do you think? Do you think that I have thought this up myself in my heart, or that I am lying about the Saviour and his desire that we go out and preach?"

Levi answered and said to Peter: "Peter you have always been hot tempered. Now I see you treating [one of our] women the same way as those that oppose us. But if the Saviour has declared her worthy, who are you to reject her? Surely the Saviour knows her and has loved her very well. He loved her more than us for she has been willing to preach openly and to go on her mission. Let us be ashamed of ourselves and not pretend that we are perfect but separate as He commanded us and go out to preach the Gospel rather than staying here making up new laws but doing so in private because we are afraid."

And when they heard this they began to go forth to proclaim and to preach.

[Chapters 1 to 3, 11 and 12 are missing, Chapter 10 was removed for separate sale]

AUTHOR'S NOTE

If you enjoyed these stories then the story of Roaring Flamebringer continues in the Chronicles of Cymbeline, duchess of Fearnost. Roaring Flamebringer is the last living descendant of the great dragon Imperial Devourer who appears in 'Alanaa the Water Element', 'Atlantis Reborn', 'The Persian War', 'The Coming of the Golden Age' and 'The Book of Knowledge'. Ra'el is the last descendant of the marriage of Alanaa, Element of Water and Crown Prince Charubus of Persia, some forty two thousand years before these stories are told.

The legend of Artor, King of Dunrovia, has taken on new significance with the discovery of a Dark Ages Royal Seat at Tintagel. Similar Dark Age findings can be seen on the pilgrim route between Vezelay and Fontenay, on the edge of the Forest d'Etapes, in sight of the hill-top City of Avallon. All of these landmarks sit on the 'Oyster Trail'.

The 'Oyster Trail' is a famous pilgrimage trail that takes in many places of worship in Europe. Significantly, this includes the burial place of Mary Magdalen and also the location of the fabled city of Camelot. The trail snakes across West Europe and reputedly finishes at the burial place of the Baron of Oysters, Baron de Scales, in Suffolk.

The 17th Baron de Scales was known at the Court of Queen Elizabeth I in England as 'spear shaker'; he won his reputation through winning jousting competitions across Europe as had his ancestor, the 13th Earl of Oxford. He was known as the Lancelot of his day *and he had a famous spear.*

His family name may have been used as the inspiration for Arthur's most loyal knight, Sir Bedevere (Be de Vere) in the Arthurian legends which are told very differently in France and Germany than in England or Wales.

The Spear of Longinus (companion treasure to the Holy Grail) was once painted as being held by a young Horace de Vere, later first Baron of Tilbury who was such a great commander that he and his brother Francis became the first non Royals to have a sarcophagus or tomb in Westminster Abbey.

The BedeVere family were linked to legends of the Holy Grail, were prominent in the Crusades, married into the de Scale and de Clare families, took on the guardianship of the 'Oyster Trail', the pilgrim way from the graveside of Mary Magdalen to the hiding places for the Sword, Blood-line, Grail, Shroud, Robe and Spear.

The de Clare family would claim to hold the Blood-line: to be the descendants of Mary Magdalen through their female line (not just the stewards of her remains) and the BedeVere, de Scale and de Clare families intermarried in the 11th and 12th centuries at a time when the Church was recognising the importance of Joseph of Arithamea's and Mary Magdalan's mission to Western Europe with the Holy Grail (Grael).

The Curtana

The Curtana is a special sword: one whose tip has been removed to indicate that justice is merciful but also blunt. It is the sword of state to be carried at all Royal occasions and is the representation of Excalibur in the medieval, Tudor and Stuart period. Today a relatively modern version of the curtana, dating to the 18th Century can be found amidst the Crown jewels. The original is lost. But it was held by the Bedevere family for 20 coronations from 1327 onwards.

From the time of Edward III, when the Legend of the Round Table and a Royal Order of Christian Knights gripped the country, the Bedevere family traditionally held the Sword of State, the '*Curtana*', the English

King's Excalibur at key meetings involving the monarch, in Battle and at coronations, partly recognising the medieval connection between the Bedevere family and the Knight entrusted by Arthur with Excalibur, namely Sir Bedevere.

Whether the Grail is the search for a dream or an ideal, a real cup, a stone that fell from heaven or the blood of the descendants of Mary Magdalen, the BedeVere family employed symbols throughout the many castles, properties and manors they owned and the church they built that are clues to the hiding place for a simple cup and spear, the resting place for the descendants of the de Clare and de Scales families, some of whom still live in France, Italy, Suffolk and North Essex today.

If the Grail is a sacred cup as accepted by the medieval Christian Church, its resting place is more likely to be at one of the major Grail pilgrimage centres as the locations in Suffolk are too obvious ... yet Suffolk meets part of the legend in which the Grail is said to be 'hidden in plain view'.

And if you visit the west door of the church built by the BedeVere family in humble prayer, wearing simple clothing, without jewellery or adornment, seeking mercy for other's and nothing for yourself, with no lustful thoughts, after a period of fasting and all night vigil then *Grail Questers* who are deemed worthy can still be granted sight of the '*Grael Vision*', beneath the cup carved into the church's great oak doors.

According to the various legends, the guardians of the Grail respect humility and chastity, the Grail was lost when one of its guardians had lustful thoughts regarding a supplicant; he was permanently wounded (the maimed or Fisher King), and only healed through the selfless love and sacrifice of Parsifal's (Percy's or Perseus') sister.

The Birth of the legend of Christ's travels as a child, Arthur and the Grail

The origins of the Grail Legend lay in the apocryphal works of Pilate and Nicodemus (4th and 5th century), the early Christian mythologies of

Beowolf (7th century), Orlando (8th century) and the Song of Roland (8th and 9th centuries) together with the verbal tradition of a holy Crusader knight, Parzefal (6th to 12th centuries), and these gave birth to the legend of a Grail (a chalice or a stone), a kingly sword and a spear.

The link with Mary Magdalen followed when de Boron spoke of Jesus visiting France and Britain as a child under the tutorship of Joseph of Arithamea, but also one re-writing of this story by Menessier talks of Mary Magdalen being Christ's guide and alternatively of being responsible for bringing Christianity to Albion.

Nearly fifty years after the establishment of a convent and abbey dedicated to Mary Magdalan (the former overrun and dispersed by Saracens), Saint Bardilo in c 830AD is said to have found the sarcophagus of Mary Magdalen in the Holy Land and to have hidden it beneath the cathedral built in her honour at Vezelay. Later, her body would be 'found' in Provence and Vezelay gradually declined as a place of pilgrimage.

The establishment of a pilgrimage centre in Provence in 1250 and the down-playing of Vezelay reflected two things:

First, the legend of Arthur, the travels of Joseph, Mary Magdalen and the young Jesus, had become accepted within the space of just sixty years (from 1190 to 1250) as **core teaching and tradition within the Christian church: no longer a story but part of the beliefs of all Christians.**

Second, Vezelay was neither large enough nor important enough to be the pilgrim centre for this rapidly growing, popular and important legend; and Vezelay was vulnerable to assault and poorly fortified.

Many believe there was a third reason, namely that the 'tomb' found by Charles the Good in 1250 was a diversion to protect the *real* hiding place from the incursions by Arab and Italian armies.

At the same time, as the legend of Mary Magdalen's and Joseph of Arithamea's travels was developing, we also have the story of Artor: a mighty Christian leader, the King of Dunrovia (one of the founding kingdoms of the House of Wessex) or a Romano-British Count, who had held the Saxon Shore protecting the Romano-British from the invasion of the Saxons. The Legend of Artor had been part of poetry and song for over a Century before Artor's battles were recorded by Geoffrey of Monmouth in 1135, sourced from French and Welsh traditions and forming part of Celtic myth, but not yet part of Christian teachings.

In a twenty year period, these stories and legends would be written down in full for the first time. The legends of Arthur, the Grail, Parsifal, the Holy Blood, the Spear, Excalibur, the Round Table and Camelot rippled through the Courts of Europe and Outremer (the Crusader kingdom) becoming the source of a new wave of romantic poetry and song.

Robert de Boron's account in 1200 would be the first to talk of Joseph of Arithamea *bringing the Grail out of Judaea* and the young Jesus to Britain. Whilst there is evidence of Christianity having a strong foothold in Britain by the second century AD, the evidence supporting a visit to either Cornwall or Glastonbury by a young Jesus in the first century AD can only be classified as fable.

Phillip of Flanders was said to be the source of the new stories, Chretien de Troyes (1190), Wolfram von Eschenbach (1210), and Robert de Boron (1200 and 1208) would each develop and then record the legend of Parsifal and the Grail between 1190 and 1210, with de Boron **linking** Grail, Spear, the sacred blood and the childhood of Jesus for the first time in 1208. The legend of the Round Table began with de Boron's reference to a table set with 14 seats but only twelve could be used.

Illuminated copies of the Welsh epic *Peredu*r, using the same sources as de Troyes, were also in circulation around 1210.

By 1230, the legend of the Grail had been accepted by the Christian church **and incorporated into its teachings.** It was no longer just a Celtic myth but rather seen as evidence of an early Christian church in Britain.

By the time of Mallory's work, Le Morte d'Artor (1470), two separate strands of legends, that of Arthur, Round Table and Sword, and that of

Parsifal, the Grail, Holy Blood and Spear had been drawn together, but with the Grail having been lost before Arthur became King and needing now to be found again.

It is possible that some great artefact that motivated the BedeVere family, the descendants of Sir Bedevere, would aid them to victories at Hastings, Lewes, Sluys, Crecy, Poitiers, Agincourt, Bosworth, Stoke Field, Blackheath and on the continent at Nieuport, Breda and Maastricht. It may have come into their hands or been re-discovered during the early Crusades. The BedeVere family's long line of victories puts Paton, Napoleon, Wellington and Marlborough into the shade.

From somewhere they found the courage to repeatedly charge against enemies larger and better armed than they and yet won! If they found that motivation through believing they held mystical Christian artefacts then even though their beliefs in any powers may have been misplaced, the resulting courage in battle was truly magnificent and helped shape the history of England, Ireland, Holland and France.

The 'Oyster Trail' shows the route that the Grail and the Spear of Longinus are said to have taken before finally arriving at one of the two places that are now regarded as their final hiding place and both protected in different ways but hidden in plain view.

Vezelay as a starting point for the 'Oyster Trail' is important as the town looks across its western valley to another town on a hill-top, and one that would have been an island some 8000 years ago. In front of that town are a lake and two rivers, the Camut and the Lot. The town on its western isle is called *Avalon*. The rivers pass a mound where once stood a Motte and Baillie castle: the Castle of Camut et Lot or Camelot.

The 'Oyster Trail' possibly ends in Hedingham, Colchester, Clare or Lavenham, although it may even continue on to the de Scale lands in central Suffolk (such as Framlingham) but is that also the final resting place of the Spear and the Grail?

Much more likely is that if they existed at all, then they were buried with the body of the last person to use the Spear and one of the last descendants of Sir Bedevere able to show their descent down the male line. This would also give some explanation to the magnificence of his tomb in Westminster Abbey, whose grandeur far outweighs his achievements but not if it is the resting place of a great artefact. The armour he wore in battle was buried with him, and it is likely therefore that his weapons which included a spear, mace, a rapier and short sword, went with him to his grave.

That then brings us to 'Excalibur', 'Calibarnus' or 'Caelicbann' to give the sword of Arthur some of its other names. The Arthurian legend has the sword being given to Bedevere as Arthur is dying from the wounds inflicted by Mordred's spear. Bedevere is said to be the last man to touch it before it was returned to the lady of the lake at Avallon. Bedevere is given three guesses to show he had thrown the sword into the lake and at his third guess perhaps he gets lucky? Did he actually throw the sword away? Or did he keep it thus accounting for the string of victories his family would then have over 1000 years of fighting?

Unlike the Spear and the Grail which are artefacts fixed in physical form, there is no evidence that the sword was unable to adapt to the different periods of its use. If such a powerful weapon existed, it would surely be a gladius in the 4th century, a long sword in the 7th Century, a broadsword or claymore by the 14th century and a rapier in the 17th or else it would have been locked away as out-moded and un-useful.

In the portrait below we can see the Spear from which the Bedevere's got their name of 'Spear Shaker', a rapier with an exquisite pommel, and hidden behind Horace is a second shorter sword, we are deliberately left by the artist to guess what it looks like but its placement *in hiding* is a significant clue to its importance and a well-known artistic devise to denote a concealed treasure ie Bedevere is not only carrying the Spear but also possesses an important "concealed sword".

Horatio Lord
Vere of Tilbury

ABOUT THE AUTHOR

I am a writer of fiction, non-fiction and fantasy. Brought up in a Christian household and community, I am of Islam, embarking on a slow and careful period of study and teaching and one that can never be fully accomplished in my lifetime given the depth and scope of my new faith. As a consequence of my upbringing, I retain a love for Christianity, Judaism and Islam, but as part of a single path towards peaceful unity and belief in one God founded on the principle of religious tolerance.

Taught in the tradition of Sufi, I am most fascinated in the early writings of the Islamic tradition, its poetry, dramas and love stories. I abhor the acts of violence and terror done in the name of my faith as showing we are not suited to be the stewards of God's creation for which task respect for **all** life is an essential part.

This is a work of fiction but as always drawn from real world experiences and so, inevitably, there is a cross-over between the fantastical and the real. Where that transition happens will be down to the reader's own belief set.

For example, does Ra'el exist? Yes and her early life reflects that of a real person but these stories are fiction. Does the Grail exist? No but something inspired the BedeVere family to levels of courage and defiance beyond that of their peers! Do dragons exist? That really depends on whether there was ever a time when our world saw the magical alongside the natural and scientific; for dragon flight is or appears to be impossible under our current understanding of the laws of physics and aerodynamics.

Did Joseph of Arimathea and Mary Magdalan ever come to Britain? There is evidence of Christianity being present in Britain from the 1st Century but it is most likely that the Word spread through the many ports and Britain's trade with the rest of the Roman Empire than it was the result of a mission.

What is perhaps more interesting is St Helena's role in the conversion of the Roman Empire in the early 4th Century AD? That she was a British princess and considered a worthy spouse for someone who already ruled half the Roman Empire suggests that the royal households in Britain were highly respected and had survived both the invasion and the rebellion in the first century AD. The lessons of the origins and causes of Boudicca's rebellion appear to have been truly learnt in its aftermath by both Rome and the British. It helped also that the new dynasty that ruled from Rome after Nero had come from the Provinces and began therefore as both more tolerant of other faiths and the middle classes and more pious than either Caligula or Nero (until the untimely death of Titus brought Domitian to the Imperium).

No doubt Boudicca would have been proud when another British princess conquered the whole of the Roman Empire only this time through love and hope, two hundred and fifty years' after her own rebellion. However, even the life story of someone so influential on world history as Helena remains in the shadows. There is no evidence to support St Helena being the descendant of Mary Magdalan.

Do not take these stories too seriously, therefore. They are stories told to put off a terrible fate for a lonely young girl caught in the grip of a monster: a fictional example of courage and grace under pressure. In the end, this is a story of hope through personal sacrifice and nothing more.

Enjoy them and may these stories bring you peace in your heart.

With all my love and prayers
Layla Ghaniyah Abrar

"Here is the House of Layla:

I walk beneath her silent tower
Kiss the clematis on her walls
Touch the trellis where the wisteria falls
But it is not love for her walls
To which my beating heart calls
SHE is the source of my desire"

(Laylo o Majnan, from the orig. Quintet by
Nizami Gandavi, modern trans.
by the Sleeping Dragon™)

ATLAS

The Cartography of Ra'el and Maria Magdalan's World

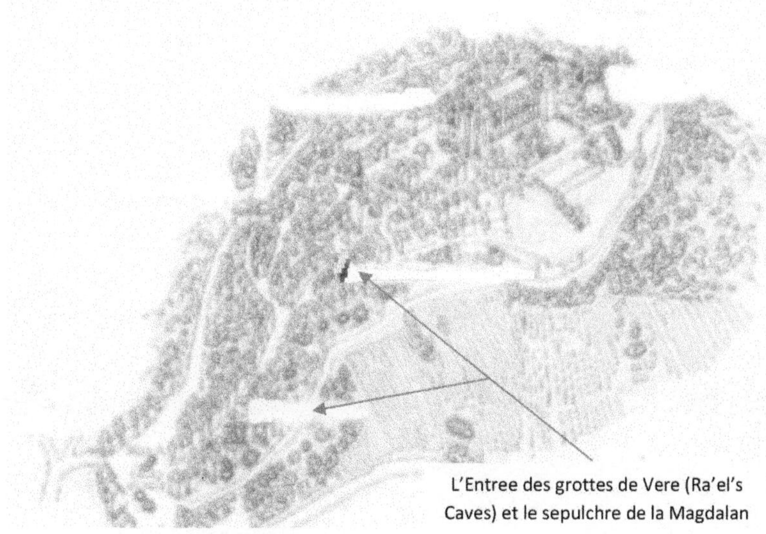

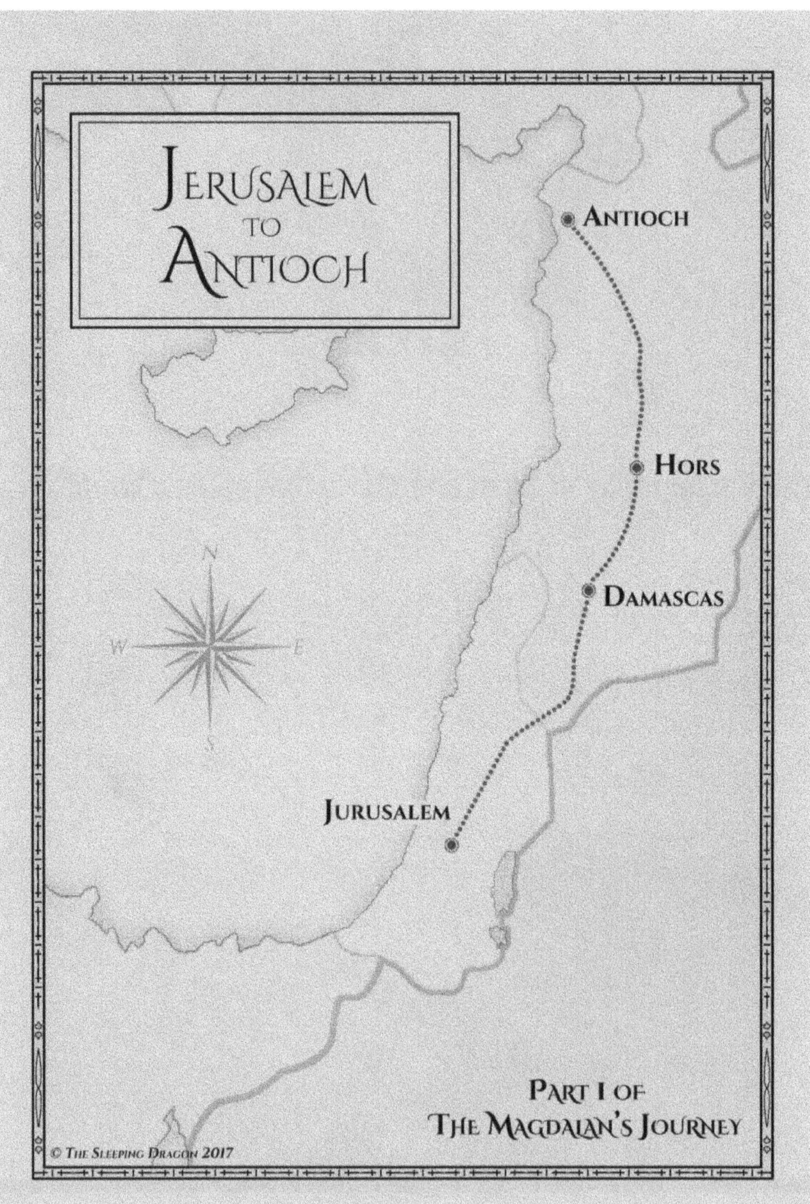
Jerusalem
to
Antioch
Antioch
Hors
Damascas
Jurusalem
N
W
E
S
Part I of
The Magdalan's Journey
© The Sleeping Dragon 2017

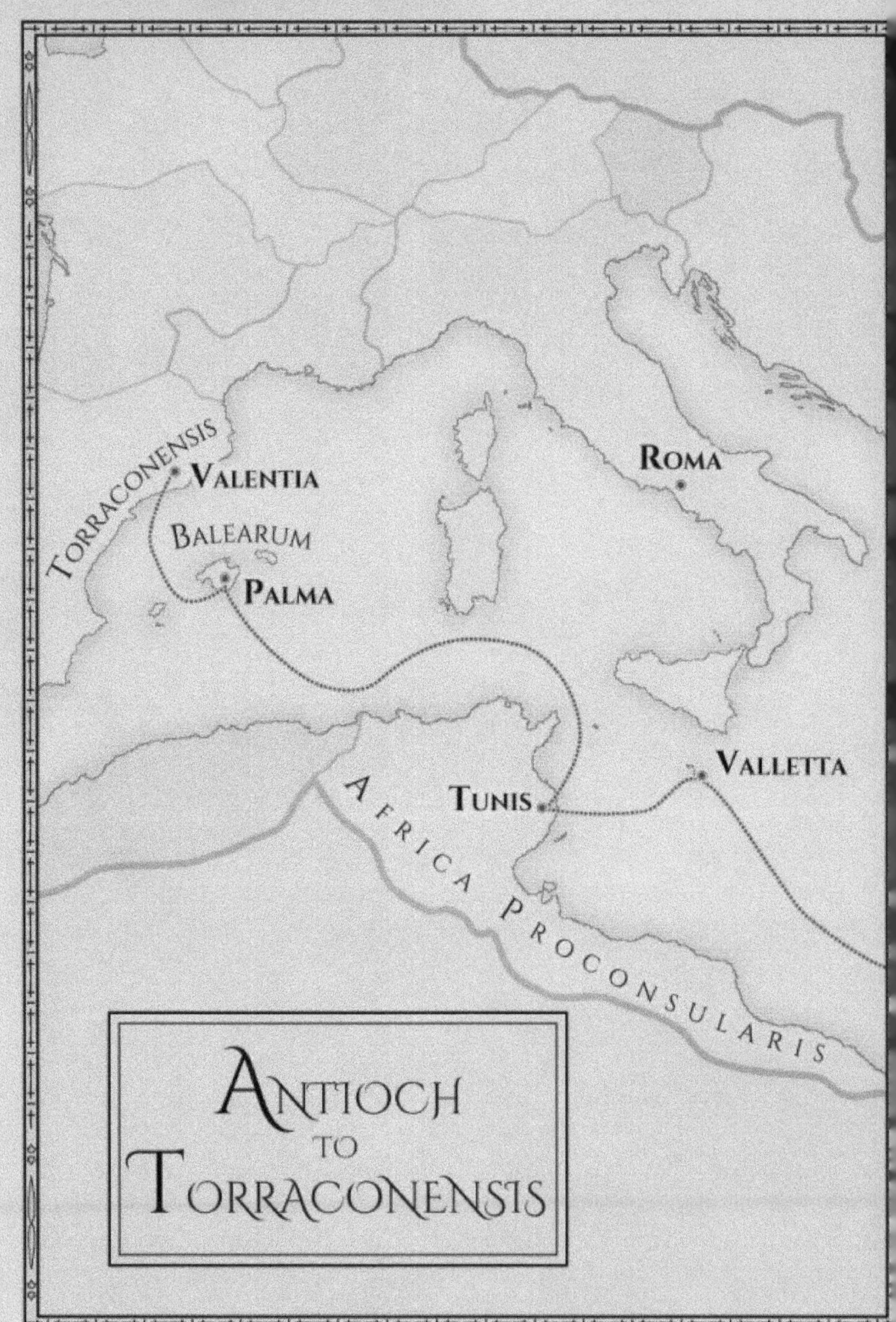
Torraconensis
Valentia
Balearum
Palma
Roma
Tunis
Valletta
Africa Proconsularis
Antioch to Torraconensis

N
W
E
S
CRETE
HERACLEA
CYPRUS
LYCAEA
ANTIOCH
CYRENE
CYRENAICA
PART 2 OF
THE MAGDALAN'S JOURNEY
© THE SLEEPING DRAGON 2017

Torraconensis
to
Sugdavellum
Britannia
South Hamm
Gallia Belgica
Caleti Sequana
Gallia Lugdunensis
Turonis
Lemovica
Torino
Aquitania
Burdigala
Tolosa
Lugdunum
N
E
S
W

Baschus
Iaenus Portus
Marsela
Bascones
Torraconensis
Osca
Caesaraugusta
Balearum
Valentia
Lusitania
Baetica
Part 3 of
The Magdalan's Journey
© The Sleeping Dragon 2017

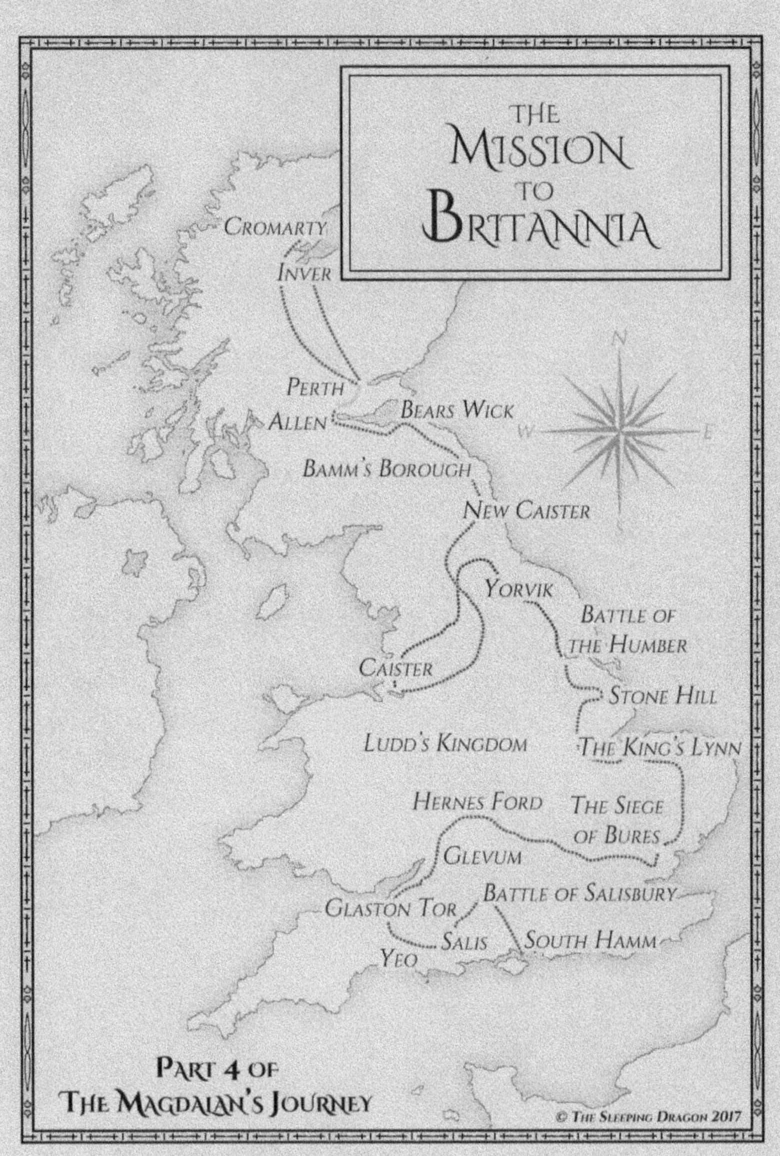
THE
MISSION
TO
BRITANNIA
CROMARTY
INVER
PERTH
ALLEN
BEARS WICK
BAMM'S BOROUGH
NEW CAISTER
N
W
E
YORVIK
BATTLE OF
THE HUMBER
CAISTER
STONE HILL
LUDD'S KINGDOM
THE KING'S LYNN
HERNES FORD
THE SIEGE
OF BURES
GLEVUM
BATTLE OF SALISBURY
GLASTON TOR
SALIS
SOUTH HAMM
YEO
PART 4 OF
THE MAGDALAN'S JOURNEY
© THE SLEEPING DRAGON 2017

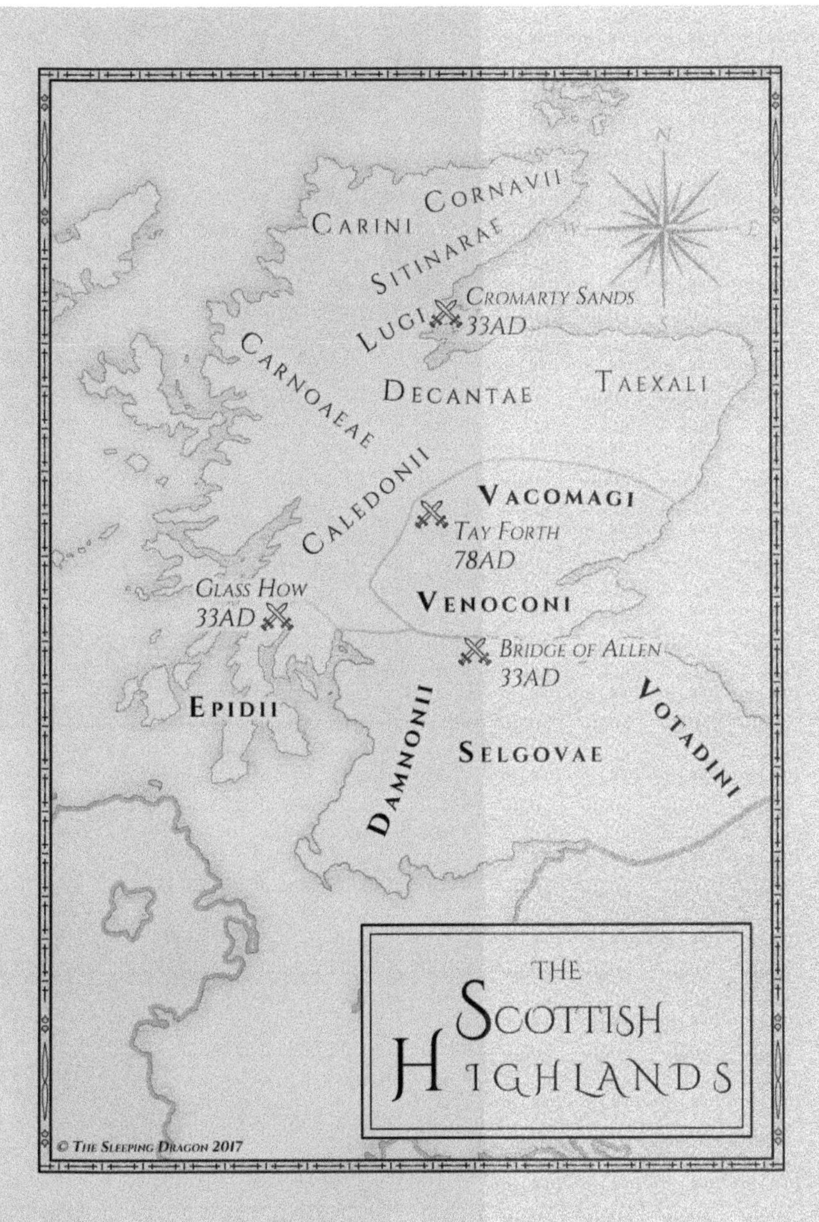
Carini
Cornavii
Sitinarae
Lugi
Cromarty Sands
33AD
Carnoaeae
Decantae
Taexali
Caledonii
Vacomagi
Tay Forth
78AD
Glass How
33AD
Venoconi
Bridge of Allen
33AD
Votadini
Epidii
Damnonii
Selgovae
The Scottish Highlands
© The Sleeping Dragon 2017

If you have enjoyed reading this book then you might also enjoy the following by the same author

An Audience with the Sleeping Dragon
Book Two: The Shroud of Turin
Book Three: The Grael Stone
Book Four: Gloria - the Final Coming

The Chronicles of Cymbeline, duchess of Fearnost
The Servers Soul
Suspended Belief

The Saga of Clan Faeron
Alanaa, the Water Element (includes the Book of Knowledge)
Atlantis Reborn
The Persian War
The Golden Age
The Death of Peleus
The Rise of Lucifer

Other stories:
Tales from the Burning Bush (short stories)
The Sacrifice of Mnesis
Castillion

Detective novels:
The Courteous Ghost
The Westerfield Mysteries

Historical accounts (non fiction):
Nothing is Truer than Truth
Instructions on the Royal Sport of Jousting

Poetry:
Incoherent weeping

Religious (non fiction):
Islam refreshed for the 22nd Century

Lightning Source UK Ltd.
Milton Keynes UK
UKHW011525140220
358721UK00012B/22

9 781546 289111